"What did you say your name was?" Tyreta asked.

"Lieutenant Stediana Walden," the woman replied. "But everyone calls me Sted."

"Did my brother die bravely, Sted?" She asked it without thinking, hoping the answer was yes. At least then she'd be able to tell her mother Conall had died for something.

"He saved my life on that boat," Sted replied. "Donan's too. But don't be too sure he's dead. I wouldn't put it past Conall Hawkspur to have wormed himself out of that fix. Most likely he's washed up on a beach somewhere full of half-naked whores and more booze than he can fill his belly with."

She didn't sound too convinced by her own words. Then again, if anyone could survive a storm at sea and come out the other side dry as a desert, it would be Conall.

Tyreta watched the streets of Candlehope roll by until eventually they left through the main gates and turned north along the coast road. To the west, in the distance, she could see a rising dust cloud as an army marched closer. Looked like they were fortunate to get out when they did.

Maybe her luck was starting to change. Maybe it was too early to tell.

As R. S. Ford

THE AGE OF UPRISING

Engines of Empire
Engines of Chaos

WAR OF THE ARCHONS

A Demon in Silver
Hangman's Gate
Spear of Malice

STEELHAVEN

Herald of the Storm
The Shattered Crown
Lord of Ashes

As Richard Cullen

THE WOLF OF KINGS

Oath Bound
Shield Breaker

ENGINES OF CHAOS

BOOK TWO OF
THE AGE OF UPRISING

R · S · FORD

orbitbooks.net

Orbit
Hachette Book Group
1290 Avenue of the Americas
New York, NY 10104
orbitbooks.net

First Edition: April 2023

Orbit is an imprint of Hachette Book Group.
The Orbit name and logo are trademarks of Little, Brown Book Group Limited.

The publisher is not responsible for websites (or their content) that are not owned by the publisher.

The Hachette Speakers Bureau provides a wide range of authors for speaking events. To find out more, go to hachettespeakersbureau.com or email HachetteSpeakers@hbgusa.com.

Orbit books may be purchased in bulk for business, educational, or promotional use. For information, please contact your local bookseller or the Hachette Book Group Special Markets Department at special.markets@hbgusa.com.

Library of Congress Cataloging-in-Publication Data
Names: Ford, R. S. (Richard S.) author.
Title: Engines of chaos / R.S. Ford.
Description: First Edition. | New York, NY : Orbit, 2023. | Series: The Age of Uprising ; book 2
Identifiers: LCCN 2022032645 | ISBN 9780316629614 (trade paperback) | ISBN 9780316629607 (ebook)
Subjects: LCGFT: Novels.
Classification: LCC PR6106.O757 E53 2023 | DDC 823/.92—dc23/eng/20220711
LC record available at https://lccn.loc.gov/2022032645

ISBNs: 9780316629614 (trade paperback), 9780316629607 (ebook)

Printed in the United States of America

LSC-C

Printing 1, 2023

*For Christian Dunn. Who published a short story
about twenty years ago and made me believe
I could actually do this. I'm still not sure he was right...*

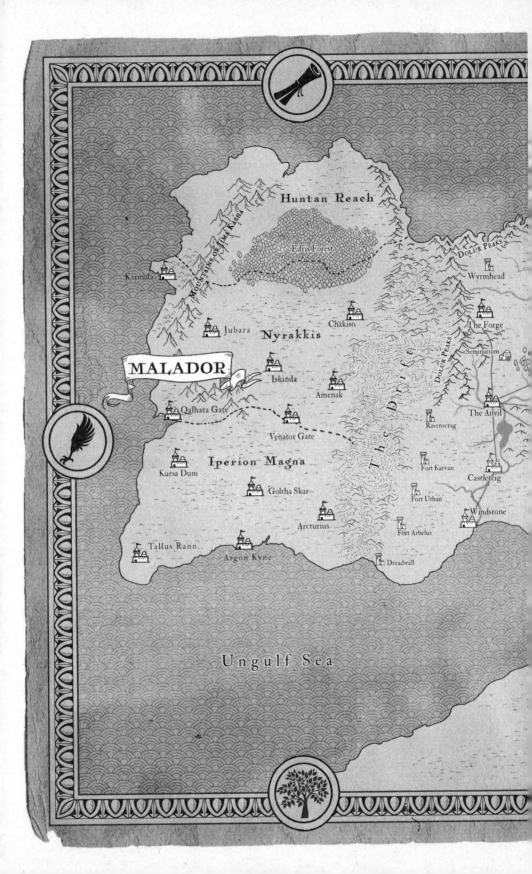

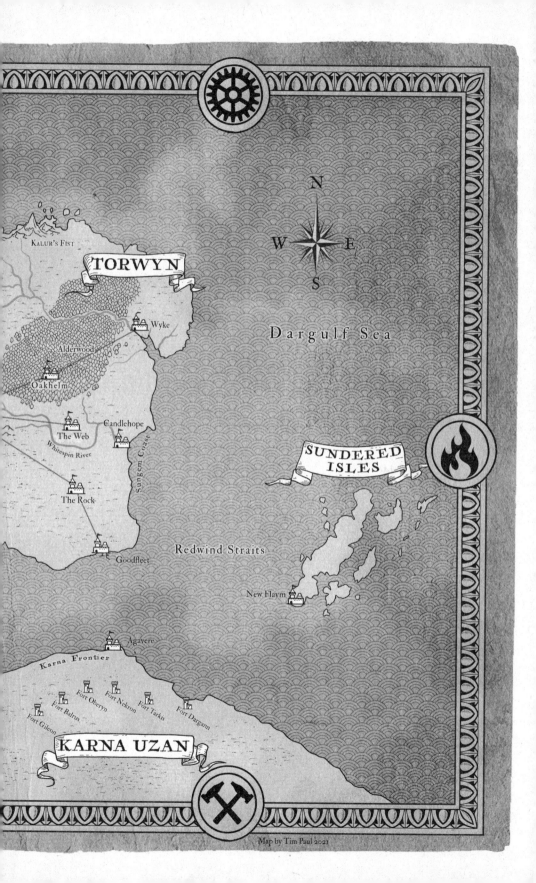

DRAMATIS PERSONAE

THE HAWKSPURS

Conall Hawkspur—Son of Rosomon. Captain of the Talon.

Crenn—An artificer.

Faiza—A lieutenant in the Talon.

Fulren Hawkspur—Son of Rosomon. A skilled artificer. (Deceased.)

Melrone Hawkspur—Husband of Rosomon. (Deceased.)

Rosomon Hawkspur—Guildmaster. Mother to Conall, Fulren and Tyreta.

Starn Rivers—Swordwright of the Hawkspur Guild. (Deceased.)

Stediana Walden—Sted. A lieutenant in the Talon.

Tyreta Hawkspur—Daughter of Rosomon. A webwainer.

THE ARCHWINDS

Ianto Fray—Imperator of the Titanguard.

Kassian Maine—Former swordwright to Treon Archwind.

Lancelin Jagdor—The Hawkslayer. Swordwright of the Archwind Guild.

Lorens Archwind—Eldest son of Sullivar and Oriel.

Oriel Archwind—Wife of Sullivar.

Philbert Kerrick—An artificer.

Sullivar Archwind—Emperor of Torwyn. (Deceased.)

Treon Archwind—Father of Rosomon and Sullivar. (Deceased.)

Wyllow Archwind—Youngest son of Sullivar and Oriel. A webwainer. (Deceased.)

THE CORWENS

Rearden Corwen—Guildmaster.

Wachelm—A junior actuary of the Corwen Guild.

THE IRONFALLS

Maugar Ironfall—Swordwright of the Ironfall Guild. Brother to Wymar.

Wymar Ironfall—Guildmaster. Brother to Maugar.

Xorya Ironfall—Swordwright-in-training. Daughter of Maugar.

THE MARRLOCKS

Borys Marrlock—Son of Oleksig and swordwright of the Guild.

Donan Marrlock—A minor member of the Guild.

Emony Marrlock—Youngest daughter of Oleksig.

Oleksig Marrlock—Guildmaster.

THE RADWINTERS

Becuma—A senior representative of the Radwinter Guild.

Jarlath Radwinter—Guildmaster.

Mincloth Radwinter—Wife of Jarlath.

Thalleus Brisco—Swordwright of the Radwinter Guild.

THE HALLOWHILLS

Hesse Fortuna—Associate of Keara. A webwainer.

Ingelram Hallowhill—Guildmaster.

Keara Hallowhill—Daughter of Ingelram. A webwainer.

Lucasta Hallowhill—Mother to Keara. A webwainer. (Presumed deceased.)

Ulger Vine—Associate of Keara. A webwainer.

THE DRACONATE MINISTRY

Ansell Beckenrike—Knight Commander of the Drakes.

Everis—A junior knight of the Drakes.

Falcar—A young and handsome knight of the Drakes.

Gylbard—Former Archlegate. (Deceased.)

Hisolda—High Legate of Vermitrix.

Hurden—A stern knight of the Drakes.

Lugard—A pious veteran of the Drakes.

Olstrum Garner—Sanctan's consul.

Regenwulf—A respected veteran of the Drakes.

Sanctan Egelrath—Archlegate.

Willet Kinloth—A junior legate.

IPERION MAGNA

Baenre Mokhtar—Servant of Senmonthis.

Mikal—Prisoner of Senmonthis.

Nylia of Amenak—Prisoner of Senmonthis and friend to Conall.

Orsokon—Warmaven of Arcturius.

Ramassen the Ox—Prisoner of Senmonthis and former pit fighter.

Senmonthis—Scion of Arcturius.

THE ARMIGERS

Draga—Captain of the Mantid Battalion.

Kagan Terswell—Frontier marshal of the Griffin Battalion.

Moraide—Captain of the Viper Battalion.

Rawlin—Drift marshal of the Bloodwolf Battalion.

Sarona—Drift marshal of the Ursus Battalion.

Sonnheld—Frontier marshal of the Viper Battalion.

Tarjan—Drift marshal of the Corvus Battalion.

Ultan—Captain of the Ursus Battalion.

Westley Tarrien—Marshal of the Phoenix Battalion.

PEOPLE OF TORWYN

Ashe Tyburn—Fugitive artificer. Lover of Verlyn.

Nicosse Merigot—Disgraced artificer. Brother of Lysander.

Grace—Daughter of Jessamine and Sanctan.

Jessamine—Lover of Sanctan. Mother to Grace.

Lysander Merigot—Disgraced artificer. Brother of Nicosse.

Verlyn—An unsanctioned webwainer. Lover of Ashe.

ORGANISATIONS OF TORWYN

Armiger Battalions—Military legions that defend Torwyn from foreign threats and protect its interests abroad. The eleven battalions are Auroch, Bloodwolf, Corvus, Griffin, Kraken, Mantid, Phoenix, Raptor, Tigris, Ursus, Viper.

Draconate Ministry—The ecclesiastic power in Torwyn, led by the Archlegate, which worships the five Great Wyrms:

Ammenodus Rex—Great Wyrm of War.

Ravenothrax the Unvanquished—Great Wyrm of Death.

Saphenodon—Great Wyrm of Knowledge.

Undometh—Great Wyrm of Vengeance.

Vermitrix—Great Wyrm of Peace.

Guilds—*The ruling power in Torwyn. The six major Guilds are:*

Archwind Guild—Most powerful Guild in Torwyn, specialising in artifice. Its military arm is known as the Titanguard.

Corwen Guild—The nation's administrators. Its military arm is known as the Revocaters.

Hawkspur Guild—Controls transit. Its military arm is known as the Talon.

Ironfall Guild—Works the forges. Its military arm is known as the Blackshields.

Marrlock Guild—Mines for ore and pyrestone.

Radwinter Guild—Responsible for farming and lumber.

PROLOGUE

The needle dug deep into his forearm, his right hand steady as he carved the last letter into his flesh. He gritted his teeth against the pain, but there was no way he'd show an ounce of discomfort in front of this gathering.

Every now and then he dipped the needle into a well of ink that pooled on top of a rock. The mark had to be permanent, had to show his commitment to this gang. Every eye watched intently as the final letter formed on his arm and the name they'd given him stood out stark against his bare skin.

Stone. It was the only word he could spell with any accuracy. This adopted family had picked it on account of his stubborn head and stout fists. His own family were dead and gone. His mother before he could remember her. His father not three winters ago. Stone could remember those last days—his father coughing up oily shit from the manufactories, looking and sounding older than his years. But the blacklung came for everyone who worked the forges and refineries sooner or later. Even now, the smog hung over them, clinging to the sky above the Burrows.

When finally he'd finished, his arm bleeding like fuck, Stone put the needle back down. Coins wiped his arm for him, round face grinning, more of a leer than a smile. Queen Clariss rose to her feet.

She was the oldest and best dressed of all of them, though that wasn't saying much. The girl sported a blue velvet jacket, frayed about the hem, stained about the sleeve, but still a sight better than what anyone else wore. Her boots were black and muddy, hair tied in a bright red band instead of a crown.

"Stone," she said, voice making a little whistle on account of her missing front tooth. "Welcome to the Clan of Bastards."

Someone started clapping and the rest joined in. Stone stood up to a cacophony of whoops and cheers, and everyone was looking at him with pride. He could put a name to every dirty face—Diamond Tooth, Jaffer Threetoes, Mad Dog Mace, Claiburn the Jester, Ranley Scars, Henny the Razor, Lysa Smokes, Vic the Shark. Now there was Stone to join those names. Another member of the Clan of Bastards, the wiliest street gang in the whole of the Anvil. Or so they told themselves. Stone knew it wasn't true. There were plenty of wilier gangs besides this, but it wouldn't do to point that out.

As he looked around at the mob standing in that old crumbling building, the skeleton of what might once have been an artisan's school or a Guild embassy, Stone felt a part of something, no longer looking in like a stranger. Now he was one of them.

Queen Clariss took her place on the cracked dais of some missing statue. There was a serious look to her youthful features.

"Now we've got that shit out of the way, let's get on to the first order of business," she said. "Our next job's gonna be big. We're gonna hit a Marrlock warehouse. There's one sitting right on the Riveryard and it's too tempting to ignore."

"Fucking Marrlock Guild?" replied Diamond Tooth, through teeth that were conspicuously bereft of diamonds. Stone could hear the fear in his voice. "That is big. How are we supposed to rip that place off?"

"I've got it all planned out," Clariss said. "Won't be nothing to it. As long as you all do your bit we can be in and out with enough pyrestone to see us all living like Guildmasters. Them Marrlocks won't even see us coming."

Stone could see some of them were up for it, their faces greedy and needy. Others weren't so sure. Least of all Coins.

"Never mind the fucking Marrlock Guild," he said in his little voice. "We all know what's waiting down at the Riveryard. And I'm not so sure I want to go strolling around in there, especially after dark."

That put a dampener on the enthusiasm. They all knew the rumours and the truth that went along with them. People had been going missing, and not the highfalutin citizens of the Anvil—the movers and shakers, the well-dressed and well-moneyed. It was people like them: the underclass, the needy and the dirty living in their hovels.

No one had a clue who was behind it. Could have been Revocaters, picking off the poor. Could have been something else. Stone had heard more than one tale about the Ghost. The spectre that haunted the Riveryard. A man or a beast that stalked the empty warehouses in the dark, picking off its prey and eating their flesh. Maybe it was just some madman getting his kicks from killing the poor. Maybe it was another gang doing its best to rid itself of competition. Whatever it was, neither the Ministry nor the Guilds seemed too keen to stop it.

"Not afraid of bedtime stories, are you, Coins?" Queen Clariss said. "We all thought you were made of tougher stuff." Giggles from the surrounding gang made Coins's round face start to redden like a tomato. "Let me worry about monsters in the dark, brother. You concentrate on not getting spotted by the guards."

They were all looking at him now, and Coins turned a deeper shade of red. It wouldn't do to show cowardice in front of this gang. That was as likely to get you cast out as anything else.

As they carried on giggling at Coins's discomfort, Stone turned his attention to something shifting in the shadows of the old building. Movement in the dark. A flash of red and yellow. Before he could shout a warning, the clacking report of splintbow fire echoed across the room.

Queen Clariss went down. She grabbed her leg, splintbolt sticking out like a broken bone, blood pouring between her fingers as she rolled off the dais. More splintbows fired their payloads across the room, but their sound was drowned out by a piercing scream.

Stone had heard people yelling before, but it never sounded so pained, like foxes fucking in the woods. Mad Dog Mace went down but didn't make a sound, body stuck with two bolts in the chest.

Stone was already moving, Coins right by his side, bare feet slapping against the loose floorboards as they fled for cover.

"Revocaters!" someone shouted. Could have been Ranley Scars, could have been Jaffer Threetoes, they both sounded much the same. Whoever it was, they were stating the bloody obvious.

Chaos spread throughout the derelict building. Revocaters burst from out of the shadows and through doorless archways. They'd been harrying the street gangs of the Anvil for years, but Stone had never seen them so determined, never known them to kill with such merciless intent.

He ducked at the sound of a splintbow close by. Heard the snapping ricochet of bolts hitting the wall beside his head. Another of his gang went down with a yelp, but Stone had no mind to stop and see who. He and Coins raced for a gap in the floor that dropped down to the level beneath. Stone's feet crunched against the bricks below, the marble floor having long since been carved up and sold for pennies.

A deep voice shouted for them to stop, but after what he'd just seen there was no way that was happening. Stone had never been able to work out why they always shouted "Stop!" It wasn't like you were gonna just give yourself up. Instinct, he supposed, just like running when someone was trying to kill you.

He and Coins sprinted across the ground level, fleeing the ruckus above, until they came out on the street. Another Revocater was waiting behind the wall opposite, looking for runners just like them, but Stone surprised him so much he emptied his clip of splintbolts without thinking to aim. As the bolts clattered harmlessly around them, they raced down the street.

More shouts followed, drowned out by the sound of the steelworks pounding, sheets of metal rolling off conveyor belts, bound for the manufactories. They raced past a wagon surrounded by workers. A couple of them glanced up with disinterest as the boys sprinted by, too preoccupied with their own drudgery to care about a couple of urchins being chased down by Revocaters.

Stone risked a glance over his shoulder. Three of them were still in pursuit, those yellow-and-red uniforms standing out starkly against the drab buildings of the Burrows. There was plenty of distance between them though. All they had to do was reach the fish market and they'd lose them easy enough. Stone could already smell it in the distance—the pungent stink of fish cutting through the acrid smell of the steelworks.

Coins went down with a yelp. Stone stumbled to a stop as his friend floundered on the ground, grasping his twisted ankle. There was a slapping report in the distance, another volley of splintbolts skittering along the ground toward them, just out of range.

Stone reached down to pull Coins up, but he could already see his friend wasn't gonna be able to run.

"Help me," Coins whimpered.

Stone saw those Revocaters gaining. He could help Coins, of course he could, but then they'd both be caught. And it didn't look like the Revocaters were gonna let them off with a slapped wrist. Most likely it would be a gallows rope.

Stone offered one last look at his friend's big round eyes in his big round head. There wasn't even enough time for him to say sorry before he set off again at a run.

If Coins shouted anything in his wake, it was lost in the noise of the manufactories. If the Revocaters were gaining on him, Stone didn't dare look back to see as he raced toward the relative safety of the fish market.

He almost stumbled as he rushed across the Parade of Builders, the Cogwheel to his right, the Whitespin up ahead. The sound of grinding machinery was quickly replaced by the hubbub of market vendors bellowing across the open plaza.

Stone tried to lose himself amid the crowd, squeezing through the press of bodies. Another shout for him to stop resounded across the marketplace, catching the attention of stallholders and punters alike. These fucking Revocaters were relentless. Didn't they know he was barely worth their time?

His way was suddenly barred by a broad-shouldered fishmonger. Stone barely had time to notice the stains on his apron before he ran right into him, a reek of fish guts on the man's clothing. He grabbed hold of Stone's shirt, the sleeve tearing as he held it in a meaty fist.

"I've got him," the fishmonger shouted. Twatting do-gooder.

Stone wasn't yet into his teens, but the Clan of Bastards hadn't given him that name for nothing. He balled a fist, planting his feet for purchase before he swung at the fishmonger's chin. The man was taller, wider, stronger, but a punch to the jaw would put anyone on their arse if you hit them right.

The fishmonger went down, almost ripping off Stone's sleeve altogether. No time to gloat. Stone was off again and this time the crowd were moving out of his way, giving him a clear path out the other side of the market, the tramping feet of the Revocaters following close behind.

Up ahead he could see the edge of the plaza dropped away to the warehouses that crowded the banks of the Whitespin. When he reached the edge, he took a breath, then used the edge of the wall to propel himself forward. Stone cleared a good ten feet of nothing to land on the roof opposite. Something whistled past his ear. Didn't take a genius to know it was a splintbolt, not that he needed any encouragement to keep moving.

His feet made a racket on the roof as he raced to the far side. A quick look over his shoulder and he could see the Revocaters were none too keen to follow him. He slowed, heaving in air, in two minds whether or not to throw them a crude gesture, but the instinct to find safety won out.

Stone clambered down the drainpipe at the other side of the roof, heart still racing when his feet touched the ground. The riverside was busy, but it wouldn't take long before those Revocaters caught up. He had to find somewhere to hide.

No one paid him much mind as he walked past the fishermen and bargemasters on the quay. He slipped into a back alley, hoping to lose himself in the thick press of warehouses. The buildings got more ramshackle the further he delved into the maze of passages until eventually he found himself outside an old storehouse. The main doors were chained shut, but if he could get inside, it would at least give him a chance to think on his next move.

At the back of the building were some boarded-up windows, and it took little effort to prise one open and squeeze inside. Stone was hit by how dark and dusty it was. A musty stench hung heavy in the air—that fusty stink of rotting wood and decay. He took a moment to gather his thoughts, trying not to think on Coins lying there in the street or what might have happened to the rest of the clan. His arm stung, and he looked down to see blood running in rivulets down to his hand before he remembered he wasn't injured—it was just the tattoo he'd given himself.

The sleeve of his shirt was hanging on by a thread, and he pulled it free, tying it around his forearm and tightening the knot with his teeth. As his eyes adjusted to the gloom, Stone could see the place was cavernous. Crossbeams had rotted away and fallen from the roof, lying aslant across the floor of the warehouse, giving it the look of a shadowy forest. As he picked his way through the enclosed space, he was forced to battle through the dusty remains of spider-webs that made it impossible to see more than a few feet.

He could hear the sound of running water and eventually saw light up ahead. As he made his way through the forest of beams he began to hear a dull thud above the sound of the river. It was rhythmic, drumming a slow, monotonous beat.

Eventually he struggled from the mass of fallen beams, seeing one side of the structure had fallen away into the Whitespin. A gap in the wall showed the river flowing past, and framed within it was a single figure stripped to the waist. He was hulking, his broad back showing pockmarks on bare flesh. With a muscular arm he reached down and plucked something from the floor before flinging it through the open gap and into the river beyond. It seemed a curious way to fish. The man didn't even attach a line to his bait.

It was then Stone saw the cleaver in the brute's hand.

Gore clung to the steel. The thing must have weighed a tonne, but in that huge ham fist it looked little heavier than a knife. Stone stood frozen as he dragged his eyes away from the dull steel to what was on the floor. Hunks of meat lay discarded like loose offal. As his eyes focused he realised this butcher wasn't carving any pig. A human hand lay grey and desiccated on the ground. Next to it was a lump of thigh. Not far from that, a severed head.

Before Stone could think on what to do, the butcher turned to face him. He must have sensed someone watching, must have known his game was up. Stone should have run, but he was trapped in the butcher's gaze. Those eyes were so small Stone could hardly see the whites.

Neither of them moved. Just stared at one another across the derelict storehouse. They were only a few feet apart. If Stone made a run for it, maybe he'd get away, but his feet wouldn't budge.

"Seen enough, little piggy?" said the butcher. "You should be careful where you tread."

Stone shook his head. Should he have nodded instead? He had no idea what the fuck to do. His feet wouldn't move and all of a sudden he needed to piss like he'd never needed it before.

"You're the Ghost," he managed to whisper.

That brought a grin to the butcher's face that didn't reach his tiny eyes.

Stone knew if he didn't get a grip on himself and run the fuck away, he was done.

He turned, racing across the storehouse, jumping a fallen beam, webs catching against his face. Heavy boots slammed down in his wake. He'd already run for his life once today, but this time there was terror to his desperation. At least with the Revocaters there was a slim chance of mercy. With the Ghost he knew there'd be none.

Ahead he could see a door hanging badly in its frame. Light shone beneath the lintel. Open air. Escape.

Stone focused on it, bare feet padding across the splintered boards. Could he wrench it open in time and fling himself into the freedom of the outdoors?

He heard the crunch of snapping wood. Felt his foot break the floorboard and slip into the gap. Stone shrieked in pain as he went down, face slamming against the ground. Dragging his foot out of the hole he saw how mangled it was, the flesh torn almost to the bone. He tried to stand, but the pain in his ankle was agonising.

Solid footsteps drew nearer. The Ghost was taking his time. No need to rush. Stone wasn't going anywhere.

He turned to see that cleaver hanging from the butcher's meaty grip. Those eyes filled with hunger.

"I warned you, little piggy," the Ghost said. "Be careful where you tread." He licked his lips, as though he might take a bite of Stone's flesh before he cut him into chunks and flung him in the river.

This was it. Nowhere to run, even if he could have. All Stone could do was crawl on his back, trying to put distance between him and this killer. The urge to piss was overwhelming, his bladder felt like it would burst, and he gritted his teeth against the pain.

"Come on then, you fucker," Stone spat. Maybe if he goaded this killer, he'd end it quick with his cleaver. At least then he wouldn't have to worry about pissing himself…

The door to the storehouse burst inward, rusted hinges springing from the wood. The light from outside was blocked by a huge figure who stooped beneath the lintel. The Ghost took a step back, looking like he might flee, but he stood his ground, gripping tight to that big old cleaver.

Stone squinted through the dark, watching as the intruder made his way in. Almost seven feet of armoured might, winged helm reflecting the sun that shone through the door, white surcoat bearing a rearing dragon.

The Drake glanced at Stone lying there on the floor, then at the Ghost. A huge sword hung from the gilded scabbard at his side, but he made no move to draw it. Stone willed him to reach for that blade and hack down the Ghost, but he stood, silent like a statue.

The Ghost's tiny eyes displayed a flicker of doubt where previously they'd shown nothing but malice. Then he squealed like a cornered animal, raising that cleaver high and lumbering forward to attack. Stone held his breath as the Drake just waited, like he wanted this butcher to hack him to pieces. At the last moment, as the Ghost sliced down with his cleaver, the Drake raised an arm. The sound of the weapon clanging off armour rang through the storehouse. One of the Drake's gauntleted hands snapped forward, taking hold of the Ghost's meaty neck. His other grasped the wrist holding the cleaver. The butcher gave off a squeak as the air was caught in his throat. He didn't look menacing anymore. As the Drake's grip tightened, the cleaver fell from the Ghost's stumpy fingers to clatter on the floor, and he grasped the armoured hand clamped tight about his neck.

"Did you think you could elude the justice of Undometh forever?" the Drake snarled from within his helm. The words were terrifying. Hate and might mixed into a single breathy voice. "Ammenodus grant me the strength to slay this villain."

The Ghost's eyes began to roll back in his head as he choked, spitting what little breath he could from his pale lips.

"Ravenothrax comes for you this day," growled the Drake. "Can you see him? Do you feel those black wings embracing you?"

The choking had stopped. The Ghost's thick arms hung limp at his sides, his tiny eyes wide and staring at nothing up in the broken rafters.

"To the Lairs with you, murderer." The Drake was whispering now, his grip still tight around the throat of the corpse. "May Vermitrix grant eternal peace to your victims."

Stone had seen enough. He flipped over onto his belly, trying his best to crawl away out of the light. With any luck the Drake would ignore him and not decide to send another sinner to the Five Lairs.

There was a thud as the body of the Ghost was discarded. Stone froze where he lay, gritting his teeth, still trying his best not to piss. Footsteps drew nearer and he braced himself, ready to feel those armoured hands clamp around his own throat.

The Drake grasped his arm and, with incredible strength, pulled Stone to his feet. He stumbled, hobbling on his injured leg as the Drake regarded him, eyes barely visible within that huge helmet.

"Rejoice, child. By the grace of the Wyrms, you have been spared a most grisly fate."

Stone glanced at the body of the Ghost. He didn't look so scary now. Just another hunk of dead meat.

"Can...can I go then?" Stone asked. Still wondering if his luck was about to change.

The Drake stared, still holding him up by one arm. "Go where, boy?"

Now there was a question. "Home," Stone replied, surprised at how small his own voice was.

The Drake reached down, grasping Stone's forearm before sliding back the shirtsleeve he'd tied around his bleeding arm. The letters there stood out stark and livid, marking him as a ganger from the Burrows.

"Do you even have a home, child?"

Another fine question Stone wasn't sure how to answer. If anyone in the Clan of Bastards had survived, they'd be scattered across the Anvil. Their home was empty lofts and cellars. How long before they were found by the Revocaters again? The answer was obvious, and Stone wasn't in any mood to lie about it.

"No," he replied. "I haven't."

Again the Drake regarded him in silence, as though weighing him, measuring him. Before the presence of this armoured behemoth, Stone could only stand and wait to be judged.

"I can offer you shelter, child. Come with me to the Mount. There will be a roof over your head and food in your belly. And perhaps you may yet gain the favour of the Wyrms."

"What would I want that for?" Stone snapped. The Wyrms had never done anything for him up to now.

"Perhaps in time you will see," the Drake replied, bearing Stone's weight as he guided him toward the light of day. "But first, let's get you home."

PART ONE

THE SPIDER AND
THE WYRM

ROSOMON

An ashen sky hung ominously over the choppy waves of the Dargulf Sea. A storm had been threatening for the past two days, the wind whipping the cliffs to the east with intermittent fury, but so far no rain. One mercy at least.

Rosomon gripped her cloak tight about her shoulders as they made their way north. It was drab brown, with no embroidery or markings. Nothing to identify her as Guildmaster of the Hawkspurs nor show she was anything but a traveller on the coast road.

For two days they had skirted the towns and villages that dotted the coastline, desperate not to be seen. They were hiding like rats from a lantern, and she was haunted by that shame, but it was the only way they might get to Wyke without incident. If the Ministry knew where she was, they would send an army to stop her, and so she walked an unfamiliar path in unfamiliar garb, surrounded by allies she barely knew.

The Titanguard had already proven themselves loyal, but they were her brother's bodyguard, not hers. Could she really trust them to serve her in the coming war? So far she had seen little reason to doubt them.

A dozen warriors shadowed her at all times, walking in tight ranks, each one a doleful giant. They wore no armour and carried scavenged weapons, but still managed to look imperious as they strode through the bleak elements. Rosomon could sense their loss—they had been tasked with protecting an emperor, trained to the peak of martial prowess, and bestowed with the mightiest trappings he could offer. In return they had failed him. Allowed him to die at the hands of a usurper. Rosomon knew all too well how they felt. She could have saved her brother if only she had uncovered Sanctan's betrayal sooner. Now all she had left was grief and hate, and a bitter thirst to avenge her slain brother.

It was a unique agony. An ache from what she had lost, mixed with a sense of foreboding at what she would have to do. Could she really order these men to sacrifice themselves and strike back at the heart of the Ministry? Could she lead them in war?

She was a skilled administrator, used to organising scouts and functionaries, but she was no general. Rosomon needed someone with her who could guide her through this. Someone who had fought a dozen battles and risen victorious from every one. She needed Lancelin.

But Lancelin was not here.

She had sent him away once again, just when she needed him the most. Were he by her side, surely this task would be bearable. But no one was here. There would be no guidance, no help. This was a task for Rosomon alone, and she would rise to it or perish. All she could do was remind herself that she was the daughter of Treon Archwind, the man who had raised Torwyn out of the dirt and forged it into an empire. Her only hope was to seize his legacy and believe he was with her, at least in spirit.

Too much had already been lost. Her sleep was plagued by visions of Fulren, of his final moments on the Bridge of Saints, sacrificing himself so the rest of them could escape. Rosomon had tried her best to rid herself of the memories, but it was an impossible feat. More than once she had hidden her face within the hood of her drab cloak and wept. Mercifully, if any of her guardians had noticed her misery, none had mentioned it.

Of Tyreta and Conall there was still no word. Every morning she had risen hoping a Hawkspur scout would return with her daughter. When they were finally united, at least a portion of her loss would be gone. As yet, there was nothing.

As for Conall—brave, handsome Conall—there had likewise been no news. Was he even now a prisoner? Had Sanctan's agents captured him? Were they torturing him as punishment for her defiance?

Rosomon gritted her teeth, clenching her fists, willing the tears away.

"My lady."

She started at the voice, forcing back her emotions, desperately trying to stay in control of them as she turned to see the brawny frame of Ianto Fray. He stood like a statue against the grey skies, his square features regarding her solemnly. The hair was growing unruly on his head and chin, but the young Titanguard still looked every inch the disciplined soldier. Despite the elements, he wore no cloak, his bare arms bulging from the beaten-leather vest he wore over his torso. It was scant armour compared to what he was used to, a garment more suited to the training yard, the cog of Archwind embossed on the chest. Where previously he would have been bedecked in the stoutest battle armour the artificers of Archwind could craft, now he stood half-naked against the wind. More evidence of how far they had all fallen.

"Yes, Ianto," Rosomon replied, relieved that her voice did not reflect her fragile state.

"The hour grows late, Lady Rosomon. It would be wise for us to pitch camp close to those woods."

He gestured inland at a thick copse of trees. It would provide shelter from the sea wind and shield them from view of anyone travelling the road.

"Of course," she replied.

Before she could give the order, Ianto turned to his men, signalling them toward the trees. They helped the few artificers travelling with them, steering their wagon from the road, pulled by the sullen mule they had borrowed from a farm in the marches.

Ianto stood by her side and they watched their tiny army move toward the woods. It was some relief to have the young Titanguard beside her. He was barely Tyreta's age, yet here he was, commanding men. It reminded Rosomon how she had to adapt if she was to lead this resistance. They had no idea what awaited them in Wyke and she had no army to fight with, other than a score of disgraced warriors. It seemed a lost cause, but she could not give in yet.

"You keep these men in good order, Ianto," Rosomon said as they watched the ramshackle army disappear into the wood. "Command much respect, despite your youth."

"I was trained in logistics and battlefield tactics from a young age, my lady. The Imperator Dominus was about to recommend me for advancement. Before..."

Ianto stopped. Rosomon already knew what he was about to say. Mallum Kairns, Imperator Dominus of the Titanguard, was dead. Sacrificed just as Fulren was. With his master, Emperor Sullivar, also slain, the notion of progressing through the ranks was meaningless.

"We will rise again, Ianto," she said. "And you will have your chance to avenge those you have lost."

She may as well have been talking to herself. Persuading herself it was true. Perhaps by saying the words to Ianto it would somehow make them all the more prophetic.

"This is all I deserve," Ianto said, still staring at the wood, now their column had disappeared into it. "We failed him. I failed him."

Rosomon glanced up at this warrior, this boy with such a weight on his shoulders. It made her feel suddenly guilty for her own indulgence. She was a Guildmaster, born to her responsibility, trained to take on the mantle of leadership. Here was a boy, carrying the burden of the Titanguard, and yet he did not shirk it.

"We have not failed him yet," Rosomon said, making her way from the road, toward the trees. "This is a long way from over."

Ianto followed close behind. Having the young Titanguard nearby made her suddenly feel less alone. Less vulnerable. When she saw their camp being so efficiently erected, for the first time she began to believe that maybe they did have a chance. Their number was small, but surely help was coming. Marshal Rawlin might yet bring more Armiger Battalions loyal to the Guilds. Lancelin could persuade Wymar Ironfall and his Blackshields to join them. Emony might even bring her father and the Marrlock Guild. She was right to say this was far from over. Rosomon had to cling to the hope that it had barely begun.

She made her way through the camp, and each Titanguard she passed stood at attention, offering a nod before going back to their work. Likewise the artificers offered her a deep bow of respect. Rosomon felt undeserving of it. She had yet to prove she was a leader worth following.

Just as she began to think there would be nothing for her to do but collapse beneath a tree and try to sleep, she heard harsh, whispered voices from across the camp. Two artificers stood at the rear of their wagon, arguing in an animated fashion. Perhaps she should have let them play out their quarrel, but she could already see they were drawing gazes from the rest of the men. Such disharmony couldn't be allowed to continue.

"It has to be kept covered," one of the artificers hissed as she drew closer. He was tiny, with wispy grey hairs poking from beneath a cloth skullcap. "Or the steel will rust."

The second artificer raised his hands in consternation, his portly figure quivering in his frustration. "The pyrestone needs to breathe," he spat beneath gritted teeth. "Leave the cover off."

"What is going on here?" Rosomon asked.

Both men turned, their expressions changing from annoyance to shame when they saw who had interrupted their dispute. The one with the skullcap wrenched it from his head and both men bowed.

"Just a minor disagreement on the storage of equipment, my lady," said the portlier artificer. "Our short supply of pyrestone has to be left uncovered in these conditions. Otherwise the damp confinement will cause it to degrade."

It wasn't any theory Rosomon had heard before. As far as she knew pyrestone was a robust power source, and she had organised its supply and transportation across the whole of Torwyn. Still, it wouldn't do to promote disunity within her ranks.

"Very well," she said. "Then I suggest you remove it from the cart and cover the rest of the equipment."

It appeared neither man had considered that as an option.

As one artificer went about struggling with a small crate of stones, the other placed his skullcap back on his head.

"What's your name?" she asked.

The artificer looked surprised at her sudden interest in him. "Er...Kerrick, my lady. Philbert Kerrick."

"Do you have a breakdown of supplies, Philbert? What resources do we have left?"

Philbert looked forlornly at the back of the wagon. There was an array of metal devices of varying shapes and sizes. "This is all the ordnance we have left. Several charges, a few splintbows and perhaps enough equipment to jury-rig a cannon or two." He looked embarrassed at the paltry display. "I am sorry, my lady."

"Don't be," Rosomon replied, though her heart sank a little at the news. "It isn't your fault."

"But I am sure once we get to Wyke you will be able to provide all the equipment we need to arm the Titanguard," he added.

Rosomon wasn't so sure. "We should have plenty of stores. But even so, all the artifice in Torwyn won't help us against the Hallowhill Guild. I watched four of them bring down an entire squad of Titanguard with little effort."

She was thinking out loud, spreading her own doubts among her followers. Treon Archwind would never have shared his fears with subordinates. Some general she was turning out to be.

Philbert's face twisted into a pained expression, his brow furrowing. "With the webwainers united against us, it does pose a significant problem. We can construct all the weapons we want, armour the Titanguard and make them battle-ready, but yes, the Hallowhills will render our artifice useless. Perhaps even use it against us."

"I hope there's a *but* coming, Philbert."

"Indeed," the artificer said, nodding his skullcapped head. "The Merigots, my lady."

"The what?"

"Lysander and Nicosse. The most infamous artificers in all Torwyn. I'm surprised you've not heard of them." He waited for a response. When Rosomon provided none, he continued. "The brothers Merigot were widely known to have developed a range of experimental artifice resistant to webwainer influence. Unfortunately their results were...unstable at best. Lethal at worst. I believe it was your father who deemed their studies too dangerous to continue, but there is a chance they can still help."

"And where are these Merigot brothers now?"

Philbert bit his lip, then shrugged. "I am sorry, my lady. They have not been heard from in years. After their experiments were effectively prohibited, both of them left the service of the Archwind Guild."

Rosomon did her best to supress a sigh. "I appreciate the history lesson, Philbert. But it doesn't help our current situation."

Philbert lowered his eyes. "My apologies."

"No. You have my thanks," Rosomon said, placing a hand on his shoulder. "You all do."

She turned, seeing Ianto waiting faithfully behind her. A man she would need. A man they would all need.

"Come," she ordered, and made her way across the camp.

Ianto followed her toward the rest of the Titanguard. They had erected their camp and built a small fire. Each one sat in brooding silence, sharpening weapons, polishing shields or dressing the wounds they had suffered at the Anvil with clean bandages.

When Rosomon appeared from the dark of the wood, the men stood to attention. They had been her brother's loyal bodyguard. Now she had to know if they could be hers.

"We have suffered a great loss," she announced. "Yet still you have all fought bravely. None of you should feel any shame. The emperor would be proud of each and every one of you. I know it is a lot to ask, but I now hope that you will follow me in Sullivar's stead. I—"

Before she could continue, every one of them dropped to one knee, bowing their heads before her. These were the best-trained warriors in all Torwyn, and now they offered their fealty to her. It was a start. It was hope.

"Ianto Fray," she said. "Rise."

The young Titanguard stood obediently. "Yes, my lady."

Rosomon took a breath before she continued, hoping this was her right, not knowing if it was even her place to command these men.

"The Imperator Dominus gave his life so that we might carry on the fight. Mallum Kairns was a hero of the Titanguard. Were he here,

I have no doubt he would have raised you to the rank of imperator and that responsibility now falls to me. Do you accept the honour?"

Ianto bowed his head. "I do, Lady Rosomon."

A wave of relief washed over her. Twenty loyal men did not seem like much, but it was all she had. The reprieve did not last, as one of the artificers rushed through the darkening wood.

The Titanguard rose to their feet as the man drew closer, gathering his breath.

"The road..." he breathed. "You need to see."

Rosomon made her way across the camp, the Titanguard following at her shoulder as she neared the edge of the tree line and squinted across the open ground. The sky was dimming beyond the cliff edge, but in the waning light she could see a trail of figures making their way south along the coast road. Many carried belongings in sacks, or crates strapped to their backs. Others carried their children, or pulled them wearily alongside. Rosomon didn't recognise any faces, but instinctively she knew where they had travelled from...Wyke. Her city.

She struck out from the copse. One of the Titanguard whispered for her to be cautious, but she ignored him, crossing the open ground to the road. Face after face regarded her with a woeful expression, but none of them knew her. Perhaps that was a mercy. Would they have blamed her for this? Spat in her face and cursed the Guilds to the Lairs? Had they been driven from their homes at swordpoint? Had there been violence? Slaughter?

As Rosomon stood, not knowing what to do, a woman broke from the crowd. She wore a plain travelling cloak, but beneath she was dressed in the tan leather uniform of a Talon scout, the Hawkspur symbol adorning her chest.

"Lady Rosomon," she said, kneeling down and bowing her head.

Rosomon grasped the scout's arm and pulled her to her feet. All this kneeling was growing tiresome. Perhaps later she'd instruct everyone to show their respect in a less formal manner.

"What word from Wyke?" Rosomon asked.

"The city is taken, my lady. The Ursus Battalion marched upon us two days ago. A huge force. We could not hope to resist. They have imprisoned many of the Talon, but allowed anyone else who wished it to leave. Wyke belongs to the Ministry now."

Rosomon felt stinging bile rise in her throat. The hope that she might be able to take Wyke swiftly and establish a base from which to strike back at Sanctan was now dashed.

"I am sorry, my lady." The scout looked close to tears. "There was nothing—"

"What is your name?" Rosomon asked.

"Lieutenant Faiza, my lady." The woman swallowed down her emotions, her jaw tightening.

"Thank you for your report, Lieutenant." Rosomon gestured toward the wooded glade. "Go to my camp. Get some rest. I will need your help soon enough."

The scout nodded and made her way toward the trees.

"What now?" asked Ianto. Her new imperator. His voice was without emotion and he offered no suggestions. Despite the training he had been given in tactics, it was clear he had no solution to this problem. It left Rosomon with no doubt as to who was in charge.

"Now?" she replied, trying to quell her fear. Letting her anger take over. Perhaps that was the wrong thing, but she was sure her father would have approved. "Now we rest." Her eyes fell on the trail of refugees, making their way south to nowhere safe. "Tomorrow we continue to Wyke."

TYRETA

The mirror was cracked, adding myriad facets to her face, but as Tyreta stared it wasn't the shattered image that made her appear strange. She looked closer, shifting her balance instinctively as the cabin lurched on yet another turbulent wave. In the mirror, her eye stared back. Someone else's eye. *Something else.*

Tyreta reached up, pulling down her lower lid. Her iris was no longer deep brown but pale green, with a dark ring about its edge. The pupil had grown elliptical, a sharp vertical slash of black staring back at her like an animal. As the sun flashed in through the window it suddenly dilated, returning to a tiny black circle.

She took a step back, trying not to contemplate what might be happening. Was this another side effect of the Lokai ritual? Was her body undergoing more change than just the scars and tattoos that marked her flesh?

As she turned from the mirror, Cat stirred in the corner of the room. When they'd first debarked from the Sundered Isles, the panther had mewled in panic, the journey across the Redwind Straits making her crouch and shiver in fear. In time, Tyreta had managed to soothe her new companion, and now she lounged in the corner of the cabin, licking her fur like any house pet. Before Tyreta could approach and make a fuss of her, there was a shout from on deck. They were nearing land.

Tyreta shouldered her bow, grabbing the quiver from where it lay on the bed and strapping it about her waist. A dozen arrows protruded from it, fletched in yellow, blue and red. Crenn had done her proud, crafting each arrowhead with a pyrestone from the ship's stores. She already knew what could be achieved with the five blue and five yellow arrows. They would react to her command with devastating effect. Crenn had also crafted two arrows from red pyrestone, but Tyreta wasn't quite so sure what she might do with those. Red pyrestone was used as a regulator in traditional artifice, able to store and distribute power in more complicated machinery. What Tyreta might be able to do with it was a mystery, but as they approached land she was sure there'd be an opportunity to find out.

"Come," she said to Cat, grasping the spear Crenn had made for her. Its steel head was fixed with pyrestone of all three colours. So far she hadn't dared test what power she could conjure at the head of that weapon.

When she climbed out onto the deck, the sky was clear, the sun brightening up a windy day as the ship cruised toward the port of Candlehope. It looked majestic in the distance, its spires built atop a huge cliff with buildings spreading down toward the seafront. Any other day, Tyreta would have been filled with joy at seeing it. At arriving home. Not this day.

The Ministry had risen up and stolen power from the Guilds. What that meant for her and her family, she could only guess. Either way, they had to approach with caution. The ship's captain had already taken down the Hawkspur colours that flew proudly at the bow and replaced them with the flag of any other merchantman that sailed across the straits. There was no telling what might await them when they reached the dock, and right now anonymity would serve them better than Guild pennants.

Part of Tyreta hoped there would be someone waiting to arrest her and take her off to a Ministry gaol. At least then she would have a chance to vent her burgeoning frustration, to fight back, make a stand, but that would have been a stupid waste. She had to think. Had to discover how the land lay. Most pressing of all, she had to find her mother.

It would have stuck in her throat were she forced to admit it, but Tyreta knew they had to be reunited. Yes they'd had their differences, yes the great Lady Rosomon had always treated her like an obsolete part in some machine, but they were family. A family under threat. She could only hope her mother had managed to escape the coup and was even now fighting back against the Ministry.

"Are you sure about this?"

The voice was raised above the wind. Tyreta turned to see the ship's captain standing next to her. His brow was furrowed as he glared across the water toward Candlehope. He had abandoned his Hawkspur uniform just as the ship had abandoned its colours.

In truth, Tyreta wasn't sure about anything. "I think this is the safest way."

"We can still turn north. Head straight to Wyke."

Tyreta shook her head. "Wyke will be the first place the Ministry attacks if my mother has managed to raise any opposition to them. It's safer for us to land here. I can make the rest of the journey north in secret."

That seemed the most sensible option, but in truth, Tyreta didn't even know whether her mother was already a captive of the Ministry. Locked away in a dungeon or being paraded by her captors as some kind of prize.

"Very well," he replied. "We'll approach with caution. But if there's Drakes waiting for us at the dock, I doubt there'll be much I can do to protect you."

"Let me worry about Drakes," Tyreta replied, half hoping they were waiting. At least then she'd find out if her new weapons were as powerful as she anticipated.

The captain nodded his agreement, and no sooner had he left than Crenn came to join her at the prow. Cat sniffed absently at the old artificer's boots, but he made no sign that it worried him. He'd grown used to the panther's attentions, and she was almost as much his pet as Tyreta's.

"What do you think's waiting?" Tyreta asked as Candlehope loomed over them, its spires casting a long shadow from up on the cliff.

"Well, it won't be bunting and a parade," Crenn replied.

That was true enough. As they cruised into the vast circular dock there didn't seem to be much of anything at all awaiting them. Where normally there'd be dockworkers and fishermen going about their business, now there was nothing but empty vessels and abandoned machinery. Loading equipment sat unused and impotent. Every sail on every moored ship was furled.

In the distance Tyreta spied two signallers from the port authority waving their flags, guiding the ship to an empty jetty. They cruised ashore, the mariners making short work of throwing mooring ropes onto the harbourside and securing the vessel in position. As soon as the gangplank was lowered, the captain made his way from the ship to where the harbourmaster waited on the jetty.

"Let's go," Tyreta whispered to Crenn, as the captain began to talk in a heated manner about delays at sea and the recent storm.

They walked by as casually as they could manage, hearing mention of ships being impounded, of orders sent directly from the Anvil, of Armiger Battalions and Ministry decrees. Her heart sank as she made her way across the dock, Cat close to her knee, Crenn right behind her. At every step she expected to be stopped by an armed guard or Armiger trooper, but no one stood in her way. It seemed with the erosion of Guild power, the authorities of Candlehope had simply given up. The entire administrative structure of the port had just drifted away into the sea like so much flotsam.

The path from the dock led up through rising levels, a wide stone staircase carving its way through bare rock toward the city on the clifftop. Where there should have been gaggles of fishermen and traders, a route bustling with activity, there was nothing but empty cages for lobster and crab, and piles of abandoned netting. The arm of a huge crane hung limp over the edge of the upper level, the gate to the harbour standing open for anyone to wander through.

Once out on the streets of the port, Tyreta saw a little more activity. A group of drunken fishermen loitered on a street corner, engaged in an animated conversation about the damned Guilds and the damned Ministry. The voices of men arguing about permits and licenses of marque grew shriller the farther Tyreta walked into the city. Every eye fell on them as they made their way into the press of streets, and at any moment Tyreta expected someone to point and shout, *There goes Tyreta Hawkspur.*

"We need to get off the streets," she said to Crenn. "I'm drawing too much attention."

"You?" Crenn asked. "Or her?" He pointed at Cat as she stalked along beside them, head moving curiously from left to right.

"Yeah," Tyreta admitted with a little relief it wasn't just her. "Could be that."

"Maybe if we put her on a leash, it might make folk feel more comfortable."

The notion didn't sit right with Tyreta. "If you want to try and put a leash on her, be my guest."

Crenn clearly didn't think it a good idea after all, and regarded Cat with a wary look before carrying on with a shrug.

The atmosphere on the streets of Candlehope grew ever more tense the farther they went. People were packing belongings and gathering their families in the streets. Carts were being loaded and horses yoked. When there was no horse to tether, anything with wheels would do to carry what possessions they could.

Tyreta glanced across the rooftops, searching for the Hawkspur passage depot. In the distance, beyond the tightly packed houses, she spied the tall aerie that overlooked the city. It did not quite reach up to the city's highest spires, but it was a large enough building to roost half a dozen eagles.

She led Crenn and Cat across the city, quickening their pace but falling short of running. It wouldn't do to bring attention to themselves, despite how distracted the city folk were acting. When they saw the entrance to the depot up ahead, Tyreta didn't allow herself to relax. There was no telling what might be awaiting them inside.

The main gate was open; a nervous-looking sentry stood barring the way. His leggings were of Hawkspur blue but his jacket had been discarded in favour of a plain white shirt. Clearly he was reluctant to openly display where his loyalties lay.

"I need to get inside," Tyreta said as she stopped outside the depot.

The sentry looked her up and down. He was barely older than she was, and his annoyance at her demand was clearly written on his pinched features.

"Depot is closed. Best you move along," he replied, before noticing Cat lurking behind Tyreta's knees. He took a step back in surprise but he still blocked the way.

Crenn leaned in. "Lady Tyreta. I think we should make our way out of the city with all haste."

The sentry's expression changed immediately. "L-Lady Tyreta? You're Tyreta Hawkspur. Of course you can come in. My apologies, I didn't recognise you looking like..."

He motioned to her civilian dress. Tyreta realised how wise it had been to change out of the animal skins given to her by the Lokai.

Beyond him, she could see there was little activity through the open gate. Normally a depot like this would have been a hive of activity.

"What's happening?" Tyreta repeated. "Why does this place look abandoned?"

The sentry glanced in through the depot doors before turning with a shrug. "We are clearing out, my lady. An Armiger Battalion has been sighted on the road to the city. Under the circumstances, the lieutenant has ordered us to empty the depot and make our way north to Wyke."

"This Armiger Battalion. Who are they loyal to?"

The sentry shrugged again. "We don't know."

"Might it have been a good idea to find out before you abandoned your posts?" she said, trying not to lose her temper with this lowly functionary. "We are a Guild of scouts, after all."

Her frustration got the better of her before he could answer, and she pushed her way through the gate, closely followed by Cat and Crenn. The sentry gave a frightened murmur as he skittered from the panther's path. Inside, the depot was all but deserted. There were less than a handful of horses still in the stable, and every administrator and scout looked to have already fled. Before she could think to shout for attention, she heard a voice echo from one of the offices.

"Don't you know who he is, you fucking dimwit? He's a bloody Marrlock heir."

It was a woman, surly and loud. In reply there was another voice, this one somewhat quieter, and Tyreta struggled to make out his words.

She crossed the courtyard toward the office. As she did so she saw a small figure sitting on the bench outside. He glanced up at her as she approached, a little embarrassed, a little mournful. His face was pale, eyes looking as though they'd seen no sleep in an age. It wasn't until Tyreta glanced down that she saw his left leg was missing below the knee, and looked to have been recently bandaged.

"I don't care what your fucking orders are," the gruff woman shouted as Tyreta reached the door and pushed it open.

Inside she saw a senior administrator sitting behind his desk. This one still wore his Hawkspur blue uniform, his face a reddening mass, sweat trickling from beneath a receding hairline.

Standing in front of him was a rough-looking woman, her face a mask of consternation, her sinewy limbs bunched as though she might leap across the desk at any moment. When she saw Tyreta, her expression changed to one of shock, and her mouth opened to reveal a set of red-stained teeth.

"Now what?" said the administrator from behind his desk. It was clear he was at his wits' end.

"Apologies for the interruption," Tyreta said, doing her best to ignore the woman. "Are you the lieutenant in charge?"

The man's jaw tightened and he clenched his fists on the desk. "Yes. I am the lieutenant in charge, for all the good it does me. Who, might I ask, are you?"

"Have you been living under a fucking rock?" the woman said, taking a step forward. "This is Tyreta bleeding Hawkspur, you dumb coot."

The administrator's expression changed from anger to confusion, then finally recognition. He rose slowly from his seat, straightening his jacket.

"Apologies, my lady. You don't look—"

"Never mind that," Tyreta replied. "I need transportation. But by the look of things that's going to be difficult."

"It is, Lady Tyreta," the lieutenant replied. "We have only one wagon left to spare. Our last eagle flew the aerie yesterday."

"One wagon will do," Tyreta said, eager to get out of Candlehope before they were recognised by less friendly eyes. Or at least before an Armiger Battalion arrived bringing the Ministry's wrath.

The administrator nodded, rushing outside. Tyreta followed as he barked orders across the courtyard, and in short order a hitched wagon was brought from a shed. While the stable hands began to harness a pair of horses to the yoke, the woman came to stand beside her.

"We're heading your way," she said under her breath, gesturing to the one-legged man sitting on the bench. He looked nervous, fiddling with the poorly constructed crutches at his side.

"And what way is that?" Tyreta replied, suddenly suspicious of this woman who'd managed to recognise her so quickly.

"I imagine you're going north. To Wyke. I reckon that's where Lady Rosomon is headed."

"Why so eager to join my mother?"

The woman stood to attention. "I am Lieutenant Stediana Walden of the Talon. Recently under the command of... of your brother Conall."

Tyreta swallowed at the mention of her brother's name, much louder than she would have wanted.

"Conall? Where is he now?"

The woman looked downcast. "We were on a ship from Agavere when we hit the recent storm. Ship sank along with most hands. Only a few people managed to get on the lifeboat. Conall wasn't one of them."

Tyreta felt her sudden elation fade, to be replaced with a dull ache in her chest. "He's dead?"

The woman shrugged. "I can't say for sure. Knowing your brother..."

It was obvious she was trying to put a shine on the fact Conall was lost. First Fulren exiled, now both her brothers gone. Tyreta had never needed get back to Wyke so badly. She had to find her mother.

The stable hands finished with the yoke and harness, before turning expectantly to Tyreta. With a nod of thanks to the beleaguered administrator, she signalled for Crenn to climb into the driver's seat. She and Cat jumped into the back, but before she could ask Crenn to get moving, her attention was drawn back to the woman and her one-legged companion.

Could she trust them? If this woman spoke true, she had been one of Conall's loyal scouts. Surely the more of them there were on the road, the safer they'd be.

"Come on then," she said. "Wyke's a long way, and the road could be dangerous."

The woman offered a nod of thanks as she helped her companion into the back of the wagon. Tyreta had to pull him up and he struggled into his seat before glaring with concern at the panther opposite him. Cat chewed at the edge of one of his crutches before he wrenched it from her jaws.

Crenn slapped the flanks of the horses with the reins, and they trundled from the depot.

"What did you say your name was?" Tyreta asked.

"Lieutenant Stediana Walden," the woman replied. "But everyone calls me Sted."

"Did my brother die bravely, Sted?" She asked it without thinking, hoping the answer was yes. At least then she'd be able to tell her mother Conall had died for something.

"He saved my life on that boat," Sted replied. "Donan's too. But don't be too sure he's dead. I wouldn't put it past Conall Hawkspur to have wormed himself out of that fix. Most likely he's washed up on a beach somewhere full of half-naked whores and more booze than he can fill his belly with."

She didn't sound too convinced by her own words. Then again, if anyone could survive a storm at sea and come out the other side dry as a desert, it would be Conall.

Tyreta watched the streets of Candlehope roll by until eventually they left through the main gates and turned north along the coast road. To the west, in the distance, she could see a rising dust cloud as an army marched closer. Looked like they were fortunate to get out when they did.

Maybe her luck was starting to change. Maybe it was too early to tell.

CONALL

His hands were bound in front of him, the rope fastened in a complex knot he didn't recognise. Conall reckoned it would be impossible to untie unless you were the sailor who'd done the knotting. Not that he'd have made a run for it, even without his hands bound—the men at each side of him didn't look like they'd brook any nonsense of that nature.

Tulsen was the scariest bastard Conall had ever laid eyes on. He walked around without a shirt, scarred and sunburned torso on display for all to see. If that wasn't intimidating enough, his face looked like it had been set on fire and put out with a mallet. At Conall's other shoulder was Broad Yon, a massive ape of a man, shovel-fisted and lantern-jawed, and only marginally less frightening than Tulsen. Conall wasn't of a mind to piss either of them off.

They led him from the harbour at Argon Kyne without fuss or bluster, and Conall risked a glance back at the ship. Despite not knowing what waited for him in this city of Iperion Magna, he was still relieved to be out of the *Grimhide*'s brig. It had been freezing at night and like an oven in the day, and stank all the way through both.

At the edge of the dock he could see Mortivern Keelrunner talking to a gaggle of robed men. Conall could only assume they were what passed for harbourmasters in this strange place. He hadn't had a chance to thank Mortivern for his hospitality and now never would, not that he'd be recommending the room service.

Whatever he'd expected to be waiting at Argon Kyne, this most definitely wasn't it. It was hot, that was for sure, and reminded him a little of the bleak landscape surrounding Agavere. But where the northern port of the Karna Frontier had been set in a red baking desert, Argon Kyne had a quaint beauty to it. Palm trees lined the main promenade from the dock and there was a sweet smell of spiced meats wafting on the air, where Agavere had only stunk of twelve-day-old shit. Yellow birds whistled from the trees and even the stray cats and dogs that stalked their path looked well-groomed. Were he here under different circumstances, Conall might well have enjoyed the place. As it was, his stomach was tied in as tight a knot as the one at his wrists.

"Look," he said to Tulsen as they bustled him farther into the city, past the whitewashed buildings that lined the street. "I tried to tell you, I'm Conall Hawkspur. Heir to the Hawkspur Guild. I'd be worth a lot to you if you sail me along the coast and drop me at Dreadwall. You don't even have to dock, I could swim the rest of the way."

Tulsen kept his beady eyes fixed on the path ahead. "You're worth enough to us here."

"No, you don't understand. I'm talking riches like you've never seen. My mother would pay a king's ransom to get me back. I can assure you—"

"You know what?" Tulsen said, dragging Conall to a stop. "You'll be more valuable to me if you shut the fuck up."

The grim sailor reached behind him and pulled a short length of rope from the back of his leggings.

"Wait—" was all Conall managed to say before Tulsen secured the rope about his mouth.

It was fastened tight, another of those sailor's knots to keep him quiet, but it didn't stop him trying. As they all but dragged him farther down the street, past an array of amused faces taking delight in his discomfort, Conall continued with a desperate tirade of muffled gibberish. As he saw what awaited him at the end of the tree-lined promenade, he finally fell silent.

The marketplace was huge. Hundreds of people milled about the vast plaza, interspersed with raised podiums on which the market's business took place. This was no trading hub for spices, or meat, or textiles. Upon every podium waited a sorry-looking slave being bartered for by the eager crowd.

Tulsen and Broad Yon dragged him forward through the throng. At the far side of the market, Conall could see a seemingly endless line of children waiting for their turn at a distant stage. Here were women standing naked, being viewed like so much meat. There were men being slapped and prodded, their teeth examined to assess how healthy they were. And surrounding them all was a menagerie of buyers, some robed, some half-naked like Tulsen. Others wore embroidered tunics, or intricately woven gowns. Everyone stood spellbound by the spectacle—this traffic of human misery, awaiting the lottery that would dictate how their lives might end.

On seeing what was in store, Conall struggled against Broad Yon's grip, but he might as well have been trying to escape an iron manacle. He squealed from behind his gag, but it was pointless. His fate was sealed, and all the whining in the world wasn't getting him out of this.

Tulsen strolled up to a short man with a bald, round head. In one hand was a sheaf of papers, which he examined closely, as though he were shortsighted but had not discovered the miracle of spectacles. In his other hand was a stylus that dripped ink like a bloody knife.

"One from the *Grimhide*," Tulsen said, handing over a docket in one meaty fist.

The auctioneer took it between finger and thumb before shaking the paper open. Through one squinty eye he read the words scrawled upon it.

"Salvage?" he said, looking Conall up and down.

"No, I'm not fucking salvage. I am Conall Hawkspur, heir to one of the greatest Guilds in all Torwyn."

His words came out as a muffled whine.

"He's a noisy one, that's for sure," the auctioneer replied.

Broad Yon took a step toward Conall. His punch to the gut seemed almost casual, but Conall doubled over like he'd been shot by a cannon. He snorted and groaned like an old pair of bellows about to give up the ghost. Broad Yon caught him before he could collapse to the ground, holding Conall up as he struggled to breathe.

"Very well," the auctioneer said, putting the docket with the rest of his papers. "My usual percentage will apply. His price will be added to the *Grimhide*'s account."

Tulsen gave a nod of acknowledgment before he and Broad Yon made their way back across the marketplace. Conall could only watch them go, no time for goodbyes, before two brawny thugs stepped from the crowd at the auctioneer's signal. They took hold of Conall's arms and none too gently dragged him toward one of the largest podiums.

He was thrust at the end of a queue, half a dozen slaves in front of him waiting for their turn on the huge platform. Though they wore no uniforms, Conall could see the peace was being kept by several armed men of all shapes and sizes. Each carried a different weapon—sword, axe, spear—but every one of them had a barbed scourge at their belt. Despite the chaotic nature of the slave market, no one had any desire to escape. It would have been so easy to make a run for it, but Conall had the feeling they were compliant for a reason. He had no desire to test out just how that compliance was enforced.

In front of him stood a huge burly man, a twisting tattoo of a demon rising up his neck, but his bearing was almost regal. Conall could only hope he would handle being sold like chattel in as dignified a manner, it was all he could do to stop himself running off like a chicken with its head severed. The longer he waited, the more the crowd shouted and haggled, the less dignified he felt.

Up on the podium more slaves were sold. The bidding was swift, the auctioneer an expert in his field, scanning the crowd with those beady eyes and somehow managing to spot every noisome bidder. The line of misery was whittled down in short order until eventually it was Conall's turn.

He was grabbed by two guards and bundled up the stairs. The platform offered him a view across the whole marketplace, and for the first time he had an appreciation for how mundane this setting was. They could just as easily have been bartering for livestock. He

had assumed the slave markets of Iperion Magna would be filled
with wailing, woeful souls, the damned and the cursed lamenting
their lot. All he saw was a mass of eager faces waiting to make their
purchase.

As he stood like a fatted calf, Conall began to work his jaw, desperate to loosen his gag. Perhaps if he could tell the crowd who he
was, what he was worth to the Hawkspur Guild, his fate might not
be so hopeless.

"Our last lot," the auctioneer announced to the onlookers.
"Recent salvage from the Ungulf Sea, plucked from the waves and
brought here by the crew of the *Grimhide*." He slapped Conall's arse
so hard it echoed across the market. "A fine specimen. Good for
menial work, or perhaps to take your pleasure with."

Conall gulped at that, working his jaw harder to release the gag.
The prospect of being sold for someone's pleasure made him all the
more eager to explain just how much he was worth.

"Do I hear thirty ounces of silver?"

No one in the crowd made a move. Not one hand was raised or
head nodded. He wasn't even worth thirty ounces of silver? It almost
felt as though Broad Yon had hit him in the gut again.

"All right, twenty," said the auctioneer. "There. I have twenty."

Conall didn't see who had bid, and didn't care. The gag was sliding from between his teeth. If he could just get it out of his mouth,
he could explain all this away. Maybe even be back home in a few
days, telling tales of the ugly fate he'd avoided.

"Do I hear twenty-five?" the auctioneer said. "There. Now,
thirty?"

As a hand went up at the back, the gag finally slipped from his
mouth.

"Wait!" Conall called out. The auctioneer turned to him with
an exasperated squint. "You're making a mistake. Listen to me, all
of you." A hush had descended over the crowd now. Conall paused,
waiting for the auctioneer or one of his cronies to lash him with a
whip, but when nothing happened, he took his chance.

"My name is Conall Hawkspur. I am heir to the Hawkspur
Guild. Grandson of Treon Archwind. I am a man of much value in

Torwyn. A prince, you might say. If any one of you were to return me to my homeland, I would see you richly rewarded. You would live like a king. A hundred ounces of silver will look like a pile of horseshit compared to the riches you'll be lavished with."

He stopped, listening to the silence that had fallen over the crowd. The auctioneer glared up at him through that one unblinking eye. The spectators in the crowd seemed to be waiting for him to say something more profound, as the other slaves looked on in confusion.

Then, as though they had just got the joke, the crowd burst out laughing. Conall wasn't sure what hurt the most, his obvious humiliation or the realisation he was not going to be saved by some rich benefactor who might sail him back home.

The auctioneer turned to the crowd as the laughing died down. "There, you see what a jester he is. Surely that's raised the price. Do I hear thirty ounces of silver?"

A dark-sleeved hand slowly rose into the air. Conall saw its owner was a tall, slender man bedecked in a gown of purple. He resembled a praying mantis made human, gazing at Conall with deep sunken eyes, yellow teeth just visible in a lipless mouth.

"Thirty ounces from Ukhtra," called the auctioneer, before turning to Conall and whispering, "He's a fucking degenerate; I don't envy having him as my master."

Conall swallowed hard as someone else raised their hand.

"Thirty-five," called a woman's voice.

He could just see her amid the crowd. She was old, her face gaudily painted with kohl, long bejewelled fingers protruding from the sleeves of her velvet gown. Not the most attractive prospect for a mistress, but it would probably be less painful than whatever Ukhtra the pervert had in store.

"Do I hear forty?" the auctioneer asked.

Ukhtra raised his hand. He and the old woman traded bids in a brief exchange. Forty-five, fifty, fifty-five, sixty.

"Sixty-five?" came the auctioneer's next call. This time the woman did not raise her hand. "No more bids?"

Conall glared at the woman, willing her to buy him, trying not to look at the hungry face of Ukhtra, desperate not to think what

might await him if he were bought by a man even this wily auctioneer thought was a deviant.

The woman looked back, and offered a nonchalant shrug.

"Well then," the auctioneer said with finality. "It looks like this
foreign jester has been—"

"One hundred ounces!" came a call from the crowd.

There was a sudden rousing among the spectators. They glanced
around for the bidder, but no one could spot who it was, least of all
Conall.

"One hundred ounces of silver," said the auctioneer. "Does Ukhtra have a higher bid?"

Please no, thought Conall. Ukhtra offered him a final look of disappointment before shaking his head.

"Then sold, to the man from Arcturius," announced the auctioneer, whilst simultaneously scrawling on his sheaf of parchment with
the over-inked stylus.

Before he could try to identify who his buyer was, Conall was
grabbed by two guards, who bundled him from the platform and
away from the crowd.

At the edge of the marketplace was a row of cages. Within them
were masses of slaves, all hunkered together, and above each cage
hung a sign bearing the name of their new owner. Conall was dragged
toward one that bore the word *Arcturius* above it in angular script. Not
someone's name. A city.

He had heard of Arcturius before—a frontier city on the edge of
the Drift, about which there were many horrific tales. It was a city
ruled by one of the four Scions of Iperion Magna, but for the life of
him Conall couldn't remember which one. If that was where he was
bound, he truly was damned.

The guards bundled him inside and slammed the cage door shut.
Mercifully, it stood in the shadow of a tall whitewashed wall, out of
the sun. Within the cage were several other figures and Conall could
only assume they had also been bought by this "man from Arcturius."

Two thin vagabonds sat in one corner, deep in conversation. They
glared at Conall as he was thrown inside, and he quickly looked away
rather than draw their attention. In another corner sat a woman, hair

tied in braids, arms crossed over her knees. She stared at the ground as though praying, but Conall reckoned they were beyond the help of the gods now.

Leaning against the side of the cage, his thickly muscled arms threaded through the bars, was a fourth prisoner. He looked across at Conall as the cage door was locked behind him, and offered a wry nod. Strange to see a friendly gesture in a place like this, but Conall still didn't have the courage to strike up a conversation. It was best to keep his mouth shut and his eyes open. Danger was everywhere, and it could come from the owner of a friendly face just as readily as a hateful one.

As the afternoon wore on and the sun went down, the slave market began to thin out. The cages to the right and left of his own were emptied, those slaves shackled together and led off to meet their new owners. When night fell, and they were the last group in any of the cages, hooded warriors approached from the dark. Conall shielded his eyes from the bright light of their torches as the cage door was unlocked.

"Out," said a grim voice.

When no one else made a move, Conall took it upon himself to be the first to obey. He was followed by the burly man, along with the woman and the two other wretches. The five of them lined up alongside each other, as a small figure stepped into the light.

He pulled back his hood reverently, revealing a round face, hair greased back in neat, slick strands, and a smile of perfect white teeth. Big friendly eyes flashed in the flickering torchlight.

"Greetings," the man said. "My name is Baenre Mokhtar. I am the man from Arcturius. You all now live at my pleasure. Your continued survival relies entirely on your obedience. I trust I do not have to explain any further what that might mean?"

There was silence. No one was stupid enough to question this man Baenre; they all knew what he was saying—try to escape and you'll die quick.

"Good. Then we have a long journey ahead of us. Arcturius awaits."

With that, the five prisoners were bundled in a row toward the eastern extent of the city. Conall could see little in the dark until they reached a torchlit space before an open gateway. A caged wagon sat waiting for their arrival, driven by a team of six bulls.

As he was forced into the back, taking his place on the uncomfortable wooden seat, Conall realised that the journey to Arcturius from Argon Kyne would take him closer to home. Something to be grateful for, at least. All he had to do was work out how to escape without being hacked to bits, then make his way across the Drift.

Maybe best to take this one step at a time. First, he had to survive the journey to Arcturius.

LANCELIN

His horse snorted in protest as he urged it onward, kicking it harder along the forest path. He had ridden through the Alderwood for almost a night and day without stopping, and knew the beast needed to rest. There was no time to tarry though, and despite its suffering he drove it to greater effort.

So far fortune had favoured him as he made his way northwest toward the Forge. Lancelin hadn't stumbled upon any patrols, nor been spotted by civilians wandering the roads. Not that it mattered, he was just a lone traveller after all. If anyone tried to stop him, if he encountered brigands or an Armiger unit, they would regret getting in his way.

As much as he tried to retain his focus, to concentrate on the task at hand, he could not remove thoughts of Rosomon from his mind. Her face haunted him, that look of loss and sorrow. For years they had snatched their moments when they could, and he had pushed down the pain of being kept a dark secret, grateful for the time they had managed to steal. Now, seeing her grief at Fulren's loss, he would gladly have sacrificed every stolen minute of joy just to see her smile. But he knew she would never smile again.

Fulren was gone. That thought made Lancelin grasp the reins tighter, digging heels to the horse's flanks. The son he had known for only a few short days, the man he might have at least shared a bond of friendship with, had been taken from him. As much as he fought against his grief, this was a battle he knew he could never win.

Lancelin shook his head, trying to clear it of those thoughts. They would only make him weak, distracted. He had to focus, had to be wary of his surroundings. Rosomon had given him another task, and again he was determined to succeed. His journey to Nyrakkis had seemed impossible, but he had overcome every obstacle. Surely this time would be easier, and the Ironfalls would gladly join them in their fight.

Before he could begin to calculate the odds, his horse galloped from the western extents of the Alderwood and out onto open pasture. The Seminarium stood not a mile from the forest, a tower reaching to the clear blue sky, dominating the landscape like a hallowed sentinel.

He reined in the horse, allowing it a moment of respite, listening to it pant and snort as he regarded the vast stronghold. It was the greatest military academy in all Torwyn, where those worthy enough might attempt to gain the rank of swordwright. Many tried. Few succeeded. Lancelin had been one of those blessed few, and the memory of his time there, of what he had suffered, of what he had sacrificed, came back to him in a wave of memories, both good and bad.

This was where he had grown into a man. Where he had learned his trade and pledged himself to an emperor. An emperor he had failed, but now was his chance to make amends. Might the Seminarium be another place to gather allies?

Lancelin kicked his horse, guiding it toward the tower at a trot. The central spire rose two hundred feet, its outer wall solid and grim against the flat pastureland that surrounded it. An imposing monolith closed to the rest of the world, but as he drew closer he saw that the main gates stood open.

Again he reined his horse to a stop. It was curious enough that the gates to this redoubt should lie open, more curious still that there was no one guarding them.

He should have moved on, should have forgotten his past and the memories of this place. Instead, he urged the horse onward through the gates to be greeted by an empty courtyard. Bushes lined a path to the doors of the tower, but there were no attendants. No serfs, no sentries.

Warily he dismounted, keeping his hand on the hilt of his sword as he tethered the horse and approached the main door. It was closed, a solid barrier of oak banded with iron. Relief carvings of the Guild symbols stared at him accusingly, as though reminding him what had happened at the Anvil, that the very foundation on which Torwyn was built lay in peril. Still he stepped forward, pushing the door, expecting it to be barred. With a creak of hinges, it opened inward.

Lancelin stepped through to see a long empty hallway. It was unadorned, bare walls, bare floor. Everything about the place was austere. A grim habitat for a grim lifestyle, and he remembered it well. All that existed in this place was the discipline of the sword, and it was taught in a climate of hardship. Its entire function was to whittle out the weak.

A staircase twisted up around the edge of the huge circular wall, but Lancelin ignored it, walking forward though the archway to the grand training yard. The Garden of Pain, some of them called it.

Abandoned racks of weapons lined the walls as far as the eye could see. Axes and polearms were interspersed between row upon row of swords—bastard, long, broad, great and rapier. Dust and leaves were strewn across the floor, where normally there would be sand to catch the blood and sweat. Not a single servant to the Seminarium remained to clear it up.

Surrounding the yard, stairs rose up to viewing galleries dozens of feet above. They ran all the way to the tower's open summit, giving the centre of the training yard the look of a huge chimney if you leaned back to view it. The sun shone down through the open roof, and Lancelin paused, letting it bathe him in light, as memories of this place flooded back.

He had been beaten here. Bled here. And in turn he had made others bleed. At first he had hated it. By the time he left a swordwright, he had grown to love it.

Unable to resist, he picked up a wooden waster abandoned on the floor. It was perfectly weighted to mimic the heft and balance of a real weapon. He had not held one in over two decades. By the age of

ten every student was made to fight with a metal blade. By the age
of thirteen they were edged. He remembered the many occasions
his blood had been spilled on the sand of this yard. The Garden of
Pain was indeed well named.

"Lancelin Jagdor."

The words echoed around the tower and up to the open roof.

Lancelin flinched, reacting on instinct, twisting to adopt a defensive stance with the wooden sword, his own blade still in its scabbard. When he saw the man standing in the entrance to the training
yard, he allowed himself to relax.

Kassian Maine was approaching sixty, but he moved with the
grace of a much younger man. A warrior born. His shoulders were
still broad, waist still slim, but the hair on his head had turned to
slate grey since Lancelin had last seen him. At a funeral in the Anvil.

Treon Archwind's swordwright approached with all the confidence his rank demanded. He knew he had nothing to be wary of,
but then why would he? This man had taught the feared Lancelin
Jagdor everything he knew.

He stopped a few feet away, and Lancelin discarded the waster to
the floor. They regarded one another for a moment, but it was difficult to read the intention in Kassian's wrinkled eyes.

"It is good to see you," Kassian said.

"Good to see you too," Lancelin replied. But was it? What was
Kassian even doing here, and seemingly alone?

"No embrace for your old teacher?" Kassian asked. One side of
his mouth turned up in a smile.

Despite his misgivings, Lancelin stepped forward and the two
men grasped each other close. It was a crushing embrace, but there
had never been anything gentle about Kassian Maine.

"I am sorry I had to wait for such dark times before seeing you
again," Lancelin said.

"*Dark times* does not come close," Kassian replied. "The slaying
of the emperor was an evil deed."

"One I should have stopped. But I . . ."

Kassian slapped him on the shoulder. "You should feel no shame.
You were not even there."

Lancelin's well of regret grew deeper. "But I should have been. Protecting Sullivar was my only duty. But I was on a mission of my own indulgence."

"And if you hadn't been, you'd most likely be dead alongside him. There is no honour in needlessly wasting your life. If you had died protecting Sullivar, who would be left to avenge him?"

Lancelin took a step back, trying not to think on the implications. Trying not to wonder if he could have stopped this before it even began. To think on those who had suffered and died because he'd left the Anvil to find his son. A son who had still perished despite his efforts to save him.

"Why is this place empty?" he asked.

Kassian opened his arms as though gesturing to the obvious fact there was no one here. "Because I sent them all away. Every student, every attendant, had their own families. It would not have been right to keep them here during such a time of strife. Though this place was built by the Guilds, many of those homed here were still pious adherents to the Draconate. Some were loyal. Some not so much. It was not my place to admonish those who would not follow the Guilds, and so I sent them away. This is the Seminarium. A place of training and learning. It is not somewhere this nation's differences should be fought out."

"And yet you stayed," Lancelin said.

Kassian shrugged. "I am swordwright to a dead Guildmaster. What other place is there for a man like me? The question is, why are you here?"

"I too am swordwright to a dead master. But I have given my support to Lady Rosomon. She is headed to Wyke to form a base from which to strike back at the Ministry. I make my way to the Forge. With luck, the Ironfalls will join our cause."

Kassian nodded at the news. "No surprise you would pledge your loyalty to her."

"And what about you, Kassian? Will you join me and fight for the Guilds?"

The old swordwright turned, glancing around the Garden of Pain. It looked like he too was considering memories of the place. "I am old, Jagdor. My master is long dead, and so is his son. And I have always prayed to the Wyrms for guidance. What reason for me to get involved in this?"

"Because they will destroy everything Treon Archwind built," Lancelin replied. It was an angry retort, and he fought to retain his composure.

Kassian regarded him with a raised eyebrow. "And that's your only reason? To preserve the legacy of the Guilds? Or do you thirst to avenge your dead emperor?"

When Lancelin did not answer, Kassian took a step forward. In this huge training yard it was as though they were the only two men in the whole of Hyreme.

"Or is it something else?" Kassian's voice was quiet, almost a whisper. "Is it for her? Don't think I don't know what's between you."

"Does it matter?" Lancelin said.

Kassian raised a smile—a rare moment of mirth from the stern swordwright. "Perhaps it doesn't." He took a step back, making his way toward the wide staircase that led up from the training yard. "So tell me, Jagdor, can you still fight?"

It seemed an odd question. "The way you taught me, how could I ever forget?" He followed Kassian toward the curving staircase. "And those lessons you forged have been tempered in battle since."

They came to a rack of swords, their edges dulled. Lancelin reached for one, expecting his old tutor to try to teach one final lesson, but Kassian shook his head.

"No. You won't need that."

He led Lancelin up the stairs to the gallery above the training floor. There was a vestibule beyond that led out onto a long balcony. Lancelin could see the treetops of the Alderwood beyond it. Kassian stopped and turned to face his former pupil.

"This should suit you better than the piece of junk you're carrying." He picked up a sheathed blade from its rack.

Lancelin suddenly felt embarrassed by the blade at his side. It had been given to him before his journey to Nyrakkis—a functional enough weapon, but nothing like his sword of office, now lost forever.

Kassian threw the sword to him, and Lancelin snatched it from the air. The pommel bore the seal of Hawkspur.

"Novik steel," Kassian said. "Newly forged."

Lancelin measured the weight and heft in his hand. Without unsheathing it he knew how well it would be crafted. The sword at his side had been given to him so he could hide his identity. He would hide no longer.

He unbuckled the sword from his belt and let it drop to the floor. Taking the hilt of the Novik steel blade, he made to unsheathe it, when Kassian wrenched the sword from his own scabbard.

"Shall we?" he said.

Lancelin glanced at the blade in his former master's hand. The pommel bore the cog seal of Archwind. With it he had defended Treon till his dying day.

"Is this some kind of test?" Lancelin asked.

"Are you refusing?"

Lancelin slowly drew the sword. It was beautiful. Considering his recent pledge of allegiance to Rosomon, it was also more appropriate than the Archwind blade he had wielded for so many years.

He barely had a chance to finish admiring the steel before Kassian struck. Lancelin parried, darting back and adopting a neutral defence. His former tutor was an exemplar of the craft. There was no telling how he might attack. Best way to combat such uncertainty was to take the initiative.

Lancelin lunged forward, desperate to read Kassian's stance, but it was impossible, and his sword came up in a swift parry that rang through the vestibule. Instead of countering, the old man danced away, still light on his feet after all these years, face a blank mask bereft of emotion. There was no way Lancelin could read this opponent, but still he had to try.

They walked out onto the balcony, keeping a wary eye on one another. It stretched away thirty feet over empty air, offering a breathtaking view of the Alderwood to the east. Lancelin allowed his guard to drop for a split second, but no sooner had he done so than Kassian came at him, sword swiping down in a devastating arc. Now it was Lancelin's turn to parry—the first stroke, a second, dodging a feint before skipping back toward the edge of the balcony.

The old swordwright still displayed much vigour, much power, but it was also controlled. Every strike of his weapon was measured, efficient. As the echo of their blades drifted over the trees beyond, a wry smile crossed Kassian's face.

"Still as focused as ever. Still in control, despite the world around you falling apart."

Before Lancelin could answer, he cut in again. Though the Novik steel blade was unfamiliar in his hand, he still wielded it as though it were forged just for him. He turned Kassian's stroke, countering without thought. The old man was at pains to lean out of range and it opened a cut in his embroidered jacket.

Kassian took a step away, examining the rent in his magnificent red garb.

"You're getting old," Lancelin said. It was a measured remark, one meant to entice, to goad. Kassian did not rise to the bait, his face adopting the fighter's mask once more.

His sword came in like a bolt from a bow, but Lancelin managed to parry it. This time his counter caught nothing but empty air as Kassian dodged to the right. Now it was Lancelin's turn to back away, the initiative lost as his opponent pressed the advantage.

Their blades struck one another, cross-guards locking. There were a dozen ways to strike from such a position, but both men knew them all, and their associated counters. Lancelin pushed Kassian back and retreated, their blades ringing as he backed away against the stone balustrade. He placed a hand on it for balance, grasping a handful of grit from the top of it.

Kassian dodged back as Lancelin flung the grit in his face, swinging his sword blindly as he maintained his balance and retreated to a safe distance. As he wiped the dirt from his face, he offered Lancelin a wry look.

"I never taught you that one," he said.

"No, you didn't. Improvisation is the mark of a poor swordsman, you always said. But I've learned a trick or two since you last instructed me."

Kassian had no answer for that as the blank mask fell over his face again. He lunged, stretching his stance to the limit. Lancelin parried and countered, stretching equally as far. His old tutor was breathing heavily, only now showing his age as he adjusted his grip, holding his sword with both hands before performing a deft sequence of swings meant to put Lancelin on the back foot.

It was as though he had already lost. As though he accepted that his former pupil had now become the master, but he would not give in, even at the end. Did he want Lancelin to strike him down? To end this with tragic finality?

One swift parry and he stepped within the old man's guard, grasping his sword arm. His blade came up quick, stopping short an inch from Kassian's throat.

They both paused in that moment, like duelling statues atop the empty tower. Kassian was breathing hard, but trying his best not to show it.

"You never answered my question," Lancelin said. "Will you join me in the fight against the Ministry, or do I have to leave you here to gather dust?"

Kassian took a step back as Lancelin lowered his new blade. "Jagdor, you may be the greatest swordsman in all Torwyn, but you're still no judge of men. I was with you the moment you walked through my door."

KEARA

It was midnight as the landship pulled into the western terminal to the sound of distant bells chiming the hour. Debarking onto the platform, Keara shivered in the chill night air, wishing she'd worn a heavier coat. Pyrestone lamplights winked and buzzed as they stepped onto the main street of the Web, their carriage already waiting for them. Once they'd climbed aboard and it trundled across the cobbled street, in time to the clacking sound of ironshod hooves, Keara couldn't help but stare out of the window.

How long since she'd last been here? Could have been a decade, but nothing had changed; the place was still a shithole, ripe with the stink of decay and degradation. The faded magnificence of the buildings could still be recognised beneath the crumbling veneers, if you had an eye keen enough to see it. It was a sad testament to a time when the Web had been a city of majesty, of prosperity. How ironic it had been named after the very power the webwainers drew on, in honour of the Hallowhills' might. Now it looked worse than any slum in the Anvil, and Keara knew who they had to thank for that. It had been drummed into her since she was a girl, the man she should despise above all others even though he was long dead. Just whispering the name of Treon Archwind on the streets of the Web was likely to get you spat on, but such was the Lord of Archwind's legacy. He alone had brought the Hallowhills low, and his heirs had only prospered from it.

Well, they prospered no more. Keara had seen to that... for all the good it had done her.

She pulled the curtain back across the window. On the opposite side of the carriage, his purple jacket open to reveal his prominent gut, sat Ulger Vine. In one hand was a vial half-full with a dull red liquid, in the other a pipette he held above his tattooed eye as he vainly tried to aim the red drop.

"As if the journey from the Anvil wasn't crap enough," he grumbled. "Now I have to suffer this fucking carriage."

Finally he managed to get the drop in his eye and he blinked, smiling at the immediate sensation. Ulger Vine could never have been described as a handsome man with his shiny bald head and the web tattooed over one eye, but his smile always brightened Keara's mood. The woman sitting next to her, not so much.

Hesse Fortuna had her legs crossed, black boots shining, purple uniform tight to her slim figure. Her pinched features showed no emotion beneath her straight-cut black hair. Even at night she insisted on wearing dark eyeglasses, which only served to enhance the impression that she was an emotionless witch.

Keara could never have imagined these two miscreants would end up her most loyal webwainers, but that's what life threw at you when the choices were slim. From the entirety of the Hallowhill Guild, these were the two who had followed her most faithfully, served her most efficiently. And in times like these you didn't get to choose who was most loyal—you just accepted it, and hoped you didn't end up being knifed in the back.

With a beaming smile on his face, Ulger offered Keara the vial. Her thirst for the high had been nagging at her all day, or perhaps she just needed to settle her nerves? She reached across the carriage and took it from him—distilled redstalk that would hit the spot quicker than chewing it. There was also the added advantage that it didn't turn your teeth red. Whether she was feeling the effects of withdrawal, or just anxious as all fuck, the red drop would ease her tension. Sprinkle a little spice on the senses. Add a teaspoon of lemondew and rosemeg to her mind.

The carriage bucked every now and again, but Keara managed to time it right, a single drop falling into her right eye.

"That's the shit." Ulger laughed as she felt the narcotic properties begin to immediately take hold.

There was a rush of sensations at first: excitement in her gut, tingling in her extremities, a pleasant fuzz about the brain. As the carriage trundled on, everything dulled around the edges, her fears quickly fading away. The more her senses deadened, the more she could feel the pyrestone emanating its power all around her. She pulled back the curtain again with numb fingers, gazing at the pretty colours as the horses pulled them past shimmering streetlights. A smile crept up the side of her face as she watched the show, mesmerised by how it danced in a kaleidoscopic burlesque. Perhaps this wouldn't be so bad after all.

With a jolt the carriage came to a stop.

"We're here," said the driver from above.

Keara was brought back to earth with a rush. She had hoped the journey might at least last a little longer. Oh well—best pull herself together before meeting the old man.

Hesse wasted no time in opening the door and stepping out into the night. Keara dragged herself out of the comfortable chair and stepped down onto the cobbled street with a shudder of cold. Before her stood the rusted iron gates of the Hallowhill estate, and she resisted the urge to shake her head to clear the fug, before marching through them with Hesse and Ulger by her side.

What had once been a well-kept garden was little more than an overgrown forest of bushes and vines. Her father had not been able to afford a gardener for years, and the results were plain to see. As she picked her way past the undergrowth, the house revealed itself up ahead.

Paint was crumbling from the plaster veneers to reveal the bare redbrick beneath. The purple paint covering it had almost completely faded, making the house a stark metaphor for the decaying power of the Hallowhills. A wasted building in the wasted city of a wasted Guild.

As Keara approached the front door it opened with an ominous creak. Standing there was a grey-haired man with an imperious expression. She recognised the high-collared jacket that marked him as steward of the estate, but she didn't recognise the face.

"Welcome, ma'am," the steward said, standing aside and allowing the three of them to enter the lobby.

The smell of mothballs and rot was almost overwhelming. Most surprising of all were the candles that had been lit in place of the pyrestone lamps. As she led her friends toward the sweeping staircase that curved up to the first-floor landing, the steward placed himself in front of her.

"Lord Ingelram has made it clear he only wishes to receive his daughter, ma'am."

Keara regarded the steward. It was nice that he obeyed her father so faithfully. Still bloody annoying though.

"Where is Gloster?" she asked, wondering what had happened to the old steward she had known since she was a child.

"He was dismissed over a year ago, ma'am," the steward replied. "As was his replacement two months later. I have held the position ever since his dismissal. My name is—"

"Then I suggest you don't get too comfortable in that jacket," Keara said, walking past him and making her way toward the curving staircase.

"You might need these," said Hesse before she could mount the stairs.

Keara turned to see her looking with those beady eyes she always kept hidden, her dark eyeglasses held out in one slender hand. Of course, it was like that after the red drop—her eye would be bloodshot. It wouldn't do for her father to know what she'd been up to. That she'd succumbed to her need for narcotic stimulation. The old bastard hated any notion of weakness, and reliance on the drop was a sure sign of that.

Donning the glasses, she made her way up the stairs, deeper into the dilapidated warren of her father's house. At the top, a long corridor led off from the landing, and on the wall still hung those dusty old portraits. Each one had been turned around, to hide the rogues' gallery it displayed. Depictions of a dozen ancient Archmages, along with a parade of Hallowhill Guildmasters, all turned to the wall.

Keara guessed that her father could no longer bring himself to look upon those faces as he stalked the halls of his estate in disgrace. Seeing those icons of the past was a constant reminder of how far he had allowed the name Hallowhill to sink into ignominy.

At the end of the corridor was the main lounge, and as Keara strode the darkened hallway toward it she could see the squalor that lay in wait. A musty room, a threadbare carpet, not a marble veneer or wooden panel left unmarred. At least there were pyrestone lights here, though they burned dimly, some of them flickering with erratic power. The plaster was chipped and falling from the walls, the old couches shabby and dust-layered. The carpet so rimed with dirt she would be sure to wipe her feet on the way out.

When she entered the lounge, she saw that there were no portraits here, just stark squares on the dirty wall where they had hung. A fire crackled beneath the mantelpiece, and before it sat her father. Lord Ingelram's back was to her, but she could see his hand clutching the arm of the chair like a veiny claw. With some trepidation, she walked forward to stand beside that battered leather armchair, waiting in silence to be received.

Ingelram stared into the flames, a crippled old man, his hair as threadbare as the carpet, the flesh of his scalp dotted with liver spots and pimples. For a moment, Keara wondered how much of a chore it must have been for her mother to bed this creature. To share her every waking moment with him as he pawed at her. She glanced to the mantel, where her mother's likeness had hung for so many years, seeing that even that cherished portrait had been removed. Her father had not once mentioned her name since she'd disappeared years earlier. Rumour was he'd had Lucasta Hallowhill murdered for her infidelity, but Keara had never allowed herself to believe that. More likely she had simply abandoned her loathsome husband. Keara liked to think her mother was living happily somewhere with a handsome, vigorous lover. Perhaps a lie she told herself, but sometimes lies were all you had to stay sane.

"So you have deigned to return home," Ingelram said, still staring into the fire. His voice was ragged, as though he had phlegm to clear from his throat but couldn't be bothered.

Keara swallowed for him. "I have. With good news, Father. Sullivar is dead. The Guilds have been overthrown. Our alliance with the Draconate has sealed us a historic victory."

"Really?" he replied, still not looking at her. Hardly the hearty congratulations she deserved.

"Yes, Father. I have achieved what no one could since Treon Archwind cast us down into the gutter. I have made the name Hallowhill one to be respected."

That was enough to turn his head. Ingelram gazed up at her with those rheumy grey eyes of his, wearing an expression that fell a little short of disdain.

"Take those ridiculous things off your face," he said.

Keara was reluctant. Should she leave them on? Defy him and spare her embarrassment? Not that she had ever defied her father's word before now.

Slowly she reached up and took off the eyeglasses before gazing back at him as confidently as she could manage, not even trying to hide her bloodshot eye and the clear evidence of what she had been up to.

"Still taking that destructive narcotic, I see." She could detect neither anger nor annoyance in his tone, as though he couldn't have cared less if she destroyed herself with drugs. "Do you think it will give you more power? More steadfastly attach you to the web? Or are you still just beholden to your hedonism?"

Keara didn't answer. There was no point. Neither excuse nor legitimate reason would change Ingelram's opinion of her. She could have handed him every Guildmaster's head on a golden platter and he would still have treated her like the disappointment she was.

"So you have achieved something none of us ever could, have you?" he said, looking back at the fire now he had seen all he needed to. "You truly think you have raised us up, back to our rightful place?"

What was she supposed to say? She had done more for the Hallowhills than Ingelram ever had. More than anyone in two generations.

"I have—"

"You have made us beholden to religious fanatics!" Ingelram spat. His phlegm dislodged as he sprayed his ire, and he hawked, spitting a glob into the flames. "The webwainers were once power-ful throughout Hyreme. We ruled as Archmages. Held this land in the palm of our hand. And now? Now we are servants, scurrying from one master to the next. We should be the ones to rule, not the Ministry or the Guilds."

"Father, this is the first step. The first victory. From here we can—"

He silenced her with a hateful look. "The first step? I command you to take the Anvil and all you can do is return to me with talk of taking a first step? A step is not enough, girl. None of this is enough. Nyrakkis has its sorceress queen. Four mighty Scions hold the city-states of Iperion Magna, and yet here *we* sit in our own filth. Tor-wyn is a nation ruled by bureaucrats, merchants and tinkers. It is the Hallowhills who should rightfully sit upon the throne."

You mean, you should, Keara thought. But she would never have the courage to say it out loud. "We have won, Father. The Guilds are beaten. The bureaucrats and tinkers rule no longer."

"No, they don't," Ingelram replied, gripping tighter to the arms of his threadbare chair. "The priests do."

"They will not rule for long. The Hallowhills will rise, in time." She was trying to persuade herself as much as her father, even though she had no idea how that might happen. "But for now we have enough. Once we—"

"Enough! Enough? That's all you can say? That's the limit of your ambition? It will never be *enough*, girl. I will not hand this nation over to dragon-worshipping zealots. I will not dethrone one unwor-thy gaggle of rulers only to see them usurped by another. It will only be enough when Torwyn sits in the palm of the Hallowhills."

He paused, taking a deep breath and raising a hand to grasp his doublet, as though feeling for the erratic beat of his desiccated heart.

Keara had wanted this meeting to go much differently. She had hardly expected him to laud her with compliments, let alone thanks, but to be berated after sacrificing so much...

As she watched this spiteful old man she was almost desperate to admit how she truly felt about him. He had no webwainer powers, as few men did. It was not he who had risked his life for their vic-tory. Not Ingelram Hallowhill who had made bargains and promises and struck deals with zealots so they might prosper. It was her. And what more did he want her to do? Open her veins to rejuvenate his dying Guild? She should have said all that and more, but Keara had never been brave enough to argue with this old man.

"What would you have me do, Father?" she asked. The words tasted sour on her lips. She sounded weak, like a lowly servant, lower even than the sycophantic steward who had let her in.

"I would have you return to the Anvil," Ingelram said, all his ire spent. "I would have you secure power for your Guild. I would have you raise the Hallowhills to prominence, even if it is on the corpse of the Archlegate himself."

Keara stifled a sigh of frustration. "And how would you have me do that?"

Her father turned to her again, those corpse-like eyes glaring right through her. His lips turned up at the edges, and she could see the rotten yellow teeth within that unholy maw.

"You are nothing if not resourceful, daughter. I'm sure you'll work it out. But to help you, I've decided a gift was perhaps in order."

He gestured with one crooked finger. Keara looked where he was pointing, across the room to a faded old cabinet. Atop it was a small wooden casket. She moved to it, undoing the clasp and opening the lid. Inside were two daggers—heirlooms she had coveted for years, ancient weapons manufactured before Ingelram's grandfather was even born. Both daggers were etched with the spider symbol of the Hallowhills, so masterfully crafted it almost took her breath away. One was straight-edged, a yellow pyrestone set in the pommel. The other was curved, blue pyrestone housed where the quillon met the blade.

"Father," she said, turning back to him. "I don't—"

"No. You don't. But you'll take them anyway and make use of them as you see fit."

He turned back to the flames, waving her off with a withered hand.

No further instruction was necessary, and Keara was of no mind to linger. She took both blades and turned, leaving the warmth of the lounge and the flickering lights. Leaving the corpse of the Guildmaster, her hateful bastard father, behind her. But she could never leave him behind. He would always be there, lingering like a ghoul. Judging. Disdaining. Infesting every scheme she could devise with doubt.

When she reached the bottom of the stairs, the steward was still waiting patiently.

He bowed. "I hope Lord Ingelram—"

"Fuck off," she breathed as she swept by him and opened the door, hearing that familiar creak of ancient hinges. Her friends were waiting outside beneath the dim porchlight.

Hesse sat silently on the edge of the stone fence, her legs crossed. Keara handed over her dark eyeglasses and the woman placed them back on her nose. Ulger leaned against a chipped marble pillar, plucking the petals from a yellow weed he had pulled from the mess of a garden.

"That was quick," he said, glancing over his shoulder. "What now?"

Keara didn't tarry, walking down the porch stairs and heading back across the garden. She gripped the daggers tight, one in each hand, feeling the weight of them, their heritage and all it symbolised.

"Now, we go back to the Anvil."

CONALL

He awoke with a jolt to bright daylight, the grumbling wheels of the cart rattling his teeth and rousing him to stark reality. Conall couldn't remember what he had dreamed about, but then he couldn't remember falling asleep either. He wiped a line of drool from the corner of his mouth with the back of his hand, feeling the ropes still binding his wrists, a reminder of his lot.

Squinting against the sun, he took in the bleak landscape that surrounded him. There was little vegetation. Little of anything. The road looked seldom travelled as it ran away in their wake, crowded on both sides by steep rocky hills.

The others in the cage still sat in the same positions as the previous night. On one side, the two wiry men sat close together in a conspiratorial fashion, talking in a strange dialect. As Conall looked over, one of them glared at him suspiciously and he diverted his gaze. Usually he had to get to know someone before their animosity developed. In Iperion Magna it appeared to be the default position. If he could avoid being strangled before they reached their destination, he'd count himself lucky.

The woman still sat at the edge of the cage, arms over her knees. She stared ahead at nothing, and it was doubtful he'd get much in the way of conversation there either.

The big man who'd deigned to offer him a nod back in Argon Kyne sat opposite. He still had a smile on his face. One of those smiles that didn't look too genuine. A smile that spoke mischief. Conall nodded in his direction, trying his best to make a friend, though wary it could just as easily turn out to be an enemy.

"Eastlander, eh?" the man said, Magnan accent thick and gruff. "You are far from home."

Wasn't that the truth. "Through no planning of my own," Conall replied. "And hopefully not for long. Do you know anything of our buyer, Baenre Mokhtar?"

The big man shrugged. "Nothing. But if we are heading to Arcturius, it is likely this Mokhtar is just a servant, rather than the buyer."

"A servant to who?"

That only prompted a laugh from the hulking prisoner. "If it is who I think, you might soon wish you'd been enslaved to that old pervert Ukhtra."

The man's eyes lit up and he laughed once more. None of the other prisoners seemed to find it amusing. As much as Conall wanted to find out who his new owner was, he didn't have the heart to pursue it. Maybe it was best he didn't know. Maybe if he could persuade Baenre it was in his best interest to let him go, he wouldn't have to find out at all.

"I am Ramassen," said the big man, slapping his broad chest. "They call me the Ox."

"It's a pleasure," Conall replied, though it most definitely wasn't. "I am Conall Hawkspur. Tell me, how did you find yourself in this cage?" He wasn't particularly interested but it might help pass the time. It might also help gain an ally, and Conall was in sore need of those.

Ramassen smiled again, clearly relishing the opportunity to talk about himself. "I have lived most of my life in one cage or another, Conall Hawkspur. From a youth I fought in the death pits of Tallus Rann. My reputation was renowned throughout the western arenas. After I had defeated all my foes, and left many a slave master poor, I was sold into the service of the Lord of Venator Gate. That was easy work. Standing around in the shiniest armour, training with the most magnificent of weapons. Strutting the streets like a king."

He stared off wistfully as though the memories gave him particular pleasure.

"Didn't work out?" asked Conall.

Ramassen shrugged. "My master was a generous lord, but even he could not suffer me fucking one of his favourite concubines. But he showed mercy, my cock and balls are still where they've always been." Ramassen grabbed his crotch as though to check he was right about that. "I was sold again. And again, and again. And eventually I found myself on the slave market of Argon Kyne. Much as you did."

"Indeed," Conall replied. "Though my route was a lot different."

He was about to tell his sorry tale when Ramassen shrugged. "I am sure."

The Ox turned in disinterest and glared through the bars. Now he had finished talking about himself the conversation was plainly over. So much for passing the time.

As the cart trundled on, pulled along by the snorting bulls, Conall found himself glancing at the lone woman. How had she found herself here among such unsavoury company? Was she also a veteran of Iperion Magna's death pits? She certainly looked as though she could fight—scars on her face, shoulders and arms swollen with sinuous muscle, and the look in her eyes told him she brooked no shit. There was a tattoo on her cheek, but Conall couldn't make out the symbol, and half her left ear was missing. It was likely she had more of an interesting tale to tell than Ramassen, but Conall didn't have the courage to ask her.

"Back at the market," said Ramassen, now bored of staring out at the arid landscape. "You said you were a prince of Torwyn. Were you lying, just to save yourself from a good fucking?"

Conall briefly thought on whether it would serve him well or ill to tell this man too much. But what did it matter now? They were both prisoners in the same cage.

"I wasn't lying, but I'm not a prince anymore," he replied. "Now I am a slave, just like you. But if I can persuade this Baenre of the truth, perhaps I have a chance at freedom. My family is wealthy. There would be a rich reward for him if Baenre were to contact my people back home."

"Then you had best persuade him quick," Ramassen replied. "For when we reach Arcturius, it won't matter if that reward is your weight in gold, or even mine, there will be little hope for you."

Conall was about to ask what he meant by that, and who was waiting for them, when the wagon lurched forward, the road sloping down into a huge quarry. They all held on to the bars of the cage for purchase as the bulls pulled them down a steep incline, and it wasn't until they reached the bottom of the ramp that the entirety of the quarry came into view.

It was a vast outpost—tents erected around the perimeter, flags fluttering in the warm breeze displaying the grim face of a demon— all fangs and no eyes in an elongated skull. Several other bull-drawn wagons were already waiting, their cages empty. Here and there along the floor of the quarry sat groups of miserable-looking slaves, surrounded by heavily armed guards.

When they drew closer, Conall could see their livery was likewise emblazoned with the eyeless demon head, shields adorned with the imagery, some showing six arms and legs sprouting from the symbol. Chains were lashed to the front of those shields and across breastplates and pauldrons. Their helms sloped to a sharp muzzle at the front, giving each one a fearfully inhuman aspect.

The cart trundled to a stop, the breathy sound of snorting bulls filling the air as the cage was approached by a group of warriors.

"Out," shouted one of them, his voice sonorous from within the helm.

The cage door was swung open and Conall rose to his feet, feeling the stiffness in his legs. He was the first to jump down, and quickly bundled across the valley floor along with the rest of the prisoners.

The other sorry-looking slaves were prodded with spears and forced to their feet, before being organised into ranks. Conall was pushed into line, with Ramassen on his left and the silent woman to his right. Glancing over his shoulder, Conall quickly counted twenty prisoners in all, surrounded by their armoured keepers. He scanned the quarry for any sign of Baenre Mokhtar, but if he was here, he had not deigned to come and greet them.

Above, several vultures wheeled in the clear sky. Could they sense impending death in the air? That idea did nothing for Conall's fast-fraying nerves as the flap of a nearby tent was pushed back.

A huge warrior stepped out into the daylight. He was stripped to the waist, olive-coloured flesh crisscrossed with livid white scars. A helm covered his head, similar to the other warriors, only his bore curved horns that swept downward over the jawline and it only housed a single socket for his left eye.

The brute strode across the sand and stopped before the ranks of slaves like a marshal on parade. One hand rested on the pommel of his curved scimitar, which sported a long ornate grip. He regarded the bedraggled prisoners for some time, his silence filling Conall with growing dread.

"My name is Orsokon. Warmaven of Arcturius." When finally he spoke, it was high pitched and singsong in timbre. That voice was so unexpected from such a beast of a man that Conall had to quell a smirk. "You are now servants of the Scion Senmonthis. Truly an honour for such pathetic scum."

At mention of the name Senmonthis, all the mirth Conall felt at that voice crumbled to ash. He thought back to his old history lessons, remembering that the Scions of Iperion Magna were legendary for their cruelty and evil. These powerful beings ruled their city-states with an iron hand, sacrificing the guilty and innocent alike in wicked blood rites. Was that the fate that awaited him? To be slaughtered on an altar for the exaltation of some ancient sorcerer? His eyes flitted around the quarry, desperate to find Baenre Mokhtar, keener than ever to explain what a grave mistake was being made.

"From here on, you will march," Orsokon continued. "The road will be hard. Not all of you will survive. Those of you that do, who prove yourself resilient enough, will be rewarded with a lifetime of servitude to the greatest Scion of Iperion Magna."

Fuck that. He was marching nowhere, and certainly not serving at the pleasure of an ageless sorcerer. Fighting back his fear, Conall stepped forward out of the line.

"There's been a mistake."

Several guards turned their helmed heads toward him before standing back at attention. The silence that followed made him realise the mistake might have been his.

Slowly, Orsokon turned to regard him through the single eye-piece in his helm. "Really?"

"If I could just speak to Baenre Mokhtar, I'm sure we can clear all this up. You see, I'm not supposed to be here. I am Conall Hawk-spur. Heir to the Hawkspur Guild of Torwyn. You'll find I am worth much more—"

Conall stopped as Orsokon moved closer. He could hear the huge warrior's breath resounding within his helm, but couldn't see his eye behind the single slit.

"Really?" Orsokon repeated.

When Conall opened his mouth to speak again, Orsokon struck him in the gut. It made the punch he'd endured from Broad Yon feel like a lover's teasing slap to the rump. The air escaped him in a single breath and his legs gave way. On his knees, Conall vainly tried to suck in air, but his lungs refused to work. All he could do was wheeze, panicking at the prospect of never drawing breath again.

There was a ring of steel as Orsokon drew his scimitar.

"My thanks for volunteering," said the huge warrior. "I will now demonstrate the price for speaking out of turn."

Conall managed to look up as the sword was raised, desperate to beg for mercy but still unable to speak. Those vultures still wheeled above, one of them squawking in anticipation of a decent meal. Orsokon prepared to strike, and in that instant Conall saw a white jewel forged into the weapon's cross-guard. It glowed with a baleful light that made Conall feel sick to his already bruised stomach.

"Wait!" a voice shouted from across the quarry.

Conall managed to suck in a little air. Not much but enough for him to breathe. Some yards away, the robed figure of Baenre Mokhtar was making his way toward them. Orsokon slowly lowered the blade, turning to face the diminutive figure. In the huge warrior's shadow, Baenre looked tiny, but Orsokon still obeyed his word.

"You have interrupted me, Mokhtar," Orsokon whined in that ridiculous voice.

Baenre grabbed Conall's arm and dragged him to his feet. "I have, great Warmaven. And for that please accept my apologies."

"How am I to instil discipline if you interfere at every turn?"

Baenre bowed his head in apology. "Surely all these recruits will be disciplined soon enough. Best we do not waste them needlessly. Especially when they might show so much promise."

Conall was flattered, but couldn't manage to speak his appreciation.

"Promise?" Orsokon said, turning his helmed head toward Conall. "I see little of that."

"Nevertheless," Baenre replied, dragging Conall away from the ranks of slaves. "I have questions for this one."

Hurriedly, Baenre guided Conall across the quarry floor, as Orsokon turned back to the other slaves and carried on his grandiose lecture. Once they were within the safety of one of the tents, Baenre lit a couple of candles before turning to Conall. There was a knife in his hand, and Conall girded himself, desperate to flee but fighting the urge.

"It is clear you have much to say for yourself, eastlander," Baenre said as he cut the ropes that bound Conall's hands.

"That's been a constant curse of mine, I'm afraid," he replied.

He hadn't realised how sharply the ropes had been digging into his wrists and he rubbed at his sore flesh. The pain in his stomach still throbbed but at least he could manage to speak.

Baenre regarded him impatiently. "You wished to speak to me. So here I am."

Now was his chance. He knew he might not get another. "I was not lying. I am Conall Hawkspur, heir to the Hawkspur Guild." He was almost getting bored of repeating himself. "My mother is Rosomon Hawkspur, Guildmaster and sister to the emperor of Torwyn. I am worth much to you alive. If you let me go, you could find yourself in receipt of a huge reward. More gold than you could carry on ten wagons." He thought for a moment about where they were bound, and it filled him with sudden dread. "Send me to Arcturius and you'll get nothing."

Baenre listened patiently, but showed no sign of being moved by Conall's generous offer. "I believe you."

Conall couldn't stifle his sigh of relief. "That's music to my ears. So you'll send me back across the Drift? Or on a boat perhaps?"

Again, Baenre displayed no emotion. "No."

Conall struggled to understand what he was hearing. "No? Did you not hear what I said? I can make you a rich man, Mokhtar. Rich beyond imagining."

Baenre shrugged. "You have no idea what I can imagine. But still, it is of no matter. You are now a slave of Senmonthis, as am I. You belong to her, as do I. Were I to cheat her of her prize for the promise of a great reward, no matter how large it was, my life would be forfeit. There would be nowhere I could spend these riches you speak of without looking over my shoulder for the rest of my days. And she would find me. That is certain."

"Then when we get to Arcturius, you need to tell her. Tell Senmonthis what I'm worth."

That brought a snigger from Baenre. "She already knows what you are worth, Conall Hawkspur. That's why I was sent to find you."

Two guards entered the tent, as though at Baenre's unspoken order.

"Wait," said Conall, as Baenre waved an arm and the guards grasped him. "What do you mean? Why were you sent to find me?"

"Talking is over, Hawkspur. And Arcturius is a long way off. I suggest you get some rest before your journey."

He was bustled from the tent before he could ask anything else. Outside, Orsokon had finished making his introductions to his new recruits, if that's what they even were. Conall was shoved toward where they sat in the open, crowded around a rock half-buried in the centre of the quarry. There his legs were kicked from under him, and he fell unceremoniously on his arse.

Everyone was eating from wooden plates, but it seemed Conall was to go without.

"How did that go, Prince Hawkspur?" Ramassen said with a grin, before licking the last morsels from his plate.

"It could have gone better," Conall replied, feeling his stomach churn with hunger.

Suddenly someone was holding a plate of grey gruel under his nose. Conall recognised the woman he'd shared his cage with all the way from Argon Kyne.

"Thank you," he said, taking what was offered.

Before he could even think to ask her name, he was shovelling the foul-tasting dreck in his mouth with his fingers. By the time he'd finished, and had lowered himself to licking his own plate like Ramassen, the sky was beginning to darken.

"I am Conall," he said to the woman when he'd finally finished.

Some of the other prisoners were already bedding down on the earth as night drew in.

"I gathered that," the woman replied gruffly. "You've been telling anyone who will listen since Argon Kyne. I am Nylia of Amenak."

"It's nice to make your acquaintance, Nylia. Although it would have been a lot nicer under different circumstances." He looked around at the guards lurking on the edge of the camp. Thankfully there was no sign of Orsokon. "So, how did you find yourself in this predicament?"

She stared into his eyes and shrugged. "Much like you, my prince. A mistake. One I may live to regret. But then again, who knows?" With that, she turned her back on him and laid herself down on the hard earth.

So much for making a new friend. With no other option, Conall lay down and used his arm for a pillow. There was a long walk coming. Friends or not, he'd best get ready for it.

ROSOMON

Their trek northward had been met by bitter winds. Even sheltered within the walls of the abandoned boatyard there was still a biting cold. She watched through the window of an administration building as her followers built a camp amid the workhouses and machinery. Every piece of artifice stood unattended, abandoned by those workers forced to flee in these uncertain times.

The Hawkspur Guildlands had grown more sparsely populated the farther north they travelled. More and more refugees filed past along the coast road, although some had abandoned their flight and joined her, swelling the numbers of her army. It would still not be enough, and now, as she stood overlooking the carcasses of half-built boats, listening to the sound of the canal as it ran off toward the sea, she could only consider the folly of all this.

No word from Marshal Rawlin, nor from Lancelin. Wyke lay less than twenty miles to the north, and still Rosomon had no idea how she might win it back. As for Tyreta and Conall, she had done all she could to exorcise them from her mind, and still they haunted her. But at least there was a chance they lived. Everywhere she looked she saw Fulren's ghost: in the face of a refugee, or one of her artificers, even when she closed her eyes. It was during quiet times such as this she doubted herself the most, but there was no way she could let her followers know it. She had to act like a general now—a warlord. Whatever that meant.

A torch illuminated the dark of the office. In the doorway she could see the bulky frame of Imperator Fray, torch in hand. He entered, illuminating the interior with the bright flame, showing the empty place in all its ignominy. This had once been a chamber of industry, and now it stood impotent and unused. Was that the fate awaiting all of Torwyn? Not if Rosomon could help it.

"My lady," Ianto said, with a curt bow of his head. "Your scout has returned."

Behind him in the shadows, Rosomon saw Faiza step forward. She knelt in front of her, bowing her head solemnly before rising.

"Lady Rosomon. I have patrolled Wyke's perimeter as you ordered, and the news is as we feared. The Ursus Battalion have consolidated their occupation of the city."

"Defences?" Rosomon asked, bracing herself for bad news.

"All entrances are guarded, the walls to north and south heavily patrolled. There is no way in without a fight."

This was no news. Rosomon had known she would face a determined enemy if she was to take back Wyke. The only surprise was they had not already been confronted by the Archlegate's servants.

"I did manage to find a number of refugees though," continued Faiza. "People of Wyke who stood against the battalion and managed to escape. I have brought them with me."

"What did they have to say about the situation in the city?" asked Rosomon, eager for any news that might give her an edge.

"They are keen to tell you in their own words."

"Very well. Let's hear what they have to say."

Ianto led her out into the main complex of the boatyard. Fires had been built and food was being shared by what passed for her army. Though their numbers had increased on the journey north, it still filled her with little optimism. Many of the refugees had joined them because they had nowhere else to go, and few of them were fighters.

They approached a fire in the shadow of the boatyard wall. Around it were hunkered a dozen men and women. Some of them had bandaged wounds, and there was little conversation as they stared into the fire, eating rations given them by the Titanguard. As she approached, one of the men rose to his feet. Before he took to his knee, Rosomon noted his neck-length hair and moustache. He had the broad shoulders of a warrior, but he did not hold himself like a fighter, his gait more lumbering.

"There is no need to kneel before me," she said. "Please, stand and tell me what you know."

He did as commanded. "My lady, I am Rasmuth Reeve. Formerly a senior landship engineer at the terminal of Oakhelm. When all this began, me and the rest of my engineering team headed straight to Wyke. We had no idea the Ursus Battalion would be so quick to follow us. We fought them, for the emperor and for the Guild." There was a sudden spark in his eye as though he had relished the opportunity.

"That was brave of you, Rasmuth," Rosomon replied, wanting to grasp his shoulder, to hug him in thanks, but she knew it would not be appropriate. She had to maintain a distant air of authority. "What happened after?"

"We stood no chance. Many of us died. Many of us were captured. They kept us in the city gaol—no food or water. If we hadn't broken out, I reckon they'd have let us starve. A patrol hunted us toward the Alderwood till they gave up. Lucky your scout found us when she did."

Rosomon felt her jaw tighten at the news. There was no way these ordinary men and women could ever have beaten the Armiger. They should have stayed in their homes and waited for help. Yet they hadn't. They had taken a stand, shown bravery, and all for her and the Guilds.

"Your courage is appreciated, Rasmuth. And that of your fellows."

"The Guilds have given everything to us, my lady. It was our duty to take a stand. We will fight for you until our last breath. The Ministry ain't never done nothing for us, and by the Guilds, we'll take the fight right back to them the next chance we get."

Rosomon was about to thank him for his loyalty, but the words stuck in her throat. All she could do was nod her gratitude and turn away. Shame began to overwhelm her as she walked from the fire. For too long she had wallowed in grief, no matter how much she told herself she was fighting it, and all the while people were dying to defend her Guild.

"Imperator," she said, as she made her way from the campfires and beyond the edge of the camp. "Your thoughts?"

The canal flowed by, singing a soft tune as the moon rose huge and fat in the dark sky.

"The engineer, Reeve, paints a grim picture," Ianto said. "We're in danger here. The city is only—"

"I am aware how close we are to Wyke," Rosomon replied, clenching her hands together for strength as much as warmth. "And I'm also aware it is a city in bondage. The odds are stacked against us, but we must act."

Ianto shook his head. "My lady, I am as concerned by the engineer's tale as you are, but we have to wait for reinforcements. We simply do not have the numbers."

"I cannot wait, Ianto. Not while my people suffer. I have to do something."

"I can't guarantee your safety if we move farther north."

"My safety is not what matters now. Too many people have already given so much. You heard him, he is an engineer but he fought anyway. People are already dying. Rasmuth Reeve is not a man of privilege or standing, and yet he stood up to the Ministry with nothing but a few of his fellows. It is my duty to do the same."

"It is not your duty to sacrifice yourself needlessly."

Ianto's words cut through the dark and struck right at her heart. He was right. She was allowing her emotions to get the better of her. Letting her frustrations force her into rash decisions. She had to think. More importantly she had to listen.

"So what do you suggest?" she asked.

The young imperator shook his head. "With the refugees we have gathered we have nowhere near enough men to stage a frontal attack. Even if we assume a modest number of Armiger troopers, they are better trained and better equipped than we are. There are simply not enough of us."

"Not yet," she said, remembering Rasmuth's tale of defiance in the face of overwhelming odds. "Were I able to slip into the city, to spread word of my arrival and grow support, we could stage a revolt. The people of Wyke would surely follow were I to lead them. There are thousands of people in the city, enough to defeat any Armiger."

Ianto considered the suggestion, his expression turning grave. "That may well ensure a victory over the Ursus Battalion, but the casualty rate would be too high. I am sorry, my lady, but considering every option, the best outcome would be to wait for other allies to arrive."

Of course he was right. Rosomon bit back her frustration, knowing her rashness had once again made her want to act before considering all the options. She was no general, and every step of her journey north had proven the truth of it.

"I am grateful for your advice, Ianto. I would be lost without it."

"Then please, my lady, heed this advice: we have travelled too close to the city already, and put ourselves in needless danger. We should retreat back along the road, find somewhere to hide—"

"No," said Rosomon. "I will not run. I have come too far to take a step back now."

Ianto looked like he might argue further, when one of the guards from the perimeter came toward them.

"Lady Rosomon," he said, "messengers have arrived in the camp. Talon scouts. They have asked for you."

More turbulent news no doubt. Rosomon felt the trepidation rise as she followed the guard to where three scouts in their Talon uniforms waited. From the looks of them they had ridden for days to get here.

The first was a tall man, his head shaved to the scalp, his eyes drawn and bloodshot. The other two were women, likewise pale and thin. Rosomon could only imagine what they had been through in recent days.

"I have news, my lady," said the tall scout. "News of your family."

Rosomon clutched at the hem of her cloak, desperate to know what this scout had to say, but she was so fearful of hearing it she could not answer.

"Then speak it," said Ianto.

The scout looked around with suspicion. He was surrounded by unfamiliar faces. "My news is for Lady Rosomon's ears alone."

"Is it Tyreta?" Rosomon managed to say. "Is my daughter safe?"

The scout shook his bald head. "We don't know, my lady. The news is of Conall, but I cannot speak it in front of so many outsiders. The wrong word in the wrong ear could put your son in a lot of danger."

"I understand," said Rosomon, desperate to know what might have happened to him. "But there is nothing you can say in front of the Titanguard that will be shared outside this circle."

The scout bowed his understanding as Ianto gestured for half a dozen of his fellow Titanguard to follow them. Rosomon led them away from the camp, with her bodyguard close by. The three scouts followed some way along the canal until they reached an isolated spot. Rosomon felt her stomach tighten as they stood in the dark.

"There's no one listening," she said. "You may speak freely in front of my men."

The scout licked his lips, glancing sideways at the towering guardians. Beside him the two women glared, giving Rosomon an unnerving feeling.

"What is it, man? Speak."

One of the women wrenched something from her jacket. Rosomon had time to see a metal sphere, much like the explosive charges the artificers had used at the Anvil, before it was flung in the air.

Blinding light heralded a dull boom.

Rosomon tried to shield her eyes but it was too late. She staggered, almost losing her footing as she heard cries of alarm from her men. Her ears began to ring as she squinted, seeing nothing but a white glare. As the world took on a dull grey hue she could just make out Ianto's hulking form moving toward her. Sparks suddenly flared. An electrical hum bursting through the ring in her ears.

Ianto screamed in pain. It wrenched Rosomon from her dazed state, her eyes starting to focus with horrific clarity. One of the scouts held a whip, the thong wrapped around Ianto's torso. Pyrestones were embedded along its length, winking blue in the night. With a flick of her wrist, the scout sent a surge of energy coursing through the whip, igniting each pyrestone, and another jolt of voltaic energy coursed through Ianto's body.

The other two barred Rosomon's path back to the Titanguard, who were still stunned by the blinding explosive. There was no one to protect her.

One of the women took a step forward, reaching into her jacket to produce a pyrestone pistol. The bald man drew a knife. Before they could take a step toward her, Ianto let out a feral cry of rage despite the charge running through his body. He lurched forward, headbutting the bald assassin and sending him reeling, before the webwainer holding the whip powered it up once more and the Titanguard spasmed in a violent convulsion.

Rosomon ran.

There was nothing she could do to help Ianto. These people had come to kill her, and she had no time to consider whether this was cowardice, whether she should have stayed to help her imperator. Instinct screamed at her to run headlong into the dark, alongside the wide canal, feet racing across the grassy field.

Behind she could hear the footsteps of the assassins, unrelenting in their pursuit. At any moment she expected to hear the shrieking snap of the pyrestone pistol, feel the shot enter her back and suck the life from her. Then, through the darkness, she spied her salvation looming up ahead.

Another building stood on the canal shore. A boathouse. Rosomon raced toward it, feet churning up the soft ground, not daring to glance over her shoulder to see if her pursuers were gaining. She jumped down onto the slipway and dashed in through the open access arch. The place was shrouded in darkness, and she stumbled up a steep staircase to the first storey. Moonlight lanced in through the windows, illuminating a barge suspended from the roof, hoisted for repairs to the hull. There was nowhere else to run.

She pressed herself against the wall, stealing breath as quietly as she could, silently chiding herself for her stupidity. She should have ignored the building and carried on into the night, at least then there may have been a way of losing her pursuers in the dark. Now she was cornered.

As she heard the sound of footfalls on the lower level, she clamped a hand over her mouth to silence her gasps. The stairs creaked, as one of the assassins made their way to the upper level, and Rosomon crept away from the stairs toward the rear of the building. Her eyes adjusted to the gloom, and she could see a wide-open space covered with benches and machinery, abandoned tools strewn all around. Not too far from her was a wrench lying on a worktop, and she grasped it, before pressing herself against a pillar.

"Come out, Lady Rosomon," called a man's voice. "There's nowhere left to run."

He was close. Too close—perhaps just feet away. They had her cornered like an animal. Assassins come to do Sanctan's dirty work. Curse her treacherous nephew to the Lairs he so loved. If he thought she would die like some cur, he was sorely mistaken.

Rosomon stepped out, raising the wrench high. She had enough time to note the look of surprise on the man's face before she brought the wrench down. It thudded against his bald head and he fell backward with a curse.

Suddenly, a pyrestone light flared in one corner of the boathouse. Then another, and another, until the whole structure was illuminated. Rosomon froze as she saw one of the assassins levelling her pyrestone pistol. Slowly, a look of satisfaction crossed the woman's wan features.

From the shadows stepped the woman with the whip, as the bald man rose to his feet, dabbing a hand to his bloody forehead before examining it in the light. His face turned to fury as he stooped and picked up the wicked knife he had dropped.

"I'd let you try and talk your way out of this," said the woman with the pistol. "But I doubt we've got time. All I'll say is, Ingelram Hallowhill has a message for you."

The man with the knife stepped forward, brandishing it with evil intent. "Why don't I fucking carve it out for you?"

Rosomon gripped the wrench tighter, gritting her teeth. She would fight. By the Guilds, she would fight to the death.

One of the lights flickered before winking out, bathing a section of the building in darkness. It was followed by an immediate staccato clap, and half a dozen splintbolts riddled the knifeman: one in the neck, one in the arm, four in the chest. Rosomon saw a brief look of surprise cross his face before he collapsed in a heap.

The lights flickered again, dimming to almost nothing. There was a flare of static as the assassin with the whip powered up her weapon and turned to face the darkness. The woman with the pistol aimed it at the shadows, eyes wide with fear.

A beast snarled from the dark, close to the whip wielder. Before she could move, her legs were taken from beneath her and she fell, losing her hold on the whip. She screamed in terror, hands clawing as she tried to grab her weapon, but something with immense strength dragged her away into the shadows.

The yelling continued, followed by the sickening sound of rending flesh and a low throaty growl. Rosomon was consumed by panic, desperate to flee, but the last assassin grabbed her about the throat, using her as a shield against whatever was lurking in the dark.

"Who the fuck's there," she snarled, sweeping her pistol from left to right, desperate for a target. "Come out now or I'll kill this bitch, I swear it."

"Close your eyes." A voice from the shadows that Rosomon was sure she recognised.

No sooner had she squeezed her eyes tight shut than a dull explosion burst close to her ear and something moist spattered her face. The assassin loosed her grip on Rosomon's throat and she darted away. When she opened her eyes she saw the woman on her knees, grasping the bloody stump where her right hand had been—her pyrestone pistol now nothing but shards.

From the dark stepped a woman, all sinewy muscle and disdain, as she reloaded a clip into her splintbow.

"Bitch!" screamed the assassin. "You're a dirty fucking bitch."

The woman shrugged. "Maybe. But I'm a bitch that's gonna live more than ten seconds."

An arrow streaked from the dark, burning bright before burying itself in the assassin's chest. A percussive blast tore through her rib cage, exposing bone and spattering innards across the floor. Rosomon looked away, clamping a hand over her mouth rather than cry out at the horror.

The boathouse was silent. She could barely catch her breath, barely believe her eyes, before another woman walked into the light.

"Tyreta," she yelled.

Rosomon raced to her daughter, grasping her tight, hardly noticing that the girl she had said goodbye to so long ago was now a woman.

"Mother," Tyreta said.

Rosomon just held on, feeling like she might never let go.

"Mother," Tyreta repeated.

Rosomon released her, stepping back, gazing at the strange marks on her daughter's flesh, sigils twisting up her neck and along her arms. Tears began to fill her eyes.

"What have they done to my girl?" she whispered.

Tyreta looked sheepish. "I can explain everything."

Before she could begin, a bestial head appeared from the shadows, padding closer, its sleek body moving with animal grace as it licked at its bloody jaws.

"What in the Lairs is that?" Rosomon breathed.

Tyreta winced. "Yeah, I can explain that too."

TYRETA

She sat within the relative safety of the compound. It used to be a boatyard, a place of manufacture, but now she couldn't tell what it was. A refuge for waifs and strays? Or the camp of an army eager for battle? If that was the case, their chance of victory looked far from promising.

Tyreta's mother had barely left her side since they'd been reunited, and now she was ordering her followers—seeing to guard positions, assessing their arms and equipment, looking over the welfare of the newcomers. Each one of them obeyed her every word without question, nodding their heads with respect, bowing, kneeling. It looked like Lady Rosomon had finally become the empress she always considered herself to be. Doubtful she envisioned it would turn out like this though, leading a sorry band of laggards through the wilds.

Of course she'd had so many questions for Tyreta, demanding to know where she had been, what she had done, how she had got here. And of course, Tyreta had obediently explained to Lady Rosomon the story of New Flaym—the uprising of the kesh, the gift they had given her that still marked her flesh, how the nightstone was a part of her now, how she had defeated a great and mighty war leader. Rosomon had listened as though Tyreta were telling her of a visit to the local fete, before she relayed a sorry tale of her own.

Fulren was dead, sacrificing himself in their fight against the Ministry. Tyreta had refused to believe it, raging, screaming, but eventually she had simply fallen silent and wept. Now she stared into the flames of the fire, her hate burning ever brighter. Sanctan would pay for what he had done, and Tyreta would be the one to punish him for it. Punish all of them—the Guilds and Armiger Battalions that had betrayed them. Anyone who'd had a hand in this treachery. Even her cousin Lorens would feel Tyreta's wrath, but for now she had to sit there in silence, while Sted relayed the story of Conall to her mother.

Rosomon listened as she was told the tale of her other brave but doomed son. Of his heroics at Agavere, and on the ship that should have brought them home if not for the storm that had raged over the Ungulf. When Sted had finished, Tyreta drew her eyes from the fire, wondering if there was any way she would be able to console her mother, perhaps even share an intimate moment, but Lady Rosomon gave no reaction. There was no wail of anguish. No tirade as she spat her hate and grief. Instead they sat around the meagre fire and watched the flames lick at the night air. Crenn ate his bowl of watery stew. Donan rubbed at his sore leg, his constant look of discomfort never changing. Only Sted looked grim, doubtless feeling guilty for the news she had been forced to deliver.

Tyreta's only solace was Cat, who lounged at her feet, licking the fur of her paws. Paws that had so recently torn an assassin to pieces. No wonder she wasn't hungry like the rest of them.

Strangely, her mother seemed to have no opinion of the animal. Tyreta had expected Lady Rosomon's chiding comments: that she found the beast distasteful, that it was dangerous, that Tyreta had no place bringing such a creature to these shores. Instead, she offered no word of complaint. It was both a surprise and a concern, and a sign that the Rosomon of old was gone. Who this new woman was, this military leader, Tyreta had no idea. And she wasn't sure if she liked it.

The silence was broken when a scout came forward, bowing before Rosomon.

"Imperator Fray is alive, my lady," the scout reported. "He is severely burned but will recover. It is all the healer can do to keep him in his bed."

"Thank you, Faiza, that is good news," Rosomon replied, though she didn't seem overly heartened by it. But what could anyone expect? She had lost two of her sons. Having her daughter returned to her side was never going to make up for that.

"Those assassins were webwainers," Tyreta said, desperate to focus on something other than their grief.

Rosomon looked up at her, drawing her eyes away from the flames and nodding. "Sent by Ingelram Hallowhill, and using the uniforms of my own scouts to lure me away. It is clear he sees me as a threat and he knows where we are. Even now there may be more enemies on the way."

Tyreta felt her stomach churn at the prospect and she glanced toward her spear leaning against a nearby wall. Let them come. She would gladly send a message of her own to that old ghoul Ingelram.

"We need to strike back before he has the chance," Tyreta said. They could not just sit by helplessly and wait for trouble to come to them. That notion, above all others, excited her. "I would happily return the favour to the old bastard."

"Don't be ridiculous," her mother snapped. There it was. There was the old Lady Rosomon, dismissing every idea Tyreta had.

She should have stood up for herself. Should have told her mother she was no longer the naive girl who had said goodbye at the Anvil. Now she was a warrior, imbued with the strength and magics of the Lokai. Filled with the power of the nightstone. But she knew she could never defy her mother, no matter what new abilities she had been granted.

"Still," Rosomon continued. "The Hallowhills are a problem that must be dealt with if we are to win this war."

War. The word hung in the air like a dark cloud. Tyreta had never considered that's what this was before, but now it seemed obvious. This was no longer a coup. No longer a usurpation of power. They would never give in to the Ministry without a fight, and war was the only thing that remained.

Rosomon raised an arm, gesturing for someone across the camp. A man quickly came forward, stooping low as though he were trying for a bow with every step. He wore the battered apron of an artificer, grey hair sprouting from beneath his skullcap.

"Artificer Kerrick. It appears the threat from Ingelram Hallowhill is more pressing than I gave it credit for. Tell me more about these artificers you spoke of the other day."

"The Merigots, my lady?" replied the artificer.

"The same."

Kerrick hunkered down beside Rosomon, making himself comfortable by the fire.

"I am not sure what to add. The Merigots engaged in unsanctioned research. Toyed with artifice in forbidden ways. Some say they even dabbled in the magics of the Archmages. Their experiments achieved some success, that's for sure, managing to counter the abilities of even the most potent webwainers, but I am afraid the details have been lost to time."

"So they kept no records?" Rosomon asked.

Kerrick looked at the ground, rubbing his chin in thought. "I cannot think of any. Perhaps if we had access to the Great Library, there might be some records. But..."

"That is in the Anvil. And you're sure there is no notion of where these brothers might have fled to?"

The artificer shook his head. "None, my lady."

Someone cleared their throat at the other side of the fire. Tyreta squinted through the flames to see old Crenn leaning forward. He had a pained expression on his face.

"Well... that might not be entirely accurate..." he said.

Crenn didn't seem to want to elaborate as all eyes turned toward him.

"You know where these brothers are?" Rosomon asked.

"I know where one of them *was*," Crenn replied.

More silence. Tyreta heard her mother's sigh of impatience and willed Crenn to reveal what he knew.

"And?" Rosomon said. "Are you going to tell me where, or do I have to guess?"

"Erm...apologies, my lady," Crenn replied in embarrassment. "Fact is, I worked with old Nicosse in Windstone for a while, before I hopped on a ship for New Flaym. I knew them both back in the day, at the academy, but it's many years since Nicosse fell out with his brother, Lysander, and they went their separate ways. Where he is, I have no idea, but unless something's changed, there ain't no reason Nicosse won't still be in Windstone."

"You worked with these men?" Rosomon asked.

"For a time." Crenn seemed uncomfortable with the fact, as though he too might be implicated in their unsanctioned activities. "Until it was clear that what those two were working on might land me in the shit. Begging pardon for the language, my lady."

Rosomon rose to her feet, not caring about Crenn's spicy turn of phrase. She looked down at Kerrick. "You're sure this man Nicosse can help us against the webwainers?" The artificer nodded, and she looked across at Crenn once more. "Tell me, what was the nature of this study? What did you learn from them?"

Crenn shrugged. "I didn't learn much. I spent a lot of time watching, and not much time understanding. But I saw some things. Some successes. From what I could tell they had pretty much figured out how to turn any normal folk into webwainers, and reduce webwainers to normal folk."

It seemed an absurd notion, but Rosomon only looked more intrigued.

"Turn ordinary people into webwainers? So with enough resources and volunteers they could build an army? One big enough to smash the Hallowhills?"

"I saw ordinary folk do some amazing things when those brothers had finished with them. But it took a toll. Twisted their minds. Sent some of them mad with rage or despair or worse. I wouldn't wish such a curse on anyone."

Tyreta's mother didn't seem to hear the last part. It was obvious her desire for victory over the Ministry clouded any other concerns. That only served to make Tyreta think on what she had done, what she had been through. What she had become. It made her realise she could perhaps make a difference in this war.

"I will find him," Tyreta said, rising to her feet.

Her mother turned with a familiar look of annoyance. "Don't be absurd."

Tyreta could feel every eye on her, embarrassment deepening. Each person around that fire had witnessed her being undermined, but what had she expected? Rosomon had not seen how her daughter had grown. Did not realise all she was capable of.

"I mean it," Tyreta said. "I can do this...I have to do this. You need an army, and this is not it." She swept a hand over the camp full of sorry refugees. "If this artificer is out there, he could give us just the edge we need. What choice do you have? Who else are you going to send?"

"I will find someone. There are more than enough men at my—"

"No!" Tyreta yelled. It silenced the camp, even her mother, but she couldn't bring herself to regret her rashness.

Lady Rosomon narrowed her eyes. "Tyreta, you are not ready."

She should have kept her mouth shut, accepted what she was told, but that was the Tyreta who had landed on the shores of the Sundered Isles. The Tyreta who had left those shores was very different.

"What would make me ready, Mother? You've always demanded I live up to my responsibilities to the Guild. That I do my duty. Well, I want to do it now. I *need* to do it. I'm not the girl you said goodbye to at the Anvil. I've had to fight for my life. And I survived. I rescued the people of New Flaym. Fought a warlord and won. What more can I do to prove—"

Rosomon raised her hand—the one that had always demanded obedience—and damn it Tyreta couldn't defy it, not even after all she'd just said.

"I'll tell you what you are," her mother whispered. "You're foolhardy. Stubborn. Rash and bloody belligerent at times." Tyreta waited for that quiet but uncompromising voice to tell her to sit down. Instead, Rosomon let out a sigh. "But very well. Go to Windstone. Find this Nicosse Merigot and bring him back to Wyke. But you must travel swiftly, and with no landships or war eagles at our disposal, I have no idea how that might be achieved."

Tyreta couldn't quite believe what she was hearing. Her mother was actually allowing her to go on a mission of her own. The only problem now was how to get it done.

"Erm..." another voice squeaked from across the fire as someone raised their hand as though asking permission for something.

It was Donan. The Marrlock Guild man. Tyreta had barely heard him speak during their journey north, but now it was obvious he had something to say.

"You have an idea?" her mother asked with some severity. Tyreta had heard that tone before, when Lady Rosomon's patience was on the wane.

"There's...there's a transport tunnel just north of the Rock," he said. "It feeds into every mining shaft and tunnel system along the route to Windstone. If we could reach it, and access the underground terminal, it would take no more than two days to reach the city."

"Can you draw me a map and show me how to use it?" Tyreta asked.

Donan nodded enthusiastically. "That I can."

"No," said Rosomon. "You'll go with her."

Donan's eyes widened. He opened his mouth to speak, then looked down at the stump of his knee. "But...my lady, I can't walk ten yards without struggling. Let alone travel leagues to the south."

The artificer, Kerrick, took a step forward, peering across the fire at Donan. "Oh, that should be no problem. I could rig a leg from the stores of this very boatyard. A hydraulic device should be able to regulate your gait. We'll have you dancing a jig in no time."

Crenn quickly stood. "No. That's a ridiculous idea." He peered down at Donan's missing leg. "You want pneumatics, not hydraulics. That's a much more effective system for constructing limbs."

As the two artificers argued, and Donan gazed at them both with a forlorn expression, Sted rose to her feet.

"I'll go too, if it's all the same to you, my lady."

Rosomon regarded the woman with some respect. She was a lieutenant in the Talon, after all, and a friend of Conall's.

"Very well," Rosomon replied. "I would appreciate it if you'd ensure my daughter returns to me safely."

"I will," the woman said. "Won't let her out of my sight."

There was a strange look in Sted's eyes. Tyreta wondered if it was determination or apprehension. Was she guilty that she had not managed to return Conall to her Guildmaster's side? Was this a way for her to make amends? Whatever the reason, Tyreta had no complaints she was going with her.

Rosomon turned to Tyreta. "And I assume you'll be taking that thing with you?" She gestured to Cat.

"I think that's best," Tyreta replied.

"Good. Then walk with me." Rosomon moved away from the fire toward a quiet spot.

With some trepidation, Tyreta stood and followed her mother. Most of the camp was sleeping, and Rosomon led her into one of the huge boat stores that jutted out over the canal. There they stood, just the two of them, listening to the water as it flowed away to the sea.

"This will be dangerous, Tyreta."

"I know, Mother. I am—"

"And difficult, despite the companions you travel with. This is no longer the country it was. If I had any sense, I'd make you stay by my side. But the closer we get to Wyke, the more danger there is for all of us."

Tyreta could see her mother was struggling with the words, wringing her hands, trying her hardest not to break down. Fulren was dead, Conall lost to the Ungulf Sea, and despite their differences, she knew she was all her mother had left. Now Rosomon was being forced to send her only daughter on a mission that may well put her in peril. Tyreta should have hugged her close, reassured her, told her everything would be all right, but that would have been a lie.

"I should command you to go somewhere safe, far from here," Rosomon managed to say. "But I know you would defy me. You never could just do as you're told, but you're a woman now. I can see that. Perhaps I've seen it for a long time."

Tyreta suddenly found it hard to swallow. She opened her mouth to speak, to tell her mother that perhaps she had changed her mind and would not leave her side after all, when Rosomon raised a hand for her to be silent.

"Just promise me you'll take care of yourself. Promise me you'll return safe and well."

Her mother was shaking, hands clasped tightly, all that fettered emotion fighting to escape—a wellspring of grief desperate to explode. Of all this, all the strife and uncertainty, that was the hardest thing to take.

"I promise, Mother," she replied.

Tyreta expected her mother to grab her and squeeze her for as long as she could. Instead, Lady Rosomon turned and left her alone by the canal.

ANSELL

It was these quiet moments he dreaded the most. Opportunities to reflect. Time to think back and lament on what he had done. Those dark duties he had performed for his master.

Ansell was a servant of the Draconate. A vessel born to carry out the will of the Great Wyrms. A righteous weapon to be wielded only by the Archlegate. Yet in performing such service, his deeds had brought with them a guilt that was often difficult to bear.

It had been on Sanctan's order that he executed Gylbard at Wyrm-head. That old man had stood in their way, his inaction threatening everything they held dear. There was no doubt it had been Ansell's duty to kill the former Archlegate, but still the shame of it weighed heavily.

Piled upon that, he had also been compelled to lead an assassination against the Maladoran emissary. That had been an easier burden to carry—or at least it would have, had the boy Fulren Hawkspur not got in the way. It was shameful enough he had been forced to act in secret like a common assassin, hiding his identity as they cut the woman down, but Ansell had paid for that all right.

He absently raised a hand, feeling the burn on his chin that would not heal, the sparse beard that refused to grow over the blackened flesh, which he dared not shave for fear his skin would slough off to the bare bone.

Both those crimes were wicked enough, but most recently of all he had murdered the emperor. Cut him down in front of a baying crowd like an executioner. And no matter how many times he told himself it was for the greater good, that he had simply obeyed the will of the Great Wyrms, Ansell Beckenrike was not sure he would ever be able to endure that disgrace.

His lips moved in a quiet prayer as he implored Vermitrix, the Great Wyrm of Peace, to forgive him. To offer some release from the pain of this guilt. He had barely begun when those whispered words were drowned out by a sudden sound from the adjacent room.

Ansell looked up from the bench in one corner of the small lounge. To his right was the front door of the manse, in front of him the door to the bedchamber. Beyond it he could hear the woman moaning in ecstasy. Or was it discomfort? Ansell found it hard to tell, but then how would he? His only experience of carnal acts was listening to Sanctan from another room. As well as her whimpers of delight, he could hear the creak of the wooden bed, the bang of the frame against the wall. Sanctan's mistress, Jessamine, was putting on quite the show.

The ignominy of sitting there, listening to all this like some degenerate, should have stung Ansell to the quick, but this was just one more discomfort he was forced to endure in his duty as the Archlegate's personal bodyguard. Even before Sanctan had been ordained, when he was still but a High Legate of Undometh, it had been Ansell's duty to see him safe as they snuck through the streets to his lover's manse. To sit in silence as his master slaked his need.

Ansell had long since stopped struggling with the hypocrisy of it, for how could he ever hope to square the circle between Sanctan's pieties and his lusts? The man was Archlegate now, appointed and ordained by the High Legates themselves. He was the Draconate's chosen, and it was not for Ansell Beckenrike to question his actions, no matter how profane they might seem.

He stretched his leg as he sat on the bench, feeling it ache down to the bone. It had been days since his battle with Jagdor, and though he knew how fortunate he was to survive it, the indignity of that defeat still bore a heavy weight. There were stitches in his arm where Jagdor's sword had breached his armour, and his eye was bruised yellow, though the blackening of his eyeball had faded. Perhaps Undometh would give him a chance at vengeance soon. Surely it was only a matter of time before the Guild resistance rose up and attacked the Anvil. Then Ansell would have his chance at a reckoning.

He was about to say a prayer to the Great Wyrm of Vengeance, remembering the words to a particular passage from the Draconate Prophesies, but they were scattered to the air as the rhythmic clack of the bedframe reverberated once more, and Jessamine's vocal performance began to reach its first crescendo.

Ansell forgot Undometh, forgot his need for vengeance, and instead thought on the wisdom of Saphenodon. Perhaps the Great Wyrm of Knowledge would allow him to understand why all this had happened to such a loyal servant. Perhaps he would also be better able to comprehend the motivations of his superiors, and why they preached sanctity one day but practised debauchery the next. Before he could begin to formulate that hymnal in his head, a small figure crept from the room to his left.

The girl was tiny and willow limbed. Ansell had never seen her before, but then this house was a new meeting place for Sanctan's secret trysts with Jessamine. Was she the whore's daughter? That was the only explanation.

As he sat in silence, the girl climbed up onto the bench beside him, staring from beneath an unruly mop of silver hair. Ansell risked a glance at her, noticing a heart-shaped face that resembled Jessamine's. Yes, the same features as her mother, apart from the eyes. They looked exactly like...

"What happened to your face?" the girl asked.

Instinctively, Ansell pulled his hood further over his head. He knew how hideous his visage was, and he would never have wanted to distress an innocent child. Strangely, this one did not seem to care

about his scars. Instead she pulled the hood back, revealing more of
his face. The awkwardness of it kept Ansell frozen to the spot. How
was he supposed to react to this? He had no experience with the
unpredictability of children.

The noise of Sanctan's coupling with Jessamine rose once more
to a second crescendo, but the girl seemed unconcerned with it, as
though it was a familiar sound to her.

"Does it hurt?" she asked.

Mercifully it didn't. It simply made him look more the monster
he often felt like. The girl clearly had some concern for him, and
may the Wyrms bless her for that, but Ansell was in no mood to
reply. As much as he was appreciative of her compassion, it was still
outweighed by annoyance at being under such scrutiny from a child.
He was a warrior born. A holy defender of his faith. Not a nursemaid tasked with entertaining an errant girl. Was this his duty now?
Was this what he was to be reduced to?

She reached out a hand, touching his necrotised flesh with one
thin finger. On instinct, Ansell swatted her hand away in annoyance,
immediately chiding himself for his rash reaction. He expected the
girl to mewl at his hasty rebuke, but she didn't.

"Sorry," she whispered, as the sounds from the next room began
to subside. "My name is Grace, by the way."

Ansell sighed at her persistence. What was he to do? Tell her to
leave him be? To go back to her childish ways elsewhere?

"You're supposed to tell me your name now," she said.

Before he could react, her foot slipped from the bench and she
went tumbling to the wooden floor. Ansell braced himself for her
yelp of pain, for her to grasp an elbow or a knee and yell for her
mother. Thankfully she did not whine as other children were wont
to, but climbed to her feet, straightening her stained frock as though
nothing had happened. She was clumsy, for sure. Ironic, then, that
someone had chosen to name her Grace.

Ansell closed his eyes, silently beseeching Ammenodus Rex to
grant him the strength to suffer this humiliation. As though in
answer to that prayer, a loud wail came from the next room as Sanctan's indulgences came to fruition.

Scant seconds later the door to the bedchamber opened. The Archlegate walked out, fastening his trews at the waist, shirt unbuttoned to the navel, his garb that of any citizen of the Anvil. He quickly grabbed his cloak from a peg where it hung by the door.

"Time for us to leave, Ansell," Sanctan pronounced.

As he rose from the bench, Ansell saw the woman Jessamine standing at the door to her bedchamber. A sheen of sweat covered her body, a white sheet trying and failing to shield her modesty. Ansell could make out the contours of her figure, the hint of her nipples beneath the linen, and he immediately averted his eyes.

"That's it," she said. Her voice was harsh, and certainly contrasted with her comely exterior. "You're gonna fucking disappear, just like that?"

Sanctan paused at the door, smile dripping with charm. "Alas, my love, I have important business to attend. My brood awaits. But know you will be in my thoughts as I perform my duties."

Grace tottered to her mother's side, and Jessamine picked the girl up. Ansell opened the door for the Archlegate before following him outside into the chill of the street.

"Bye-bye, Ansell," Grace shouted, her voice echoing from the small house as he closed the door behind him. He felt his teeth grind in annoyance.

Both men raised the hoods of their cloaks before making their way along the streets of the Burrows. They moved north through darkened alleyways toward the Mount, the citizenry ignoring them as they did so. Despite what had happened in the Anvil so recently, it looked like little had changed for most of its inhabitants.

Or had it?

Could Ansell feel an underlying air of tension? Were people looking at one another with more suspicion than they would have before? Were their conversations more hushed, as though they feared being heard? In fact, there was little talk at all. Little industry, little bustle.

A beggar called to them for alms as they passed the corner of a street, but Sanctan ignored the man, increasing his pace. Ansell tried not to look at the wretch, wondering if the poor soul would soon see any benefit from the new power the Ministry had over this city. Over this nation.

The Mount reared up ahead of them, and immediately Ansell felt relieved. The place stood like an oasis in this sea of woe, and out on the streets, bereft of arms and armour but for the blade he hid in his cloak, Ansell felt virtually naked.

When they drew closer, he could see hundreds waiting outside. They clamoured together in reverential quiet, every eye turned to the huge edifice of the Mount, waiting for the way to be opened so they could flood inside and hear the words of the Archlegate, as he preached to them of better days to come. It had been a daily occurrence, and Sanctan had gleefully risen to the task. Even now he moved with utmost haste to a side entrance, where he was allowed inside by two of Ansell's brother knights.

The door slammed closed behind them, and Ansell followed the Archlegate deeper into the bowels of the Mount. Torches lit their way, and for the first time that morning Ansell found himself breathing easier. Down they rushed, level after level until Sanctan finally reached his vestibule. Here, temple serfs were already awaiting their master—four of them, heads bowed, piously waiting to robe their Archlegate in his vestments of office. No one thought to question him on where he had been, but Ansell knew. For a moment he began to wonder if they would be so dutiful if they realised what he had been up to not so long ago. If he told them, would they so readily tend to him like the saint they believed him to be? But Ansell would never tell them.

Instead, he scanned the antechamber for any danger, but what danger would there be here in the Archlegate's own lair? The place glittered with opulence—a chalice shining gold and bejewelled as it was filled by one of the attendants, a glittering bowl brimming with sanctified water in which to wash him. It was a stark comparison to the hovel they had just come from.

Sanctan spread his arms, and his attendants unclothed him with expert efficiency, nimble fingers untying his trews and unbuttoning his shirt. No sooner was he naked than they daubed him with flannel and sponge.

"Did you see them, Ansell?" Sanctan asked. "Waiting on our benediction? Is it not glorious to see how far we have risen in so short a time?"

"Glorious indeed, Archlegate," Ansell replied, though he saw little glory in any of this. Standing in a dungeon in the Mount, watching men who were little more than slaves wash the stink of a whore from their master's flesh.

Sanctan smiled the wider, lifting a leg as the serf tended to his nethers with the cloth. "We have brought down an empire. The people of Torwyn have risen up and cast down their false idols. Released themselves from the shackles of the Guilds."

Was Sanctan practising his speech to come, or was he merely basking in his own victory? Either way, Ansell knew better than anyone what they had won...and the price he had paid for it.

Two serfs took up their cotton towels and, with ceremonial reverence, dried Sanctan's naked body before dressing him in silken undergarments. It was a new type of vestment for a new Archlegate. His traditional robes of office were cut from rough cloth, and every former Archlegate had suffered them with stoicism. Sanctan, however, had insisted on the luxury of silk to diminish their discomfort.

"Torwyn has entered a new age," he said. "There is much to look forward to in the seasons to come. Seasons that will see us all rise. Together."

As the attendants pulled the Archlegate's robe over his head, Ansell found himself unable to share in Sanctan's optimistic view. Surely they had merely gone back to the days when the Draconate was a dominant force, before the Guilds had built this land anew with their engines and artifice. Change was coming, but whether it would be for the better was not something anyone could predict. Nevertheless, it was not Ansell's place to question the words of the Archlegate.

When he was finally dressed, Sanctan stood in front of the huge, gold-framed mirror that was nailed to one wall, adjusting his cuffs and rolling his shoulders, inspecting his magnificence.

"That's what I like about you, Ansell," he said. "Our conversations always have breadth and depth." He turned, patting Ansell on the shoulder as he walked by. "Let's do this again soon."

With the serfs scurrying after, Sanctan left Ansell alone in the chamber. A candle sputtered in its sconce, as though urging Ansell to leave. He took the hint, walking the long route back to the Mount's dormitories, passing some of his brothers as they made their way to the nave so they might listen to the Archlegate. Ansell did not envy them. Though he would have never said it, he had heard more than enough of Sanctan's prating for one day.

Due to his position of privilege as knight commander, Ansell had his own private chamber. In reality, it was little more than a cell. There was no adornment, no window, no shelves of screeds, nor even a mirror. All he owned was a simple table, a bowl to wash and a pallet bed. Upon his feather pillow lay a copy of the Draconate Prophesies—everything he would ever need to know written within those well-thumbed pages.

But nothing that was written in that book had prepared him for the things he would have to do. For the things he had seen and endured. The things he would continue to suffer.

On its stand hung his armour of office. On the shelf beside it sat his dragon helm. The dent in the side, where Jagdor had dispatched him so deftly, had already been worked out by a smith, and the helm bore a smooth finish once more. The rent in the sleeve of his hauberk had been neatly stitched after the sword blow to his arm, and no one would even know it had been torn. Leaning against the wall beside it was his sword. The sword he had wielded when he slew an emperor.

Perhaps he should have donned that armour and joined the rest of his brothers in praise. It would have shown devotion to stand with them among the pious citizens of the Anvil, and listen to their Archlegate.

Instead, Ansell closed the door to his cell, shutting himself inside his prison. He pulled the shirt over his head, discarding it on the floor before reaching beneath the thin straw-stuffed mattress and pulling out the scourge he kept hidden there.

It was such a simple device, stout of handle and wicked of barb, yet it had become of such particular use in recent days. Ansell knew no amount of pious observance could rid him of his shame. Sanctan's holy words would not free him of his guilt for the deeds he had done, even if those deeds had been in the name of the Draconate. But the scourge...

He knelt in the centre of his cell, and began.

CONALL

He fell again, grazing his knees on the stony ground, grunting in pain, heaving in breath. His leggings were in tatters, the soles of his boots almost worn through. How many times had he fallen now? How many more before they reached their destination? If they ever did.

Someone grasped his arm.

"You have to get up," Nylia said, face stern, jaw set. "Just keep moving, Hawkspur, or you'll be left to rot."

As much as he wanted to lie down and use the sand as a pillow, he couldn't let the wasteland take him. Instead he wearily took her arm and she pulled him to his feet, before they stumbled onward.

How many miles had they walked now? How many more to go? How long before they gave him something to eat or, by the Wyrms, let him drink? Not in his worst moments in the Karna had his mouth been so dry or his legs so tired.

None of them had spoken, but then why waste the energy on that? What would they talk about anyway? Even Ramassen had been mercifully silent as he lumbered on through the desert. Of the twenty who had set off from the outpost, only a dozen remained. The others had collapsed, left for the vultures as warriors on horseback urged the rest on through the arid landscape.

Ahead of them rode Warmaven Orsokon, his hulking frame absurdly large atop his lean desert steed. Conall would have laughed at how ridiculous the towering warrior looked, if he'd had any strength left for mirth.

As they approached another rise up ahead, Orsokon reined in his horse and turned to face them.

"Not much farther," he barked, that singsong voice resounding from within that horned helm.

He reached to his saddlebag, taking a waterskin and tipping back his helmet to reveal a lantern jaw. Conall watched, licking his dry lips, as Orsokon gulped down a draft of water, letting it spill down his chin, splash off his saddle, and drip onto the dry earth.

Not much farther. How many times had Orsokon said that on their journey? Half a dozen? Ten? Twenty? Was he trying to give them hope that this torture would soon be at an end? Or was he simply tormenting them? Whatever the reason, it wasn't fucking helping.

The warmaven kicked his horse and trotted over the brow of the hill. The rest of the captives stumbled in his wake. Just one more hill. Just one last effort. Clawing at the incline, feet slipping on the scree. When Conall crested the ridge, expecting to see more miles of bleak land, what lay ahead made him gasp in relief.

Arcturius loomed ahead of them, rising from the dirt and rocky earth like a giant monolith. It was an ugly edifice, made from the same grey stone that dotted the landscape, but to Conall's weary eye it was the most beautiful thing he had ever seen.

A curtain wall surrounded the city, huge angular spires peering from beyond its crenellated summit. At the centre rose a single enormous tower, and standing atop it was a foreboding statue, there to remind anyone who cared to look who ruled this place. A vast stone demon stood at its apex, six limbs sprouting from an armoured torso, a huge eyeless head atop it. Myriad chains connected the statue to the surrounding towers and for one terrifying moment it looked as though a real demon stood proudly above its bastion.

Just beyond the city, the ground fell away into a deep canyon. They were truly at the edge of the Drift, and all that lay beyond it was Torwyn. Conall's home. He was so close, yet so impossibly far away.

"Keep moving," bellowed one of the riders, and they stumbled on, heaving in breath, newly invigorated now the end was so close.

As he willed one foot in front of the other, staring at the ominous black gates set in that stone wall, Conall couldn't stop thinking about what lay waiting within. The Scion Senmonthis was fabled to be a demon herself. An Archmage from the Age of Insurrection, who betrayed Obek and forged her own kingdom in southern Malador with three of her fellow traitors. Beyond that, Conall knew few details, and he began to regret paying little attention to his history tutors in Wyke. If only he had been a more attentive student, he'd know what to expect within those grim walls.

When they staggered to within a hundred yards, the gates began to slowly open. The horsemen wrangled them ever closer, while Conall and the others shuffled, exhausted, toward the darkness that loomed ahead.

He spared a glance upward as they neared the threshold, seeing carvings of demons staring back down at him. If they had been placed there to strike fear, it was most definitely working.

When they had stumbled through into a wide courtyard, and the horsemen reined in their mounts, the gates were pushed closed behind them by thickly muscled slaves. Each one was chained to the gate, their only purpose to open and close the entrance to the huge walled city. Orsokon jumped down from his steed as though he had been out for an afternoon jaunt, gesturing toward a shallow well twenty feet across.

"Your reward," he said. "Go ahead. You have all earned it."

Conall wanted to wait, to see if this was a trick of some kind, or perhaps a test, but he was so thirsty he lurched forward with the rest. They swarmed around the well, dipping their heads into the tepid water and drinking deep. He didn't give a shit what it tasted like as he gulped it down. It could have been poison for all he cared, he just had to slake his endless thirst.

Nylia finished dunking her head and sat with her back against the well. "So, we get to live," she breathed.

Ramassen looked up from the other side, his face dripping. "For now."

It was an ominous prospect none of them needed reminding of.

Conall glanced around the courtyard when he had drunk his fill. It extended a hundred feet in every direction, the walls rising to open air fifty feet above them. There was no sign of Baenre Mokhtar—or anyone he might be able to reason with. No way to talk himself out of this one. Not that his attempts to lure Baenre with the promise of immeasurable riches had borne fruit so far.

Before he could dunk his head in the well once more, the guards surrounded them, jabbing with the butts of spears and urging them to their feet. Conall dragged himself up and followed the others as they were ushered deeper into the complex. An archway flanked by more leering demons led to a dark tunnel, its roof an iron grille through which more guards glared down, jeering at them as they were corralled along. He could hear distant voices crying in pain, wails of anguish mixing with the distant ring of steel.

The corridor ended in a shadowy chamber, a musty stink hanging in the air. Here, the only sound was that of a dozen exhausted prisoners gasping in the dark.

Orsokon strode in after them. He gripped a pair of prisoners, standing them side by side in front of double doors set in the far wall. Then another pair, and another until the dozen were standing side by side in a wretched line. Ramassen stood beside Conall, his confidence gone, eyes glaring pensively. In front of him were the two wiry men he'd been caged with at Argon Kyne, and in front of them was Nylia next to a tall rangy man, grim about the face but doleful about the eyes.

No sooner had they been arranged in ranks than the double doors were thrown open. Conall squinted in the sudden brightness as the first pair of prisoners were ordered to follow Orsokon, and the doors were closed behind them.

He listened to muffled orders from beyond the door but couldn't quite make out the words. Immediately after, he heard a telltale ring of steel.

"What the fuck is going on," he breathed at Ramassen, like he didn't already know the answer.

In reply, one of the guards jabbed him with the butt of a spear, demanding his silence. The sound of combat was brief, punctuated by the occasional pained grunt. It ended mercifully quick, and the doors were immediately thrust open. Conall caught a brief glimpse of what lay on the other side—a high-walled arena, blood on the sand—before Orsokon loomed in the doorway.

"Next," he said in a nonchalant tone.

Now it was Nylia's turn. She glanced back at him, though there was no way to read her expression. If she was afraid, she didn't show it. Conall would have wished her luck, but he was too scared to utter a word. She walked through the doors with her dolorous partner and Orsokon slammed them shut once more.

The sound of clashing blades lasted longer this time. Conall could hear Nylia's voice bellowing a cry of frustration, or was it pain? Whichever it was, ominous silence quickly followed.

Again the doors opened, again Orsokon's singsong voice demanding the next two combatants step through—those two wiry men who could have been brothers. They did not hesitate, walking forward to meet their fate as Conall realised it was his turn next.

This battle seemed to last an age. With every passing second and every ring of steel, Conall fought to quell the panic within him. He knew what was coming, but still tried to put it from his mind as the fighting sounded increasingly desperate, the guttural voices getting louder and angrier. Through a narrow gap in the doorframe he could see the shadows of the two men as they fought, trying his best not to look at the hulking figure next to him.

"I am sorry I will have to kill you," Ramassen whispered as there was a loud cry from beyond the door.

In the silence that followed, Conall realised the chance of him being ransomed was most definitely off the table, and he would have to fight or die. The doors were flung open, and he squinted in the brightness once more.

"Next two," Orsokon said, as though inviting them to a country dance.

Ramassen strode forward and Conall managed to force himself out into the light before the doors were slammed behind him.

They were in a circular arena, with no spectators but for the guards who stood about its perimeter. The sun shone down on them, and

Conall could just see the spired towers peering over the edge of the rooftop. A body was being dragged across the sand by two shirtless attendants, leaving a trail of crimson in its wake. It was unceremoniously flung into a pit at the centre of the arena, before a trapdoor slammed shut over it. Conall couldn't see any sign of the victor.

"Your final test," said Orsokon, a sword held casually in each hand. "Only one of you will walk from here alive." With that he threw the swords across the arena, one landing at the feet of each fighter.

For an instant, Conall considered leaping for his blade and attacking Ramassen while he was still unarmed, but as the huge warrior casually strode forward and picked up his weapon, he dismissed the idea. May as well do this right, he thought, picking up his sword and turning to face his opponent.

Ramassen regarded him with a note of pity to his eyes, but there was still a degree of steel behind them. Conall recognised his opponent for the seasoned gladiator he was.

"They call me the Ox," Ramassen reminded him. "I was champion in the death pits of Tallus Rann. Victor in a hundred battles, and I offer you a quick and clean death, eastlander. If that is what you desire?"

It was a generous proposal, all things considered. Conall thought about announcing his own title. Telling anyone who cared to listen that he was Conall Hawkspur, son of Melrone, trained by the swordwright Starn Rivers in all matters of martial prowess. But what would have been the point?

"If it's all the same, I will have to refuse," Conall replied. "But thanks anyway."

Ramassen shrugged, offering a nod of respect. "I thought it only polite to ask."

The grin faded from his face, and he crouched in an attacking stance. Conall suddenly felt exhausted at the prospect of battle, but he settled on the balls of his feet, raising the sword defensively just like Starn had taught him all those years ago. The only duel he'd been in since his training was with Marshal Beringer, and that had ended with him sat on his arse in the dust. He could only hope this time things would go better, otherwise he'd have more than a bloody lip and damaged pride to contend with.

Ramassen advanced. Conall had expected him to be a lumbering brute, but the Ox was light on his feet, more dancer than warrior. When he was within range, he attacked without pause or remorse, sword striking in swiftly. Conall was at pains to parry, looking for an opportunity to counter, but Ramassen left no opening, forging ahead, pressing Conall back with a series of lethal swings and feints.

Conall darted away across the arena as their swords rang, desperate to block his opponent's steel, fighting the urge to panic in the face of such an onslaught. He could almost hear Starn grunting at him as he did. *Don't let your enemy dictate the terms. Take the battle to him. Find his weakness. Watch. Anticipate.* It was a mantra Starn had repeated time and again, but it was one thing hearing advice...quite another heeding it.

One last wild swing, and Conall dodged away from Ramassen, more stumbling retreat than graceful withdrawal. After putting some distance between them, he managed to finally catch his breath.

"Nowhere to run," Ramassen said, taking a measured step forward. "You should have accepted my offer."

Maybe he was right. A quick look around the arena and Conall could see no way to escape. No chance of a reprieve. Orsokon was looking on impassively from behind his helm, hand on the grip of the curved blade at his side. He was like a statue in the midst of the arena and there would be no help there.

Conall braced himself as Ramassen advanced relentlessly. He needed an edge against such a brutal and experienced foe, but his sword felt heavy, the tip trailing in the dirt.

Before Ramassen could attack again, Conall swept the blade through the sand, sending a cloud of grit toward Ramassen's face. His opponent's hand came up swiftly to block it, his advance halting before he backed away.

"Do you think no one's ever tried that before?" Ramassen asked. "I have fought in a dozen pits across the Magna. I can see you haven't, boy."

Of course he hadn't, but now wasn't the time to tally up their victories. Conall darted forward, swinging his sword in an arc, before changing his approach and lunging in with a low thrust. It was

Ramassen's turn to parry, deflecting the strike with ease, and leaving Conall with the feeling there might be no weakness he could exploit.

The Ox came at him again, and it was all Conall could do to keep that blade at bay. He grunted, froth gathering at the edge of his dry mouth, arm growing tired, a dull ache in his shoulder as Ramassen beat at his weapon again and again. His foot caught on something, and he lost his balance under the onslaught, sword falling from his grip. Conall was on his back, ground rattling at the impact and he realised he'd fallen over the trapdoor at the centre of the arena.

Ramassen towered over him, taking no time to gloat, raising his blade high to finish this swiftly. Conall's hand touched a ring of metal...the handle of the trapdoor. He gripped the handle, rolling aside and wrenching the trapdoor open, desperate to shield himself from the killing blow. Ramassen's blade swept down, slamming into the edge of the door. The sword sank deep into the wood, wedging the blade tight, and Ramassen grunted as he tried to wrench it free with both hands.

Conall glanced to his fallen sword. He scrambled across the sand, grasping it, swinging with a growl and feeling satisfaction as it sank into the meaty flesh of Ramassen's thigh.

The Ox bellowed, clutching his leg, forgetting his weapon still wedged in the trapdoor as he fell to the ground. Conall rose to his feet, looking down at the man he had bested. Or was his luck the only victor here?

Ramassen looked up at him, spittle flecked across his lips, hands vainly stanching the blood that ran through his fingers. "You fought well, eastlander. It takes a mighty warrior to bring down Ramassen the Ox. If only there had been a roaring crowd to witness it."

"Finish him," Orsokon ordered.

The words distracted Conall from the rapture of triumph, as he realised what he had to do. It should have been so easy; his enemy was helpless. But this was no enemy. This was a man enslaved, just like Conall. They had been forced into this, and Ramassen had done nothing to deserve death.

"I said finish him," Orsokon repeated.

Conall shook his head. "I can't."

Orsokon strode forward, but Conall stood firm. He was done with cowering. Done with obeying this bastard's every word. No matter the consequences, he would not murder a helpless man.

He tensed every muscle as Orsokon bore down on him, expecting him to wrench that curved blade from its sheath and execute them both. Instead, he snatched the sword from Conall's hand and turned on Ramassen.

Without a word, Ramassen let go of his leg. Raising his head, offering his neck as an easy target. Orsokon grasped the sword in both hands and sank the blade into Ramassen's shoulder just above the clavicle. It was a gladiator's death, puncturing the heart and killing the giant fighter instantly. Conall stared as Ramassen's corpse collapsed to the dirt.

Orsokon flung the sword away in disgust. "At least one of you deserved a warrior's death."

Conall tensed his gut, expecting another solid punch from the warmaven. Instead, Orsokon grasped his throat in both hands. Conall clawed at those thick wrists, but it did nothing to stop his airways being closed.

"The next time you disobey me, it will be you in that pit." Already the attendants were making their way across the arena to dispose of Ramassen's body, but Conall was more focused on trying to snatch a breath. "Baenre is not here to save you, boy. You are mine now." He jerked his head closer until Conall's nose was almost touching his helm. "Can you see?"

Just as Conall thought he might pass out, Orsokon released his grip. He collapsed to his knees, gasping for air as his arm was firmly grasped by an attendant and he was ushered to a doorway at the far side of the arena.

He didn't struggle, allowing himself to be dragged away, no fight left in him. Once he was through the door, it slammed behind him, and he welcomed the quiet confines of the dark.

As his eyes adjusted, he could see other figures lurking in the shadows. Three of them: the arena's other victors. Each one sat in silence, in shock at what they had been forced to do. Relief at surviving. Conall was pleased to see Nylia's face among them.

He sat beside her, noting she nursed a wound in her forearm, though she offered no word of complaint. He would have tried to help her, but what did he know of the healing arts? He had already demonstrated he knew little of combat. Little of anything at all.

Instead, he gave a nod of acknowledgment as they both sat in the dark, listening to the sound of other prisoners dying in the arena. She didn't return the gesture.

LANCELIN

They rode in silence most of the way north, but neither man had ever been known for skill at conversation. The Seminarium had fresh steeds, despite the lack of stable hands, and they covered the distance to the Dolur Peaks at a gallop, only stopping briefly at night to allow the horses some rest. After two days, the mountain range appeared before them, consuming the grey skyline. As the path became more strewn with rock they reined their horses to a steady walk. It wouldn't do to have the animals go lame so close to their destination.

"Do we have a plan?" Kassian asked when they were within a mile of the Forge. "Wymar Ironfall is an unknown quantity in this."

Lancelin had no idea what he would say when they reached the Forge. The fact he could be riding into mortal danger had played on his mind since he started this journey. Nevertheless, he had to try, for the sake of Torwyn.

"No, I have no plan," he replied honestly. "I will ask Wymar to join us. He will fight for the freedom of the Guilds, or he won't."

"Aye, it could be a short conversation. What if he's already sided with the Ministry?"

Again, Lancelin had considered the idea. "Then I imagine Wymar will say no."

Kassian nodded matter-of-factly. "And we'll both end up prisoners of the Draconate."

"I'll be no one's prisoner," Lancelin replied.

Kassian laughed so unexpectedly it made Lancelin's horse start in fright, and he had to wrestle with the reins to bring it back under control.

"Still the old impetuous Lancelin Jagdor," Kassian said. "For all that stoic, focused exterior you still have the heart of a rebel."

Of all the things he had become in the years since his studies at the Seminarium, impetuous was the last thing he considered himself. Clearly Kassian had a different view of it, but before he could argue the old man was wrong, they cornered a bend in the mountain pass and the Forge revealed itself before them.

The city was hewn from the mountainside, rock face shaped into myriad towers and walkways. At the centre was a huge cave mouth flanked by giant statues of armoured warriors. For a moment Lancelin thought how much they looked like Wymar and Maugar, but they had been carved into the solid rock many centuries before either of those men were even born. Clearly the appearance of the Ironfall Guildmasters had changed very little over the years.

Through that yawning entrance lay the city proper. A warren of streets and dwellings that ran deep into the labyrinthine cave network of the Dolur Peaks. Even from a distance Lancelin could hear the sound of forges echoing from within, as smoke streamed out through a hundred chimneys, belching a grey trail up to the clouds.

The uneven mountain path led to a solid road, a thoroughfare that ran right up to the entrance. It stretched almost as wide as it was long, and Lancelin felt surprised to see how scantly guarded it was. There were fewer than a dozen Blackshields, the warriors of Ironfall, moving to greet them as Lancelin and Kassian reined their horses onto the path.

He could feel himself growing tense. From the corner of his eye he saw Kassian leaning forward, seemingly relaxed in his saddle, but his right hand teased the cog pommel of his sword. For his part, Lancelin sat back, keeping his hand well away from the hilt of his new weapon, keen to show he was no threat.

As two of the Blackshields approached, Lancelin nodded in greeting. They were bedecked in heavy steel plate, though they wore no helms. Each one had hair swept back in a topknot and darkened with pitch, in much the same fashion as the Guildmaster and swordwright of the Ironfalls.

"I am Lancelin Jagdor..." he began, but the Blackshield held up a hand before he could finish his introduction.

"We know who you are," he replied. "Our spotters have had eyes on you for the past five miles. Hand over the weapons, and we'll talk."

Not the best start. Lancelin glanced to Kassian, who offered him a simple shrug to indicate he was happy to follow Lancelin's lead. If Wymar had already thrown his lot in with the Ministry, it wouldn't be a good idea to proceed unarmed.

"I have come to speak with Lord Wymar," Lancelin said.

The Blackshield tipped his head to one side. "No shit. We know why you're here, so hand over that pretty sword and we'll see what we can do."

That was the thing with sentries—always so annoyingly vigilant.

Before Lancelin could refuse, there was movement within the huge cave mouth. A procession of Blackshields was led out by the formidable figure of Wymar Ironfall. Over his back was slung an axe and at his side a thick-bladed broadsword. His armour was resplendent by comparison to his men, who had taken to covering the steel in soot from the forges. Emblazoned on his breastplate was the flame of Ironfall, cast in gold and shining in what little daylight crept through the clouds.

As Wymar approached, Lancelin resisted the urge to slide his hand closer to his blade. Instead he sat and watched, trying to read the stern expression on Wymar's face until he reached them and stopped, regarding both men impassively.

"Lancelin Jagdor and Kassian Maine," Wymar grunted. His men had not drawn their weapons, but they still looked ill at ease. "Nice of you to visit." With that, a grin spread across Wymar's bearded face. "Well, climb down off those horses and greet me like the friends we are. Your arses must be numb from all that riding."

His men visibly relaxed as Wymar stepped forward and opened his arms in welcome. Lancelin saw Kassian raise an eyebrow in pleasant surprise, before both men climbed down from their horses.

Wymar held out his arm, and Lancelin gripped it in greeting, before he was pulled closer and crushed in a friendly embrace. As he released Lancelin and approached Kassian, the Guildmaster of Ironfall called the swordwright an "old dog," before moving in to hug him like a brother. Had Kassian known this would be Wymar's reaction all along? If so, he might have mentioned it sooner.

Wymar turned back to Lancelin, his brow creasing in concern. "I am sorry to hear about Sullivar. He had his faults, but he was a good man at heart."

Lancelin felt that familiar clutch of guilt and remorse. "He was. His loss is difficult to bear."

"It is a loss to us all," Wymar replied, guiding them toward the yawning entrance of the Forge. "Those bastard zealots will not be satisfied until we are all under their boot. That little shit Sanctan should have been throttled in the crib."

Lancelin followed, thinking on all the things he should have done. Had he not left to rescue his son, none of this might have happened, but he knew deep within that he would never have refused Rosomon. Even had he known what would happen—that Sullivar would be overthrown and Fulren ultimately perish—he was not sure he would have taken a different course.

"What do you intend to do about it, Wymar?" Lancelin asked. "I assume you aren't just going to barricade yourself in the mountains and wait for this to blow over?"

"Of course not, Jagdor," Wymar replied with a knowing wink. "The Ironfalls go to war. And we do not go alone."

He gestured ahead, and Lancelin could see two figures waiting at the vast entrance. One was tall and imposing in his dark armour, the other was a diminutive woman standing in his shadow.

"The Griffin Battalion have already joined our cause," Wymar said as he mounted the slope to the cave entrance. He raised his voice as the sound of the forges grew louder. "Let me introduce Frontier Marshal Kagan Terswell."

The man stepped forward to greet them. He had long hair and a beard, giving him the look of an Ironfall but for its deep auburn colour. His armour was burnished iron, one shoulder bearing a steel lion head, the other an ornate paw, grey surcoat displaying a yellow griffin rampant on the chest.

"Lancelin Jagdor," Marshal Terswell said with a curt bow of his head. "Your reputation precedes you."

Lancelin returned the gesture. "As does yours. You're a long way from the Karna, Marshal."

"When this whole sorry affair began, I was already on the shores of Torwyn. Once the Anvil was taken, I knew it was best to make my loyalties known, and I brought what men I have here to the Forge."

"And he has brought artificers loyal to the cause," Wymar said, gesturing at the woman beside him. She was short, wiry, with a scar below her left eye. "They have been most helpful. Already reduced inefficiencies in my forges, and improved output by quite a margin. Soon our automation will be second to none, and productivity increased fivefold."

Lancelin could feel the thrumming vibration of machinery and the heat from the fires emanating from within. "More equipment and materiel won't help us if we don't have the fighters to use it."

"We will," Marshal Terswell replied. "When the rest of my battalion gets here."

"And what of your men, Wymar?"

The Lord of Ironfall grinned, his black beard spreading like a huge bush on his face. "Oh, we have already taken the fight to the Ministry. A contingent of Blackshields heads north as we speak, led by my brother, Maugar. He aims to take Wyrmhead. Once the tower falls it will be the first punch to Sanctan's gut."

"You sent Maugar away?" Lancelin asked, unable to hide his frustration. "He should be here, protecting his Guildmaster. Fighting by our side. Wyrmhead holds no strategic significance; it is a waste of good warriors."

"Maybe you're right, Jagdor." If Wymar thought Lancelin had overstepped his bounds, he made no mention of it. "But my brother is an impulsive man. When his blood is up, not even I can curb his anger. But fear not, I have a more than suitable replacement by my side."

"Really? Who?" Lancelin could think of few who would have done Maugar's job as well.

"His daughter, Xorya, now acts as my right hand. My niece is more than up to the task while her father exacts his ire. Just ask Kassian, he taught her everything she knows."

Lancelin glanced to Kassian, who nodded his head. "She is a more than capable sword. One of my best students."

Lancelin wasn't so sure. "You think an untested trainee will compensate for Maugar's absence?"

"I can see you're not convinced," Wymar said, as he led them deeper into the complex. "Why don't I introduce you?"

Lancelin entered the city in the mountain, quickly remembering what a marvel the Forge was to behold. Across a cavern he could see hundreds of workers labouring at the colossal forges. The grind of gears and pistons was deafening, along with the heat of the furnaces that towered on the periphery. Huge chimneys reached up to the cavernous ceiling, funnelling smoke out through the mountain, as turbines fed cooling water along canals before flushing out wastewater through sump pipes. Spread throughout the whole complex of machinery were vats of oil feeding the ancient engines as they smelted ore into workable metals.

Wymar led them across bridges that fell away to nothing on either side, past soaring towers that reached up into the dark. On every granite surface had been hewn a frieze of immense detail, showing the history of the Ironfall Guild and its famous luminaries.

Lancelin could barely hear himself think as they delved ever deeper into the subterranean city, until they finally reached a vast open plaza. From his elevated position Lancelin could see over a thousand Blackshields arrayed in disciplined ranks. They practised their shield wall formations, as functionaries fired missiles at them or charged at them with pugil sticks. Each of them was an armoured behemoth, but together they struck a formidable force of arms. With such warriors as this beside them, Lancelin began to think they might actually have a chance of defying the might of the Ministry.

In the centre of this maelstrom stood a tall young woman with short black hair, barking orders that were immediately obeyed. She strode from rank to solid rank, seeming to instinctually know how to adjust their formations for better efficiency, pointing out in no uncertain terms where their weaknesses were.

Wymar paused for a moment, smiling at what he saw, before he led Lancelin and Kassian down onto the training plaza. As soon as Wymar appeared, the Blackshields dropped to one knee and bowed before their lord. Only the woman remained standing. At first she fixed Lancelin with a stern expression, but as her eyes fell on Kassian that look softened.

"Master Kassian," she said, before she too dropped to her knee and bowed before the swordwright of all swordwrights.

"Xorya," Kassian replied. "It is good to see you putting all I have taught to good use."

The young woman quickly rose to her feet, hand gripping the ornate longsword sheathed at her side. "This is just a warm-up. I'll be happy to put all I have learned into practice when I get a chance to face those Ministry fuckers."

"I'm certain you'll get your chance," Kassian replied.

Xorya glanced to Lancelin, taking a step forward and looking him up and down. A challenge, perhaps?

"And I'll look forward to seeing if the great Jagdor's reputation is well earned. Or just bluster."

Yes. Definitely a challenge. But Lancelin was willing to overlook her youthful exuberance. He'd faced many a challenge, and put down many a challenger, but he doubted this was the time or place.

Before he could speak for himself, Wymar barked a laugh. "You see? Impulsive, just like her father. But maybe we could work on the manners a bit. Carry on, Xorya. We'll need these men fighting fit in the days to come."

With a bow to her uncle, Xorya went back to barking at her men. Lancelin and Kassian followed Wymar back up the stairs from the plaza.

"You see? I told you, Jagdor, she has as furious a nature as my brother. And twice his spirit."

"I do see," Lancelin replied. "But fury only gets you so far. If she's to lead those Blackshields in battle, she'll have to learn more than how to fight, spit and swear."

"She will," said Kassian. "She has time. I don't remember you being a great leader of men at her age."

"No. But I learned fast. Just as she'll have to." He turned to Wymar. "Lord of Ironfall, what is your next move? You must have a plan?"

Wymar nodded. "Indeed. My next move is to march on the Anvil. What other tactic could there be? The sooner we wrench back control from Sanctan, the better."

"A sound strategy. But I am here to tell you that will fail. You don't have enough men to launch a siege, no matter how well drilled they are. And neither do we know the Ministry's strength yet. Sanctan could have any number of Armigers ready and waiting for you to march on the capital. The better option is to join Lady Rosomon at Wyke. There we can unite our forces and create an impregnable bulwark from which to strike back at the Draconate."

Wymar spread his arms wide. "What is more impregnable than a mountain, Jagdor? You've seen my Blackshields, seen how fearsome they are, and with the help of the Griffin Battalion there is no way the Ministry can stand against us."

"If it were just the Ministry you faced, then I might agree. But they have the support of the Hallowhills, and who knows how many others have flocked to their call. An attack on the Anvil would be a rash move. Come with us to Wyke. Help us take the city and hold the northern Guildlands. Once we know how many Armigers have declared for us, then we can take the Anvil."

Wymar stroked a meaty hand through his beard before scratching his chin. "That makes sense. But who will defend the Forge if I come with you?"

"You can leave Xorya to defend the Forge. We will take Wyke, consolidate our forces, then march on the Anvil."

Wymar gazed at them both, then slowly a grin crossed his face.

"Very well, Jagdor. I will come with you and take Wyke. Then we will see what this Archlegate is made of when I stamp his skull into the dirt." His eyebrow rose, and there came a sly aspect to his face. "But first...first we will feast in honour of our coming victories."

The thought of feasting at such a crucial time filled Lancelin with dread. But if he knew one thing, it was that there was no denying Wymar Ironfall when he offered a man his hospitality.

ANSELL

He knelt in prayer, bedecked in armour, helm by his side. Surrounding him were his brothers, each one offering their benediction before the altar. Upon it stood simple depictions of the Great Wyrms, flanked by a candle on each side. Humble idols, there to remind them all of their place within the Draconate.

The Sanctum of Drakes was a vault within the Mount where brother knights could pray, meditate and reflect. There were no High Legates here. No serfs to interrupt them. It was a holy place reserved solely for the martial brotherhood that held the Draconate together.

In the shadows, Ansell could hear his brothers at prayer, some mumbling their litanies with serene calm, others snarling them through gritted teeth. It had been a turbulent time in the Anvil, indeed throughout Torwyn, and each reflected on their deeds in a different way, finding solace however it suited them.

Closest to Ansell was Regenwulf, gripping his sacred blade, head resting against the cross-guard, eyes closed as his lips moved beneath a drooping moustache. He was one of the oldest knights among the Drakes, old enough to have fought in the Battle of Eight Warlords, when a war-host had risen from the Drift and threatened to conquer the entire nation. He had been left a gruesome scar from forehead to chin during that conflict, and he often reminded every one of his brothers where it had come from. A show of pride, which was easy for them to forgive.

In front of him was Lugard, a pious veteran, raising his saturnine features to the ceiling, arms held wide as he reflected in silence. His sword was nowhere to be seen, though his skill with it was only rivalled by his pious observance of the Draconate. Beside him was young, handsome Falcar, blond head bowed, gauntleted hands clasped together. Ansell could only wonder how long those chiselled features would stay so unblemished—among the Knights of the Draconate, no one stayed unscarred for long.

Behind him knelt Hurden, as wide and implacable as Ansell was tall and stern, and beside him, Everis, the youngest of their number, still inexperienced but admired nonetheless. He displayed much mirth on occasion, and no amount of admonishment could mar his smiling face. Ansell could only think he would learn piety and sternness with age, but for now his occasional levity acted as a tonic to them all. Ansell was sure it would not last. Not if what they faced in the days and weeks to come was as grim as they all feared.

Each of these warriors was allowed to perform their observance to the Great Wyrms in his own way. In the Sanctum of the Drakes there was no judgement, and not even the Archlegate would dare besmirch such sanctity. They said their prayers to whichever of the Great Wyrms they wished without fear of reproach.

For Ansell, there was none other than Ammenodus Rex whose favour he would call upon. What other would he need in such a time of strife? Despite the fact that the streets of the Anvil were quiet, he would need the Great Wyrm of War's favour soon enough. But was his god even listening? Certainly the steel statue that sat on the altar gave Ansell no clue, and he had received no benefit so far.

Had Ammenodus been watching over him when he fought the swordwright Jagdor? The wounds that still plagued him were testament to the contrary. Ansell could only hope he would be watched over more vigilantly when the Guilds rallied. When they began to fight back in earnest. Though he did not know when, it was certain that day could not be far away.

A gust of air besmirched the purity of the chamber as the door opened behind them. No one moved in their observance, no one turned to see who had intruded on their prayers. Ansell opened his eyes, hearing the quiet shuffle of sandals on the stone floor, before someone came to stand at his side.

From the corner of his eye he could see someone fidgeting with the sleeve of their grey robe. A legate, here in the lair of the Drakes. A brave one. Or stupid. Or perhaps too fearful of disobeying an order to worry about a reprimand for his trespass here?

Ansell turned his head. The legate was young, a crop of unruly fair hair atop his shaved temples. There was something familiar about him, but Ansell could not quite place it. His fearful eyes confirmed the fact he was anxious to be here.

"Knight Commander Beckenrike," he said in a quiet whisper. It destroyed the serenity of the place, and he may as well have shouted the words from the bottom of his lungs. Regenwulf halted his prayers, turning his grizzled visage on the legate, who swallowed audibly. "My apologies for the disturbance, but the Archlegate has requested your presence in the vestibule."

Ansell nodded, ceasing his prayers and rising to his feet. He followed the legate as he hurried from the Sanctum, wondering once more where he had seen this young acolyte before.

Taking his sword from where it knelt against the wall, he closed the door behind him, leaving his brothers to their prayers. He could only hope they had more luck than he in asking for a blessing.

As the skinny legate led him up from the vault, out through the soaring arches and grand halls of the Mount, Ansell remembered where he had heard tell of this boy before. He had recently returned from the Drift, from his time administering at one of the forts. Rumour had spread that the boy had seen a demon in the wastes, and tried to tell anyone who would listen that there was something evil on the horizon for them all. His story had been deemed little more than the fanciful tale of a coward, and he was admonished for his hysterics. What was his name? Kenlith? Konlath? Something similar? When they neared the door to the vestibule of the Archlegate's personal chambers, Ansell put those thoughts from his mind.

The young legate stood to one side as they reached the door, bowing his head respectfully as Ansell entered the chamber. Heads turned toward him expectantly as he strode in, but when the occupants realised it was just one of many anonymous Drakes, they turned their attention back to the table.

Ansell moved to the periphery of the room. It had once been a vestibule—a chamber for quiet contemplation—but now it was the Archlegate's war room. The place he would meet with his "generals" to formulate their plans for domination.

A long oak table sat at its centre. At the head of it was an empty chair, carved with the likenesses of the Great Wyrms. Sanctan's chair in pride of place, and larger than any of the others. Only one other chair sat unoccupied at the table, but Ansell was under no illusions it was for him.

Present at this meeting were the great and good of Torwyn, the influential figures who had planned this rebellion and succeeded in bringing the Guilds low.

Prince Lorens sat in the seat closest to that reserved for the Archlegate. He looked nervous, out of his depth, but then that was only to be expected. He had helped bring this about by betraying his own father, the emperor of Torwyn, who Ansell had cut down at the Cogwheel. Did the boy know it was Ansell who had killed him? Did he even care? No matter, it was not as if Lorens was in a position to seek revenge. He had been carried along with this insurrection like a helpless rider on a rampant steed. If he was harbouring any second thoughts regarding his involvement, he was too craven to speak of it.

Beside the boy sat Drift Marshal Tarjan of the Corvus Battalion. He stared ahead as though sitting to attention at some military court-martial, his slim face impassive, bald head shining in the torchlight, dark beard impeccably trimmed and waxed to a point.

Opposite him was Marshal Sarona of the Ursus Battalion. She reclined in her armour of office, bear symbols embossed into the dark steel, furs adorning her broad shoulders. Her hair was shorn at the sides, leaving a short greasy mop on top, and she drummed her fingers impatiently on the tabletop. It was clear she was a woman unused to being kept waiting, but then she was here at the Archlegate's command, and would wait for as long as it pleased him.

At the other end of the table sat Darina Egelrath and Rearden Corwen. They leaned into one another, talking quietly. All Ansell could hear was a conspiratorial whisper. Perhaps they were making plans of their own. Or maybe they were just talking about the weather. Either way, it was of little concern—both were invited out of courtesy, he was sure. What more could Sanctan want from either of them now he held total control of the Anvil?

Last was Olstrum Garner, seated on his own at the far side of the table. The former consul kept his eyes focused on the one window that looked out onto the Anvil. Of all the conspirators who were present, this was the one Ansell was most suspicious of. He had betrayed his emperor, risked his life for profit. Such a man could never be trusted, but the Archlegate had seen fit to keep him for his usefulness. Only time would tell whether that was a mistake.

Ansell assumed the one empty chair was reserved for the Hallowhill Guild. They had been key to all this, but where their representative was, he had no idea. Doubtless Sanctan would be displeased with the absence.

Before he could think further on it, the door opened. Sanctan Egelrath smiled at the gathering as he entered, as though greeting his brood with unparalleled grace. His white vestments looked different to Ansell's eye. Had he added embroidery to the humble garment about the cuffs and collar? And the opulent gold chain he now wore was no symbol of the Draconate.

"Thank you all for attending," Sanctan said as he eased himself into his large chair. He looked tiny in it, as though he had sat himself upon the throne of Torwyn rather than a seat in the vestibule.

None of the others acknowledged him as they sat waiting for him to speak. It seemed this was not a formal gathering, although it was unsurprising no one knew how to proceed. The Archlegate was unused to hosting such a gathering for war.

"And congratulations to you all," Sanctan continued. "We have achieved something not seen in this kingdom for a hundred years. We have given the people hope. We have returned—"

"We are a long way from victory," Marshal Sarona interrupted, raising one of her dark eyebrows. "It might be premature to start congratulating ourselves when there is still much to do."

If he was annoyed at the interruption, Sanctan didn't show it. Instead he inclined his head, before raising a hand and cocking his ear to the open window.

"I'm sure that is true, Marshal, but do you hear that?" Silence but for the chirruping of birds in the eaves of the Mount. "The clamour of dissention on the streets? The sound of revolt? The citizenry rising up to demand the reinstitution of the Guilds?" More silence. "No, I don't hear it either. We *have* won a great victory. One we should be proud of."

Sarona let out a disconsolate sigh. "I have received word that the Kraken Battalion have claimed Windstone for the Guilds. War has erupted in Castleteig. The Ironfalls, Marrlocks and Hawkspurs have still not formally surrendered to us. We are indeed a long way from victory."

Sanctan's assured smile wavered just a touch as he traced something on the tabletop with his finger. Keeping himself in control perhaps? A sign of his pride being hurt? As much as Ansell obeyed the Archlegate without question, he could not help but think it an advantage to have someone speak against his overconfidence.

"As long as everyone here holds to their tasks, victory will be assured. We knew this was never going to be easy. The Guilds would not simply roll over and allow their lands and assets to be taken, and their titles to be withdrawn. But progress has been made, Marshal Sarona. Your own battalion has already taken Wyke. The Rock will not stand for much longer and neither will the Forge."

"And when they fall? What then?" Sarona sounded unconvinced of the Archlegate's plans. "How do you intend to ensure the people will follow? The Anvil may be quiet now, may be cowed by your Drakes and Rearden's Revocaters, but what of the rest of Torwyn? Once you destroy the Guilds, what of their artifice? What of the engines that power this country? What will you do to feed your people?"

Sanctan dismissed Sarona's concerns with a wave of his hand. "The Guilds will not defy me for long, and with them gone there will be no dissent. The Ministry holds the hearts of all the people of Torwyn. It always has. We have merely been silenced by charlatans. Once the artifice falls and the Guilds are no more, the scales will fall from their eyes. There will be no turning back."

Marshal Tarjan leaned across the table, his well-oiled beard shining, his crisp uniform creaking, it was so tightly tailored. "Once the artifice falls?" he asked. "And how would the Hallowhills feel about this?" He glanced furtively at the empty seat.

Sanctan followed his gesture, glancing at the chair that should have been filled by a representative of the Hallowhills. For a moment, Ansell thought he saw a glimmer of doubt in Sanctan's face, before he reclined in his huge wooden throne and waved another dismissive hand.

"The opinions of the webwainers are nothing to be concerned with."

"Really?" Tarjan replied, raising a sharp eyebrow. "You expect Ingelram Hallowhill to roll over so easily? After all he has sacrificed to secure your victory? With the others subdued, his Guild will become the most powerful organisation in Torwyn. Ingelram will finally hold the power he has craved for so long. He and his webwainers control all the artifice. One man will be in charge of the most valuable commodity in all Torwyn."

"Not for long," Sanctan replied casually, as though Tarjan's concerns were of no matter.

He let his words linger for a moment. The tension in the air was palpable as they thought on the prospect of Ingelram Hallowhill controlling the country's artifice and what it might mean for each of them.

"All right," Sarona said eventually. "I'll bite. Why would it not be for long?"

"Because I intend to strip this nation of its accursed engines and dump them in the deepest pit. The use of artifice will be forbidden throughout Torwyn. Its machinery smashed, to be replaced by the vigour and labour of its people. No one will be permitted to use it, on pain of death. By decree of the Draconate Ministry."

Again, Sanctan let his words hang in the air. No one seemed of a mind to speak as they processed what had just been tabled. No more artifice. The repercussions would be widespread and devastating. Whole industries would collapse.

Rearden was the first to find enough courage to speak. "Archlegate," he said in that crowing tone of his. "I...must object. I do not think you appreciate the consequences of such a decree. Its effect on the country's economy. On its people. Thousands will starve. There will be rioting in the streets."

"And it will be quelled," Sanctan replied, as though it were obvious.

"I am sorry, Archlegate, but I cannot sanction this. I doubt any of us could. We agreed on a transfer of power to curb Sullivar's excesses and protect us from threats across the Drift. Not for the whole infrastructure of Torwyn to be put in jeopardy, from the smallest farm to the largest manufactory. You must think again."

Sanctan glanced up from examining his fingernails, and fixed Rearden with a nonchalant smile. "Must I?" he said, before gesturing toward Ansell with the slightest raising of his chin.

It was the smallest of signals, but Ansell had long since learned to read his Archlegate. He took a step forward, towering over Rearden, who glanced back over his shoulder, seemingly unimpressed by the threat.

"Sanctan," he breathed. "We have known each other too long to engage in such pointless theatrics. Empty threats of violence—"

Ansell grabbed Rearden's thinning hair in a gauntleted fist. The Guildmaster had a chance to emit an effusive squawk before Ansell slammed his head into the hard oak table. He paused, considering slamming it twice for good measure, but a pitiful burble from the Guildmaster made it obvious he had learned his lesson.

"You all have your jobs to do," Sanctan said, all his good humour now faded away. Ansell could see that Marshals Tarjan and Sarona were little impressed with the violent display, but the rest looked shocked as Rearden bled profusely from his now-crooked nose. "I suggest you all get on with them. My decree will be made public by the end of the day. I expect it to be supported by you all."

The Archlegate had no more to say. If anyone objected further to his plans for the country, they did not see fit to speak it.

Rearden rose gingerly, gripping tight to his bloody nose as he staggered from the room, closely followed by Lorens. The marshals likewise stood. Tarjan offered a curt nod to Sanctan before leaving, where Sarona did not offer so much as a second glance. Only Olstrum and Darina remained.

"You will set in motion the dismantling of the city's artifice," Sanctan said, still examining his fingertips. "I am relying on you to organise this as efficiently as possible."

Olstrum nodded his assent, but he could not hide the reluctance in his eyes. "As you command, Archlegate. I will set about the task immediately. But...might I take this opportunity to enquire as to the health of—?"

"The health of...?" Sanctan raised his brows as though the question were a stupid one. "You should think more on your own health, Olstrum."

The consul sank visibly, lowering his eyes for a moment before glancing Ansell's way. "As you command, Archlegate," he said, sliding back his chair and slinking from the room like a dog that had just been kicked.

Now only Sanctan and Darina remained. The Archlegate's mother glared across the table with a disapproving expression, but Ansell could not remember her looking much different any other time.

"You are making a mistake," she said, the stark words ruining the calm of the vestibule.

Sanctan sighed like a child told it was his bedtime. "I disagree."

"You are moving too fast. Trying to bring about too much change too quickly. It will not—"

He slammed his hand on the table. "I will not be contradicted!"

The words echoed through the room. Darina looked distinctly unimpressed with her son's fury. She watched him without emotion, before glancing toward Ansell.

Did she expect him to approach her and offer the same harsh lesson he'd given Rearden? Was that Ansell's purpose now, to threaten and beat old men and women?

Without another word, Lady Darina rose imperiously and turned to the door. Ansell expected her to throw a final barb at her son before she left, but she kept her peace as she closed the door behind her.

Sanctan let out a long sigh, before standing and stretching his spine. He turned toward the one window, shaking his head.

"They do not share my vision," Sanctan said to no one in particular. "But I will make them see."

Ansell could only ponder what that meant. Would the Archlegate grant his brood enlightenment? So far he had forced everyone around him to accept his will with duplicity and violence. It was certain that would carry on well into the future. And Ansell had little doubt what his part would be in the days to come.

KEARA

She was over a day late, but with the red drop tingling its way through her system she couldn't have cared a shit. Any repercussions there might have been for upsetting the Archlegate seemed almost inconsequential. Besides, it was such a beautiful day, why waste it worrying on things that hadn't happened yet?

From the observation deck of the landship, the Anvil looked stunning—coruscating lights winking on those soaring white towers, the skytrain line encircling it like a lambent halo. Keara would have smiled in delight, but all the mirth was gone from her. All the joy leached from her body as her father's words echoed in her ears, no matter how much narcotic she dripped into her eyes.

Through the haze of the red drop, she noticed the forge fires of the Anvil no longer burned. There was no pall of smoke drifting on the southern wind, and the city looked quiet, like an ancient monument to a time long dead. But Keara knew the old regime was not dead yet. There was still much work to do before that day came.

As she leaned against the gunwale she watched Ulger standing to the fore. His bald head was tilted back as he let the wind rush past him, arms outstretched to embrace it as it blew through splayed fingers.

Hesse stood to the rear, eyes concealed behind her dark eyewear, hair billowing. She looked discomfited, nervous even, and it served to bring Keara crashing down from her high.

"What's your problem?" she called across the observation deck.

Hesse chewed at her lip before saying, "We're late."

Of course they were late, but wasn't it Keara's prerogative? A little demonstration that she was an ally to the Ministry and not its servant.

"Let the Archlegate wait," Keara said. It was defiance, pure and simple, but when she said the words, she didn't quite feel their conviction. No matter. What would Sanctan Egelrath do anyway? He needed her, and her Guild. He was hardly going to punish her for tardiness, like an apprentice late for tutelage.

As the landship crossed the boundary of the city she could see workers busying themselves in one of the manufactory yards. They were dismantling a section of hulking machinery, the sounds of their hammers and blowlamps rising above the din of the pyrestone engine.

The closer they came to the landship terminal, the more activity was evident, until eventually she could see the platform up ahead. Where previously there had been rows of landships maintained by crews of artificers, now hulking workmen were stripped to the waist, breaking up the great engines and reducing them to scrap.

"What's going on?" Hesse asked as the landship began to slow.

Keara shook her head. "I have no idea."

"Don't you think you ought to find out?"

The notion she should be concerned by all this sat ill in Keara's stomach, but she didn't reply. As the landship slowed to a stop that ill feeling set like stone, foreboding clouding her mind as the ecstasy of the red drop began to wane.

Her nausea persisted as the three of them debarked and made their way through the terminal. There weren't many other passengers, nor much in the way of security as they proceeded through the building and out into the city. The streets were all but deserted, with the odd sad-looking stallholder touting their meagre wares. As Keara led the way toward the Cogwheel, Ulger picked an apple from the stall of a fruit seller, not bothering to toss him so much as a copper coin before he raised the apple in thanks and took a bite. The fruit seller didn't utter a word of complaint that he'd just been robbed, and Keara didn't feel the need to chastise Ulger for the theft. This was their right after all. They owned this place now.

In the distance she could make out the ruin of Archwind Palace, its magnificent facade lying open like a corpse on a slab, ribs splayed to reveal its innards. The cog symbol that used to adorn it was now so much rubble. The Bridge of Saints was likewise smashed and broken—a monument to the battle that had taken place across its hallowed span. A reminder of the sacrifices made to secure their victory. Keara had seen so many die that night, so many webwainers giving their lives for the glory of the Ministry. People she had known. People she had called friends.

Before she could lament further on that loss, she heard a noise carried on the wind. The closer they came to the Cogwheel, the louder that noise got. A single voice was raised, but she couldn't make out the words, before a cheer echoed along the promenade. As they crested the lip of the rise, she realised why the streets were mostly deserted.

A huge crowd was gathered about the Cogwheel. At its centre, elevated above the throng on a podium, was a single High Legate, flanked by half a dozen Drakes. Her black robes marked her as a devotee of Ravenothrax the Unvanquished, the Great Wyrm of Death, and as she spoke she beguiled the crowd with her every word.

"As they have fallen, so shall their symbols fall," the High Legate cried.

A pitiful squeal pealed over the crowd as the Drakes pulled on chains, dragging a war eagle onto the podium. It was huge, feathers ruffling as it struggled against its bonds. The Drakes held firm and the creature was helpless before the murmuring crowd.

Keara sensed what was coming, as the spectators began to bay in anticipation. Ulger took another noisy bite from his apple as the black-robed High Legate raised her arms for the crowd to be silent.

"We have been ground beneath the boot of the Guilds for too long. Oppressed by their idols and kept in thrall to their craven images. These beasts are symbolic of that tyranny, the great war eagles with which they controlled the skies. But you will be freed from their despotism. The Archlegate has decreed it so."

As the High Legate spoke, the sick feeling in Keara's stomach intensified. The beast struggled against its chains as one of the Drakes hefted a mighty axe.

"Behold," the High Legate continued. "This is the way you shall be freed from the yoke of the Guilds. This is the road to your emancipation."

Keara held her breath as the Drake raised his axe high. It seemed the crowd shared her trepidation. Some of them even turned their eyes away before the axe slammed down. Keara forced herself to watch the grim spectacle, as a single blow took the head from the eagle with a resounding thud. A moment's pause before the crowd howled its approval.

"Brutal," Ulger said above the sound of cheers, before taking another big bite of his apple.

"A fucking waste," Keara replied, turning away from the crowd.

Hesse was still watching. As usual there was no expression to suggest how she felt about the needless slaughter. Before Keara could think to ask, she saw someone heading toward them through the press.

Olstrum eased his way from the crowd, slithering past like the snake he was. As he moved closer, Keara could see his expression was not quite as self-assured as usual. The man looked worried, fearful even. His eyes searched the crowd conspiratorially, and as he came to stand in front of her, they shifted furtively toward her companions.

"You're late," he said. "And you know how he hates to be kept waiting."

"How did you know where to find me?" she replied.

Olstrum simply shrugged. "I know everything that goes on in the Anvil. It's my job."

"If that's true, then what in the Lairs is going on here? Why are these creatures being slaughtered in front of a baying crowd?"

Olstrum glanced toward the podium as another of the great war eagles was dragged forward in chains. "The Archlegate has decreed the symbols of the Guilds be dismantled, along with its artifice."

Keara wasn't sure she'd heard him right. "With its artifice? But that's just madness."

"You are to meet him at the Guildhall."

Changing the subject. Clearly the consul wasn't of a mind to question the Archlegate's decision.

"Why there? Why not the Mount?"

Olstrum shook his head. "I don't ask the reasons. I just deliver orders."

She should have arrived in the city a day ago. What else had she missed?

"What's going on? Is there something you're not telling me?"

Olstrum took a step closer. "I suggest you don't keep him waiting any longer, Hallowhill."

As much as she hated this simpering coward, she knew it wouldn't be wise to ignore his advice.

"Very well, let's go," she said to Hesse and Ulger.

Olstrum raised his hand. "You are to see him alone."

More bad news, but again it would have been foolish to ignore Olstrum's instructions. "Very well. Alone it is."

From the look on Ulger's face he was none too pleased with the notion, but Keara offered him a nonchalant wink before making her way from the Cogwheel.

There wasn't so much as a stray cat on the street as she walked toward the Guildhall. When it came into view, Keara remembered the last time she had entered its illustrious confines. It had felt like she was trespassing, the right to enter denied to her bloodline for too long. Had Treon Archwind not brought her Guild low, her father would have had his own seat there. Instead, it felt as though she were some disgraced serf, grovelling for forgiveness at the feet of her betters.

Only Sanctan had not treated her as such. He had offered her Guild redemption, and they had long spoken of raising a new empire—one with the Hallowhills at its epicentre. Now it seemed all that might have been a lie. If his plans to destroy Torwyn's artifice came to fruition, what of the Hallowhills? Without artifice what need for webwainers?

Surely there was some misunderstanding. She had been made promises. And despite the gains the Ministry had made, it could not hope to succeed in its crusade without continued help from her people.

When she finally made it to the Guildhall, the entrance yawned open like the mouth of some beast—one of the Great Wyrms ready to consume her. There were no guards outside, but her nerves still began to jangle as she neared the dark archway, the carved symbols of the Guilds that were hewn above it glaring admonishingly. Everything about this felt like a trap.

There were no torches to light the passageway, and Keara was shrouded in darkness, her nerves starting to fray, all her confidence vanishing with the light. But there could be no turning back.

When she entered the main hall, it was dimly lit by torches, the bright pyrestone lights that normally illuminated the place having been removed. The sigils of the six most powerful Guilds had been torn down, and on the seat reserved for the emperor lounged Sanctan Egelrath.

He squinted at his fingernails as though there was something there he couldn't quite dislodge, one leg slung over the armrest. At the bottom of the stairs leading up to that throne stood a single Drake guarding the way. Keara recognised him as Sanctan's personal bodyguard, the one with a chin scarred black, despite vain attempts to hide it beneath a wispy beard. She'd never bothered to ask his name, and he'd certainly never offered it. The Drake regarded her as she moved forward, and there was an almost sympathetic look to his sad eyes, as though he were sorry she was being subjected to this indignity.

"Good of you to finally join us, Hallowhill," Sanctan said, not deigning to look up from his troublesome fingernails.

The implication was as subtle as a brick to the head. "My apologies, Archlegate. I—"

He looked up from his fingers and regarded her with a raised eyebrow. "You were supposed to be here yesterday."

Keara dared a glance toward that Drake. Suddenly he didn't look so sympathetic. "I had important business at the Web."

"More important than attending a meeting of our new council? Plans are afoot, Hallowhill. Plans you and your webwainers are critical to."

"Really? Do those plans involve executing more helpless animals? Or destroying more artifice?"

Sanctan shrugged as though it didn't matter a damn. "Those things are necessary. A demonstration of intent."

"A demonstration of power," Keara replied, instantly regretting it. She was speaking her mind too readily, most likely a result of the red drop that still lurked at the edge of her senses. It was a dangerous game to play with Sanctan.

Nevertheless, he seemed unconcerned by her candid opinion. "And we have only just begun. We must push ourselves to greater efforts. This nation has not been brought to heel yet. Demonstrations of power are not enough, we must dominate. For that to happen you will need to play your part." He was staring at her now, all his arrogance sloughed off, replaced by steel. "Castleteig is under siege. You will send more of your webwainers to help bring order to the city. It must be taken. Wyke is under our control, but if my guess is right, it may soon come under attack. You will also send your people there to ensure it remains under my control."

My control. Not *our* control. Sanctan was making it crystal clear who this was all for. Who this would benefit.

"My webwainers are at your disposal," Keara replied. "But how are they to be effective without artifice?"

"Rest assured they will be provided with stormhulks, and all the materiel they require for the task."

"That's all well and good, Archlegate, but what happens when all this is over? What happens when my webwainers finally seal your victory and there are no more battles to fight?"

A smile rose on one side of Sanctan's mouth. It was obvious he knew what she was implying. That she knew his real plans. That she could see an end to the Hallowhills' usefulness when all this was over.

"You need not concern yourself with that," the Archlegate replied. "We face a stubborn foe. The priority for now is to see our enemies defeated."

Keara should have kept her mouth shut. There was no way she should question this man, poke the lion with a stick, but the future of her Guild was under threat. Hadn't her father warned her of this very thing?

Once again her eyes flicked to the brooding knight who stood scant feet away. She knew he was here more to intimidate her than to protect Sanctan. If she went too far, would he be ordered to demonstrate the might of the Ministry? Keara was past caring.

"I've witnessed how you intend to destroy the Guilds, Archlegate. How you intend to eradicate the very infrastructure this country is built on. The Hallowhills are also a part of that infrastructure. Will we be cast aside once you've achieved your goal? Tell me, Sanctan, what fate awaits us when you have what you want?"

That smile crept up the side of his face again. "Why, Keara, it is the same fate that awaits everyone. You will exist in a state of grace beneath the watchful gaze of the Great Wyrms." The smile fell away, those eyes regarding her with renewed intensity. "Or you will be burned in their righteous breath."

But of course. What answer had she been expecting?

Sanctan shifted in the throne, rising to his feet and walking down the stairs to stand before her. "Do you doubt my word? I would hate to have to convince you of the right path to take."

The Drake behind him hadn't moved, but the threat from Sanctan was convincing enough. Still, she had no answer. The red drop inside her gave enough courage not to throw herself to her knees and pledge fealty to the Ministry, but neither did it give her the strength to speak.

Sanctan tilted his head, regarding her with that benevolent expression that might at any minute turn to menace.

"Saphenodon teaches us that there is courage in defiance. To stand by one's convictions is the noblest of traits. But she also teaches us that there is wisdom in obedience, even when it appears that to obey goes against our own interests. Ultimately, wisdom is the key to faith, and faith is the path to deliverance. Do you understand, Hallowhill?"

Keara wasn't entirely sure she did, but now wasn't the time to question the Archlegate on scripture. "Of course. Thank you for the lesson."

"Good," he replied. "I would hate to have to teach you the word of Undometh. The Great Wyrm of Vengeance is a much more unforgiving tutor." He let that one hang in the air for a moment before the smile was back on his face. "Together we have achieved a great victory, but there is still yet more to do. The rewards for your support will be ample. The punishment for betrayal..."

"I get it," she whispered.

"Of course you do. I didn't ask for your help because I thought you were stupid. And just in case you think I'm being unfair, I have a very specific task for you. Repairs to the Bridge of Saints and the palace are underway, but I'm finding the labourers lack a certain... motivation. I'll be putting you in charge, and your webwainers will be key to restoring this city to its former glory. If that's all right with you?"

It most certainly wasn't. She was heir to a Guild, not a glorified foreman. "Of course it is."

"Excellent."

With that he walked away, leaving her to ponder how far she'd fallen. The Drake followed him, not deigning to offer her a second glance. She waited until they had left the hall, and when she was sure she was alone, Keara let out the breath she had been holding.

All this she suffered on the promise of power, but now the folly of that decision was becoming more obvious with every passing hour. *The rewards for your support will be ample?* That didn't look bloody likely. With each new revelation it was becoming clear that Sanctan was rendering her Guild obsolete. Perhaps her father had been right, and she had made them beholden to religious fanatics. That notion stung most of all.

Outside the Guildhall the streets were still deserted, but to her relief, Ulger and Hesse waited patiently for her.

"So how did that go?" Ulger asked.

"It could have gone better," Keara replied, failing to mention that it could also have gone much worse. "I'm starting to think we've made a fool's bargain. We've replaced one set of overlords with another, but at least with the Guilds we were useful. Soon, a day might come when we have served our purpose."

That seemed to worry Ulger, but Hesse was less concerned. But then she never seemed concerned about anything much.

"So what now?" Hesse asked.

Keara regarded those eyes hidden behind her dark glasses.

"Now? We bide our time. And wait for an opportunity to present itself."

LANCELIN

He rose from the oaken bed, taking another opportunity to appreciate the stout polished veneer and the craftsmanship that had gone into its construction. His chamber was carved from the bare rock of the Dolur Peaks, and might otherwise have been a depressing cell, but it was well lit with torches, a fire glowing perpetually in the hearth. On every wall were bookshelves built into the bare rock, and as he stood, Lancelin regarded those shelves as he had every morning, marvelling at the array of tomes. As well as ancient codices on the techniques of forging, there were also books on poetry and philosophy going back to the Age of Kings. He could only marvel at what a contradiction these Ironfalls were—at once boorish, ale-swilling ruffians, while at the same time warrior poets, artisans and minstrels.

Lancelin would have to think on that contradiction later, for today they would leave for Wyke. He was quick to don his travelling clothes, buckling the sword belt around his waist so the blade sat comfortably at his hip. As he ran a thumb over the Hawkspur sigil that adorned the pommel, he considered once again what a precious gift Kassian had given him. If only he still had a Guildmaster to wield it for.

But then, he did. Rosomon was waiting for him, and she needed him now more than ever. He knew that he would never truly be whole until he could return to her side, but she in turn must be suffering—struggling to deal with the loss of Conall and Tyreta. The death of Fulren.

Lancelin found himself gritting his teeth at the thought of his son. No one would ever ask him about the pain he felt. No one would ever know of Lancelin Jagdor's grief, but then he had spent a lifetime ignoring his own losses.

A rap at the door sharpened his focus. Lancelin opened it, expecting some Ironfall serf to be waiting with slabs of cooked meat for him to break his fast, but instead he was greeted by the stern features of Kassian Maine. Lancelin had known him long enough to discern the subtle details in that grim face, and he could tell his old sword master's brow was furrowed deeper than usual.

"There is trouble," Kassian said. "You need to come with me."

"What kind of trouble?" Lancelin replied, following Kassian along the corridor.

"The Griffin Battalion is leaving."

Lancelin asked no more questions as he followed, though the implications were dire. The thought of losing a valuable ally so early in their campaign against the Ministry was a blow.

When they reached the cavernous entryway to the Forge, troopers of the Griffin Battalion were already filing out in disciplined ranks. To one side Frontier Marshal Terswell was engaged in heated conversation with Wymar, their discussion growing ever more animated.

Both men were flanked by their lieutenants—stern-looking Blackshields and Griffin Battalion troopers glaring at one another, waiting for their leaders to give them reason to begin fighting. Lancelin approached them as quickly as he could.

"You're a bloody coward, Terswell," Wymar barked. "Curse you. And curse *me* for ever trusting you."

"Watch your tongue, Ironfall," growled the frontier marshal. "I'll not be lectured in bravery by a man who hides himself away in a bloody mountain."

"What's going on?" demanded Lancelin, as he came to stand with the men. He was tempted to get between them, but he doubted it would stop them if they came to blows.

Wymar pointed an accusing finger. "This craven bastard is running away. He made his promises to the Guilds of Torwyn and now he's backing out."

Lancelin expected Terswell to deny it, but his silence spoke more than words ever could.

"Why?" Lancelin asked. "Why now?"

He could see a flicker of shame in Terswell's eyes, before the marshal regarded him with a steely gaze. "Travelling to Wyke is folly. By now Sanctan Egelrath will have dispatched every Armiger Battalion loyal to him. They will be marching on Wyke as we speak. There could be ten thousand troopers already in the Hawkspur Guildlands; it would be suicide to oppose him."

"We already agreed on this. You knew it would be difficult, Kagan, but we made a pact. You stand for the Guilds, not the Ministry."

"I am sorry, Jagdor. If it makes a difference, I do not stand for the Ministry either. I just can't sacrifice my troopers for a cause that may already be lost. I would help if I could, but I have my men to think on."

"So where do you intend to go? Nowhere in Torwyn is safe. Bleat about neutrality all you want, but you'll have to fight eventually."

Terswell tightened his jaw, regarding Lancelin with resignation. "Good luck to you, Jagdor."

He spun on his heel and walked away with his lieutenants. Lancelin expected Wymar to spit some insult in the frontier marshal's wake, but instead he stood in silence, bunching his gauntleted hands into fists.

Lancelin felt compelled to do something, anything. Rosomon had sent him to recruit as many allies as they could find, and here he was, failing at the first test. Should he have gone after Terswell? Grabbed him by his throat and squeezed compliance into the cowardly bastard? He took a step after Kagan, but a hand on his arm kept him in place.

"I know what you're thinking," Kassian whispered close to his ear. "But his mind is made, and it would be foolish to start a fight right here. If we have to face the Griffin Battalion later, then we will do it on our terms."

It was the first time anyone had mentioned the notion of war to Lancelin. Before he had seen this as an insurgency, a coup, but it was clear what they faced now was civil war, pure and simple.

He turned to Wymar. "What now, Ironfall? Do you still stand with us?"

Lancelin could feel himself bristling at his failure, and tried his best to subdue the anger in his voice. For his part, Wymar narrowed one eye and offered a bearded grin.

"I told you I would come to Wyke by your side, Jagdor, and the Ironfalls are a Guild who keep their word. My Blackshields are more than a match for any Armiger. Come, I will show you how dedicated we are to this cause."

Lancelin cast one more glance toward the troopers of the Griffin Battalion as they marched away, before following Wymar and his shield men deeper into the Forge. A clamour of noise echoed up to the high cavernous ceiling as they approached the sprawling courtyard at the centre of the mountain city. There waited rank upon armoured rank of Blackshields. As soon as their Guildmaster showed himself, the warriors fell silent, standing to attention as the refineries continued their clangour in the background.

Wymar drew his eye across the rows of shield bearers, their spears rising like a forest of dark iron.

"Warriors of the Forge," he pronounced, his deep voice resonating throughout the cavern. "By now you know that the cowards of the Griffin Battalion have turned tail and fled. They have run from this fight before it has even begun."

A discontented murmur reverberated through the ranks of the Blackshields, and Wymar raised his thick arms for silence.

"We of the Ironfall Guildlands were tempered in hotter fires than those mere mercenaries. For centuries my ancestors have stood as stalwart as the mountains we now call home, loyal to Torwyn and its people. As have each of yours."

Now the stirrings of displeasure turned to approval, as the dark-haired warriors of Ironfall nodded their agreement.

"For one hundred years we have carved out our place in this nation. Forged its raw material into steel and iron, refined oil into the blood that runs in this country's veins. The Ironfalls have fed this nation's prosperity. We are the backbone of Torwyn's industry. Without us, Torwyn will only fall. But we will not hide. We will not retreat. We will face this uprising and stamp it beneath our ironshod boots."

A cheer rose up, echoing throughout the cavern. As it did so, Lancelin's eye was drawn to the edge of the cave behind them. Someone was moving in the shadows, clinging to the rock wall as they slipped from one tunnel to another. He caught a glimpse of a woman's face, one he was sure he recognised. With such an auspicious speech taking place it seemed odd to him that someone would be slinking about in the dark, and he took a step toward the figure as it ducked into a dark passageway.

"Where are you going?" Kassian asked above the cheering of the Blackshields.

"I'll be back," Lancelin said, moving from the raised dais and toward the tunnel.

"Our legacy is now under threat," Wymar continued, as Lancelin made for the passage. "Which of you will stand alongside me? Which of you will face the tyranny of the Draconate Ministry by my side?" Another cheer, drowning out the tolling sound of the forges. "Will you fight to restore Torwyn to its once-great status?"

As those cheers became deafening, Lancelin slipped into the passage, illuminated by pyrestone light. He could see the shadowy figure just up ahead, a woman from her gait and stature, head bowed but walking with purpose. She led him on a circuitous route further into the bowels of the mountain. With every yard, the hotter it got, and the more pungent the stink of the infernium refineries that resided below.

Eventually he was led into a huge chamber containing an intersecting system of pumps and storage cylinders, rising thirty feet to the roof. Pressure gauges and steam outlets were rigged via myriad pipes to an intricate web of machinery. At the far side of the chamber he spied the woman tinkering with some device attached to one of those pipes.

With so loud a din deep in the bowels of the Forge, the woman didn't notice she had been pursued until Lancelin was almost upon her. He grasped her shoulder, spinning her around, and recognised her pinched face, that scar below her eye. This was the artificer Marshal Terswell had been with when he first entered the Forge. But if the Griffin Battalion had already left, what was she still doing here?

Her face turned to panic on seeing him. She'd been manipulating some pyrestone gadget chained to one of the refinery pumps.

"What are you doing?" he demanded.

She opened her mouth to answer, before ducking under his arm and dashing for a nearby tunnel. Lancelin grasped her cloak as she fled, but only managed to tear it from her shoulders.

With a last glance at the device, its red pyrestone winking furiously in its midst, he gave chase. Damn she was fast, tearing through those corridors as though Ravenothrax himself were closing in with gnashing jaws.

He almost lost her as she ducked left along a smaller passage, the noise of the clanking refinery echoing with a relentless dull boom. As she crawled up a steep flight of rough-hewn stairs, Lancelin fell upon her, grabbing her wrist, slamming it against the stair, expecting her to be holding a weapon of some kind, but she was unarmed, eyes wide in fear.

"Don't kill me," she screamed above the deluge.

"What have you done?" Lancelin snarled. "What was that device?"

"We have to get out of here," she said desperately. "Those charges are planted throughout the refinery. They cannot be stopped. We have to get out or we'll both die."

"What have you—"

She fixed him with a fierce look. "This stairway is the only way out. We have to run or we're both dead, swordwright. Make your choice."

He glanced up the stairs, seeing the enticing glow of daylight from just beyond its lip. Whatever this artificer had done, it might spell doom for the Blackshields, for the whole of the Forge. Lancelin could not let that happen—he could not fail Rosomon, not again.

He grasped the artificer by the collar and dragged her back the way they'd come, his only thought on saving the men who might fight alongside the Hawkspurs. Once more he plunged into the deafening noise of the passage, desperate to remember the way he had come, to retrace his steps through this cloying labyrinth.

Every chamber looked the same, each one deserted, no one to ask if he was taking the right route back to the cavern in which Wymar was stirring his army into a frenzy, to fight a war they might never see. At each step the artificer struggled, but he dragged her along like a rag doll, determined she would meet either justice or the same fate that awaited everyone in the Forge.

At the end of the passage was torchlight, a cacophonous roar echoing as the Blackshields cheered for their lord. Lancelin burst out into the cavern, seeing Wymar with his arms raised as the Blackshields continued to shout their approval at his speech. Whatever words he had said had whipped them into a frenzy. Kassian turned as Lancelin appeared, his face creasing in concern.

"We have to get out," Lancelin yelled, but his words were lost amid the cries of Wymar's men. "There is something—"

A seismic vibration snatched the cavern in its fist, shaking it as though the whole mountain were about to collapse. Lancelin was thrown to the ground as a rumble of thunder consumed everything. Heat raged, a dozen refineries combusting on the periphery of the cavern, sending a devastating wave of fire throughout the Forge.

Rocks crashed down around him, and Lancelin covered his head. He could hear screaming, the yells of a thousand men suddenly caught in a deluge of stone and debris. The ground cracked, fissures opening up to consume anyone unlucky enough to be standing nearby.

Lancelin gritted his teeth, eyes clamped shut as dust and soot filled the cavern. He could barely breathe, bracing himself for the inevitable impact of a falling rock.

Then silence. A hand gripped his, pulling him to his feet, and he saw the grim eyes of Kassian looking on with concern. He had been struck in the head, a trail of blood running from his scalp and through the grey dust that covered his face.

Lancelin glanced about the raised dais, seeing the armoured form of Wymar lying amid a pile of rubble. From the blank stare on the

Lord of Ironfall's face, it was obvious he was dead. Of the treacherous artificer there was no sign.

Some of the Blackshields on the square below were rising to their
feet, though most of them had been consumed by the mountain.
Above them, the rocky rooftop suddenly cracked.

"Run!" Lancelin shouted.

A few of them staggered toward the entryway of the Forge, as the
roof began to collapse, pitching black rock onto their heads. Another
explosion burst from an interior passage as Lancelin and Kassian
stumbled toward their only escape. Fires burned, corpses littering
their path, as they desperately picked their way across the debris.

The arch leading out to the road east had mostly collapsed, almost
sealing them in. All that remained was a wide slit in the rock, smiling like a demon's maw, letting in what little sunlight it could. Some
of the Blackshields raced ahead, desperate to escape the dust-filled
cave before they were entombed.

Lancelin and Kassian followed, climbing over the fallen statues
that once stood as a proud testament to the might of Ironfall. No
sooner had the first of the Blackshields reached the narrow gap than
they were met by the staccato clap of splintbow fire.

Lancelin ducked as a relentless volley met the remaining Blackshields. The dull snap of a longbarrel echoed from outside, pyrestone-
fuelled shot humming overhead, puncturing the armour of one hapless
warrior.

"This way," Kassian growled, grabbing Lancelin by his jacket and
dragging him out of range of the splintbows.

A passage led upward, and Lancelin could only hope it would take
them to freedom and not a dead end. Behind, he heard some of the
Blackshields bark in pain and fury, their lust for vengeance overtak-
ing their sense, as they ran headlong into the fusillade, desperate to
take the fight to the Griffin Battalion.

"We cannot help them," Kassian urged as he led the way, up the
tunnel to a stout oaken door.

He shoved it wide, and Lancelin stumbled after him, sucking in a
purging breath of fresh air as they were struck by sunlight. He stopped,
blinking in the brightness, only to see that they were surrounded.

Half a dozen troopers of the Griffin Battalion had taken positions upon the surrounding rocks. Each one had a splintbow levelled, and Lancelin swiftly assessed their chances. If he and Kassian acted quickly enough, at least one of them might draw his sword before the troopers opened fire. Maybe one of them would even cut an enemy down before being killed.

"What do you think?" Lancelin asked.

A wry smile crossed Kassian's stony features. "I think our chances are slim."

"Who knows, maybe they want to take us alive."

Kassian shook his head. "What did I always teach you?"

He remembered well enough. A swordwright would never have let himself be taken prisoner. The only question was, which of these men to kill before he was shot down like a pig in its pen?

Before he could decide, a dark shadow dropped from the rocks above to land amid the troopers. Lancelin could barely focus on the blade as it swept the air, but he did see the head fall from the first of the splintbowmen, a second run through the chest.

It was all the distraction he needed, and he wrenched his sword from its sheath, leaping up to the rocks as one of the troopers turned to face this new assailant. He almost managed to bring his splintbow to bear, before Lancelin's blade opened his throat.

There was a sudden snap of bolts, quickly drowned out by a cry of pain. Lancelin turned, seeing their rescuer's blade flash again. One of the troopers lost a hand, his splintbow firing errantly. The man next to him was struck by three bolts before he fell silently. One last thrust of a blade, and Kassian had downed the final ambusher.

Xorya Ironfall looked down on the dead as though she were sorry they had fallen so quickly. Her teeth were clenched as she offered Kassian a nod and wiped her blade clean.

"Shall we get the fuck out of here?" she asked.

Neither of them needed asking twice.

CONALL

Every day repeated itself—rising before the sun, a bowl of gruel, rigorous training, more gruel, more training, sleep. Standing within the circular arena, he could only dream of a cold drink on a balmy autumn night in Wyke. It was so bloody hot he could feel the sweat running in rivulets down his face, down his back, into the crack of his arse.

Conall held his form, sword gripped tight, blade pointing straight from the hip in a rigid horizontal brace. It was the heaviest weapon he'd ever wielded, wood carved around an iron core to give it weight, simulating the real thing. There were a score of them in the circle, all holding their swords just the same, all silent as they had been, for what, an hour? Two? Twenty-odd captives in a pit, all in this together and yet he barely knew any of their names. But then they'd been forbidden to speak for the most part. No stories of previous lives. Nothing to mark them apart but for the strange symbols sewn into the breast of their tunics.

Conall wasn't one for making friends with just anyone; he'd always picked and chosen his compatriots with care. Who would make him laugh, who would watch his back, who had the high enough status. Right now he would have started a conversation with any of these ruffians given half a chance, but when their training was finished for the day he would be too exhausted to even try. All they had the energy to do was eat, drink and sleep, before the next day began anew. It was an existence of laborious misery, one he'd spent his life avoiding. Then again, at least no one else had died.

The memory of Ramassen's corpse flashed in front of his eyes and he gritted his teeth at the thought of it, muscles tensing that little bit more. Conall's guilt had faded a little every day since he'd watched the man die, but then he'd had his own misery to think on instead. At least the Ox didn't have to suffer this damned torture. He wasn't caged in this accursed city being trained for the Wyrms knew what.

This whole place was designed to plague the mind as well as the body. Somewhere distant, a tune was playing. Strings and pipes issuing a lilting refrain, but so far he had seen no sign of minstrels.

Though they were caged within a training yard with thirty-foot stone walls, there was no roof above them. Lifting his eyes, Conall saw a flock of birds making its way east across the clear blue. He swallowed down his jealousy as he watched them fly from view, desperate to be atop a war eagle taking him anywhere else but here.

His arm suddenly stung as he was struck with a stick. One of the instructors glared at him from within a full helm. Conall raised the sword, biting back the insult he wanted to spit. For good measure, the instructor slapped Conall's inner thigh, spreading his stance wider. His muscles protested at the sudden strain, but he suffered it in silence. There was no way he was pissing any of these mad bastards off when all he had to fight with was a heavy wooden stick.

Others had complained in the early days, barking displeasure at their foul treatment. It hadn't ended well. It had only taken a handful of them to be left bleeding and pleading on the ground for the rest to get the message. As a consequence, Conall had accepted his lot—tried to concentrate on what few positives there were to this imprisonment.

He was leaner for one, and definitely stronger. Over the days of relentless training, he had learned a number of new sword forms he was unfamiliar with, and despite the difficulty of the training, every day was becoming a little easier to bear. But none of that was much consolation for the way his mind was being altered. Twisted by Arcturius and the fanatics who ran it. Then again, even that was becoming easier. Was he beginning to accept what was happening? Would he eventually become one of them? Another drone enacting the will of the hive?

As he glanced across the training yard, he could only wonder if anyone else was thinking the same thing. Nylia was standing not ten feet away. Of all these prisoners it seemed, to Conall at least, that she was adapting the best. She offered no word of complaint as she performed every task demanded of her. Conall had tried to attract her attention on more than one occasion in the days since they'd arrived, but she had ignored him, and any hopes he might have harboured to make a friend in this place had faded away.

A foreboding shadow fell over Conall, and his eyes shifted to take in the towering figure of Warmaven Orsokon. The brooding beast of a man leered over him, or at least Conall assumed it was a leer—it was hard to tell since the bastard never took off that one-eyed helmet of his. All he could hear was the warlord's breathing. Hopefully he wouldn't speak in that stupid high-pitched voice. That might only serve to tip Conall over the edge, and the last thing he needed was to get beaten to snot for laughing.

Instead he stared straight ahead, holding his form as best he could, until Orsokon moved on to someone else. Slowly he let out a breath. This couldn't go on. Whatever these devils had planned, Conall couldn't be here when it came to fruition. He had to escape, and soon, but to do that he'd need help. But from who?

None of his fellow captives seemed of a mind to flee this place, not that he'd had a chance to ask any of them. There had been no sign of Baenre Mokhtar for days, and though the prospect made Conall want to puke, it looked like he'd have to make it out of here on his own.

"To rest!" Orsokon's squeal of a voice echoed through the circle.

As though on instinct, Conall entered a neutral stance, holding his wooden sword vertically in front of him. Everyone else did the same, standing in silence as the echo of Orsokon's words faded, and Conall felt immediate relief in his aching limbs and overstretched tendons.

"I am pleased with your progress," Orsokon said, as he paraded in front of them. Despite how much he hated the feeling, Conall couldn't help but be proud that the warmaven was happy with their performance.

"Soon, just as you have in body, you will progress in mind. There is a great awakening in store for each of you. One for which you should feel privileged. For now, you will fuel your bodies and rest."

Conall had no idea what *great awakening* meant, but he was too tired to think on it as they were ushered from the yard. They filed through the huge double doors in strict ranks and Conall knew the drill well, following along a series of labyrinthine passageways, led by a withered old slave master. They took a different route every day, sometimes bisecting the same tunnels, squeezing up cramped stairways or down into subterranean vaults. All the while that music was piped in from somewhere, playing its beguiling tune as though lulling them into a stupor.

This time, they moved upward onto an open walkway that revealed the clear blue sky. It funnelled them along until they reached the summit of a towering bastion that looked out over the surrounding country. Conall was overcome with awe as, for the first time in days, he was greeted by the vista of Iperion Magna. It swept from west to east, a sprawling desert with mountains to the north that crawled to the lip of the Drift.

As the others carried on following their slave master, he stopped, taking an opportunity to breathe in the sight, not knowing when he would get another chance to view it. His eye was suddenly caught by another flock of birds in the distance, that envious feeling creeping up on him once more.

"Have you ever noticed they often fly past, but never land here?"

He glanced over his shoulder to see Nylia standing close by. She was also watching those birds, a look of longing in her piercing eyes.

"I don't blame them," he replied. "I wouldn't be here if there was any choice in it."

He took in the view of the city from their elevated position. Arcturius was a solemn edifice carved from the grey stone of the surrounding land, that huge statue of the chained and eyeless demon towering over it, a brooding sentinel meant to strike awe. Despite the myriad towers and walkways, the city looked all but deserted, and Conall began to wonder where everyone was. His eye was drawn to a road across the city's eastern wall. It led directly to the Drift, as though it might have been a trade route. From everything he knew, the Drift was not inhabited by anything that could be considered "civilisation," yet here was a main thoroughfare leading right into its heart.

"Keep moving."

He flinched as he was struck on the arm with a wooden baton. Days ago he might have whined at the affront, might have complained. Not now. Instead, he and Nylia followed the rest of the prisoners down into the interior of the bastion, along the winding corridors until they reached their garrison building.

The charmless bunkhouse did little to fill Conall with any relief. Stone pallets for sleeping lined three of the walls, and a single table squatted in the centre. Some of the other recruits immediately collapsed on their bunks in exhaustion, but Conall took the opportunity to sit close to Nylia.

As a group of thralls entered, carrying food and water for the group, Conall leaned in close to her. "Tell me about your homeland," he asked, desperate for some connection. Anything to break this monotony.

She regarded him suspiciously. "You are a curious man. Why ask that question in such a place as this?"

Conall shrugged. "It's better than silence, don't you think? Banal conversation is a popular pastime where I come from."

She leaned in closer to him, as though offering some kind of challenge. "In Nyrakkis we have little time for the banal. Does that make you think ill of it?"

He smiled for the first time in what seemed an age. "I don't think ill of Nyrakkis because it's banal. But I've heard dark tales that would make anyone wary."

"And I have heard much the same of Torwyn."

"I'm sure," he replied. "Dragon worshippers and the like? At least we aren't slaves to evil gods."

That made her laugh, and the sound of it was much better music than any he'd heard since he came to this dread city. "Where I am from, there is more fruit in the trees than we could eat, and the water from every spring tastes better than wine. Can you say the same about Torwyn?"

Before he could answer, one of the thralls handed him a plate of thick gruel and a hunk of bread, along with a wooden cup filled with tepid water. Despite the meagre offering, Conall smiled his thanks at the old man. "Much appreciated."

The wrinkled old thrall gave no answer, returning to the table to deliver more slop.

"I've always preferred wine to water anyway," Conall said, looking down at the cup. Something hairy floated in it, and he dipped his finger in to fish it out.

In contrast Nylia drank from her own cup with gusto, before saying, "I have come to appreciate in recent years that every meal should be regarded as a feast."

With that she dug deep into her gruel with the hunk of bread, before taking a bite and chewing as though she were eating the finest cut of meat. Not for the first time, Conall felt somewhat resentful at himself for not having appreciated the little things when he had them in abundance. He pushed his gruel around with the bread, but couldn't bring himself to eat, despite his hunger.

"I imagine being enslaved here is not much different to Nyrakkis," he said quietly.

She turned on him with a frown. "We are not slaves. We serve our gods and our queen for the betterment of the land. And are your people not slaves to their dragons?"

Conall sighed. "There are no dragons. No one knows if they were real or just legend, but whatever the truth of it, the Guilds have set Torwyn free from their priests. I am proud to have been a part of that."

"Ah yes. When you were a prince."

Conall knew he had been no prince. Even if he had, this was as far from a royal court as he could possibly get. "For all the good that did me."

"I think perhaps our lands are not that different after all," Nylia replied, her eyes showing a strange kind of mischief. "We too have our noble houses. Lords raised in status above the rest of us."

It sounded as though she were accusing him. Conall would have told her that was not how things worked in Torwyn. How the Guilds had been established for the benefit of all, but before he could formulate the argument, an imposing figure entered their chamber.

The atmosphere turned forbidding as Orsokon appeared. He regarded them, his nasal breath resounding from within his helm. "Do you all enjoy your feast?" he squeaked.

When no one answered, Orsokon reached out an arm and pushed a thrall out of his way to grasp a tankard from the table. The old man slipped and fell, wincing and moaning as he struck his arm on the stone tiles.

"You should be grateful for such precious bounty," Orsokon proclaimed, pouring the tankard onto the ground where it spattered on top of the old man.

Conall gripped the side of his bunk. The sight of that old man's pain made him want to rage, even though he knew it was pointless. There was no way he could beat Orsokon in a fight, and even if he could, there were a dozen more like him ready to beat Conall to shit. Nevertheless, he found himself rising, glaring at the warmaven.

As soon as he stood, he realised his mistake. No one came to stand by his side, no one daring to support him in his defiance. He was alone against an insurmountable enemy, but he had stepped in the arena now and there was no going back.

"What kind of coward pushes an old man around?" he said. There was no waver in his voice, so that was something to be grateful for.

Orsokon regarded him through that dark slit in his helmet. "I have fought in every great city of the Magna," he replied gently. "The number of foes I have killed is beyond remembrance. How could such a man as I be a coward?"

So Orsokon lacked the ability for nuance. That certainly put a different spin on things.

"Who other than a coward would be so afraid to show their face. Do you wear that thing because you're so damned ugly?"

"Ah." Orsokon nodded. "You are mocking me. I understand now. Base insults, is that all you are capable of?"

"Oh, I'm capable of more than that," Conall spat, preparing himself for the inevitable. He was done being ordered around by this bastard. Time to fight. Time to die. How could that be any worse than being imprisoned in this asylum?

The huge warrior unravelled one of the chains bound about his forearm, and wrapped it around his fist. As he did so, Conall felt his nerve begin to wane. If there'd been anywhere to run, he would have darted for it, but there was no escaping this.

Well, he'd been flogged before. Now he'd find out what a punch in the face with chain-wrapped knuckles was like. Brief, he hoped.

Orsokon took a step forward, and Conall raised his chin to take his punishment like a true heir of his Guild. Instead of striking, Orsokon stooped and picked up the old man by the scruff of his tunic. With a resonant thud he hit the man in the face. Conall held his breath as he saw blood smear the old thrall's nose before he was struck again. A third blow and the man's head lolled backward. He hadn't made a sound. When Orsokon was finished, he dropped the old man in a bloody puddle.

"What the fuck is wrong with you?" Conall blurted, unable to take his eyes from the thrall, who lay unmoving on the floor.

"Are you not hurt by this?" Orsokon asked. "I assumed this punishment is more effective than physical pain. For you to know that your actions have led to the waste of this pitiful life. You are weak, eastlander. Have I not guessed correctly? Compassion is your downfall. But fear not, I will drive it from you, no matter how many thralls I have to kill. Can you see?"

With that he turned and left, striding from the room as though nothing had happened. Conall stood and watched while the other thralls dragged the old man from the chamber, leaving a smear of blood in their wake.

As the candles on the wall sconces flickered in the silence, Conall sat heavily on his bunk.

"I've had enough of this shit," he whispered. "I have to get out of here. This is a madhouse."

"That is impossible," Nylia replied. "Our every move is observed, even if we cannot see the watchmen."

"We have to at least try. We're going to die in here, or worse. Be driven insane. Listen to that bloody music droning away day and night. It's enough to drive anyone to insanity. And we haven't even met Senmonthis yet. I for one have no intention of waiting around for that introduction."

"Very well, Conall. Then we must find a way."

He turned to her, expecting to see enthusiasm, but was met by her usual cold stare. "You mean it? You'll come with me?"

Before she could answer, another of the prisoners moved closer to them, one of the men who had travelled with them from Argon Kyne. All three regarded one another for a moment before the man said, "If you're getting out, I'm going too."

Conall raised a smile. It seemed his plan was gaining traction. "All right. You're in. What's your name?"

"I am Mikal," the man said, offering a nod to them both.

"Nice to finally meet you, Mikal. Now, let's all get the fuck out of here."

ANSELL

Another day in the Burrows, forced to once again repeat his most humiliating of duties. If the ignominy wasn't bad enough, Ansell could barely stand the boredom. He had committed to memory every detail of the manse, from its intricate coving to the patterns painted on its cabinets and bureaus. Every crack in the skirting, every curled and mouldy sheet of paper on the wall. At least there was silence. Even with the window open it was quiet, only the birds singing outside, oblivious as the rest of Torwyn burned.

He should not have been here. It was a waste of his time. As knight commander he should have been performing his duty in some corner of the Guildlands, fighting for the Ministry. But the Archlegate had given his orders, and here he was, waiting in a small room outside a woman's bedchamber as Sanctan Egelrath took his pleasure.

It was unusually silent in that chamber, but Ansell guessed he should have been thankful for that mercy. He didn't have to listen as the most pious man in all Torwyn exercised his lusts.

He let out a long low sigh, almost chiding himself for such thoughts. Who was he to question the Archlegate? Then again, wasn't it his right to do so? Surely this again demonstrated weakness on Sanctan's part? Sin? And was Ansell just as culpable for allowing it to happen? But he was one of the Archlegate's brood, and by dint of that fact his servant in all things. He could never question his master's motives.

Ansell cast his eye across the room. Grace sat in one corner, her tongue sticking out as she concentrated on her child's work. In one smudged hand she held a stick of charcoal, on the floor a pile of vellum, a gift from Sanctan, on which she scribbled frenetically. An artist at their easel. A monkey let loose in a paint shop, more like.

She looked up, catching Ansell's eye before he could turn away. So far all had been quiet, but now it was inevitable that he would be—

"Ansell?" she crooned.

"Yes, Grace," he answered, knowing from hard experience that ignoring the girl would do no good.

"Do you have a wife?"

The notion was preposterous, but then how would this child know of his sacred vows? It was an insulting question to a man such as Ansell, but he had to remember from whom it had come. She meant no harm by it.

"No," he replied, hoping that would satisfy.

"Why not?" she replied.

Foolish of him to think that would be the end of it. "Marriage is a privilege reserved for other men."

As soon as he said those words the questions surfaced again in his mind. He was held to a particular standard, forced to deny himself such mundane pleasures, and yet they were sacrifices the Archlegate did not appear to share. Best not to question. That was not his place. Better to simply obey.

"Will I be a wife one day?" she asked.

How was he supposed to answer that? He was no augur, but he had to remind himself once again that this was a child.

"To me, that sounds a shallow ambition for one so young. You could achieve anything you wish to, Grace."

The girl brightened at that, before looking up to the ceiling, searching out inspiration for her next question.

"So could I be a Guildmaster?"

Clearly she was reaching for the stars. Besides, if the Ministry had its way, there would soon be no rank of Guildmaster to aspire for.

"Perhaps another vocation might be more…realistic."

Grace shrugged before going back to her scribbling.

There was a muffled noise from the bedchamber. The sound of a deep voice answered by another, more shrill one. The creak of a bedframe that made Ansell wince. Still, it was mercifully quiet by comparison to previous occasions.

"Have you ever been out of the city?" Grace asked, her attention still on her drawing.

Ansell felt his hands tighten into fists. Curse the curiosity of infants. It was all he could do to quell the sudden memories such a question inspired. Of his days as a neophyte, not yet fully ordained, when he had been sent with so many others to Dreadwall. They had faced a host of Magnan pirates over the space of six days. Fleet after terrifying fleet had come to raze that city on the coast, and take its entire populace as slaves. Ansell had learned the meaning of righteous slaughter during that time, and been forged as a true warrior of the Wyrms. It was a time he would sooner forget.

"No," he replied.

"Neither have I." She stopped her work and looked at him. "Do you think I ever will?"

Another question impossible to answer. "Perhaps."

Her face widened into grin, one tooth missing at the front. "Would you like to come with me?"

As he looked into those hopeful eyes all he could see was innocence. How could she know the dark vagaries of the world they lived in? Its hardships and its iniquities? Despite her annoying inquisitiveness, she was at heart a good child. Kind above all else.

"Perhaps," Ansell said again.

"Could we go and see the sea?"

"Yes," he replied, not thinking it too fanciful an idea.

"And the mountains? I would like to go see the snow and the mountains."

"Yes," he said, again without considering the implications of making such promises, or that he might have to one day honour his word. But what did that matter? She was but a child, and it was a promise he would never be called upon to keep.

When she went back to her charcoal and her vellum, Ansell couldn't stop himself asking, "What are you drawing, Grace?"

She stopped what she was doing, her eyes rising to regard him with a look of embarrassment that was out of place on her young face. Slowly, she raised the yellowing paper to reveal the figure upon it.

"I was drawing you," she said quietly.

It was the simple likeness of a brutish face, but what could he expect? The more he looked at what she had drawn, the clearer it was to see sadness in those crudely rendered eyes. A hideous reflection of himself in the mind of a child. The last thing he might want to witness.

"Do you like it?" she asked hopefully.

"No," he replied. Perhaps harsh, but then the truth should always be the first thing from the mouth of the pious.

Her inconsolable expression was not what he expected. Surely she should have appreciated his candour, not taken it as a barb. His honesty was a sign for her to strive harder. He was only trying to encourage her to greater effort. Still, Ansell could not quell the feeling of guilt that suddenly rose within him. Clearly there was some knack to speaking with children he had no talent for.

"It is not a very good likeness," he said, struggling to find the words that might give her some kind of hope. "But it shows promise."

"Maybe I'll do better the next time," she said.

"I am sure you will."

"Do you want to draw with me?" Grace asked, offering up her charcoal in one dusty hand.

Ansell would normally have scoffed at the idea, but he managed to subdue that reaction. "I do not have the talent for it," he said, hoping that would be enough to extinguish the idea.

"Then what do you have the talent for? Everyone is good at something, Ansell. What do you do?"

What should he say now? He was the righteous sword of the Great Wyrms, but it was doubtful a child would appreciate such a position of honour.

"I am...a shepherd," he answered, offering a silent prayer of thanks for the sudden flash of inspiration.

That answer seemed to delight her, and she beamed at him. "Oh, I love sheep. How many do you have? Can I see them?"

Her delighted reaction had a strange effect Ansell had not felt for as long as he could remember. Suddenly his mouth was sore, the burn around his chin reacting to the fact he was smiling.

"Fuck you, Sanctan!"

Both of them looked toward the chamber from where Jessamine had wailed. There were no muffled murmurings now. Every word was clear as a bell.

"Jessamine, we have talked about this, and at length." The voice of the Archlegate, as though he were preaching at the podium.

"I will not be treated like some dirty secret. I am not your fucking whore." Jessamine's voice had reached a pitch that suggested she didn't care who heard.

"Jessamine, my love—"

"Don't give me that *my love* shit. You don't love anyone but yourself. I've had enough of this. I'm gonna tell. Anyone and bloody everyone. See if I don't. I'm no one's whore, Sanctan, and I won't be kept a secret forever."

Ansell glanced down to see Grace staring forlornly at that door. She had forgotten the charcoal and her drawing. Forgotten about sheep and shepherds. All she heard was her mother's wrath.

"Grace, can you sing me a song?" Ansell asked her.

She looked up at him despondently. "I don't know any songs."

Strange that a child so young would not know even the simplest lullaby, but all thoughts of that were shattered by the sound of something smashing in the bedchamber. Ansell rose to his feet as a scream emanated from within, though whether it was of fear or fury he could not tell. He should have entered, his first duty was to protect the Archlegate after all, but Sanctan had ordered Ansell not to disturb him under any circumstance.

Grace stared at the door, her lip quivering, eyes glistening with tears. It was silent in the room, and he began to feel more unnerved with every passing second. The least he should do was find out what was happening, or even intervene, if just for the girl's sake. As the silence wore on it frayed at his nerves more than the sound of their quarrel.

Ansell took a step toward the door. It opened before he could reach it. Sanctan stood there, donning his civilian garb, a look of shock to his face, blood running from a scratch on his neck.

"Time we left, Ansell," he said. He was trying to remain calm but there was a tremor to his tone.

Ansell looked past him, into the room. Lying on the tangled bedding was Jessamine. She lay on her back, dead eyes staring at the ceiling, one of those sheets pulled tight around her throat.

"What have you done?" Ansell said, but the answer was plain for anyone to see.

Sanctan moved to block his view. "Remember to whom you speak. I am the Archlegate, and I have given you an order. Now come . . . and bring the girl."

Before he could pick her up, Grace rushed toward the bedchamber. Ansell managed to grab her before she could reach it and see what lay inside. Sanctan was already at the door to the street outside, and just as he opened it, Grace gave out a wail.

She struggled in Ansell's grip, squirming like an eel, but he managed to cling on to her, carrying her from the manse. With Sanctan leading the way, they walked along the high balcony and down to the street. Mercifully, there was hardly a soul to witness them as Grace continued to struggle in his arms.

"I want my mama," she demanded, clawing at his shoulder, desperate to escape.

Ansell did all he could, but calming a hysterical child was yet one more skill he had never attained.

"Keep her silent, will you," Sanctan hissed as he hurried along an alleyway.

Ansell grasped the girl tighter, shaking her as gently as he could when she would not be still.

"Grace," he demanded. "You have to be quiet now."

She wailed in reply, and he cast a glance over his shoulder in case they were seen. Might someone think they were abducting the child? But wasn't that what they were doing?

"I said, keep her silent," Sanctan repeated, this time more urgently.

What to do? What to say? This was a child in distress, and Ansell was unused to consoling such people. Or any people. He was the righteous hand of the Great Wyrms, not some assuasive priest.

"Where shall we go, Grace?" he whispered, trying to soothe her with gentle words. "When we have seen the mountains and the sea? Then where will we go?"

Grace calmed, looking at him earnestly with her tear-filled eyes. "I don't want to go anywhere. I just want my mama."

"She is sleeping, but you will see her later. For now, we are going on an adventure."

He surprised himself at how easily the lie slipped from his tongue. Now he could add flagrant deceit to the other sins he had committed in the name of the Draconate, all done at the behest of his Archlegate.

"Do you promise?" she asked.

"Yes," he replied, feeling the chains of yet more guilt pile upon him, weighing him down like a drowning man.

It seemed to mollify her enough that she laid her head against his shoulder and quietened. He could feel her occasionally let out a sobbing breath, but as they continued through the streets she was mercifully calm. No one offered them so much as an accusing glance as they carried on, Sanctan with his hood drawn tight over his head, Ansell carrying the girl as though she were his own slumbering child.

He felt relief wash over him when they eventually neared the Mount, forgoing the main entrance to make their way to the rear and be let in through a well-guarded gate. More secret ways, more slinking into their temple like robbers in the night, after stealing a girl away from her mother. Her murdered mother.

The thought of that began to plague Ansell as he made his way through the torchlit corridors toward Sanctan's vestibule. Though Jessamine had not died by his hand, Ansell still felt culpable for the killing. He had, after all, done nothing to stop it.

Sanctan threw off his cloak, fixing Ansell with a dour look. "It was an accident. You understand that?"

"Yes, Archlegate," he replied, though he could comprehend little of what was happening. Surely if the Archlegate said it was so, there was no denying the truth of it. But then, he had heard with his own ears what happened.

Before he could think to question the facts, the door to the vestibule opened and Regenwulf entered, a rosiness to his cheeks as though he had travelled with all haste.

"Archlegate," he said, bowing briefly. "There is news from the Forge."

Sanctan seemed to forget recent events as he raised his chin expectantly. "Speak it."

"The Griffin Battalion have enacted their plan. The Ironfalls are defeated."

A grin spread across Sanctan's face so fully, Ansell thought he might punch the air at the news. "And so, Wymar is removed from the game. Not long before the rest will fall. These are great tidings, Regenwulf. Ansell, see to the girl, then return to me in the war room. We have much more to discuss."

Ansell bowed, avoiding the confused look Regenwulf gave him as he left the vestibule like some nursemaid, and carefully made his way down toward the Mount kitchens. Grace stirred at his shoulder as he did so, looking about the place in confusion.

"Where are we?" she asked.

"This is my home," he replied, with no idea how else to describe it.

"Are your sheep here?"

Ansell shook his head as they reached the kitchen. There was much bustle as cooks and servers performed their daily chores. The smell of fresh bread was fading, to be overtaken by the welcoming aroma of a spitted pig. He sat Grace at the nearest table and took a cloth from where it lay next to a stove.

"Dry your eyes, girl," he said, offering it to her.

Grace did as she was asked, and Ansell glanced about the kitchen. For the most part the scullery serfs went about their business, heedless of the interruption, but some of them looked at him with fearful curiosity. It was doubtful they had ever seen a Knight of the Draconate looking after a child in such a manner.

"Are you hungry?" he asked.

Grace shook her head, still wiping her face.

"Thirsty?"

"No," she replied. "I just want Mama."

She spoke the words quietly, as though she knew deep down her wishes would not be met.

"I told you," he said gently. "We are off on an adventure. We will see her later."

"Where are we going?"

Where indeed. "If I told you that, what kind of adventure would it be?" Perhaps he was getting better at this. One lie following the other, as though they were the most natural words he had ever spoken. "But first you will have to rest. Then later, adventure awaits us."

Did he see a trace of a smile on her face? Or was she only humouring him, this child who had just lost her mother?

Ansell turned to the nearest maid, who gazed back at him fearfully. "You. Look to the welfare of this child. See her cared for and given lodgings within the Mount. And keep her away from the other orphans."

The woman nodded obediently, and Grace allowed the maid to take her in her arms.

"Her name is Grace," he added, as the pair made their way from the kitchens.

He watched them go, feeling some relief that this duty was over. But with the end of one task there would be the start of another. The Archlegate would have more duties for him to perform, perhaps even more dire than this one.

TYRETA

The wagon trundled ever southward. For the most part it was a peaceful journey, interspersed with the odd curse from Sted every mile or so as she drove the stubborn mules. When they hit a particularly violent bump in the road, she would loudly lament the soreness of her arse. Other times those mules would veer off the road, despite Sted's noisy ministrations, and she would level a cacophony of profanities at them.

At first Tyreta had found her griping funny, but now it was starting to grate on her nerves. The gravity of their mission began to weigh heavier, and with every mile south they travelled the more likely it was they'd come up against an enemy patrol. Add the fact that their supplies were already dwindling, and she was beginning to wonder if this had been a good idea at all. With luck, Donan's plan to take the underground transport tunnel would see them reach Windstone before they were forced to forage for food.

Even if they did reach the city without starving or being caught by a patrol, was there any guarantee that this Nicosse Merigot would even be there? Tyreta tried to put the thought from her mind. Best think on what she could control and not worry about the worst of all outcomes.

Across the wagon from her sat Donan, a glum look on his face that she had grown so used to. He seemed in constant pain, though to his credit offered no word of complaint. Beside him was Crenn, tinkering with the metal leg he was crafting. He twisted in a screw, before jamming the screwdriver in his mouth and tightening a nut with the wrench. When satisfied it was secure enough, he flexed one of the joints, listening closely to the squeak and hiss of pneumatics, before massaging oil onto the sprocket wheel at the heel joint. It was a marvel to see him at his craft, and at least one of the group had something to occupy them as they travelled.

Cat was ranging somewhere in the wilds. She had spurned the discomfort of the wagon, choosing to prowl beside it for miles, before disappearing into nearby woodland. Tyreta couldn't see her, but she had a strong notion Cat was somewhere close by. Perhaps another consequence of her new powers that went along with the improvement to her senses.

With luck, if they encountered an Armiger patrol, they'd look like any ordinary group of travellers. So far on this lonely road they'd seen only a few wayward refugees, the odd horse-drawn cart or lone rider. It struck her as odd when the strangers they passed offered a friendly nod or wave, seemingly untroubled by the chaos that had erupted across Torwyn. As though the whole country hadn't all of a sudden caught flame.

"Fucking cocksucking mules," Sted barked suddenly. "This bastard road goes on forever and my arse is killing me. Fuck my luck."

Tyreta found herself cringing at the outburst but nobody else seemed to even notice. She leaned closer to Donan.

"Has she always been like this?"

Donan nodded. "Pretty much. At least since I've known her."

"How is your leg?" Tyreta asked, concerned at his discomfort.

He looked down at the stump despondently. "Mostly it's just a dull ache, but sometimes it itches something awful."

Sted twisted in her driver's seat, fishing for something in her shirt pocket. "Try this, Marrlock," she said, tossing a stick of redstalk over her shoulder. "That'll help, trust me."

Donan picked the redstalk up from where it had landed on his lap. He held it for a moment, regarding the pungent root with reluctance, before shoving it in his mouth.

"Thanks," he said.

Tyreta turned to Crenn, who was still tinkering with his artifice. "Do you think Nicosse will help us if we find him?"

The old man shrugged. "I don't see why not. He was always an amiable enough chap, and held no love for the Ministry, that's for sure."

"What about the Guilds?" she asked.

Crenn winced. "I'm fairly sure he don't love them neither. He and his brother were treated like outcasts. Pariahs even. Pretty shoddy behaviour on the part of the Guilds if you ask me. No offence to you, obviously."

"None taken," she replied.

"Anyway," Crenn said, closing one eye and sighting along the length of the metal leg. "How are you holding up?"

"I'm fine," she replied, though with everything going on she felt far from it.

Crenn stopped what he was doing and turned to her with an earnest look, seeing through her dismissive answer. "You've been through a lot in recent days. I've noticed the change in you. I first met a young girl flush with mischief. Now you're different, and I don't just mean those eyes of yours."

Instinctively she looked away to hide them from him. "I'm dealing with it, Crenn. Best I can, same as all of us."

"Just so you know, you're not alone."

She appreciated the thought, but Crenn was wrong. She was alone. Everything had changed, not just in Torwyn, but inside her own body and mind. There wasn't anyone who could help her with that.

The wagon suddenly bucked as they hit another pothole in the road. Sted cursed again, this time loud enough to set a flock of birds to flight from a nearby tree.

"Maybe we should stop here awhile," Tyreta suggested, eager for the distraction, no matter how brief. "I think we could all do with a break."

Sted didn't argue with that and did her best to direct the mules from the road. Tyreta was first to jump down, stretching her aching back and walking toward the distant cliffs. The sea had been their one constant companion on the road as it stretched out to the horizon. Beyond it, somewhere off into the far distance, were the Sundered Isles. As Tyreta stood, letting the sea air brush through her hair, she wondered if she had made the right decision in leaving. As much as she didn't belong there, did she really belong here anymore?

As she stared out across the endless waves, Tyreta began to feel strange, and not for the first time. Her peripheral vision darkened, focusing her eyesight so that she could see far out across the waves. Saliva filled her mouth, and with it came the taste of blood on her tongue.

A soft purring alerted her to Cat stalking toward her. The panther had returned with something in its mouth, something feathered and most certainly dead. As the beast's jaws cracked the bird's bones, Tyreta felt it too, raw meat in her mouth as sweet a morsel as any she had ever tasted.

She shook her head, trying to rid it of the sensation. How she had managed to conjure such an intimate connection with the panther she had no idea, but of all the changes she had endured since returning to Torwyn, this was the most unnerving.

Her stomach rumbled as she blinked away the dark shadows cast around her vision, and Cat continued to tear at her prey. One of them would have a full belly at least.

"You'd best eat," Sted said, as though reading her thoughts.

Tyreta turned to see her holding out some dried meat and an apple. She took the food with a nod of thanks, taking a bite of the apple, thankful as it washed the ephemeral taste of blood from her mouth.

"This is a brave thing you're doing," Sted said, as she too looked out onto the sea.

"It is my duty," Tyreta replied, finishing the mouthful of apple and taking another bite. "I don't have much of a choice."

Sted smirked. "We all have a choice. And you've made a courageous one. In fact, the more I get to know you, the more you remind me of Con."

Tyreta wasn't sure if she believed her. Maybe she was just trying to say the right thing—although from what she'd experienced, Sted was most certainly not in the habit of shining anyone's ego.

"I'm not sure how true that is. Conall was always so cocksure.

Always so confident. I don't have a damned clue what I'm doing half the time."

That made Sted laugh. "Conall Hawkspur didn't know what he was doing *most* of the time. He got through life on a smile and a wink, and if that didn't work, he'd be running like the wind. But there was no other man I'd rather have been stuck in a fix with."

"Sounds as though you liked my brother. One might even say respected him?"

Sted's brow darkened as she regarded Tyreta. "I owe your brother my life. So does Donan. Guess we'll never get to thank him now though."

The reminder of her missing brother cut Tyreta deeper than she expected. As she swallowed down the last piece of apple and pitched the core into the sea, she suddenly regretted not spending more time with him when she'd had the chance. From what Sted had just said, she never really knew her older brother at all. It was always Fulren she'd been close with, and he too was gone to the Lairs. Both of them had left her alone, and the reality of that was hard to swallow.

"Shit, I'm sorry," Sted said, seeing her obvious sadness. "Didn't mean to upset you. I'm subtle as a brick sometimes; I didn't think about how much you must be hurting."

"It's all right," Tyreta replied, doing her best to show her resolve. Especially in front of such a tough woman. "I shouldn't let it get to me. There's so much we have to do. Grief seems like a luxury none of us can afford right now."

"Nah," Sted replied. "Grief is never a luxury. And we don't get to choose when we feel it."

That seemed an oddly insightful thing for her to say, but before Tyreta could agree, she heard Donan whine behind them.

"Come on now," Crenn said, crouching in front of Donan, who sat on the back of the wagon. "We're gonna have to get this over with sooner or later."

He was trying to strap the metal leg to Donan, who looked none too happy about it. No sooner had he tightened the buckles that secured the device to Donan's waist and thigh than he began making final adjustments with his wrench.

Donan looked unsure. "I don't think this—"

"Then don't think," Crenn said, rising to his feet and hauling Donan from the rear of the wagon.

Donan hissed in discomfort as he put weight on the stump of his leg. The redstalk was still in his mouth, but clearly its medicinal properties were insufficient to the task. Crenn took a step back, encouraging Donan to take a step forward, but he only managed to stagger into Crenn's arms.

"I can't do it," he wailed.

Sted guffawed at the sight. "You look like a newborn foal."

Donan regarded her angrily, before setting his jaw. He tried to walk again, but only managed to stumble before Crenn held him steady. When Sted found that even funnier, he turned on her.

"Will you just fuck off," he snarled. "Do you think this is a joke? Do you think I asked for this? To have my leg cut off?" With that, he took an unsteady step toward her.

The humour drained from Sted's face. "What were we supposed to do? Leave you to die on that ship?"

Donan looked incensed, taking another step. This time he found his balance and Crenn moved away from him. "That's what I told you to do. It would have been better than this." Another step toward her. "I wouldn't have been left helpless. Useless." One more faltering step. "I can't even..."

He stopped when he reached her, their noses almost touching. From what Tyreta had seen Donan was no fighter, but right now he looked ready to throttle someone.

"Can't even walk?" Sted asked.

Donan's frown faded as he looked down at his new leg. The leg that had allowed him to walk all of ten feet. A smile spread across his face and a tear ran down his cheek.

"I...I don't..."

Sted slapped him on the arm, which unbalanced him for a moment before he steadied himself. "No need to apologise, Marrlock. Now, let's get the fuck out of here, before I get all teary-eyed."

As Donan mumbled his thanks to Crenn, they climbed back into the wagon, and Sted urged the mules back onto the road. Tyreta could only marvel at Donan's recovery as he babbled a litany of questions at Crenn on how he'd been able to construct such a mechanical marvel. Crenn could only shrug most of his answers, unable to explain the intricate workings of artifice to a layman.

As the afternoon wore on, they reached the brim of a hill that looked down onto wide-open pastures. In the distance, Tyreta spied the telltale chimney of a refinery, though there was no smoke billowing from it. Sted craned her neck before turning to Crenn.

"Pass me the monocular," she said.

Crenn took out the contraption from his bag of tricks and offered it to her. Sted adjusted the focal lens and looked through it with one eye.

"That's what I feared," she mumbled. "Trouble ahead."

Tyreta moved up beside her. "What is it?"

Sted offered the monocular. Through it she could just make out armed troopers milling about a settlement less than a mile down the road. "Armigers," she breathed.

"Can you tell which battalion?" asked Sted.

"No. But it makes no difference. We have no idea who's loyal to the Guilds or the Ministry. Should we risk going through anyway? Try and pass ourselves off as refugees?"

"No," Donan said, not even trying to mask the panic in his voice. "If we're caught, who knows what they'll do to us."

"So what's the alternative?" Sted asked. "Jump in the sea and swim by them? This road is the only route south. If we have to go around, it could add a couple of days to the journey, and time ain't on our side."

Donan stood in the back of the wagon, looking up and down the road as though trying to gauge his bearings. "If we head west from here, I'm sure there's a Hawkspur barge station only a mile or two down the path. Takes ore up and down the river to the landship terminal bound for the Forge. Maybe that would be a quicker way?"

Sted rubbed her chin as though considering it, but Tyreta knew they couldn't spend all day deciding. Someone had to take charge of this.

"We'll do it," she said, wondering if Sted might argue.

Instead she shrugged. "Okay, if you say so. I'm just about sick to the high teeth of these damned mules anyway."

Without further fuss, Sted went about unhitching the mules from the wagon before leading them to open ground just off the road. She was surprisingly tender as she bid goodbye to them, in contrast to the way she had berated them for their entire journey.

When they'd gathered their supplies, they struck out west, Donan leading them on a circuitous route, every step on his new leg becoming more assured. Tyreta could tell he was still in discomfort, but he looked determined to get them to their destination.

"Are you okay?" she asked as they made their way through a patch of dense woodland.

He had almost chewed Sted's redstalk down to the nub. "I'll be fine." From the sheen of sweat on his brow he looked anything but.

"We can stop and rest if you need to."

Donan shook his head. "I can rest when we reach the barge station. And I need to get used to this thing." He gestured to the pneumatic leg. "Crenn might be a genius and all, but I doubt he's tried one of these things out for himself. Hurts like a bastard."

She left him to it, and it wasn't long before he led their motley group from the trees, the river running north to south ahead of them. Downstream they could see the barge station in the distance, and Donan quickened his pace, urging them onward. Sted stopped him before he could rush farther along the river path.

"It's right there," he said. "We've made it."

Sted shook her head. "Not yet we haven't. There's no telling what might be waiting for us in that station."

Tyreta could see outbuildings along the riverbank and a row of boats. From their position upstream it was impossible to tell if any Armiger troopers were hiding within.

"Looks deserted enough," said Crenn. "Can't see any Hawkspur rivermen nor any troopers."

"Well, we can't wait here all day," said Sted. "Guess one of us should scout ahead."

She was already checking the clip of her splintbow, preparing to strike forward.

"Wait," Tyreta said, glancing toward Cat, who sat patiently on the riverbank. She thought back to the feeling she'd had at the seashore—that weird sensation of oneness with the panther. "I think I have a better idea."

She knelt down before Cat, who stared back into her eyes. They focused on one another, as Tyreta began to block out the group's confused chuntering. The web began to coalesce around her, the connection to this animal growing stronger, their bond tightening. In a sudden blur her consciousness was dragged toward that feline head, and as she began to focus, she realised she was seeing through Cat's eyes. Her limbs felt stronger, body lighter, lither, keen for the hunt.

Tyreta began to move swiftly along the canal path toward the barge station, only it wasn't Tyreta, it was an unnatural symbiosis of the two. Cat and Tyreta moved as one, smelling, tasting, experiencing everything through feline receptors.

Was she the panther? Or was she just seeing through her eyes, experiencing the world from the animal's perspective? The farther she crept through the undergrowth, the less it seemed to matter, and she proceeded, hidden from sight, hearing the flow of the river, sensing every scrabbling creature in the undergrowth and quelling the desire to hunt it down and consume it.

When she entered the perimeter of the boat station, her ears pricked up, sensitive to any sound, nostrils flaring, sniffing the air for the scent of human flesh. All she could sense was the distant aroma of her companions drifting on the air. The boat station was abandoned.

Tyreta opened her eyes, her connection with Cat dissipating like a hazy memory. Everyone was looking at her strangely.

"It's safe," she said, rising to her feet.

Donan raised a hand, pointing directly at her. "Your eyes."

Tyreta remembered what she had seen in that cracked mirror on the boat, and she turned away, not wanting anyone else to see the feline aspect her body was adopting. Without a word she led them down the canal path to see Cat waiting patiently in the gateway to the boat station.

Sted moved toward one of the riverboats moored in the tiny dock. "Anyone know how to get one of these things working?"

Crenn shrugged as he jumped from the jetty onto the boat. "I can have a bloody good go," he replied.

When they'd climbed aboard, Tyreta was relieved that no one questioned what she had just experienced. Doubtful they'd stay quiet for long though; they still had a long way to go. Hopefully, by the time she had to answer any questions, she'd have a better idea herself.

ROSOMON

Shutters rattled in the wind as she sat at a table on the first floor of the aerie. Through the broken slats of the eastern window, she could spy nothing but the roiling sea, and through the western was the Alderwood stretching across the Hawkspur Guildlands. The aerie marked the most southern extent of her homeland. She had never thought to return in such ignominy.

This tower was a symbol of Hawkspur might. A beacon on the coast from which war eagles would have been sent to the far corners of Torwyn. Now it stood as a reminder of her Guild's loss.

Ianto was close by—her constant shadow, one she was grateful for. He still bore burns on his flesh where the pyrestone whip had scorched him, but he had made no mention of his ordeal. Rosomon had been surprised at the speed of his recovery, and despite what he'd been through, he still refused to leave her side.

At the sound of hoofbeats approaching along the road, Rosomon rose. She walked to the northern window in time to see a lone horse and rider making their way along the coast. Faiza. The lieutenant had proven herself a capable scout over the past few days, and Rosomon was finding herself relying more and more on the loyalty of strangers. If only she could offer them something in return. If only she was the general they needed her to be.

A clattering of boots on the stairs as Faiza rushed up to the first floor of the aerie, before bowing.

"Lieutenant," Rosomon replied. "What have you to report?"

"The Ursus Battalion have shored up defences around the city," Faiza replied. "The walls are manned. The populace kept in their homes. However, they do not seem to have any scouts posted on the outskirts of the city, and do not range any distance into the surrounding countryside. If we approach at night, and with stealth, we should be able to breach their perimeter and be in the heart of the city before they can mobilise their force."

Some good news at last. It seemed Rosomon's plan of attack had already been formulated for her.

"Do we have anyone within the city who will join us? Could we recruit a force large enough to face the Ursus?"

Faiza looked doubtful, pausing as though she did not want to deliver the bad news. "There are a few loyal members of the Talon still at liberty in the city, my lady, but mostly those who remain are ordinary city folk."

As Rosomon had feared. She turned to Ianto, hoping he might offer some words of encouragement. "What are the chances we could strike back against an Armiger Battalion with a civilian army? We already have a decent complement made up of refugees."

Ianto's jaw worked as he clenched his teeth. Rosomon had already learned that was a sign of bad news.

"Even if we outnumber the battalion forces ten to one, we would still need a huge amount of luck. And sacrifice."

Rosomon turned to Faiza. "Can you estimate the Armiger numbers?"

"Perhaps two thousand, my lady."

"And how many citizens left in the city?"

Faiza screwed up her nose as though it might help her guess. "Twelve, maybe fifteen thousand."

Rosomon turned back to Ianto, hoping his jaw had stopped its clenching. "Is that enough?"

His downcast expression told her it wasn't. "Against a force of two thousand Armiger troopers, most likely those people will be slaughtered."

For a brief, mad moment, Rosomon considered whether the casualties might be worth it, just to show their mettle. Just to spit in Sanctan's eye with this one show of defiance. But the sacrifice was not something she could suffer. These were the very people she was fighting for. Sacrificing them to seal herself a victory over the Ministry was not an option.

"Then we wait," she said, despite how frustrated she felt. Then again, perhaps there was something she could do, a way to turn this to her advantage. "Or I could go into the city myself."

Ianto shook his head. "You can't think—"

"I will present myself to the marshal of the Ursus. I will explain the folly of her actions and persuade her to abandon any notion of loyalty to the Archlegate. The Ursus must join the Guilds instead."

"No, my lady, you would just be putting yourself in needless danger. At best you would be surrendering to the Ministry. At worst..."

"We are all in danger, Ianto. Every one of us. I cannot be protected, no matter how much you try."

Ianto opened his mouth to argue, but there was another creak of the stairs. Rosomon turned, expecting one of her Titanguard, but instead it was a diminutive figure, her blonde hair dishevelled, her face flushed from the cold.

"Emony," Rosomon said.

"My lady," the girl replied.

Before Emony could bow, Rosomon threw her arms around her, almost lifting her into the air. "It is so good to see you." She let go, seeing the look of embarrassment on Emony's face. "Did you manage to find your father?"

Emony nodded. "I did. He took some persuading, but in the end he saw the sense in joining you."

"Where is he?" Rosomon asked.

Emony turned back to the stairs. A whiff of pipe smoke heralded more footsteps ascending the aerie. Rosomon did her best to calm herself as Oleksig Marrlock mounted the stairs, pipe in hand. He regarded her with a nod—not quite the same greeting she'd had from his daughter.

He was portly about the middle but broad shouldered. A man

who had always led by example, toiling in the mines for years along-side the workers of his Guild. Despite being well past his prime, he still posed a striking figure, and bore a permanent scowl atop his low, grey brow.

Behind him came a man who looked much similar, albeit younger and more physically imposing. Borys Marrlock was swordwright of his Guild, and Oleksig's eldest son. As Oleksig sat himself at the table in the centre of the room, Borys leaned against the window ledge, hand resting on the pommel of his blade. He at least offered a bow to Rosomon, if not a word of greeting.

"Hello, Lady Rosomon," Oleksig said, leaning back on the chair while resting his foot on another. "Been a long time."

"Too long, Oleksig. I did hope to see you at the Anvil some months ago, but you clearly had more pressing matters."

"And good that I did. Might have been me who was imprisoned."

But it wasn't. He had sent his daughter instead, and in hindsight it was good for Rosomon that he had.

"I am grateful you have come now."

Oleksig shrugged, lazily moving his foot from the chair before standing and stretching his back. A back bent and crooked after so many years of hard labour. "Can't say I'm happy about it. The Rock is all but abandoned now, left for the Armigers to fight over. I'll admit, I almost didn't come, but my daughter was insistent we help you in any way we could. So here I am."

"And I know you are not an easy man to persuade. But this is the only way we can beat the Archlegate."

Oleksig nodded, giving his pipe another puff before realising the pipeweed had extinguished, and placing it in his pocket with a shrug. "When I heard your brother had been murdered, I was dis-gusted. Me and Sullivar had our differences, but he was a fair man. Fairer than your father anyway. Besides, the Marrlock Guild has no standing army as others do. We needed to unite with someone and it weren't gonna be the Ministry, that's for sure."

"I appreciate your candour," Rosomon replied at his unexpected honesty.

"And I'd appreciate knowing what your plan of attack is."

Straight to the point. But then what could she have expected from Oleksig Marrlock.

"Right now I am waiting on word from Wymar Ironfall, and the Armiger Battalions still loyal to the Guilds."

"How many Armigers do we have?"

Rosomon shook her head. "I don't know yet."

Oleksig didn't even try to hide his disappointment. "And what of Rearden Corwen and Jarlath Radwinter? Can we expect help from them anytime soon?"

"We will receive no help from Rearden. He has succumbed fully to Sanctan's poison. As for Jarlath . . . it is unlikely."

Oleksig sighed at the news. "And why aren't you in Wyke yet?"

He asked the question as though he already knew the answer. That made Rosomon all the more reluctant to tell the truth of it.

"Wyke has been taken. By the Ursus Battalion."

Oleksig reached a hand to his waistcoat pocket again, putting the pipe in his mouth despite it having gone out. Clearly it was a crutch for him, a habit he found hard to break. "So you have no army. And no base of operations when . . . if it ever . . . arrives?"

"I was considering a parley. I could meet with the Ursus. I could negotiate—"

"Out of the question," Oleksig said. "We do not negotiate with murderers and usurpers. We have to drive them out. We have to fight."

"Then we will have to wait," Rosomon replied. "I do not think it will be long before we receive word—"

"We will not wait."

Rosomon had no idea what Oleksig was talking about now. Did he mean to leave? To run?

"Without an army we cannot hope to take on the Ursus Battalion. They are dug into the city. If we attack with what forces we have, even if the people of Wyke rise up, we will suffer too many casualties."

"Perhaps your army is already here, Rosomon," Oleksig said, offering a smirk to Borys, who displayed no emotion in return.

"Oleksig, you already said your Guild is made up of miners, not warriors."

"As far as the Marrlock Guild is concerned there's no difference. Come. Let me show you."

He turned to the stairs that wound up through the centre of the building like a corkscrew. Rosomon followed, past the empty pens of the war eagles that would once have resided here, up to the summit of the aerie. The wind blew violently, and she had to grab her cloak and pull it about her before it blew away on the breeze.

Oleksig walked to the southern edge of the bastion, leaning against the parapet of the tower and gazing out over the scene. Rosomon joined him, and for the first time she began to feel something unfamiliar inside. Something she hadn't felt for the longest time...hope.

There were thousands of them, making their way north along the road. Banners flapped in the breeze, their myriad sigils denoting the different mining leagues. Men and women milled together in Marrlock grey, and those who did not carry flags or pennants held the tools of their trade—hammers, pickaxes, shovels. Many had even brought musical instruments with them—drums, horns, pipes— and she could only imagine the din they would make when raised together in a chorus. It looked as though every miner in the Rock had taken up arms and joined Oleksig's crusade.

"Where did they all come from?" Rosomon asked, unable to drag her eyes away, feeling more hope with each passing moment.

"I put the word out to every league in Torwyn. More still will be making their way here, if they're able. Here's your army, Rosomon. Here's how we win back Wyke."

She turned to him as she thought on the grave consequence of what he suggested. "There's an Armiger Battalion waiting for us, Oleksig. They are not just workers with a cause. They are a trained mercenary force, bred to fight. To kill. I cannot let these people sacrifice themselves for their Guild. We should be putting ourselves at risk for them. That is the reason we were given this responsibility."

Oleksig looked down at her, one bushy eyebrow raised. "You can't fight this war yourself, Rosomon. If we do nothing, there will be no Guilds left. And then what? The Ministry takes over and everything the Guilds have built collapses to rubble. Who knows what future awaits these people. Yours and mine. They may not be warriors, may not be an army, but they will throw themselves on the Ursus Battalion like hounds on a bear."

She wanted to argue, to tell him the sacrifice would be too great a price, but she knew this was the only way. If the Guilds fell here, at this first step, it would be the dawn of a new age for the Ministry. A dark age, where everything the Guilds had built would be cast into shadow, replaced by the rambling vision of a mad priest. She had seen Sanctan's zeal firsthand. He could not be allowed to take control, no matter the cost.

"What do you think, Ianto?" she asked.

He gazed out over the leagues of miners with little emotion. "I think I see an army."

"But is it one we can use to win back Wyke? Should we not wait for more soldiers?"

Ianto shook his head. "Every day we wait, the more the Ministry tightens its grip on the Guildlands. We have to strike now."

Rosomon turned back to Oleksig. "Very well. Your Guild will have its chance to prove itself an army. We will march on Wyke, and the miners of the Marrlock Guild will strike the first blow."

That pleased Oleksig, and he clapped his son Borys on the shoulder before heading off to spread the news to his followers. As she gazed down on the men and women of the leagues, Rosomon could only hope Lancelin, and those Armigers loyal to her, would hurry to her side. As convinced as she was of their support, it still might not be enough to face the might of the Ursus Battalion.

KEARA

Growing up within the cloistered surroundings of her father's manse, she had never been exposed to an excess of manual labour. Not even wandering the cobbled expanse of the Web had she seen an abundance of men and women hard at work, toiling in the streets. That was hardly surprising, since nothing had been done to renovate the crumbling facades of her city for decades.

Keara had always mixed with other webwainers, always benefited from the privileges of her position. It had never crossed her mind to try to expand her cultural horizons until she'd done her stint on the Karna Frontier with the Armigers. Even then, she'd seldom spent time fraternising with the rank and file. As much as she hated to admit to herself, that kind of thing was beneath her. She was a Guild heir, born for greater things than toiling among the masses. Now though, it appeared she had been cast down with the rabble.

She gazed across the Bridge of Saints. It looked a damn sight better than it had the day the Guilds launched their attempt on Sanctan's life. When they had attacked Archwind Palace with all the fury and artifice they could muster. It had been blown apart and washed away on the Whitespin, but now the Archlegate was determined to return it to its former glory.

Cranes had been erected at both sides to lift the heavy masonry that was to replace its old marble bulwarks. A huge frame of steel and iron now spanned the gap in its centre. Sanctan had said that her webwainers would be instrumental in rebuilding the city, but as far as Keara could see, it might have been more appropriate to recruit some of the poor from the Burrows. At least it would give them something to do, rather than venting their ire at the Ministry and rioting on the streets. Offer them some kind of purpose now their manufactories had been shut down.

She turned away from the bridge, toward Archwind Palace. The debris and smashed masonry had been cleared away, and what remained of the lower levels was little more than a skeleton. Three stormhulks stomped along the parade in front of the palace, carrying their heavy burdens and shifting the piled debris. It was an ignoble use of these machines, and even more humiliating for their pilots. But what choice did they have? Refuse the Archlegate's demands?

Despite the sorry state of the palace, Keara could tell it would soon be a very different edifice from the one that had stood before. Gone would be the Guild regalia, the grand architecture, and in its place...perhaps best not to think on that. Dwelling on what Sanctan was planning for this monument to the Guilds might only make her weep.

As one of her sisters toiled within her stormhulk, Keara felt a strange pang of envy creep up on her. The task might well have been beneath her, but at least it was honest work. Her sister got to bond with the machine, feel the thrill of the web, the power it conveyed. It was a pleasure she would have given her weight in pyrestone to feel right now. Instead, for Keara Hallowhill there was only the banality of carrying out Sanctan's wishes.

The foreman approached, cradling a vellum scroll in the crook of his arm. Yet more schematics for what they were building? Or more accurately, what they were rebuilding. And now she had to give her approval, no doubt. The foreman didn't need her to sanction every cornice and strip of coving, but still, it made her feel somewhat better to know she was in charge. At least for now.

"New plans," the foreman said, slapping the schematics down on a crate beside her.

"What do you mean, *new*?"

He sighed in consternation. "Look, I don't draw them, I just build them. This isn't my doing. I'm only here to do my—"

Keara held her hand up to curb his protest. She'd heard him whine long and loud about every aspect of the palace renovations. If the plans had changed, it wasn't his fault. Nor hers for that matter.

She looked down at the schematics. A quick glance showed her that Sanctan's original intentions for the building, that it be constructed anew to represent the union of Hallowhill, Corwen and Ministry, had been cast asunder. Now any trace of the Guilds had been eradicated, to be replaced by symbols of the five Wyrms. It would not just be the Mount standing proud amid the streets of the Anvil, but the palace would also represent the dominance of the Draconate.

Sanctan really was bringing about a new order.

Keara stretched the crick from her neck. How she would have loved to take some of the drop right now, to blot out the world for just a spell, but there was none to hand. And where were her bloody friends when she needed them? No sign of Hesse. Less sign of Ulger. Clearly they were even more averse to mundane work than she was.

"All right," she said to the foreman. "If that's what the plan is, that's what we'll do."

No point making his job any harder. Or complaining to Sanctan. What would she do? Have him rewrite his plans and ensure that the Hallowhills were at their forefront? After everything he had told her of obedience, after all his veiled threats, it was probably best to just suffer in silence.

As the foreman beckoned over some of his labourers, Keara turned and slipped away before she became embroiled in the details. They didn't need her input. Her position overseeing this was all for show. To give her something to do, and keep her occupied while the rug was pulled right out from under her. And she was helping them do it.

She walked into the hollow shell of the palace, remembering it of old. How it had struck wonder in her every time she entered. They had cleared the wreckage, the bodies, cleaned up the blood. This truly was a carcass of a building. As she made her way up the stairs she realised it was not just the debris that had been cleared.

Everything that represented the Guilds—Archwind, Hawkspur, and the rest—had been torn down, plastered over and planed to nothing. Even the memory of them was being eradicated.

Up she walked, along a staircase that had previously been lined with portraits, sigils, tapestries depicting ancient victories, now seeing nothing but bare walls. She climbed so high she could barely catch her breath, aimlessly wandering the corridors of a dead emperor's castle. But no, it wasn't aimless. She knew exactly where she was going.

The throne room was shrouded in darkness. She remembered a huge pyrestone chandelier had hung at its centre once, brightening the opulent surroundings. Now, four braziers cast ominous shadows across the floor. But even in dark she could still see the throne in front of her.

There she stood for a moment, filled with longing, gazing at it, breathing it in. Keara couldn't help but think how good she'd look sitting on that throne. Then it would be Sanctan doing the bowing and scraping. Doing the shit-work, just like he deserved. How great Torwyn would truly become were she the one living in a palace. An empress, benevolent when called upon, ruthless when necessary.

But dwelling on it wouldn't get her anywhere. Not that it seemed planning would either. She still had no idea how she was going to turn this around, how she would fulfil her father's ambitions and drag the Hallowhills to the top of the heap. Or drag herself there, more like.

She left the throne room before the temptation to sit herself on that exalted seat became too much to bear. There was no point trying it on for size now, it wasn't hers...yet.

Beyond the throne room was a huge wide-open hall, dotted with thirty-foot columns rising to the ceiling, each one hewn like the bole of a tree and surrounded by twisting vines. It would have been beautiful, but for the gouges in those columns and the smashed tiles that peppered the floor. It was here that Sanctan's Drakes had done battle with the Titanguard on that fateful night. How she would love to have seen that. To watch as they fought each other with all their power and fanaticism. It would have been quite the show, but now the hall was quiet. There was nothing here but...

He stood at the edge of the hall, gazing through the wide opening as a breeze drifted in and tousled his black curls. Lorens had his back to her, and there was no way to tell if he knew she was there. He just stood, staring out of that opening where once there had been a window of stained glass. What must he have been thinking? Did he too have designs on the throne? Was he looking out at the Anvil and wondering when the city would be his?

No, had he sided with his father he would have inherited that throne eventually. Lorens had proven himself a more loyal member of Sanctan's brood than any of them. He'd turned his back on the old ways, to embrace the new. Just like her? Was Lorens some kind of kindred spirit she had yet to form an alliance with? Only one way to find out.

She approached him, letting her heels click on the marble floor, lest she surprise him. She didn't want to get a reputation for creeping around like a ghost in the walls. Even so, Lorens didn't turn around at her approach, just kept staring out onto the city.

"Taking in our new empire?" she asked.

He offered her a sideways glance. She'd been half joking, but clearly he didn't see the funny side. There was only suspicion in the slight twitch of his eyebrow.

Lorens gazed back out onto the city. "You know as well as I do, the empire is no more. You helped see to that."

Indeed she had, and her contribution had been greater than most. "You played your part, Lorens."

He offered a curt nod. "Indeed I did."

Was there a note of regret in that remark? "It cannot have been easy losing your father like that."

She ground her teeth as soon as she said the words. Perhaps insensitive? But then sensitivity had never been one of her talents.

The trace of a smile crossed Lorens's face. The last thing she had expected.

"My father never saw the bigger picture."

Lorens must have been calculating to have condemned his own father, but that was a surprising response, even to someone who hated her own father. "That's all you've got to say on it? It was the Ministry who killed him. The Ministry you serve."

"We all serve someone."

Was this the fanatic talking? Somehow she didn't quite believe his conviction.

"But you could have inherited the throne. Become an emperor."

"Sacrifices have to be made. Everyone will pay a price eventually. That's just the cost of change."

Keara had heard some cold things in her time, with a father like hers of course she had, but that beat anything the old crow Ingelram Hallowhill had ever said. Was this honesty? Or was he just saying what he thought he should? Was he really one of Sanctan's fanatics? Keara began to wonder if it had been a good idea starting this conversation at all.

"She won't speak to me anymore," Lorens said. "My mother."

Keara could hardly blame her. "It must be hardest of all for her, to accept the new way of things."

"The way of things?" More gazing through that window. More regrets, perhaps? "Yes, I think we can safely say she is struggling. I imagine it's so much easier for you. Your father was a part of all this from the beginning, part of the big plan. The casting off of old traditions."

If only he knew. There were some old traditions her father would happily have seen restored. He would have liked nothing more than to go back to the days when mages had ruled all of Hyreme. Ingelram Hallowhill would have happily seen the return of Cornelium Obek and his demonic reign if he thought it would give him just a whiff of power.

"Everything changes eventually," was all she managed to say.

"That's true. And it's hard. Hardest of all for those who might force that change."

He was saying all the right things, but she could tell there was just a slight lack of conviction, like an actor not entirely convinced of his script.

"It will be hard for us, but in the end the reward will be worth all that sacrifice."

Now it was her turn not to feel the conviction of her words. From the wry look on his face, she could tell he felt it too.

He turned, looking down at her with a lingering gaze. When she was a girl, Keara had once read a book about lovers and their lingering looks. How they would drink each other in, before the inevitable kiss. This could have been a moment from that book.

"I wish you well, Keara Hallowhill," Lorens said. "May the Wyrms protect." Then he turned and left her.

He looked lost just before he walked from the hall. Like a child abandoned at a fayre by his parents. But in reality, it was Lorens who had abandoned them.

Keara always had Ingelram, she had not been abandoned, but still she envied Lorens his loss. If only that twisted old bastard had left her at a fayre, her life might have worked out a little bit easier.

Lorens was alone because of his choices, and look where it had got him—a hollow spectre of a man. As she watched him go, she promised herself that would never happen to her.

Now it was Keara's turn to look out through the window and down onto the Anvil. Change was happening, right in front of her eyes. Transformation. The last remnants of magic and artifice being used to lay the foundations for a new order. And if she didn't do something fast, she might just end up buried beneath them.

ANSELL

Beneath the Mount stretched a labyrinth of passages and cavernous chambers. Soon after the Age of Insurrection they had been used for rituals and rites that were now forgotten, even by the most learned of High Legates. Now, the Archlegate had put these forgotten chambers to a much different use.

Ansell was stripped to the waist, his labours leaving him dripping with sweat. This cave deep beneath the ground was stifling, stinking of unwashed bodies and misery. To one side stood Sanctan, bedecked in his robes of office, looking every inch the beneficent priest, unaffected by the grime and the filth.

"I admire your resilience," the Archlegate said. "But it will ultimately serve you ill."

Dangling from chains bolted to the roof was a sorry figure. He did not answer, just hung there, his breath coming in shallow gasps.

Sanctan offered a long sigh. "This is just becoming a waste of everyone's time. There is no need for you to suffer like this. All you have to do is give us the names we have asked for. Someone must have been behind the riot. Once you have identified the leaders, you may go on your way, brother."

The man on the chains managed to raise his head. His face was blackened with bruises, left eye swollen shut, lip cut, nose leaking blood. So far he had uttered little other than the odd grunt of pain, but now it seemed he might be ready to talk.

"Go and fuck yourself," he managed to say.

Sanctan looked untroubled by the insult, offering the slightest nod of his head.

After rolling his stiff shoulders, Ansell moved forward. He regarded the man, helpless as he was, unable to defend himself. Then he punched him in the gut. The prisoner's muscles were already tensed in readiness and he took the blow with little more than a grunt, as he had so many others. Ansell did not relent, punching again, and again, though his knuckles were already sore. With every blow the man issued a wheezing breath, but he took the punishment with such resolve, Ansell could only admire him for it. With a final blow, Ansell heard the crack of a rib. He stopped, stepping back into the shadow, short of breath himself. The man on the chains took the opportunity to gasp in some air.

This was what he had been reduced to now—acting as an inquisitor's brutish hand. Surely this was a job for Revocaters, but instead here he was, the defender of a holy faith, demoted to the status of torturer.

Sanctan took a step forward, regarding the man in his sorry state. Was there some sympathy to his expression? Ansell thought not. It was most likely an affectation. A ruse to make the victim think this was for his own good. That it pained Sanctan to inflict such agony.

"All you have to do is give me the names of the heretics who plotted your little failed uprising. Even now my followers are scouring the Burrows. Sooner or later they will find the ones I seek. All you are doing is prolonging the chase, and your own suffering."

The chained man raised his head. From the one eye not swollen shut, he regarded Sanctan with as much hate as he could muster. Ansell saw the steel behind that gaze, the prisoner clinging onto his dignity, despite his precarious position.

"We are not heretics. We are just ordinary folk, making a stand against a tyrant."

That brought a smile to Sanctan's face. "Anyone who defies the authority of the Draconate is a heretic, whether they believe themselves so or not. They must all be dealt with in the same manner."

"We just want to protect our families. Keep a roof over their heads. Now the Guilds are gone, and you've outlawed artifice, what work do we do to keep ourselves fed? What are we to live on?"

Ansell could only think the man had a point. It was true, they had been dismissed from the manufactories, and with no work to speak of they received no pay. The Ministry had certainly not compensated them, and so they had risen in protest. A violent cry for help, perhaps? But the Archlegate had labelled them as heretics, and surely that was all that mattered.

Sanctan had no answer for the man and took a step back. He raised one hand, a flick of his finger, signalling for Ansell to begin again. This time he tried to avoid looking the man in the face—best not to regard him as human. As he pummelled the man's torso with his fists once more, he tried to ignore that wretched wheezing, tried to imagine he was beating a slab of meat rather than a man. When he heard another rib snap, and the resulting squeal of pain, he stepped away.

The man's breath was fevered, and he spat out a gob of blood that splashed on the stone floor.

"You will not win," he gasped. "You cannot feed the poor on faith alone. We will not sit back and do nothing while our children starve."

"You are wrong," Sanctan replied. "There might be much pain in the coming weeks, much suffering before we enter an age of green pastures. But be assured, that age of plenty will come. Unfortunately, some will feel more pain than others."

"And how much pain have you suffered?" the man spat.

Sanctan's serene countenance darkened. The prisoner had clearly hit a nerve. Rather than spitting back his anger, Sanctan signalled once again.

Ansell could see the man tense every muscle. It was doubtful he had many ribs left to break, and all Ansell could think of were the merciful tenets of the Draconate he had learned. Saphenodon's treatises on forgiveness and understanding. This man had suffered enough. Surely this was butchery for butchery's sake?

A solid punch to the jaw, and Ansell offered the gift of oblivion to the prisoner. It would end his pain, for now at least. On seeing the body go slack on its chains, Sanctan stepped forward, glaring in frustration.

"Disappointing. We were just starting to make progress. No matter, there will be time to continue this later."

Ansell bowed, picked up his shirt and opened the door to the cavernous chamber. Serfs were waiting outside ready to unchain the man and ensure he still lived—at least long enough for his interrogation to continue. Ansell could only hope there would be enough of the man left to tend.

As he made his way up from the maze of tunnels, leaving Sanctan behind him, he tried to purge his thoughts. He had done his duty, but it had been a shameful one. Yet another task for the Archlegate he could not justify. Even thinking such things—that the Archlegate might be wrong, that he could be overstepping his bounds—was heresy. No matter how he tried to rid himself of those feelings they would not leave, plaguing him every step, until he finally left the fusty subterranean tunnels behind and managed to breathe clean air.

Perhaps he should return to his chamber to purge himself with the lash. Maybe the pain of that would rid his mind of seditious thoughts. It had, after all, been many days since he had felt that exquisite rush.

No. Perhaps there was a different way.

Ansell walked through the halls of the Mount, then down to the kitchens secreted at the southernmost point of the vast warren of corridors. He had not seen Grace for days, but had heard this was the place she had taken to playing in when not in her chamber. It was only right that he should check on her well-being. After all, it was he who had brought her to this place. In part, she was as much his responsibility as anyone's.

When he reached the archway to the kitchen, he paused. Only two cooks were present, and he had made great efforts to remember the names of both. Patris was preparing a leg of mutton at his bench, jowls wobbling as he rubbed lard into the skin. At another bench stood Joye, chopping vegetables for a broth. Between them both sat Grace, her head bowed as she fiddled with something on her lap. It seemed she was up to no mischief. Happy enough, he supposed.

Ansell was about to leave when Grace said, "Joye."

The woman smiled at hearing her name, replying, "Grace."

The girl repeated Joye's name, and the cook replied in kind, until the two were trading words as though throwing a ball to one another. Before he realised it, Ansell found himself grinning at their childish game.

"What do you want, Grace?" Joye said eventually.

"Nothing," Grace replied.

Patris looked up from his mutton, laughing at their banter. Ansell could only imagine this was a game they had repeated often to divert from the monotony of their work. Odd that adults would find mirth in something so childish. And yet, Ansell found it just as infectious.

He stepped into the kitchen. Patris turned, his smile fading. He stopped what he was doing, wiping greasy hands on his apron before bowing in respect.

"I assume she is giving you no trouble?" Ansell asked.

Patris shook his head. "No, none at all."

Ansell doubted the man would admit it, even if she was. "Has she been fed?"

"When we can get her to eat. She doesn't really want much at all, despite Joye's pestering." He leaned forward before whispering, "I think she misses her mother."

That only served to make Ansell feel all the more guilty. He was complicit in that woman's death—only right that he make amends any way he could.

"Hello, Ansell," Grace called from across the kitchen.

He hadn't meant to draw her attention, but little he could do about it now.

"Hello, Grace," he replied, crossing the kitchen to stand in front of the girl. She was busying herself tying beads to a cord. A pile of them sat in the nest of her skirt, and her tiny fingers fumbled as they tied them together.

"When are we going on to the mountains?" she asked without looking up.

Ansell had hoped she would have forgotten about his talk of adventure, but clearly it had stuck in her mind.

"Soon. There are many things I must prepare before we can leave."

Grace looked up at him, one eye squinting in suspicion. "You promised, though. Remember?"

He could remember no promises, but then Grace clearly had the better memory of it. "We will go soon. As I said we would."

"There's nothing to do here. It's boring."

He could well imagine it was, for such a curious child. Perhaps it would be better to place her with the other orphans, so she could at least make friends. Then again, she was his responsibility now, and he thought it best to have her close by for as long as he could.

"I will bring you charcoal and paper. You like to draw, don't you? I seem to remember you had some talent for it."

"I'd like to see the mountains more," she replied.

"I don't doubt you would," he said, unable to stop himself smiling once again, and feeling the sting of it on his tender flesh. "What are you doing?" He pointed to the pile of beads.

Now it was her turn to smile. "I'm making something for you."

"For me?"

"Yes," she replied, tying off the last knot of the cord and holding it up for him to see.

Ansell took it from her. Five beads were tied to it, a letter scratched into each one to spell *Ansul*.

"Thank you," he replied, though he had no idea what he might do with such a thing.

He glanced to his left, seeing Joye had stopped her chopping and was looking at him with wide eyes. He could only imagine how it might appear—a fearsome Knight of the Draconate being given such a heartfelt gift by a child. Joye was quick to refocus on her labours as soon as Ansell met her gaze.

"I have one too," Grace said, holding up her tiny arm. To her wrist was tied a similar cord with five beads, the letters of her name scratched upon them. At least she had managed to spell it correctly.

No one had ever given Ansell such a thing before. It was a small gesture, but perhaps to Grace it was the most generous gift she could offer.

"I have to go," he told her.

"Why?" she asked.

"I have business to attend."

Grace brightened for a moment. "And then can we go to the mountains?"

"Soon," he replied, before turning and making his way from the kitchen as fast as he could.

He gripped that bracelet tight in his meaty palm as he made his way back to his chamber. When he entered his spartan room, he slowly unclenched his fist and looked down at the tiny gift. *Ansul.* She had done her best, he supposed. But more importantly, what did it mean? As a Knight of the Draconate, Ansell was forbidden from owning any trinkets or bearing any symbols not bestowed by his order. His sword and armour were the only things he could call his own, and those had been gifted by the Archlegate himself. Perhaps he should throw the bracelet away. It did, after all, break the code of knighthood to covet such a thing.

"Is all well, Beckenrike?"

At the sound of his name Ansell placed the bracelet within the open pages of the book on his table before closing it—his copy of the Draconate Prophesies. He turned, seeing Regenwulf standing in his doorway.

"It is, brother," he replied.

"Only your door is usually closed. It's not often I see you standing in silent reflection. Something troubling you?"

Ansell shook his head. "No, I was merely about to wash. The stink of the day's labours still clings to me."

Regenwulf stepped inside his chamber, pushing the door closed behind him. "Yes, I heard the Archlegate picked you for a grim duty. It cannot have been easy. I also notice there is a new orphan in our care, and you have shown her much attention. I wondered if that was on your mind also?"

Immediately Ansell began to wonder how much Regenwulf knew of her. Had he learned of her mother's murder? Did he know who her father might be?

"Since I brought her to the Mount, I have felt it my responsibility to watch over her, that is all."

Regenwulf ran a hand over his thick moustache. "You know

there are others who can bear that responsibility. It is not your obligation to look after the welfare of every waif under our roof. You should not forget who you are, or what your real duties demand."

Ansell was well aware of his *real duties*. He had been performing them all morning, and still felt the ache in his knuckles.

"Of course not," he replied, absently flexing his shoulder, feeling the tug of the wound in his arm that had barely healed.

"That cut still bothering you?" Regenwulf asked.

"It is nothing. Merely a reminder. There will be a reckoning for it soon enough."

Regenwulf grinned. "Don't feel too bad for losing to Lancelin Jagdor. He is a breed apart, it could have happened to any of us. Did I ever tell you I served alongside him at the Drift? That man was a demon with a blade in hand."

Ansell knew well enough about Jagdor's abilities, but it did little to quell his humiliation. Neither did it help him forget what the swordwright said when they had fought. *Sanctan is not worth your life.* Those words had plagued Ansell as much as the pain of his wounds.

"Tell me, Regenwulf—what do you think of our Archlegate?"

Regenwulf shrugged. "He speaks with the tongue of the Great Wyrms. He is our guiding flame in the dark, as was Gylbard before him, and every Archlegate before that."

At the mention of Gylbard, an unwelcome memory cast its shadow over Ansell. He remembered driving his blade into the old man's back at the summit of Wyrmhead. Watching him die on that balcony in the frigid cold. All at the behest of Sanctan. But then, he had been persuaded that Gylbard's death was the only way they might rise. The only way they could step out from the shadow of the Guilds and defend Torwyn from its real enemies in the west.

"I did not ask what you think of his office. I meant as a man. What do you think of Sanctan Egelrath?"

Regenwulf's brow furrowed. "It is not my place to question the man who calls himself Archlegate. Nor is it yours. It is our place to serve."

It was the obvious answer, one any Knight of the Draconate would have repeated if asked. Ansell could see he had raised some suspicion in Regenwulf, and nodded his agreement. "Of course, you are right."

"Why do you ask such questions?"

There were so many reasons. Ansell could only wonder if Regenwulf knew the depths to which he had sunk in serving that man. The vows betrayed. The iniquities he had seen, as well as done.

"Sanctan is young, that's all," Ansell replied. "We follow a man with little experience of the world. I wonder...if he is up to the task."

"Age does not matter. He was chosen by the High Legates and, in turn, by the Great Wyrms themselves. And he has not led us wrong yet. We have risen far in a short time, to finally reclaim our place in the hearts of Torwyn's people."

Ansell could only wonder at the truth of that. Had it been the case, those workers living in squalor at the Burrows would not have risen up against them.

"Of course, you are right, brother," he replied.

"You know I am, Beckenrike. Now, I must leave you. I suggest you reflect on your scripture, and should you still harbour doubts, we can discuss this later."

Regenwulf gestured to the Draconate Prophesies on Ansell's table, before turning and leaving him alone. Ansell looked down at that book, wondering if there were any answers within its pages. Any solace for his doubt. Or perhaps whether the lash might be a better choice to purge him of his reservations.

Instead he opened up the book, seeing the bracelet where he had left it, and before he had time to think on what he was doing, he had fastened it around his wrist.

CONALL

He had lain awake, listening to that music, fighting the urge to sleep. Despite the exhaustion, he forced his eyes to remain open, waiting until he had counted five thousand before deciding it was time to go. As those strings and flutes played on, Conall slid from his bed, still wearing the grubby clothes he had trained in the day before. Beyond the room, through an archway, a single torch burned on its sconce, casting only a little light on the corridor. There he knelt in a sea of shadow, watching, waiting.

Someone crept closer. He held his breath until he recognised the face that peered at him from the dark. Nylia looked scared, her eyes fixed on that archway. Conall allowed himself a long low breath, opening his mouth to ask her what next. Before he could utter a sound, she clapped her hand over his mouth, as Mikal tiptoed his way closer.

This was madness. If they were caught, the repercussions would be dire. He'd already seen an old man murdered for nothing, and here he was defying Orsokon once again. But what was the alternative? Wait around to become another casualty? See what the Scion Senmonthis had in store? No, they were getting out of here, or they would die. He would not remain an inmate in this asylum for one more day.

As Nylia led them through the arch from the chamber, Conall

forgot all his trepidation. They had to do this, and damn the consequences. He was a Hawkspur, an heir to his Guild, and there was
trouble in Torwyn that required his attention. If nothing else, it was
his duty to escape this infernal place. Not that duty had ever meant
anything to him before. Strange how such things started to seem
important when you had a prison to escape.

The light was brighter in the passage. Conall fully expected to
see a roaming guard, or one of the thralls going about his business,
but the corridor was empty. It felt as though they were inviting him
to escape, and the further Nylia led them through the labyrinth,
the more he felt surprise at how poorly guarded it was. Arcturius
seemed all but abandoned.

The deeper they delved down twisting corridors, the more Conall
began to wonder if they were hopelessly lost. He was blindly following this woman, but Nylia did not pause or wait to consider her
route. Who was he to argue with confidence like that? At least one
of them seemed to know what they were doing.

Eventually the corridor led them upward, the roof opening up to
reveal a sea of stars. Nylia paused, regarding the constellations with
wonder.

"We are almost at the eastern gate," Conall whispered.

She nodded. "Not far now."

"But how do you even know the way?"

She turned to regard him, a trace of a smile on her lips. "I pay
attention, eastlander."

A slight? Harsh, but probably fair. "I suppose it's a good thing one
of us does."

Before she could answer, Mikal urged them on with a frantic gesture, his face twisted in panic. Without another word they delved
back into the maze, and it wasn't long before Conall began to smell
something enticing on the air, along with a faint noise in the distance. When they reached the end of the corridor it opened out onto
a mezzanine, and Nylia paused at a ledge in front of them. Conall
looked down to see a vast kitchen sprawling below. A score of thralls
went about their duties, stirring pots of gruel, hacking at root vegetables and sawing hunks of bony meat.

As he began to wonder if they should steal some food for their journey east, Nylia tapped him on the shoulder before motioning to the top of a nearby staircase. There he saw a row of grey thrall's robes hanging from hooks. He got the message, leading them across the mezzanine before the three of them cast aside their tunics and donned the robes.

This time Conall took it on himself to lead them, walking down the stairs and into the kitchen with head bowed, making his way past the cooks as though he belonged there. Not one of those thralls looked up from their work, and he began to feel excitement fluttering in his gut at the prospect of this actually working.

He pushed open a door at the far end of the kitchen, feeling a gust of fresh night air as he walked out into a courtyard. Any confidence he might have been feeling washed away as he almost bumped into one of those overseers. His helmed head turned as Conall moved out into the torchlight, and he froze, gawking, unable to think, unable to move.

"You're late," stated the overseer. "Get moving or you'll feel the whip."

With that he cuffed Conall about the head, propelling him farther into the yard. Ahead was a huge gate yawning open to the east. Before it waited a sturdy-looking wagon, loaded to the gunnels with sacks and wooden boxes, a row of thralls unloading it with silent efficiency.

Surely it couldn't be this easy? There was no way his luck could change so quickly. It would have been stupid to question it though, and he made his way to the rear of the wagon, grabbing a heavy sack and throwing it over his shoulder.

Nylia and Mikal did likewise, and the three of them began unloading that wagon as though they were born to the task. As he returned for the third time to grab a wooden crate, he caught Nylia's eye and she flashed him a wink. Time to get out of here.

Mikal was the first to climb into the back of the wagon under the guise of collecting sacks from deeper within. Then Nylia did the same, before handing Conall a cage full of fluttering fowl. He turned, walking to the side of the yard, where he stacked the birds with the rest of the supplies. The overseers weren't watching as he made his way back to the wagon and began to climb aboard, at any moment expecting to be stopped. He gritted his teeth as he entered the dark confines, casting a brief glance back to make sure he hadn't been spotted.

Nylia was already hiding under a pile of empty sacks, Mikal concealing himself behind a crate. Conall hunkered down in the shadows, clutching his knees, trying to make himself as small and inconspicuous as he could.

A single thrall peered into the wagon, seeing it was empty before squinting into the shadowy depths. Had he spotted them? Would he give them away if he had? Just as Conall thought he might call out to the guards, the thrall swung the wagon door closed and bolted it shut.

The only sound was heavy breathing as they waited in the dark. Time stretched out as that incessant music played in the distance. Then, with a snap of reins, the wagon trundled off.

"That was too bloody easy," Conall breathed, not yet allowing himself to feel safe.

"You think that was easy?" said Mikal. "I thought I might shit. Truly we are blessed by the gods to have escaped."

Nylia shook her head. "I think you are both forgetting something. We are headed toward the most dangerous place in all Hyreme. Who knows what awaits us there. Let us not laud the gods just yet, not until we are far from here, and the Drift."

The wagon clattered along the uneven road. It was cool inside, and Conall would have loved to put his head down and sleep, but the roiling unease in his gut wouldn't allow it. His every nerve was on edge, his senses prickling with anticipation, with fear. After they'd been travelling for what seemed an hour, Mikal tried opening the back door, but it was bolted from the other side.

"Looks like we're stuck in here until we reach our destination," he said. "Wherever that may be."

"And neither do we know who might be waiting at the other end," said Nylia. "As soon as this wagon stops and that door is unbolted, we should all rush out. Make a run for it."

"A sound plan," Conall agreed, though it sounded like the most reckless plan he'd ever heard. But what other option did they have?

The journey could have taken hours, but with nothing to mark the passage of time, Conall wasn't exactly sure. Despite the gnawing fear and the rumbling of wheels, he eventually found his head nodding as he succumbed to sleep, before being jolted back to reality every now and again. When finally they slowed to a halt, he felt Nylia's hand on his shoulder, shaking him awake.

"We are here," she hissed.

Conall rose to his haunches, listening for any sound that might offer a clue as to where they were or who was waiting. All he could hear was the whickering of the horses.

There was a snap as the door was unbolted. Conall didn't wait for anyone to swing it wide, surging forward and slamming his weight against it before stumbling out of the wagon, managing to keep his footing, blinded by the glaring torches. He blinked, trying to focus, looking for an escape route, but as his eyes adjusted to the light, he realised there was nowhere to run.

They were back in the courtyard at Arcturius.

Nylia and Mikal jumped down beside him, stopping when they realised they were surrounded. Armoured overseers leered at them from behind their ugly helms, torches in one hand, whips and blades in the other.

As Warmaven Orsokon stepped from the shadows, all Conall could do was breathe, "Fuck."

He felt his bowels twitch as the warlord loomed over him. "Did you enjoy your little journey?" he asked in that singsong voice that had no business coming from such a beast.

Conall could only reflect on his disappointment. "Well, the wagon was a little stuffy, and the view was nothing to write home about, but all in all—"

An iron-hard punch to the gut. Conall dropped to one knee, doing his best not to puke as he fought for air.

"Was that levity?" Orsokon asked. "Only with you I am often unsure."

Conall tried not to panic as he staggered to his feet. This was the end, but that realisation only served to make him angrier. More defiant.

"That's because you're a humourless twat," he managed to say, staring at Orsokon, refusing to be cowed. "Maybe you'll find it funny when I stamp that fat head into the ground. Would you like that, you cowardly fuck?"

"A threat of violence?" mused Orsokon. "Anger to mask your despair. Your fear. Do I understand that right?"

If Conall could see behind that helm, he was sure Orsokon would have been smiling.

"Understand this . . . I'm going to kill you."

Before he could try to make good on his threat, he was grabbed by the arms. Nylia was next, struggling vainly against the overseers, but Mikal was faster, dodging aside and striking one of those helmed heads with his fist. To his credit it made a resounding clang and the overseer fell backward, but two more rushed forward, one of them hitting Mikal with a baton to the back of the legs. More overseers surrounded him, steel-shod boots kicking him to piss as one of them lashed him again and again with a whip.

When they were done, Mikal wasn't moving, and Conall could only wonder if he'd be next in line for a beating, but before anyone could turn their eye on him, there was a call from the dark.

"What's going on here?"

Baenre Mokhtar walked into the yard, a furious look on his face. The overseers seemed wary of him, but Orsokon was not so easily intimidated.

"These recruits decided to spurn the benevolence of our Scion. I was simply teaching them the benefits of remaining here."

"They escaped?" Baenre replied. "From Arcturius? How did this happen?"

Orsokon shrugged his muscular shoulders. "Because I allowed it. And it amused me."

"And now you're going to beat them to death?"

Orsokon turned his huge head to regard Conall. "No. Senmonthis has decided they are to be inducted, immediately."

Baenre seemed to accept Orsokon's words with resignation,

bowing his head and nodding his agreement. "Perhaps a little premature, but very well."

"What does that mean?" Conall blurted. "What does he mean, *inducted*? Inducted into what?"

Baenre regarded him with regret. "I am sorry, Conall Hawkspur, but I cannot help you. There is more to this than you realise, but soon you will learn."

Before Conall could ask what in the Lairs that meant, he was dragged through the gaping doors by overseers. He managed to steal one last look at Nylia, before they were pulled into different passageways.

He could barely see a thing in the torchlight until he reached half a dozen robed figures, faces hidden behind stone masks, iron armour beneath their hooded robes. As the overseers handed him over to them, he was hit by a rank smell that made him gag.

The robed men dragged him to a cavernous chamber, lit by torches flickering with strange blue flame. Something was written on the walls, but he barely had time to take in the alien script before he focused on the slab that sat in the centre of the room.

He had no strength to resist the stinking bastards as they chained him to that slab, securing manacles about his wrists and ankles. Without a word, they left him there to strain against his bonds.

Silence permeated the dark. He stewed in his own fear for what seemed an age, considering all the ways he would be tortured despite his best efforts to clear his mind of it. All he could hear was his own fevered breath—even the lilting music that had plagued him for days had fallen silent.

A whisper from the shadows. He couldn't make out the words, but he definitely heard something—some disembodied voice he was sure mentioned his name.

"Who's there?" he called out to the dark.

He was answered by a second whisper, this time closer to his ear, but he still couldn't make out the words.

"What do you want?" he shouted, desperate to dispel the eerie quiet of the chamber.

This time a hiss. Though it sounded inhuman, he could somehow understand its implication. It wanted him. Yearning for him with unyielding desire.

"Why?" he asked. "Why me?"

Your part in this has been foreseen, came that whisper, clear in his head like a hollow breeze.

"My part in what? What are you talking about? What is going on?"

She will rise against us. She must be stopped.

Conall gritted his teeth against the fear, desperate to understand but failing. It felt as though the shadows themselves were talking to him, but he was somehow managing to understand their infernal words.

"Who will rise? What do you mean?"

A cold wind shifted through the chamber, and with it a single word... *Mother.*

Mother? Whose mother? His mother?

"Rosomon? Do you mean Rosomon Hawkspur?"

She must fall. And you will aid us in this.

Conall shook his head at the notion, trying to expel it of the disembodied whisper as well as the idea that he would betray his own kin.

"No. I won't help you. I will not turn against my family."

She murdered your father.

Conall felt the pain of that like a dagger through his ribs. It was all he could do to stifle a sob.

"No. I will have no part in this. She did not kill my father; she would never have done that. There's an explanation. For Jagdor. For all of it."

But even as he said the words he knew the simplest explanation was most likely the truth. He had always suspected his mother's infidelity. Now it seemed those fears that she had plotted his father's death were not just the fanciful musings of a child.

None of this is by chance. This was always fated.

Conall gritted his teeth, trying to expel those foul thoughts, trying to block out that ephemeral voice. The compulsion to agree with this demon was overwhelming, and he was consumed by guilt, by old hatreds he had so desperately tried to quell.

Follow us, and you will become a legend. Your name will be spoken in the histories, and you will be granted everything you desire.

"What does that even mean?" he pleaded, but deep down he knew what the voice was offering. Aspirations he had kept hidden. Dreams of power and respect and unrivalled might that he had locked away. Now he was being offered the key to open them.

You will become greater than you could ever know.

Conall screamed, straining against the chains. "Fuck you. I will die before I betray my mother. I will fight. Show yourself and I will kill you. Take these chains off me and I'll damn well prove it."

We will see.

Quiet fell over the chamber. The oppressive sense that he was being watched by some malevolent being left him in an instant. When he moved his arm, he realised the chains that had bound him were no longer there. The shackles at his ankles had likewise vanished, and he sat up, shivering in the cold now the sweat had soaked though his thrall's robes.

"Why have you released me?" he asked quietly, feeling the dread rising once more.

What need has Senmonthis for chains? came the reply. *You are powerless. But I can give you power. More than you could ever comprehend.*

Conall looked up to see a darkness within the shadow, a void so black he thought he might fall into it and never find his way out. It had no eyes, but it was watching him, seeing into his soul. Feeding on his terror.

When it came for him, he barely had time to scream.

TYRETA

Their stolen boat puttered south along the river. The sun shone on what could have been any ordinary day, with the birds in the trees twittering along to the soft chugging of that engine. Cat lounged on the deck, occasionally swiping a paw at the buzzing flies as they teased her shiny nose.

It wasn't any other day though. Tyreta could feel tightness in her gut, her innards tied in knots as she flinched at every movement on the riverbank. Sted stood at the prow with her splintbow, one foot on the gunwale, glaring out at the idyllic view as though daring someone to attack. It was doubtful she was appreciating the view.

"All clear?" Tyreta asked.

"As far as I can bloody see," Sted snapped. Her jaw worked as she ground her teeth frenetically, bereft of the redstalk she usually clamped between them. She'd chewed her last stick to mush the day before, and it was pretty obvious she was missing the buzz.

Tyreta would have used her powers to speed up the boat and get this over with quicker, but the engine was already working at full capacity according to Crenn. If she tried to engage the pyrestones, it would likely blow the conversion shaft—whatever that was. He'd been tinkering with the engine since they set off, but the fastest they'd managed was a few miles an hour.

"Do you think we're close?" Tyreta asked.

Sted pulled a face as though working out some tricky equation. "I reckon we can't be far off. Just a few miles north of the Rock, unless I've missed my guess."

"Do you think—?"

Sted raised a hand for her to be quiet, peering forward over the prow. There was something up ahead that had most certainly caught her attention, though Tyreta couldn't see what.

"Cut the engine," Sted hissed.

Tyreta rushed to the cabin. Crenn was inside, working away as usual, and when he looked up, she motioned a hand across her throat. He understood, stretching over to the control board and pulling a lever to slow the boat. As the engine sputtered and died, Tyreta crossed the deck to stand at Sted's side. Slowly she unshouldered her bow and nocked an arrow.

The boat drifted downstream for a few yards, Donan holding the tiller straight and keeping them in the centre of the river as best he could. They didn't have to go far before Tyreta saw what had grabbed Sted's attention.

A corpse was strung up in one of the trees on the bank. He swung gently, the purple skin of his gawping face reflecting the sunlight. A wooden plaque had been tied around his broken neck, letters scrawled across the front spelling out the word *Heretic*.

"Those fucking Wyrm-loving bastards," Sted snarled.

"I wonder what he did," Donan said from the rear of the boat. "To . . . to deserve that."

"Didn't have to do nothing for those fanatics to hang him. Could have bad-mouthed the Archlegate. Could have forgotten to say his daily prayers. World's gone so mad it wouldn't matter either way."

Tyreta was pretty sure that wasn't quite the truth. More likely that man, swinging for all to see, had remained loyal to the Guilds. Loyal to her and her mother. There was no doubt he was there as a reminder not to defy the Ministry. It only reminded Tyreta how important it was she succeed in her mission.

"Look," Donan said, pointing farther downriver.

Above the distant trees that lined the bank, they could see a grey pall of smoke rising into the clear sky.

"Where is that?" Tyreta asked, feeling that dread knot tighten in her stomach.

"It's the Rock," Donan replied, his voice almost breaking. "My home. They've just...just burned it all down."

"I'm sorry, Donan." It was all she could think to say.

If he heard her, Donan had nothing to add. She turned to look at him, and even from across the boat she could see the tears gathering in his eyes.

"Nothing we can do about that now," Sted said. "Besides, we're here."

She gestured to a jetty that poked from a bend in the river up ahead. Crenn powered the engine once more, and Donan guided them toward the bank. The side of the boat scraped the wooden landing, and Tyreta jumped ashore, taking a rope and fastening it to the mooring. Cat immediately leapt onto the jetty and dashed off into the underbrush.

"Thought you could control that thing," Sted said as she stepped off the boat.

"Apparently not well enough," Tyreta replied, wondering where the panther was off to.

Donan was helped onto the jetty by Crenn, before he nodded along the river path. "Transport station is a couple of miles down the road."

Tyreta could see he was still shaken by what was happening at the Rock, but she just didn't have the words to console him. Trying to ignore the plume of smoke as it consumed the southern skyline, she followed Sted along the river path.

There was no sign of the enemy, but Tyreta found herself gripping her bow, just in case. The group walked in silence for a mile or so, before the telltale slag heaps of a huge quarry came into view past the woodland. Beyond them, metal cranes had been erected like spindly statues, leering down at the earthworks.

"It's this way," Donan said eagerly, leading them off the main path and through the trees.

Soon they came out on a road running parallel to the river, the gates to the quarry visible to the south. As they were about to approach, that knot in Tyreta's stomach took on a more sinister aspect. She was struck with an overwhelming sense of nausea, her gut cramping so tight she had to grit her teeth against the pain. An eagle screeched as it soared over their heads, and she almost staggered at the deafening noise.

Was it a warning? Some portent granted by the nightstone that was now a part of her essence?

"Wait," she said, grasping Donan's arm before he could stride any closer to the gates ahead of them.

"What is it?" asked Sted, frowning at her with concern.

"It's just...I have...I have a feeling."

Sted's frown turned to raised eyebrows. "A feeling? And what does the feeling tell you?"

"I—I'm not sure. I think there might be danger ahead."

"So there *is* danger, or you're not sure?"

"I don't know," Tyreta growled. "Just give me a moment to think."

Sted glanced impatiently up and down the empty road. "Time isn't a luxury we can afford. We can't stand around all afternoon and wonder what's waiting for us. Where's that panther of yours? Can't she check the way ahead?"

"She...I don't know where she is."

That eagle shrieked again, a piercing cry of warning. There was no other way to interpret it.

"So what do we do?" asked Sted.

Tyreta raised a hand for her to be quiet, closing her eyes tight. She began to focus, hearing the wind rustle through the trees, smelling the pollen on the air. The circuitous strands of the web coalesced, and she began to feel for what lay along the road ahead with nebulous fingers. Despite her best efforts, her senses couldn't penetrate more than a few yards. But maybe there was another way.

She stood tall, raising her face to the sun, feeling it bathe her in a cleansing light. One deep breath and she let her consciousness soar. Up she rose, lifted on the air like the petal of a flower. When she

opened her eyes, they were seeing with the vision of the eagle far
above.

Tyreta soared on the thermals, across an open field with the woodland to her left. In front was a huge gash in the earth, the quarry running deep, flanked around its edge by those metal statues.

She dived, feathered wings fluttering faster as she wheeled between
the towers. On the floor of the quarry she could make out figures:
horned helms atop their heads, others wearing yellow uniforms. Rising on the thermals, she circled the largest tower, spying someone
hidden within its summit. A single gunman, longbarrel gripped tight
as he ranged for a target through its monocular scope...

When she opened her eyes, Tyreta almost cried out at the thrill of
her experience.

"It's not good," she gasped.

Sted was holding on to her, making sure she didn't collapse.
"How not good?"

"Auroch Battalion. And Revocaters, I think. There's a sniper, up
in the nearest tower."

"That's definitely not good." Sted had a wonderful way of stating
the obvious. "At least now we know the Auroch Battalion is in the
pocket of the Ministry."

"Do you think they might be looking for us? Know we're on the
way?"

Sted shook her head. "I don't see how. But it's not like I'm just
gonna stroll up and ask. We might need to come up with a new
plan."

"Maybe not," said Tyreta, already turning toward that tower.
"There might be a way we can get in without being seen."

"How? You just said they had a lookout in the tower. Even if we
could avoid getting shot, they'd still raise the alarm."

A smile crossed her face. "Don't worry. I think I have that
covered."

Crenn was already scanning the towers with his monocular. "I
don't see what you can do. You're a good shot with that bow, but I
can barely make out the sniper from here. Even if we can get within
range for you to loose an arrow, we'll be spotted for sure."

Tyreta was already moving closer, taking an arrow from the quiver at her hip. One set with a red pyrestone at the tip.

"No one could make that shot," Sted said. "I've seen you do some things, girl, but that's impossible."

Tyreta shushed her. "I need to concentrate."

She closed her eyes, nocking the arrow. There was a moment of pause as her senses began to tingle with anticipation. Or was it reluctance? Taking a life wasn't something to be done lightly, but as she remembered that body hanging by the river she raised her bow, letting out a long cleansing breath.

The string creaked as she drew it as far as she could. With her eyes still closed she loosed. The red pyrestone in the arrowhead flared, light flashing behind her eyes as she connected with it, and the landscape moved past her lightning fast. She was soaring, not with the precision of a hawk, but the burning fire of a pyrestone, spinning in flight until she exerted her will. The arrow turned, her powers altering its trajectory as the tower grew larger in her panoramic view. She spied the sharpshooter growing larger, becoming her only point of focus. At her command the arrow streaked through the air, hunting its target, homing in until it entered the tower, a red bolt of web-fuelled energy that sank deep into his body.

Tyreta opened her eyes. Turning, she saw Crenn still looking through the monocular, his mouth agape.

"By all the bloody Wyrms," he breathed.

Sted took a step forward, much less impressed. "All right, when we've finished patting ourselves on the back, we still need to get to the underground station without being killed by a battalion of Armigers."

Tyreta pushed down the thrill of what she'd just experienced. Sted was right.

"Follow me," she said, drawing another arrow from her quiver, keeping her eyes fixed on the road ahead.

The gate lay open, abandoned mining carts forgotten along the side of a path that curved down into the quarry. Conveyor belts sat immobile, ore strewn across their length as they arced down to the shaft entrances at the base of the huge mine. Industrial hulks sat powered down like sullen sculptures, long abandoned by their pilots.

Two Auroch troopers stood guard a few yards down the path, and Tyreta signalled for her group to duck down behind a conveyor before making their way past. The guards didn't seem to be expecting much trouble, and they managed to sneak by them without being seen. Maybe this wouldn't be as difficult as she thought.

In silence they followed the path toward the base of the quarry. Just as they reached the bottom, Donan tapped Tyreta on the shoulder. He gestured across the quarry floor to a wide entrance. A sign hung above it depicting the carriage of a landship—the entrance to the underground terminal.

Twenty yards away, between them and the entrance, stood a dozen Auroch troopers. One of them, a lieutenant from the white chevron on the arm of his uniform, was engaged in a heated debate with a yellow-clad Revocater, red plume designating her as a captain.

With the guards occupied by their quarrel, Tyreta crept toward the entrance, crouching behind piles of discarded ore and debris. The others followed, and the closer they got to their goal, the louder the argument became.

"But this is our jurisdiction," barked the Revocater, her plume agitating with anger. "Rearden Corwen himself has ordered this place be left intact."

"My instructions come directly from the Archlegate," countered the Auroch lieutenant. "This facility is to be destroyed, with immediate effect."

Tyreta had almost reached the entrance, the latent energy of the pyrestones within the mine teasing her senses. Before she could dart through the dark opening, there was a metallic clank behind her. She turned in time to see Donan fall to the ground, his metal leg caught on the track of a mining wagon. The guards ceased their quarrel.

"What in the Lairs was that?"

Sted cocked her splintbow, rising up from behind their cover. "Fucking run!" she bellowed before unleashing a volley toward the arguing troopers.

Tyreta had time to loose a single arrow before sprinting for the cave, not even bothering to see if it hit a target. Corrugated stairs led down into the dark and she stopped just inside the entrance as Crenn and Donan stumbled after her.

"Get to the terminal," she ordered, nocking another arrow. "Start up the transport."

As they both clattered down the stairs, she took a breath before Sted dived into the tunnel, bolts ricocheting around the entrance behind her.

"Better move, Hawkspur," she shouted, running right by and following the others deeper into the cave. "They're pretty pissed off."

Tyreta backed away, bow still trained on the gaping entrance as she made her way down the stairs. The light from outside was suddenly extinguished as a hulking figure advanced toward her, his bulk taking up most of the tunnel—an Auroch trooper, heavily armoured, shield braced. He had a steamlock carbine levelled over the top of his shield, pointed straight at her.

She loosed, the blue pyrestone in the arrowhead bursting to life as it struck the shield. Light arced across the metal, sparking with energy, but still the behemoth kept coming.

Tyreta reached for another arrow, but the trooper had her in his sights, the carbine aimed right at her chest. There was nowhere to dodge, no way to stop him before he fired.

A roar echoed through the tunnel. Cat leapt from out of nowhere, clawing at the trooper's back. He fell under her weight, his single-shot carbine firing wildly, blowing chunks of rock from the wall.

The panther locked her jaws on the armour, claws leaving divots in the iron, but she couldn't get to the flesh beneath. Tyreta shouted for Cat to follow, before turning and running after Sted down the stairs and into the tunnel beyond.

The passageway sank deeper into the earth before levelling out. She rushed through it, bursting out into the underground terminal. At the far end sat the transport conveyor Donan had told them about, Crenn already on board, frantically fumbling at the dashboard while he tried to couple together a mess of bare wires.

"Get a move on, old man," Sted snapped just as Tyreta reached them.

"We need to go," Tyreta cried. "Now."

Crenn fixed her with a dark look. "I'm bloody working on it."

Tyreta turned back to the entrance, seeing Cat burst from the tunnel. Behind her clattered half a dozen troopers, weapons raised. Sted fired her splintbow, and those troopers scattered, leaping for cover.

A volley of bolts snapped back at them, one thudding into the carriage right by Tyreta's head. More of them were pouring into the terminal—a score of troopers and Revocaters, all armed to the teeth, all bent on stopping their escape. She reached to her quiver but realised there wouldn't be enough arrows to bring them all down.

There had to be another way.

She could feel the overwhelming presence of pyrestone in the air, that heady stink of power making her head spin. More bolts streaked past her face, another steamlock carbine bellowing from the far end of the terminal, shot ringing off the side of the conveyor. Sted ducked, hunkering in the engine's cabin, screaming for Tyreta to "Get down!"

She ignored the warning. There was a thick seam of pyrestone down here. An untapped resource hidden among the rock above them. Their only chance.

Tyreta raised a hand as a score of enemies took aim. She could feel the latent power in those stones, just waiting to be harnessed. Her hand trembled as she reached out, fuelling the pyrestones with her will, making them glow within the rock face—making them burn.

The first one exploded, sending shards of rocks tumbling atop the heads of the troopers. Then another, more and more, a cacophony of explosions, stone after stone erupting, dislodging the rock above and sending it crashing down on their hunters.

"I've got it!" Crenn yelled above the deluge.

The engine whined as turbines fired, the conveyor jolting forward. Tyreta felt a hand on her shoulder, dragging her into the cabin where she toppled, falling on her arse as the engine steamed off along the underground rail, gaining in velocity with every second.

Hot air began to blow along the tunnel like a gale, riffling Tyreta's hair as she turned to see Sted glowering.

"Do we have to do everything by the skin of our shitting teeth?"

"Honestly?" Tyreta replied. "I think that went well."

As they sped southwest to Windstone, Sted didn't seem to share her view.

ANSELL

He stood alongside his brothers, behind a phalanx of impenetrable shields. A wall of steel that would have struck fear in any foe, but it was no army they faced. In front of them, blocking the throughfare, was a mob of ordinary folk. They had flocked from every corner of the Burrows to spit their rancour. To swarm through the city streets, to burn and smash, and spread their misery throughout the rest of the Anvil. It could not be allowed, and so here they were, shields braced, swords drawn, ready to slaughter their own people once the order was given.

Regenwulf was to his left, Falcar to his right. Their presence did little to make him feel better about any of this. Every part of it was wrong. Ansell should not have been here quelling the citizens of the Anvil. He should have been facing the tyrants of the Guilds—his blessed blade cutting through the ranks of the very people who had held these folk in chains for so long. But this was a situation that required restraint, a cool head above all else. Listening to the din, Ansell could tell there were few cool heads here, other than his own.

Behind him was rank upon gaudy rank of Corwen Guild Revocaters. He and his brothers were all that stood between them and the bellowing crowd, and Ansell could sense the tension brewing among those Revocater lines. Swords were already drawn. Trembling hands fumbled at the stocks of splintbows. Some of them gnawed at their lips as they nervously prepared themselves to face battle. Things were going to get out of hand, and the mob weren't about to make this precarious situation any better.

They were just yelling for now, but they wouldn't stand there bellowing and waving those placards forever. At first they had chanted in unison. Demanding that they be fed, that the manufactories be reopened, that they be allowed to return to their labours so they could provide for their families. All that had ended, and now their chants had turned to snarling rage. Only a matter of time before...

The first rock was thrown. It clanked harmlessly off a shield, nothing to be concerned with, but Ansell knew it was just a start. Another flew, then another, playing that tinny tune. He remembered how the crowd had gone mad at the Cogwheel when he'd cut down Emperor Sullivar. The sound of raining stones had rung like the bells of an orchestra. It only took a couple of those stone throwers to embolden the rest, before it began to rain.

Stones turned to bricks, turned to boulders. Shards of metal and wood clanked off those shields. The placards on which they had scrawled their ire now so much ammunition for the mob. Their voices were raised as they raged, but they weren't the only ones. Behind him the Revocaters began to growl and bellow. Working themselves into a fury. They would not stand idle for long.

"Shoot the bastards," said one of them.

"Give the order to bloody fire," snarled another.

Still Ansell and his fellow Drakes stood impassively, holding the line.

No one had charged at them yet. No one had dared. He could only hope it stayed that way before these people were cut down by volley after volley of splintbow fire.

Unlike his brothers, Ansell had kept his sword sheathed, but his hand lay on the hilt. He suddenly remembered the bracelet on that wrist. Grace had gifted it to him for his kindness. He didn't feel too kind now, but it served to remind him that he was a good man. Here to serve the people, not slaughter them. It appeared those Revocaters had a very different idea of service.

"All right," said a voice behind him—a voice he recognised. "Make sure your clips are loaded. We have our orders."

Ansell turned to see the Revocater captain parading along the front rank of his men as they checked their weapons. This was it—the slaughter about to begin. A part of him could hardly blame them, as a piece of wood sailed over the front rank to hit one of the Revocaters in the face, his howl of pain lost amid the din of the crowd.

Ansell couldn't just stand there while they shot down these people. All they wanted was food. A chance to earn their living.

He took a step back from the shield wall, ordering Regenwulf and Falcar to plug the gap, before he strode toward the captain, who was even now pulling his blade free of its scabbard.

"I have not given the order to fire," Ansell announced.

The captain was young, clearly inexperienced, but he fixed Ansell with as imperious a gaze as he could muster. "You're not in charge here, Drake. I take my orders from Rearden Corwen. This unrest is to be quelled no matter the cost."

Ansell would have warned him that cost might be too much to bear, but he doubted it would have done much good. Instead he leaned in close, glaring from behind his dragon helm. "My orders come from the Archlegate. That puts *me* in charge."

He let those words hang in the air, among the din and the raining missiles. The Revocater captain worked his jaw, trying to think of the best way forward. Could he lose face in front of his men? Should he stand up to this Knight of the Draconate and risk the ire of Sanctan Egelrath?

"Do you think your Archlegate would sanction rioting in the streets?"

"These people are starving," Ansell replied. "All they want is—"

Something heavy struck him in the pauldron. The captain took a step back, shaking his head.

"I've had enough of this," he growled, turning to his men. "Prepare to fire!"

Ansell's time had run out. If he didn't do something, dozens of innocent people were going to die. These were not enemies they faced; they were just workers, common folk who had kept Torwyn's wheels of industry spinning for year after toil-filled year.

"Lower your weapons," Ansell growled at the front rank, his voice resonating from within his helmet.

Some of the Revocaters paused in response, unsure of who to obey. The captain took a step forward, jabbing his finger against Ansell's breastplate.

"I told you—I give the fucking orders."

Ansell glanced down, seeing that finger besmirching the sacred purity of his surcoat. Raising a gauntleted hand, he grasped hold of it. A brief look of panic crossed the captain's face before Ansell squeezed.

"Touch me again and they'll be the last orders you ever give," he said.

He could feel the grinding of finger bones in his fist, and the captain's eyes widened. He gritted his teeth against the pain, and to his credit managed to stifle his yell of protest.

Some of the Revocaters lowered their weapons. A couple of others levelled them right at Ansell. This whole situation had slipped beyond his control. Now it seemed he would be forced to slay the very men he had come here to keep peace with.

"Look," shouted one of the Revocaters, before Ansell could consider further violence.

One of them was pointing over the phalanx of knights. Every eye focused beyond the shield wall, and Ansell turned to see a single figure slowly moving between the row of shields and the rioters. He squinted, not quite believing what he was seeing—a diminutive, white-robed man, walking without fear as the mob's rage gradually subsided.

They ceased flinging their missiles, their bellowing rage diminishing as they saw the Archlegate—the man who should have been the object of that wrath. He was the one they had blamed for their troubles, and Ansell felt panic grip his guts.

He rushed back toward the shield wall. "With me," he ordered, pushing past Falcar in his haste to reach Sanctan. The Archlegate was exposed, he had to be protected, and it was Ansell's job to see that task done.

Before he could reach him, Sanctan raised a hand. Ansell halted in his tracks. It was silent now on the street. Every eye was on the Archlegate, who stood with nothing but his white vestments to protect him against the rage of the Burrows.

Sanctan regarded the crowd. Gazing over them with such benevolence, such sympathy. "Who will speak with me?" he asked. His voice was quiet, but everyone heard his words.

Nobody moved. Nobody dared, so struck were they by his presence. He had liberated them from their yoke, but was now the object of their hatred. In his zeal to remove all memory of the Guilds he had forced these people to scrabble in the dirt for scraps. Still, no one had the courage to tell him to his face.

"Will none of you step forward and trade words with your Archlegate?" he asked again.

Just as Ansell thought no one might be brave enough, a woman pushed her way from the crowd. She was short and wore a red rag about her hair, grey unkempt locks sprouting from beneath it. Her face was lined with age and wear, and everything about her smacked of someone who had seen hard toil for all the long years of her life. Despite that, she carried herself with dignity, and Ansell was sure he recognised some wisdom in those dark eyes of hers.

Sanctan smiled as she came nearer to him, but Ansell gripped tight to the hilt of his sword. It was a futile gesture—if she meant to do the Archlegate harm, he would never stop her in time.

"Thank you for speaking with me," Sanctan said.

The woman raised an eyebrow. "Doesn't look like I have much choice."

"We all have a choice, my child."

Her lips twisted into a sneer. "Not all of us. And I'm not your child. If you think you can make us go back home with a wave of your hand and a blessing, you've got another thing coming."

"That is not my intention," he replied.

"So what is your intention? You gonna set your Drakes on us? Like we haven't suffered enough. You've already made us destitute.

We can't feed our children. What are we supposed to do now we have no way to make a living?"

Sanctan sighed, long and deep. "And I am sorry for it, truly, but you direct your anger at the wrong people. It is not the Ministry that has brought you to this. You know as well as I do that the Guilds have held you all in chains for decades. Now that I have cast them down, they have cut off our supplies, and we fight for our freedom still. I have sent my warriors to every corner of Torwyn to eradicate their insidious influence, but they are a powerful enemy. They still control much of the nation, while our resources dwindle. But a reckoning is coming, and soon there will be enough for everyone to eat. To feast."

"That's all well and good," the woman replied, seeming unmoved by Sanctan's reasoning. "But what do we do when all this is over? You've closed down the manufactories. The machine yards. Smashed every piece of artifice you could get your hands on. What are we supposed to live on now? What are we supposed to do in a year, in five years? How are we supposed to feed ourselves when you've destroyed any way we had to survive?"

Sanctan took a step closer to her. Ansell yearned to move forward and stand in his path, but he could sense the anger of the mob was barely held at bay. Any moment it could boil up once more, and slaughter would be inevitable. He could do nothing that might provoke them.

Instead he watched as Sanctan laid a hand on the woman's shoulder. "Change is coming, for all of us. It will not be easy, but we must learn to embrace it."

Before the woman could answer, someone shouted from the mob, "We want our lives back!"

There were grumblings of assent from elsewhere in the crowd. In reply, Sanctan raised his head, peering over them.

"Do you?" he asked. "Do you really? You want more years of endless drudgery, during which you don't even see the light of day? You want to return to a time when you would work till you could work no more, and then die from the blacklung? In the new age that I will build there will be no more of that. You will all be given your own holdings in greener pastures. Your own fields to tend.

Your own rivers to fish. You will feed yourselves, your families, and live in abundance. No stomach will grumble in hunger. No throat be left parched and ragged from the manufactory smoke. I did not make this world. The Guilds made it. It is they who are responsible for your hardship. I would only release you from that."

Ansell could see his words moved the crowd, and some of them nodded in response. Even the woman in front of him had lost her sneer, and now she gazed at him with hope.

"You'll give us all land to live on? And teach us how to work it?"

Sanctan nodded. "That was always my intention. It is no less than you deserve. For decades the Guilds have jealously guarded their ownership of the land. Have used you all as little more than slaves. When finally I have defeated them, I will set you free."

The woman frowned, as though trying to see through his lie, but was unable. "We'll hold you to that. Don't think we won't."

Sanctan leaned close, looking deep into her eyes. "All you need do is trust me."

She didn't say another word, but then Ansell supposed she didn't need to. She would find out eventually if the Archlegate spoke truth. When she turned back to the crowd, he wondered if trusting Sanctan was the right thing to do.

Despite his own doubts, Ansell could only feel relief now it looked as though the riot was over. The crowd turned despondently, most of them sloping off toward the Burrows, shoulders sagging, all their anger fled. Others still looked up for a fight, but with most of the mob now done with their protest they didn't have the courage to stand by their own convictions.

Ansell moved closer to the Archlegate. Sanctan watched as the crowd left, a smile of serenity on his face, appearing almost joyous that his words had managed to quell any potential for violence. This man, who Ansell served faithfully, was indeed a storm of contradictions.

As the Revocaters lowered their splintbows, their captain came forward. Sanctan turned to regard him with some sympathy. The captain gripped tight to his hand, but if any bones were broken, he made no fuss about it.

"My thanks, Archlegate," he said with a bow. "Once again you have demonstrated the strength and wisdom of the Ministry."

"No, Captain, it is you who should be thanked," Sanctan replied. "You and your men acquitted yourselves well, and I shall ensure that Rearden Corwen hears of your faithful service."

For a moment the captain glared at Ansell, before nodding his appreciation and returning to his men. Ansell was joined by Regenwulf, Falcar, and the rest of his brothers as Sanctan spread his arms, welcoming them closer.

"Kneel," he asked.

As one they obeyed, leaning on their shields and bowing their heads.

"A blessing upon you all," Sanctan said. "You have served each of the Great Wyrms well this day. You have shown restraint. Mercy. You should be proud of all you achieved. You have averted what could so easily have become a slaughter, and demonstrated the compassion of Vermitrix herself." He took a step closer, lowering his voice. "But do not forget that each of you is a warrior born. You are the axe and blade of the Wyrms. The sons of Ammenodus Rex. When called upon, you will no longer need to hold yourselves in check. When I unleash you upon the Guilds, you will be my divine vengeance. Is that understood?"

"Yes, Archlegate," they all answered as one.

With that, Sanctan bid them rise. He turned, making his way back along the abandoned street toward the Mount, surrounded by four of Ansell's brothers.

He watched as the man who had so recently murdered an innocent woman left them alone. Sanctan had saved lives today, but did that assuage him of the sins he had already committed?

A gauntleted had slapped against Ansell's armoured shoulder. Regenwulf had removed his helm, and a grin beamed on his moustachioed face.

"Good work, Ansell. We should be proud of what we achieved today, and the Archlegate has once again proven himself worthy of his position. His compassion is able to quell even the most unruly of his brood."

True perhaps, but there were deeper truths only Ansell knew. If Regenwulf's eyes had seen what Ansell's had, he might not have thought Sanctan so saintly.

"Do you not agree, brother?" Regenwulf asked in response to the silence.

Ansell took the helm from his head. It was stifling in his armour, and all he wanted to do was undress and cast it aside.

"We showed mercy today," he replied. "And the Archlegate, wisdom. It remains to be seen whether the people of the Burrows will truly benefit from it in time."

Regenwulf's dark brow creased. "Of course they will, brother. We will all benefit from it. Once the Guilds are quelled, Torwyn will become the nation it was always meant to be."

Ansell looked across the street at the abandoned placards. Things could indeed have been much worse. The riot could have spread throughout the city, buildings burned, innocents murdered. Perhaps it may even have reached the Mount. Ansell could only think that perhaps Sanctan had risked himself for his own benefit, and not for the benefit of his brood. But he could never tell Regenwulf that. He could not shatter his brother's illusions, or reveal his own doubts. They were Knights of the Draconate. Faithful to the end. Instruments of the Great Wyrms.

"You are right, brother. Of course."

Ansell placed the helm back on his head, before the doubt reached his eyes. Perhaps silence was best. For all of them.

KEARA

The bells rang out their monotonous drone, again and again across the city rooftops. Clanging above the spires, chiming up through the redundant halo of the skyway. It was a reminder to everyone in the Anvil who was in charge. Though the Mount was a mile across the city from the Hallowhill embassy, the sound still drove a nail through Keara's head. Maybe she should have closed the shutters to drown out the noise, but right now the prospect of rising from her chair and crossing the room seemed a titanic effort.

Ulger started to laugh, a long low rumble in his chest. Next to him, Hesse didn't even react, sitting still as a mannequin. For all Keara could tell, she was asleep behind those dark lenses of hers. Ulger stopped laughing as quick as he'd started, before tipping back his bald head on the cushions of the couch and opening his eye wide. With a steady hand he held up a pipette to drip a single dot of red drop in his tattooed eye.

And why shouldn't he? Why shouldn't any of them?

Cloistered as they were in the upper chambers of the old building, there was little else to help pass the time. The Archlegate had given his orders and she had obeyed. The rebuilding of the palace and Bridge of Saints progressed without incident. Webwainers had been dispatched across the Guildlands to help in the war effort. Now all they had to do was wait for victory. So what if they were perhaps celebrating it a little too early.

Looking at the plaster crumbling on the walls and ceiling, they should maybe have put their efforts to something more useful. Like decorating. Hopefully, when victory was finally sealed and Sanctan provided the rewards he'd promised, they could afford the services of a paper hanger and a few painters to spruce up this shithole.

But no. Keara had no intention of waiting on victory. She had to act, and soon. If the Hallowhills were to rise to the position her father demanded, Sanctan would have to fall. Then she could afford her own bloody paper hangers. Only problem was, how to achieve it? What could Keara Hallowhill do to bring down both Guild and Ministry so that she might grasp the advantage? Right now, letting them both fight out their war seemed the most expedient course.

In the meantime she'd sit and wait in this relic of a building, a place that mirrored her father's crumbling manse. A grim reminder of how far her Guild had fallen. They would rise again, of that she had no doubt. She just had to await the right opportunity.

"Don't use all that," she chided, as Ulger raised the pipette for a second time.

He paused, grinned, then stoppered the vial before tossing it across the room toward her. Keara snatched at it, missed, and it fell to the floor. It took a huge effort to lean over and pick it up off the stained carpet, before she leaned her head back and plopped a drop in her eye.

Almost instantly those droning bells sounded like sweet music as the potent narcotic began to tease her senses. Monotonous clang transformed to lilting tune, ringing a sweet melody in her fuddled head.

"Did you hear about the riot down in the Burrows?" Ulger asked, his voice sounding muffled as though she were listening through a wall.

"No," she replied, her own voice echoing a little too loud to her ear.

"Thousands of them, kicked up a right stink by all accounts. I'm surprised we couldn't hear them across the city. Started off as a protest over the shutdown of the manufactories. Then the rioting started. Threatened to set fire to their own homes, fucking idiots."

"Is that what you think? That they're idiots?" she asked. Ulger just shrugged as though he couldn't have cared less one way or the other. "Those people have no work. No work, no money. No money, no food. The Ministry has destroyed their livelihoods without a thought to how they'll replace them. People can't live on prayers."

Ulger shrugged again. "Neither can you live with a splintbolt in your neck. Not that it came to that. Sanctan himself turned up. Talked them down with a few calming words, I hear. Like charming the birds from the trees... or the flies off of shit."

At that, Hesse gave out a giggle before clamping a hand over her mouth. Ulger looked at her, before grinning from ear to ear. Keara just watched them from across the room. The red drop was having a much different effect on her. She didn't find any of this funny.

Sanctan Egelrath was slowly tightening his grip on everything. He had destroyed the Forge, and most likely the Rock was next. Without those industrious cities there would soon be no artifice to speak of. The Hallowhills would see their power dwindle, when all she wanted to do was rise from the ashes of this war and drag her Guild with her. How could she do that with the whole of Torwyn in the grip of a man who would send them back to an age of stone and wood? Add to that the fact her father would brook no failure, and she found herself in a very uncomfortable place indeed.

"Listen," Ulger said.

Hesse had stopped her giggling. Keara turned her head toward the window, realising all had gone silent.

"The bells," Keara said. "Why have they stopped?"

Ulger shook his head. "No idea. Maybe someone got as pissed off as us and stabbed the bell ringer?"

Hesse guffawed. Ulger hissed a laugh through his teeth.

Someone knocked at the door.

They both stopped laughing, as the echo of that knock faded. Keara didn't move from the comfortable chair, hoping she had only imagined it. Then someone knocked again.

"Shouldn't one of us get that?" Ulger asked, clearly meaning anyone but him.

Hesse didn't seem like she was moving anywhere either. Curse her ill luck and her lazy bastard friends. With some difficulty, Keara eased herself out of the armchair, but before she could take a step toward the door, it opened.

An armoured giant stepped into the room. Keara had spent a lifetime trying not to be intimidated by anyone, but even she was unsettled by this vast beast striding in like he owned the place. She was heir to a Guild, but the Drakes were a law unto themselves, further empowered by the rising dominance of the Ministry. And you rarely saw their faces, that unnerved her even more than the imminent threat of violence that accompanied these bastards wherever they went.

Behind the first Drake came a woman bedecked in a blue robe. A High Legate, bearing all the quiet confidence her rank bestowed. Then another Drake, closing the door behind them in a surprisingly gentle manner.

"Please," the High Legate said with a smile. "Don't get up."

Keara eased herself back into the chair, guessing the woman's words were meant as an order, rather than a polite instruction. It would be foolish to stand now though; that would only suggest indecision, and Keara knew she had to at least appear confident, even if she didn't feel it.

Across from her, Ulger shifted uncomfortably as one of the knights crossed the room to stand behind the couch. He still had a shit-eating grin on his face though, the red drop doing its bit to relax him. Behind her dark eyeglasses it was impossible to tell if Hesse was intimidated or not.

"My name is High Legate Hisolda," the woman said. "No need for introductions, I already know who you are."

"To what do we owe this honour?" Keara asked, trying to sound as sober and sincere as she could.

"I have been sent by the Archlegate. He has a mission for you. One suited to your particular...skill set."

So she was being given orders by lackeys now? Why wasn't the Archlegate here to tell her himself? Was Keara Hallowhill not an important enough name to warrant a personal audience?

"And he sent *you* to tell me?" she asked, unable to hold back her displeasure.

"As you know, the Archlegate is a busy man." She offered a smile, though the effort looked like it hurt.

"Aren't we all," Keara replied.

Hisolda glanced about the room, at the dirty shelves and the threadbare rug. At the two webwainers sitting in a slovenly stupor. "Yes, so I see. But still, it falls to me to relay your new orders."

As she spoke she ran her finger across the mantel, before inspecting it closely. Whatever she saw revolted her, and she quickly rubbed it away with finger and thumb.

"So what does he want me to do?"

Immediately Hisolda's expression changed from disgust to sincerity. "We have been apprised of the fact the resistance may be attempting to contact an artificer last known to reside in Windstone."

"Who?" Keara asked, increasingly annoyed that this sounded like nothing to do with her *particular skill set*.

"A man named Nicosse Merigot. Are you aware of the name?"

Before Keara could answer, Ulger let out the boyish giggle he had been at pains to hold in.

Yes, of course she'd heard of him. The Merigots were well known to have disgraced the Archwind Guild. Nicosse and his brother had conducted forbidden experiments that might well have destroyed the Guilds entirely.

Keara shrugged. "I think the name rings a bell."

Hisolda peered at her seriously. Could she see through the lie?

"Does it ring a bell that Merigot was developing artifice that could nullify your Guild's link to the web? That he could render your powers worthless?"

"Those are just rumours. There is no evidence that—"

"Evidence or not, the Archlegate has deemed this man an

immediate threat to the new order. He wants Nicosse found, if in fact he still lives."

Ulger giggled again, this time receiving an annoyed glance from Hisolda.

"I'm sorry," Ulger said, desperate not to laugh. "It's just these two are making me really uncomfortable." He gestured to the Drakes, neither of whom had moved a muscle since taking up their positions at the edge of the room.

"Why do you need me for this?" Keara asked. "Surely the Revocaters would be more suited to tracking down a fugitive."

"We have received other information," Hisolda replied. "Our source tells us that Tyreta Hawkspur has been sent by her mother to find this artificer. She is herself a webwainer of remarkable talent, by all accounts. The Archlegate is very keen to be...reacquainted with his cousin. Who better to secure her capture than another webwainer? Send a thief—"

Ulger guffawed so loud it made Keara flinch. Hisolda turned her head slowly, glaring at him as he grinned like a boy caught with his hands somewhere they shouldn't be. She gave the slightest of nods to the Drake behind the couch, and he stepped forward. Ulger let out a choking sound as the Drake closed a gauntleted hand around his throat.

Keara nearly rose to her feet in protest, but she was rooted to the spot, her arse stuck to that armchair like she'd been glued there. Ulger most certainly wasn't seeing the funny side anymore, and he struggled like an eel in a trap, kicking his legs as the Drake lifted him bodily from the chair, slamming him against the wall so hard shards of plaster fell away. Hesse didn't even move as he was dragged from the couch beside her.

The pyrestone lights suddenly winked in agitation as Ulger tapped into the web, desperate to save himself, but flashing lights wouldn't stop the armoured giant that held him in his grip.

"Don't be too put out," Hisolda said, ignoring the violence. "These knights and I will be accompanying you on your little jaunt to Windstone, so you won't have to do all the heavy lifting. And who knows, perhaps this is all just conjecture. Maybe Merigot isn't even there, and all we'll have wasted is time." She smiled. Keara had never seen anything so condescending in her life, but what could she do? This woman spoke with Sanctan's voice, and Keara was in no position to ignore it. Not yet at least.

"When do we leave?"

"First light tomorrow," Hisolda replied. "So I suggest you get plenty of rest before the journey."

"We'll be ready," Keara replied, though she had no idea how. The red drop left you with a heftier hangover than any liquor.

Hisolda looked unconvinced too. "I'm sure," she replied, before turning away.

The Drake next to the door opened it for her, and she walked out. The second Drake pushed Ulger to the ground before the two knights marched from the room, closing the door as gently as when they entered.

Ulger bolted to his feet, straightening his ragged tunic. "Fucking twats. Who does she think she is?"

Keara let out a long sigh of resignation. "She thinks she is the voice of the Archlegate."

"And what does that make us? His fucking puppets?"

As much as she wanted to disagree, she couldn't help but think Ulger was right. "For now."

"So what? We're just going to go along with everything that bastard says? Run off to Windstone on some mad errand to nothing?"

"That's exactly what we're going to do." Keara forced herself from the chair, listening to the sound of silence from outside. "It's time we got our shit together and started acting like we know what we're doing."

Maybe this was the chance she had been looking for. If Tyreta Hawkspur was gallivanting around the countryside in search of ghosts, it would be the perfect opportunity to capture her. With a Guild heir in her clutches, Keara might gain some much-needed leverage in this nightmare of a conflict.

Hesse leaned forward in her chair. "Red drop anyone?" She waggled the vial enticingly.

Keara knew it would have been stupid to go for another dose.

Especially on the eve of a mission she had been handpicked for. This could be the one opportunity she needed to get ahead. If she messed it up, that chance might be gone like piss on a breeze.

"Fuck it," she said, plucking the vial from Hesse's hand. "Why not?"

ROSOMON

From the southern ridge of the great valley, Rosomon could see the entirety of Wyke stretching from the coastline in the east toward the Alderwood in the west. There was no one to stand in their way, no sign of battalion troopers, no artillery, no cavalry or archers, and yet fear still gnawed at her.

"I can't see anyone," Ianto said, lowering the monocular from his eye. "Not so much as a single sharpshooter. It's as though the city has been abandoned."

He offered Rosomon the monocular. Through the scope she could see the city in minute detail, every street empty. If the Ursus Battalion were still there, they were well hidden. Neither were there any city folk going about their daily business. Every window and door of every house had been closed, every shutter barred to the daylight.

Wyke lay at the bottom of a deep valley, hunkering amid two high ridges. To the east stood the giant dam that held back the Dargulf Sea, funnelling the River Taine from the west. Along its majestic span were the myriad waterwheels and pump stations that kept the city fuelled. Just north of the river Rosomon could make out the landship station, a single engine sitting quiet and unmoving. It gave her a strange sensation of loss. For the longest time all she had known was the buzz and hum of transit running in and out of that

station. Keeping Wyke connected to the rest of Torwyn, carrying
trade goods to its great cities and in turn transporting commodities
out into the sea and along their nation's coastline.

Now there was not a single ship in the bay beyond the dam. Each
of the four huge aeries, situated at cardinal points on the outskirts of
the city, stood empty. There were no shrieking war eagles preparing
to send word across the length of the Guildlands. All that remained
was an unnerving silence.

When she had seen enough, Rosomon handed the monocular to
Oleksig. He took it in one meaty hand, removing the pipe from his
mouth with the other. As he surveyed the city, Rosomon turned to
look over the army he had brought, if army was the right word for it.
Thousands of men and women stood in disciplined ranks, the pennants of the mining leagues whipping and snapping in the wind. She
could see some zeal in their determined faces, but also fear. These
were not trained killers like the army they faced. Yet here they were,
ready to throw themselves on the enemy to defend their Guild.
Their way of life. That is, if there was even an enemy to face.

"What do you think?" she asked Oleksig.

He lowered the monocular with a shrug. "I think this looks like a
trap, if ever I've seen one."

Oleksig was no battlefield general, but she knew he was right.

"It may well be, but we can't wait here forever," she replied. "Trap
or not, we have to enter the city. The longer we wait, the greater the
chance Sanctan will send reinforcements, and the initiative will be
lost."

Oleksig nodded his agreement. "I was getting bored up here anyway." He turned to Borys. "Tell the bands to strike up a rousing
tune. Let's at least make ourselves sound fearsome while we march."

Before Borys could give the order, Rosomon spied someone at
the bottom of the ridge. A rider galloped from amid the narrow,
cobbled streets, mounting the hill and driving their steed upward. A
cloak of Hawkspur blue flowed from her back, and it was with some
relief Rosomon recognised Lieutenant Faiza.

"Wait," Rosomon ordered, as Faiza drew closer before reining in
her horse.

"My lady," the scout said. "The Ursus Battalion…they have made ready to leave Wyke. Their captain wishes to speak with you before they go."

Rosomon took a moment to take in what Faiza had said. They had come all this way, prepared for battle, and now they were to take back Wyke without a fight? It seemed unlikely.

"Where is this captain?"

Faiza gestured behind her. "On his way now, my lady."

Rosomon squinted down the ridge. There was another rider, this one armoured, though it looked like he carried no weapons. Could this be the miracle they had all hoped for? It certainly seemed too good to be true. When she glanced at Oleksig, he looked anything but convinced.

"If I suspected they'd set a trap before," he said, "I'm pretty sure of it now."

Ianto nudged his horse forward. "I should go ahead and question the truth of this captain's word."

"I appreciate your concern," Rosomon replied. "But no. Let him come. I doubt he would intend to take on an army alone." She looked toward Oleksig. "Would he?"

Oleksig shrugged before drawing on his pipe once more. The lone warrior was moving closer now, driving his steed up the ridge as though eager to greet them. From the intricate dark armour he wore, and the bearskins across his shoulders, it was obvious he held a senior rank. Despite the opulence of his dress marking him an officer, he looked young and fresh faced, with a flush to his cheeks below a thick mop of dark hair.

He reined in his warhorse in front her, before nodding in respect. "Lady Rosomon. I am Captain Ultan of the Ursus Battalion. I am sorry we couldn't meet under better circumstances."

Was he nervous? He certainly didn't bear the arrogance demonstrated by most Armiger officers she'd met before. Despite his polite greeting, she felt anger welling up inside her. He had come here to subjugate the people of Wyke for the betterment of a fanatic. Nevertheless, she fought down the urge to spit her ire in his young face. She had to stay in control—lives might depend upon it.

"Are you ready to leave my city, Captain Ultan?"

"Indeed, my lady. We received word from Marshal Sarona this morning ordering us to withdraw."

Rosomon could hardly believe what she was hearing. There was no way this could be so easy. "And may I ask the reason for this sudden change of heart?"

Ultan winced, suddenly looking very much his age. "My apologies, I was not given any further details. Were I asked to guess, I would suggest that the marshal has reconsidered where her loyalties lie."

It might have been much better had she considered her loyalties when all this began. Many lives might have been saved. Nevertheless, Rosomon could not spurn this chance to retake Wyke without bloodshed.

"Whatever the reason, I am grateful for it, Captain Ultan. Please convey my regards to your marshal when you next see her. I do hope the two of us might speak further, and at length, some other time."

"I am sure you will, my lady." He glanced uncertainly over his shoulder toward the city. "As you can see, Wyke remains unmolested, despite some initial resistance. Please believe that I did my best to ensure casualties were kept to a minimum."

Rosomon had heard much different, but she could not make issue of it. Not when they were so close to ridding themselves of these intruders. "And where are the people of my city now?"

"I thought it best if they remained in their homes while we concluded our business. For their own safety. I hope you will allow us to withdraw from the city without further hostility."

Ultan's amiable nature was disarming, and Rosomon felt her anger waning, but still she felt the need for a reckoning. But no. He had offered a show of conciliation, and she had to do the same.

"You may leave, Captain. But might I suggest you do it quickly?"

With another bow, Ultan spun his horse, riding back down the hill. Rosomon watched from atop her steed as he disappeared. For days she had anticipated battle, slaughter, but perhaps the tide was turning. Sanctan's grip already slipping, and all she had to do was wait until his inevitable fall. Just hand the bastard enough rope and he would surely hang himself.

"That went well," Oleksig said, glaring in Ultan's wake. "Part of me is a little disappointed we didn't get a chance to teach those bastards a lesson."

"We haven't taken the city yet," she replied, turning to Ianto. "Take your men and see the way is safe. Make sure the Ursus have left Wyke for good."

Her imperator nodded, signalling for the rest of the Titanguard to follow him. They rode down the sloping valley and through the main gate of the city. As Rosomon watched them go she couldn't shake the dread feeling that had followed her north for so many days. This had been so easy. Too easy.

Before long, she could see far to the west that Captain Ultan had kept his word. A column of armoured troopers were streaming from Wyke's western gate. They raised their bear pennants proudly, though Rosomon could think of little they had to be proud of. They had come here to conquer. To tighten a madman's hold on his realm. They should have hung their heads in shame, not marched like heroes.

Ianto trotted out of the gate at the bottom of the valley, raising his arm to signal all was well. Still Rosomon sat, gripping her reins, reluctant to move forward, wary of the sight that might greet her when she finally returned to her home.

"Can't sit around here all day," Oleksig said, kicking his horse forward.

Borys followed, along with some of their senior league officials. It looked like she had no choice but to face what waited below, and she put heels to her horse's flanks. All the while she kept her eyes on Ianto, who waited patiently at the gate.

"All is well?" she asked, when finally they reached him.

"As far as we can see, my lady. The Ursus have gone, but there is no one yet on the streets."

Rosomon proceeded through the gate and along the road that led toward the River Taine as it wended through the centre of Wyke. The rest of them followed her, but even the presence of her Titanguard did little to allay her fears. As they plodded through the outskirts she found herself gripping the reins so tight it hurt her palms, but she could not turn back.

Ianto was right, the streets were empty. Not so much as a stray dog. She couldn't help but feel relieved. Had she been greeted by the wailing masses, it might have broken her. Might have made her heart crack in two, made her hate herself all the more for the part she had played in this. Thankfully all that greeted her was the peaceful sound of the river.

When finally they reached Wyke's centre, she stopped not far from the riverbank. Ianto and the Titanguard reined in beside her, sitting in the eerie silence.

"It's like nothing ever happened," she said, to herself as much as anyone else.

She started at the sound of a creaking door. A woman appeared from a house nearby, clutching her child close. From an adjacent window, a man peered out fearfully. Seeing the Ursus had gone, more people came out of their homes, calling to one another, their voices filled with the joy and relief of liberation.

As they began to fill the streets, hugging one another in reconciliation, someone pointed in her direction. "That's Rosomon Hawkspur!"

"She's saved us," said someone else.

"The Guilds be praised," cried a third.

She could only watch from atop her horse as the burgeoning crowd began to move closer to thank her for their salvation. An old woman gripped tight to her skirt as though she might fall if she let go. A man wept uncontrollably, unable to speak so overcome was he with emotion. Every face looked up to her, every voice raised in thanks.

Rosomon climbed down from her saddle, smiling through the attention, nodding in acknowledgment of their praise, though she felt thoroughly underserving of it. She had not masterminded some cunning liberation plan. It was the Ursus who had taken it on themselves to leave, all she had done was allow their retreat.

As she made her way along the river the crowd followed. Women hugged her with tears in their eyes, men gently patting her shoulder, lips trembling as they held in their emotions. To the east, the great temple bell began to ring out chimes of freedom.

"My lady." Ianto's voice rose above the hubbub. The imperator and his Titanguard began to push their way through the crowd. She was suddenly surrounded by her bodyguard and bustled away from the throng, north over the bridge. "It is still not safe. We must get you somewhere secure."

"Take me to the Hollow," Rosomon said. She could see the ancestral home of the Hawkspurs in the distance as it clung to the side of the northern ridge, looking down over the city.

As Ianto and his men led her closer, she began to dread what she might find in there. Had it been ransacked by the Ursus? Defiled in the name of the Archlegate? It felt so long since she had last been home, she'd forgotten how far the path to its gate twisted up through the city streets. By the time they reached it, she was quite out of breath, bracing herself for what she might find.

"I will go the rest of the way alone," she said to Ianto, not wanting him to see how she might react when finally she made it home after so long. Thankfully, he nodded in respect, and she carried on without her Titanguard.

At the end of the cobbled path stood the wrought iron gate to the Hollow. Above it the sigil of the Hawkspur Guild stood proud, its blue paint crumbling. Had that happened recently, or had Rosomon just never noticed how it had become tarnished by the years?

As she entered the circular courtyard she was hit by a sudden rush of memories. The first time she had come here it had been as Melrone's new bride. It was a day she should have cherished, but Rosomon had always carried a bitter seed of loss, even on that first day. Back then, her hopes of being with her true love had been dashed, and she was resigned to the reality of her position—to live out her days with Melrone, and to perform her duty to the Guilds.

At first this place had been more prison than home, but over the years, and with the birth of her children, she had grown to accept it as her own. Now the future was more uncertain than ever.

When she took in that wide yard with its high walls and the vines that covered them, she forced herself to focus on happy memories. Of Tyreta climbing the trees that lined its edge, and Fulren laughing at her antics. Of Conall regaling his friends with one tale or another as they reclined in the summer sun.

Now her boys would never return, and those untroubled days
were dead and gone. All she had left was Tyreta, but Rosomon had
sent her away on a mission that might have put her in mortal peril. It
had been foolish, but what could she have done? How could she ask
her daughter to take on the mantle of her Guild, but still protect her
from every danger?

The ancient oaken door opened before she was halfway across the
courtyard. From inside came an old and familiar figure. Amalric
was steward of the Hollow, who had served Melrone and his father
before him. When Rosomon had first come here, feeling nothing
but loneliness and isolation, Amalric had shown her kindness. There
had been days when only he would speak to her, and she had grown
closer to him than anyone else in Wyke.

"My Lady of Hawkspur," Amalric said, in a voice that creaked
like the wood of an old ship. He bowed as low as his stiff back would
allow.

She could have run to him and squeezed that old man till he
burst. Instead she offered a bow of her own. "It is good to see you,
Amalric."

"And I'm sure it is good to be home. Lord Oleksig already awaits
you in the upper library."

Of course he did. While she was being regaled by the grateful city
folk, Oleksig would doubtless have wasted little time finding the
most comfortable place in the whole city. With a nod to her steward, she made her way into the Hollow, past the dark wood veneers
and through the stone arches. Hunters' trophies hung on every spare
inch of the bare stone walls, animal heads glaring, their marble eyes
shining in greeting.

On reaching the library, Rosomon found the door lay open, and
a fire had been lit in the huge hearth. Borys stood beside it, offering
the slightest of bows when she entered. Through the open doors that
led to the balcony, she could see Oleksig looking out over the city.

When she joined him, she could hear the sound of rejoicing from
the city far below. The bells of a temple ringing in the distance,
echoing through the valley. That noise marked her fledgling victory, but still those bells rang hollow.

"Congratulations, Rosomon," Oleksig said. "The first blow is struck."

"Doesn't feel like it," she replied. "I didn't do very much of anything."

He took the pipe from his mouth and banged it on the oaken balustrade. "Right enough. But you should still enjoy it. From here on, I doubt things will be so easy."

"Don't worry, Oleksig. I'm under no illusions as to the weight of the task in front of us."

"Then it might come as a surprise when I suggest our first move is to do nothing. We should stay here. Shore up the city's defences and make it a haven for anyone in Torwyn still loyal to the Guilds."

Rosomon turned to face him. "We cannot just sit here and wait. If nothing else, we'll give our enemies an easy target."

"So what is your plan? To unite the ordinary folk of Wyke with my miners before you head west? Take the fight to the Anvil? Bring down the Ministry with their pitchforks and shovels?"

Before she could answer, she saw a rider galloping west along the river road. Narrowing her eyes, she was sure she recognised the rider as Faiza. It struck her as odd that her lieutenant would be leaving the city in such haste, when it was celebrating such an auspicious day. She dismissed the thought, turning back to Oleksig.

"Yes, if that's what it takes, then that is what I will do. I can't just sit here while war rages throughout the nation. While others fight in my stead. Rest assured we will gather allies on our journey, Oleksig. We will not have to weather this storm alone."

"And what if they don't come? What if we are the only ones left to face the Ministry?"

Rosomon shook her head. "I don't believe we're the only ones who want the Guilds to win this. When people hear that we have retaken Wyke, that this city is a beacon of hope, they will flock to our side."

As she said the words her eye was drawn to yet more riders, but this time entering the city along the main road. There were three of them, racing alongside the river, driving their steeds as hard as they could.

"Who is that?" Oleksig asked, seeing the same thing.

No sooner had he asked the question than Rosomon recognised the lead rider. Lancelin, returning to her side after too long. But where was the army she had sent him to gather?

When he looked up the side of the valley toward the Hollow, Rosomon raised her arm in greeting. In reply, Lancelin pointed east toward the dam. He shouted something but he was too far distant for her to hear. Whatever he said, it was urgent. A warning perhaps?

"What's going on, Rosomon?" Oleksig said.

Lancelin's companions veered off, riding over the bridge and shouting warnings at the milling citizenry.

"Something is wrong," Rosomon said, remembering Faiza's desperate gallop from the city. "We've been betrayed. We have to—"

A dull boom resounded from the east. No sooner had it echoed along the valley than Rosomon felt the balcony shake, dust dislodging from the rafters.

A scream pierced the air, long and loud as though someone had been murdered.

Then the dam broke.

She barely had time to see the towering stone barrier collapse, water cascading down onto the city, before Oleksig grabbed her arm and dragged her inside.

"We have to get out of here," he snarled, pipe still clenched between his gritted teeth.

Rosomon couldn't speak, the shock stunning her to silence as she was dragged away from the balcony and through the library. Borys was already leading the way, wrenching the door open, his hand gripping the sword at his side.

"Wait," Rosomon gasped. "We have to do something. We have to help those people."

Oleksig stopped, fixing her with a determined glare. "We have to get out of here or we'll be drowned alongside them. Think, Rosomon. There's nothing else we can do."

He was right, and she hated him for it. She hated herself for following him as he led her out of the library, through the wood-panelled corridors as Borys strode at the fore. All her anger, all her despair at their betrayal began to roil, but she had to push it down. Now all that mattered was that they survived. This was Sanctan's doing. The bastard had led her into another trap and she had fallen for it yet again. There would not be a third time.

They reached the vestibule to the Hollow's great feast hall. Beyond it was the northern entrance to the Hollow—a bridge that would lead them out onto the summit of the valley and to safety. Amalric stood by the door to the room, his eyes betraying confusion.

"My lady," he said. Rosomon could see his hands shaking as somewhere else in the huge mansion a woman screamed. "We...I—"

Borys pushed past the old man, throwing open the doors to the great hall. Rosomon took Amalric by the arm.

"Come with us," she said, leading him after Oleksig and into the vast chamber.

Through the soaring glazed windows she could hear the tumult as the waters of the Dargulf flooded over the broken dam and consumed the city of Wyke. The foundations of the Hollow shook, and she had to steady Amalric as he almost stumbled.

A wooden table cut through the centre of the hall, fifty feet long and flanked by more chairs than Rosomon had ever taken the time to count. She remembered well the banquets that had been held here—the setting for Melrone's many excesses. Her dead husband had entertained his lackeys for days on end in this place, and for years Rosomon had avoided it like the plague. After his death she'd had every gaudy portrait and grim hunting trophy burned. She had kept a few scant reminders—swords and shields of the Hawkspur line, an antique pistol here, and longbarrel there. Now it was an austere monument to his debauchery. A mausoleum dedicated to his memory—and if they didn't escape soon, it might become a tomb to them all.

There were three doors ahead of them, and Borys stopped before growling, "Which way?"

"Here, my lord," Amalric said, loosening Rosomon's grip on his arm and shuffling toward the northernmost door. He gripped the iron handles, straining his old bones as he pulled the doors wide. "This one leads to the—"

She heard a staccato clap from the other side of the doors before Amalric straightened. Rosomon recognised the sound, knew what had happened but was frozen by the dread of it.

As Amalric stumbled back, his chest riddled with splintbolts, Borys wrenched his sword from its sheath. The sound of it ringing clear shook Rosomon from her daze, and she rushed forward to stop Amalric from falling. She was vaguely aware of armoured men pushing their way into the feast hall, but her focus was on Amalric, who stared blindly at the timber ceiling. His legs gave way and Rosomon couldn't hold him up, cradling him as she fell to her knees. The old man was already dead.

"On your feet, woman!"

Oleksig bellowed the words in her ear, dragging her up as the sound of clashing metal echoed through the huge hall. Violence, cold and brutal, flashed in front of her eyes. Half a dozen Ursus troopers were fighting their way through the doors, but Borys held them at bay with clinical thrusts of his sword.

She backed away to the wall, Oleksig at her side. He chuntered about knowing this was a trap all along as he glanced up and down at the array of weapons mounted along the wooden panelling.

Rosomon could barely catch her breath as she watched Borys hold back the heavily armoured troopers who were determined to break through the door. He could not fight them off forever.

"Do any of these work?" Oleksig snapped, wrenching an old pyrestone pistol from its stanchion.

"Yes," she replied. "I think so."

A huge Ursus trooper parried a mighty swing of Borys's blade, as another of them darted through the breach. He hefted an axe, eyes glaring at Rosomon as he rushed to attack.

Oleksig raised the pistol like a duellist of old, squeezing the trigger as though the weapon had been uniquely crafted for his own hand. There was a resounding click, but nothing happened.

"Shit!" he spat, flinging the pistol aside and wrenching a long-barrel from the wall. He raised it just in time to parry the charging trooper's axe. "Run!"

As he wrestled with the Ursus trooper, Rosomon rushed to the huge table that ran along the centre of the hall. She grabbed one of the chairs, grunting as she hefted its weight, raising it as high as she could.

The trooper had Oleksig by the throat as he raised his axe again. Rosomon brought the chair down with all her might—surprising herself when it cracked across the trooper's back but did not break. He sagged, falling to his knees as Oleksig swung the longbarrel and cracked him in the head with the stock.

As the trooper fell, Rosomon could see Borys was still fighting desperately. The rest of the Ursus troopers had poured into the hall and he fended them off with precise strokes of his glimmering blade.

"Are you sure these work?" Oleksig growled, raising the longbarrel and sighting along it.

"Yes, damn it," she growled back. "Are you sure you can shoot?"

Oleksig paused for a moment. "I can't hit a cow's arse with a banjo... but I do like the noise."

He pulled the trigger. This time the pyrestone hissed and a puff of smoke issued from the breech, but still nothing happened.

"Cock!" he snarled.

Two troopers broke from the fray as Borys fought on. He was surrounded by shield men, content to keep him occupied as the others came for her and Oleksig. Rosomon picked up the chair again, the only weapon to hand as Oleksig fumbled at the firing mechanism of the longbarrel.

She swung it as best she could but the first trooper was ready for her attack. One swipe of his sword and the chair broke into kindling; Rosomon was left with a single wooden leg in her grip.

The other trooper bowled into Oleksig and both men fell back, grappling one another in savage desperation. Before she could think what to do the first trooper grasped her arm, all but hauling her off her feet as he dragged her toward the open doors.

"I have her," he cried above the din of battle.

More troopers poured into the hall. Borys saw her being forced toward the rear doors, but he was surrounded by hulking men in armour, powerless to help. Two troopers lay on the ground, surrounded by pooling crimson, but no matter how precise his strikes Borys could not bring down the rest.

Rosomon struggled, but two more troopers surrounded her. Her arms were taken and she was bundled through the doors and out into bright daylight. The sound of the torrent was deafening, her cries of fury drowned out by the deluge that was even now consuming her adopted city.

The bridge lay ahead, crossing a narrow gorge to the northern gate. There she could see riders, waiting to carry her off, and Rosomon knew where. Far to the west, Sanctan was waiting for her at the Anvil. And now it seemed he would finally have his prize.

LANCELIN

Noise reverberated across the valley, ground rumbling beneath his horse. It reared, hooves churning the path as it wheeled in panic. A sequence of explosions erupted across the top of the dam, one after the other, blasting the summit to shards, water exploding forth in a torrent.

He was too late. Their mad dash from the west had been in vain, and now Lancelin had failed to warn Rosomon of the danger. He would not be too late to save her.

Across the river stood the Hollow, atop the valley side. She was still there, standing at the balcony that looked down across her city, and he had to reach her, nothing else mattered. Looking back, he saw Xorya and Kassian had reined their panicking steeds to a halt.

"Get up the valley to the south," Lancelin shouted, above the din. "Save as many as you can."

"You have to come with us," bellowed Kassian, gesturing to the wall of seawater cascading onto Wyke. "There is no surviving this."

Lancelin shook his head. "I'm sorry, old friend. I have no choice."

Kassian made to argue, but thought better of it and instead offered a curt nod. He knew Lancelin would have swum every sea in Hyreme to be by Rosomon's side. He had always known.

There were no more goodbyes, as he kicked his horse vigorously, reining it toward the river. Already a deluge was washing across the city, crushing every tower and tenement in its path. Screams of terror pealed out as men, women and children were consumed by the waters that had been held back for so many years by that dam.

He galloped along the riverbank to a bridge, still kicking his horse, yelling out his lungs and urging it to move ever faster. Hooves clapped against the wood of the bridge, but the sound was lost to the deafening rumble of the flood now consuming the valley. People raced past, overcome by panic, desperate to get up the hill and escape the rising tide that threatened to sweep them away. Lancelin could not pause, could not even consider helping these people. He had to get to Rosomon.

As his horse finally traversed the bridge, taking the cobbled path upward, he spied the tide crush a bridge farther up the valley to the east. Carnage was falling on the city, the press of water collapsing what remained of the dam, a huge slab of it falling onto the few buildings that still stood in its shadow. A bell tower was caught in that titanic wave, the majestic structure crumbling under the weight. As it fell, the vast bell chimed its doom before crashing into the water, sending more ravenous waves forth to devour the smaller structures.

He growled deep in his throat, heels slamming into the horse's flanks, like it needed further urging as the city swiftly drowned about them. Rosomon was up the valley, waiting at the Hollow, and he had to reach her. It was all that mattered. Not the broken dam, not the thousands about to perish in the squall. His only thought was of her.

The gates to the Hollow lay open and he galloped through, pulling hard on the reins, his steed skidding on slick cobbles. No sooner had he jumped from the saddle than a servant stumbled through the open doors, his face twisted in terror. He raced past and out through the gates as though what lay within the huge manse was more terrifying than drowning.

Lancelin pulled his sword free of the scabbard as a woman came rushing from within. She stopped in front of him, tears running down her cheeks.

"They're inside," she blurted, pointing back the way she had come. "The bastards are inside."

As she fled, Lancelin crossed the threshold and was immediately consumed by the darkness within. It was all he could do to quell the panic. There was no doubting what she was talking about—the Ursus Battalion had been waiting. They had to be behind this atrocity. This diversion. Sacrificing the lives of hundreds, thousands, so they could murder one woman.

He didn't have to stride far into the wood-panelled confines before he heard sounds of violence echoing along the passageway. A clash of metal and the grunts of fighting men urged him to increase his stride. Gripping his weapon tighter, Lancelin kept his breath even. He could not let his rising dread force him to act rashly—anyone could be waiting in the shadows of the Hollow's polished corridors.

The echoes grew louder as he approached the feast hall. Lancelin had been unlucky enough to visit once before, when Sullivar was meeting with his sister. Rosomon had sat in silence then, as Melrone entertained his cronies, all but ignoring his esteemed guest. As he approached the turbulent noise, Lancelin could only think that this time the din was much similar.

The door to the hall lay open. A sword rang against a shield. The distinctive regalia of an Ursus Battalion trooper shone in the light of the gaudy windows. As Lancelin stepped through the door he saw Borys Marrlock surrounded by hulking shield men, his sword ringing, but making barely a dent in their armour. A grunt to his right, and Lancelin saw Guildmaster Oleksig was faring much worse than his son.

He was driven back across the feast table, the stock of a longbarrel all that stood between him and the sword that threatened to cut his head off. Oleksig's teeth were bared, his trademark pipe still clenched between them. The trooper above him was pressing down with all his might, sword nudging ever closer to Oleksig's neck.

Lancelin covered the distance in a second, sword thrusting into the back of the trooper's knee where there was no plate to protect him. He howled in pain, throwing his head back before he was silenced by a blade across the throat.

Oleksig took Lancelin's outstretched hand, nodding his thanks as he was hauled off the table. Before Lancelin could think to help Borys against his numerous foes, Oleksig tightened his hold.

"They've taken her," he snarled.

"Where?" Lancelin replied, feeling the chill of panic.

"To the northern gate. Go. We'll deal with this."

Oleksig was already checking the breech of his longbarrel, as Lancelin turned to see the doors to the north lay open. He rushed across the hall, ignoring Borys and his desperate fight against the Ursus, his thoughts once again only of Rosomon.

He cleared the stairs to the door in one bound, racing out into the bright daylight, hearing the torrent from the sea as it overwhelmed the collapsing dam. Above that sound there was a sudden clap—a staccato drum, shrill and familiar. He had no time to regret his rashness before he felt the impact.

Fire bloomed in his left thigh and he clapped a hand to it, feeling the shaft of a splintbolt and the slick warm blood pouring from the wound. The second bolt, the one that hit him below the ribs, didn't hurt at all, but it halted him in his tracks.

Then he heard her—that voice unmistakable as she yelled in grief. He had heard it before on the Bridge of Saints, when her son had been taken from her. His son. Now she only cried out for him.

He squinted in the sun, seeing her at the other side of the bridge, only a few yards. One trooper was desperately reloading his splintbow, another struggling with her, barely able to hold on to Rosomon as she fought. Beyond them were horsemen, waiting to carry her off to the Anvil, no doubt.

One step forward and he felt the pain in his leg sear its way up through his thigh. His teeth gnashed as he resisted the pain, defying it as he limped to close the gap. Those horsemen were dismounting now, desperate to claim Rosomon for that bastard Sanctan. The splintbowman still struggled to get his clip in the stock, barking at the swordsman, who nodded his assent, before throwing Rosomon to the ground and charging at Lancelin.

The brightness of day was dimming as Lancelin advanced. Sweat dripped down his face, his breath coming at a wheeze. All he could focus on was the trooper, who raised his sword and screamed his challenge, voice dulled from within his helmet.

Lancelin raised his own blade, parrying, slipping to one side more clumsily than he'd have liked. When the impetus of the trooper's charge put him off balance, Lancelin struck the killing blow to the back of his neck.

Focusing back along the bridge, he saw three of them were coming, one taking the time to chide the splintbowman for his fumbling fingers as they rushed past. Rosomon was gripping the side of the bridge, pulling herself to her feet, but Lancelin could not think on her now. Could not let her distract him. His breathing was laboured. The bolt in his gut starting to ache, the one in his leg ablaze. And he still had men to kill.

His wounded leg would throw him off balance and he would have to compensate. Already he could tell he was losing blood, his vision growing more blurred by the second. Most likely his reactions would be slow. Maybe he'd faced worse odds and won, but he couldn't think when. Hardly mattered now.

An axe came at his head, the wielder silent, eyes determined within that bear helm. Lancelin dodged, ignoring the pain, the axe-head only just missing his face, but his sword did its work. The force of the blow shuddered up his arm as he caved in the back of that helm, and he was already moving to face the next—

A sword pierced his ribs, almost dragging the last wheezing breath from his body. He staggered back against the edge of the stone bridge, heavily enough that he thought he might have broken something. The one who'd stabbed him drew back his blade to finish it, and it took all Lancelin's resolve to duck.

That blade swept close, most likely shaving a few hairs from his head, but he was quick enough to counter. His sword punctured the trooper's gut below the breastplate, sinking almost to the hilt. He heard the man gasp, and knew he'd never pull his blade free in time before the last trooper was on him.

Instead Lancelin lurched forward in time to grab hold of him before he could strike. The trooper struggled, trying to bring his axe to bear, but Lancelin managed to shove him back. They fell against the other side of the bridge, grunting in rage, teeth gnashing. He was getting weaker by the second—there was only one way this would turn out if he didn't end it quick.

Lancelin butted him, full in the helm, feeling the stark shock as his head struck metal. It was enough to stagger the man, and Lancelin was quick to grab the lip of the bear helm and wrench it from his head. Then he swung. A clang as the helmet stoved into the side of the trooper's skull. Another swing and he felt the man's legs give way. One more and the trooper was laid out at Lancelin's feet.

He looked up, fighting the grogginess. There was blood in his mouth, and he had to squint to focus. But through the haze he could see her, running, face still beautiful despite her anguish. She reached out, and he reached right back, desperate to hold her, before he felt the thump in his chest.

His legs went from under him and he was suddenly sitting back against the stone wall of the bridge. A quick glance down at his chest and he could see another shaft right in the middle. That was it.

Rosomon grabbed his hand, mouth opening to speak, but what would she say about this? His lover's tearful words couldn't spare him in the end. Nothing would.

A shadow fell over them. A hulking figure blocking the sun. Rosomon looked up, cursing the final trooper as he tried to move her aside, but she refused. The splintbowman looked down from his scarred face. A hard face you only got if you were a veteran. There was no remorse there, but Lancelin had always known the last face he'd see would be one just like that. The trooper offered the slightest of smiles as he raised his splintbow.

"I killed Lancelin Jagdor," he said, relishing the moment.

Then the side of his head exploded.

An echo rang from the direction of the Hollow—a long, low blast that resounded above the distant noise of the deluge cascading onto the city of Wyke. Lancelin struggled to turn his head, seeing Oleksig standing at the door to the feast hall, longbarrel levelled, stock still smoking.

Rosomon touched his face, hands so gentle. Lancelin struggled to hear what she was saying, tried to answer, to ask her to repeat it, but the words would not come. He could see she was weeping, those tears running in a relentless tide, tracing the line of her cheeks. How he hated to see her this way. He would have given anything to take away this woman's pain.

Lancelin reached up a hand, the effort almost beating him, as he wiped away the tears from her cheek. It only left her with a smear of crimson to replace them. She took his hand, heedless of the blood.

Rosomon forced a smile, and he remembered how he would have gladly walked a thousand miles just to see it. To keep her safe. To make her happy. It was all he had ever wanted...

CONALL

He clung on to the wall as though hanging from the edge of a cliff. A desperate man riven by a howling gale, and that wall was all he had for purchase. Naked. Shivering. Alone. But perhaps being alone was a small mercy. Better isolation than to face the creature that had plagued his every waking hour, and every fevered dream.

Light lanced in through a hole in the ceiling, doing little to illuminate the shadows. He dared not look at them lest something be peering at him from the black. Something that might creep upon him with scratching claw and chattering tooth.

Fear was all he had to distract him from the hunger and thirst. Hope all but forgotten, even though he had not been tortured by that thing for so long. Had it finished with him? Would he be left to starve now that it was done tormenting him?

The metallic clack of a bolt made him flinch, the whimper that issued from his mouth the only sound he had made in what seemed like days. Light lanced into the chamber as the door opened.

"No," he moaned. All he could think to say, not that it would do him any good. Begging had not stopped that thing from the dark torturing his mind to satisfy its own vile cravings.

He clawed at the rock, his fingernails scratching at the wall, cheek pressed against the cold stone. His breath became more fevered as he heard echoing footsteps drawing closer.

"I am sorry to see you like this."

It was not the voice he had heard again and again for what had seemed like an eternity. It was a different voice. A human voice.

Slowly he turned, forcing himself to look, hoping beyond hope he would see the person he expected, and not the demon in the dark.

Nylia leaned against the stone slab that sat in the centre of the chamber. Her arms were folded, face hidden in shadow. By the light shafting into the room he could see she wore a greatsword across her back. Slowly she leaned forward, exposing her face to the light. Over her right eye was a leather patch.

"Do not be afraid, Conall," she whispered gently.

He squinted in confusion, not quite believing it was her. "What did they do to you?"

She gestured casually to the patch over her eye. "It is merely a gift. One I am glad to have received. And now, it is your turn."

"What do you mean? What kind of gift?"

She smiled, but it looked out of place. Insincere. "The gift of greatness. Right now, you are merely a man. Soon you will become as a god."

"No. I don't want to be a god. I just want to go home."

Nylia shook her head and tutted as though he were a stubborn child refusing to sleep. "Come now. You have always aspired to greatness. Even as a boy, you knew what was destined for you. And every day since you have tried to prove yourself worthy of that destiny. Now, all you need do is stand up and walk with me."

Walk with her? Where? What would they do to him? Conall's mind reeled, fear of the fate that awaited him more terrifying than the torture he had already suffered.

"Just let me go. I'm nothing. No one. I'm not worth anything to you."

Nylia looked disappointed at that. "We both know that is not true. You are worth a great deal, Conall Hawkspur. But we have no more time to discuss it. You have to come with me. Now."

"Fuck off," was all he could think to say, and he clamped his eyes shut, pressing his face to the wall again. He heard her move closer, and braced himself for the pain.

"I am sorry for this. Truly I am. But they will not wait."

She grasped his arm, that grip like a vice, hauling him to his feet. He tried to pull away but her strength was incredible. Had he grown so weak, or had she somehow become inhumanly strong?

Nylia dragged him across the chamber and toward the door. He desperately tried to plant his feet, to resist her in any way he could, but he just skidded across the moist stone floor. Panic, cold and hard, began to boil up from his gut. He issued a growl, but it came out as more of a squeal, his hand clawing at hers, trying to loosen her grip, but it was impossible. All the while she ignored his pitiful attempts to fight, forcing him out of the chamber and into the corridor beyond.

In a final despairing show of defiance he threw himself at her, fist flailing. Nylia ducked the blow, hand clamping to his throat, raising him up almost to the roof of the corridor. He grabbed her wrist, fingers snatching at her face as she tightened her grip. As he flailed desperately, the patch was torn from her eye. Had Conall the air to breathe, he might have gasped at the sight.

Her right eye was gone. In its place sat a dull red pyrestone, sunk deep into the socket. For a moment light winked in that eye. A baleful light that spoke only malevolence.

She lowered him to the ground, but still held tight to his neck. "I didn't want it to be this way, Conall."

All he could do was stare at the light in her demonic eye, shivering, naked, pathetic in the face of that unspeakable evil. Before he could protest, she dragged him farther along the corridor, past a row of stinking robed figures standing like a guard of honour.

At the end of the corridor was a vast cavern, its roof hidden in the blackness above. A host of voices were chanting quietly. The noise seemed so far away, but it resonated through the floor, the walls, permeating the chill air. In the centre of the chamber stood a huge stone slab, manacles affixed to its four points. Conall knew he was bound for it, and began to struggle again, resisting any way he could, but Nylia gripped him all the tighter.

"Wait," he managed to murmur, as she slammed him bodily atop the slab.

He tried to fight, to hold her off, but those robed figures were already surrounding him, grabbing arms and legs that were weakened by so many days of inaction. His wrists and ankles were secured into the manacles with an ominous clicking sound, and he was left to writhe in frustration.

"Stop this," he cried. "Please, Nylia, help me."

She stepped away from him, disappearing into the shadows. The last thing he saw was a shining red light glaring from the black, before that too disappeared. As those stinking robed priests also disappeared into the darkness he could feel their eyes on him, watching like spectators at a puppet show. Still, Conall had never felt so alone.

He shivered in the cold, his breath misting in the winking light of distant torches. All he could hear was the beat of his heart drumming in his ears, and the far-off chanting that droned on and on. As the darkness suddenly churned above him he held his breath.

Something was moving about the ceiling, something vast, as though the entire roof of the cavern was convulsing. It roiled like the sea, shifting like some leviathan just beyond his focus. Liquid dripped down to land on his chest, warm and oily against his naked flesh, before a tentacle unfurled from the shadow, looming huge and terrifying. Conall couldn't tell if it was alive or some kind of mechanical construct, its surface reflected the light in such a strange manner. Was this metal or flesh? As more appendages followed the first, he stopped caring. All he could do was open his mouth wide and scream.

One of the tentacles ran its bulbous length across his leg, hard and cold and blubbery, leaving a slick trail of black grease behind it. The others writhed before him in an obscene dance, as though trying to entice, lure, seduce, and it sickened him to his stomach.

From their midst came another probing feeler, this one bearing a five-pronged pincer at the end. Conall screamed his throat hoarse as it gripped his head, holding it so tight he thought his skull might crack. From its centre protruded a sucker, twitching like a palsied mouth, before it clamped itself to his eye. He gritted his teeth, feeling minuscule tendrils work their way beneath his eyelid, forcing it open.

A squeal deafened him as it reverberated in his skull. The unmistakable sound of an artificer's drill, but this one spinning so fast and so close it felt like his head would explode with the pressure. Bright light bathed his face, but held in those pincers he could not close his eye against it. Tears streamed as he saw another tentacle, smaller than the rest, at its tip a spinning drill, corkscrewing toward his open eye. He screamed again as it got closer, the prospect of mutilation chilling his bones.

The pain was almost unbearable as he was blinded. No amount of screaming could subdue it, as the drill bored into his wide-open eye. He felt the hot spatter of blood on his cheeks, before more tendrils reached into the socket and plucked the orb free.

Conall tried to thrash, tried to bellow his fury, but he was helpless. He could barely manage a whimper as another writhing tentacle moved closer to his face, a red pyrestone winking in its steel-fingered grip.

"No, no, no," he pleaded, but there was no mercy here.

The pyrestone slipped into his vacant eye socket with a sickly, moist sound. No sooner was it in place than he could feel it burning, seeking, probing. The tendons in his eye socket began to mesh with the orb, grafting themselves to it, splicing with this alien artefact that was fast becoming a part of him. Gradually, through the pain, Conall could see again, only this time a red hue covered everything, as though he were staring through stained glass.

The pincers holding his head in place suddenly released, and he gasped in relief. As one, those writhing tentacles retreated back into the black cavernous roof, leaving him alone with nothing but the distant chanting of bastard priests.

Beneath him, the slab began to move, turning on its axis with a dull grating noise. An overpowering stench spread through the cavern—a noxious stink that burned his lungs and made him drowsy.

Conall tried to resist it, to stay awake, but he was failing with every breath. As he began to lose consciousness he knew there was no fight left in him, and he was forced to give in to the mercy of oblivion...

The plain swayed gently, fronds of grass appearing desiccated and grey under a dark sky. A thunderhead was rolling in. He was alone amid the flat land that stretched for miles in every direction. Was he lost?

I see you.

The words were so clear. So close. So inhuman. But he was alone... wasn't he?

"Who's there?" *he asked. The voice had been right behind him, but he dare not turn around for fear of who he might see.*

Where are you, Conall Hawkspur?

An easy enough question. An innocent question. But as he looked at his surroundings, he began to appreciate the cryptic nature of it.

"I—I don't know."

When are you?

Damn this voice. Damn his memory.

"I don't know," *he shouted in frustration.*

Look. Up the hill.

A hill? He had seen no hill. This was a flat plain in every direction, but as he turned his head he saw what the voice spoke of. The ground rose up to a ridge that hadn't been there before. Atop it was a tall tower, one side crumbled away to reveal innards of rotten timber.

Go.

He felt compelled, turning without any thought of resistance and walking up the rise toward the tower. All the while he was mindful there was someone behind him, dogging him as he pushed himself on through the long grass.

In the shadow of the tower he was greeted by the din of battle. Looking out from the ridge, he saw into a huge canyon in which two vast armies were locked in combat. One he thought he recognised, the other alien to him. On one side flew innumerable pennants bearing the serpent, the mantis, the bear, and so many others. Among them were symbols of cog, forge fire, winged talon. They mostly carried shields and wore outlandish armour, but among them were warriors with bows, or crueller weapons spewing molten shot. Cannons blared, sending volley after volley into the enemy. An enemy that, though they fired no missiles, were still the more fearsome to behold.

Each one of them was a black-armoured beast—a towering giant, horn-helmed with shield, and a blade of molten fire. At their fore stood a mighty warlord, raising a sword with a baleful white jewel in its midst. Rallying his horde with the power of that demonic gemstone.

A shadow fell over Conall, heralded by a gust of beating wings. He looked up to see a huge flying reptile overhead, white as snow, swooping down toward the battle. As it soared over the valley, roaring its challenge to the dark warlord, he spied a woman on its back—silver armoured and white haired.

"What is this?" Conall asked. "What have you brought me to see?"

Just watch.

The beast crashed down among the enemy horde, scattering iron-clad knights in the wake of its vast bulk. In response, the warlord charged, meeting those ferocious jaws with molten steel. The beast reared, head snaking back to strike, but the warlord was faster, his aim true as he lashed out with his mighty blade.

Blood flew. The wyrm bellowed before falling dead amid the carnage, but the woman atop its back leapt clear, rising up like some saint of legend to face the demonic warlord.

Even from such distance, Conall thought there was something familiar about her. An aspect to her bearing he knew all too well, but could not quite place.

Rather than fight, the woman chose to kneel before this warlord as both armies watched on. In response the warlord raised his sword. As he struck that white-haired head from the woman's body, the canyon erupted in a cheer.

"What is this?" Conall repeated, feeling sick to his stomach at what he was being forced to witness.

All his anger fled, as he felt a hand touch his shoulder. It chilled him, freezing him to the spot, along with the dread realisation that he was no longer in control of his fate.

You will learn...

He shivered as he awoke once more in his lonely cell. The slab still sat at its centre, the shaft above offering him just enough light to see by.

Conall raised a hand to his face, feeling the blood dried on his cheek. He could see at least, but he knew all too well he had been cursed in a much more profound way than blindness.

His fingers delicately probed at his right eye, and he could feel the hardness of the pyrestone that was now part of his body. Then he noticed the mirror hanging on the wall opposite. A new addition to his cell. A way for him to see what he had become? Was this all part of the transformation? A trick that would force him to accept what he was?

He pulled himself up the wall until he stood on trembling legs. Slowly, reluctantly, he walked to the mirror, terrified of what he might see looking back at him. His body was naked, withered, but his eye...looking back at him were the blue eyes he had always had.

Take it.

That voice, so close in his ear. The one that had plagued him for so long. Tortured him. Tormented him. It was here.

Conall slowly turned, but instead of a demon in his cell, he saw a gift lying on the slab. A sword. Its blade artfully forged, a hand-and-a-half at the hilt. And set in the cross-guard was a single white jewel. As he watched, that jewel roiled with expectation, the smoke within it churning in response to his attention.

Take it.

"No," he replied. Desperate, fearful, and not caring who knew it.

You must.

"I—I won't."

But he was already moving toward the slab. Already obeying in body, where his mind refused.

His hand trembled as he reached out to take hold of the grip and lifted the blade from its resting place. It felt good in his hand. Light. Perfectly balanced. More a part of him than any sword he had ever held. And he was more a part of *it*.

This was right and true, of that he could not doubt.

Turning back to the mirror, he saw how he looked with that sword. Powerful. Indomitable. This time though, when his reflection stared back, his right eye shone red.

"No!" he snarled, flinging the blade back onto the altar. "I won't. You can't make me."

He staggered back, falling to his knees. Conall had gambled enough times to know when he was being played. There was no way he'd fall for this, no way he'd just let himself be suckered. If he took that blade, he was theirs—that was one thing he knew for certain.

There was silence in the chamber. No disembodied voice compelling him to obey, no demon in the shadows to turn his every waking moment into a nightmare. It was just him and that sword.

It pulsed with power in time to the throbbing ache in his eye. Well, let it. He was still Conall Hawkspur, heir to his Guild. They could torture him all they wanted, he would never become a slave to these bastards no matter how long they kept him here.

We shall see.

Conall flinched at the distant whisper, resisting the urge to bite back, to tell it where to go. Instead he closed his eyes, trying to block out the pain, the fear, the despair. He had no idea how long they might keep him here. All he could do was prepare himself for a long ride . . . and hope the journey didn't drive him insane.

ANSELL

The Sanctum felt cool for a change, helped by the fact that none of them were wearing armour. They waited patiently as the legate entered, head bowed, a roll of parchment clutched in one hand.

Lugard stood at the front, chin raised, glaring at the legate as though he had made some indiscretion, but as far as Ansell could see the young man was merely performing his duties. Falcar was there too, his handsome face looking on with disinterest, as was Hurden, watching the proceedings from beneath his grim brow. At the periphery of the chamber stood Regenwulf. They had not spoken since the riot at the Burrows, and there seemed an air of tension between them now. But then so much had been left unsaid. Truths that Ansell could never admit to.

The legate unrolled the parchment, squinting at it in the sparse candlelight. Ansell recognised him—Kinloth—that nervous young priest. He often looked like there was something he wanted to say but he was too afraid to say it. At least now they would find out if he was any good at reading from a script.

"Thank you for coming, brothers," Kinloth said, his voice barely audible, intimidated by such auspicious company.

"Speak up, man," Lugard ordered, empathetic as ever.

Kinloth cleared his throat, raising his chin in an attempt to comply. "The Archlegate has asked me to apprise you of our recent victories across the Guildlands. As some of you may have heard, the Forge has fallen, and by now Wyke along with it." There was some murmuring from within the room. Clearly none of them had heard about Wyke. "We have received news from Oakhelm that the Radwinter Guild has not yet offered its allegiance to the Ministry, but the Archlegate is confident it won't be long before they abase themselves in the light of the Wyrms." Kinloth cleared his throat again, perhaps growing in confidence. "The Rock has likewise fallen, and the Armigers have claimed victory in the Marrlock Guildlands. However, there is still resistance across Torwyn. Windstone stands for the Guilds. In Castleteig war continues to rage."

As he spoke the last words his voice went quieter, his confidence waning. They were far from victorious yet, and it was grave news to deliver.

"We should mount a crusade," Lugard said, the legate all but forgotten. "Sweep into the south and level the place. The breath of the Wyrms will consume all who refuse to bow before the Draconate. These traitorous Armigers must be forced to show fealty."

"As for the Anvil," Kinloth suddenly said, determined to finish. It silenced Lugard's rant, but the knight regarded the legate with yet more disdain. Kinloth carried on regardless. "The populace is suitably compliant since the recent riots in the Burrows were pacified. All is well within the capital."

With that he lowered his parchment and looked up apologetically, as though he were sorry for wasting everyone's time. If Lugard was offended by the boy's interruption, he made no issue of it.

"Thank you, Legate Kinloth," Regenwulf said. The young priest nodded his appreciation as Regenwulf turned to address the room. "You all heard those words. There is still much to do. Torwyn needs us, and we must keep the faith until this is over. Soon the Ministry will hold sway over all its brood. Now, you know your duties. I suggest you go about them."

Silently the rest of the Drakes began to file out of the Sanctum. Ansell was one of the last to leave, and as he moved past Regenwulf he offered a curt nod. To his surprise, Regenwulf reciprocated as though there had been no awkwardness between them at all.

As he made his way back to his chamber, he could feel doubt gnawing at him. Things had changed, everything had moved so fast and so far, Ansell could barely keep a grip on his notion of right and wrong.

Once back in his chamber, with the door closed behind him, he could not take his eyes off the armour on its stand. It awaited him, as though the suit had expectations all of its own. When he donned it, he would become a different man. Ansell Beckenrike would cease to be, and the knight commander was in his place. A tool. A servant. A slave?

He took a step toward it, ready to don his regalia and take up that mantle, but stopped. There was no serf to help him dress—Ansell had long since forgone that privilege. No one was here to disturb him. Would anyone even notice if he was to abandon his duties? If he was to slip away without a word instead?

That idea had plagued him for days. Surely he would not be missed? As he'd listened to Kinloth's report, he realised he was needed less than ever. The Ministry was gaining dominance everywhere. This sorry business was almost done. They had accomplished what they set out to do, and Ansell had contributed more than anyone to that victory.

But it would never be enough. Not until he died in service to the Draconate would his responsibility be fulfilled. And so, perhaps for the first time in his life, it was time to make a decision for himself.

He glanced at his armour one last time before reaching beneath his pallet bed and grasping the bundle of clothes he had hidden away days ago—plain traveller's garb. Ansell could barely think as he quickly donned the humble trews, boots, shirt, cloak, desperate to quell the sense of wrongness. He fought that feeling, swallowing it down, quashing it to nothing, so that when finally he stood dressed as any normal man, he knew with utter certainty that this was the right thing to do.

Before he could leave, he spied the book lying open on his desk. The Draconate Prophesies had given meaning to his life. For as long as he could remember he had read those pages and taken solace from the message within. Now, as he prepared to leave, he knew he was rejecting those lessons. Did that make him one more heretic? A sinner? If it did, he was no greater sinner than the man he had followed for too long.

His hand had strayed to the beads at his wrist. Ansell looked down, reading that misspelled name. That simple gift. It was the most precious thing he had ever owned. It held more meaning to him than any book or sword.

Giving it no more thought, he picked up the haversack he had prepared with spare clothes and a blanket for the road, and left his chamber for the last time. That armour, that sword and shield, were not him anymore. He was no longer the knight commander of the Drakes. He was just Ansell.

Peering out into the corridor, all was quiet. With haste he made his way toward the stairwell, at any moment expecting to run into one of his brothers, but there was no one to bar his path. His heart began to beat the faster as he considered what might happen were he to run into Lugard or, the Wyrms forbid, Regenwulf. How would he explain himself were he caught wearing the clothes of a traveller?

With every step toward the ground level of the Mount he thought on what excuse he might make when the inevitable happened, but it seemed fortune was with him. Ansell reached the kitchens without crossing paths with another soul, and he paused on the threshold, feeling the rapid drumming of his heart gradually slow.

It was ridiculous that a warrior such as he should be afeared like a rabbit in flight. He had faced the greatest fighters in Torwyn, and lived to tell of it. Fought bandits on the Drift and risen victorious. Now it seemed his greatest foe was the doubt that stopped him walking away from this place.

Ahead of him was the usual kitchen bustle as half a dozen serfs went about their business stirring pots and slicing vegetables. Beyond them, the door to the courtyard, and the servants' gate beyond that. The door stood open, beckoning him, but still he felt frozen.

Slowly he forced himself to walk across the kitchen, head bowed, trying to look as insignificant as he could. Not one of the kitchen serfs turned their head to look at him, before he finally reached the open door.

Outside, he could see Grace sitting on a barrel in the shadow of the yard wall. On her lap was some parchment he had found for her, and in her hand a piece of chalk. She went at the parchment like an artist at the canvas, though he could well imagine her drawing was far from a masterpiece. Ansell stood and watched, wondering whether he should go to her, say his goodbyes, tell her how sorry he was to leave her behind.

But could he leave her in this bear pit? Or should he take her with him, far away from here?

"She's been much happier in the past couple of days."

The voice at his shoulder made him turn, and he recognised the cook—Joye—her rosy cheeks flushed with her labours.

"Been asking after you," Joye continued. "I weren't sure what to tell her."

If she thought anything of his mundane garb, Joye did not mention it. And curious that she no longer appeared to be afraid of him. Perhaps because he was without his imposing armour and the broadsword at his side?

"Will you continue to care for her?" Ansell asked.

Joye nodded. "I wondered if you were going somewhere. Not that I'm surprised." She gazed deep into his eyes as though searching for something in them. "I've seen the change in you."

Ansell appreciated her honesty, but it felt strange that, until now, he had sensed little change within himself.

"You should at least say goodbye to her," Joye said.

Ansell glanced across the yard again, seeing Grace still at her work. The thought of bidding this child goodbye filled him with more dread than he could have imagined. He had no idea why.

"Very well," he replied, before making his way toward her.

As he did so, Patris, the cook, entered through the servants' gate. He smiled at Grace, calling her name and waving. The girl looked up and returned the gesture. When Patris saw Ansell approaching, his expression changed, as though he had spied some malign spectre come to drag him to the Lairs. It seemed not everyone had changed their opinion of him. Perhaps when he finally managed to escape the Mount, he would no longer see such daunted looks.

"Ansell," Grace said as he approached.

"Grace," he replied, remembering the playful banter she had with Joye some days before.

"Where are you going?" the girl asked, seeing the pack slung across his shoulder.

"I have to leave," he replied.

"But...you promised you'd take me on an adventure."

Ansell shook his head, feeling the regret rise within. "I cannot take you with me this time."

"But why?"

Why indeed? The more he thought on it, the more difficult a question it was to answer. Would taking her away with him be any worse than leaving her in this place? But then, he had no idea what he might face outside the city. Here she would at least be safe.

"There is much danger beyond these walls," he replied, hoping that might at least placate her. "These are troubled times. It is not safe for a little girl on the road."

"I don't care. I can be brave."

That was the thing he liked most about her—she never failed to make him smile. Such a rare thing. "I know you can. But you will be safe here. There are people who will care for you. I am not suited to that task."

She looked back down at her parchment, on which she had scribbled a scene of such complexity he had no idea what it depicted. "Do you promise you'll come back?" she asked quietly, clearly expecting an answer she would not like.

Ansell knew once he left he could never return, but the truth of it would only have hurt her. "Yes," he said, but what did one more lie matter now?

She brightened at the news. "Are you going to see the mountains?"

"First I think I will go and see—"

"The sea," she said quickly.

He ruffled her tangle of hair. "Yes, I will see the sea."

Grace took on a serious look. "And when are you coming home?"

The question took Ansell by surprise. He had always understood the notion of home, but never considered the Mount to be his. He had not yet left this place but already he knew he would not miss it.

"Soon," he lied again, and it slipped from his lips far too easily.

Before she could question him further, there was a slam as one of the double doors to the yard was thrown wide. Ansell turned to see half a dozen men, along with one woman, entering the yard. Their grim expressions put him immediately on his guard.

The gate had been left unguarded, and he cursed himself for not noticing sooner. It was too ignominious a task for any of the Drakes, but the temple guards whose job it was to keep this area secure were not at their posts.

As soon as they saw Ansell standing at the edge of the yard, the intruders stopped in their tracks. Even without his armour, Ansell struck an imposing figure. He could see by the waning aggression on their faces that they had not expected someone of such intimidating stature to be here. Even so, he had no weapon. If they had come to do mischief, it would be a hard task to stop them. When one of them glanced at Grace, his face growing more determined, Ansell realised what was happening.

"Stay behind me," he said, turning to face the group.

They must have known. Someone had told them who Grace's father was, and they had come to do her mischief. To send a message from the Guilds perhaps? The whys and wherefores did not matter now.

Ansell took a step toward them. "If you leave now, there will be no vengeance sought against you."

One of the men, a dark scar running straight across his forehead, glanced at the woman nervously. She returned his gaze, her brow furrowing as she did so. Another of them pulled a knife, more suited to the kitchen than the battlefield. Another slid a wooden bat from within his sleeve. One on the periphery stepped to the side, planning to outflank Ansell once the violence began. It was this one he had to watch the closest. The cleverest foe was always more dangerous than the strongest.

"Fucking get him then," another man blurted.

Ansell could hear the fear in his voice. None of them seemed too keen to be the first to attack.

"Leave now," Ansell replied. "Or I will kill you all."

It seemed only fair to make his intentions clear, since he was in no doubt what these people had come for. And for a moment it seemed they might do as he commanded...until he felt the blade slide between his ribs.

The sensation was unmistakable—he had felt it before. As the strength in his legs gave way, Ansell reached out, grasping the wrist that held the knife. He fell to one knee, glaring up to see it was the cook Patris who had plunged that knife so deep.

On seeing Ansell wounded, the group reacted quickly, and rushed forward. One of the men grabbed Grace, as the others brandished their weapons threateningly at the rest of the kitchen staff. Ansell heard her scream his name, but all he could do was grip on to Patris's wrist, squeezing as tight as he could, trying to wrench the weapon free of his side. The cook's face twisted in pain for a moment, before Ansell felt the strength sapped from his limbs. He loosed his grip on the knife, falling forward, unable to move.

He could only watch as Patris ran for the gate, before a scream rang through the yard. Joye yelled with all her might as she chased after Grace's kidnappers, but she would never be strong enough, never be quick enough. Ansell felt a strange swell of admiration for the woman, before she was struck over the head with that wooden bat.

He tried to crawl after them as the yard darkened around him. Joye was lying on the ground, unmoving. The kidnappers had run off through the wide-open gate.

Grace was gone...

ROSOMON

The wind gusted in off the coast, but she could hardly feel it. The world had collapsed around her and here she was, standing on the precipice, little more than an empty shell.

Rosomon vaguely heard the sea crashing against the cliffs and the blustery wind shaking the branches of a thousand trees in the forest to the west. Years ago she would have taken pleasure in it. The solace of this place had always brought her comfort—an escape from the loneliness of the Hollow. Now it felt like the loneliest place in all Hyreme.

Was she selfish to feel this way after so many others had perished? So many other corpses. Hundreds? Thousands? Far too many to count with any precision, all drowned in the waters of the Dargulf, consumed in the dark black torrent.

She imagined what that might feel like. Gasping for air, clawing at the light, knowing your end was near. Despite the bright sunshine, Rosomon felt as though she had been submerged, hearing nothing, seeing nothing but the body of Lancelin laid out before her. She was so desperate to scream, but the sound caught in her throat. It was impossible to believe that this was the end.

They had built a modest pyre, though Rosomon was unsure if this was how he would have wanted it. Lancelin would have preferred to be buried alongside the others; despite how far he had risen, he always considered himself an ordinary man. Maybe it would have been more fitting for him to be laid alongside the other victims of Wyke. But no. Rosomon would say goodbye to him in her own way. Let the other survivors grieve over their dead—this was hers alone.

He lay wrapped in linen upon a stack of logs packed with kindling. Had it been up to her, she would have seen his body paraded through the streets of the Anvil as an orchestra played its dirge. Her lover should have been celebrated across all of Torwyn for the sacrifices he had made for their nation. A statue built to his memory on the Bridge of Saints. Instead they would burn him on a hill just north of Wyke, with only the wind blowing in his honour. But not yet.

She took a step toward the pyre, looking down at what remained of all her hopes. Was it even Lancelin anymore? Or just the shell of what he'd been?

With a trembling hand she reached out, pressing her fingertips to his chest, feeling the linen that clung to his body. So cold. There was no beating from the heart beneath it. A heart she had for so many years hoped to claim for her own, and treasure for the rest of her days.

Gently she unwrapped the covering on his face and touched his cheek, feeling the roughness of his beard, before moving an errant strand of hair from his forehead. He could have been sleeping. All she had to do was quietly whisper his name and he would open his eyes for her. Smile at her. Tell her how much he had missed her.

Rosomon bent forward, pressing her face to his, feeling his flesh cold against hers when it had once warmed her, thrilled her, filled her with such yearning. It was all she could do to hold her scream of anguish inside. To stem the tears that threatened to flood from her eyes.

They had been destined to die in one another's arms. None of this was supposed to happen. She had denied herself for too long for it to end like this, but now those distant dreams she had clung to so covetously were gone. Shattered like glass and driven through her heart.

She pressed her lips to his. One last icy kiss to freeze her inside, before she covered his face once more and took a step back.

Ianto was at her shoulder, holding the torch. It shuddered in the breeze, and she could feel it warm her face. When he handed it to her, she paused, knowing it was what she had to do, but still unable to light that fire. Once the pyre was lit she would never see Lancelin again. Instead, she wanted to stand here with him until that flame died. Until the end of time if she had to, but Rosomon knew there was no time left. *Nothing was forever.*

The last time she had thought that was the night she'd sent Lancelin away to bring their son home. Now both of them were gone. All for nothing.

When she stepped forward and ignited the kindling, she was conscious of the others watching. It should have brought some comfort that she was not alone in mourning her lover's passing. Still, as the flames took, she felt like she was the only person on that lonely hill. Hers was the only grief that mattered. Selfish again, but then she had already sacrificed so much. Selfishness was her due.

The wind suddenly struck up, adding fuel to those flames. In seconds they had consumed the pyre, consumed Lancelin. For a moment she watched as it burned higher, a black trail of smoke signalling to the world where Lancelin lay. Then she turned, leaving the flames behind. Not looking back lest she finally break, and stand there until her own heart stopped beating.

She passed Oleksig, standing hands clasped. He had a black eye from his fight in the feast hall but looked otherwise unharmed. She ignored the warriors kneeling in honour at the passing of one of their own. Borys had his sword drawn, head pressed to the pommel. Beside him were two others—Kassian and the girl Xorya. They had travelled here with Lancelin to warn her of the danger. Too late.

Ianto walked close beside her as she made her way back down the hill toward Wyke. Or at least what remained of it. The sea had consumed the city, swept its people away so all that remained was devastation. Even now they were picking through the ruins, trying to recover what they could. For Rosomon there was nothing left to salvage but vengeance.

Ianto leaned close to her as they were buffeted by the wind. "I am sorry, my lady, but there are things we must address."

She barely heard his words, as though he spoke to her through murky waters, his deep voice carrying an unusual softness with it.

When she did not answer, he continued. "Our scouts report that the Ursus Battalion continues its march west toward Oakhelm. We must assume they will garrison there and await reinforcements from the Anvil. We should plan our contingencies accordingly."

They had been betrayed. Rosomon had trusted too many people and they had all thrust their knives into her back. She had failed to learn her lessons and this was where it had got them. She had killed those people in Wyke as surely as if she had forced their heads beneath the water with her own hands.

"Did you find Faiza?" she asked.

Ianto paused. A sure sign it was not good news.

"Our scouts have reported no sign of her."

Our scouts. Were they really hers? Any one of them could be loyal to the Ministry, Faiza had already proven that. Any number of Oleksig's miners. The Titanguard even. Perhaps Ianto was one of them. She could trust no one. Fulren had told her that even before all this began, and still she had been fooled.

"Do we have a casualty report?"

"The vast majority of the dead were ordinary citizens of Wyke," Ianto replied. "We lost six of our Titanguard."

Rosomon stopped, taking a breath, letting the wind wash over her. Wyke was ahead of her, that watery graveyard. A shrine to her failed hopes of rising up against the Archlegate.

Oleksig made his way closer. He was not smoking his customary pipe, perhaps out of respect for her loss. Maybe out of respect for the dead, not that pipe smoke would bother any of them now.

"The leagues had not yet entered the city when the dam blew. We still have our army."

"But there will be no help from the Forge," said Ianto. "Lancelin arrived at Wyke bearing ill tidings from the mountains. There was a massacre. Wymar is dead, along with many of his Blackshields."

"We have ill news from the Rock too," said Oleksig. "My city is in flames. Many people have been lost or placed in chains."

Everything had collapsed. Rosomon found it hard to believe all her hopes had been dashed so completely. As well as losing Lancelin, it appeared she had lost this war before it even began.

Oleksig took his pipe from the breast pocket of his waistcoat. As he struggled to light a match in the wind, Rosomon could only admire how unmoved he was by all this tragedy. Perhaps he might have been the better choice to lead them? Not that she was about to offer him the chance.

She turned to see Kassian Maine approaching—her father's swordwright—and beside him Xorya Ironfall. What must they have thought of her? That she was weak? Unsuited to her position? She couldn't let paranoia cloud her judgement. She had to stay in control, just as Lancelin would have wanted.

"Imperator." At her word, Ianto stood to attention. "We will press on toward Oakhelm as planned. It is time we learned once and for all where Jarlath Radwinter's loyalty lies. If he has already offered the Ursus Battalion shelter, we have our answer."

Before Ianto could acknowledge her, Kassian took a step forward. "I am sorry for your loss, Lady Rosomon. I know you and Lancelin were..."

He paused, unsure how to say it? Clearly Kassian was not suited to offering condolences, but then Rosomon already knew he was unsuited to anything other than killing.

"Lovers?" she answered. There was little point in hiding it now. Half of Torwyn probably knew. The swordwright cast his eyes down as though the notion embarrassed him. She had never taken him for a prude. "Why are you even here, Kassian?"

"I was your father's swordwright. This is—"

"I remember. As a little girl I would often see you following him faithfully. And I remember how swiftly you left when he died."

And that was not all. She remembered the stories Lancelin had told her. Of how brutal his time had been at the Seminarium under Kassian Maine's tutelage. How this man had tried to remove any vestige of emotion from Lancelin and forge him anew. Rosomon had been grateful her lover had still managed to retain some of his humanity, if only for her.

"And you are a little girl no longer," said Kassian, looking her straight in the eye. "There is much still to be done, Lady Rosomon. Forget your grief, you have an army to lead, and must rise to that task."

All her fury boiled up in that instant. All her hate and disdain for this man who had stolen her lover away. So many precious moments she might have spent with Lancelin had been taken, and this man was responsible, at least in part.

She bolted forward, hand lashing out to strike him across the cheek. He caught her wrist in a steel grip before she could touch him.

Ianto's sword was halfway from its scabbard but Kassian held up his other hand in a gesture of warning.

"That's not worth it, son." He was still staring defiantly at Rosomon.

She wrenched her wrist from his grip, taking a step back before raising a placatory hand. Her bodyguard slid his sword back in its scabbard.

"So are you here to help?" she asked.

Kassian glanced toward Ianto and Oleksig as though weighing their worth. "Of everyone present, I am the one best able to help you against what's coming. I was your father's sword. He trusted me with his life."

"And why should *I* trust you?"

Kassian's stern expression did not waver. "I served your father until his death. Since then I have trained every swordwright that's ever risen to the rank. I was born to defend the Guilds. Just like Lancelin."

Don't you dare speak his name, she wanted to yell, but managed to hold her peace. Rosomon had feared Kassian as a girl. Had grown to hate him as a woman, but now she was being called on to trust him.

"Then you'll get your chance," she whispered, before gesturing to the grim-looking woman standing tall beside him. She was young, but carried a sword at her waist and muscle about her shoulders that commanded respect. "I take it this is Xorya Ironfall?"

The girl bowed. "It is, my lady."

Rosomon had to think back a long way, but she remembered Maugar's daughter from a trip to the Anvil. She had been a child then, but still stern about the eyes. Clearly she had inherited her father's grit.

"You've grown into Maugar's image. Where is your father now?"

"North," she replied. "At Wyrmhead. He and his Blackshields intend to take the Draconate bastion in the name of the Guilds."

A bold ambition, and one that might have served them well had they the men to spare. But Rosomon knew she needed fighters at her side here and now.

"You must travel to find him with all speed. Persuade him to abandon that endeavour and return south. We are bound for Oakhelm, and he should meet us there." She turned to Ianto. "Still no word from Marshal Rawlin?"

The imperator shook his head. "None, my lady."

"Then we will proceed without him. Speed is of the essence."

Oleksig blew out a long draft of smoke. "We could still stay here. Fortify the city."

"There is no city. Wyke is no longer the stronghold it once was. We have been flushed from our lair. The only option we have now is to take the fight to the hunter." She turned to Kassian. "Do you agree?"

If he was surprised at being asked his opinion, he did not show it. "I do, Lady Rosomon."

"Then I hope, for now, I have risen to the task enough to satisfy you."

She did not wait for his answer, and marched toward what remained of Wyke. There was no more time for grief, Lancelin would have told her that were he still alive. He would have wanted her to fight, to die if that's what it took. Rosomon would not let him down.

It would be her last gift to him.

VERLYN

The windmill spun slowly in the breeze, issuing its rhythmic whoosh and grind as it turned and turned. She gazed up at it, letting the sun bathe her, those sails revolving in the clear blue sky. It usually brought a smile to her face, but today Verlyn knew there was little to smile about.

They'd renovated that old mill from a wreck. Spent weeks building it from rubble, and now it was theirs. The place had been abandoned for decades after all, who else had the right to lay claim now she and Ashe had sweated and bled to rebuild it? Verlyn knew full well who, and the thought of it ruined what should have been a perfect day.

She closed her eyes, tapping into the web, seeking, searching, until she connected with the pyrestones within the mill. Though the wind did its job keeping those sails spinning, the pyrestones brought the engine to life, turning the main shaft night and day, threshing the wheat, separating the chaff, winnowing the grain, and performing the work of five millers. Even now she could feel the power in those stones waning. It wouldn't be long before the light winked out in each one of them.

Where they'd get more, she had no idea. Pyrestone was expensive enough in times of plenty. Now the edict had come down from the

Ministry that artifice was to be banned, it would only raise the price on the black market, if there was even a market at all. Even if they could replace the stones, how long before the Revocaters came and tore the place down?

Verlyn shook her head, turning away from the windmill. No use worrying on a thing that hadn't happened. There was enough to worry on already.

She walked to the end of the narrow lane, flanked by hedgerows on either side, until she saw the field. It should have been a beautiful day with the sun shining so hard, but that shadow from the north hung heavy and dark over everything. There had been much strife at the Anvil, everyone knew it. How long before it spilled out from the Archwind Guildlands and made its way south to their farm? She'd already heard tell that half of Torwyn was in flames, and it looked like most of the trouble had passed them right by. But surely they wouldn't stay shielded from it forever.

She reached the field, pausing at the edge to look out onto their acreage. Verlyn had never worked out how much land they had, but it rolled off as far as she could see. Crisscrossing the fields in an intricate web were row upon row of irrigation channels funnelling water right from the Serpentspin. The crop was doing well at least, and she listened to the sway of the corn, interspersed with the intermittent clack of the irrigation pipes and the occasional drizzle of water as they fed the land. A living, breathing marvel, not yet choked to death by the Ministry.

Her hand brushed the ears of corn as she walked by. In another life, Verlyn had never had the time to appreciate quiet moments like this. She had been all but a slave to her position, her duty, and now she was free. When she and Ashe had escaped all that, it had seemed they would be running forever. She never saw this coming, though. Never thought a farming life would suit her so well. It was a pleasant surprise when it did, and it beat being slave to a Guild, any way she looked at it. Now, with the Guilds gone, it should have been one less thing to worry over, but with the end of one problem, there'd risen another one much bigger—and this one had scales and teeth and hot fiery breath.

When she came to the field's far edge, she could hear the snuffling and grunting of the pigs in their pen. Those animals never failed to bring a smile to her face, which was ironic considering how often they had to butcher one of them.

Here too was more artifice keeping the water butts and feeding troughs filled from the mechanical rig that squatted over the pens. Verlyn closed her eyes, reaching out to the red pyrestones within their conversion chambers. With a click of gears and a hiss of pneumatics, the shaft opened to allow the feed to slide down into the trough. The pigs squealed in excitement, barracking one another in their haste to feed.

With that minor chore seen to, she walked up the ridge that looked out over the lake. It was so wide she could only just see the hills as they rose beyond the eastern shore. Looking north, there was still no sign of any boats. When she and Ashe first found this place, there had been a constant convoy of traffic to and from the Anvil, but now nothing. The only thing that had floated down from the capital in recent weeks had been corpses. Well . . . mostly corpses.

Not for the first time, Verlyn felt grateful for this isolation. With the Guilds in charge, life had been tough for a fugitive webwainer. Now, who knew what might happen if her talent was discovered. Would the Ministry impose more laws that harkened back to when they persecuted mages as heretics? Hangings, burnings, who knew what might come. They could have run, of course, but where would they go? Besides, they were both getting too old for running.

Once again she tried to convince herself not to worry over things that hadn't happened, but there was only so long she could ignore the inevitable.

Leaving the lake behind, she made her way south toward the farmhouse. The path ran along the western bank of the lake, then down into the shallow valley in which she and Ashe had made their home. The house was modest enough—a couple of rooms, a kitchen with a stove Ashe had built from nothing, and even a tin bath with functional taps. At the edge of their fenced-off holding was a single shack. It looked so innocent from the outside, but within was a veritable treasure trove.

Verlyn opened the door and stepped inside. In the light of a dangling pyrestone lamp, Ashe was busying herself at her worktable. She'd been tinkering with that device for days, something to make their meagre pyrestone supplies work more efficiently, but Verlyn couldn't help thinking it was all in vain. As much as she loved this farm, and loved Ashe, they had to come to terms with the fact that before long they might lose it all. Not that there was any convincing Ashe. She had always been hopeful, seeing the best in people, no matter what danger or hardship they faced.

Ashe didn't notice she was being watched, so preoccupied was she with her work. She ministered to that little device as though caring for some poorly piglet rather than a machine, massaging it to life with tender hands.

The whole workshop was filled with delights, not that Verlyn had any idea how half this junk was built. She was just the operator, using her gift to add a spark of life. Ashe was the crafter, condemned to create but never to use. That was their curse—to be drawn together and then forced to live in two separate worlds. But then, Ashe and Verlyn had not just been drawn together as artificer and webwainer.

Verlyn kissed Ashe gently on the back of her neck. She didn't even pause in her work, but the trace of a smile crept up one side of her mouth.

"Is everything all right?" Ashe asked, still probing at the device with some kind of plectrum.

"Everything is exactly as it should be," Verlyn replied, but she couldn't help but wonder how long it would stay that way.

"Did you find anything else washed up on the shore?"

Verlyn hadn't even looked, not relishing the prospect of finding any more corpses. "No."

Weeks ago a battle had been fought in the Anvil all night long. Even though they were miles south of the city, they could hear it raging and see the flashes of light in the northern sky. In the aftermath, detritus had been washed down on the current, much of it running aground on the shores of the lake. Among the wreckage had been bodies. But not all of them dead.

"How is the patient?" Verlyn asked.

Ashe looked up from the device, nonplussed. "Maybe you should go and find out?"

Busy, as always. Ashe had transformed this place from a barren, abandoned ruin to a verdant farm. She never laboured the point that she'd done the lion's share of the building, but still, she wasn't shy about letting Verlyn know when she should pull her weight.

Sticking out her tongue, Verlyn left Ashe to her device and walked out of the workshop to their farmhouse. It looked humble enough from the outside, so any normal traveller might pass by without offering it a second glance. Just the way they liked it.

Verlyn entered, and with the slightest touch of her powers a grid of pyrestone lights flickered to life on the ceiling. She passed through the kitchen, then the sitting room, stacked high with books, and on to the smallest room at the back of the house.

She could hear him breathing, even before she pushed the door open and tiptoed into the tiny bedchamber. Why she bothered being so quiet she had no idea—he had not woken since they found him.

By the light from the corridor she looked at that boy in his bed, feeling a familiar sadness at what he had suffered. Both his legs were gone—one of them already severed when they'd pulled him from the lake, the other too mangled to save. His left arm was likewise missing below the elbow.

How he had managed to survive so long neither she nor Ashe could guess, but he was the only one of those floating bodies they had fished from the lake alive. Verlyn had been sure they would wake one morning to find he had finally given up, but he had clung on to life despite his grievous injuries. She should have admired him for it, but his stubborn refusal to die had only made her suspicious that there was something unnatural keeping him from the Lairs. And that was not all.

There were markings on the back of his neck—strange sigils that spread from the top of the spine and out across his shoulders. She had never seen such things before, and neither had Ashe, even with all her scholarly knowledge. Of course, Ashe had just thought them harmless tattoos—the product of some fanciful artist. The more Verlyn had examined them, the more she could sense a darkness emanating from those weird symbols. A fell power beyond her understanding.

That unease had grown so intense she had all but begged Ashe to hand him over to someone. Who that might be, she couldn't say, but still Ashe had refused. She would never abandon him now. Broken things fascinated her, and she was determined this boy would be fixed, no matter the danger.

Verlyn reached out a hand, running a finger across that fevered brow and touching the scarred flesh around his eyes.

"What have you been through?" she whispered. A question she had asked countless times since they'd found him.

The boy's eyes flicked open.

Before Verlyn could step back in shock, he grasped her wrist with his one remaining hand, sucking in a gasp of air as though he'd been drowning.

"Ashe," she yelled, not knowing what else to say, what else to do.

The boy's eyes darted around the dark room as though searching for someone, staring through her like she wasn't even there. He squeezed her wrist tighter, and Verlyn tried to pry his fingers from her arm, but he held on as though he might fall to his death if he let go.

The pyrestone lights in the corridor winked and fizzed, as though sensing her panic. Or was it something more? Was it this boy's doing? There was a strange power emanating from him, permeating the air, making her nauseous.

"Water," he managed to say, squeezing her wrist so tight she almost cried out in pain.

"It...it's all right," she gasped. "You're safe now."

He squeezed even harder. Verlyn opened her mouth to scream, still clawing at his fingers, when a vision flashed in front of her eyes—an image of violence, the swift screech of a beast in her ears.

"Stop," she managed to gasp, but the visions would not obey.

Verlyn was dragged from the room, soaring on hot winds, flying on eagle's wings, borne aloft on the thermals, high over blasted landscapes that stretched to every horizon. Then blackness.

Her senses were nulled, no sight nor sound.

Another flash of violence, staring into the maw of a screaming demon as it spat its venom into her face . . .

"Verlyn!" The word was shouted into her ear as she fell back into Ashe's waiting arms. "Are you all right?"

Verlyn nodded, though she wasn't sure it was true. Her mind reeled from the vision, her wrist numb, but both sensations faded fast. She stared at the boy, his eyes still searching the shadows for something.

"Yeah, I'm fine. Not sure if he is, though."

"He's awake," Ashe said. "I can't believe it."

She moved to his bedside. Verlyn wanted to tell her to be careful, but whatever sensation she had experienced was now gone—not even a shade of it remained. Whatever dark magic the boy had conjured had disappeared as fast as it arrived.

"Here," said Ashe, grabbing a cup and filling it from the jug of water she kept by his bedside. "Drink."

She pressed the cup to his lips and he gulped down the contents. "Just breathe. You're safe."

He lay back on the bed, his one good arm probing at his body. They both watched helplessly as the realisation dawned on him. The extent of his horrific wounds. He would never walk again. Never see again. At first he seemed to accept those facts with resignation, until he let out a strangled sob.

"It will be all right," Ashe said soothingly, stroking his hair. "We'll take care of you."

How typical of her, always looking on the bright side.

"Who won?" he asked. He could only be talking about one thing.

"You mean the Ministry and the Guilds?" Ashe said. "No one yet. But it doesn't look good for the Guilds. From what we know, they're in retreat. The Armigers are still fighting though, but no one knows how that's going to end."

"Were you a soldier?" Verlyn asked, keen to know more about him. "Whose side were you on?"

The boy shook his head. "I'm no one."

That was hard to believe. Even if he wasn't a soldier, he was definitely *someone*.

"What's your name?" Ashe said.

He paused, considering the question. Verlyn presumed he was wondering if he was safe. If it was worth telling the truth.

"My name is Fulren," he whispered.

"I'm Ashe. And this is Verlyn. You're on our farm and you're safe now."

"Thank you," Fulren said. "What . . . what will you do with me?"

"Don't worry about that," Ashe said. "Just rest. We can talk later."

Fulren closed his eyes, as though he'd been waiting for permission. Exhaustion took him, and he issued a long sigh as he gave himself over to sleep. Ashe turned, taking Verlyn's arm, and they made their way outside into the welcome sunlight.

"We have no idea what we've brought into our home," Verlyn said. She resisted the temptation to tell Ashe about the shocking visions she had seen.

"Whoever he is, he's no danger to us now."

"I still have a shitty feeling about this."

Ashe smiled and kissed her on the lips. "You have a shitty feeling about everything. Trust me. It'll be fine."

Verlyn shook her head. "I love you, Ashe Tyburn, but you're stubborn as a goat. We need to get rid of him as soon as he's well enough."

"No," Ashe replied, in a tone that brooked no argument. "He washed up on our shore. He's our responsibility now."

With that she made her way back to the workshop, leaving Verlyn with nothing but growing frustration. So typical of Ashe, always desperate to fix everything.

Maybe she was right—maybe this wasn't a curse. But as Verlyn remembered the visions she had seen, the visions he had given her, she found that hard to believe. There was trouble coming. But with Ashe so determined to keep that boy under their roof she supposed that, as with so many other things, she'd just have to deal with that when it happened.

PART TWO

A LEGACY OF HATE

CONALL

He could barely remember how long since he'd last seen the sun. That shaft of light lancing in through the centre of his cell never darkened, whatever cast it was from no natural source. It offered no clue as to how much time had passed since he'd been mutilated by the demon beast they set upon him. Since that baleful jewel had been forced into his skull.

Now that he was being fed, all notion of demons, time and even freedom had escaped him. All he thought on was shovelling gruel in his mouth one filthy handful at a time, snaffling at it like a pig. Conall had long since stopped caring about airs and graces, or any of that meaningless shit.

He paused long enough to look up over the edge of his bowl, seeing Orsokon watching him as he gorged himself like an animal in a zoo. The huge warlord was silent, sitting on a stool too small for his bulk.

The urge to scream his hate was almost too strong to quell, to rise, to leap at that bastard and tear the helmet from his head. But he could not allow himself that luxury. He had to survive.

In his periphery he could see another figure watching him. Just like Orsokon she offered no pity. Days ago Conall would have felt humiliated that he looked so pathetic in front of Nylia. Now he had lost any sense of worth. So what if he looked like a beast at the trough? At least he was alive.

As he scooped more of the tasteless slop into his mouth, Nylia pushed herself away from the wall and picked up a cup from the altar at the centre of the cell. She approached warily, as though he might lash out, before gingerly offering him the cup.

"Take it," she said. "Drink."

He ignored her, concentrating on the food, trying to shove in as much sustenance as he could. There was no telling when he'd be fed again. Besides, he had no desire to look Nylia in the face, to see the patch she wore over her right eye, to be reminded of what lay beneath it.

"Here," she said, more gently this time.

As much as he wanted to pretend she wasn't there, his thirst wouldn't allow it. He stopped eating and reached out, taking hold of the cup but managing to avoid her gaze. It took all his will not to snatch it away from her and pour the whole lot down his throat. Instead he tentatively put it to his lips and took a sip. What was he so afraid of, poison? If they wanted to murder him, surely they'd have done it already. On tasting how refreshing that water felt as it slipped down his throat, he took another gulp.

"That's it," Nylia said. "Get your strength back. You'll need it for what lies ahead."

Despite the fog clouding his mind, Conall read the insinuation in those words... *what lies ahead*. He knew what it meant, that he'd have to give in, give up, hand himself over to whatever thing they had forced into his skull. Everything about this was designed to make him weak, susceptible. The mirror nailed to the wall of the cell, tempting him to look upon his weakened body and his jewel of an eye. The distant droning chant that called to him in a strange language, lulling him, drawing him to its dark power.

"You know she is right," Orsokon said.

Conall regarded the warlord, not deigning to respond. A few feet away from him was the sword lying on that altar, so tempting, so alluring. He felt the desire to reach out for it rising up from deep in his gut, and he wasn't sure how much longer he could resist.

"It can be yours," Orsokon continued, "just take it. Then we can do away with all this nonsense. There is no point in—"

Conall snarled as he threw the cup straight at the warlord. It clanked off his helm, splashing its contents across Orsokon's chest before spinning off into the dark.

"I would rather fucking die," Conall bellowed as loud as he could. It wasn't as loud as he wanted.

Orsokon made no move, and if Conall hadn't known better he'd have thought he was smiling behind that one-eyed helm as he said, "Stop acting like you have a choice."

That only served to infuriate Conall more and he threw away the wooden bowl along with the rest of his gruel. "I have every choice."

Orsokon shook that big head. "You will join with us eventually."

"I told you—I'll die first."

Conall would never have believed it of himself, but as he said those words he had never been so certain he spoke the truth.

Orsokon looked less convinced. "You will not die. You will join us. Perhaps even become the best of us. But don't take my word for it." The warlord rose up to full height, and from his knees he looked to Conall like a giant of legend. "If I cannot persuade you, then perhaps *she* can."

Conall glanced at Nylia, but as she turned her back it was obvious Orsokon wasn't talking about her. She opened the door to the cell and they left him with nothing but the echo of it slamming behind them. Conall opened his mouth to protest—the last thing he wanted was to be alone in the darkness with nothing for company but silence. The company of his captors was far preferable to being abandoned with that mirror and that sword, and the solitude of his own thoughts.

He stifled a sob, clenching his fists. Waiting. Any second he was sure that door would open again, and this time whoever came in would be a far more fearsome torturer than Orsokon.

Senmonthis. One of the four Scions. The most powerful beings in all Hyreme, able to reduce a man's mind to slop with nothing but a word. He'd endured much these last days, but Conall was damn sure he wasn't ready for that.

He screwed his eyes shut, girding himself for whatever was coming. When he opened them again, he saw the circular shaft in the
ceiling wasn't the only source of light that now illuminated his cell.
There was light from behind him, shining bright as day.

Slowly he turned his head, holding his breath. Where before had
been nothing but a brick wall, now the side of the cell was open onto
an immense cavern. Braziers burned at the entrance to the opening,
illuminating a huge ziggurat that squatted in the cavern's midst. A
single bridge led to the monstrous construction, spanning a chasm
that fell away to nothing but blackness. It was an invitation he had
no choice but to accept.

Conall rose to his feet, staggering through the opening and stepping onto the bridge. Something fluttered up amid the stalactites,
and he could only hope it was bats, and not something more sinister.
The stone bridge was supported by chains suspended from the roof
and thick as a man's waist. At the other side the ziggurat loomed, and
through an opening he could see fires burning within it, beckoning him forward, luring him like a single lantern on a storm-tossed
beach where he might break upon the rocks. But Conall knew he
had no choice in this, there was no alternative than to press forward.

He made his way across the bridge, not daring to peer over the
sides lest he lose his nerve and fall quaking to his knees. It was bad
enough he was being forced to meet his fate; having to crawl there
like a penitent would be a humiliation too far. She was waiting in
there—he knew that much for certain—and with every step his
mind raced faster. It screamed at him that this was wrong, that he
should turn and run as fast as he could. But where would he go?
There was only the cell. Only that sword. Only the mirror to show
him what had become of his eye. To remind him of what lurked
within, waiting to tear the very soul from him.

When finally he reached the ziggurat, he was almost quaking
with dread, but he stepped within those menacing confines anyway. The chamber that greeted him was huge, rising up to a vaulted
ceiling. On its periphery knelt a host of robed priests, more than he
could count. Each one had their head bowed, gauntleted fists pressed
against the floor as they chanted in unison to their living god.

And in the centre of the chamber, there she sat...an old woman.

Conall couldn't quite believe it as he watched her sitting there on a little wooden stool, wicker basket on her knees as arthritic fingers interwove a spindly nest of reeds.

What the fuck was this? A dream? Had he finally gone out of his mind?

She looked up at him, eyes bright within her wrinkled face, and she smiled before beckoning him closer. There was no arcane compulsion, no aggression, just a simple invitation that Conall found impossible to resist. He walked forward, wondering if this truly was Senmonthis, or merely one of her servants. But who else could it be?

She carried on weaving that basket as he came to stand before her. "I am sorry for what you have been through, Conall Hawkspur. Truly I am."

It was a kindly voice, like one of the nursemaids from his childhood at the Hollow. He was taken aback by the sincerity of it.

"No need to apologise," Conall replied in a hoarse whisper. "Just set me free and we'll say no more about it."

She laughed, as though she had a throat full of phlegm. "That's not possible, I'm afraid. You are extremely valuable to me. Wheels have been set spinning beyond the walls of Arcturius. They race to secure the fate of every soul in Hyreme. A game is being played for the highest stakes, and I require pawns aplenty if I am to win. You are a link in a chain beyond your comprehension."

"Oh, I can comprehend well enough," he said. "Trust me, I'm cleverer than I look. So feel free to explain exactly what it is you want from me."

She smiled up at him with those piercing eyes, and gently laid the basket down at her side. "Very well. An age-old feud has been put aside. Alliances have been made. And now, war is coming. A great war that will eventually involve your homeland. Before that happens, Nyrakkis will fall. And after—"

"Let me stop you there. None of this has anything to do with me," he said, sounding more desperate than he'd have liked. "Your war doesn't interest me. I'm nobody. I'm no general, no warlord. I can't help you with any of it."

"Oh, but you can. For now your mother fights the dragon priest. Should she fail, Torwyn will fall to the zealots who would see your nation dragged back to an age long dead. In which case it will be easily swept away by the coming tide. But should she prove victorious, she will become the most powerful woman in all Torwyn."

"How do you know all this?"

The woman gestured with one wrinkled arm to the priests who knelt on the periphery of the chamber. "My augurs have foreseen it, of course."

They continued to chant, their droning voices almost giving him a nosebleed. "I still don't understand what I have to do with any of this."

But he did. They had already told him, and even through his delirium he remembered. Still, Conall refused to accept it, and he could only hope he had misunderstood.

The old woman regarded him solemnly before a smile crossed her wrinkled face, revealing a crooked row of yellowing teeth. "All I want you to do is kill your mother."

Conall felt bile rise from his gut, the gruel that had been so tasteless on the way down now burning the back of his throat. "I can't do it."

"I see that," she replied, pointing an arthritic finger at his face. "But the gift I have given you, the power within, will ensure that you can."

Conall gritted his teeth, subduing the rage rising up inside. "I've resisted it so far. I'll never give in to it. I will not let it win."

Her grin only widened. "Yes, it certainly appears that you are strong-willed. Stronger than I could have anticipated for one so prone to indulging in his vices."

"Then you should just let me go," he said. "I'm not worth your time. I don't belong here and there's no value in keeping me."

"Don't fret, child. I fully intend to let you go. Just not yet. Not until you have accepted your fate."

"My fate is my own, you rancid fucking hag." He took a step forward, his fists bunched. If this wrinkled old cow would not listen to his words, he'd shake his point into her decrepit old limbs.

Before he could reach her, she rose to her feet. At the same time every priest surrounding them likewise stood. Their chanting ceased, and it was enough to stop Conall in his tracks.

The woman's mirth had fled, those eyes no longer kindly. That might have been enough to quench Conall's ire, but there was more—a sensation he could feel deep within his chest, an aura of insurmountable power exuding from her delicate frame. He felt the sudden urge to take a step back, to turn, to run, but he was rooted to the spot. All around the chamber he could feel that aura spreading as those robed priests stood upright, trembling, opening their arms to their matriarch.

The first gauntlet hit the floor, ringing off the tiles, the echo resounding through the chamber. Then one of those robed figures collapsed with a cry of anguish—or was it ecstasy?—leaving nothing but empty cloth and plate armour. One after the other those priests fell, and with each crumpled body the old woman grew, twisted, changed into something new...something malevolent.

Those bright eyes of hers retreated back into a skull that was already elongating, the flesh sloughing away to reveal bare bone. Her legs twisted into equine hindquarters, arms extending, thickening into solid muscle, knuckles teasing the floor. Horns sprouted, furling into a crown upon her head, and all the while Conall fought the urge to scream. But he couldn't stop himself falling to his knees and trembling in the face of such a formidable being.

"There is no way to resist," said the fiend before him. The voice was no longer that of some quaint old lady—now it reverberated through the chamber, filling it with malice. "You are a worm before a god. All I require is time, and then you will be mine. Time is something I have in abundance, while for you, Conall Hawkspur, it has all but run out."

The chamber started to grow painfully hot, and Conall squeezed his eyes shut rather than look upon the thing that loomed over him. He clenched his jaw, sweat pouring down his face, down his arms, his back. His flesh burned as he was consumed in an all-powerful conflagration, eating away at him until all he could do was open his mouth and scream...

When he opened his eyes, he was alone in his cell once more, shivering in the single shaft of light. The sword still lay on its altar as he whimpered in the dark, unable to comprehend if what he had experienced had been real or some sorcerous nightmare.

"Can you see?"

For a moment he didn't recognise that voice, thinking Senmonthis might still be lurking somewhere in the dark ready to eat him whole. Then his blurred vision began to focus, and Orsokon stepped into the light. Despite the hate he bore this bastard, he still felt relieved it was no demon coming at him from the shadow.

"What now?" Conall managed to say, once he'd regained enough breath to speak.

"You know what now," Orsokon replied. "You can either give in willingly, or compliance will be torn from you like flayed flesh."

Conall wanted to defy him, to tell him that they could flay him to the bone if they wanted and he would still never give in. But he retained that instinct to survive, and just enough sense to know he should keep his defiance to himself.

"Tomorrow we go to the Drift," Orsokon continued.

Conall grasped his knees, still shivering, unable to get warm. "Why?"

"To prove your worth, of course. To face the denizens of that wasteland."

"But why?" Conall demanded, more forcefully this time. "You already know my worth."

Orsokon leaned forward. "Because the trials you will face there cannot be overcome unless you give in to the gift we have given you. When you face the Drift, you will not refuse its help then."

"We'll see," Conall hissed from the dark.

Orsokon only laughed at that, before turning and leaving him alone in the chamber.

The memory of Senmonthis had left an indelible stain on his mind, and no matter how tightly he squeezed his eyes shut, he couldn't seem to get rid of it. Alongside the image of that inhuman form, he remembered the collapsing robes and fallen armour— more priests than he could count, sacrificed just so their Scion could demonstrate her power. If he didn't give in soon, maybe that would be his fate. To become an empty shell left to rot.

No, he had already said it once—Conall Hawkspur would make his own fate.

Even if he had to cross the Drift to do it.

TYRETA

They made their way through a labyrinth of service tunnels, unused for years from the rust and mould clinging to every surface. Donan led them on as though he knew this subterranean system like the back of his hand, but Tyreta was beginning to wonder if he had any idea where they were going. Still, it made more sense than walking out through Windstone's terminal, which was no doubt guarded. The fewer questions they had to answer, the better.

When they finally reached the end of yet another ancient corridor, they were met with an iron door. In the light of their pyrestone lantern it looked rusted shut, and probably hadn't been opened in decades.

Donan tried turning the circular handle, but it was stuck fast. Sted shoved him out of the way, grabbing it and straining as hard as she could. When it wouldn't budge, she slammed her shoulder against the door with a curse.

"Great work, Donan," she hissed. "We'll be down here forever at this rate."

Before she could berate him further, Crenn gently moved past, brandishing his wrench. He went about loosening a bolt here, forcing a nut there, and in moments the door swung wide with a drawn-out squeak. He treated them all to a smile before being the first to go through. Tyreta couldn't help but grin at his mischief, but when she smelled what waited on the other side it was all she could do not to puke.

"What a magnificent stench, Donan," Sted said as they came out in what appeared to be a dumping ground for all sorts of waste, both industrial and organic. "You bring us to all the best places. Remind me *not* to accept your invite for a night on the town."

They were at the edge of the city. By the direction of the sea wind that was blowing across the junkyard, Tyreta could tell it was most likely on the eastern side.

"How was I to know we'd come out in a dump?" Donan lamented.

"It's all right," Tyreta replied. "You got us here, and we're all grateful." She raised an eyebrow at Sted, who didn't look the slightest bit grateful. "Crenn, you said you could find this Nicosse?"

"Sure," said the old artificer. "If he's still there. Bridgeside is west of here. Follow me."

He led them across the junkyard, past the rotting fish heads and torn netting that lay among stacks of broken furniture and masonry. Donan retched more than once at the stink, attracting a scowl from Sted every time he did it.

Once within the city proper the air was somewhat fresher, but not by much. Filth lined the streets, and Tyreta could sense a grim atmosphere. It took her a while before she realised it was similar to what she'd experienced in New Flaym after the kesh had left it battered and broken. A mournful pallor hung over the place, and the few people they passed eyed them warily.

Eventually Crenn led them to the main square. The statue of a ship stood at its centre, the marble carving marred by gull shit, the stone mast long since broken off. In its shadow stood a tall man in a bright red robe, surrounded by a crowd of onlookers. He was young for a city crier, but Tyreta supposed you didn't have to be old to parrot the news.

"...and so, for the third day, thanks to the valiant intervention of the Kraken Battalion, we have seen peace on the streets of Windstone," he called in a monotone. "After the defeat of the Raptor Battalion, there is no sign of Ministry incursion at our gates."

Some of the crowd spat on the ground at mention of the Ministry. "But farther north, battle still rages. Castleteig has become a killing field, where the brave forces of the Viper Battalion fight for freedom against overwhelming odds. At the Anvil, the servants of the Archlegate hold sway. A decree has been laid down that all artifice is to be destroyed, its use deemed as heresy..."

Tyreta had already seen exactly what the punishment for heresy was along the southern canal. Now it seemed Sanctan wanted to abolish artifice altogether—yet more signs of how urgently she had to find Nicosse.

"Let's move," she said, having heard more than enough.

Crenn led them on, and as they left the square she moved closer to him.

"What do you think the chances are this Nicosse will even help us?" she asked.

Crenn shrugged. "I know him from old. He was always amenable enough."

Sted eyed Crenn with suspicion. "Just how well do you know him?"

"We were apprentices together at the Anvil. He was a little older than me, but we always got on all right."

As they walked, Tyreta noticed they were being watched suspiciously by more than one passerby, and once again she was conscious of how much attention Cat was bringing them. Though the panther walked close to her thigh, she could understand the alarm a wild animal would provoke in an urban environment.

"We need to find a quick way out of the city. A way back north. Donan? Any ideas?"

He stuck out his bottom lip in thought. "Well, we can't go back the way we came. The landship line north would be the quickest way."

"Do you know anyone who could help us with an engine?"

He raised his hands as though it was obvious he did. "I have associates in every major city in Torwyn. I'm sure I could—"

"Fine. Look into it and get us a way out of here as soon as you can. When we have Nicosse, we'll meet you back at the square."

Donan nodded his agreement and made his way off northward. Crenn continued to lead them west through the city, where the press on the streets grew thicker. The presence of the Kraken Battalion also grew more numerous, and with every corner turned Tyreta found herself feeling more conspicuous.

"We're drawing too much attention," she said to Crenn.

He nodded knowingly. "This way. Bridgeside isn't far."

They followed him down a passage off the main throughfare that led down a flight of weathered stone stairs. The sound of the Serpentspin grew louder as they made their way into the lower part of the city. Here the houses had been carved into the sheer black rock that made up the coastline, and the wind became whippier, reminding Tyreta of why the city had been given its name.

Their route opened up on the banks of the river as it flowed down a series of weirs. To the north, several bridges spanned the falls, to the south the estuary opened out into a huge harbour. There were no ships docked, all trade having been stopped by the recent conflict.

"Are you sure we're in the right place?" Sted asked, looking around at the rickety houses built precariously into the rock. "Seems a bit of a dump for a legendary artificer to be living in."

"Nicosse had quite the fall from grace," Crenn replied. "He may have taken it very hard."

"How hard?"

Crenn sucked a little air through his teeth at the prospect of giving bad news. "Well, his wits might not be all they were."

Sted started to curse under her breath. "So we've come all this frigging way, and you're telling us that this man, who could turn the tide of the uprising, might not even remember his own name?"

"All right," Tyreta said. "Let's just find him and get this over with."

Sted quit her griping, but Tyreta knew she was only voicing everyone's fears—that this mission might have been a waste of their time and effort. Nevertheless they followed Crenn along the bank. On one side was a stone bulwark guarding against the rushing river, and they could barely hear a thing as they made their way up it. Soon they came to a door set beneath one of the bridges that spanned the rushing falls. It looked rotted by moisture, hinges rusted, as though it might fall from the frame at any second.

"Oh, this looks promising," Sted growled over the noise.

Crenn ignored her, stepping up to the door and rapping on it with his fist.

There was silence but for the rushing water, until they heard a distant voice call, "What do you want?"

"It's Crenn," he replied, as loudly as he could.

More silence. Had the man inside even heard?

"Don't know a Crenn," answered the voice finally. "Piss off."

"We were apprentices together at the Anvil. I was a couple of years younger. You remember the academy?"

"Sure I remember, but I don't know any bloody Crenn." If indeed it was Nicosse inside, he sounded more exasperated by the second.

Crenn turned to them, looking a little embarrassed. He hesitated before turning back to the door. "Monkey Knuckles. It's Monkey Knuckles."

Sted blurted out a throaty laugh, before slapping a hand over her mouth. There was a sudden snap as a bolt was slid aside, and the door opened just wide enough for them to see an old bearded face glaring out.

"Now that name I remember. So, what do you want?"

Crenn smiled as wide and toothy a greeting as he could. "Nicosse. We've come to talk. We need your help."

Nicosse thought for a moment, eyes raised as though his answer might be written in the air.

"No," he snapped, before slamming the door shut again and dislodging a few drips of moisture from the lintel.

"Yes, you were right," said Sted. "He's very amenable."

Tyreta had seen enough, and stepped forward. Crenn moved from her path as she banged against the door with the flat of her hand. "Nicosse. Nicosse Merigot, we need your help. My name is Tyreta Hawkspur, and I've come a long way to find you. I think you might be able to turn this war in our favour, and I'm not leaving until you've heard us out."

She stepped back, staring at that rotted wooden door, surprised as any of them when Nicosse opened it again. His face bore a grave expression.

"And why should I help you? A Hawkspur?"

"If you let us in, I can tell you. Wouldn't that be better than standing on the street so the whole city knows our business?"

Nicosse considered it for a moment, before taking a step back and opening the door wider. They entered one by one, and Tyreta had to hunch her shoulders to avoid hitting her head on the low roof. As Cat padded inside, Nicosse glared at the panther with reservation.

"There's nothing you can offer that will persuade me to help you," he said, still staring at Cat. "So say your piece and get lost."

Sted took a step toward a nearby sink set in the wall. Crockery was piled up around it, and an iron kettle sat amid the mess. "Look," she said, gesturing to the kettle, "why don't we all have a nice cup of tea and talk it over?"

She picked up the kettle, then looked around for a stove to put it on. If there was one, it was buried beneath the clutter.

"Never mind bloody tea," Tyreta said. "We need you to come with us, Nicosse. If the Guilds fall, then Torwyn falls with them. The Hallowhills have joined forces with the Ministry and we believe you might be the only one who can stop them. Somehow. The rumour is you know a way to render them powerless?"

Nicosse sat himself down in a dusty old chair, crossing his legs. "Even if I wanted to, there's no guarantee. It's been a long time since I even looked at my old schematics."

"So you can do it? You know how to stop the webwainers?"

He brightened a little at the prospect. "Oh yes. I developed nullification artifice years ago. My experiments bore a lot of fruit. That was until Treon Archwind and Ingelram Hallowhill stuck their beaks in. I was reprimanded, forbidden from experimenting further, and eventually cast out. Although that last part was probably more to do with my brother Lysander's experiments than mine."

"If there's any chance you can help, you have to come with us."

Nicosse furrowed his grey brows. "I don't have to do a damn thing. I owe the Guilds nothing."

Tyreta let out a long slow breath, trying to curb her frustration. "And what do you owe the Ministry? They've already put out a decree that the use of artifice is to be forbidden. Torwyn's entire infrastructure will collapse and they'll throw us into a dark age. People will starve."

He shook his head dismissively. "I am done with the Guilds, and with the Ministry. None of this has anything to do with me."

"This is pointless," Sted said. "This old man's just wasting our time. I knew this was a shit idea. What the frig is nullification artifice anyway? Anyone heard of it?"

Nicosse rose to his feet, glowering at Sted. "Just because you haven't heard of it, doesn't mean it's not a thing. My experiments were curbed before I had a chance to perfect the science, but it's real all right. And devastating. It can block any webwainer's connection to the web. It renders them toothless."

"Yeah?" she said, rounding on the old man. "Bloody well prove it."

Nicosse was bristling, and Tyreta marvelled once again at Sted's ability to get a rise out of even the most placid person. The old man turned to her.

"You have the gift, I take it?"

Tyreta was surprised at his powers of deduction. "Yes. How did you—?"

Nicosse gestured to the spear slung at her back with pyrestones set in its head. "I assume that's not just for decoration, girl. Your work, I assume, Monkey Knuckles?" Crenn shrugged modestly. "Not bad craftsmanship, crude but effective I suppose. So why don't you humour me? Use it."

"Now?" Tyreta asked, as the old man moved to a worktable and began to rifle through the mess.

"No better time." He found what he was looking for—a small innocuous-looking device no bigger than an apple.

Tyreta unslung the spear, holding it in one hand. Immediately she focused on the tip and the three pyrestones inlaid into the steel. They began to respond to her will, burning, glowing, sending heat and light dancing along the spearhead.

Nicosse manipulated the device in his hand, before setting it down on a table and taking a step back. No sooner had he retreated to a safe distance than prongs snapped open on the housing.

There was no sound, but Tyreta felt a seismic wave of energy fill the small room. Instantly her connection to the web was silenced, the stones at the tip of the spear winking out in an instant. She staggered back with the shock of it, and if Sted hadn't caught her she might have tripped on her arse.

"I trust that's proof enough?" said Nicosse, smiling behind his bushy grey beard.

"More than enough," Tyreta breathed, staring at that little device. That source of so much potential. "You have to help us. You could end this war."

Nicosse picked up his tiny device and reset the prongs. "For years I have been forced to live in this hole." She could hear the bitterness in his voice. The disdain. "I know who you are, Tyreta Hawkspur. I know where you're from. Your grandfather is part of the reason I am here. So why should I even give you the time of day?"

She could see his point. Nicosse had been wronged by her family, but none of that mattered now. Some things were more important than the feuds of old men. Then again, maybe she could use that to her advantage.

"Because my grandfather is dead. But Ingelram Hallowhill is still very much alive. Didn't you say he was part of the reason you're here too? His alliance with the Ministry is a threat to everyone this side of the Drift. Wouldn't you want a chance to bring him down?"

Nicosse stopped fiddling with the nullifier. Slowly, a contemptuous smile spread across his face.

"Yes. I imagine a reckoning with that twisted bastard is long overdue. A prospect I may well relish."

"So you'll come?" Tyreta asked, not savouring the prospect of forcing him. If they had to kidnap this bitter old man, she'd have even more problems.

Nicosse nodded. "Aye, I suppose I will. Even if it's just to see the look on Ingelram's face when I force his webwainers to their knees."

"Thank fuck for that," said Sted. "Can we all get out of this hovel now? I'm going mouldy just standing here."

"I need to gather some things," Nicosse replied. "Then I'll be with you."

"What things?" Sted was clearly eager to be away from this dump.

"Every artificer needs his bag of tricks." Nicosse dragged a large haversack from within an overfilled cupboard, and began stuffing it with various devices and bits of paraphernalia.

Sted turned to Crenn. "Where's your bag of tricks, Monkey Knuckles?"

Crenn didn't rise to the gibe, and merely looked down his nose at her before patting the trusty wrench at his belt.

Eventually, Nicosse finished stuffing his bag before hefting it over one shoulder. He looked much more spry and eager than when they'd first arrived. The prospect of settling scores with the Hallow-hills had clearly filled him with unforeseen vigour.

"That's everything," he said.

Sted swung the door to the tiny house open, and Tyreta led them out onto the path by the weir. Crenn guided them back up through the streets, taking as many back alleys as he could find until they were at the central square once again. She was surprised at how normal everything seemed. Everyone going about their business as usual, the crier now gone from his spot beneath the statue, and instead Donan waited patiently in the shadow of that marble ship.

"Any luck?" Tyreta asked as they approached him.

He nodded enthusiastically. "I spoke to a contact of mine who owes me a favour at the landship depot. All journeys north have been stopped."

"Shit," Sted snapped. "What do we do now?"

"It's okay," Donan replied with a grin. "He told me there's still a functional engine at the maintenance yard."

"Won't it be locked?" Tyreta asked. "How are we supposed to get in?"

Donan's grin grew wider, and he held up a set of keys that dangled from an iron ring. "As I said—he owes me a favour."

Sted stepped forward, glaring right at Donan. "I could kiss you, little man."

The smile fell from Donan's face at her threat.

"Let's save the kissing until we're a long way from here," Tyreta said. "The Kraken Battalion might have declared for the Guilds, but the sooner we leave Windstone behind, the better."

They quickly moved north, ignoring the strange looks they were getting as they walked along with their pet panther.

"There is still war in Castleteig," said Donan. "I'm not convinced this is the best idea."

Tyreta knew he was right. "We don't have much choice. A landship north is the quickest way back to my mother. And time is against us."

Donan eyed Nicosse, who huffed under the weight of his pack. "I hope all this was worth it."

Tyreta remembered the power of his device. How it had cut her off from the web in an instant. "Believe me, it will be."

They made their way through Windstone as fast as they could. All the while, Tyreta couldn't believe how normal everything seemed. Despite having to fight off an Armiger Battalion, the place looked relatively unmarred by this war, where so many other places were left in flames. It didn't seem fair, but then none of this was. Tyreta had little time to think on the justice of war, as the maintenance yard came into view ahead of them.

It was unguarded, and Donan made quick work of opening the main gate. Nicosse began to look unsure as they moved through it, and hopefully when they got out of the city Tyreta could put his mind at ease. After all, he was only making artifice for them, not being asked to take on the Drakes single-handed.

Ahead was a huge administrative building, and Tyreta assumed the yard was beyond it. They stopped at the door, and Donan fumbled his keys in the lock before realising it was already open.

"Not locked," he said with a shrug. "Guess there's not much to steal."

"Guess not," Tyreta replied, pushing the door open and walking inside.

She was greeted by a huge landing, with doors to either side, a wide staircase leading upward. Crossing the lobby, she suddenly stopped, a dread feeling manifesting in her gut. The same feeling she'd felt back at the quarry.

Danger.

Before she could shout a warning, a huge armoured figure loomed from one of the adjacent rooms. He was seven feet of brute, dragon helm ducking below the lintel, shield and sword bigger than anyone had a right to lift.

A second Drake made his way down the staircase, sword ready to strike, shield braced in front of him and bearing the dragon symbol of the Draconate. From the other room walked a woman, hair long and curly, hands on her hips as she smiled a greeting.

"Hello, Tyreta," she said, as though they were old friends.

Tyreta could sense the power in this woman. Although she didn't wear the uniform, there was no doubt she was a webwainer of the Hallowhills.

"Run!" Tyreta yelled, hefting her spear. In an instant the spearhead glowed with angry light, sparking like her fury.

Undaunted by the display, the Drakes moved in...

KEARA

Those knights attacked with all the disciplined might she would have expected from holy warriors, but Tyreta faced them with a fury that came from nowhere. Keara watched as that spear whirled and flashed, bouncing off their shields, narrowly missing their faces, legs, arms. One of them hacked downward with the speed of a war eagle, but Tyreta had already dodged out of the way, seeming to know where the Drakes were going to strike before they did. Pyrestone energy surged through the corridor, burning with incandescent light as the spear sparked and hummed. Keara could have watched the spectacle all day, but she had her own job to get on with.

The others were already fleeing, racing up the stairs of the admin building. Keara ran after, not caring where Hesse and Ulger were. The artificer was her target, her way to end this quickly, to prove her worth and that of her Guild. But which one of those men was he?

She ducked past the battling Drakes, skipping away from the thrashing spear and up the wide staircase. Tyreta's four companions were already nearing the top—the one-legged man, the rough-looking woman and the two old goats, though one of them seemed pretty damn spry for his age.

They disappeared over the lip of the stairs, and Keara did her best to speed up, hands going to her hips, resting on those blades, ready to unleash all the power her Guild could muster. She took the stairs two at a time, feeling the excitement blossom inside, barely able to stifle a laugh as she hunted down her prey.

No sooner had she reached the top step than she was greeted by the echoing report of a splintbow. She ducked, feeling the sharp whip of a bolt narrowly miss her head. Off balance, she tumbled back, sprawling in a heap and cursing her eagerness. An eagerness that had almost got her killed.

She kept her head down as the splintbow unleashed its volley. Then the telltale click of an empty bolt clip echoed from above the staircase followed by the ping of a spring jettisoning the spent cartridge.

Only a few seconds before it was reloaded. No time to think. Time to move.

Keara pushed herself to her feet, wrenching the daggers from the scabbards at her hips. Her hands buzzed as she felt the power they held, their pyrestones pulsing as she fuelled them with energy. Her right hand heated up as flames sheathed one naked blade, her left buzzed with voltaic power as electricity coruscated along the length of the other.

The woman was already sliding the clip into the stock, pulling the bolt handle, raising the muzzle. Keara wasn't going to make it. She'd never have time to reach her before the woman let off another volley. All she could do was stare down the barrel of that splintbow and wait for a bolt to the chest.

Flame blossomed in front of her. From an adjoining passage burst a gout of fire that almost consumed the entire corridor. Before the woman could shoot she was forced to duck, twist, and dive from the path of the flames.

Hesse strode out in front of Keara, carrying some huge industrial welding tool, a canister slung beneath it, containing what Keara could only assume was infernium. A rictus grin spread across Hesse's face as she gleefully aimed the welder, agitating the pyrestones within and transforming it into a powerful weapon in her webwainer hands. Keara had no idea where Hesse had found the bloody thing, but was grateful she had.

Pyrestone energy bloomed as Hesse charged the welder again. The woman with her splintbow sensed what was coming, leaping over a balcony as Hesse sent another streak of fire after her. The dark glasses on her face reflected the flames, giving her the look of an insane artificer wielding a weapon of most devious construction.

Up ahead, the three others were still running—two of them dragging a bearded old man with them. That one had to be Nicosse.

Before Keara could continue her pursuit, there was a blast in her ears and smoke filled the air with the stench of black powder. Ulger appeared at her side, laughing gleefully. In his hands was an old steamlock carbine, which he hastily broke before slotting another shell in the breech. He rushed ahead, caught up in the zealous pursuit.

Keara followed him as the three men dashed down another flight of stairs, the one with the metal leg losing his footing when they reached the bottom. Nicosse ignored his plight, fleeing toward a door at the far end of the corridor, but the spry old codger stopped to help.

"Just run!" the foundering man shouted, looking over his shoulder, seeing Ulger gaining ground with that carbine aimed right at him.

The wild-looking old man didn't move, refusing to leave his friend. Ulger slowed, lowering his carbine, aiming it at the two fugitives as though he wasn't sure which to shoot.

"Wait," Keara shouted.

Ulger turned to her with a frown, like a child who'd had his toys taken away. "For what? We're here to kill these bastards."

"They could be—"

A snarl. Guttural. Inhuman.

Keara lurched back on instinct as a muscular beast, dark-furred and fast as an arrow, leapt from behind her. Ulger had no chance to react as it pounced on him, claws raking his face, fangs tearing at his shoulder. The carbine went off in his hand, firing wildly, almost as loud as his scream. She watched, stunned, as the beast tore the flesh from his face, ripping an eye from its socket, rending his arm at the shoulder. He tried to fight back, but it was impossible against such a snarling tempest.

Keara felt the daggers still humming in her fists. She had to act. Had to overcome her shock and help Ulger.

Biting back her fear, she leapt forward, desperately avoiding those flashing claws. The blue pyrestone flashed, blade slashing the beast's flank at the same time a trail of lightning danced across the creature's hide.

It hissed, leaping away from Ulger's prone body, before turning, lips pulled back in a snarl. She felt useless in the face of that beast, her weapons seeming wholly unsuited to the task of killing it. To her relief, the great cat roared, before running off after the others.

Keara watched them flee, the one with his metal leg, the old man helping him, the panther running after. She should have chased them down, should have slaughtered them all, but she heard Ulger groan at her feet.

Keara looked down reluctantly, unsure of what she might see. Blood was pumping from Ulger's neck in time to his waning heartbeat. The side of his face was a bloody mess. Where his eye was, she had no idea. He tried to speak but all he managed to do was cough up blood. Slowly he raised a trembling hand, a last plea for her to grasp it, to comfort him in his final moments. As much as he was her friend, Keara couldn't bring herself to do it as her stomach lurched and she swallowed down the bile in her throat.

She sheathed her knives before picking up his carbine. There was a belt around his waist with ammunition, and she wrenched one of the projectiles from it, ignoring the smear of blood it left on her hand.

Loading the carbine, she strode after her quarry, suddenly feeling cold to her bones and fighting the urge to vomit. The door opened onto a huge engineering yard. Landship carriages sat in rows among the maintenance rigs and loading machines.

There, about to disappear into the maze, were the three men. Maybe Ulger had the right idea all along—they were here to kill these bastards. She raised the carbine, sighting along the barrel. Steamlock weapons weren't that accurate, but by the Lairs she'd do her best to bring one of them down.

Shattering glass threw off her aim. She barely had time to dodge aside as one of the Drakes came tumbling from a first-storey window and crashed to the ground where she'd been standing. After him leapt Tyreta Hawkspur.

She landed deftly, rolling, rising to her feet, that humming spear flashing brightly with pyrestone energy. Keara raised the carbine, taking aim. There was no way she'd—

The clapping report of a splintbow, and she ducked, bolts whistling past her head. The carbine slipped from her hands as she scrambled for cover, looking up in time to spy the rough-looking woman racing past, joining Tyreta as they sprinted across the engineering yard after the men.

Hesse kicked open the door to the terminal, her teeth still clamped in a rictus grin, only now she looked distinctly less amused. The pilot flame on the welder she carried winked out, and she flung the heavy tool to the ground in disgust.

At the far side of the engineering yard waited a single landship, and they were headed right for it. Could she even stop them in time? Keara scanned her surroundings, seeing a heavy loader standing not far from the waiting engine.

As the second Drake staggered out of the terminal, she grabbed hold of Hesse's shoulder and pointed to the loader. "We have to stop them. Use that." Then, turning to the Drake, "You, come with me."

Then she was off, chasing her quarry, hearing the clank of the Drake's armour as he followed close behind. Tyreta and the splintbow woman were only thirty yards ahead but the three men had already climbed into the rear of the landship carriage.

Tyreta glanced over her shoulder, seeing they were being pursued. With frightening swiftness she plucked an arrow from her bow, nocked, fired. Keara barely had time to dive for the ground before the flaming arrow streaked overhead. There was a dull metallic clang as it struck the Drake's shield, then a deafening boom as the pyrestone arrowhead exploded.

He was flung back several feet, but Keara was already rising, already running those women down. They clambered up onto the rearmost carriage and disappeared inside, making their way toward the engine at the head of the landship.

Keara felt a thrum of energy as the engine powered up a hundred yards down the track. Black smoke billowed from its exhaust vents as the power core fired. At the head of the snaking vessel the engine moved, pulling the carriages after it, their couplings tightening as the landship prepared to leave.

She was too far away; she'd never reach it before it escaped from the yard and disappeared north along the track. But maybe there was another way.

Keara stopped, holding out her hand, shutting her eyes tight as she reached out, her powers stretching along the web to tease the engine's power core so many yards away. The pyrestones burned bright in her mind's eye, and she forced them to dim. There was a whine as the stones broke their connection with the landship's network of artifice, and the engine slowed.

Something fought her. A power greater than her own. A feral manifestation of the webwainer gift that began to neutralise her hold over the power core. Despite her command of the web, the engine revved once more, motors roaring, pyrestones igniting. But who could have...?

Tyreta.

Keara yelled in frustration, opening her eyes to see the carriages moving away. In her rage she sprinted after the landship, but it was gaining speed with every laboured step she took. She would never catch them now.

A squeal of hydraulics pealed out, louder than the landship engine. From the corner of her eye, Keara spied something moving, swooping overhead to latch on to the last carriage. Motorised arms contracted like the claws of a huge talon as the heavy loader grasped the landship. Its wheels spun on the tracks, pistons protesting as it tried to escape, but it was held firmly in place by the huge machine.

Hesse stood atop a pile of loading crates, her arms raised theatrically as she brought the loader to life, imbuing it with raw energy and forcing it to grip tight to the landship. Typical bloody Hesse—always making a show of things.

Keara was almost at the rear carriage, about to jump aboard, when one of the Drakes raced past her, steel-shod boots pounding the ground, eating up the yards to the landship. She could hear him growling in his throat, refusing to be beaten as he gripped the doorframe, sword in hand, hauling himself inside.

She clambered up behind him, squinting through the dark, seeing nothing but his metallic bulk in front of her. The clap of a splintbow broke the silence of the carriage, the sound of bolts clanging against steel made Keara duck on instinct, but the Drake endured the volley without a word, his armour protecting him from harm.

He rushed forward, and Keara watched in awe as he batted the woman with the splintbow aside. She went crashing through a partition wall, the Drake not even halting his advance.

The carriage was suddenly lit up by the spear in Tyreta's hand, those stones glowing angrily as she thrust the weapon at the Drake. He deflected it with his sword, countering, but far too slowly. Tyreta dodged the blow that would have cut her in half, bringing the spear up and connecting with the Drake's breastplate. He was blasted back in an incandescent flash of light, sparks flying. Keara could only dodge his vast bulk as he was flung backward.

The deafening sound of grinding metal echoed through the carriage. Above her head, the teeth of the loader finally lost their grip on the carriage roof, ripping half of it away and allowing light to stream in, along with shards of twisted metal that landed on top of her. The landship bucked as, finally released, it continued its journey along the tracks.

"Come on," one of the men shouted from up ahead. "Get to the engine."

Tyreta helped the dazed-looking woman to her feet, and they began to move up through the adjoining cars. Keara clambered from the wreckage, trying to keep her balance in the bucking carriage. She pulled her knives, stalking after them, tasting blood in her mouth. They would not escape, she would not allow it, not after what they'd done to Ulger.

Up ahead, Tyreta wrenched the carriage door open, pulling her friend through and striding across the gap between the cars. She offered a quick glance before slamming the metal door closed.

Keara rushed to it, grasping the handle, wrenching it open. Instantly she felt something alarming—a prevailing sense of pyrestone, powering up to a tumult—but all too late. In the next carriage, Tyreta glared at her. Beside her was one of the old men—the one she'd assumed was Nicosse—offering a strangely satisfied smile.

Before she could rush forward to attack, something whined at her feet, rising in pitch. She looked down, seeing a device placed next to the carriage coupling. It winked at her frenetically.

She leapt back just as the explosion blew her into the carriage, smashing her through a wooden partition. Dust filled the air, the stink of charred wood and singed metal. Her ears rang, a copper tang on her lips.

Keara rose to her feet slowly, feeling the ache in her limbs. Blood was running from her scalp, but she ignored it as she glared through the twisted devastation that had been the front of the carriage. In the distance, powering its way along the rails, was the landship. She had time to see the panther that had mauled Ulger leap through the open rear door, before the vessel disappeared from the yard.

Gingerly she turned, limping back through the carriage. The Drake was already rising from the carnage, offering no words as he retrieved his sword from the debris. Keara could sense where her knives were among the wreck, and managed to sheathe them before she clambered down from the back of the carriage.

This would not stand. They had escaped toward Castleteig, she knew that much. And that city would not be as welcoming as this one. Rage bubbled inside her so violently she almost forgot... Ulger.

Keara ran back toward the terminal. Outside it, the Drake who'd been flung from the window was dragging himself groggily to his feet. These knights hadn't been much use to her so far, but by the Lairs they were tough bastards. Hesse was waiting for her by the door to the admin building, and she followed as Keara made her way inside. Ulger was still on the ground where she'd left him.

She knelt by his side. The one eye he had left in his head was staring blankly, the arterial pumping of blood had stopped and now he lay still in a sticky pool of red. Reaching out a trembling hand Keara closed that staring eye. She gazed over his horrific wounds, the rents across his chest and arms, until her eyes came to rest on the pocket at his hip. Her hand went to it, feeling the vial of red drop within.

It would do him no good now. It would do her no good either, but still she fished in his pocket and took the vial. As she secreted it in her jacket a shadow fell over Ulger's body.

"I take it they've escaped?" asked Hisolda.

Keara stood, turning to see the High Legate regarding Ulger's corpse. "What do you think?"

"No matter. We should be able to catch up with them in Castleteig."

Her lack of remorse made Keara bristle, and she took a step closer. "We need more men."

Hisolda regarded her without emotion. "We don't have that option. Though we may encounter a battalion at Castleteig loyal to the Draconate. Perhaps they might help us."

"This is not what I signed on for," Keara snapped, gesturing at Ulger's body. "This has got out of hand. It's too dangerous."

"And yet we have no choice in the matter. Tyreta Hawkspur has found her man. This mission just became more important than any of our lives."

"Tell that to him," Keara snarled, pointing at her dead friend.

Hisolda seemed unmoved. "I am more than willing to say the proper rites of passing for your associate."

"Feel free. For all the good it will do him now."

Keara turned, suddenly needing some air. Or maybe something more potent.

ROSOMON

She'd almost forgotten the beauty of the Alderwood. It was a dense forest of ancient oaks, home to deer and wolf, and all manner of birds. A far cry from the filthy stone and bustle of Torwyn's crowded cities. Here the air was worth breathing, but Rosomon remained mindful this was no time to enjoy the ambience.

They travelled the road southwest, following the abandoned landship line, a furrow that cut right though the dense forest for miles. Rosomon had been just a child when the construction of this great thoroughfare had started. Mile upon forested mile had been cleared to make way for the route that would connect Wyke with Oakhelm and then the Anvil. Back then, the Radwinter and Hawkspur Guilds had worked together, united in a clear purpose—a union that had achieved the seemingly impossible, for the greater good of all. As she rode that old path, Rosomon wondered if those days were gone.

There was no telling what lay ahead in Oakhelm. Jarlath had not declared his loyalty to the Ministry, but neither would he be keen to stand against them. Rosomon had her suspicions, and he had already cooked his books to dupe the Guilds. Who knew what his motives were in doing that? To line his own pockets? Or those of the Ministry? Rosomon was determined to discover the truth, and she had brought what passed for an army to help her do it.

At her side rode Ianto, her ever-present shadow. Behind was Oleksig at the head of his miners, who marched proudly, their banners unfurled. The people of Wyke were here too, the survivors having formed a militia only too eager to exact their revenge.

Would they be enough? Or was Rosomon simply leading them into yet more danger? But would it have been any less dangerous to leave them in the flooded remains of Wyke?

A horse and rider trotted out of the woodland farther along the path. On seeing them, Ianto shifted uneasily in his saddle, but Rosomon lifted her hand to calm him, recognising the blue uniform of a Talon herald. It was no guarantee they were loyal though—Faiza, her own lieutenant, had betrayed them, and she had thought that woman trustworthy. Nevertheless, what danger could an army be in from a lone scout?

The rider reined his horse to a stop and Ianto kicked his own steed forward to greet the man. They exchanged brief words before Ianto took a rolled scroll from the scout's hand. He unfurled it, reading briefly, before returning to Rosomon's side.

"News from the Anvil," he said, holding out the scroll to her.

"Give me the gist?" she said, in no mood to read yet more bad news.

"It appears a group loyal to the Guilds has managed to kidnap Sanctan's daughter. They have her at a secure location within the Anvil, and want to know what to do with her."

"A kidnapped child?"

Ianto nodded gravely. "It appears so."

What had they become? What had Sanctan sparked within people that they would resort to abducting a little girl? Something twisted deep within her gut, sharper than a knife, colder than the grief and hate she had been forced to endure. It was the loathsome realisation that this might be to her advantage, and that perhaps she should use it.

"What would they have me do about it?" she asked. "I never sanctioned this."

"Yet they await your order. Perhaps they want help in seeing the girl spirited away from the city."

"And what then? What am I to do with her? Threaten her life so Sanctan ends this uprising and sets things back the way they were?

He knows I would never carry through any threat to an innocent child."

Or would she? The more she thought on it, the more the prospect of holding some leverage over Sanctan began to appeal. A notion of making him suffer as she had suffered. Of snatching away something *he* loved.

Rosomon gritted her teeth against the thought. What was she becoming? Some kind of monster? But there would be many more unsavoury acts she might be called upon to perform before this was over. Many more innocents would have to die before the Ministry was purged, and it would all be on her order.

She turned to the scout, waiting patiently atop his horse. "Relay the message back. The girl is to be released immediately. We will not deal in the suffering of children, no matter how far we are pushed."

With a nod, the scout spun his horse and rode off through the trees. Ianto crumpled the paper in his fist and stuffed it into his pocket. He was silent as they continued.

"Do you think that was the wisest course?" Rosomon asked. "Or should we have harnessed the advantage?"

"I think you are a general, my lady. I think your orders are to be obeyed. But..."

"But what?"

He turned to face her. Was that sorrow in his eyes? Resignation? "Mercy has not served us well so far."

Ianto was not wrong about that. So far mercy had only seen thousands of her people killed. Trust had been the bane of her leadership, and yet here she was, still forced into it.

She glanced over her shoulder, seeing Kassian Maine atop his horse not too far behind. He rode alone, even his former pupil Borys Marrlock seemed in no mood to disturb his solitude.

"Tell me," she asked Ianto. "What do you think of our new ally, the former swordwright?"

"I never met him in the flesh before now, but I always knew of his reputation. He was a loyal servant of your father. A loyalty that was never in question."

"So you think we can trust him?"

"As far as we can trust anyone."

Not the answer Rosomon was looking for, but what else could she expect from her pragmatic bodyguard? And he was right, Rosomon had been betrayed by people she thought loyal more than once. More than bloody twice, so what did that say about her naivety? Athelys, Starn, Lorens and now Faiza. Every one of them had stabbed her in the back, and she had not seen so much as a flash of the knife when it was plunged in deep.

Before she could chide herself further, they caught sight of more scouts on the road. One of them approached, holding up a hand for the column to stop. Rosomon reined her horse to a standstill, as Ianto shouted at their followers to halt their march. Another call echoed back along the woodland trail for the army to rest.

Two Talon scouts moved forward, wearing green cloaks to blend into the surrounding woodland, splintbows slung low so they could raise them quickly if needed. The first looked up at Rosomon, his face covered in mud to better hide the shine of his skin in the shadowy forest.

"My lady, there is a Radwinter contingent on the road ahead. We made contact, and it seems they would speak with you before your arrival at Oakhelm."

She turned to Ianto, hoping for advice, but he simply shrugged. "Do you wish to proceed?" he asked.

"I doubt I need to tell you it could be yet another trap," she replied.

The scout shook his head. "It is a small contingent. We have searched the surrounding woodland. They are alone, and poorly armed."

"Very well." She turned to Oleksig. "Shall we?"

He took a disinterested puff on his pipe. "Any excuse to get down off this bloody horse."

Kassian nudged his steed forward. "I would accompany you also. If it please?"

It didn't, but perhaps this way she'd find out one way or another if he could be trusted. "Very well. Let's go and see what this Radwinter has to say."

They urged their horses forward. Ianto and Kassian rode at her side, with Oleksig and the ever-present Borys behind. The trail cut through the woodland, and on either side Rosomon saw her scouts at the edge of the tree line. They offered some reassurance on the road, but when she spied the small contingent awaiting them up ahead, Rosomon realised she was most likely worried over nothing.

Veiled from the sunshine beneath a cloth awning awaited half a dozen green-garbed Radwinters. A table had been set in the shade, with a woman seated beside it. As Rosomon drew nearer she saw most of the contingent were wearing simple labourer's garb, but one figure stood out among them. Thalleus Brisco—swordwright of the Radwinters—waited at the rear, a head taller than the rest. He was almost as old as Kassian, though his hair was still dark. His narrow, pinched cheeks looked as though they'd never been creased by a smile in his life.

When they were within a dozen feet of the awning, the woman seated beneath it stood and moved into the sun. Rosomon saw a face she recognised, and immediately remembered the name.

"Becuma," she said. "We meet again."

She well remembered the girl Jarlath had sent so many weeks ago. Back then she had tried to deceive Rosomon, but had been beaten to the punch. Now they would see if she had improved her talent at negotiation.

Becuma bowed. "My lady. It is an honour to see you again." Rosomon found that hard to believe. The last time they'd met, Becuma had all but called her a bitch. "Please, join me at the table. I've brought a vintage I think you'll be impressed with."

Rosomon swung her leg over the saddle and slid to the ground. As she did so, Becuma uncorked a decanter on the table and filled two crystal glasses with deep-red wine. Oleksig and the others like-wise stepped down from their horses, standing behind her as she took a seat.

Becuma smiled, sliding one of the glasses across the wooden table. Rosomon smiled back, reaching forward and taking the glass that Becuma had kept for herself.

"Leaving nothing to chance," Becuma said, picking up the other one. "As ever."

Rosomon nursed the glass on her lap. "Where is Jarlath?"

"For his own safety, the Guildmaster has sent me to parley. He thought it best he speak through an intermediary before you reach the gates of Oakhelm. Just so we all know where we stand."

"I'm sure. And what awaits us in Oakhelm? The Ursus Battalion. More Armigers? Drakes?"

Becuma looked almost insulted by the insinuation. "Jarlath remains faithful to the Guilds, as he always has been."

"And yet he does not act in their defence."

"He has merely been awaiting your arrival before exposing his Guild to the wrath of the Ministry. We have no army in Oakhelm, no way to defend ourselves against the Archlegate and his allies. And we are so very close to the Anvil. Had we risen against him, how would we have defended ourselves in those first days? Surely Sanctan would have set the whole Alderwood aflame."

Rosomon glanced around at the trees. "And yet I smell no smoke. So you remain untroubled, despite Sanctan's eagerness to bring us all low. How do you explain that?"

Becuma shrugged her round shoulders. "I can only assume the Ministry has bigger problems than farmers and lumberjacks to consider. We pose little threat to Sanctan Egelrath when he has you to contend with."

Flattery. That was a new one, and a tactic Rosomon had hardly expected.

"Jarlath could have told me all this himself, and yet I have to march a hundred miles to hear it from you."

"And for that, Jarlath sends his apologies. But he is more than happy to make amends. Hence the reason for this little meeting."

"How very cordial." Rosomon glanced at the guards surrounding Becuma until her eye fell on the Radwinter swordwright. "So cordial he sent Thalleus Brisco as part of the reception committee."

Becuma glanced nonchalantly over her shoulder to where the imposing figure stood, still unmoving. "He is merely here for my protection. Though looking at who you've brought, I doubt he'd be much use were things to go...south."

"So what now?" Rosomon asked.

"Now? You may proceed to Oakhelm. Jarlath is waiting to

welcome you. And he's more than happy for you to send scouts ahead and ensure the city is safe for your arrival. We have nothing to hide."

Rosomon rose to her feet. "Oh, he can be sure I will." She raised the glass of wine and downed it in one hearty swig. "Tell Jarlath I will see him soon."

Ianto handed her the reins to her horse and she mounted, taking the path back northward without turning around. Making a determined exit was just as important as a purposeful entrance, or so her father had once said.

When they'd ridden a hundred yards up the path, she turned to Oleksig. "Your thoughts?"

He puffed on his pipe, before letting the smoke surround him in a thick grey fug. "I don't think it takes an old miner to work out we'd be walking right into a trap. Letting scouts in to look around in advance of our arrival is all well and good, but what if there's something they miss? I've never met a scout who can sniff out poison. And an assassin can take many forms, as you're well aware. I don't have to remind you what happened the last time we went strolling into town with a welcome invite."

"Agreed," said Ianto. "This is far too dangerous and puts you at extreme risk."

Rosomon nodded at their advice. "But we need allies, and I can't help but think dismissing Jarlath would be a mistake. What is our alternative? To skirt Oakhelm altogether and head straight to the Anvil? Hope someone will flock to our banners on the way? We cannot hope to take back the capital without help."

Ianto gripped his reins tighter, clearly fighting his frustration. "We have already taken too many risks without placing ourselves in more needless danger."

"This is all a risk," she replied, letting her frustration brim to the surface and instantly regretting it. "I know Jarlath. He has never been a pious servant of the Wyrms. I don't believe he would throw away everything he has built just to serve the Draconate."

"Perhaps not," Oleksig said. "But then he won't have to. Under the rule of the Ministry, the Radwinters and their infrastructure would be needed more than ever. They use little enough artifice as it is. The new regime will only see his power and influence grow, just under a different leader."

It all seemed so obvious. Rosomon had been blind to it before, but now the truth was clear: Jarlath would betray them one way or the other.

"Kassian, what do you think?" It pained her to ask his opinion, but she needed every one of them to contribute. Right now she could see no way around her problem.

In return, Kassian raised an eyebrow, surprised he had even been asked his opinion. "I think Marrlock is right. We will be betrayed. But there is one card in our hand that perhaps Jarlath does not anticipate."

"And what is that?"

"Thalleus Brisco's loyalty is beyond question."

"Jarlath's swordwright? You mean his loyalty to the Guilds?"

Kassian shook his head. "No. His loyalty to me."

That did little to reassure her. Even if Brisco was more dedicated to Kassian than his master in Oakhelm, it still did not solve the issue that Rosomon didn't trust any of them.

"How will that help me if Jarlath intends to betray us?"

Kassian turned to her. He looked earnest enough, but Rosomon had already learned the hard way that appearances meant little in these fractious times.

"The swordwrights are taught unyielding loyalty to the Guilds. But when required, they will choose what's best for Torwyn over the needs of their masters. Even their Guildmaster. If we need him, he is ours."

"So how do you explain Starn Rivers?" Rosomon bit back, remembering well the day her own swordwright had tried to kill her for the Ministry. "He alone disproves that theory, Kassian."

"Starn was an anomaly. And he graduated the Seminarium long before my time as tutor there. He should never have been given the Hawkspur sword."

Rosomon could only think that a meagre excuse. She herself had managed to persuade Lancelin to abandon his emperor in the search for their son. He had left the most important duty in Torwyn to satisfy the woman he loved. And where had it got them?

They had almost reached their encampment now. Rosomon could hear the lilting sound of Marrlock minstrels drifting through the forest. As they arrived and dismounted, Ianto took her reins from her.

"So what are your orders, my lady?" he asked.

She turned to look back along the road to Oakhelm. "We will proceed to the city. Let's see what hospitality Jarlath has in wait for us."

Ianto sighed, clearly unhappy with the idea. "And how will you make him prove his loyalty?"

Rosomon shook her head. "I have no idea. But he will do it. Or he will bloody well die."

Or at least, one of them would.

CONALL

He'd heard tales of the Drift since he was a boy. An expanse of dead earth, stretching from north to south and filled with the most diabolical of creatures. Conall had never intended to poke so much as a toe in it before, but now he was here, he couldn't help but feel a little disappointed.

The land was dead all right, but if there were fiendish beasts waiting to consume anyone foolhardy enough to trespass here, they were well hidden. So far, all he'd been met with was a dusty expanse of nothing. Their trek through the wasteland was so bereft of incident, he was beginning to yearn for some fanged monster to leap out at them, just to break up the monotony.

Orsokon led the way, his rangy stride eating up the miles at a frightening pace. Every now and then he would kneel, fist always resting on that huge curved blade, as he grasped a clod of sandy earth and pressed it to his helm, sniffing like a bloodhound. He was definitely searching for something, but what it might be Conall had no idea. And neither was he much concerned. More pressing was the need to rid himself of this cursed eye.

It plagued him every step, and he could barely resist tearing off the bandage and clawing at the socket. He gritted his teeth against the constant itch, but was sure to make no complaint about it. He didn't want to be the only one in the group griping and moaning as they travelled this desolate shit-scape.

Only slightly less maddening was the heavy sword strapped to his back. He had feared it at first, shivered like a coward as they'd forced him to carry it, but after the first mile of trekking through the waste he'd realised there was nothing to be afraid of. Though that baleful jewel was still set in the hilt, it had done nothing to curse him. No disembodied demon had beseeched him to serve it on pain of death. It was just a heavy lump of metal weighing him down as he sweated.

Each one of his companions likewise bore a massive weapon— sword or axe—the gems set into their blades covered with bandages, much like their right eyes. Conall could only wonder whether that was for their own benefit, to shield them from the evil that lurked in those noisome white gemstones, or for some other nefarious rea- son. Either way, he wasn't of a mind to ask—it wouldn't do to mark himself out as a troublemaker. He was done with resisting. At least for now.

Up ahead, Nylia was dogging Orsokon's tracks like a faithful hound. She at least was taking to this task with relish. As for the rest, they had accepted their gifts with a mixed reception.

Conall tried keeping a wide berth between himself and the rant- ing maniacs, spitting nonsense through gritted teeth or staring at the sky in wonder, as though they'd never seen it before. Others were silent, staring ahead in a stupor, and Conall wasn't sure which reac- tion unnerved him the most. Mikal was with them too, but he no longer seemed to recognise Conall, every now and then trembling as though momentarily afflicted with a palsy.

As for Conall, he felt much the same as always, but for the itch in his eye. He couldn't help but think that wouldn't last. Would he be suddenly stricken with madness? Or would he simply accept his fate like Nylia?

"Wait here," Orsokon hissed from up ahead.

They had reached the bottom of a ridge, and the dozen or so hunters stopped obediently as the warmaven scrabbled up the rise. Conall gazed around at the group, this gaggle of lunatics, and won- dered how he'd ever ended up here, before he eased his way to the front of the group and stood by Nylia's side. At first he was unsure of what to say, but then anything was better than this silence.

"You have no need to fear, Conall." She spoke first, offering a sideways grin.

He couldn't quite believe what he was hearing. It was as though she'd gone through a very different experience than him. As though she found this to be a boon rather than a curse.

"No need to fear? We've been mutilated. Violated. No need to fucking fear?"

She grasped his shoulder and pulled him close, before whispering, "Be careful. You do not want to be overheard saying such things."

"Overheard by who? Orsokon? I don't give a shit if he hears me or not."

Nylia shook her head. "I do not speak of Orsokon. It is not he you must be wary of now."

He could guess well enough who...or *what* she was referring to. But Conall wasn't worried about that yet; there had been nothing so much as a whisper from the demon they'd put inside his skull since they left Arcturius. Lucky for him, he supposed. From the corner of his eye he could see one of the others slapping his head as though he was squashing lice, while another drooled onto his leather breastplate.

"Beautiful, aren't they," Nylia said, as though complimenting a newlywed couple. "Each one blessed in their own way."

"Blessed? Are you insane? Is that what you think this is? A blessing?"

Her brow furrowed. "Of course. We have been given a gift. You will see."

Was that her talking, or the thing that possessed her? Was she just making the right noises, going along with this for her own sake? Or had she truly succumbed to the allure of the demon within?

"Is any of the real Nylia still in there?" he hissed through gritted teeth.

That brought a wide grin to her face. "You never really knew the real Nylia."

"No, I suppose I never did. And now I guess I never will."

"On the contrary," she replied, offering an earnest look. "You will know me better than anyone ever has. We are joined by a bond stronger than mere kinship. We are a part of the great beast."

Before he could ask what that even meant, Orsokon scrambled back over the rise. He stood before them, regarding them all from within that one-eyed helm.

"We are not far behind our quarry. Come, we must hurry."

He led them back up the hill, and they all scrabbled after like a pack of hungry wolves. Some of the group looked more eager than others, shaken from their malaise by the smell of their prey. Others were reluctant, looking scared, spurred on by fear rather than zeal.

Once over the rise, Conall saw more miles of nothing spreading out to every horizon. This was a world away from the Drift he had expected, a place of danger at every turn, but then perhaps that was a good thing. Maybe soon this sparse land would offer him a chance to escape.

A hairy, bare-chested maniac began to chatter frantically, grunting like a beast, jumping from one foot to the other. He pointed a hairy-knuckled hand toward the distance. Conall could see dust rising through the heat haze—something moving through the wastes.

Orsokon didn't need to speak, instead he casually gestured toward the distant caravan. The mob of crazed fighters began to lope toward their quarry, growling their eagerness as they chased down the travellers. As much as Conall would have liked to leave them to it, he was compelled to follow. There was no voice in his head, no demon possessing him, driving him forward, but still he moved along in the wake of that hunting party, wondering what in the Lairs he was supposed to do. Whatever it was, he thought perhaps he might fare better with a sword in hand, and pulled the demon blade free of its scabbard.

The hunters churned up the barren land, closing the gap like hounds on the hunt. When they were within two hundred yards, he could see a convoy of covered wagons rumbling along the dirt road. They were pulled by a combination of bull and sorry-looking horse. Surrounding each of the wagons were lumbering guards carrying crude but wicked-looking weapons—serrated glaives, spiked mauls, hammers. The muscular warriors would have struck fear in him, if Conall hadn't been more afraid of the predators he was with.

He had no idea where this caravan was headed out here in such barren land, and neither was there time to ponder. The hunting pack did not wait, did not try to formulate a plan of attack, before they fell upon the enemy, howling like animals.

Some bloody ambush, but Conall found himself caught up in the furore as he watched Mikal sprinting at the largest of the guards. They saw him coming, forming a rank of sorts to meet the oncoming attack, but Mikal ducked the clumsy swing of a maul and struck back with frightening speed, hacking the leg out from under the brute with his blade.

Then the pack was on them. The sound of clashing steel echoed through the waste. Conall stumbled to a stop some yards back as a score of masked guardians met the attack. A huge hammer caved in the head of one of his fellows, knocking him back to the dry earth, blood saturating the parched ground. Nylia leapt at the lead wagon, blade striking swiftly, impaling the driver's midriff and halting the caravan where it stood.

A scream was cut short by the sickening thud of another huge weapon. The slash of a serrated edge opened a corpulent belly, spilling guts and shit to the ground. A mouth opened impossibly wide, yowling in pain or fervour or fear, it was impossible to tell which. Horses reared and bulls lowed, squeals of panic and furious curses filling the air with a clangour.

All the while Conall tried to resist the urge to join this needless slaughter. This madness. But the blade in his hand was insistent. He could feel it trembling with anticipation, with yearning.

Fight.

He took a faltering step forward. A cloud was forming ahead of him, kicked up by the violence. He had nothing against these travellers. Why would he—

Fight.

No. He could not succumb to this. He was Conall Hawkspur. His mind was his own. He was not a—

Fight.

This was not him. It went against everything he had ever been taught. Still, he took another step, glaring at those warriors, desperately defending whatever was in their wagons. He could resist, he could resist, he could—

Fight.

Conall ran. His lips parted, teeth grinding as he snarled, clutching that demon blade in both hands. He plunged into the dust, and the frenzy of combat.

One of the huge guardians loomed from the cloud, maul raised high above a head covered by a dome of iron, eyes glaring yellow through the slits. Before that maul could strike, Conall had already dodged to the side, faster than he had ever moved in his life. The sword in his hand slashed upward, carving a groove in the guard's distended gut, and forcing him to stagger back. His downswing took off that huge helmed head.

A leaner figure jumped down from a nearby wagon—the driver, knife in his hand, long and evil and covered in rust. Conall staggered away as the driver slashed with that blade, barely avoiding its keen edge.

Kill.

He would not.

Conall stepped back out of the driver's reach. "Wait," he said, holding a hand up to calm him, but the man was in no mood for clemency.

He darted at Conall, slashing with that knife again. The demon sword shook in his hand, hungry for blood, but Conall grasped it tighter, subduing its urge to strike. He tried backing away, but his foot caught on the rocky ground and he stumbled on his arse. The driver took his chance, raising the knife, ready to plunge it down.

A sword drove straight and true through the driver's neck. His eyes widened in surprise before the blade twisted and exited his throat at the front, spraying blood that spattered Conall's face. He could taste it, warm and bitter on his lips.

As the driver fell, Nylia looked down at Conall, her face filled with relish at her deed. She said nothing, no quip, no demand for him to get on his feet and fight, before she plunged back into the fray.

He staggered to his feet, backing away from the wanton slaughter, staring as the last of the guards were driven into the dust. The slaves of Senmonthis did not stop at victory, venting their fury on the corpses and hacking down the beasts of burden that had pulled these wagons along the lonely road. It felt like he was watching through an unfocused lens, not wholly a part of this unbridled slaughter, but neither wholly apart.

The sword in his hand was silent. He looked down at it, seeing the blood on that blade. Was it there because of him? Had Conall Hawkspur caused that brute's death, or was it the voice in his head, spurring him on? As much as he wanted to assuage himself of the guilt, he knew he was not entirely innocent. That demon had only stirred a need within him, not controlled him like a puppeteer.

Was this how it would always be now? A harrying voice urging, suggesting, teasing him with promises of violence? And in return, what? His soul?

The carnage subsided, the cloud of dust settling to reveal a mess of corpses. Every bull and horse lay slaughtered. One of his fellow hunters dancing gleefully from one prone guard to the next, making sure they were dead before taking a grisly trophy—an ear, a finger, it didn't seem to matter what.

Two of them threw open the back doors of a wagon, and Conall gazed into the empty confines. There was nothing inside. No prize of gold or even supplies. They had done all this just for the joy of killing. So many dead in such a senseless act.

Nylia stood silently to one side, watching with a smile. Nearby, Mikal had reverted to twitching and mumbling to himself. One of the others, a heavyset warrior whose eyepatch had slipped from his face, sat in the dirt and blood, rocking back and forth as he pulled at his receding hair. Another danced about the wagons as though he could hear a band playing its merry refrain. Most of the others just glared, empty-eyed, as shocked at what they had done as Conall.

"Children of Senmonthis."

He turned at that weird voice that had plagued his nightmares. Orsokon was some way distant, not having lifted a finger during the fight. At his words, the rest of the fighters stopped their lamenting or their revelry, and moved closer to him.

"Let us give thanks," said Orsokon, gesturing for them all to kneel.

The dozen or so still alive dropped to their knees, bowing their heads, only too eager to obey. Conall reluctantly joined them.

Orsokon cleared his throat. "Though you are still worms, you have been granted an auspicious victory. Such a passionate display has ensured your survival. Rejoice. You have been offered a great gift. Accept it as part of who you are now. This is just the beginning, but one day, if you are blessed enough, you might rise to become one of the most exalted. A warrior unbound by earthly limit. Arise."

Obediently, the rest of the group jumped to their feet. Conall stood gingerly, feeling none of the vigour the rest of this mad cohort displayed. All he could do was stand and watch as they followed Orsokon on through the wasteland.

They had left devastation in their wake, and for nothing other than to prove they could kill. Was this his fate? To follow this Scion, and fight or die in its service? Conall tried not to think on it, as Nylia walked after the others.

"Thank you," he said to her.

She turned to him. "For what?"

"For saving my life. If you hadn't intervened—"

"Don't thank me, Conall. Just accept what you are. Then perhaps next time, I won't have to intervene."

She walked away after the others, leaving him among the corpses with that blade in his hand. As he wiped the blood from it, he hoped it would be some time before he had to use it again.

FULREN

He was lost in the silent dark. Floating in an ocean, with nothing but a starless sky above. There was no pain at least, but was that a reason to be thankful? Pain would have given him something to feel, a distraction from the endless void he was thrust into.

A whisper.

Was that the women somewhere close by? Or was it something far worse beyond a door he could not see? Watching him. Waiting for its moment.

Fulren fought against the fear, against the isolation. He could feel the shade of his lost limbs. Ghosts haunting him, taunting him, reminding him what he had lost. At the end of his left arm he could still feel his hand. He clenched it into a fist, but knew there was nothing there but empty air. Likewise, he could wiggle his toes, his mind giving the order, his nerves and tendons responding, but in reality they were gone. He would never walk again.

So what now? Was he to give in to despair? Let it consume him, and eat away at what little remained? Or could he resist?

But how?

There was nothing left but a shell. A shadow of Fulren Hawkspur rotting in some bed. Death would be his only release. He had come to terms with that over the last few days, at least when his thoughts had manifested some kind of clarity. Despair was all that remained. He knew he had to end this, but how was he to do the deed in such a helpless condition?

You cannot die yet.

The words were whispered in his ear. He felt the breath of it against his cheek, and it made the gooseflesh stand livid on his skin.

"Who's there?" he called to the darkness.

No answer. Nothing coalesced in his room, no shade of anything human or otherwise. He was alone in that ocean, adrift on the flotsam of his own misery. But deep down, Fulren knew he was not truly alone.

Was something coming for him? Something diabolical creeping through the black to devour him? Perhaps that might be a better fate than the one he was condemned to.

He lay back, trying to fight the fear, fight the misery. He listened out for another whisper, another fetid breath against his ear, but all he could hear were distant voices chattering. The two women who had fished him from the lake? Or was it something more fiendish? As much as he strained his ears he could not tell.

Fulren remembered the warning Wenis had given him what seemed a lifetime ago ... *It will open a door that can never be closed.*

It had been a dire warning, made in the most serious terms by a woman who treated everything with levity. And she had been right. He was now experiencing those consequences, but Fulren would not shy away from them. Perhaps he should even embrace them— what did he have to lose now?

Closing his useless eyes, he tried to focus, fighting through the torpor imbued by whatever drugs the women had administered. As he did so he felt himself sinking further into that ocean of calm, listening, opening himself up to that voice. Something was calling from somewhere, trying to break through, and if he allowed it to come...

There. In the far distance.

He could not make out words, could not even tell if they spoke a language he understood, but he could hear them beyond the veil. The more he tried to focus, to comprehend what was happening, the further the voice seemed to slip away.

This was out of his control and that notion frustrated him most of all. More than the loss of his body, his sight. Would there be nothing he could harness to his advantage? Not even the cursed necroglyph at his neck was under his command.

He lay back, trying to relax, trying to let go of that resentment. The past few days had gone by in a whirlwind of fleeting sensations. Perhaps if he could piece together what had happened, bring his mind into focus, he could make some sense of this.

His mother's tears were the last thing he remembered. Her grief so stark in his mind. Jagdor had stood beside her, that implacable guardian. Had they managed to escape? Were they even still alive?

And what of his brother and sister? In all this mess had they managed to avoid the attentions of the Ministry? Tyreta had been safe in the Sundered Isles, Conall in the Karna. Had the Ministry's insidious influence stretched that far? If the Guilds had truly fallen, what fate awaited them if they tried to return? Fulren could only hope they would flee to somewhere safe, lest they share a similar fate to his...or worse.

But what could be worse than this? And how would he help them now he was little more than butchered meat?

Hate welled up, his teeth gnashing at the injustice, the betrayal. A tingling heat began to tease the nape of his neck. That old familiar feeling of warmth increased, burning, searing. The necroglyph began to spread its power, but where before he might have tried to stop it, now he allowed it to shine, to burn, to overwhelm.

Lights coalesced in his field of vision, a starfield of red, blue and yellow. Nearby he could feel the burgeoning power of a pyrestone light within its housing. A light bloomed, brighter than the rest, a sun amid stars. This was no dream, no illusion brought on by narcotics. This was oh so real, and Fulren almost laughed at the joy of it.

A light shattered.

He was sprayed with glass as quickly as he was plunged into darkness. The searing pain in his neck dulled to numbness as he lay there in that sea of black once more.

"What the shit is going on!"

The words spoiled the sanctity of the tiny bedchamber. Fulren heard footsteps, the door swinging open, sending a welcome billow of air across his perspiring body.

He saw light in the doorway outlining the image of a woman. Must have been a webwainer, her latent energy glowing bright against the dark. Was she afraid? He couldn't sense it, but her reluctance to approach suggested she was wary of him, despite how unthreatening he was.

Another shape pushed past her, indistinct against the black. She entered the room, moving to Fulren's bedside.

"The pyrestone has blown its housing," she said, and he recognised her voice from what could have been a fever dream. Was she called Ashe? Yes, he remembered her telling him.

"Be careful," said the one at the door. Her light was becoming agitated, that webwainer power coursing through her body, reflecting her temperament. She was powerful, and Fulren wondered if she could sense his power in return.

"Don't be such a wimp," Ashe said. "It's only a bit of glass." She leaned in closer to Fulren, so close he could smell her breath. Had she been drinking? "Are you okay?"

"Yes," he replied. "I'm fine. It just..." But how would he explain this? How would he tell them he had been cursed in the land of Nyrakkis? He could already see the light within the woman at the door changing from yellow to red as her unease grew. What was her name? Verlyn, that was it. The last thing he needed was for her to be suspicious of him. He was lying here helpless—he could not make an enemy of these women.

"Go and find something to clean this up with," Ashe ordered, already picking pieces of glass from the bedsheet. "This has made a right old mess."

Verlyn moved back from the doorway, plunging Fulren's field of vision back into darkness. He could still sense Ashe close by, muttering fretfully as she brushed off the debris.

"Must have been a faulty connection in the conversion chamber. I've tried my best to make everything as stable as possible, but we're short on resources. I'm sorry if it frightened you."

He tried to focus on her, but it was difficult in the blinding dark. "Are you an artificer?"

She stopped what she was doing, most likely looking at him. Was she impressed with his assumption? Was her face filled with pity? He could only guess.

"I was," she replied.

"What happened? I take it you've no affiliation with the Archwind Guild."

"No. Never did. I learned my trade the old-fashioned way—at the knee of my father. When he died, I fell in with a bad crowd, you know, the usual story. Ended up making dodgy devices for even dodgier people."

"Is that why you ended up living along the Serpentspin, miles from anywhere? You're running away from someone?"

She sighed, as though not wanting to be reminded of it. "I guess so. We needed to start a new life and here seemed as good a place as any."

Light intruded on the bedchamber once again as Verlyn returned. Fulren noted the fiery red motes that whirled within her had dimmed to orange. He could only hope that was a good sign.

The two women began to clear up the mess, shovelling the broken glass and pyrestone shards into a bucket. While they worked, Fulren got a curious feeling from them—their affinity with one another, their affection. Simmering below it though was the unmistakable sense of Verlyn's caution.

As they worked, Ashe pulled his bedsheet aside and it snagged on the stump of his left leg. He winced, grunting in pain.

"I'm sorry," she said. Before he could tell her it was all right, she backed away. "I think he needs another one of my cocktails."

"Yeah, I think that's a good idea," Verlyn answered. "You'd best be quick."

Ashe hurried from the room, and he was left alone with the webwainer. She stood looking over him, and he wondered if she knew he could see her, or at least her fluid image.

"So what's in this cocktail?" Fulren asked, keen to break the silence.

"Oh, the usual," said Verlyn. "Touch of poppy essence, dab of sea snake venom, pinch of ground redstalk."

"I'm sorry I asked."

She reached forward to pick an errant piece of glass from the bed and he reached out to touch her arm. She snatched her hand away before he could.

"You don't have to be afraid," he said, eager to put her at ease. Perhaps too eager.

He could see those lights within her roiling in a sea of combative colours, shifting and turning. It was beautiful to watch.

"I'm not afraid," she said.

He could sense she was lying, and that only served to make him feel more guilty. These women had saved his life and here he was, striking fear into one of them. But what could he do? He would have run away, as far as he could get, rather than place either of them in danger, but there would be no more running for Fulren Hawkspur.

"Here it is," Ashe said as she came back into the room.

The women helped him into a sitting position, Ashe fluffing the pillows so he was more comfortable. Gently she raised a cup to his mouth and he took a sip of the tincture she had prepared. It was like rancid oil at first, but the aftertaste left a honeyed sweetness on his tongue.

"Thank you," he said.

Within a moment he felt the pain in the stump of his leg begin to dull, along with the numbness of the necroglyph at his back. He swallowed down the rest of Ashe's cocktail, before settling back on the bed.

"We should let him rest now," Verlyn said, only too eager to leave the room.

"I'm not so sure," answered Ashe. "He's awful pale. Maybe we should take him outside, get some sun on his face. Can't do him any harm, can it?"

"What's the point in getting sun on his face, he can't bloody see—" Verlyn stopped, realising she was being insensitive.

"You could always just ask me," Fulren replied, ignoring the awkwardness. "I'm blind, not deaf. And I'd love to go outside."

"That's settled then," Ashe said. "Get these sheets off him and get him on the porch."

She began to fuss with the bedding. Verlyn moved closer, but there was a reluctance there, as though she were still afraid to go near him.

Ashe helped him sit up, and with some difficulty he managed to position himself at the edge of the bed. With the cocktail numbing his senses, Fulren could barely feel any discomfort in his legs.

Both the women managed to pick him up, and Fulren realised how little remained of the man he'd been. He must have weighed as much as a child as they carried him with ease through the house. A light breeze brushed against his face as they made their way outside and placed him gently in a chair.

It was peaceful, a few birds tweeting nearby, the murmur of grass in the wind. There was also a pretty unpleasant stink of shit, which made Fulren screw up his nose.

"That'll be the pigs," Ashe said, seeing the look on his face. "You'll get used to it."

"Earthy," he replied, and was heartened when she giggled in response.

As his senses became accustomed to this new environment, he began to feel another sensation. The essence of pyrestone drifted on the air, and he turned his head toward it. Through his murky vision, he could just make out the glittering of artifice in the distance.

"Where did you come from?" Ashe asked suddenly, breaking his connection with the stone.

He turned his head toward her voice, wondering whether it was worth lying. But what did it matter now? "I was born in Wyke."

"You're a long way from home, Fulren."

Wasn't that the truth. "I'm not sure I have a home anymore. Who knows what the Ministry has decided to do with it. Burn it to the ground more than likely."

She placed a hand on his shoulder. "If it makes you feel better, I know how you feel."

"Why? Is this not your home?"

She let out a long sigh. "I guess it is now."

Ashe squeezed his shoulder, and he felt suddenly grateful for the gesture.

"Home is where you make it," Verlyn said matter-of-factly.

Through the dark he saw her move forward to touch Ashe's hand.

For a moment they stood in quiet reflection, and Fulren could only envy that intimacy.

He turned his attention back to the dark, where he could just see those distant pyrestones twinkling. Perhaps he was not so lost after all.

"You said you were an artificer?" he asked. "I assume you've got a workshop? Or at least something similar?"

"I still dabble," Ashe replied. "Do you know anything about the art?"

"A few bits and pieces. How about you take me to your workshop?"

"What for?" Verlyn asked.

"Don't be so miserable," Ashe chided. "What harm could it do?"

She took hold of the chair Fulren was sitting on, and reluctantly Verlyn grasped the other side. Carefully, they carried him across a wide expanse of dark until Fulren could see those winking lights more clearly. When Ashe opened the door to a barn, he was hit full in the face by dazzling light.

The stench of oil and lubricant hung heavy in the air, along with the crackle and fizz of pyrestones in their conversion chambers. A long-forgotten memory of his own workshop flooded back.

"Trust me," Ashe said. "If you could see this, I'm pretty sure you'd be impressed."

But he already was. Even though he could not see, could not walk, was imprisoned in this broken shell, Fulren knew he could no longer despair.

There was work to do.

ANSELL

He gripped the edge of the bed, straining with all his might, trying desperately not to grunt as he heaved his legs over the side. The stitches pulled at his wound, teeth grinding as he quietly prayed for them not to tear. Sweat was dripping from him, breath coming in heaving gasps. This was not his first visit to the infirmary, not his fifth for that matter, but this time felt worse than ever before. Was the wound infected? Had he been stricken with fever?

Across the sweet-smelling chamber, he heard a moan. In a bed at the far side of the infirmary was another patient, a legate from the frailty of his body. Ansell had no clue what afflicted him, but he could only hope it was nothing contagious. He already had enough ailments to consider.

Birds tweeted from beyond the window, the sun lancing in through the shutters and giving the room an aspect of purity. It wouldn't do for the sick to waken and find themselves in a grimy dungeon of a chamber. The pleasantness of the surroundings was something to be thankful for at least.

With great effort he managed to stand, taking a moment to find his balance, before staggering toward a nearby table. There was water in a jug, wooden cups set beside it. Ignoring the cups, he picked up the jug and gulped down the contents, relieved when none of it leaked from the hole in his side.

Where were the temple serfs? Surely they should have been waiting in attendance for him to wake. Had he been forgotten?

Ansell placed down the empty jug and stumbled toward the window. When he opened the shutters, he was bathed in bright sunlight, breathing in a lungful of purifying air. It took him a moment to realise the usual cloying smog that pervaded the city was gone. With the manufactories closed down, the stench that hung over the Anvil had disappeared. At least some good had come from it.

The city sprawled out toward the teeming rathole that was the Burrows. As he cast his eye over the various districts, he could only begin to wonder where those brigands might have taken Grace. How would he find her in such a maze? Was he even capable?

He should have left the city days ago, and taken her with him when he had the chance. Should have predicted the danger. At that thought he pressed his fist against the stone balcony, feeling the pressure begin to bruise his flesh, resisting the urge to smash it until his knuckles bled and broke.

"Good to see you on your feet, brother."

Ansell turned to see Regenwulf standing in the doorway. For a fully armoured Knight of the Draconate he moved with surprising lightness of foot when it suited him.

"This?" Ansell replied, gesturing to the bandaged wound at his side. "Nothing more than a trifle, brother. We have both suffered much worse during our service."

And it was true, but the pain deep inside Ansell was like nothing he had ever felt. There was an ache in his heart, as though part of it had been stolen, and the only way he might feel whole was for it to be returned.

"You almost died," Regenwulf said. "That wound was deep. Another inch either way and I'd be saying the rites of Ravenothrax over your corpse right now."

Ansell knew he had been lucky. His attacker had tried to strike a fatal blow, and it was only fate that had spared him. Unlike Fulren Hawkspur, who he had aimed to wound rather than kill. Just the memory of that filled him with yet more regret—more shame piled with the rest like wood for his pyre.

Regenwulf took a step forward, glancing around the room to ensure they weren't overheard. "Where were you going, Ansell?"

He found himself reaching to his wrist, for the bracelet that lay beneath the cuff of his gown. Upon finding it still there, he felt an unusual sense of relief.

"What do you mean?"

"When we found you in the servants' yard, you were wearing the garb of an ordinary citizen. Were you sent on some mission I was not told about?"

How to explain it? The truth might have dire consequences, but could he deceive one of his brothers?

"Yes. That was it." The lie slipped from his mouth easier than he could have anticipated.

Regenwulf's dark brow furrowed at the answer. "Is there something I need to know? Something you have to confess?"

Ansell should have felt guilt, but all that remained in his heart was a growing anger. At himself, at the injustice inflicted upon Grace. "If I need to confess, I will find a High Legate."

Regenwulf's expression softened. "I have noticed the change in you, Ansell. Ever since the emperor was slain, you have not been the man I knew. If you are troubled, you can unburden yourself to me. We are still brothers."

It was tempting. He could so easily have told his old friend about all his doubts, his fears. But how would Regenwulf ever understand his lack of faith in their Archlegate? It went against everything they had been raised to believe.

"Do not worry yourself on my account. There is nothing wrong. Apart from a new scar, I am still the man you have always known."

That seemed to satisfy Regenwulf and he nodded his understanding. "There is no shame in what happened, Ansell. It was an ambush; any of us could have fallen foul of it. Do you have any idea who those brigands might have been?"

Ansell knew all too well they had come for Grace, and her alone. They were Guild sympathisers, perhaps even sent by the Guildmasters themselves to gain leverage over Sanctan.

"No. I have no idea."

Regenwulf opened his mouth to ask something more, but instead he turned, his keen ears hearing someone's approach. Footsteps echoed along the corridor outside, polished boots carrying a lean figure into the infirmary. Olstrum Garner entered with little ceremony, regarding them both in that friendly manner he often bore. They were not friends though, and Ansell was about to chide him for disturbing them, when Sanctan also entered the infirmary, his sandalled footsteps inaudible on the tiled floor.

As soon as he appeared, Regenwulf dropped to one knee. Ansell struggled to kneel, feeling the wound pull at his side as he fought for balance.

"Brother Regenwulf," Sanctan said. "I would like to speak with Brother Ansell in private."

Regenwulf stood, offering Ansell a brief nod before bowing again to the Archlegate and leaving them alone.

"Please," Sanctan continued, gesturing for Ansell to rise. "You must be in great discomfort."

He struggled to his feet, gritting his teeth against the pain. As he did so, Olstrum closed the door, shutting out the rest of the world. Sanctan peered over to where the legate lay in his sickbed, but the old man was still now, not making a sound. Satisfied they would not be overheard, Sanctan turned back to Ansell.

"This is all such sad business. I was very fond of that girl. Grace." He added her name as though there might be some doubt as to who they were discussing.

"I am sure the culprits won't have gone far," Ansell replied. "We could track them down. Dispatch the Revocaters—"

"And why would we do that?" Sanctan looked genuinely bemused at the suggestion.

"Because she is your—"

"My what?"

Ansell knew he could not answer. To suggest the Archlegate had sired a child would have been heresy. Breaching his vows of chastity was reason enough for him to be cast down from his position. For a moment, Ansell began to wonder if it was Sanctan, and not the Guilds, who had ordered the girl's abduction. It would certainly have rid Sanctan of his problem. But even he would not have sunk so low... would he?

Olstrum stepped forward, an insipid smile on his face that Ansell would have happily wiped away with a swipe of his hand. "There have been a number of spurious rumours spread about the girl's lineage in recent days. Most likely by the kidnappers themselves. We all know those rumours couldn't possibly be true. Unfortunately, as much as we would all like to see the girl returned to the welcoming embrace of the Mount, such efforts would only serve to fan the flames of idle gossip."

Not for the first time, Ansell found himself reaching a hand to the bracelet beneath his sleeve. "Then what is to become of her?"

Sanctan shrugged. "I am sure, in time, her abductors will realise she is not my... issue. Then they will tire of her and release her back onto the streets of the Anvil. You never know, Grace was always such an affable child—perhaps they'll develop some affection for her and adopt her themselves."

Ansell fought back the panic. They couldn't just abandon her to the whims of her captors. There was no telling what they were capable of.

"We have to do something."

Sanctan's expression darkened, and he took a step closer. "Do not forget who you are, Ansell Beckenrike. And who you serve."

For the longest time he had struggled with that question. Everything he'd ever known had been tested, all the faith he'd ever had brought into doubt.

"I serve the Archlegate," he replied. How easily those words came to him, despite their lack of sincerity.

"Good," Sanctan replied cheerily. He smiled, looking Ansell up and down as though seeing him for the first time. "I know I speak for everyone when I say how relieved we are to see you recovering so swiftly."

Even if he believed Sanctan's sympathy was genuine, it was more concerning that he had forgotten his daughter. Abandoned her to the city's underbelly. There had to be a way to find her. Ansell's eye fell on Olstrum—a man who had his dirty fingers in dirtier pockets all across the Anvil.

"When may I return to my duties?" he asked.

Sanctan shrugged. "Whenever the apothecaries of the Mount deem you fit."

"And what then? Will I be given a chance to redeem myself? Sent somewhere key in securing our victory over the Guilds?"

Sanctan narrowed his eyes. Did he suspect some subterfuge? "You are needed here, Ansell. By my side."

"I am the gnashing tooth and rending claw of the Wyrms. I should be sent to fight alongside my brothers. Perhaps the consul could advise me on where might be the most fitting deployment?"

Sanctan turned to regard Olstrum, before looking back at Ansell with a twitch to his eye, as though he was sure he was being toyed with but couldn't quite work out how.

"Perhaps," he said with a shrug. "Olstrum, I suggest you apprise our brother with an update on the latest manoeuvres. Then later, we can decide where his skills might be put to best use."

With a sweep of his long white robe, Sanctan made for the door before leaving them both alone. In the confines of the infirmary, with just Ansell for company, Olstrum's insipid smile wavered slightly.

"Well," he said, unable to hold Ansell's gaze. "Not much has changed since before you were…erm…incapacitated. Armiger Battalions loyal to the Draconate still fight on several fronts. We do plan to deploy contingents of your knights in a number of areas. Perhaps—"

He stopped as Ansell took a step forward, looming over him. Even wounded, and in a plain linen gown, he was an imposing figure—especially to a worm like Olstrum.

"I am aware you are a well-connected man, Consul. With many resources at your disposal."

Olstrum looked up at him, unable to disguise the worry in his eyes. "What—? What do you mean?"

"Eyes and ears throughout the Anvil and beyond. Ways and means."

Olstrum swallowed. "Yes…yes I have some contacts who occasionally provide me with information."

"So you could find her if you wanted to?"

"The child?" he replied, his eyes widening. "But the Archlegate has expressly—"

"Don't be concerned with what the Archlegate has said. Be more concerned with me. And her name is Grace."

"But... I cannot go against the word of the Archlegate."

Ansell leaned in closer. "My word should be the one you worry about."

Those beady eyes of his opened wider, before Olstrum clenched his jaw and narrowed them again. A display of courage perhaps? "No. I will not defy his orders."

Ansell reached out, taking Olstrum by the collar of his pristine jacket. He felt the wound in his side sting in protest at the exertion, but still he lifted the consul off his feet and slammed him against the wall.

"You will find her. You will use all your cunning, all your guile. Bribe every spy and informant you know in this city, if that's what it takes, but you will find her."

Rather than look cowed, Olstrum struggled against the iron grip. Ansell felt the sharp tear of stitches in his side, and loosed his hold. Olstrum managed to struggle free, wrenching the cloth of his jacket from Ansell's hands.

"No," he cried. "I said bloody *no*." Olstrum backed away, wiping a tear from his eye with the back of his hand. His face looked mournful and he shook like a man pushed to his limit. "I have been stretched like a traitor on the rack. Dangled like a morsel for wolves. Lashed to strings and forced to dance like a marionette for two masters. I may have betrayed my emperor, but I will not make an enemy of Sanctan Egelrath."

Ansell took a deep breath, resisting the urge to clamp a hand over his wound, despite feeling it bleed beneath his gown. "And yet you have no fear of making an enemy of me."

"Kill me if you want," he replied, walking forward, arms wide as though presenting himself for the execution. "I don't care anymore. It would be a mercy compared to what Egelrath will do."

"You really would have me end your life right here? And yet... you have never struck me as the kind of man who doesn't care if he lives or dies."

Olstrum's shoulders sagged. "Some things are more important."

Ansell could see he was tormented by something. "Tell me."

Olstrum set his jaw, staring at Ansell with more grit than he had ever seen from the man. "I have a family."

Now it all became clear. "And the Archlegate will harm them if you do not obey his every word. I understand. And I too know what he is capable of. Nevertheless, you will help me find Grace, or you will die."

Olstrum nodded. His options were few, but from what he had just revealed, they had been all along.

"All right," he said. "But in return, you must make a vow to see my family safe."

It sounded like such a simple promise to make. Perhaps it would be a simple thing to do. Perhaps not.

"Agreed."

Olstrum took a step forward, his mask of indifference returned. "I said vow it."

What did it matter now? Ansell had broken so many oaths already he did not know which still stood and which he'd abandoned.

"I swear by the Great Wyrms if you find Grace, I will do all I can to see your family returned to you unharmed."

Olstrum let out a long low sigh. "Then I'll do it."

He turned, and left Ansell alone in the infirmary with the slumbering legate in his sickbed. For a moment, he wondered what he had just agreed to. But then, it was only one more burden to pile with the rest.

CONALL

The place was a hive. No, a menagerie. Or was it a warren? Whatever it was, he'd never seen anything so debauched—and he'd seen some pretty off-colour shit in his time. However it might be described, Conall couldn't tell if he was aroused or repulsed.

The deeper he wandered, the more extreme the catalogue of grotesquery grew. Or was it an orgy of misery? He stopped trying to find the words and paused for a moment. Drinking it in. Breathing deep of it, smelling the sweat and the blood. Hearing those whispered groans of delight and agony. Of ecstasy.

Close to his feet a couple rutted for all they were worth, trading grunts as though in competition with one another. Above him someone hung from a chain, hooks piercing the skin of their back, stretching the flesh, but the look on their face spoke only of a quintessential frenzy. A few feet to his right, a crowd had gathered around a stone altar, bent over it like pigs at a trough, snuffling as they feasted on the innards of some poor unfortunate. As the blood and gore ran down their chins, Conall began to wonder what their victim had done to warrant such a grim fate. Then the head of that body turned and regarded him with a bloody smile.

He balked, reeling back from the horror, only to be greeted by half a dozen bodies nailed to a wall, while a group of emaciated women performed lascivious acts on them. Conall gritted his teeth, squeezing his eyes shut, reeling from the stink of incense, and fumes of a far more narcotic origin.

Isn't this what you wanted?

The voice was close to his ear, but when he opened his eyes, there was no one there.

It can all be yours.

He turned but there was no one behind him.

"I never asked for this," he hissed.

The noise of the crowd fell silent, as though he had been invisible until he opened his mouth to speak. A dread feeling grew as he regarded the deviant host. The hairs stood on his neck when he realised that every eye in this endless cavern of filth was staring at him. Their ecstatic looks were gone. Now they stared blankly, chilling him to his loins.

Conall turned, ready to flee into the darkness, anywhere but this, when a score of hands gripped his arms, his neck, his face, before he could take even a single step. He was dragged into the melee, consumed by the gleeful groans of delight that infested his ears.

Powerless to resist, he was hoisted in the air, paraded through the cavernous orgy, spinning, falling...

He woke with a sharp intake of breath, surrounded by darkness, and for a moment he thought he was still among that orgy. It took some moments to realise the bandage that covered his pyrestone eye had slipped down to cover both. He tore it from his face, and was greeted by the sight of the winnowing fire. Stark wilderness surrounded them, and Conall had never thought he'd be so relieved to find himself in the Drift.

Most of the others were still sleeping. He could see them in the faint dawn light, some plagued by fitful dreams, others in a deep slumber, as though they hadn't a care in the world. Nylia was close to him, but her back was turned.

At the edge of the camp stood Mikal. He stared out into the wild, keeping watch against the denizens of the Drift. Every now and again his shoulder twitched, and he would mutter softly to the still air. Of Orsokon there was no sign.

Had the warmaven left them alone to fend for themselves? Conall didn't really give a shit. This was the best chance he'd have. It was madness to stay here, to suffer in this way and be forced to mindlessly slaughter for the sake of some maniacal god-mage.

Gently he pulled aside the woollen blanket and rose to his feet. No one else stirred, and Mikal still gazed into the dawn. Even the voice in his head remained silent. Whatever demon was plaguing his dreams did nothing to deter him. Carefully, he placed the bandage back over his eye, covering the pyrestone, hoping that perhaps it would keep the voice silent for now.

Looking out into the darkness, he couldn't see a thing. No landmarks to speak of, no mountains or ziggurats of wind-blasted stone. It was just him and the endless waste of the Drift.

A quick glance at the sky and the few waning stars showed him the way east. It wasn't much to go on, but it would have to do. He took a step toward the edge of the camp before stopping. His sword lay by his bedroll. That baleful gem set at the cross-guard still wrapped in a tight linen binding.

Should he take it? Or should he leave that fell blade and its cursed demon behind? Facing the vagaries of the Drift unarmed would be a foolish move, but taking that weapon might put him in even greater peril. Not much time to make up his mind.

He picked up the blade, dismissing the thought of the evil it harboured. Slowly he crept away from the camp, leaving the dying fire and those slumbering warriors behind. The sun would rise soon, and he was determined to put as much distance between them as he could before anyone knew he was even gone.

At the edge of the camp, as he cast one last look toward the fire, he saw Mikal standing, staring right at him. Conall froze, expecting him to bellow from the bottom of his lungs. Instead his left eye twitched, the corner of his mouth turning up slightly, before he turned his back.

There was no time to think on the reason. Conall seized his chance and took his first tentative steps toward freedom.

Do you think yourself brave or stupid?

It was a distant whisper, teasing him like a seafront whore. Conall did his best to ignore it, relieved it was not screaming in his ear, compelling him to obey.

When he was far enough from the camp, he opened up his stride, his flight turning from gentle lope to full-on sprint. Soon his lungs were almost bursting, the sword feeling heavier in his grip with each laboured step.

This is futile. You cannot resist.

"Get out of my fucking head," he gasped, running on, not daring to stop lest he give in to the entreaty.

Where do you think you are running to, Conall Hawkspur?

"I'm going home."

Silence as he ran. Or was that the sound of distant laughter?

And what do you think waits for you there?

Conall thought immediately of his mother, of his festering resentment. Quickly he tried to shatter those thoughts with memories of his brother and sister. Fulren's naive adoration of him. The wilfulness of his sister that he had always admired. But they were gone, split apart by the Ministry, and Conall didn't even know if they were still alive.

If his family couldn't help him, surely there would be someone else. What about his friends in the Talon or the courtly sycophants he had cultivated in Wyke? There had to be someone.

There is nothing for you there. No one who can help you. Your only salvation is to give in. Accept this, as you would the coming of night and the breaking of dawn.

He tried to run faster, eyes locked on a horizon now illuminated by the rising sun. In the distance he could just make out a landmark, a crumbling tower listing under the weight of a sand dune.

Conall slowed, risking a glance back and seeing nothing in his wake. Perhaps he was safe now. Maybe when Orsokon found out he was gone he would abandon him to the Drift. It was a small hope, but the only one Conall could cling to.

When he eventually reached the ruin, it looked ready to fall, the crumbling walls giving no clue as to its origin. It was a remnant of a kingdom that died a thousand years before, but now it was the only shelter he might find in this blasted place.

You will never make it across the Drift.

The words were hissed as he passed beneath a crumbling arch, the keystone rotted to dust.

You are not strong enough, Conall. You never were. If you accept me, you will become greater than you ever imagined. I can show you such sights as you can only dream of. The rewards for submission would be more than anything you can comprehend.

He reached a stairwell, dragging himself up the worn stone. It was hard to breathe, as though his lungs were filled with smoke, and when he reached the first floor, he dropped to his knees. With a trembling hand he took the bandage from around his head.

Have you always been so weak?

Conall closed his left eye. The view through the right was painted crimson, a kaleidoscope of blood-misted facets. His hand began to shake wretchedly as he reached for the socket, fingers pausing before they touched the pyrestone, now as much a part of him as his drumming heart.

You are not strong enough for this, Conall. You never have been.

He sobbed. It was right. He had never been strong enough, not for this nor any other damned thing. But perhaps it was never too late to prove someone wrong. Even yourself.

A scream, long and loud, issued from his mouth. It hurt his throat, hurt his ears, but he needed it to fuel him as he plunged his fingers into his eye. They probed into the socket, and he cried all the louder from the pain. He managed to wedge a thumb behind the pyrestone, feeling the tendons and veins that connected it begin to protest as he pulled.

Blood ran down his cheek, his scream turning to whimper, fingers growing slick with his own juices. Conall tightened his grip, teeth gnashing, spitting his desperation. He fell forward, red spattering the ground, and with a last bark of pain-fuelled hate he ripped the pyrestone from his head. There was a tearing noise in his ears, searing agony driven like a lance through his brain, and he almost lost consciousness.

The stone made a hollow clatter as it hit the ground, and he whimpered again, looking down at that little red crystal. He was free.

Hands still shaking, he pulled the bandage back over his eye in a vain attempt to stem the tide of blood that ran down his cheek, spattering his leather jack. For a moment he paused, waiting to hear that mocking voice in his head, but all was silent. Reaching down with a trembling hand, he picked up the pyrestone, squeezing it in his fist as though he might shatter it with nothing more than rage.

"Where are you running to?"

He didn't have to look up to know who had spoken. That melodic voice could only belong to one man.

Gingerly, Conall placed one hand on his sheathed sword, still grasping the pyrestone in his other fist as he rose to his feet. Orsokon stood at the top of the stairs, his huge bulk blocking the morning sunlight that streamed in through a skewed window frame.

"Please. Just let me go," Conall said. It wasn't a request though; he spoke it like an order.

Orsokon shook that huge helmed head. "You will never be free. No matter how hard you try to resist. No matter how far you run. Stop all this, just accept who you are now. You belong to Senmonthis. An eternity of glory awaits you in her divine shadow."

As though to labour the point Orsokon took a rangy step forward, towering over Conall. He could hear the warlord's breath resounding within that helm, and smell the fusty stink of his unwashed body. Despite how intimidated he was, Conall refused to show it, and he raised himself tall and proud, staring back with the one eye left in his head.

"You're making a mistake," he said.

Orsokon's head tipped to one side like a curious dog. "And what mistake might that be?"

"To think me a slave to your bitch mistress."

Orsokon grunted in amusement. "Enough of this." He held out his hand as though Conall might take it and be led away to accept his fate. "Come."

Conall reached forward, placing the red pyrestone in Orsokon's outstretched palm. "Can you see?"

The warmaven looked down, a strange squeak issuing from within his helm as he reached for the curved blade at his waist. Conall's hand was faster, and he wrenched his sword free of the scabbard before plunging it through Orsokon's bare midriff. The warlord gripped the blade that now transfixed him, letting out a strange choking sound that heralded a drip of blood down his chin.

Conall snarled, tearing the blade from Orsokon's flesh before he swung it in earnest, taking the bastard's head right off his shoulders. The helm fell to the ground with a clang before the body collapsed, staining the dry floor with blood.

He stared at that body. That vile insurmountable beast he had feared, now dead at his feet. It made him smile. A smile that turned to a grin, before he was laughing so hard he almost slapped his thigh at the joy of it.

"Fuck you, bastard. Weren't expecting that, were you?"

A tear ran from his eye and he quickly wiped it away. Next to the body lay the red pyrestone. That tiny thing that might as well have been the most indomitable gaol. It would cage him no longer. But just to make sure, best put some distance between him and it.

Conall turned, almost tripping over himself to dash down the stairs. He managed to pause long enough to clean the length of his blade on the sleeve of his jerkin, before sheathing it again. At the bottom of the stair he saw the bright light of day just through the door. He was free of this now. Free of it all. The only thing he had to do was—

The sun was blotted out by a figure moving to block the doorway. Conall stumbled to a stop as Nylia barred his escape, staring at him, but offering no word of challenge.

"Please don't do this," he breathed.

Her lip trembled. A moment of doubt, gone as soon as it came. "You cannot hope to escape, Conall."

"I can bloody well try," he replied, gripping the sword he had only just sheathed.

"There is no running from this. You are bound to it until your dying day."

He reached up to the bandage over his right eye, lifting it for her to see the bloody ruin of his face.

"I beg to differ."

All it did was bring a smile to her face. Not quite the reaction he'd been looking for.

"Do you think it is so easy? The change in you is more profound than a red jewel. You are bound by more than that."

"I've rid myself of it, Nylia. I am a slave no longer. And I can free you too. Together we can both tear that accursed thing out of your head."

A flicker in her human eye. The shadow of doubt perhaps? For the briefest moment it was as though she was back, fighting it, resisting with all her will.

"You have to run, Conall," she spat, as though the words were a knife in her side. "As far and as fast as you can. There is no way to know how long I can keep the voice quiet."

She gasped her last words, stumbling from his path.

Conall stepped out into the light, pausing for a moment, watching as she fought a battle in her mind. If he left her now, it would haunt him forever. If he stayed, he knew it was only a matter of time before the demon in her head regained control. Then they would both be lost.

Without a second look, he raced off to the east.

ROSOMON

T his had to be the most grotesque mockery of a throne room
she'd ever had the displeasure of sitting in. Jarlath had clearly
modelled it on the emperor's chamber in the Anvil, though where
Archwind Palace was a soaring construction of marble and iron,
here was only oak and pine.

A vast wooden table sat in prominence at the centre of the circular chamber, surrounded by a dozen chairs of polished alder. At
the head, a gaudy throne of dark oak sat awaiting the master of the
house to take his place. It was clear from all this that Jarlath considered himself emperor of the whole Alderwood.

Rosomon sat as far from that oak monstrosity as she could get.
Oleksig not too far to her right. On her order, their scouts had
searched every last inch of the city, sweeping through each mitred
nook and dovetailed cranny, but finding no sign of enemy agents. If
Jarlath had allowed assassins from the Ministry within the boundary of Oakhelm, they were nowhere to be seen, not that it put
her imperator at his ease. Even now Ianto was somewhere in the
city, diligently searching for anything he or his men might have
missed.

Still, Rosomon did not sit comfortably in her chair as she waited
on the Guildmaster of Radwinter. There had been no sign of him

since they'd arrived, and as they continued to wait it only made her
suspicions grow.

"This is unconscionable," grumbled Oleksig, chewing on the stem
of his pipe and puffing pungent smoke into the air. "That *we* should
be kept waiting like common serfs."

Rosomon glanced over one shoulder, seeing the imposing figure
of Borys standing close to his father. His sword was unbuckled, the
sheathed blade held in front of him, easier to draw if needed, Rosomon guessed. Likewise, Kassian Maine stood close to her, appoint-
ing himself her protector should trouble arise.

"Jarlath has always considered himself a man apart," she replied.
"Above the rules that govern the rest of us."

"Not too far above, I hope. For our sakes as well as his."

Rosomon reclined in her seat, trying to appear relaxed even if she
didn't feel it. "I am sure there is some reason for his absence. Perhaps
an innocent one. If Jarlath wanted to betray us, surely he would have
done it already. We would have faced resistance on the long road
from Wyke, rather than been welcomed into the city."

Oleksig looked unconvinced, and she couldn't blame him.

The main doors opened, swinging on well-oiled hinges. The
carving of the Radwinter tree sigil that was wrought upon it split in
two as half a dozen men marched through carrying the axes of Guild
lumberjacks. As they took up places around the wooden throne,
Thalleus Brisco strode in behind them. His eyes took in the room,
and the four people waiting inside. If he was concerned at facing
two fellow swordwrights, his expression didn't show it, though his
eyes lingered for a moment on Kassian Maine. Was there something
between them, this former master and pupil?

Before she could wonder further, the stomping gait of Jarlath
Radwinter entered through the doors. There was a wide smile visible through his bushy beard, clearly the gravity of their current situation lost on him. Had she not known Jarlath of old it might have
further deepened her suspicions, but Rosomon was well aware of
the man's flippant temperament.

"Greetings, all," he said. "Welcome to my humble meeting hall,
and apologies for the tardiness."

Rosomon rose to her feet, but before she could begin to question him, Mincloth entered behind her husband. The woman was small and rosy cheeked, looking more fishwife than mistress of a Guild. She rushed forward, taking hold of Rosomon in a tight embrace, though her head only came up to Rosomon's chest.

"Oh, I am so sorry, my dear. For all you have lost."

Though taken aback by Mincloth's informality, Rosomon patted the woman on the back. "And I appreciate your sympathy."

Mincloth released her and backed away to take her place at Jarlath's side. Rosomon noted her kindly expression was quick to fade.

"Please sit, my friends," Jarlath said, gesturing to their chairs before taking a seat on his own huge throne. He turned toward the door, and Rosomon recognised another newcomer. "Becuma, see our guests are given refreshment."

The woman did as she was bid, but Rosomon could tell from her frown she was none too happy about being ordered to perform a servant's work.

"Shall we proceed?" Rosomon said, keen to move on to the business at hand.

"Of course, of course. There is much to discuss. This has been a very trying time for all of us, Lady Rosomon."

More trying for some than others, it seemed. Indeed, Jarlath appeared wholly unaffected by the recent tumult—his people unmolested and his city still in one piece.

"Before we begin," Rosomon said, trying to keep an even tone. "Where have you been? We would have expected you to greet us at the city gate, and yet we were kept waiting."

"Ah yes, my apologies. Despite the recent upheaval, there is still much to do throughout the Alderwood, Lady Rosomon. Our industry does not stop. It cannot be allowed to. I am still required to perform my Guild duties."

Oleksig leaned forward over the table. "So much so you cannot even meet with your fellow Guildmasters? And especially at a time like this? We are at war. After what happened at Wyke we are no longer sure who can be trusted, Jarlath, and you choose now to see to Guild business?"

Jarlath began to bristle at the insinuation, but managed to curb his anger. "Again, I can only offer my apology."

Oleksig shrugged. "Never mind. We are all here now. And there is much to discuss. The most pressing matter is what we intend to do when the Armigers and the Archlegate's Drakes fall on this place like wolves on a lamb. We need to know the numbers in your army, a full inventory of troops, arms, armour."

Jarlath glanced briefly toward Becuma, who moved uncomfortably from one foot to the other as she poured wine from a decanter. It was obvious he was not about to deliver good news.

"I understand your eagerness to know such things," he replied, fiddling with his cuff. Rosomon could see it was threadbare—almost as though he had picked at the lining for many days. "But what I have to report is more important than numbers. Much has happened since we all last met. Many things for me to ponder."

Rosomon braced herself for the worst. This was what she had feared, but surely if Jarlath meant to betray them, he would have done so.

"Ponder?" Oleksig spat, slamming his pipe down on the table and spilling ash on its polished veneer. "What could you possibly have to ponder, man? Our emperor has been murdered. Our nation burns, and all you can do is ruminate over the bloody ruins?"

Jarlath clenched a fist, ignoring his worn sleeve. "I have been forced into an awkward position. You must understand, I am not happy with this. It's not what I wanted, but ultimately I must do what is best for the nation. And for my Guild. I understand what you have both lost but..."

Rosomon realised her nails were digging deep into her palms. She briefly glanced to Kassian on her left, but he seemed unmoved by what Jarlath was suggesting—that he had done what they all suspected and made some kind of deal with Sanctan. Chosen the Ministry over his fellow Guildmasters. Somehow, Kassian's lack of emotion made her even more uneasy. Had she walked straight into another trap?

"What position are you talking about, Jarlath?" Oleksig spat. "If you've betrayed us, I swear—"

Jarlath shook his head. "It is not a betrayal. It is…the most practical course. And I am a practical man, you both know that."

He raised a hand, the one with the ragged cuff, and at his signal Becuma moved to the door. She opened it with some reverence, almost ceremonially, before taking a step back.

"I would ask that you not overreact," Jarlath said. "We are all just here to talk, and must view this situation with pragmatism."

Rosomon held her breath as she watched Lorens walk in with that little smile. On seeing he had the audacity to be wearing Archwind red, she almost threw all pragmatism to the wind. Two Armiger troopers walked in behind him, black Corvus uniforms tight to their frames, splintbows lowered, but at any moment they could raise them and pepper the room with bolts.

She reclined in her chair, desperate to stay in control. Here was the boy who had betrayed his own father, and as a result the empire of Torwyn hung in tatters. Her son was dead, her lover dead, and all because this boy had been seduced by the power of a madman.

Lorens took his seat as though he had not reduced their lives to embers. "It's good to see you all." His eyes fell on Rosomon. "You most of all, Aunt. I hope you're well."

She could not answer him, gritting her teeth lest she scream. Instead she glared at Jarlath, who eventually managed to meet her gaze.

"I knew you would do this," she said, desperate to keep a calm tone to her voice. "I should never have come here hoping for friendship. Hoping that you would remember your loyalties. You have betrayed everything we stand for, Radwinter. I should have burned this place to the ground before thinking I could ever trust you."

Jarlath reclined in his pathetic throne, as though he suddenly realised the deck was stacked in his favour. "Please don't dramatize, Rosomon. And spare me your threats. I was left with no choice, and so I made the most expedient decision. You should both have done the same; it would have saved a lot of lives. Soon the Ministry will have complete control of the Armigers. Control them and you control the country, no matter how powerful your Guild."

Lorens leaned forward, and Rosomon found herself glaring at him, resisting the urge to claw out his eyes. "Aunt Rosomon, the

Forge has already fallen. The Rock along with it, and we all know what happened to Wyke."

"It is time we accepted the reality of things," Jarlath said, as Becuma placed a glass of wine in front of him. "Appeasement is the only way. Sanctan is a reasonable man. He will not allow Torwyn to collapse into anarchy. He needs us. He needs our organisations and will allow us to operate much the same as before. What matter who sits on a throne, or whether we call ourselves an empire?"

She felt sick to her stomach, but managed to swallow down the bile fast rising in her throat. "You are both fools to think Sanctan will allow you your freedoms. He will not stop until the whole country is crushed beneath his heel. Eventually he will have no more need for either of you."

"Fools, Aunt Rosomon?" Lorens looked genuinely offended. "On the contrary. Jarlath has shown more wisdom and foresight than any of his fellow Guildmasters. He is wise enough to know the Archlegate cannot be stopped. Sanctan is a man of purpose, driven by divine right. But you should know the truth of it—there are two Armiger Battalions waiting just to the west, ready to fall on Oakhelm and crush any resistance. They have the support of a contingent of Drakes, along with the Hallowhills. What do you have, Aunt Rosomon? A few Talon scouts, miners and the citizens of Wyke at your beck and call?"

She stood up, her chair clattering to the floor behind her. Rosomon had tried to stay calm, to suffer this with dignity, but now her fury would not stay chained.

"Your father was murdered by these people. Your Guild crushed. Everything you were born to inherit has been reduced to cinders, and you sit here like a compliant little serf at the behest of a tyrant."

"No!" replied Lorens, more forcefully than she expected. "I have gained much more than mere titles and privilege, Aunt. I have come into the sight of the Great Wyrms. I have been blessed. I have been saved." He took a breath to calm himself. "The only reason that our army has not fallen on the city already is because I ordered them to wait. We are family, Aunt Rosomon. I am offering you a chance to end this peacefully. I'm offering you a chance to live."

She glared back at that stupid boy, swallowing down her bile. "Is that a chance you offered your father?"

Lorens slammed a hand on the table. "That was not meant to—"

"Enough!" Jarlath rose from his throne, hands raised in a placatory gesture. "Please, let us stay calm. Now is not the time for hot heads. None of this can be solved with further violence. We have already lost too much. There is no sense in further defiance. Let's not draw this out any longer than necessary. Rosomon, you have to understand, it's over."

She fixed him with as firm a look as she could muster. Rosomon had to stay calm, had to wrest control of her anger.

"No. You're wrong, Jarlath. It is far from over."

The two Corvus troopers levelled their splintbows, one of them right at her chest. Rosomon raised her chin, almost daring him to shoot.

Thalleus Brisco drew his blade with a long ominous hiss of steel. It did more to fill her with dread than the thought of being shot down by splintbolts.

"Rosomon," Jarlath said, his tone measured. "It would be a shame for you to die here. Please, see some sense."

At a word she could have ordered Borys and Kassian to draw their swords, but what then? She doubted even swordwrights would be able to make it across the room before they were shot down. Even if they survived, they would have to face the skills of Thalleus and half a dozen axemen.

For his part, Oleksig sat back, watching the proceedings with interest as he puffed on his pipe, like this was all some play and he the only spectator.

Kassian stepped forward, to stand alongside Rosomon. He made no move to draw his blade as he held Thalleus in his gaze. The two troopers tightened their grips on those splintbows, but just as Rosomon thought surrender might be their only option, she saw Kassian offer the briefest of nods from the corner of her eye.

Thalleus moved with blinding speed. His blade swept left then right, a blur of steel, a spray of red. Both the Corvus troopers fell before they could think to fire their weapons.

Borys reacted like a sprinter off the mark, tearing his sword free of its scabbard. The first axeman barely had time to heft his weapon before he was beheaded. A second at least managed to raise his, before his chest was run through. The third bellowed, charging forward, but Borys ducked his sweeping blow, then gutted him.

Seeing their fellows bested so brutally, the rest of the axemen fled the throne room, one dropping his weapon in his haste.

Mincloth screamed a howl of terror, and Rosomon saw that her face had been spattered with blood. Becuma stumbled back, desperate to escape the butchery, but only managing to slip on the slick floor. Rosomon almost laughed as Jarlath's aide squirmed through the blood to crawl beneath the nearest table.

Lorens had already shot to his feet, his chair bouncing on the wooden floor behind him. He took a step back, looking for somewhere to run, but there was no way to escape without going through Borys.

Thalleus grasped hold of Jarlath's collar, driving his master to his knees. The Guildmaster of Radwinter had a desperate look to his eyes, but he stopped short of begging for mercy.

With one hand still holding Jarlath, and the other on his sword of office, Thalleus looked up at Kassian, awaiting the order.

Kassian turned to Rosomon. "Your instruction, my lady?"

It had all happened so fast she could barely think. The tables had turned, that much was obvious. Jarlath gazed up at her as he floundered on his knees. Mincloth and Lorens likewise gaped at her. Oleksig had not even moved from his chair, though now he smiled as though pleased with the grim spectacle. It seemed she now held the high cards.

"Please," Jarlath said. "Forgive me, Rosomon. I did what I thought was best...for all of us."

But she knew it was one more lie. Jarlath had done what was best for *him*. And Rosomon Hawkspur was all out of forgiveness. She looked at Thalleus, who gazed back with emotionless eyes.

"Do it," she ordered.

Jarlath had no time to plead, no time to shout for someone to save him. Thalleus swept the head from his shoulders in one swift motion, as Mincloth screamed once again. Her howl echoed though the throne room of Oakhelm, a bitter and grievous cry of anguish. It should have cut Rosomon to the quick. Instead, she felt nothing.

Slowly she walked across the room, ignoring the corpses, and the blood fast pooling on the polished wood floor. Lorens watched her with every step, his jaw tightening. Was he resisting the urge to beg? Or was he really this brave? He did not look ready to die, either way.

"You will go back to your master, Lorens. And you will tell him what you've seen here. There will be no surrender. The Guilds do not kneel."

He nodded, unable to speak, before taking an uncertain step back. "Thank you, Aunt Rosomon."

"And, Lorens. If you ever stand against me again, you will regret it."

All he offered was a nod, before turning on his heel and marching from the chamber with as much dignity as he could muster.

It was silent in the room, but for the quiet sobs of Mincloth as she knelt over the body of her headless husband. Thalleus loomed over them both, wiping the blade of his sword clean with a rag. It seemed that Rosomon's suspicions regarding Kassian had been unfounded. There was one man she could trust at least.

She made for the door, with her new swordwright at her shoulder, but paused at Mincloth's side. The woman looked up, anger and terror and grief in her tear-streaked eyes. Rosomon stared back, remembering the woman's insincere words.

"I am so sorry, my dear. For all you have lost."

Then she left without looking back.

FULREN

He wobbled precariously, legs trembling. Or at least what legs he had left. Fulren was strapped into leather braces, which were in turn attached to pneumatic stanchions compensating for his lack of balance. Ashe told him they would stabilise him, but it felt as though he might topple over at any moment. And he had...more than once.

The contraption was belted to his waist, with a sleeve buckled up to the nipples. He leaned on a wooden crutch, gripped tight in his one remaining hand, which was all he had to stop him planting face-first into the ground. With his left arm gone he felt out of kilter. And he couldn't see a thing. This whole rig was like some torture device, but he had to get used to it. Had to triumph over it.

"Come on," Verlyn said from across the yard. "This time, Fulren. You can do it."

He tried to focus on her voice. She wasn't far away, but it felt like he had an ocean to cross. As he shifted his weight, the pneumatics built into the left stanchion responded with a huff of air, articulating in response to his movement. The metal foot slid forward a few inches across the ground. It immediately put him off balance, and in a panic, he shifted his weight again so the right foot moved. He teetered, grasping the crutch tighter, finding his centre again. This time he didn't fall.

One step. One single step. A small achievement, but an achievement nonetheless.

"That's it," Verlyn said. "You're bloody walking."

Buoyed by her encouragement, he shifted his weight again. This time the metal foot on his left moved a little further, a little easier. Fulren gritted his teeth, swaying for a moment before shifting his balance to the right, the other leg moving in response.

He laughed, his heart filling with hope as he carried on the momentum, weight shifting back on the left leg. His foot responded, but this time the steel tip of his toe clipped a rut in the ground. All of a sudden his equilibrium was shattered and he leaned heavily on the wooden rod. It wasn't enough to stop him falling.

The ground hit him all too quickly, and not for the first time.

"Shit, shit, balls," he spat at the dirt, punctuating his words with a punch of his right fist. It hurt, but not as much as the humiliation.

He pushed down on the ground, desperate to right himself, desperate to stand, but it was an impossible task. Strapped into that steel rig, lost in the dark, he may as well have been chained in a cell.

"It's okay," said Verlyn, kneeling beside him and trying to turn him over like a floundering fish. "Don't feel bad. You're getting better at this."

"Just get the chair," he snapped.

Before he could apologise for his ingratitude, she left his side. As he lay there he desperately tried to quell the rage, quell the tears. Fulren seethed in his pain and frustration, unable to stop it eating him from the inside.

A whisper in the distance...

The words were indistinct, but they breathed a promise from across aeons. Tempting him. Drawing him into their web with an offer he could barely resist.

Give up, Fulren Hawkspur. Let me in and I can make all this go away.

The necroglyph tingled at his neck.

I can make this right again. You will need no stick to walk with. There will be no more shame. You will run like a wolf on the plains.

It was a hushed invitation...a seduction. And for the first time, as he lay there in the dirt, Fulren realised that offer might be all he had left.

The dull ache in the stumps of his legs turned to an itch. He could feel where his flesh pressed against the metal of the pneumatics, and he sensed a sudden roiling beneath the scarred skin, as though the severed sinews yearned to regenerate and entwine with the artifice. He could become as one with this machine—a cauterised symbiote of flesh and steel. All he had to do was believe, to think those new limbs into existence, and it would make them real.

"Here we go."

Verlyn's voice dragged him from the fugue of temptation.

She'd brought the contraption Ashe had constructed from a kitchen chair and the wheels of an old handcart. Fulren tried to shake the memory of that whisper from his head, as Verlyn unbuckled the leather straps that bound him to his metal legs. As she heaved him in the chair he said, "Thank you."

"Think nothing of it," she replied, patting him gently on the shoulder.

Verlyn's attitude had softened over the past few days, but he could tell she was still wary of him. And with good reason. Fulren was fighting a battle in his mind with an entity he had little understanding of, and he suspected that Verlyn could sense it.

Across the yard he heard Ashe come out of her workshop. "You're doing well, Fulren. Don't be too disheartened."

He nodded his thanks at her encouragement, but her words did little to make him feel better. How long would he be able to resist the lure of that voice? And even if he could, what would become of him now he was only half a man?

"Why don't you come inside," Ashe said. "I might have something to make you feel a bit better."

Verlyn wheeled him across the yard. He was helpless to protest as he rumbled over the uneven earth and into the workshop. But what else could he do? These women had shown him nothing but kindness, it was only right he should humour them, no matter how pointless it felt.

Inside the workshop he could see the glow of pyrestones, bright in his field of vision. In the light they cast were the outlines of various devices, though he couldn't tell what the contraptions were for.

"There's something I wanted to try," Ashe said.

He heard her rifling on her workbench before she moved closer. There was a telltale hiss of hydraulics to his left. Then, with Verlyn's help, Ashe strapped something to his shoulder, and buckled it to the stump of his arm, much like the pneumatic stanchions she had rigged for him to walk.

More experiments. As grateful as he was, he would have told her it was useless, that he would be a worthless lump of meat for the rest of his life, but again he humoured her. Whatever she had strapped to him was heavy on his shoulder, but as Ashe adjusted various straps and braces, it felt more and more comfortable.

"Now," she said. "Can you feel anything?"

"Yes," he replied. "Instead of nothing at the end of my elbow, now it feels like I'm carrying a boulder."

He heard her tinker with something. Reaching across with his right arm he could feel a metal device attached to him—a mechanical arm of sorts.

"What about now?" asked Ashe.

Fulren moved his shoulder and upper arm. In response, he heard the artifice in the stanchion respond. Reaching across with his right hand, he could feel the metal arm articulate, bending in response to slight movements of his muscles.

"That's..." He didn't know what to say.

"That's a good start, is what that is," Ashe said. He could sense the delight in her voice.

"What's this?" Verlyn asked from across the workshop.

Through the inky dark, Fulren could make out her silhouette. She was holding a dome of bevelled metal in her hand, and inside shone the distinctive glitter of pyrestones.

"That," Ashe replied, "is not quite ready yet."

"But what is it?"

Fulren heard Ashe sigh. "All right, since you asked. I rigged it from parts of a communication array in one of the stormhulk wrecks we found. I didn't know whether to try it out yet."

"Try it out for what?"

"Well, it might help Fulren to see."

Just the thought of it made him stifle a gasp. He might never walk, never use his left hand again, but being able to see like before would be a greater gift than he could ever have hoped for.

"Let's try it out then," Verlyn said. "How does it work?"

"That's the thing," Ashe said. "It needs the powers of a webwainer to activate it. Fulren has no link to the web, so I'll need you to help channel the artifice in the helmet. What do you think? Want to give it a try?"

It took him a moment to realise Ashe was talking to him and not Verlyn. "I've got nothing to lose, I guess. What's the worst that could happen?"

Verlyn handed the glowing dome of metal to Ashe, who then carefully placed it over his head. It fit snugly, coming down to touch the tip of his nose. With that helmet on, the ambient light from the workshop's pyrestones suddenly dimmed. All he could see were the various stones within the helmet shining brightly in his field of vision. They melded together to form a kaleidoscope of colour that danced and twisted as he moved his head.

"So?" Verlyn asked. "What do you see?"

"Absolutely nothing," he replied. Not strictly true, but he wasn't comfortable trying to explain that the necroglyph allowed him to see shades of light.

"Verlyn," Ashe said. "Try and activate the artifice. I've used the optical relay from the stormhulk, so you should be able to manipulate the output."

Fulren braced himself, unsure of what to expect. He had seen his sister use her gift more times than he could remember, and there was nothing remarkable to it. She had told him it was like touching raw energy with your fingertips, but he had never really understood the experience until he had been given his necroglyph.

The kaleidoscope of colour suddenly shifted. As he watched, the muddle of contrasting light began to coalesce. He could see the hard surfaces of the workshop become clearer. Where before there had only been monochrome silhouettes, now he was dazzled by the spectrum morphing before his eyes.

"Anything changing?" Ashe said.

"Yes," he replied, hearing the excitement in his own voice. "It's working."

Before he could try to focus further, he heard a dread sound in the distance. A whisper that had become so familiar. As it spoke, the faces of the two women grew clearer, both of them staring at him—Ashe with gleeful expectation, Verlyn with rapt concentration.

The rest of the workshop came into razor-sharp focus. Tables covered in an array of clutter, tools hanging on the walls, lights dangling from rafters on threads of wire.

He looked down, seeing the sorry stumps of his legs. The missing arm still strapped to that hydraulic device, the claw at its end lying open as though he were begging for alms.

Let me in.

The voice echoed in his head, deafening like a knell. He gritted his teeth against the cacophony, seeing Verlyn suddenly stagger back, covering her ears.

The room was doused in black once more, the light from the pyrestones winking out to nothing. Fulren heard muffled voices, like someone talking in a different room. It took him a moment to realise it was Ashe and Verlyn, but as he listened their conversation was gradually consumed by that far-off whisper. Though it did not speak in any coherent language, he knew what it wanted...his permission.

All he had to do was let it in. Just accept the gift it offered and all his suffering would be over.

The helmet was wrenched from his head, and he heard Ashe's voice all too clearly.

"Are you all right?"

He shook his head, trying to clear it. "Yes...I think so."

"What in the Lairs was that voice?" Verlyn asked. He could hear anger, but also fear.

"I...I don't know," he gasped.

But he did know. It was something he had awakened in far-off Nyrakkis. Something that offered him sweet release from the nightmare he was trapped in. Fulren knew that the price he might have to pay for that was far worse than what he suffered now.

"I could hear it," Verlyn said. "Calling to us...calling to *you*."

Fulren had no idea how to explain it. He had been offered shelter by these women and now it seemed he had put one of them in danger.

"It's all right," Ashe said, placing a hand on his shoulder. "It was probably just a reaction to the artifice. When a webwainer tries to channel through someone who doesn't have the gift there's bound to be weird side effects."

"Yeah, maybe," Verlyn replied. "I think I need some air."

Fulren heard her leave as Ashe squeezed his shoulder once more. "I'd best go and see if she's okay. You be all right for a second?"

He nodded, sitting quietly as she left him alone in the workshop. When they were gone, he could hear their muffled voices—Verlyn anxious and fearful, as Ashe tried to soothe her with calm words.

What had he done? Brought a curse all the way from Nyrakkis, right to the doorstep of the very people who had saved him from certain death? If he could have fled this place, he would have, but trapped in this chair, blind, useless, he knew he could never escape. Not from them, and not from that fell voice in his head. He could only hope that Ashe was able to work her artificer magic and get him walking again. At least that way he'd be able to run away. It might be the only way he could keep them safe. It was the least he owed them.

CONALL

Walk far enough toward the east and he'd make it home. That was all he thought—his one mantra as he trod the endless waste using his sword as a crutch. He relied on the sun to guide him during the day, the stars at night, though for all he knew out here in the Drift those stars were just toying with him. Laughing as they made him wander in ever wider circles.

Birds cawed far above. He looked up to see them wheeling. Vultures? They certainly weren't like any birds he'd ever seen before. Best not to think on what they were, or what they were after. They'd have to wait if they wanted to pick over his bones, though not that long from how thirsty he felt.

The pain in his eye had reduced to a dull ache and the bleeding had stopped. Dry blood was caked to his face, the patch over his eye crusted to his skin. He tried not to think on the prospect of infection, of fever, of dying in a hole in the Drift, shivering out his last breath.

Conall stopped, leaning on his sword and wiping his greasy brow. The sun was at its zenith, casting a haze on the far horizon, but squinting through his one eye he was sure he could see something. A perimeter wall? A town? Civilisation at last?

Spurred on by the prospect of being saved, he quickened his pace, churning up the distance, sword clanking in the dirt with every laboured step. The closer he got, the more he realised his hopes of salvation were dashed. The distant wall was crumbled to nothing in places with huge breaches all along its length. Through those holes he could see ruined dwellings, half reclaimed by the barren land.

When he eventually reached it, he crept through one of those gaps, seeing the remains of the city sloping down into a valley. The buildings had been arranged in neat concentric circles, and by the looks of it this had been a burgeoning community once—temples, market squares, statues long since blasted smooth by sandstorms. Perhaps it was a mercy this place was abandoned. So far the only people he'd met in the Drift had tried to kill him.

He staggered down the street, surrounded by ancient buildings on both sides. What once had been a teeming metropolis was now nothing but a graveyard of rotting stone and dust. At least there were no grim remains, no bones clawing at the sky, or skulls grinning in welcome.

His eye was suddenly caught by a stone structure squatting in the centre of the road ahead. Could it be . . . a well? He almost dropped the sword in his haste to reach it, stumbling to his knees at its edge. Most of the stones around the circular rim were crumbled to nothing, and as he peered over the edge he could see only darkness below. Beside the well was a metal bucket on the end of a chain. It seemed odd that amid this city consumed by the Drift was an item that had not corroded to rust. Perhaps someone did live here after all. Or something.

Who cared? His thirst was too torturous for him to think on it further and he grabbed the bucket, frantically lowering it on its chain. Eventually it slackened as the bucket hit something below— the unmistakable sound of sloshing water. Eagerly he hauled the bucket back up, relieved and excited when he realised it was much heavier than it had been on the way down. As he pulled it from the well, Conall's eagerness waned.

It held water all right, but it was brown and sludgy, as though someone stricken with disease had voided their bowels into it. It didn't smell too rank though, and what choice did he have anyway? Risk disease, or die of thirst.

With some difficulty he lifted the bucket to his lips, letting the brown water run into his mouth. He could taste grit and sand, but still he swallowed it down, gulping till he could gulp no more. When he'd drunk his fill, he rested his back against the well, gasping in relief.

At least it wasn't thirst that would get him. Not yet anyway. Looking back along the path he had taken, he began to wonder if he was still being followed. It would take a fanatical hunter to track him across that desolate waste. And for what? He wasn't worth anything to Senmonthis anymore, now he had rid himself of her demonic influence.

The sun was dropping toward the horizon. He would have to find shelter soon, and days out in the Drift, sleeping in gullies and hunkering next to rocks, had given him an appreciation for a roof over his head.

Using his sword for leverage, he staggered to his feet and limped deeper into the city. As he passed ruin after ruin he began to wonder how much farther he'd have to travel before he saw the forts of Torwyn looming on the horizon. Imprisoned in Arcturius, that prospect had been nothing more than a distant dream. Now it seemed his fortunes had changed, but he was not home yet.

The path opened out into a circular plaza, a weathered plinth standing at its centre that might once have been the base of some towering statue. Dilapidated streets led off from it in all directions, but on the western side was a building taller than the rest. It looked alien among the ruins—its walls and roof intact, red stonework still visible, where all the others were crumbling and grey. It looked to have been some kind of tower, perhaps a temple, or the manse of an ancient magnate. The fact that it still stood where the surrounding buildings had been reduced to dust made Conall think perhaps it had been the home of some long-dead mage. Whatever it had been, it was his best prospect for shelter.

The door had rotted off its hinges and he entered through a wide archway. Light lanced down through the structure, and narrow gaps in the ceiling offered a view to the tower's upper level. Conall spied a bell at the summit and could only wonder how long it had been hanging silent out here in the waste. And what had it been used to summon a thousand years before?

The thought made him shiver, but he forced himself to dismiss it—all that mattered now was survival. He climbed the stone stairs to an upper floor, a huge window offering a view out over the city. Detritus was slung in every corner of the chamber, covered in a film of dust, and his eye fell on the remains of a skeleton, peering from the garbage. Had this been the building's previous owner? If so, he doubted they'd mind if he took shelter for just the one night.

As the sun dipped below the craggy rooftops, he leaned his sword against the wall and searched among the junk for kindling. There were enough rags and desiccated wood to start a fire, and after a significant degree of effort he managed to get a flame. By now darkness had fallen over the city, casting a vast shadow across the ruins. Conall hunkered in the dark, wondering what he might do when he got home. Whether there would even be a home to get to. Had the Guilds already managed to beat down the Ministry's uprising, or had they failed completely?

Even as he thought on that grim prospect, he found his eye drawn every now and again to the sword leaning against the wall. The cloth binding still hid that loathsome white gem set at the crossguard, and he could only thank the Wyrms that he had rid himself of the red pyrestone that was twinned with it. It had been agony at the time, but worth it, just for that croak of surprise from Orsokon before he took the bastard's head. The memory of that brought a smile to his face.

"I won," he whispered at nobody.

And yet you will still need me.

Conall jumped to his feet, staggering through the detritus, away from the demon blade, till he was backed up against the window frame. Raw, cold terror racked his body, the hairs standing on his neck, breath caught in his throat.

"No," he gasped.

Don't be afraid of me, Conall Hawkspur. There is danger close by. You have much more villainous foes to think on.

"Shut up," he snarled, trying to mask his fear with anger. "Just shut the fuck up and get out of my head."

He stared at that sword, the white gem still hidden, but he knew it could see him, hear him, read every thought. But how? He had torn the pyrestone from his head, the conduit for its power, surely he had exorcised whatever spirit tormented him.

You must flee. Forget your fear of me, and run.

"What are you talking about?" he snapped, unwilling to believe the deceitful fiend that plagued him like a waking nightmare.

You should not have built the fire. It will only attract them.

He glared at the winnowing flame in the centre of the room that still cast flickering shadows onto the walls. "What do mean? Attract who?"

The window, Conall. Look out of the window.

Slowly he turned, glaring into the darkness, feeling the night air blow gently against his cheeks. The moon shone bright through scant clouds, and he could see the distant rooftops framed in silver. At first, all he could make out were those grim buildings, the crumbling legacy of a long-dead age. Then, in the shadows at their base, he spied movement. Focusing, he could make out a silhouette just a few streets away, moving closer, clinging to the darkness. Then there, in an adjacent street, another outline, darting from ruined house to ruined house, creeping through the night toward his tower.

"Shit," he breathed.

With growing urgency he moved to the skeleton still buried among the clutter. Grasping its arm he twisted, mumbling an apology to the long-dead corpse as he tore the bone free. After ripping a ragged strip from his shirt, he quickly bound the end of the bone before plunging it in the fire. It would burn, but not for long.

Conall made for the stairs, before stopping in his tracks. He turned, seeing the sword still leaning against the wall. He should have run, left that accursed thing where it was, but if those things approaching through the shadows meant him harm, how would he fight them? Better to face them with a smile and sword than just a smile.

He rushed across the room, grabbing the blade before stumbling down the stairs. Out in the open he caught sight of half a dozen figures wreathed in shadow, peering at him from the edge of a nearby street.

This was most definitely no time for introductions, and he rushed northward, away from whatever was so desperate to make his acquaintance. He hadn't got far before he noticed more of the things shambling from the black, determined to block his escape. He raised the torch, already sputtering out in his hand, casting light on the nearest of the figures. It immediately scurried away from the flame, but not before he saw its pallid flesh, spindly arms tipped with jagged nails, mournful eyes like a damned spirit locked in its rotting shell.

Give me control.

"No," Conall snarled, looking around for a route to escape, but all he could see were yet more of the creatures emerging from the dark, blocking off the streets.

I can save you.

"Fuck off."

He turned to the east, seeing a long road illuminated by moonlight. At the end of it a wide stairway rose up to a crumbling monolith. It was his only clear path.

Before he could run for it, one of the dead things darted at him from the dark, face a dead-eyed mask, yellowing fangs bared. He thrust the flame at that hideous face and it recoiled, murmuring and spitting like an old man in his cups. Though it looked like he could keep the things at bay with fire, the makeshift torch wasn't going to last all night.

You do not have much time. The fire will die, and these fiends will feast on your flesh until the sun rises to bleach your bones.

Conall tried not to listen, already running toward that vast stairway in the distance. He loped along as fast as his tired legs would carry him, waving his flame at anything that moved. Before the stairs was what remained of a bridge spanning a dried-out riverbed. As he stumbled across it, more clawed hands grasped its edge, pulling themselves up to join the hunt. Once across, he reached the bottom of the stair, daring a glance over his shoulder, seeing the horde of ungainly bodies following in his wake.

He hadn't taken three steps before one of them came at him from the dark. This time when he raised the flame the creature hissed, swatting the torch from his hand and sending it spinning off into the night. Conall felt claws rake at his arm, tearing his sleeve, opening his flesh. A snarl of pain issued from his throat, and he managed to clamber up a few more stairs away from the thing.

Let me in, Conall. Or you will surely die.

A wave of ghouls had reached the stairs now, clambering over one another in their eagerness to reach him. Conall wrenched the sword from its scabbard, hefting it in both hands.

"Stay back," he called, more a plea than an order. "I don't want to hurt anyone."

Either they didn't hear him or didn't care. The sound of their hungry murmuring grew louder, surrounding him as they clawed their way closer. He could see hollow eyes, recognising their hunger, and knew they would not stop until they had devoured their quarry.

"All right," Conall whispered. "Do what you have to."

The sword bucked in his hand, almost jolting itself from his grip. His arm moved of its own accord, wrist twisting. Instinct took over as he adopted a defensive stance, but not one he had ever been taught by his Guild's swordwright.

As soon as the first ghastly face loomed at him from the dark, the sword responded, hacking its head from bony shoulders. There was no arterial spray as the head bounced down the stairs, the body falling limp like an empty sack of sticks.

The sword swept left and right, blade slicing through shrivelled flesh, arms and heads sent flying into the night. Conall could only stare in horror, his body no longer his own, as the things were hacked asunder and reduced to crumbling bone, as though they'd been dead as long as their city.

He retreated up the stairs, all the while that demon sword cut a swathe around him. The creatures seemed unaffected by the death of their brood, but then he supposed they were already dead—what would they have to fear?

The ground flattened out as Conall reached the top. He was at the summit of a huge structure, walls rising high behind him, but through a narrow corridor he could see the structure fell away into the night.

Below, the creatures hesitated, unable or unwilling to follow beyond the summit of the ancient temple.

You have to run now.

Conall stared back into the dark, into the wastes beyond. Gritting his teeth, he ran through the gap in the wall before leaping into the night.

The ground hit him almost instantly, but he had no time to think, no time to rest, and he was on his feet, ignoring the bruises, the gash in his arm. He risked a glance back to see if he was being pursued, but nothing dared follow him beyond the boundary of the city.

Then he turned and ran, letting the night take him.

TYRETA

Despite the liberal attentions of Crenn's wrench, the landship limped north at a slug's pace, engine protesting with every laboured mile. All the while, Tyreta tried to stay focused on the task at hand, but she couldn't stop thinking about what had happened at Windstone.

How had the Ministry learned of her mission? Was it a spy in her mother's camp? However they had found out, the Ministry obviously felt this important enough to send webwainers and Drakes to stop her. She could only hope they were long gone, and whatever waited in Castleteig was an easier obstacle to overcome.

As the landship crested a bridge across the Serpentspin, those hopes were quickly dashed.

Above the sound of the whining engine, she heard the dull boom of artillery to the north. Gripping the bulwark of the engine's observation platform she spied the city in the distance—smoke rising from its broken towers in long grey plumes, casting a dark haze across the horizon.

Sted was by her side, squinting through the stiff breeze. "That doesn't look good."

"No, it doesn't," Tyreta replied. "But we don't have any choice but to enter the city. We need to reach the northern terminal and find a landship that'll take us as close to my mother as possible. If we have to travel on foot, it'll take weeks to reach her, and we might already be too late."

Sted shrugged. "All right. I'm sure you know what you're doing."

She didn't sound too sure at all. A voice behind them bore even less confidence.

"You're mad if you think I'm walking into that. I never agreed to go into battle."

Tyreta turned to see Nicosse staring ahead fearfully. He was pulling on his beard with one liver-spotted hand as though it was trying to strangle him.

"It's our only option," Tyreta replied.

Nicosse shook his head. "I left all this behind years ago. I shouldn't even be here. If I'd known what was waiting, I'd never have agreed to come. This war has nothing to do with me."

Tyreta took a step toward him, doing her best to quell her frustration. "This has everything to do with you, Nicosse. You have to pick a side. If the Hallowhills aren't stopped, Torwyn is doomed. Do you want to live under the rule of the Ministry? Do you think they'll let you live in peace once they find out what you're capable of?"

"Even so, he does have a point," Sted said. "We're walking straight into a bear pit. It won't do us any good if we're captured by a battalion faithful to the Ministry. Maybe we should enter the city after dark, rather than just rolling up to the terminal."

That was uncharacteristically cautious of her, but Tyreta couldn't disagree.

"All right. Let's see what we can do here..."

She looked out from the observation deck. Though the sound of bombardment had all but cleared the skies over Castleteig, she spied a crow perched on a tree next to the river, watching their landship roll by. Tyreta closed her eyes, focusing her power, trying to home in on the creature. She connected in an instant, her consciousness sliding along the web at shocking speed, so that she was peering from the creature's eyes faster than she'd ever thought possible.

With a flap of wings the crow took flight, gaining altitude as it made its way toward Castleteig. The closer it got, the clearer the devastation became. Half this once-great city had been reduced to rubble. The crow's keen eyes could see cannon emplacements on the northern bank of the Serpentspin as it wended its way through the city, lobbing munitions across the span of the river.

She urged it to wheel about, swooping low across the shattered rooftops toward the city's southern extent, dropping toward the landship terminal. A few Armiger troopers patrolled the area, and she recognised a tattered banner emblazoned with a writhing snake.

Tyreta opened her eyes, cutting off her connection with the bird. "The Viper Battalion holds the southern half of the city."

Nicosse looked a little relieved at the news. "I hear they are still loyal to the Guilds."

Sted nodded her agreement. "They've always been staunch allies. I can't imagine they've gone over to the Ministry, not yet anyway."

Tyreta turned her head north, toward the broken buildings looming ever larger in front of them. "We'll just have to take the chance. And hope they can help us get north of the city."

The three of them made their way down into the landship. Crenn and Donan waited in the engine room, while Cat sat patiently in the corner. Her hackles were up, and she had hated every moment of the deafening journey.

Through the viewing port, Tyreta could see they were approaching a tunnel that led to the terminal beyond. The landship was suddenly shrouded in darkness, the whine of the engine momentarily amplified, before they emerged in the city. Crenn eased back on the throttle, and the engine cruised to a standstill at the platform.

Tyreta was the first to peer out of the engine door. The air was thick with cloying dust, and the distant rumble of artillery. Through the curtain of smog she could see the engine was surrounded by troopers.

"Here we go," she said, stepping down from the engine. "Nice and easy."

None of the troopers made a sound from within their viper helms as Tyreta raised her arms. The others debarked behind her, likewise holding up their hands to signal they were no threat. Even Sted had her hands up as she chewed her lip frantically in place of her usual stick of redstalk.

Cat jumped down from the engine, moving to stand at Tyreta's leg. Immediately, half a dozen splintbows were levelled at them, and Tyreta lifted her arms higher.

"Wait," she said. "My name is Tyreta Hawkspur. We are here on a mission for my mother, Lady Rosomon."

One of the troopers stepped forward, a captain from the green snakeskin band on her upper arm. She wore no helm, and Tyreta saw fresh scars on her cheek and forehead.

"What kind of mission?" she asked, glancing nervously at Cat. After what had happened at Windstone, Tyreta had no idea who she could trust. "I—I can't tell you. I'm sorry."

The captain raised her splintbow. "You've got about three seconds to tell me what you're doing here, or you *will* be sorry."

Before Tyreta could think of something, a cloaked figure stepped forward to speak in the captain's ear. There was a hint of blue beneath the dirt on his grubby uniform. A Talon scout.

"All right," the captain said, after listening to the man. "You'd best come with us, Lady Tyreta. The frontier marshal will want to see you."

The rest of the troopers lowered their weapons, and the captain led them out of the terminal. Sted offered a reassuring wink as they moved north, but it did little to allay Tyreta's fears.

The wide stairs up from the platform emerged on a scene of utter carnage. Through the eyes of the crow, Tyreta had thought the devastation shocking. Up close it was nothing less than sickening. Almost every building along the parade had been destroyed. The distant drawl of artillery frayed at her wits, and she had only been here a few short minutes. She could scarcely imagine what it would do to anyone forced to endure it for days on end.

Smoke hung heavy, carrying the stink of death with it. The farther along the street they went, the more hunkering figures were hidden in the shadows. Ordinary folk caught up in the carnage. A stark reminder of this war's consequences. More evidence of why the Ministry had to be stopped.

The Viper troopers seemed unmoved by the sight. Tyreta could barely imagine what they had suffered over the past days.

"How long have you been fighting here, Captain...?"

The woman glanced back over her shoulder. "Captain Moraide. And we've been fighting pretty much since the day we got back from the Karna. We pushed north as far as we could, but the Tigris Battalion had already beaten us to Castleteig and claimed it for the Draconate. We engaged, and were doing well too, until the Phoenix Battalion got here. Since then it's been a battle of attrition. Lines are pretty much drawn along the Serpentspin, but it's not looking good for us. Word is the Hallowhills are sending more 'wainers. That means more artillery, more stormhulks. Unless we get some reinforcements soon, we'll lose the city altogether."

"Has no one come to help you? No one from the Guilds?"

Moraide shook her head. "We've sent requests to Windstone, to the Rock, anywhere we could think of. So far nothing. And so we fight alone."

"I know my mother is grateful for the support you have shown us. As are the other Guildmasters."

She offered a wry smirk. "Gratitude is all well and good, but it's not going to win this war. And not every Guildmaster still stands for the Guilds. Ingelram Hallowhill for one."

"If I succeed in my mission, Ingelram Hallowhill will become a distant memory," Tyreta replied.

"Tell that to—" She stopped, raising a closed fist.

No sooner had she done so than someone screamed, "Incoming!"

The troopers scattered. Tyreta grasped hold of Nicosse and pushed him toward the cover of a nearby wall. She felt the pyrestone missile before she saw it plummet into their midst, bouncing once before coming to rest in the middle of the street. There was a surge of energy, followed by a seismic blast that threw Tyreta to the ground.

Her ears rang, dust filling her lungs, but she managed to stagger to her feet. Nicosse was curled up in a ball, hands clamped tight over his ears. There was no sign of Cat or Sted, but hunkering behind a slab of fallen masonry was Donan. He managed to give her a reassuring nod, before she heard the distant whistle of more missiles.

This time she did not cower. Tyreta stepped out from behind the cover of the broken wall, glaring up into the sky. Her vision dimmed, darkening at the edges, allowing the light of the approaching pyrestone device to glow distinctly against the shadow.

Raising her hand, she channelled all her energy, all her anger, toward that flying missile. It shuddered in the air before she sent it flying down an abandoned street with a sweep of her arm. The sound of the detonation echoed from between the ruined buildings, and there followed an ominous silence.

Sted and Crenn crept from their shelter, as did Captain Moraide and the rest of her troopers.

"Any casualties?" called the captain.

Her men began to sound off, calling their names until they were all accounted for. Nicosse brushed himself down, and Donan breathed out a long sigh of relief. Of Cat, there was still no sign.

"How did you do that?" Moraide asked when she was satisfied no one was hurt.

Tyreta could only offer a shrug. "It's a long story."

"Then I guess it'll have to wait. We need to keep moving."

The deeper they moved into the city, the more vigilant the troopers became, aiming their splintbows at every darkened alley for fear of attack. Tyreta followed as the street rose to reveal a devastated amphitheatre. She had heard of the tiltyard of Castleteig before, of how tourneys had been held here since the Age of Kings. Warriors still fought every year, some even riding their steeds at one another with lances, as they had done a thousand years past. Now it was little more than smashed rubble.

From their vantage point she could see the city dropped away to the river below, marking the Viper Battalion's forward defensive line where hundreds of troopers manned stout barricades. The two bridges across the Serpentspin were blockaded with huge rocks, and every jetty looked to have been smashed and cast into the river.

"We've held this position for more than a week," said Moraide. "No telling how much longer we can defend it, and we don't have the munitions to bring down the bridges."

Tyreta could offer no words of advice. She had no idea if her mother had even retaken Wyke. If she could get Nicosse back north, maybe they'd have a chance to turn this tide, but until then there was nothing she could say to reassure Moraide that help was coming.

The Viper troopers moved swiftly down the hill toward the river, passing several hovels that had been requisitioned as barracks. The stink of decay was ripe, and Tyreta couldn't bear to look at the soldiers as they lay festering in their wounds. At the riverside, the ashen faces of the defenders looked more determined. She could only hope they would hold out long enough for the Guilds to strike back.

Moraide led them down to a makeshift bunker—what might have been a two-storey house a few days before, but now the upper levels were little more than smashed brick.

"The rest of you will have to wait here," she said, before beckoning Tyreta to follow.

Inside, three armoured warriors glared at a table on which was unfurled a weathered map of the city. The most striking of the trio stood well over six feet, bedecked in scaled armour of bronze, hands resting on the two swords at his waist. There was a long, jagged scar running through his left eye, which was bright blue, the other deep brown.

Moraide stood quietly for a moment, but none of the men noticed her as they pawed over the map.

"Frontier Marshal Sonnheld," she said eventually.

The man with the mismatched eyes glanced up with a severe expression. He was clearly unused to being interrupted.

"What is it, Captain Moraide?"

Moraide stood to even sharper attention. "This is Tyreta Hawkspur."

The severe expression drained from Sonnheld's brow as he looked Tyreta up and down. Then he bowed formally.

"Lady Tyreta. What are you doing here? This is far too dangerous a place for a Guild heir."

She took a step forward, trying to ignore another explosion that detonated all too close to the bunker. "I am on a mission for my mother."

"Might I ask its nature?"

Tyreta wondered if she could trust this man, but from what she had seen so far the loyalty of the Viper Battalion was without question. "I am accompanying an important artificer north."

"To where?" he asked.

"To Wyke, at first. Where my mother awaits us."

Sonnheld looked gravely back at the map, gripping tighter to the swords at his waist. "Then you haven't heard."

"Heard what?" Tyreta began to feel a dread knot tighten in her gut.

"Wyke is no more. It was destroyed over a week ago."

That knot tightened yet further. "What? Destroyed how? What about my mother?"

"All I know is the city was flooded. The great dam sabotaged. The deluge claimed the lives of thousands. Of your mother we have received no word."

She suddenly felt faint, the stench of smoke and rot making her head spin. How could Wyke be gone, just like that? And what of her mother? If she was dead, then who would lead them against the Ministry?

No. Until she knew better, she had to assume her mother had survived. Tyreta would finish what she had started.

"I still have to complete my mission," she said, doing her best to sound determined but sure she was failing. "There is a landship terminal to the north of the city. I must reach it."

Sonnheld shook his head. "Out of the question. Our enemy holds all the territory north of the river. It would be too dangerous to risk—"

"From what I've seen it would be more dangerous to do nothing, Frontier Marshal. If I don't succeed in this mission, that danger only gets worse. The artificer I have with me could hold the key to defeating the Hallowhills. Without them, the Ministry will be severely weakened. I'm sure you would agree."

As though to punctuate her point, more munitions blasted their tune outside the bunker. Sonnheld sighed, looking to the two officers standing beside him, but neither had anything to contribute.

"Very well. Captain Moraide will see you safely across the river. But you will have to navigate the rest of the way yourself. I can spare no more troopers for the job. There is no guarantee there'll be a landship that's operational, even if you do make it to the northern terminal."

"That's a risk I'm prepared to take, Frontier Marshal. You have my thanks."

"Then I suggest you rest here for the time being and wait for cover of dark. Good luck to you, Lady Tyreta. May the Guilds guide you."

She nodded her appreciation and left the bunker. Outside, the rest of her sorry band were being fed and watered with what little provisions the Viper troopers could spare.

"What's the verdict?" asked Sted. "Are we ploughing on to certain death?"

Tyreta could only nod. "We leave at dark."

She considered telling Sted about Wyke, about the devastation of their city, but what good would it do now? They all needed to hang on to as much hope as they could. There was no telling how long before it ran out completely.

KEARA

They drifted along the river, no one making a sound. The put-
tering of the boat's engine had been silenced a while back, and
now there was only the occasional swish of an oar as the Drakes rowed
them along the Serpentspin and into the city. Night was falling, but
Keara could still see the devastation wrought upon Castleteig. Blasted
buildings squatted on both banks, not a window intact, not a roof
without shattered slates.

To the north the shore had been marked with flying pennants—
the spider, phoenix and tiger staking their claims. On the other side
of the river fluttered the lonely flag of the Viper Battalion, marking
its tenuous hold on the south. From the state of that territory, it was
obvious which side was winning.

Keara had pursued her quarry from Windstone, quickly finding a
boat at the northern quay and claiming it, despite the bargemaster's
protests. They'd made haste northward before he could summon the
Kraken Battalion to stop them.

She had always hated boats, but to her surprise the journey would
have been almost pleasant if not for the gnawing sense of urgency.
Hesse had coaxed the engine to greater effort and their vessel had
eaten up the miles northward. It had almost thrilled her, being so
unfettered, speeding along that river. Now, as they rowed gently into

the ruin of Castleteig, she was forced to turn her thoughts back to the task at hand.

Keara had underestimated Tyreta Hawkspur. She would not do so again. Remembering the raw power she had encountered, Keara absently touched fingertips to the knife at her right hip. Her father had gifted these heirlooms that they might help her raise the Hallowhills to their rightful position. So far she had failed him. Failed her Guild. The knives she wore proudly only served to remind her of that failure. Of the sacrifices that had already been made. Would her father even appreciate her efforts? Fat chance.

Hesse sat at the bow, those dark lenses covering her eyes despite the drawing of night. Was she thinking about Ulger? Had she even given him a second thought? Did she blame Keara for what happened to him? None of that seemed likely, but Keara doubted she'd ever find out. Hesse had never been the greatest at conversation, and it was a rare privilege to know what she was thinking. Most likely that was the reason for those eyeglasses—to hide her thoughts from anyone. Maybe she had the right idea. As much as Keara had always tried to do the same, she knew sometimes it was impossible. Her passions often rose to the fore—her hopes, her dreams, her sadness. Her grief. She wiped a tear from the corner of her eye before anyone noticed, annoyed it was even there.

"I do hope you're not losing your nerve."

Keara turned to see Hisolda peering at her from the shadow of the cabin. Her immediate reaction was to snarl her defiance, to pull her knives and show this woman what real nerve was. She hadn't contributed to their encounter back in Windstone—she'd just stood by while everyone else fought. While one of them died.

"Do I look like I've lost my nerve?"

Hisolda took a step closer. "I hope not," she whispered. "The Archlegate will accept nothing short of success. Now we know that the Hawkspurs have found their man, there's no telling the damage they could do."

"This is just as important to the Hallowhills as your Archlegate. Maybe even more so. There's no need to question my commitment."

Hisolda nodded. "Then perhaps commitment is not the right word.

Commitment is for children and worker bees. What I require is your unwavering determination to find this artificer. I need you to show me how strong you really are."

Was this some kind of motivational talk? Right now it was the last thing Keara needed to hear.

"I may not share your fanatical dedication to the Ministry, but I am as determined to succeed in this mission as you and your knights. Don't doubt my resolve. I have more to lose from failure than any priest."

That seemed to amuse Hisolda, a trace of a smile crossing her lips. "I'm glad. I just wonder if you're willing to do exactly what it takes. To make the necessary sacrifices when called upon."

Keara clenched her fists, resisting the urge to grab this woman by her blue robe and throw her in the river. "I have already sacrificed one of my men. Was that not enough for you? When we catch up to Hawkspur, you'll see just how far I'm willing to go. Don't worry yourself on that score."

She turned, making her way back toward the prow, just as the two Drakes were guiding them toward a jetty. A dozen troopers waited on the shore, all armed and ready, but in the twilight she couldn't make out which battalion they belonged to.

On seeing the two Drakes, they quickly grabbed the mooring ropes and secured the boat. Hisolda stepped toward the gunwale and was gently helped onto the jetty. As soon as she set foot on dry land, the Armiger troopers knelt in fealty, leaving the rest of them to struggle ashore on their own.

"Take me to your commanding officer," Hisolda demanded.

One of the troopers nodded, leading the way. Keara could see they wore the uniforms of the Phoenix Battalion, dark half plate with a red flash at the shoulder, rising phoenix emblazoned on the chest. Hesse stuck close to her as Keara followed Hisolda up from the shoreline. From the boat, the carnage on the bank had seemed horrifying. Up close she got to see exactly what havoc this war had caused.

Not an inch of land was unaffected. The cobbles and slabs on the street were blown apart, and they were forced to slog through shards of rock embedded in the mud. A rancid stink of death and embers filled the air. Bodies had been left to rot; if they were lucky, their faces had been covered. Stray dogs picked their way through the devastation hunting for scraps. When she saw what looked like a row of heads mounted on spears, peering at her from the night, Keara had to fight the urge to vomit.

Hesse appeared completely unaffected by the devastation, and for a second time Keara regretted not having a set of dark spectacles of her own to hide her feelings. Instead, she set her jaw, trying to ignore what had happened to this once-vibrant city. Trying to forget her part in it.

They didn't have to walk far before they reached a section of headland jutting over the river. It was heavily guarded, splintbow-wielding troopers standing alongside artillerymen sighting their cannons across the Serpentspin. Beyond them, at the edge of the bastion, stood a tall young man glaring over the river through a monocular. It must have been impossible to spy anything, so black was the southern bank, and not a single fire was lit to mark an enemy position.

Hisolda moved toward him, the Phoenix troopers standing aside to allow her onto the platform with her Drakes close behind. Keara followed, conscious of the mistrustful way she was regarded by those troopers. As though they blamed her for their lot.

"Acting Marshal Tarrien," Hisolda said. "How nice to see you again."

The trooper turned, lowering the monocular, and on seeing her offered a brief bow. "It's just Marshal Tarrien now, High Legate. And this is an unexpected honour. I would not expect to see such a valued servant of the Ministry in a blighted place like this."

"Trust me, I wouldn't be here if it were not on a matter of the utmost importance. But needs must, and the Ministry sends its servants where they can be of most use." She turned, gesturing at Keara. "I am here with important members of the Hallowhill Guild on a mission for the Archlegate himself. We seek fugitives from Windstone. There's every chance they intend to cross the river and continue their flight north from here. We would appreciate your help in apprehending them."

Tarrien nodded his understanding. "I'm sure these fugitives are

important to the Ministry, but as you can see I have my own problems to deal with."

Keara stepped forward, none too keen to be left out of this. "One
of the fugitives we're after is a Hawkspur. We need to find her and
the artificer she is travelling with."

Tarrien regarded her closely, his interest piqued. "A Hawkspur?
Which one?"

"Tyreta. She is—"

"It doesn't matter which one," Hisolda interrupted. "What matters is we track down the enemies of the Draconate with all haste.
The last we saw, they were heading north from Windstone on a landship. They would have reached the southern terminal of Castleteig
by now."

Tarrien nodded. "Yes, I received reports a landship had docked
at the terminal this morning. But no one has yet crossed the river.
We'd have seen them."

"That must be her," said Keara, excited at the chance to redeem
herself. A chance to avenge Ulger.

"Indeed," said Hisolda. "And if they do plan to cross the river,
they'll do it under cover of dark, perhaps even tonight. We have
to cordon off the northern perimeter of the city. They cannot be
allowed to escape again."

Tarrien nodded. "I can offer a unit of troopers for the task, but I
can't spare more than that. I suggest you wait at the north terminal,
that's where they're likely headed. I'll see you're given safe passage
through the city."

Keara felt herself begin to panic. "No. One unit won't be enough.
The Hawkspur girl is more powerful a 'wainer than I've ever seen.
We'll need more men if we're to stop these fugitives."

Tarrien shook his head. "I'm as keen to see the Hawkspurs fall as you
are, but there is a war to fight, and I need every last trooper I have."

Keara stepped forward, desperate for him to understand, but Hisolda
moved in her path. "Thank you, Marshal Tarrien. The Ministry appreciates your cooperation in this matter. A small contingent of troopers
will more than suffice."

Tarrien bowed his respects. "You're welcome to take a look at the stores in the armoury. Hallowhill Guilders might find something useful in there." With that he gestured to one of his men, who stood to attention beside Keara.

"Thank you again, Marshal Tarrien," said Hisolda. "I'm sure we'll find something of use."

She turned to Keara, nodding for her to follow Tarrien's trooper. As much as she wanted to argue that it wouldn't be enough, Keara knew it was pointless. Besides, Tarrien was right—he had a war to fight, and by the looks of it he was on the brink of victory.

She and Hesse followed the trooper north, through the packed encampments where Tigris and Phoenix troopers prepared for the next assault. They were brooding, sullen, the past days of fighting leaving many looking broken. None of the camaraderie Keara had been exposed to during her time at the Karna. Clearly this conflict had been gruelling for all of them.

They were led to a well-lit building that was plainly a tavern before Castleteig had become a battleground. The trooper entered, opening the door wider to let the stink of the unwashed leak out onto the street. Keara followed him inside, and as Hesse closed the door behind her, she saw a gathering of bedraggled troopers sitting in the candlelit interior. Some of them drank and engaged in hushed conversation, others merely stared into the dark as though remembering the gruesome acts they had seen...or done.

"This way," the trooper said, leading them further inside. Barely anyone offered them a second glance, and Keara was glad of the sudden anonymity.

At the back of the inn was a huge storeroom. The beer barrels that would once have been piled here were missing or broken open, their contents strewn across the damp floor. Stacked in their place was an array of weaponry, most of it mundane—swords, axes, splintbows—but it was what lay on a table in the far corner that caught her eye. This was gear she could put to good use.

Keara picked up a pyrestone pistol, but a quick examination showed the conversion chamber was damaged and would not channel the stone's energy well enough to fire. Next to it lay a longbarrel with a cracked stock. Before she could look at anything else, Hesse picked up a volt gun from the far end of the table, a smile crossing her lips. It was a heavy weapon, the barrel tipped with four thick tines in the shape of a claw.

"Is it operational?" Keara asked.

Hesse smiled, and Keara could feel her connecting with the web. In response, sparks danced between the clawed tines. Were she to focus her powers, drive the blue pyrestones along its barrel to greater exertion, she could have lit up the entire room with deadly energy.

Keara looked at the trooper. "Is this all you have?"

"There is one more thing," he replied, gesturing for her to follow him to a door at the rear of the storeroom.

It led out into a cluttered yard, and Keara's attention was immediately drawn to the single stormhulk sitting idle in the middle of it.

"This any use to you?" he asked.

She moved closer, touching the purple armoured plate, sensing the pyrestones lying dormant within. One of its huge arms had been converted into a splintcannon, the other a heavy longbarrel. This was indeed a devastating machine of war.

"I think it might come in handy," she replied.

THE BATTLE OF
OAKHELM

She felt a reassuring hum within the stormhulk's cockpit. A welcome familiarity to her surroundings. The untapped power at her fingertips. Eldryd watched through the viewing port, staring at the panoramic of Oakhelm's western wall and the gate that rose from its midst. It was beautifully carved in the shape of a giant tree, leaves and branches rendered in minute detail. It wouldn't be long before she'd have to smash it to kindling.

This was what they'd been waiting for—to corral the resistance in one place, to strike the final blow. Once they were crushed, it would be time for the Hallowhills to ascend. A new age in which the webwainers could take their rightful place at the head of this nation. But first there would be battle.

Beside her at the vanguard were other hulks. Eldryd could faintly hear her Guild sisters preparing themselves in their own ways. Colwen was reciting a canticle to the Wyrms, Arianne humming some tune or other, Gwenlan breathing so heavy it almost drowned out the others, Marica silent and reflective. They had all fought for the Guilds before. Shed blood for them. Now it was time to see them destroyed.

In the distance, resounding from within the city walls and filtering through the steel chassis of the stormhulk, she could hear music. Did they have any idea what was waiting beyond the gate? They soon would. Eldryd and her sisters would play them a song all right. Their stormhulks would compose a symphony to quake the earth, a choir singing the name of the Hallowhills, never to be forgotten.

She closed her eyes, making those final checks, probing with her connection to the web, ensuring the pyrestones were reactive. Eldryd could feel the hydraulics of her hulk's arms and legs hissing with anticipation. The engine yearning to strike forward. Her body one with the steel, breath growling through its vents.

"Are we ready?" Marica called out through the cockpit's voice link.

"Here we go," Gwenlan replied, all too loud.

Eldryd could see the Armigers preparing themselves to follow in the wake of the stormhulks. Ursus and Corvus pennants flew as troopers checked their weapons, splintbows loaded, shields braced.

There, Lorens Archwind striding to the fore. He gazed up at the stormhulks, his eyes glaring intensely before he raised on arm. Eldryd held her breath in the moment before he signalled toward the gate. Their cue to begin.

"Come, sisters," Colwen growled. "Unleash the breath of the Wyrms."

Eldryd could barely focus as she advanced. Her excitement and trepidation merging into a heady cocktail. Marica and Arianne powered their stormhulks forward, levelling their heavy cannons. Eldryd felt the sudden spike of pyrestone energy as those weapons powered up before balls of molten fire burst forth to smash into the gate. The flash was blinding, and when Eldryd could see once more through the viewing port, the gates had been blown from their hinges, the intricate craftsmanship reduced to burning embers.

Gwenlan was already striding through the breach, and Eldryd exerted her will over the steel chassis surrounding her, driving herself forward, quelling the fluttering excitement as she followed through the wreckage of the gate.

As her stormhulk powered through the dust and smoke, the army they faced was finally revealed. Thousands stood against them across a killing field of fifty feet. Open ground cleared for their arrival.

Eldryd braced herself for the onslaught, confident that the armour of the hulk would shield her from whatever they could throw. But looking at the defenders arrayed in front of her, she quickly realised there was nothing to fear. These were not warriors. It was no Armiger Battalion across the way, but ordinary miners of the Marrlock Guild, some of them still holding tight to their musical instruments. Their lilting refrain had stopped now though.

Gwenlan laughed through the voice link on seeing what awaited them. The Marrlock Guild must have thought they would be well protected by the walls of Oakhelm, not realising the fury that was to be unleashed upon them. Eldryd paused for a moment, wondering if it was even right to inflict slaughter on these pathetic miners. Surely they should be given the chance to surrender? But her mind was immediately made for her.

Missiles rained in from the enemy lines. A dull explosion burst close by, as ordnance was flung across the open ground. In return, the sound of Arianne's heavy longbarrel began to pump in a dull rhythm as she fired into those hapless miners.

Eldryd strode ahead. Her left arm was fashioned into a crushing claw, the right an infernus cannon welded at the elbow. With no long-range weaponry she would have to close on the enemy to unleash the fury of the Hallowhills.

Her hulk's metal feet pounded the earth, closing on the grey-garbed miners. Among their ranks she could see artificers frantically moving along the front line, marshalling the firing of their ordnance from mortar and cannon. Her sisters howled their glee as they too advanced on the enemy, feet stomping the open ground before them.

Forty yards to the enemy. Thirty. Twenty.

Eldryd concentrated on the pyrestones in her right arm, nourishing them with her gift, feeling heat bloom as though she were holding her hand close to a hearth. The infernus cannon spat a gout of fire, oil spewing on the ground, the weapon's will becoming one with hers.

Then she fuelled it with her rage.

The cannon sprayed bright-yellow flame at the enemy, searing flesh, burning them where they stood. They must have been screaming in terror, but she could barely hear it above her own cry of fury.

As the firestorm died away, she saw the charred mass in front of her. She should have been shocked at what she had done, but her lips were pulled back, teeth set in a grin of glee, revelling in the raw power.

The rest of the Marrlock miners were already fleeing, racing away by the score toward a row of wooden buildings in the distance. It should have been reward enough to see them run, to know how dominant she was, but Eldryd would not stop—she would burn them all, burn this whole damned city to the ground.

"Come, sisters," she screamed. "They won't escape us."

Arianne and Gwenlan yelled in wordless accord, the five storm-hulks continuing their advance across the open ground. This was all too easy.

As she stepped forward in pursuit, the ground beneath her felt soft underfoot. Another step and she heard a crack of timbers. She willed the hulk to a stop, pressing her senses, feeling energy well up from the ground around them.

"Wait," Eldryd cried.

Too late.

Intense heat burst up through the earth. Pyrestone charges detonated beneath them, the ground blossoming in a sequence of stark explosions.

Arianne's scream echoed through the voice link as her hulk was pitched into a deep pit. Gwenlan cursed, and Eldryd would have shouted another warning but her own machine was already tipping, falling. She could not retain her balance, reaching out with her huge clawed hand, but there was nothing to grasp before she was consumed by the earth.

"Now!" Philbert cried.

He fought the instinct to stay hidden beneath the grass-covered awning pitched against the northern wall. It hid a score of artificers, along with a few engineers they had instructed on how to activate their pyrestone devices.

Someone kicked over the wooden shield, light and smoke assaulting his senses. He stumbled out, seeing the scorched carnage in front of him, hearing the wheeze of engines and the moan of pneumatics as the stormhulks foundered in the pit. What a stroke of genius. A perfect trap sprung with particular cunning—but at what cost? So many dead already, and Philbert was so close to being among that number.

As the others rushed forward he found himself caught up in the terror of it. His heart racing as he ran after them, the pyrestone explosive cool in his palm. It was heavy, instilled with the power to blow those infernal machines to scrap, and he was determined to see it done.

Who would have thought that he, Philbert Kerrick, would hold such a key position in all this? It was an honour—one he was determined not to squander.

They were only a few feet away now. Above the lip of the pit he could see one of the stormhulks reaching up with a clawed hand, carving divots in the turf, desperate to pull itself free. There was a pilot in there, a human being, but he couldn't allow himself to think about that. These blasted machines had to be destroyed, and quickly if there was any chance they were to live through this.

He felt his exhilaration growing with every step. This was what it must have felt like to be a warrior, to be a swordwright at the vanguard. For so many years he had been cloistered in the Titanguard workshop, such rousing sense of purpose alien to him. He could see how a man might get used to it.

He twisted the trigger coil on the device, hearing the buzz of the pyrestone within as it activated, knowing he only had mere seconds. Someone ahead had already lobbed their explosive into the pit and was retreating backward. Philbert could see the hulks below, the huge steel beasts scrabbling in that hole, desperate to escape.

They were monsters. He could not think of them as people.

With all his might he flung the device, watching it arc through the air and drop into the pit. Part of him wanted to stay, to watch, to see the result of his labours. Instead he turned, seeing Jakob standing there, eyes wide with...fear? Shock? Elation?

"Have that, you bastards," Jakob screamed into the hole.

Elation then.

Philbert grasped his arm. "We have to run!"

"Bastards," Jakob shouted, refusing to move, overcome by his thirst for vengeance.

"Jakob, come—"

The first blast echoed violently, sending shards of metal hurtling into the air. Philbert tried to duck but the second blast sent a seismic wave surging from the pit, blowing him off his feet. The world turned on its head. He had time enough to think, *Shit*, before he struck the ground, landing in a heap.

A high-pitched screech rang in his ear. Philbert couldn't move. Was his body broken? Was he paralysed by shock? Jakob lay nearby, head twisted at an awkward angle, eyes staring at nothing. The bitter tang of infernium fuel hung heavy in the air and he could feel something warm trickle from his ear.

Someone grabbed him, turning him over. He heard them speak through a thick wall, that shrill whistle drowning out the words. A big man loomed over him, a face he recognised. Rasmuth Reeve, one of those engineers.

"On your feet, man," he bellowed, dragging Philbert up.

The world around him gained a sudden sickening clarity. He managed to stand, feeling the strength return to his legs, a sense of urgency fuelled by his panic. He'd lost his skullcap. He'd always treasured that thing, but it didn't seem important now as Rasmuth dragged him away from the pit. Philbert staggered through the smoke, feeling the fire raging from within that deep hole, that grave of stormhulks.

He stumbled, desperate to keep up, seeing the others were fleeing— a horde of miners and artificers and ordinary folk, eager to escape what was coming. Rasmuth paused ahead of him, turning, opening his mouth to urge him on. Something whistled past Philbert's ear, hot and swift. A hole burst open in Rasmuth's chest and he was flung back by the force of it. Philbert stopped dead in his tracks, staring down at the body before glancing over his shoulder.

Pennants flew high as the Armigers charged through the breach, in the wake of those stormhulks. Splintbolts fired a raging volley, peppering the ground at Philbert's feet. He could see more weapons being levelled—steamlock and longbarrel, field guns carried by teams of cannoneers.

He had to move. Had to run or he would surely die. Philbert had to forget the horror—*don't think, just move.* He had never been a fit man, never thought to train his body as well as his mind. It had never seemed important before, but as he fled after the others he suddenly regretted those sedentary years.

The crowd ahead raced along Oakhelm's main throughfare, and he struggled to keep up. Someone fell nearby, a bolt in the back. In his periphery he caught sight of a head explode, skull opening up to shower the street with blood and brain.

Philbert wheezed, willing his legs to greater exertion. There had been a plan—an intricate one—but now it seemed scattered to the winds as they all ran headlong across the city. At the edge of the street was the huge main square. It had been cleared but for the massive oaken statue that stood proudly at its centre. Hundreds were sprinting past it, a full-on rout across the open ground.

He chanced another look back over his shoulder, seeing the Corvus and Ursus in swift pursuit. A flash of steel and a glimpse of a dragon helm told him that there were Drakes among their number. How could they have hoped to win? It was doubtful they would even survive the day.

As he turned back, he almost fell over another corpse. A young boy, still clutching the pipehorn he had brought. Was he dead? Should Philbert try to help? By the time he made up his mind, he had already staggered past.

Up ahead he saw the edge of the square. Shields blocked the whole of the eastern extent—a paltry defensive line in the face of such an onslaught, but it was all they had. When he spied the Titanguard standing behind the solid defence, he thought perhaps he might be saved, if only momentarily.

Philbert almost fell as he staggered to the other side of the shield wall. He gripped his knees as the way behind him was sealed, panting hard, desperate not to puke. His leggings felt moist. Had he soiled himself? No surprise there.

As he panted for breath, waiting for the advance of the enemy, he wondered if this was how it felt to be a warrior. If so, they could bloody well keep it.

Lorens pushed his way through the lines of troopers. His eyes stung, the pit in which the stormhulks had fallen giving off clouds of acrid smoke that had begun to choke the western end of the city.

Captain Ultan stood at the edge of Oakhelm's massive square, flanked by troopers of the Ursus who hunkered behind their huge shields. Not far down the line stood Lugard and the other Drakes. Behind came the Corvus. Despite the loss of their Hallowhill allies, they were still more than equipped to crush this resistance.

"Why have we stopped?" Lorens demanded.

Ultan gazed across the square toward the enemy line. Rows of shields were braced between a makeshift barricade. Piles of lumber had been stacked to defend the eastern side of the square, with rows of abandoned tenements blocking access from north and south.

"Because they have cleared a killing ground," Ultan replied. "If we charge across it without support from those stormhulks, we're exposing ourselves to whatever they can throw at us."

"So we just stand here?"

Ultan regarded him with a raised eyebrow. "If you want to lead the charge, be my guest."

Lorens felt himself bristle. Was that a barb? An insinuation that he was a coward? For a moment he thought that he might just do it. Charge ahead with the Corvus and claim this victory for himself. Then he saw her.

His aunt Rosomon walked to the fore, stepping through a gap made in the shield wall. Of course she stood tall and proud. Goading him. Yet again reminding him of what he had done. He clenched his fists against the shame of it.

"Perhaps there's another way this can be ended," Lorens said.

He pushed his way past the heavily armoured Ursus troopers, and out onto the square. Even from a distance he could tell she had seen him, though he couldn't quite make out her expression. Was it one of sorrow, or hate? Only one way to find out.

"Shall we talk, Aunt Rosomon?" he called across the open square.

She didn't answer, but took a step forward. One of her men, a hulking brute with a seven-foot spear, reached out to stop her but she shook off his hand. A word from her and the warrior stepped back into the defensive line.

They both walked toward one another as an eerie hush settled over the square. The closer they got to the huge statue standing in its centre, the less confident he felt. By the time they were within the shadow of that giant wooden axeman, any doubts about her feelings were expelled. Rosomon barely tried to hide her loathing for him. Nevertheless, it was his duty to at least try to end this peacefully.

"It would be such a pity for us to ruin this beautiful day with yet more slaughter. For so many to die beneath the shadow of this proud statue. I am still willing to accept your surrender, Aunt Rosomon. There's no shame in it."

She gazed up at the wooden effigy before letting out a long sigh. "You know I can't do that, Lorens."

He had always known she was stubborn to the last. She would sacrifice herself and so many others just to beat him. To humiliate him.

"It was foolish to think you could ever defy the might of the Draconate."

Rosomon shook her head. "No. You were foolish to return here when I told you not to."

Lorens clenched his teeth. Now even his aunt was trying to shame him. To suggest he should be afraid. He was not afraid. He was *not*.

"Empty threats are pointless now. Will you surrender or do I have to wipe out your pathetic excuse for an army?"

She looked suddenly sad, as though she pitied him, which only served to stir his anger further. "How did it come to this? Was your father not hard enough? I think maybe he spoiled you too much, because our own father treated him so harshly. Sullivar never wanted you to feel the way he did when he was a boy."

"Enough of this," Lorens spat, fists clenched, knee suddenly trembling of its own accord. He didn't need reminding of his father. Didn't need to be excused for his actions. "You *must* surrender."

Rosomon was unmoved by his outburst, glancing up casually to a flock of blackbirds flying low overhead. "No. I don't think I will."

Lorens took a threatening step forward, but she didn't move an inch. "Then you will die here, and so will everyone that follows you. I was trying to be reasonable."

She was so close to him now, gazing up into his eyes as though searching for something in them. "You really are still that little boy. You haven't learned a thing. If only I'd known how you would turn out, I would never have spared you my hand."

"*Your* hand?" he snarled, and before he knew it Lorens had slapped his aunt across the cheek. It turned her head, hair falling across her face.

When she slowly looked back at him, he could see it was all she could do to contain her fury. Silently he chided himself for losing control. For allowing her to shame him. To humiliate him.

Behind her he could see some of the shield men had moved forward, her huge bodyguards striding toward their mistress, but she raised a hand and they halted obediently. Lorens glanced back to see if weapons within his own lines were being aimed, but no one had moved a muscle. Not one of them seemed to care whether he was in danger.

Rosomon gently swept the hair from her face. "You will never raise a hand to me again."

He should have told her he would do as he pleased, that he had the right to strike anyone he wished, but the look of steel in her eyes made the words dissolve on his tongue.

"You should have surrendered when you had the chance," he said instead.

He waited for her to turn, to make her way back to the relative safety of her army, but she did not move. Lorens could have drawn his weapon right here. Could have ended this futile resistance with one sweep of a blade.

Instead, he turned away, walking the long path back to where the Ursus waited. As he reached the line of shields, he could see them watching him from beneath their visors. He could imagine them smiling, holding back their mirth, judging him for striking a woman— and his own kin to boot. They would not judge him for long.

Ultan stood waiting on the other side of the shields.

"I have been granted seniority here by the Archlegate himself,"

Lorens said, trying hard to control his voice, and for it not to crack. "Are we at least agreed on that?"

Captain Ultan conceded with a nod. "We are."

Lorens leaned in close, so their noses were almost touching. "Then do as you're told and begin the fucking attack."

He gripped tight to his sword, but it remained in the scabbard. Even when that little bastard had struck Rosomon across the cheek he'd held himself in check. Kassian Maine had always been a man of singular purpose, but even he was struggling to keep his anger at bay.

They were all hidden within the tightly built wooden tenements that lined the southern end of the square. Cramped together, breathing each other's air, watching, waiting. Standing alongside those battalion troopers, all the old memories started to flood back. Old feelings. Old desires. Days when he had fought on every frontier. Duelled a dozen enemies. Won tourneys. Won adoration.

Those days were behind him now, and he had long since taken on the mantle of teacher. Today he would have the chance to impart a singular lesson.

The shout went up from the western side of the square. Grunts of assent bellowed from the Ursus Battalion as they marched, shields braced, spears jutting forward like the spines of an ancient beast.

Through the tenement building, Kassian heard whispered orders given for cannon and mortar to be loaded. At the lip of the windows in front of him troopers readied their splintbows, gently releasing safeties and cocking breeches. Marshal Rawlin was closest to the door, glimpsing through the spyhole he had bored before all this began. He slowly raised a hand.

Kassian's grip tightened on his sword. His teeth were grinding and he made a conscious effort to stop it. No matter how many times he had been in this position, there was still no way of completely mastering the fear. It just had to be managed. Controlled.

When the Ursus had reached the shadow of that wooden statue, Rawlin lowered his hand in a slicing motion. The building shook as a cannon, positioned at the far end of the room, fired into the flank of Ursus troopers. The clacking report of splintbows resounded, immediately drowned out by mortars firing from the level above.

Rawlin wrenched open the door and Kassian heard a bellowed cheer. He was right behind the marshal of the Bloodwolf as he raised his sword and charged. Troopers poured from the row of wooden tenements, through the pall given off by the cannon volley.

To his right, Kassian saw the miners and civilians yelling at the first blow struck. As he cleared the smoke cloud, he wrenched his sword free, seeing the bodies ahead. The Ursus reeling in panic. Someone shouting for them to rally.

Beyond the ranks of enemy troopers, more ordnance was being fired from the tenements that lined the square to the north. A missile whistled overhead, superheated shot smashing into the ranks of troopers desperate to raise their shields and defend their flanks.

Rawlin led the Bloodwolf troopers into the fray. He wore no helm, sword raised aloft. The marshal was brave, but headstrong. Just the kind of shining example most fighters needed in battle. Kassian had seen his like many times—leaders more likely to die gallantly than survive the day. Not that Kassian hadn't run headlong into his share of battles in the name of Treon Archwind.

As he raced after the vanguard he could only think this was what he had been born for, trained for. His duties at the Seminarium had been noble work, but they paled next to the glory of taking on the Magnan Fleet, or defending Tyndur Pass against the Huntan tribes before it was finally sealed.

All thoughts of nostalgia evaporated as he ploughed into the melee. An axe swung, just missing his head, swords clashing so near they almost burst an eardrum. The battle swiftly reduced to a grunting, tooth-grinding slaughter, but for Kassian Maine there would be no such exertion. His craft was one of precision—to assess the opponent and react with deadly accuracy. The minuscule brushstrokes of a swordwright were designed to paint in sharper colours than could be daubed with brute force. But most of them were still red.

He scanned the battle, wary of any attack. If he could find Lorens, strike quick and fast, it might not end this conflict but it would at least avenge Sullivar. His eyes flicked from one frenzied face to another, but among the fray it became obvious he would never find Treon's grandson. Before he could even think on his next move, an errant splintbolt ricocheted off his shoulder guard.

Kassian staggered, fighting to control himself—his fear, his anger. Some might have said he was too old for this—Rosomon for one. He could have stood on the edge of the battlefield, offered his advice, but that had never been his strength. He was a killer. The best in all Torwyn in his day. He had nothing to prove, but still...

A powder blast shook him from his reverie as a steamlock carbine was fired all too close. A Bloodwolf trooper fell dead at Kassian's feet and he realised he had to focus. Had to make himself of use.

Maybe he *was* getting too old for this. Perhaps he had overestimated his ability. There was only one way to find out.

He squinted through the smog settling over the square, as he tried to find the most fearsome foe. Show his worth. The fighting was brutal, no weft nor wain, just pitiless carnage. Amid it all he saw a giant black-armoured beast in the bearskin of the Ursus. He wielded a maul, laying low all comers, and Kassian was moving toward him before he could start to think it was a stupid idea.

He slipped through the slaughter, ignoring all else as he stalked the behemoth. As low and swift as his old legs would carry him, he made his way past sword strike and barrel blast until he was within only a few feet of his prey.

A space had opened around the Ursus trooper, no one daring to get close enough to face that swinging maul. Kassian could see the dents and scorch marks in his armour where it had resisted splintbow and longbarrel alike. As soon as he stepped forward, the warrior locked eyes with him, glaring from behind the bear helm. Those eyes narrowed as he saw his foe, some old man. He had no idea who he faced. That would be to Kassian's advantage.

With a muffled grunt, the trooper raised his maul and charged. Kassian awaited the attack, reading the trooper's stride, working out when he would swing long before he did it. At the last moment he stepped aside, not as deftly as he once would have, but it was fast enough to avoid that vicious maul. As the iron weapon struck the ground, Kassian swept his sword down, clanging it off the back of the trooper's helm.

Not powerful enough to strike a fatal blow, but it would make him realise he was in a fight.

With a snarl the trooper rounded on Kassian, swinging wildly, exposing a gap in his armpit where backplate and breastplate met. An easy target. Perhaps too easy. But Kassian was not here to toy, he was here to kill.

Lunging forward, he extended his thrust as far as he could. The tip of his blade pierced the hauberk, driving through padding, into flesh, over the rib cage, severing arteries, slicing organs. No sooner had he wrenched the weapon free than the trooper staggered back, his maul falling from numb fingers.

Kassian didn't even wait for the man to fall before he was searching the square, peering north as another wave of ambushers charged toward the fray. The banners of the Mantid Battalion flew high and proud. Their enemy would be crushed between a tide of armoured might.

But first there was work to do.

A pungent cloud had settled over the square, the noise of battle still cacophonous. Cannons had stopped firing from their hidden positions to north and south, but now the Corvus and Ursus were caught between the jaws of the Mantid and Bloodwolf. Ianto longed to rally his Titanguard, to march them forward and bring the emperor's vengeance to those Armigers who had come here seeking murder, but his duty to Rosomon was more important than his own desire.

Marshal Rawlin had only returned with one other battalion to face the might of the Ministry, but the Mantid were proving more than up to the task. Now, as the smoke was settling, and the frenzied cries of those warring factions drew closer, it looked like they might have won the day.

"We should retreat to a safe distance," he said to Rosomon above the sound of battle.

She couldn't take her eyes from the fighting, peering over the shields of the men in front of her. "No, I need to stay. I have to see this."

Ianto took a step closer. "It would be foolish to risk yourself when we are so close to victory. There are too many people relying on you; your safety is paramount."

He could see her jaw working frenetically as she fought with the urge to stay and watch—to see her plans come to fruition. "Very well," she said eventually, dragging her eyes away from the fighting. "Lead the way, Imperator."

Ianto breathed a quiet sigh as he pushed his way through the crowd, with Rosomon close behind. Instinctively the rest of the Titanguard, a dozen men who had been his peers not too long ago, moved from their positions and followed. They were all armed with shield and spear, the best they could scavenge. He would have been much more comfortable in his Archwind battle armour, but since leaving the Anvil they had learned to make do.

Quento took the lead, striking forward as the rest of them surrounded Rosomon with a wall of shields. A command post had been secured at the northern landship terminal, and it would be safe there until the fighting was over. The streets of Oakhelm were eerily quiet as they made their way north, though the sound of the fighting still resonated along the tightly packed lanes.

He should have been in the midst of that battle. Should have been leading his brothers in combat, but not for the first time Ianto reminded himself of his solemn duty. He had failed one master. He would not fail the second.

Quento stopped in his tracks, raising a hand for them to hold position. Ianto froze. Above the sound of the battle, he could hear nothing, but something had clearly spooked his fellow Titanguard. He was about to call to Quento, to ask him what was wrong, when a noisome blast echoed from up ahead.

Quento was thrown to the ground as a missile struck his shield. Before he could rise, there was a sharp staccato rap, and he was riddled with splintbolts. Feet pounded along a nearby alleyway, and the Titanguard braced their shields to face the oncoming foe. A giant Drake bowled from the shadows, smashing himself into their flank, hacking with his huge broadsword. In return he was struck by a crescendo of spearheads, but his armour turned every strike.

A second Drake, then a third, appeared from the dark streets, heedless of the Titanguard and their weapons. Ianto cursed himself for falling into an ambush, but he had little time to wallow in guilt as Armiger troopers of the Corvus filled the road ahead. Lorens was among their number—that cursed traitor—and on seeing him, Ianto had to swallow down his bile. He had to stay in control, had to protect Rosomon at all costs.

The Titanguard grunted as they deflected the wide-bladed swords of the Drakes, and Ianto weathered the assault, his shield struck by one powerful blow after another. Rosomon was close to his shoulder, safe for now, but when the Corvus reached them, they would surely be overwhelmed.

"Hold the way," Ianto barked, grasping Rosomon's arm and dragging her from the fighting.

As one, the rest of the Titanguard moved into a tight formation, standing shoulder to shoulder, shields locked as the Drakes continued to rain blow after hacking blow. Pulling Rosomon away from the fight, Ianto didn't look back lest he feel compelled to help his brothers. He could only envy them the chance to fight. It should have been him spitting the righteous hate of his emperor at the bastard enemy, but he had to get Rosomon out of there.

They left the skirmish behind, racing along a narrow alley, splashing through the rank puddles. Behind, he could already hear the sound of approaching feet, the lumbering steps of a heavily armoured warrior in their wake.

"In here," Rosomon said, pulling her arm free of Ianto's grip and heading toward a huge mill standing tall amid the surrounding buildings.

Ianto followed her through the wide-open doors, casting a glance back to see the imposing sight of a Drake in pursuit. The interior of the building was cast in shadow but Ianto could still make out the machinery—chippers, planers, barkers and saws of all kinds. He led Rosomon deeper into the dark, and they both hunkered down behind a long stack of timber.

Two figures were silhouetted in the doorway—one the hulking armoured knight, the other slighter with a fine sword in his hand.

As he peered through the dark, Ianto recognised Lorens, most likely come to ensure the death of one more of his kin.

Ianto gripped tight to his spear, desperate to hold himself back. One throw and he could enact Sullivar's vengeance, but then he would be left to face the Drake with only a sword, and he had to keep that behemoth at a distance—at least long enough for Rosomon to escape.

"You have to run," Ianto whispered. "I will hold them here."

Rosomon glared at him through the dark before shaking her head. "No. Ianto—"

"Get to the northern terminal." He gripped her arm tight. "Run, and don't look back. There is no dishonour in this. It makes the most tactical sense."

She looked like she might argue, but he returned her glare with as much determination as he could, until she nodded in agreement. It was the only signal he needed.

Lorens and the Drake hadn't encroached more than five feet into the mill before Ianto stood, presenting himself as an easy target. Lorens looked reluctant to advance, but the Drake strode forward to challenge him. As he did so, Rosomon burst from cover, sprinting for the door. Lorens saw her, moving to intercept, but Ianto had already drawn back his arm, and flung his shield. It clanked dully as it struck Lorens on the side of the head, and he fell in a heap as Rosomon fled the mill.

The Drake watched her go, before bracing his shield. He knew if he turned his back, Ianto would be on him. Instead he presented a wall of impenetrable steel, but Ianto was buying time, not looking to win a victory.

He jabbed with his spear, trying to hold the Drake at bay, but it rang off that shield, barely making a scratch. The Drake advanced, forcing Ianto into retreat toward the bottom of a staircase. It led up to a mezzanine above, and he slowly walked backward, rising up the stairs with his spear braced as the Drake came after, increasing his stride, keen to end this quickly.

No sooner had Ianto reached the top of the stairs than the Drake raised his sword. Ianto jabbed again, but the spear tip slid off the Drake's breastplate. A swipe of that blade and the shaft broke, leaving him with little more than a useless wooden rod.

Ianto wrenched his own sword from its scabbard. "For the Guilds!"

He flung himself at the Drake, sword crashing against shield. Every swing was met by the knight, his blade and shield absorbing each deft attack, and he resembled a machine as much as anything else in this mill. Still Ianto rained blow after blow, exhausting himself with his relentless onslaught. He knew this beast wanted him to tire, to slow, but every second he kept the Drake occupied was one that Rosomon could put distance between them.

A final swing of Ianto's sword was batted aside by that huge shield. The Drake struck with his helm, slamming forward to butt Ianto in the face. He staggered back against the wooden banister, sword falling from his hand. A feral snarl from the Drake as he battered Ianto with his shield. The banister cracked under his weight, wood breaking as he was smashed backward, and he fell, guts lurching before he slammed into the ground.

The wind was punched from his lungs. He tried to gasp but the air wouldn't come. His eyes filled with tears, mouth filled with blood, and all he could hear was the ominous tread of the Drake descending the staircase.

He braced himself for the final strike. The last swing of the sword that would take his life. Instead, the Drake strode past and rushed from the mill, leaving Ianto helpless on the ground.

The warrior lay foundering. He was brave, but ultimately weak when faced with the fury of Ammenodus Rex. Finishing him might have been a mercy, but Lugard had other things to think on.

Quickly he checked on Lorens. The Prince of Archwind bled profusely from the head but he still breathed. Some help he had been— but then Lugard needed no one else to help him with this task.

He dashed from the darkness of the mill into bright daylight. The sound of the battle had subsided, more than likely his allies had been defeated, but there was still time to strike one final blow for the Ministry.

There—footprints in the soft earth. His heavy boots echoed along a narrow, abandoned street, as he focused on his quarry. The armour of the Draconate was heavy, but fitted Lugard like a second skin, and he could run in it for almost an hour without need to stop for breath.

Ahead he spied a flash of blue disappearing down a nearby alley-way. Rosomon had a head start but Lugard would not be denied. She led him northward, but he was gaining with every stride. He could not lose her.

A landship terminal stood at the northern extent of the city. Rosomon raced across open ground toward it, stumbling up the stairs before disappearing through the open archway.

Lugard leapt the stairs in one, slowing as he reached the threshold, and peering into the dark interior. He was breathing heavily, sweat pouring down his back as he hefted his shield, wary of anyone lurking in the shadows.

The terminal was spacious, a gargantuan hall for loading lumber, but he could see little in the dark. This place was as abandoned as the rest of the city, another monument to the Guilds that would be left to rot once the Ministry finally closed its grip on Torwyn.

"Rosomon Hawkspur," he called into the black. "Come out, and I will end this quickly. The Archlegate has decreed your end, and his word must be obeyed."

Something scraped on the floor nearby and Lugard spun, holding his breath, eyes straining through the dark. The hiss of a taper made him turn again, and he saw a flame ignite before a torch sparked to life. In the light of that fire he realised his mistake.

Surrounding him was a score of shields, warriors with swords and spears, domed helms with bearded faces beneath. Blackshields.

Another torch was lit, then another, and Lugard realised he had been drawn into a trap. He gritted his teeth, trying hard not to curse himself for a damn fool as a hulking figure stepped forward—Maugar Ironfall, the swordwright. Beside him stood his daughter, though Lugard could not recall her name. This would likely be his end, but all was not lost—at least he might be offered the chance to die on the blade of a worthy opponent.

"Shall we begin, Maugar?" he said, hoping his challenge would be accepted.

"No," said another voice from the dark, before Maugar could answer. Rosomon pushed her way past the shields. "This needs to end."

Lugard lowered is shield. "You do not get to dictate how I die, Hawkspur."

"Is that all you want? A righteous death?"

"I serve the Great Wyrms. It is the only death I could ever hope for."

Rosomon shook her head. "But this is not service to your Wyrms. You are here at the bidding of Sanctan Egelrath."

"And he is my Archlegate. As such, he speaks with the mouth of the Wyrms. His word is to be—"

"His word is a lie!" Rosomon snarled, viciously enough that Lugard almost took a step back.

Was she trying to pour poison in his ear? Did she think to turn him from his faith?

"You speak heresy, and I will hear no more of it. Kill me if you wish, but I will not listen to your sedition."

Maugar slid his blade from its scabbard, but Rosomon held up a hand for him to hold.

"Your army is defeated," she said. "What service is there in death? What good will come of it? If you are so keen to enter your Lairs, I will grant you a swift journey. But if you choose to lay down your sword, you will live. And perhaps gain the chance to atone for your failure. That much I promise."

Was her offer genuine? Even if it was, should he accept? Lugard's sole purpose had always been to die in service to the Ministry. Dying at the hand of Maugar Ironfall would indeed be glorious, but there had been something to her words. Something that rang true in Lugard's head.

He had always suspected Sanctan unworthy to hold the seat of Archlegate. He had watched as that man coveted power. Curated support. Seized control and used it to strike terror in his brood. Lugard had seen firsthand what happened when the man was defied—the merciless destruction of Wyke was a testament to that.

Gylbard had always been suspicious of him, but no one had listened, and when he eventually died there had been whisperings of foul play. Ansell had become a changed man, and he spent much time with Sanctan. Had he been tarnished by the stain of their new Archlegate?

By a man unworthy of the position? And now here was Lugard, prepared to die for him.

His shield clanked as he dropped it to the ground. When he took the helm from his head, he could finally breathe more easily. He sheathed his sword before unbuckling the belt at his waist, then, with reverent care, laid it on the ground.

There would be disgrace in surrender. But perhaps the Hawkspur woman was right, and Lugard might yet gain the chance to atone. For the Archlegate, as well as himself.

Rosomon nodded at Maugar, who signalled for some of his Blackshields to take the Drake. Thankfully, the knight offered no resistance as Maugar's men bound his hands and led him away.

"Could be a mistake offering mercy," Maugar said as they both walked from the darkness of the terminal. "Xorya tells me it didn't go so well for you last time."

"Enough people have died today. Besides, it may come in useful having one of Sanctan's faithful as a prisoner."

Maugar and Xorya stayed close as she made her way back toward Oakhelm's main square. An eerie quiet had descended on the city, but she was still grateful for the Blackshields that accompanied them. When three of her Titanguard appeared on the street ahead, she allowed herself to relax, if only a little.

"My lady," said one of them breathlessly, dropping to one knee. "The enemy has been defeated. Many have surrendered at the central square."

"Where is the imperator?" she asked.

Before she could answer, she saw Ianto being helped toward her by two of his brother Titanguard. He looked in a bad way, gripping tight to his ribs, but he was alive at least.

"Are you all right?" she asked him as he limped closer.

"Just need to catch my breath," he replied. It looked like he would need much more than that.

"This is the second time you have almost died trying to save me, Ianto. Next time—"

He straightened. "There will be no next time, my lady. I won't fail you again."

"You haven't failed me yet, Ianto, but might I suggest you rest awhile, before returning to your duties?"

"If that is your order." He looked relieved at her suggestion.

She and Maugar carried on toward the square. As they drew closer she could hear music playing as loudly as it had earlier in the morning. This time though, rather than a heady lament, it was a cacophony of rousing tunes all fighting for supremacy. By the time she reached the square, Rosomon could barely hear herself think.

The place was devastated, some of the tenements to the north still on fire. Despite the blaze and the carnage that surrounded them, some of the Marrlock miners were dancing a jig around row upon row of bound prisoners.

All at once, the music faded as a single violin began to play a lilting version of "Auld Molly Sprite." It had been her father's favourite, and she had not heard it for the longest time. Suddenly the strain of what she'd been through these past weeks seemed to overwhelm her and it was all Rosomon could do to fight back the tears.

Still she walked on, past the raised standards of the miners leagues fluttering alongside those of the Mantid and Bloodwolf. Captured weapons were being piled high as surgeons treated the wounded out in the street.

Marshal Rawlin approached. If he was pleased with his victory, he did not show it.

"My lady," he said, dropping to his knee in an unexpected show of respect. "We have captured over a hundred prisoners of the Ursus. Captain Ultan among them. Your nephew, Prince Lorens, is also in our care, though most of the Corvus Battalion have fled."

"Thank you, Marshal Rawlin," she replied. "We shall see that justice is done."

A cheer went up, and Rosomon looked to the north of the square, where Oleksig was celebrating along with his miners. She had never seen him so animated as he danced atop one of the barricades, a jug of frothing ale in his hand. Borys stood nearby, looking on with his usual lack of emotion, and Thalleus Brisco was not too far away, cleaning his sword with a Corvus pennant.

Some of the miners began to chant above the sound of the rousing violin. "*Guilds, Guilds, Guilds*" repeated over and over until it dominated the square. It filled her with such hope she thought she might faint from the relief of it.

As she watched them, Kassian Maine came to stand by her side. His scant armour was spattered with dark crimson and there was a cut on his forehead, but he looked more invigorated than she had ever seen him.

"You performed well today," she said. "For an old man. Though you did leave it rather late to make your appearance. I thought I might have to fight the Armigers on my own."

That raised a grin on one side of Kassian's face. "Doesn't matter when the trap's sprung, my lady, as long as it's laid right. We all have you to thank for that."

She didn't know how to respond. They had lost many good people today, and it would be indulgent to congratulate herself when there was still so much to be done. Before she could answer Kassian, some of the miners spotted her from across the square. The cries for the Guilds faded, to be replaced by another call.

As the name *Hawkspur* echoed through the city of Oakhelm, Rosomon only wished Lancelin was here to see this. But he was not here. He was ash, along with so many others. And for that, she would still have her reckoning.

FULREN

"All right, Fulren, you can do it."

As much as he appreciated Ashe's words of encouragement, his confidence was waning. She let go of him, casting him adrift, and he immediately tensed every muscle, fighting to stay on his feet. Despite that, he managed to find his balance, letting himself trust in the pneumatic rig that passed for legs. Across the yard, only a few feet away, he could make out Verlyn's outline silhouetted against the dark. She seemed so far away across that sea of nothing.

"Come on. Just like last time," she called to him. "Only maybe with less falling over."

Fulren gritted his teeth, shifting his weight and moving the left stanchion of the rig. It articulated with a whisper, Ashe having oiled and bevelled and filed out the imperfections, so it performed with a smoother action. That single step was a vast improvement on last time, and it served to embolden him a little. He braced his weight on the left side, before shifting the right leg, managing to stay upright. A real step. An actual, honest-to-goodness step.

He laughed at his success, but that only served to unbalance him slightly. Best concentrate. Don't go dishing out the medals just yet.

He held himself in place for a moment, trying to find his centre. Over the past few days he'd learned to compensate for only having one arm, and the natural imbalance it gave him. Now he just had to—

I can make this so much easier.

A breath on the breeze that brought a nauseating wave. He tried to ignore it. To not give in to that temptation. It haunted him more vividly with every passing day, becoming so much harder to resist. But he had to resist it.

"Fuck you," he mumbled through gritted teeth.

The sudden anger made him more determined to do this on his own. Damn that voice. Damn the curse of Nyrakkis. He could make it without the necroglyph's power.

Another step forward on his left leg. This time increasing his stride. He'd show it, whatever it was. He'd prove he needed no help.

No sooner had he moved his right leg, he felt himself begin to waver. His arm shot out to find purchase but there was none to grasp. The rig began to topple and he braced himself for yet another meeting with the cold autumn ground.

Verlyn grabbed him before he fell, Ashe holding him too, keeping him steady. As he reeled in the dark he gritted his teeth against the frustration.

"You're getting there," Verlyn said. "Every day there's real improvement. Don't beat yourself up about it."

Fulren tried to relax, to let the scowl recede from his brow, but he was shaking with such rage it almost brought him to tears.

"This would be a lot easier if we used the helmet," Ashe said.

He could see sparks of red light course through Verlyn's body at the mention of the pyrestone helmet. "It didn't work last time."

"Nonsense," Ashe replied. "We just didn't give it a chance. Besides, I've made a few modifications. This time it'll perform better. You'll see."

Before Fulren could protest, Ashe let go of him, rushing toward her workshop. The memory of what he'd seen with that helmet had filled him with hope, but he also remembered the consequences. It had summoned that voice to the fore, linked him with whatever fell power the necroglyph bore. Verlyn had felt it too.

"I think it's best if we don't try this again," he said. "You know... after last time."

"Yeah. Maybe you're right."

He could hear the reluctance in her voice. "When we used it last, you . . . you heard it too, right?"

"I don't know what I heard," she replied. "But I'm damn sure I don't want to hear it again."

"So maybe one of us should tell Ashe it's a bad idea."

"Yeah," she said. "Bad idea. But I think it would be best coming from you."

He could hear Ashe making her way back from the workshop. "Here we go," she said, sounding excited at the prospect of giving her device another try. "Let's see if we can get the thing working properly this time."

"I'm not so sure," Fulren said. "I'm a little beaten from using this rig. Must have covered at least ten feet today. I don't think now's the right time to try the helmet."

"What are you talking about? Don't you want to see? This will make everything easier."

"No," he answered, a little too forcefully. "Look, I'm blind. Nothing's going to change that."

"Horseshit. Don't be so defeatist. You've come such a long way since we found you. You're getting stronger every day." She laid a hand on his shoulder. "I know you're scared, but I know you're brave too. Just think about the scariest thing you've ever faced. This'll be nothing compared to that."

Fulren was suddenly reminded of the scariest thing he *had* ever faced—the jaws of Ghobeq yawning wide. The last thing he had ever seen with his own eyes. "I just don't think that—"

Ashe leaned in closer. "It's not gonna be as bad as Verlyn's cooking, is it? Just give it one more try. If it doesn't work this time, I won't ask again."

Before he could think of another excuse, he heard the sound of hooves approaching from along the road. Neither Verlyn nor Ashe said anything at the noise, but he could feel the immediate tension. Verlyn turned to look north, the dim light inside her body suddenly agitating.

"Who is it?" he asked.

"Revocaters," Verlyn replied.

He felt Ashe grip his shoulder tighter. "Should we hide him?"

"Too late for that. Just get him in the chair."

He heard Ashe move the chair closer, the wheels trundling across the yard, and she gently helped him into it. No sooner had she placed a blanket over his lap, perhaps trying disguise the steel rig about his legs and waist, than he heard those hooves gallop to a stop in the yard. The horses snorted and whickered, perhaps three of them in all.

"Good day to you," said a man's voice. "The Wyrms have truly blessed us with a fine autumn morning."

"Yes," Verlyn replied. "I suppose they have."

Fulren could sense the foreboding. Verlyn was standing stock-still but the webwainer light inside her was roiling like a thousand frantic fireflies. As the man climbed down from his horse, moving closer, those lights became ever more turbulent.

"Blessings of the Wyrms to you," Ashe said as some kind of after-thought. "What can we do to help such esteemed agents of the Corwen Guild?"

"Ah, but we are all servants of the Great Wyrms now," the man replied. "The Guilds are no more. We are here at the order of the Archlegate himself."

"And what business would the Archlegate have with a little backwater farm on the edge of the Serpentspin?"

There was a pause, before he said, "Just standing here I can see there is a lot of unsanctioned artifice on this property."

"It's a farm," Verlyn said, as though she were talking to an idiot. "There's only the two of us here. How else are we supposed to run the place if we don't have artifice? We supply grain and swine to three towns. How do we do that without—?"

"That's not my problem," the Revocater replied. "All I know is, by decree of the Draconate, the unsanctioned use of artifice is now prohibited within all former Guildlands. It is to be dismantled with immediate effect."

"Who's the cripple?" said one of the other Revocaters from atop his horse.

"This...this is my nephew," Ashe replied. "He's been like this most of his life. Can't move nor speak. No use around the farm."

"Be easier if you got rid of him then. One less mouth to feed."

Fulren bristled at the insinuation. Before Ashe could say anything, the first Revocater took a step closer.

"Your problems with productivity are of no consequence to the Ministry. I have my orders. All this machinery has to go. Take on extra labour if you have to. There'll be plenty of bodies making their way down from the Anvil now the manufactories are closed. I'm sure they'll work for cheap."

"We've been living on this farm a long time," Verlyn said, almost spitting the words. "Just the two of us. It's taken a lot of sweat and blood to build this place. Do you think we're just going to tear it all down for the sake of the Ministry? Throw it in the Serpentspin like trash?"

"I don't care what you do with it." The good humour had gone from his voice now. Fulren could sense an edge of menace. "Artifice is forbidden."

"Since when?"

"Since the Guilds thought they could bury the Great Wyrms beneath their boot, and were shown the error of their ways. See to the dismantling of this unsanctioned shit, or you'll suffer the consequences of defying the Archlegate."

Fulren saw Verlyn take a step closer to the Revocater. Ashe's hand tightened on his shoulder. He would have called out, told her not to do anything stupid, but these Revocaters thought him mute. He couldn't do anything to antagonise them.

"Why don't you all go and get fucked," Verlyn spat.

Fulren heard the slap, before Verlyn staggered backward. Ashe gasped at the sudden violence, but Verlyn was boiling, rage bubbling over so that all Fulren could see was a red storm inside her.

"No," Ashe shouted, but Verlyn was past hearing.

She shot forward, fist swinging, but the Revocater was faster. There was a sickening thump, Verlyn groaned, and he saw the red light in her wink out momentarily before she fell to the ground.

There was a clank beside Fulren as Ashe dropped the pyrestone helmet she'd been holding. "Get your hands off her," she screamed.

A scuffle, and one of the Revocaters shouted a word of warning.

Fulren gripped the arms of the chair, desperate to know what was happening, but all he could make out was a whirlwind of activity, wisps of light, horses stamping nervously. He should have shouted at them, told those Revocaters who he was, if only to distract them.

Something hit him in the side of the head, so hard he toppled over, wheelchair and all clattering to the earth. As he floundered, the clacking report of a splintbow cut the air.

For a moment he heard nothing. Feeling the cold wind brush against his cheeks before Verlyn screamed, high and long and loud.

"Verlyn?" Fulren gasped. "Ashe?"

He lay there for a moment, listening to someone sobbing. One of the Revocaters hissed a curse as wind rustled through the trees. Somewhere in the far distance, it whispered to him. That demon in the dark, teasing him, as though it had been waiting for just this moment.

"Bastards," Verlyn growled. Her silhouette was a baleful red, scintillating lights churning in a storm cloud. A starfield of red planets swirling like a tempest. "I'll kill you all."

Fulren was overwhelmed with nausea, feeling sickness grasp him in a cloying embrace as he fought back the urge to vomit. He heard one of the Revocaters snarl, saw Verlyn fighting with someone against the field of black.

"Get off her," he shouted, still fighting the urge to puke. "Let go of her."

He reached out, hand nudging something cold and hard on the ground. His fingers clasped the steel edge of Ashe's pyrestone helmet. As they did so, the necroglyph seared at his neck.

Could it work? Even without Verlyn's webwainer gift to draw out its power, could he use it to see?

Yes.

Fulren shook his head, trying to dispel that fell whisper. Verlyn grunted like an animal as she fought with the Revocaters. He heard the hiss of a sword being drawn. The clack of a splintbow clip being loaded into the stock.

All the while that whisper grew in volume, pounding in his head, and he resisted the urge to clamp his right hand over his ear.

Walk, Fulren.

Heat welled up in his legs from thigh to foot. *But he had no bloody feet.* His hand shook as he ignored the pain, raising the helmet and placing it over his head.

The world solidified, almost blinding in its clarity. Verlyn struggled with one of the Revocaters. Another sat atop his horse, splintbow in hand trying to aim but unwilling to shoot. The third had dismounted, sword drawn, ready to cut Verlyn down.

As his rage burned so did that necroglyph, more intensely than ever before, fuelling him, urging him. Making him whole.

His knee bent, the pneumatics of the rig that secured his lower body hissing in protest at the sudden movement. Fire seared all the way down to his ankle. For the first time in days, Fulren managed to push himself up with one arm. He bent his metal legs, raising himself up until he managed to stand. At first his knees shook—knees he had felt no sensation in since before they'd pulled him from that river. Through the eyes of the helm, he saw the Revocater holding Verlyn look toward him, mouth gaping open.

"Let her go," Fulren commanded.

The Revocater shoved Verlyn aside, drawing his blade. A challenge. *Face him.*

Fulren looked toward the cold earth. Ashe lay there, unmoving. Her eyes were open to the clear sky. Two splintbolts in her chest.

The necroglyph sparked. Feeding on his sudden rage.

Fulren stepped toward the first Revocater. The man looked panicked, shocked that this blind cripple had risen from the dirt, and he raised his sword to attack. Fulren ducked to one side with unnatural speed, the rig hissing as he moved, perfectly balanced, the machinery acting in symbiosis with his broken body.

His one remaining hand snatched forward as the sword swept by, plucking the blade from the Revocater's hand. A precise backswing took the man's head from his shoulders.

From the back of his horse, the one with the splintbow took aim, but his movement was laboured. He pulled his trigger, unleashing a storm of bolts. Fulren swayed to the side, three of those bolts flying wide. The last soared toward his chest, but he brought the sword up with the swiftness of a hunting bird, striking the bolt from the air to spin away harmlessly.

The pneumatics of his legs whined, one of the bolts securing a panel pinging away under the strain, as he powered himself toward the rider. The man's hand fumbled at his side for another splint-bolt clip, but before he could grasp it, Fulren had run him through where he sat.

He turned to face the last Revocater, who was already charging. Everything had slowed, and he took in the look of menace on that man's face, watched the sword arcing down toward his head, the glint of the sun on the blade. Fulren stepped aside, his weapon flashing, the Revocater's throat opening up, spraying an arc of red droplets.

The man staggered back, sword slipping from his hand. He clawed at the mortal wound, knees buckling. As Fulren watched him fall, all the tension seeped out of him. The rig felt suddenly heavy once more, his balance shifting awkwardly.

There came a roar in his ears like an ocean swell. A wall of noise that threatened to burst his skull.

Fulren wrenched off the helm before he toppled. His head struck the earth, and he saw Verlyn, shining against the dark as she moved toward him. She called his name, but another voice spoke much louder than her...

At last...

TYRETA

The oars whispered as they cut through the water, almost inaudible, but the noise still served to fray at Tyreta's nerves. Her eyes were locked on the far bank, and at any moment she expected battalion troopers to shout out a warning, for splintbow fire to strafe them as they sat helpless in the boat. So far her keen eyes had spotted nothing awaiting them in the dark.

Captain Moraide sat at the prow, jaw set, eyes scanning the bank. Tyreta could only admire the woman's grit—it was all she could do to not pitch herself over the side and swim for safety.

"This is fucking nuts," Sted hissed in her ear. In contrast to Moraide's calm exterior, Sted was glaring at the far side of the river like she hated it.

"We don't have any choice," Tyreta replied, desperate to keep her voice down. "We need to get Nicosse to my mother as quickly as possible. The landship terminal is the fastest way."

"And if there's no landship?"

"We'll work something else out, I guess. You know you don't have to be here."

Sted raised an eyebrow, suggesting that was bullshit. It wasn't. Tyreta had given them all a choice, and made it clear they didn't have to accompany her north of the river. There was every chance they wouldn't all make it through alive, and she would never have forced them to come. But they'd stood by her. It had given her a shred of hope that she might succeed in her mission. Not so much hope that she wasn't terrified—but if a shred was all she had, she'd cling on till it frayed to nothing.

Moraide held up a hand for them all to be silent as the boat cruised toward the bank. The troopers raised their oars as the vessel slipped up to the side of the jetty. Moraide was quick to step on land, holding the mooring rope steady as Tyreta and the rest of them debarked.

"Good luck," the captain whispered once they'd all stepped ashore.

Tyreta offered her a grateful nod, and Moraide climbed back on the boat before silently ordering her men to cast off. Once they'd disappeared into the night, Tyreta led her friends through the dereliction. No one uttered a sound as they pressed northward, not even so much as a squeak from Donan's mechanical leg.

Things were as ruinous this side of the river as on the south, and it looked like both armies had done their darndest to destroy the other. The only good thing to come from it was an abundance of cover provided by the burned-out buildings as they worked their way up through the enemy's lines, easily skirting the guards posted near the river.

Tyreta could sense every movement, hear every sound from some yards away. Her eyes penetrated the darkness almost as though the path ahead was lit up with lanterns, and she was learning to accept her burgeoning talents rather than question them. When she eventually sensed something approaching, she held up a hand for them to stop, trusting to her instincts.

Sted gripped her splintbow tighter, eyes scanning the oppressive darkness. The others froze where they stood as Tyreta nocked her bow, resisting the urge to pull the string tight.

Cat appeared atop a nearby ridge, licking her mouth and purring a greeting. Tyreta let out a breath, dropping to her knee as the panther jumped down and padded toward her.

"Where've you been, girl?" she whispered, as Cat rubbed her head against Tyreta's face.

"Can we save the reunions for when we're far from here?" Sted asked, taking the lead.

She had a point, and Tyreta followed her farther into the city.

"Where is everyone?" Tyreta asked as they made their way along an unlit street, passing open doors, revealing no one at home.

"Most likely all the normal folk fled a while back. Avoided the killing. Would you hang around here with all this going on if you didn't have to?"

Not likely. They'd reached a rise that offered a view of the northern half of the city. Crenn was quick to take his monocular and scan the distant winking lights.

"Can you see the terminal?" Tyreta asked.

"Yep," Crenn replied. "And it looks like there's a landship. Whether it's operational or not is anyone's guess."

"What about security?"

"Can't see anyone. I guess they're more concerned with what's happening at the river than their northern perimeter."

"Could be a trap," Tyreta said.

Crenn shrugged. "Could be. But what do we do about it?"

"We do our best not to fall right in," she replied, taking the lead again.

The others followed, unperturbed by the prospect of another encounter with the Ministry. Donan seemed to have grown fully used to his leg now, and moved with as much resolve as the rest of them, pushing on through abandoned street after abandoned street.

They weren't half a mile from the terminal when Tyreta suddenly felt that familiar sensation of dread. She stopped, holding her hand up to stop them all.

"What?" Sted asked.

"Something's not right," she replied.

"You mean, 'we're in danger' not right? Or 'you've stepped in shit' not right?"

Before she could answer she felt a surge of raw energy. A dozen pyrestones ignited beyond the wall to her left, powering up with fiery intensity. The wall exploded, a high-pitched screech of turbines defiling the quiet sanctity of the street as a massive stormhulk powered itself forward, foot slamming down a few yards away and cracking the paved tiles beneath it. There was a whine as one of its arms aimed a weapon, pyrestone energy blooming.

The group scattered as Tyreta dived out of the way, feeling a molten ball of pyrestone-fuelled ordnance strafe past her head and smash through the window of a nearby building. Her bow fell from her grip, but she was back on her feet in an instant. Before she could retrieve her weapon there came a telltale *clack* as bolts were fed into the breach of the hulk's splintcannon.

She ran, dodging to one side as a fusillade of missiles smashed into the paving where she had been standing. Instinct took over, the urge to flee, and she leapt toward the nearest house, desperate for cover. Her shoulder smashed into the front door, and it burst inward with the ping of a breaking lock. Tyreta almost went sprawling, but managed to stay on her feet, dashing across the lobby and into an adjacent passage.

Behind her came the sound of smashing glass and collapsing brick as the huge stormhulk burst through the wall, intent on hunting her down. She could feel the intensity with which its pyrestones were fuelled. Whoever was piloting the thing was one powerful webwainer—perhaps more powerful than any she'd ever encountered.

As she ran through the house and out onto the street at the other side, Tyreta grabbed the spear strapped to her back. She should have run, hidden from this behemoth, but there was a feral need growing inside her. An urge to suppress her flight instinct, to turn and face this foe. To prove she could not be beaten.

The stormhulk smashed its way from the house, pneumatic legs kicking aside the brickwork, vents spewing black smoke as the pilot pushed the machine to its limit. Tyreta felt the energy swell as the heavy longbarrel began to charge, readying to fire another volatile round straight at her.

She drew back her arm, fuelling the spear with all the power she could muster. The spearhead glowed white-hot, electricity dancing along its length as she threw. It streaked through the air like a bolt of lightning, aimed at the heart of the machine. At the last second the pilot turned the vast engine, dropping the huge shoulder, which took the brunt of the spear's impetus. It ignited with voltaic energy, so bright Tyreta had to shield her eyes.

The hulk staggered, the arm that carried the longbarrel sheared off completely, but the thing still moved, staggering after her, levelling its splintcannon. She was dead in its sights, an easy target for the next volley of bolts, but she refused to run. Instead she raised a hand, probing with her senses, connecting with every pyrestone that powered the devastating machine.

Gritting her teeth, she ignited them with all the hate she could muster—overloading those stones with her rage, her will, her defiance. A series of metallic explosions rang out before the splintcannon could unleash its deadly volley, smoke billowing from a dozen joints beneath the armoured plates of the hulk. It whined as it tried to move, but with its power source dead, there was nothing the webwainer could use to power it.

The cockpit hissed as it was released, smoke billowing in an acrid cloud. A woman crawled out, the one she had seen back in Windstone—the one who had pursued them all so doggedly. She all but fell from the dormant hulk, hitting the ground awkwardly while she coughed a string of bile from her lungs. Tyreta should have run, fled this city as fast as she could, but she was shaking with fury, with the overwhelming urge to kill this foe.

The woman glared as she approached, raising a hand for mercy, unable to speak as she hacked a cough. The broken haft of Tyreta's spear lay on the ground, and she picked it up, feeling the weight of it in her hand. It was not the magnificent weapon it had been but it would still do the job.

She raised the shaft, ready to smash her enemy's skull to pulp, but stopped before dealing that killing blow. This woman was helpless. Beaten. What was she even thinking?

Incandescent light burst to her left, followed by a jolt of sparking energy. Tyreta was struck by a thunderous torrent and flung like a rag doll across the street, where she landed in a heap.

Her flesh sparked as she tried to rise. It felt as though she'd been grasped in the fist of a storm. Across the street was a second woman, another webwainer from her powerful aura. She held a huge weapon, the end shaped like a talon, energy still sparking between its claws.

Tyreta struggled to stand, bracing herself for another shot of that volt gun, when someone rushed to her side. The clack of a splintbow rattled in her ear, and it was the webwainer's turn to jump for cover.

"Come on," Sted said, dragging her to her feet. "We have to get the fuck out of here."

Tyreta stumbled after her, away from those webwainers toward a path that led northward. Crenn was waiting up ahead, brows furrowing when he saw the state Tyreta was in. Donan was already urging Nicosse to get moving.

Together they stumbled along the street. A glance over her shoulder and she could see the two webwainers still in pursuit. The one with the volt gun strode ahead like some kind of emotionless golem, while the other woman drew the two knives at her side, blades radiating pyrestone energy.

Sted slammed another clip into her splintbow, turning, firing indiscriminately and forcing their pursuers to dodge for cover. Tyreta's head spun as she staggered on, still reeling from the raw energy that had jolted through her every fibre.

When they made it to a crossroads, Tyreta had to stop, leaning against the wall, her breath shallow and ragged.

"Come on," Sted urged. "We can't hang around, we don't know how many more—"

"Just wait," Tyreta gasped. She knew how hopeless this was—they were being hunted by powerful enemies and had no weapons to fight with other than a single splintbow. But there was one weapon they hadn't used yet.

She closed her eyes, trying to stay calm and centre herself as she reached out with her senses. There, not more than a hundred yards away—Cat stalked after them through the dark. Tyreta pressed her will, her consciousness flowing across the web like a whirlwind to join with the beast.

The furore as she connected almost took her breath away, and she could suddenly see through Cat's eyes, feel the strength in her limbs, the speed, the urge to hunt. She moved across the urban landscape as easily as any jungle, clinging to the shadows as she stalked the webwainers. They were not difficult to find, their scent heavy on the air, their clumsy advance across the city echoing like the beating of a drum.

There, one of them stumbled along, holding a pair of knives in limp fingers. Lips curled back from Tyreta's fangs as she slowed, moving ever closer for the kill. The woman stopped, as though sensing the panther's approach at the last second. Fear glinted in her eyes, exquisite terror upon seeing the beast stalking toward her. Days ago she had wounded Cat with one of those knives. She would not do so again.

Tyreta stirred the creature's natural instinct to hunt. Cat moved at speed, senses afire at the prospect of rending with tooth and claw, but as she came within five yards of the woman, every muscle tensed to leap, something enveloped her body. It was heavy, shining with myriad tiny jewels. Tyreta barely registered it was a net, before she felt energy course through every strand. Pyrestones burned bright all along the netting, sending energy streaming through Cat's body, and she was struck rigid, stunned by the electrical current. It was all Tyreta could do to sever her connection, before the panther lost consciousness.

She sucked in a sharp breath of air. "We have to run. Get to the terminal. Now!"

Donan urged Nicosse onward, the old man huffing as he clutched his bag of tricks. Tyreta had no time to consider if there was anything in there that could help them as they ran northward, at any moment expecting more webwainers to charge at them along the dark streets.

"There," Sted shouted, pointing to a sign brightly lit by the moonlight.

The landship terminal. Only one street away.

"Keep moving," Tyreta gasped. She wanted to turn back and find Cat, but she had to keep going, had to get Nicosse on that landship.

Ahead pyrestone lights glistened, illuminating their escape route. No sooner did Tyreta feel a swell of hope that they might just make it than two hulking figures stepped out of the shadows to block their path. Sted skittered to a stop in front of the Drakes, who stood shoulder to shoulder, swords drawn. She raised her splintbow, firing off a volley, the staccato clack echoing along the street before the bolts rang harmlessly off that impenetrable armour. Sted reached for another clip before realising there were none left.

"I'm out," she hissed, stating the obvious.

"We need to find another way," Tyreta said, grabbing her and dragging her back along the street.

She had no idea where to go, or even if there was another route to the terminal, but there was no way they were going through two armoured knights. Before she could even think where they might run to, Crenn and Nicosse skittered to a stop in front of her. Beyond them stood one of the webwainers—the one with the volt gun. She was smiling, delighting in this moment before the kill. As her weapon powered up, ready to unleash its fury on them, Tyreta thought about subduing the woman's abilities, but her head was still pounding, her connection to the web hazy and erratic. There was nothing she could do to stop her.

Donan screamed, throwing himself at the woman. She barely had time to level the volt gun before he grabbed hold of her, fumbling for the weapon in her grip.

"Run," Sted shouted, dashing forward to help Donan.

Crenn was already pulling Nicosse away from the fight as the knights strode purposefully toward them. Tyreta resisted the urge to take on those Drakes; they had to get the artificer away, that was more important than anything else.

With a last look back at Sted and Donan still struggling with that woman, Tyreta staggered after the two old artificers as they ran through the abandoned streets. Her senses were on fire and she could feel the hum of a nearby pyrestone light throbbing like a migraine. Breath came laboured, her limbs numb as she fought to keep up.

Nicosse and Crenn were blurred in her vision, but as she watched them she was assailed by an overwhelming sense of danger nearby. Crenn stopped, turning to face her, urging her forward, his words muffled in her ears.

"Wait," she gasped. "There's—"

A figure stepped from the dark, twin blades in her hands. Tyreta tried to shout a word of warning but the woman was too swift, and one of those daggers sank between Crenn's ribs. He staggered, legs failing him as Tyreta raced forward to help, a cry of anguish caught in her throat. The woman backed away, glaring at Tyreta, goading her with a smile.

She stumbled over the debris, desperate to reach him, but as she fell to her knees by Crenn's side his eyes had already glazed. She grasped his hand, but she could sense it was too late. All she could do was watch as he struggled to breathe, his grip growing weak in hers.

"Crenn?"

That single word was a plea—imploring him to stay with her. Instead, he slipped away with a quiet sigh. Tyreta had brought him here all the way from New Flaym. Crenn had saved her life there and accompanied her on this mission. Now he had given his life for it, and it was her fault.

But no. It wasn't just her fault.

Fire ignited within her, embers growing to cinders, bursting to flames. Nicosse cowered in the shadow of a derelict house. It was her mission to protect him, but all thought of that was misted red as she looked up at that woman, still walking away, keeping her eyes fixed on Tyreta.

A growl issued from her throat, a sound no human could ever make. She felt a feral power welling up inside, a seed planted in the jungles of the Sundered Isles now bursting to life. Her hands twisted into claws, the nails at the ends of her fingers pushing through flesh, extending to talons. Her vision sharpened as she watched her prey, that fogged focus sharpening with nothing but the urge to kill.

The woman ran.

Tyreta glanced down at Crenn, his chest not moving, blood running black in the moonlight. She should have stayed at his side, she owed him that much, but the overwhelming urge to hunt forced her to rise, to follow. That webwainer was only fifty yards ahead, ducking into a derelict building. Tyreta gave chase.

Her senses felt more heightened than ever as she reached the threshold, slowing, straining her ears for any sound that would give away the woman's hiding place. It was almost pitch-black inside, but her eyes easily adjusted to the gloom. She reached out with her powers, trying to locate the source of pyrestone set in that woman's blades. There was a dull thrum of energy, but it was indistinct within the walls of the building.

"You should give yourself up, Tyreta," said a voice, echoing through the run-down house. "I admire your loyalty to the Hawkspurs, but there's no way you'll defeat the Ministry."

There...just up the stairs. The woman was on the upper floor, and Tyreta made her way up, moving on all fours, stalking her like a beast in the forest. On the landing she paused, glaring through the dark, sensing that source of energy. At the end of the corridor was a wall, and through it she could see one blue and one yellow pyrestone winking in the dark. The webwainer's daggers.

Tyreta ran, feeling the unfettered power in her limbs, every muscle and sinew straining as the growl in her throat grew to a roar. She smashed into the wall, plaster shattering, wood splintering as she burst through, ready to rend with tooth and claw.

There was no one there—just two pyrestones sitting on top of an abandoned cabinet in a corner of the room.

Movement, swift and precise. Tyreta saw a flash of steel before a blade pressed to her throat. The woman grabbed her hair, wrenching her head back. One cut with purpose, and Tyreta's neck would be opened to the world.

"You know, you're pretty predictable," the woman whispered.

Tyreta felt her rage simmering, but she had to admit that had been a clever move. The woman had taken the stones from her weapons and left them as bait.

"Do it then," Tyreta snarled, barely recognising her own voice. "Take your victory for the Ministry. The Hallowhills have always been slaves, what difference whether to the Guilds, or to Sanctan Egelrath."

The woman grasped Tyreta's hair tighter. A raw nerve perhaps? "I am Keara Hallowhill, and I am no fucking slave."

"No? And yet you serve the Draconate as faithfully as any Drake."

Keara's hand was trembling, that blade poised to strike. All the while, Tyreta closed her eyes and focused on the yellow pyrestone sitting not five feet away on the cabinet.

"The Hallowhills will rise. We will become the greatest power in all Torwyn. If you're lucky, maybe you'll live long enough to—"

With a surge of effort, Tyreta fuelled every last ounce of energy into the stone and it exploded—filling the room with blinding light, stunning the woman long enough for Tyreta to shake off her grip.

Anger surged up again, her hand striking out before Keara could try to stab her. Razor claws slashed the woman's cheek and she screamed, staggering back. Tyreta was on her, another swipe of those claws and she'd knocked the dagger from her hand, one more and she'd torn three stripes in the arm of her jacket. A sharp kick and Keara fell back, head slamming against the wall.

As she lay dazed, Tyreta picked up the fallen dagger. It was beautifully worked, made by a craftsman for a deadly purpose. Standing over that woman it was all she could do to stop herself putting it to use.

Keara looked up, a gallows' smile on her bloody face. She was beaten and she knew it.

"Go on then, Hawkspur. Let's get this over with."

Tyreta should have done it. One quick strike, just like the one that had ended Crenn. Every fibre of her being screamed for her to do it. She was the victor, and this was her right. The law of the wild.

But Tyreta Hawkspur was no animal.

She drove the blade deep into the wall, noting the look of relief on Keara's face before she slammed her foot down. Keara's head cracked into the wood floor and she was still. Tyreta made her way back down the stairs and out into the night to be greeted by the sight of Crenn lying on the other side of the street, Nicosse still cowering nearby.

"Get up," she said. "We need to—"

He looked terrified. Gripping his knees and shaking like a leaf. Tyreta didn't even hear the brute move in on her, barely felt the first blow. Her teeth clacked together as the gauntleted fist struck her jaw. She fell, tasting the blood on her tongue, trying to rise, but all the energy had been sapped from her body with that single punch.

Other figures moved from the shadows, splintbows trained right at her. There were perhaps a dozen of them, phoenixes emblazoned on their armour. As Tyreta's blurred vision began to focus, a woman walked into the light. This one wore a blue robe—a High

Legate—and she gazed down at Tyreta with what could have been sympathy.

"An admirable attempt to escape, girl," she said, before all the sympathy melted away. "But you cannot escape fate."

Sanctan must have thought Tyreta a particular danger if he'd sent such a loyal servant to stop her. But stop her he had.

ANSELL

The cloak was drawn tight, hiding his face from the sorry gathering that surrounded him. Beggars hunkered together all along the street, desperate to ward off the encroaching cold. They had regarded him warily when he first joined them, wondering who this giant was and how he had fallen so low. Within an hour it was as though he were one of them—just another forgotten drifter left to the vagaries of the streets. Now he sat on the cold cobbles, hidden in the shadows, one more vagabond waiting for alms.

Olstrum had kept his promise—a simple piece of parchment left in Ansell's chamber. A street name, a house number. Of course it was in the Burrows, that had come as no surprise. He always knew he'd have to pursue these heretics to the least salubrious end of the city to find Grace.

He had not questioned Olstrum's information, but neither did he trust it completely, and so he waited here in the dark, among the sorry wastrels of the Anvil. His backside was almost numb, but as night had begun to fall he grew certain this was the place.

Cloaked and furtive figures came and went from the house all day. Ansell had seen them waiting at the door, glancing about nervously, looking to see if they were being spied upon, with no idea that one of those beggars might be watching their every move. Then they had knocked, that same knock every time—three, then one, then two. The hatch in the centre of the door would snap open and, after showing their faces, those cloaked figures had been allowed inside. If this was not the place he was looking for, then it was most certainly used for some other illicit purpose.

The old man sitting beside him shuffled uncomfortably, mumbling some lament as his grog-stinking breath steamed in the cold night. Not for the first time Ansell began to question why he was here, and the consequences he might face if he was discovered.

Just by investigating the place he was defying the explicit instruction of the Archlegate—heresy in itself, but his mind was made. Ansell Beckenrike was no man's puppet, not any longer. He had come here for Grace. To liberate an innocent child used as a pawn in other men's games.

And the reason? Was it to wash away his previous sins? Would this one act redress all the evil he had perpetuated in the name of the Draconate? He had murdered an Archlegate so that Sanctan might rise. Had slain an emperor to protect the man he now disobeyed. Would saving this girl from her fate put him back in the graces of the Great Wyrms?

Did any of that even matter now?

Surely he had been punished enough for his sins. His chin itched maddeningly, the scabs from whatever spell Assenah Neskhon had cursed him with refusing to heal. The stab wound he had suffered mere days before ached, worsened by the cold, the stitches barely holding the laceration closed. The various wounds inflicted by Lancelin Jagdor were still a reminder of the ignominy he had suffered at the swordwright's hands. Perhaps that humiliation was the worst wound of all. The deepest cut that could never be stitched.

A cart rumbled toward them along the cobbles. Ansell pulled the hood lower over his face as it trundled past, the man in the driver's seat glaring at the row of beggars with disdain. He hawked and spat, narrowly missing Ansell's foot.

The driver's callous gesture angered him more than it should. If not for a twist of fortune, it might have been him sitting in the dirt. He was spitting at his own people, albeit the forgotten and waylaid.

Surely they should have been helping one another, and yet the
Guilds had made them selfish. Made them think only of their own
betterment.

Ansell had seen good people in the short time he had sat here—
acts of benevolence as the poor spared what few coins they could.
It had heartened him somewhat, but he was not here to lament the
struggles of the poor, nor think on the goodness in people's souls.
He was here to punish evil.

A cloaked man hurried along the street, stopping outside the door,
a quick look to left and right before he knocked—three, one, two.
He shuffled impatiently as he waited, turning to see if he was being
watched, the moonlight illuminating his face. Ansell recognised
him immediately. The cook. Patris. If there had been any doubt this
was the right place, it was expelled in that instant of recognition.

The hatch in the door opened, before Patris was allowed inside.
No sooner had the door closed than Ansell rose to his feet, stretching
his numb legs. He paused, quelling all doubt. There was no use in
waiting any longer, it would gain him nothing. He had no weapon
at his side to loosen in its scabbard, nor even a knife. He would
face this trial unarmed, and learn, one way or another, whether the
Wyrms were truly watching over him.

The beggars murmured behind as he crossed the cobbled street.
There was no more traffic, no rumbling carts, no one to see but the
vagrants wallowing in their misery. In the distance to left and right,
lanterns burned on their stanchions. No pyrestone light winked in
the Burrows lest it be cracked open and the precious stones within
stolen.

At the door he was bathed in shadow. One last pause. One last
chance to abandon this folly. To return to the Mount and forget his
disobedience.

He clenched a fist and knocked. Three. One. Two.

Muffled voices beyond the door. Footsteps approaching. The
hatch slid open and a frowning face peered out through the gap.
Ansell thrust his hand inside, grasping the man's throat. He didn't
even have time to give an awkward squawk before Ansell's fist tightened. The man struggled, grasping Ansell's wrist with both hands,

trying to loosen that iron grip, but it would never work. He kicked at the door in his panic, but that only urged Ansell to greater effort and he squeezed all the tighter.

The man went limp, falling from Ansell's grip, and he took a step back, raising a foot, smashing it against the lock. With a resonant *ping*, the door flew open, halted by the fallen body. Ansell braced a shoulder against it, shoving it open, striding inside.

A shout of anger to his left, a feral cry of rage. Ansell braced himself as the man raced along the corridor, a sword already raised. His attack was easy to read, and Ansell stepped aside as the blade missed him by an inch, before he grasped the man by the neck. Aided by the impetus of his charge, Ansell thrust his attacker's head into the wall, the sword falling from his hand. Grabbing a fistful of hair, he smashed that head into the wall again and again and again until the body went limp in his hands.

The clap of a splintbow. Ansell turned, raising that ragged body as a shield, feeling the impact as it was riddled with half a dozen bolts. Once the clip emptied, he dropped the corpse, seeing a hawk-nosed man atop the staircase desperately fumbling more ammunition into the stock. Ansell was already moving, taking the stairs three at a time, just as the man slid the clip into place. He levelled the splintbow, but Ansell managed to grasp the stock, turning it away as the weapon fired wildly, peppering the ceiling with bolts.

With a grunt, he wrenched the bow from the man's grip, flinging it down the stairs. As the man went for the knife at his belt, Ansell clamped a hand over it before butting him in the bridge of that big nose. The man sagged against the wall. Ansell punched him full in the face, wood panel cracking as the back of his head smashed into it. Again he struck, the panel giving way. Once more and that head disappeared into the splintered hole.

Ansell was breathing heavily now, stepping away from the body in time to feel the sharp sting of a blade in his shoulder. He reacted on instinct, grasping the hand still holding tight to the knife, its blade still sunk in his flesh. A woman screamed in his face, trying to wrench her weapon free, but Ansell was stronger, slowly pulling it from his shoulder. She carried on screaming, rage and hate in her eyes, spitting phlegm in his face. Ansell shoved the knife deep into her throat, seeing her hate turn to surprise as she choked on the steel.

It didn't take long for her to spit her last, coughing blood all over him, before he let go and she collapsed at the top of the stairs. Blood was pouring from his shoulder as he staggered the rest of the way up and leaned against the wall of a corridor. The stitches had torn again in his side, and he could feel the warm sensation of yet more blood beneath his shirt. One of his sleeves hung ragged from the fight and he tore it free, wrapping it around the fresh wound in his shoulder and tying off the knot with his teeth.

The house was quiet now. Nothing but the sound of his own breathing. He took a step along the corridor, with doors all along its left-hand side. Gently he pushed one open to find an empty room—just a bed and a piss-pot, but no one waiting to kill him.

"Grace?" he called.

No answer. Perhaps she was not even here. Perhaps he had killed those people for nothing. Then movement at the end of the corridor, a shadow flickering in the candlelight before Patris moved into view. In front of him was Grace, his hand clamped over her mouth, a knife in his hand, poised at her throat.

"Don't come any closer," the cook said. A tremble in his voice. Normally fear would be Ansell's friend, but not now. Patris was holding a blade to Grace's neck, and fear might encourage him to open it up as readily as make him surrender.

"Let her go," Ansell replied as gently as he could manage.

Grace was staring at him, not making a sound, no sign that she was even scared.

"I'm not stupid," Patris spat. "As soon as I let her go you'll fucking kill me."

He was right about that.

"Give her to me and you won't be harmed."

Patris shook his head. "You're lying. I know you people. I've toiled at the Mount for years, and I see you. All your self-righteous horseshit. Even your Archlegate stands behind a pulpit of lies. And here is the evidence." He pressed the knife to Grace's neck. "He pretends to be so pious and yet he lays with whores."

"Just let her go. I won't hurt you."

"Liar! You have to swear it. Swear it on your fucking gods."

As much as Ansell yearned for his reckoning, he knew there was no choice about it. He had already given an oath to Olstrum so he could find this place, what difference to do it one more time?

"All right. I swear by the five Great Wyrms that if you give the girl to me, I will not harm you."

Patris glared, his eye twitching as he considered the words. Ansell thought perhaps it would not be enough, that Patris would be too scared, that he would kill the girl anyway out of spite. Then, ever so slowly, he lowered the knife and took his hand from Grace's mouth.

Ansell beckoned to her, and she walked forward, not rushing, not panicking, taking everything in her stride as she came to stand before him. He knelt.

"Hello, Ansell," she said.

"Are you all right?" he replied, looking over her little body but seeing no sign she had been harmed.

"Yes."

He wanted to grab her, hold her close, make her feel safe, but there were still things to be resolved.

"Wait for me outside," he said.

With a nod she walked past him, and Ansell struggled to his feet, feeling the ache in his side and in his shoulder. Blood still trickled from his wounds and he would need attention from the apothecaries again, but there was time enough for that later. He walked toward Patris who, to his credit, stood his ground despite his obvious fear.

"We didn't hurt her," said Patris, still holding tight to that knife. "We were never gonna do her any harm."

"And yet you took her anyway."

"You swore," said Patris, holding up the knife. "You said—"

Ansell snatched his wrist, turning it, twisting it so the knife fell from his fingers. His other hand grasped Patris's throat before he could mewl any more excuses.

"I am the divine hand of the Wyrms," Ansell snarled, tightening his grip. "It does not matter if I offer mercy, for *they* will grant you none. Ravenothrax comes for you this day. Can you see him? Do you feel those black wings embracing you?"

Patris made no sound as his eyes bulged, his pallor turning dark. His mouth was open, but with his throat so constricted he could plead for mercy no more. That fat tongue lolled as Ansell tensed every muscle, feeling his wounds cry but ignoring their pleas until Patris sagged in his grip.

He dropped yet another body to the floor before turning, staggering, holding out a hand to steady himself against the wall. Slowly he worked his way back through the house, now a charnel pit of corpses. He spared no pity for these people. Their intentions had perhaps been high minded, but they would be judged in the Lairs just the same.

At the bottom of the stairs he took a cloak that still hung from a hook, before making his way outside. The cold air filled his lungs and he breathed it in for a moment, seeing Grace waiting just as he had asked. Kneeling, he wrapped the cloak about her shoulders.

"Are you sure you're all right?"

She smiled and nodded. "Yes. I'm hungry though."

Ansell could only marvel at her resilience, at how unaffected she was by this whole experience. Gently he picked her up, feeling the twinge in his side and shoulder more keenly than ever, before walking back through the Burrows toward the Mount.

Grace leaned her head on his shoulder. Glancing down at her, Ansell realised for the first time how much she resembled Sanctan. Those eyes were the same, but also her seeming disregard for the violence that had just taken place. She had walked through a house of corpses and made no mention of it. If any of those abductors had shown her an ounce of affection, she most certainly didn't reciprocate. But then she was a child. Ansell knew well that despite their vulnerability, children could also demonstrate remarkable resilience.

"Are we going on our adventure now?" Grace asked quietly, close to sleep.

"Have you not had adventure enough for one day?" Ansell replied.

Grace didn't answer, resting her head on his shoulder and falling asleep.

The spires of the Mount appeared above the distant rooftops. He knew there would be consequences for this, for defying the Archlegate's word and returning his daughter. Perhaps Grace was right, and it was time for another adventure. Maybe he should just take her as far from this place as he could. Start his life anew...

But that was a dream for other men.

KEARA

S he walked past a line of troopers on guard, each one at rigid
attention. None of them so much as looked at her, but by the
state of her face, it was doubtful anyone would pay her much attention ever again.

Three gashes across her cheek, sewn up as well as the battalion surgeon could manage. She hadn't dared to look at the wound, avoiding
mirrors like the plague. Her cheek throbbed, but a little touch of the
drop had dulled her senses enough to bear it. Whether she'd be able
to bear the scars was another story.

She gritted her teeth at the prospect of a mutilated face as she
made her way through the old building. It had been a gaol before all
this started. Fitting then that it should be used to cage their prisoners.

Moving up through the tight warren of stairwells and passages,
she came out onto a balcony that ran along the northern wall. There
was a yard below, and bastions from which the gaol guards could
shoot down at any prisoners unruly enough to provoke them. Now
that yard was empty, but the balcony wasn't.

At the far end was a cage, a beast thrashing and hissing within.
That panther had almost been the death of her, but now it was helpless. Hesse had found a stick and was teasing the hapless creature. It
clawed at the bars while she tormented it, but if she was deriving

any pleasure from the sadism, she showed no sign—her face a blank mask, eyes hidden behind those dark lenses.

Keara left Hesse to her amusement, ducking back into an adjoining corridor of dark stone, cell doors on either side, a row of Phoenix Battalion troopers lining the way. At the far end one cell door was open, and Keara took a deep breath before walking in.

She tried to keep a straight face, hiding her delight at seeing the prisoners she had managed to capture. Tyreta was shackled to one wall, her eyes regarding Keara with ill intent. Opposite her was the old artificer—the one that had survived. Nicosse looked weary and terrified, and Keara almost felt sorry for the poor wretch. Did he even realise what he had got himself involved in?

Slowly she moved toward Tyreta. Though it was sad seeing such a capable woman in chains, Keara had to remember the danger. This woman gifted the scar on her cheek, but then spared her life. Should she have been grateful for that?

She knelt down, just far enough away so Tyreta couldn't get to her. Keara had seen firsthand how fast and strong she could be, and whatever sorcerous powers she had harnessed had given her claws that could easily rip out a throat. Tyreta just stared back, her eyes resembling those of an animal. A panther perhaps? In the dim light of the cell it was difficult to tell.

"This is nothing personal, you know. If things had been different, if this whole uprising had never started, we might even have ended up friends. As it is, fate has put us on opposite sides."

"I'd never be friends with a strung-out drop addict like you," Tyreta hissed through her teeth. Teeth that looked inhumanly sharp.

Keara realised her left eye must have been bloodshot after she'd dripped the last of Ulger's stash into it. "It might be wise to show a little more gratitude for keeping you alive."

Tyreta's mouth twisted in a mocking smile. "Don't worry yourself about me. I'll be just fine."

"Will you? Why? Because the Archlegate is your cousin? Do you honestly think that will spare you? Familial loyalty counts for shit right now. Sanctan didn't care about family when he tore your bastard Guild apart."

That hurt her, Keara could tell from the creasing of Tyreta's brow. "Why do you hate us so much?"

Why indeed? The fact Tyreta didn't even know made it taste all the more bitter in Keara's mouth. "Because the major Guilds have treated the Hallowhills like serfs for decades. No, you said it yourself, more like slaves. Now it's time for all that to change."

Tyreta shook her head as though she could hardly believe it. "And so you crawled into bed with a fanatic like Sanctan? You stabbed an old man and left him to die in the street because your pride is hurt?"

Keara rose to her feet. "You murdered one of mine first. I'd known Ulger for years. He was a bastard sometimes, but he was *my* bastard. A friend. And now he's dead—torn apart by your fucking pet."

"Crenn was a good man, you mad bitch," Tyreta snarled back. "He'd never done any harm to anyone."

Keara drew in a breath, trying to calm herself down, to quell the rush of the red drop and take back control of her emotions. "Then I suppose we're even."

Tyreta narrowed those feral eyes. "I should have killed you."

Keara smiled back. "Yes, perhaps you should. But maybe you just don't have that killer instinct. Despite the claws." Absently she raised a hand to her face but stopped short of touching the stitched wounds on her cheek. "That's why you're in chains, and I'm standing here."

"I won't be in chains forever. When I get out of here, you'd best watch your back, because I'll be coming for you."

Keara wanted to laugh in her face. Wanted to tell her how pathetic she sounded, but there was something in those eyes. Tyreta meant every word, and it made a little shiver work its way through the numbing effect of the red drop and course down Keara's spine.

Turning her back on Tyreta, she walked to where Nicosse was chained. He didn't look much. Just an old man, pathetic and wretched.

"Are you really what all this fuss has been about?" she asked.

He looked up at her mournfully, beard all matted as he shook his balding head. "None of this was my idea."

She could well believe it. "If it makes you feel any better, it wasn't mine either. I'd rather be shacked up safe and warm at the Web, waiting for all this to blow over."

"I have nothing to do with any of this," he pleaded. "I'm nobody really. You could just let me go."

As pitiful as Nicosse looked, Keara was all out of mercy. "It's a little too late for that, my friend. I couldn't let you go, even if I wanted to. But I don't want to. I've heard you're a talented man. A legend, depending on who you ask. Forbidden experiments. Heretical rites. You could save us a lot of time by telling me all about it."

Despite how fearful he looked, Nicosse smirked. "It would be too complex a thing to explain. Even to a webwainer."

"Try me," she replied, trying not display her annoyance.

"Oh, I can build things you wouldn't believe. Things that would change Torwyn for good. But it was my brother who was the true pioneer."

"Ah yes, Lysander." She leaned in closer, smelling the old man's stale odour. "I heard he was a degenerate too. What he'd be worth if he were here in your place. Is he even still alive?"

The old man looked away with a sad expression. "I have no idea. But if he were here, I doubt you'd be so confident."

Keara held up her arms, glancing about the cell as though looking for someone in the shadows. "But he's not here, is he. No one has heard from him in years. And if he could achieve half the things people say, then why hasn't he risen? Seized control for himself? Or are the legends just so much pigshit?"

Nicosse looked at her, bushy grey brows creasing into a dark frown. "If my brother had chosen to rise, decided to claim what was well within his ability to take, you webwainers would have become obsolete. He could have forged a power that would have brought Torwyn to its knees."

"So why didn't he?" Keara asked, tiring of the old man's rant.

"Because he recognised the danger in it. Combining the power of pyrestones with magics far darker could mean the destruction of all Hyreme. An age of apocalypse."

She almost laughed at his fanciful claim, but something in his tone, in the surety of his words, made her wonder if he was telling the truth. Though she would never admit it, the notion frightened her. But also thrilled her. What she might learn from this man, what she might gain if only—

"Amusing yourself, Hallowhill?"

Keara turned to see the sweep of a blue robe. Hisolda entered the cell with two Phoenix Battalion troopers at her back, shooting Tyreta a disdainful glance before focusing on Keara.

"Apologies," she continued. "I may have previously neglected to thank you for your role in all this. You have been a great help. I'm sure the Archlegate appreciates your...contribution."

"What does that mean?" Keara replied.

"It means your services are no longer required. I can take things from here."

She could take all the credit, more like. Keara was not of a mind to let that happen, but right now she couldn't work out quite what to do about it.

Hisolda took a step toward Tyreta, gazing down with unbridled joy. "The Archlegate is so very much looking forward to his reunion with you, girl."

To her credit, Tyreta said nothing. Not even deigning to look up at the woman. Keara doubted she'd have shown as much reserve in Tyreta's position.

When she could see she would get no rise from Tyreta, Hisolda turned her attention to Nicosse. He struggled to look up at the High Legate, almost as though he could sense something bad was coming.

"Ah, the heretic," Hisolda breathed. "Do you have any idea what I've been through to find you?"

That sounded a bit rich considering she'd barely lifted a finger. It was Keara who'd sacrificed, Keara who'd bled, and here was Hisolda only too eager to claim the reward.

Despite his fear, Nicosse managed to raise his head and look at her. "You needn't have bothered to exert yourself on my account. I am no threat to the Ministry."

Hisolda nodded her agreement. "Not anymore, you're not. And in a short time, no artificer will be." She turned to regard Keara with a solemn look of sincerity. "You know I've always had a grudging respect for webwainers. The Guilds have turned them into the beating heart of our society, with their industry and their clever little inventions. And in turn, you have become their unwitting servants. Used and abused."

Keara began to wonder what Hisolda was getting at, when the woman turned back to Nicosse with a sneer. "But artificers. They are a different breed altogether. Hunkering in their workshops like rats. Devising. Plotting. Scheming. Seeding Torwyn with their infernal machines. Stripping the land like locusts. Making the labour of good honest people obsolete."

She clicked her fingers. One of the troopers stepped forward, holding out his splintbow, and Hisolda took it from him. She looked over the weapon with an odd kind of reverence.

"Take this," she continued, running a hand along the weapon's stock. "Such an ingenious feat of engineering. An intricate combination of parts, but at the same time oh so simple to operate. Does not require a pyrestone or a webwainer to use, and yet bestows the power of life and death unto even the weakest of hands. All down to artifice." She smiled down at Nicosse. "But soon, none of this will exist. We will stride into an age of renewed faith. The machine age will be consumed in the breath of the Wyrms. Until then..."

Hisolda levelled the splintbow at Nicosse. Keara opened her mouth to shout for her to stop, but she'd already pulled the trigger. The clack of the splintbow echoed with dreadful clarity as Nicosse was riddled with bolts, convulsing for a moment, before slumping in the corner of the damp cell.

Tyreta screamed, "No!" but it was too late. Keara could only stare at the murder in front of her, as Hisolda casually tossed the splintbow back to its owner. She hitched up her blue robe before kneeling next to Nicosse's corpse.

"Now we have no more problem."

Keara took a step toward the priestess before stopping herself, not for the first time desperate to contain her emotions. "No more problem? Have you any idea what we could have learned from that man? He might have been able to help us in our fight."

Hisolda rose, turning to regard Keara with a grave look. "We need no help from artificers."

"My Guild—"

"Your Guild only exists because the Archlegate allows it. You retain what little power you have through the grace of the Ministry. If you want to keep it, I suggest you don't question me anymore."

Keara's fists were bunched, jaw squeezed shut so tight she could feel the stitches pulling in her cheek. "And what about Tyreta? Are you going to execute her too?"

Hisolda glanced over to where the Hawkspur knelt in the corner of the cell, staring in disbelief at the artificer's corpse. "No. She will be taken back to the Anvil. She may be just the leverage we need to end Lady Rosomon's little resistance movement. I suggest you make ready. A landship is being prepared to take us north by sunset tomorrow."

She had to keep her emotions in check, just for a short while until...what? Keara had been rendered surplus to requirements already. With one last glance at Tyreta, who glared with unmasked loathing, she marched from the cell and out into the corridor.

This could not stand. Nicosse might have been able to help her, the Hallowhills, her father, but now he was dead in a cell. All Keara had left to show for her efforts was Tyreta, but even she was being stripped away and gifted to the Ministry.

Or perhaps not.

She took a deep breath as she made it out onto the balcony. Hesse was still there, still tormenting that panther, though it looked like it was losing interest in the stick she was poking it with.

"Leave that fucking thing alone and come with me," Keara ordered.

Hesse regarded her blankly before flinging the stick over one shoulder and following her along the length of the balcony.

"Can we go home now?" Hesse asked.

"No," Keara replied, stopping when she was sure they were out of anyone's earshot. "We need to fix this. We need a renegotiation of terms. The dice have been loaded against us."

Hesse looked at her from behind dark lenses. Then raised an eyebrow. "What?"

"I mean, we need to get different dice. Understand?"

Hesse nodded as though she did, before raising her other eyebrow. "What the fuck are you talking about?"

"I'm talking about that Hawkspur bitch," Keara hissed, desperate not to raise her voice. "Once she's handed over to Sanctan, this will all be over."

Hesse shrugged. "But that's a good thing, isn't it? We can go—"

Keara grabbed her by the shoulders. "When the Ministry have everything they need to end this war, they won't need us any longer. Do you understand that?"

Slowly Hesse nodded. "So what do you want to do?"

"I want to solve that problem."

Hesse opened her mouth and raised her chin as though she understood completely. "So new dice?"

Keara grinned, feeling her cheek ache but starting to enjoy the pain. "Exactly that."

FULREN

He was trapped in a maze of steel and iron, cloying, crushing. The noise was deafening, the hiss and clank of machinery squeezing him as tight as the structure that surrounded him, but still he crawled through the labyrinth, the heat of outlet pipes burning his flesh, stifling the air in his lungs. On he moved, somehow finding the will to squirm through the darkness, wriggling within the shadows of this infernal manufactory for all he was worth. He could hear himself groaning, moaning, but he could not give in. Not yet.

Salvation lies ahead, Fulren Hawkspur.

He resisted the urge to curse that fell whisper. To tell it he would not succumb. How he yearned for someone to help, but there was no one here. No one to offer him just a sliver of reprieve from this torment. Had he been damned to the Lairs? Was this his ultimate fate?

No. He had to keep going. To resist that urging in his ears. His only redemption would be of his own making.

Give in to me.

He screamed above the sound of the voice. Above the beat of that clanking machinery, the grinding of cogs, the piston hiss of the engine in which he was trapped.

I could save you, Fulren. I will offer redemption where no one else can.

That voice boomed in his ears, and he gritted his teeth against it.

He almost wept at the prospect of what would happen if he offered himself up to that voice. To give himself over to it. To damn himself.

A hiss of steam seared his back and he cried out, a pitiful sob lost among the noise. He stretched out an arm and burned it on a white-hot pipe. There was a buzz as a razor-edged conveyor passed overhead and his back was lacerated.

You are pathetic without me. A shell. Be a man and accept what can be yours.

He gritted his teeth against the pain, but tears still flooded out. There was no way to resist this. No other way to be saved. He had lost everything. His sight, his limbs...his sanity.

For what was this if not madness?

He had to give in to it. To death, if nothing else. But there was still so much for him to do. He would not succumb. He would endure. Rise...

And you will rise, Fulren Hawkspur. All you need do is accept what is offered.

As the machine beat and drummed and echoed around him, he stopped. There was no fight left, he knew that. No matter what he did, he could not defeat the thing he had become. A sightless, crawling worm of a creature, flailing in the dark against the inevitable. The whisper was right. He could only give in.

"Take me," he said. A quiet request, little more than a beggar beseeching alms.

I cannot hear you.

"Take me!" he screamed. "I give in. Have me. Do what you will, but release me from this nightmare."

Very well.

The hissing stopped. The thud of turbines and the whine of engines ceased their incessant din. He felt the slither of cold metal run over the back of his hand as tendrils of copper wire wrapped themselves around him. Fulren resisted the instinctive urge to panic, allowing himself to succumb to the machine as it began to enfold him in its embrace.

Plates pressed to the flesh of his torso, hissing as white-hot steel cauterized, armouring him in a metal skin. He gritted his teeth against the searing pain but could not quell a scream of agony. Pain engulfed him as fronds of molten iron bored their way into the stumps of his

missing limbs. As his body was grafted to a metal structure of whining pneumatics, so his head and face were covered in molten fluid
that solidified to his skull.

Light blinded him. A prism of colour in his line of sight and no
way to shut his eyes against it. He couldn't breathe. Couldn't think.
The Fulren of old melted away to be replaced by an engine of diabolical origin.

A golem of steel and flesh.

The scream caught in his throat as he opened his eyes. All he could
see was the blackness of the bedchamber, the faint echoes of the
demon engine fading in his ears.

Fulren was drenched in sweat, the light cotton bedsheet wrapped
around him like a shroud. Struggling for air, he wrenched the sheet
to one side, momentarily forgetting his lost legs, his missing arm, as
he clawed his way from the bed. The floor hit him, the resounding
thud sending a shock wave through his body.

Each breath was laboured. He reached out his right arm, clawing
at the floorboards, inching his way across the room until he managed to grab the doorframe and pull himself into the corridor. The
house was silent, a cool breeze blowing down the passage and offering a moment's release from the cloying tomb of his nightmare.

He had to get outside. Girding himself, he continued to crawl,
shifting his broken body until he reached the front door. It swung
gently in the breeze, the cold making him realise it must have been
the dead of night.

Eventually he managed to shift himself through the door, reaching the porch. There he paused, raising his head long enough to see
a swirl of light in the distance. Verlyn.

She was standing stock-still at the edge of the yard, head bowed
from what he could see. He would have called out to her, but as the
memory of the previous day began to dawn, he realised that this was
a solemn moment. Fulren had no right to intrude upon it.

Before he could shift himself to the step of the porch, Verlyn
turned. Slowly she made her way closer, before kneeling beside him.

"You look like shit," she said quietly.

"I feel it," he replied.

"Let's get you in the chair."

She stepped onto the porch and he heard the creak of the chair's wheels as she moved it beside him. With some effort she helped him sit.

"I was just saying goodbye," she said.

Her voice sounded small and she appeared so lost, but Fulren had known enough loss of his own. It could break anyone, no matter how strong they were.

"I'm sorry," he said, gesturing across the yard to where she'd been standing. "May I?"

Without a word she pushed the chair across the cold ground of the yard until he came to a stop at what could only be a graveside. Though Fulren couldn't see into it, he knew that Ashe was lying in the ground. He should have said something, some words of solace, but what could he say? The feeling that this was all his fault began to creep deeper into him, and it was all he could do not to weep.

"That's enough," Verlyn said eventually.

Without asking she grasped the chair and pushed it back toward the house. Once inside the kitchen, she picked up the iron kettle, heating water on the stove. He supposed it was as good a time as any for tea.

"What will you do now?" he asked, as she placed a warm cup in his hand.

"It's obvious I can't stay here," she replied. "Those Revocaters will be back in numbers, now a group of them has gone missing. I've buried the bodies, but it still doesn't solve the problem that the farm runs on artifice. I doubt we'll be able to take on a dozen of them even if you are..."

She stopped short of saying it. Fulren remembered how he had felt when that arcane energy coursed through him. When he gave himself over to the voice, and was rewarded in kind.

"You don't have to take me with you," he said. "You should just run. As far from here as you can get."

"And leave the son of Rosomon Hawkspur to the mercy of the Draconate? Then this would all have been for nothing."

Fulren gripped the cup tighter, despite how hot it was. "You...
you know who I am? But when did you..."

"Not at first, but we worked it out eventually. It's pretty obvious
you're highborn from the way you talk. Everyone knows Fulren
Hawkspur was exiled to Nyrakkis, and you didn't get that mark on
the back of your neck anywhere in Torwyn. Besides, you talk in your
sleep. A lot."

"You knew who I was all this time? And never said anything? But
you must have realised the danger you were putting yourselves in."

"Ashe knew the dangers, but she didn't care. Guess that's just the
person she is...she was. She would never have abandoned you, after
turning up on our doorstep like a helpless kitten. Ashe always did
the right thing. Even if she knew it would have consequences."

Fulren could hear the regret in her voice. The loss. "And what
about you? If you'd known the consequences, would you still have
helped me?"

She drew in a long breath. "I never had as pure a soul as Ashe.
Always surprised me what she saw inside. But things can't be
changed now. And Ashe would never forgive me if I just walked
away and left you to the Revocaters."

"I—I don't know how to thank you for what you've done for me.
What you've both done."

"I don't need thanks. But I do want answers. This power you
have—where does it come from? What's that mark on your neck?"

For so long Fulren had been desperate to keep it a secret. To keep
so much to himself, if only to protect these two women from...
what? The truth? Or what he might be capable of? None of that
seemed to matter anymore.

"When I was exiled to Nyrakkis, I was condemned. The only
way I could survive was to embrace their demon sorceries. I was
cursed by them, but even I don't fully understand what's happening
to me."

That was truth enough. There would be no benefit in mentioning
the voice whispering in his ear and plaguing his nightmares.

"That explains a lot," Verlyn said. He was relieved at how little she seemed concerned by the confession. "I could tell you were

dangerous. I just didn't know how much. And if I had any sense, I would get as far from you as I could."

"Then why don't you?"

"Well, firstly I don't have much sense. I mean, I'd like to think I don't scare easy, but you, Fulren. You scare the shit out of me. But you know what... I've got nothing left to lose now."

For a moment, Fulren thought that perhaps she did. That by staying by his side she might be in danger of losing her soul right along with him. Hopefully he would find some way of controlling the demon inside, so no one ever got hurt by it again.

"So what do we do? Where do we go?"

"We find someone who can help us. Or more to the point, help you. Someone who knows what's happening to you and can fix it."

"That sounds like a tough ask. I don't even know myself. I can't imagine any way to fix this other than just not use it."

"I don't know either. But I know someone who might."

That was hard to believe. He doubted even the sorcerers of Nyrakkis could understand what was happening to him. It certainly seemed alien to everything he had seen in Torwyn or Malador.

"Who?" he asked.

"Ashe and I have an old friend. He helped us when we were first on the run, but I haven't seen him for a lot of years. He might have moved on since we last met. What's certain is he holds no love for Ministry or Guilds, so there's no guarantee he'll help you once he knows your heritage."

"But what makes you think he knows what to do?"

"I don't for sure, but there's no one else. He's the only chance you have, even if it's a slim one."

It seemed there were only slim chances left. Better than none. "All right. It looks like we have no choice. Let's meet this man and see what he can do. But when?"

"No time like the present," Verlyn replied. He heard the scraping of her chair as she stood. "I'll get some supplies together. We have a wagon, and thanks to those Revocaters, we've got horses to spare."

She left him alone at the kitchen table while she went to prepare.

All the while he could only wonder if this was the best option. Ashe was dead and now he was only putting Verlyn in more danger. But she was stubborn. He doubted there'd be any talking her out of it.

If there was any chance he could learn to control this power, he had to take it, before it consumed him whole. With any luck, he would be able to harness it for the good of his Guild. He had no idea where his mother was, but he had to do something for her. She would be fighting, and if he could help, even in a small way, he had to try.

It wasn't long before Verlyn returned. "Time to go."

As she wheeled him outside he could hear the horses snorting and shying in the cold night air. He grasped the side of the wagon and she heaved him up onto the seat. A breeze blew in his face as he sat up on the wagon, and she stepped up beside him, pulling a cloak around his shoulders.

There was silence but for the sound of the horses, and Fulren could see Verlyn's distinct outline as she milled about the farmhouse. Before long, he began to see the faint flicker of yellow light, then the warmth of a fire brushed against his face. Within moments those flames were billowing, the wood of the house crackling as it caught aflame.

"What have you done?" he asked as she climbed up onto the wagon beside him. "This is everything you and Ashe built. All you owned."

"And I'm not leaving it for anyone else. When this is nothing but dust on the breeze, there'll be no reason for me to come back here."

"I'm truly sorry," he said, as the flames grew higher.

"Nothing for you to be sorry for. I never wanted to pick a side. Even when I knew that no good would come from the Ministry being in charge, I was determined to stay out of it. Now the side's been picked for me, and I'll fight the Ministry as long as there's breath in my body. And from what I've seen so far, you might turn out to be the best weapon I've got."

She snapped the reins, and the horses began to pull the wagon away from the warmth of the fire now raging through the old farmhouse. As he pulled his cloak tighter around his shoulders, Fulren felt far from a weapon. All he felt was scared at what might lie ahead.

Perhaps the man they were going to meet would help, or maybe he would turn out to be just another dead end. Then all Fulren would have left was that voice in the distance. That tempting whisper calling on him to give in. And there was no way of knowing how long he'd be able to resist it.

TYRETA

Death permeated the air. She tried to block it out, that feeling of imminent destruction, but it had filtered into every brick of her cell, every link of her chains.

Reaching out with her power she had tried to touch a rat scurrying in the shadows, a cockroach skittering along the wall, but with the distant sound of artillery, and the cloying haze that pervaded the chamber, it was all she could do to keep breathing.

At least she could breathe. Nicosse Merigot would never draw breath again, and she had been the one to lead him to his fate. She might as well have pulled the trigger herself. Not only had she failed her mother, but she'd got that old man killed in the bargain. And Crenn. As soon as she thought about him it was all she could do not to weep. He had followed her all the way from the Sundered Isles, only to die on the end of a dagger. Tyreta would have her reckoning for that all right, but chained up in a shitty cell it seemed all but impossible.

The only good thing to come from this was knowing her mother had survived the devastation at Wyke. The legate who'd murdered Nicosse had said as much. Not that it mattered now. Tyreta was nothing more than a burden—a bargaining chip they could use against Lady Rosomon.

"These squalid accommodations must be hard for someone like you to stomach—highborn heir such as yourself."

Tyreta flinched at the voice. Keara stood at the end of the cell, leaning against the wall, half hidden in the shadows. Silently Tyreta cursed herself for not having sensed her, but with such calamity tearing Castleteig apart, her senses were befuddled.

"Why don't you unlock these chains. That'll make me comfortable enough."

That brought a wry smile to Keara's face. She stepped out of the shadows, looking down with something close to pity.

"Maybe. But first those nails of yours will have to be clipped." She absently raised a hand to the scar on her face. An indelible mark Tyreta had gifted to her. Not much to repay her for Crenn, but it was a good start.

"Come to gloat? While you can?"

Keara shook her head. "I came to express my condolences for yet another loss. And to tell you it was not my idea. I never wanted any of this."

"Fuck you," Tyreta spat. "You murdered Crenn. And Nicosse is dead because of you. This is all down to the Hallowhills and your blind ambition. You helped make this happen."

Keara crouched down beside her. "Are you telling me you've never done anything against your better nature for the good of your Guild?"

"We all perform our duty. But some of us don't resort to murder to do it."

"You've killed plenty, you just choose not to call it murder. But whatever helps you sleep at night. Personally, I think we're more alike than you'd care to admit."

"I'm nothing like you!"

The words left her lips before she had a chance to think on them. Before she had a chance to consider Keara might be right.

"I think what's obvious is we'd both go to great lengths for the Guilds we serve. And right now, letting you go might be the best way for me to serve mine."

Was this some kind of trick? Letting her go made no sense, but was Keara really cruel enough to dangle that in front of her?

"What are you talking about?"

"I'm talking about unchaining you. But on the condition you leave this city as fast as you're able."

"You think I'm stupid, right? You think I'd believe you're just going to let me go?"

"Whether I think you're stupid or not isn't the issue here. It's whether you want to get out of this shithole or not."

"What about my friends?"

Keara rolled her eyes as though talk of friends bored her. "Already released, and waiting for you just beyond the Armiger garrison."

"All this sounds too good to be true. Shame I just don't trust you."

Keara sighed. "Then you have a problem, Hawkspur. Because you can either choose to trust me, or you can stay here and await your fate at the hands of the Ministry. Who knows what your cousin Sanctan has in store for you at the Anvil. But don't think on it too long. Tick-tock, and all that."

Tyreta didn't like the prospect of that either. "Then I guess my fate is in your hands, Hallowhill."

That brought a smile to Keara's face, and she snapped her fingers, conjuring an iron key in her palm like some backstreet charlatan. She unlocked the manacles at Tyreta's wrists before standing up and turning to the archway that led from the cell.

"Come on, Hawkspur. We don't have much time."

Tyreta leapt, grabbing Keara's hair and slamming her head into the rotten brick of the wall before kicking her legs away. Keara fell, and Tyreta was on top of her before she hit the ground, claws already extended from her fingers.

"I should kill you right now," she snarled.

Keara's mouth twisted into that insipid smile. "Think about it. Do you really believe I wouldn't have a contingency? If you show your face beyond the walls of this gaol, and I'm not with you, those friends of yours won't last a second."

There was every chance she was lying. But every chance she wasn't.

Tyreta stood, calming herself as best she could as her claws retracted into her fingers.

"What the fuck happened to trust?" Keara said as she rose to her feet and brushed herself off.

"I'm finding these days it's in short supply," Tyreta answered.

"I know exactly what you mean—trust hasn't served either of us very well. But we have a chance to make a difference now. If the Ministry prevails, we're both doomed. Our Guilds will be destroyed and everything our families have built ground into the dirt. We have to work together, whether we like it or not."

Despite the aching need to kill this woman, Tyreta knew that if the Ministry was to be destroyed, they would have to form an alliance, no matter how much they might hate one another.

"Where's my panther?" she asked. "I won't leave here without her."

Keara shook her head. "No panther. It's too dangerous."

"I said, I won't—"

"This is not a discussion. Forget that beast and take your win, Hawkspur. We have to go. Now!"

The notion of leaving Cat behind was unthinkable, but Tyreta had to pick her battles. From the look on Keara's face, it wasn't something she'd compromise on.

"All right. Let's go."

Keara led the way through the winding corridors of the old gaol. She'd planned her route well, and they didn't encounter a single trooper as they made their way through the oppressive building and out into the yard. All the while Tyreta had to resist her instinct for revenge. This woman had killed Crenn, and so casually. Stuck a knife between his ribs and left him to bleed his last. How Tyreta would have relished a chance at vengeance, but she had Donan and Sted to think on.

They squeezed through the open gate at the end of the yard, hugging the shadows as they worked their way up through the urban landscape. When they reached the edge of a long avenue of sparse trees, Keara signalled for her to stop.

"Go to the end of this street," she whispered. "Your friends are waiting. And mine is there too. If she doesn't come back to meet me here, your panther's head will be mounted on my wall by sunrise."

For a second, Tyreta considered thanking her, but that would have only rubbed salt deeper into her bitter wound. Instead she moved along the avenue without a word, wary of an ambush as she tried her best to stay out of the light. At the far end she saw the webwainer from the fight days earlier leaning against a wall, arms folded, eyes shielded behind black lenses despite the dark.

"Where are they?" Tyreta asked.

The woman reached to her side, unclipping a monocular and sighting back down the avenue. When she was satisfied Keara was in one piece, she beckoned to someone behind the wall. Sted and Donan walked into the open, their hands bound. Sted looked furious but with a gag across her mouth she was unable to fill the air with the usual colour.

With frightening swiftness, the woman pulled a knife and cut their hands free. Then, as she backed away she offered Tyreta a jaunty waggle of her fingers before she was gone into the night.

"Are you both okay?" Tyreta asked.

Sted wrenched the gag from her mouth. "I've been fucking better."

"We're fine," Donan replied. "Where's Nicosse?"

Tyreta just shook her head. "Dead. We have to get to the land-ship terminal as quick as we can. There's not much time before they realise we're gone."

"What's going on?" asked Sted. "Why did they let us go? And more to the point, why did they let *you* go?"

"I'm not sure. That Hallowhill is up to something. Whatever it is, I'm happy to try and work it out when we're a long way from here."

As though to press her point, a patrol of troopers made their way across the street ahead, and Tyreta signalled for them to get down. They were practically invisible on the unlit street, but she held her breath as those troopers in their tiger-shaped helms walked on by.

Once they'd gone Donan crept up beside her. "What do we do without Nicosse? I can't believe we went through all this for nothing."

"Shut up and move," Sted hissed, before Tyreta could answer.

It saved her telling him that she had no idea what they'd do. They'd come so far, lost so much, and all for nothing.

As she led them on, she felt a growing ache within her—an over-whelming sense of loss nagging at her insides. It was more than grief, more visceral, as though part of her had been left behind in that cell.

It took a moment for her to realise that the missing part of her was Cat. It had seemed the right decision to leave her behind to save her friends, but now it hurt her more deeply than she could ever have imagined. She and Cat shared a connection—a bond forged in the jungle. How could she just abandon her?

"Are you all right?" asked Sted, when they got closer to the terminal.

"Yes, I just... We need to keep moving."

Tyreta forced herself to press on, and within minutes they could see their destination ahead. They stopped in the shadow of an old clock tower that overlooked the terminal.

"Doesn't even look guarded," Sted whispered.

Tyreta could sense her excitement. They were almost free of this damned place, but she couldn't shake that overwhelming feeling of loss, like a thread knotted tight in her gut.

"You have to go," she said. "Find a landship and get out of here."

"What the fuck are you talking about?" Sted demanded. "We all have to—"

"No," Tyreta snapped. "I have to go back for her."

Sted's brow furrowed in anger. "For the panther? You're risking your life for a dumb animal?"

Tyreta grasped her by the shoulders. "I can't leave her here."

"And I can't leave *you* here," Sted replied. "I have a duty to my Guildmaster. There's no way I'm gonna stand in front of Lady Rosomon and tell her I left her daughter behind because of an overgrown house pet."

Sted was a stubborn one, that was for sure. As for Donan, he looked scared, but she was sure he wouldn't leave without her either.

"All right," Tyreta said. "All right, let's go."

Sted breathed a sigh of relief before Tyreta led them closer to the terminal. She reached out with her senses, quelling the ill feeling inside her, and she couldn't detect anyone waiting for them, no danger hiding in the dark. They rushed through the abandoned terminal, relieved to see a single landship engine standing on the platform.

"Let's hope it's operational," Sted said, jogging along the platform and stepping up onto the driver's cabin.

Donan hurried along behind her, but it was all Tyreta could do to put one step in front of the other. She was almost in tears, gritting her teeth against the grief she felt. Why had she done this? She should never have agreed to Keara's demands.

Sted was already doing her best to power up the engine but her efforts yielded nothing. Donan pushed past her, pulling the activation lever and imbuing life in the central core.

"Here we go," Sted said, unable to mask her excitement.

Tyreta grabbed her, one arm about her throat, the other locked around the back of her head. Sted struggled, but despite her sinewy strength, she could do nothing to stop Tyreta as she gently squeezed, blocking off her airway. Donan watched in horror as Sted's struggling grew weaker and she sagged in Tyreta's arms.

Gently she laid Sted on the floor of the engine and looked up at Donan. "Get as far north as you can, but make sure you stop short of the Anvil. Then head northeast and find my mother. Tell her... tell her I'll see her soon."

Donan nodded, before gesturing to Sted lying prone in the cabin. "She's gonna be really pissed off when she wakes up."

Tyreta glanced down at Sted's unconscious body. "Yeah. Do your best to apologise for me."

"Shouldn't we just wait for you?" Donan asked.

That would have been nice, but she couldn't risk it. She'd lost too much already. "I can take care of myself, Donan. Wouldn't be surprised if I reach my mother before you do."

He smiled, but it trembled slightly on one side of his mouth. She tried a smile of her own, but it wouldn't come. Instead she turned, racing back through the terminal, back along the street, hugging the shadows, feet padding silently on the cobbled path.

The farther she went, the stronger the pull inside. Cat was waiting for her, and with every step Tyreta felt that connection grow. She moved more like an animal with each passing yard, feeling the claws ready to spring from her fingertips, seeing everything with crystal clarity despite the darkness. When a patrol wandered nearby, she easily avoided it, stalking through the night as they moved past only a few feet away, completely unaware of her presence.

She had no idea what was happening to her, but neither did she care. All that mattered was finding Cat. And when she released her, they would escape together and go on the hunt. Eat their fill.

The gaol came into view up ahead. Tyreta sprinted into the abandoned yard, hearing the noise of troopers within, laughing and joking, unaware they were being stalked by the most ruthless predator. She reached the bottom of the tower, leaping up and grasping the brickwork with her fingers. Nimbly she scaled the wall, hands probing for purchase, feet finding every nook to push herself higher.

At the lip of a balcony she paused, hearing the steel-shod feet of a trooper marching by. She should have let him go, should have spared him and concentrated on her task, but she was overcome by the need to hunt, to kill. No sooner had he marched by than she launched herself over the edge, falling on him like an unsuspecting doe. The splintbow fell from his fingers and he opened his mouth to shout in alarm, but her claws had already grasped his neck. She squeezed, feeling warmth gush over her fingers before she ripped out his throat.

He choked, desperate to breathe, drowning on his own blood. Tyreta reeled backward, staring down at what she'd done as her prey convulsed, arteries in his neck pumping a steadily ebbing stream. She was horrified and thrilled all at once. A sight that should have sickened her only filled her with the hunger for more.

Tyreta picked up the splintbow, checking it was loaded and primed, before creeping farther along the balcony. Hissing from nearby told her she was in the right place as she peered around the corner.

A cage sat at the far edge of the raised bastion. Tyreta issued a hiss of her own as she spied a trooper taunting Cat with his dagger. The panther snarled, clawing at him, and he laughed at her distress.

Tyreta could not hold herself back, stepping out from cover, aiming, firing. The trooper fell under a hail of bolts, and Tyreta dropped the bow before dashing to the cage. It was padlocked, a brief search of the trooper revealing no key. She desperately looked around for something to prise open the lock, spotting the trooper's fallen dagger.

Before she could even reach for it, she sensed danger from inside the building. Footsteps approaching up the staircase. Someone was coming, and there was nowhere to hide. She had to be swift, and

every muscle tensed as she prepared herself to leap on the approaching trooper.

The dragon helm of a Drake appeared from below. As he stepped
up onto the bastion, Tyreta snarled in challenge, but the Drake was
unperturbed, not even bothering to draw his sword as he advanced.

She leapt, high and fast, claws raking his armour, managing to
score a deep three-grooved divot in his helm, but he had already
grasped her, throwing her bodily against the wall. Her teeth clattered as she smashed into the brickwork and fell to the floor.

She howled in fury, leaping to her feet. He stood waiting, and it
only amplified her frustration when he still refused to draw his blade.
Did he not think her worthy? She would show him his mistake.

This time as she leapt he lowered a shoulder. She clawed at the
edge of the plating, trying to slash at the flesh beneath, but he managed to grasp her arm, dragging her off him and slamming her to
the ground. She scraped her nails across his breastplate but may as
well have fought a golem of steel. One punch of his gauntleted fist
and she felt the world spin.

Cat howled, thrashing in her cage as the Drake pressed his steel-
shod boot against her neck. She grabbed it, writhing on the ground,
desperate to get up again, but constricted as her throat was it took all
her effort to fight for air.

Tyreta wanted to spit her hate, but with a boot on her neck she
was growing weaker with every second. Another Drake appeared
next to the first and they both watched as that boot on her neck got
heavier, her thrashing growing weaker. The animal inside wanted
to fight, but her body would not obey. Still she thrashed, still she
raged, until she could fight the black no longer...

KEARA

It was only a matter of time until she'd have to face what was coming. Her plan was in tatters, and there'd be consequences for sure. Troopers were dead, Tyreta was still in chains, and they would want to know who set those prisoners free in the first place. Keara wanted to head straight back to the Web, but that would only have led to a dozen fingers pointing her way. Better just to sit tight and hope the wave of shit that was coming washed right by.

The waiting was the worst part of it all, but wait she would. At least it was comfortable in this little house. Whoever owned it had kept a small but decent wine cellar too. Not her usual vice, but it would have to do now the red drop had run out.

She rose from the couch, leaving the little fire to crackle in its hearth. Hesse was sitting in an armchair, feet up on a stool reading some book or other. Whoever owned this house had a decent library. If they ever returned, they'd at least find all their books still here—but not so much the wine.

"Should we have run?" she asked.

Hesse didn't look up from the book. "I don't know. I'm not in charge."

"But you must have an opinion."

Hesse sighed, looking at Keara from behind those dark lenses. "I know you're probably fucked, whether you run or not."

That wasn't the help and advice she'd been hoping for, but it was honest at least. Any plan she might have had for setting Tyreta free and gaining the good graces of Rosomon Hawkspur were now crushed to powder. She took a sip of wine. Fuck she needed some red drop.

The door to the little house opened, agitating the fire with a breath of cold air. Keara was about to tell whoever it was to piss off, when she saw a glint of steel and a white surcoat. Those knights always gave her the creeps, looming around like statues, never speaking. Now was no exception.

He stood for a moment, letting the warm air out, surveying the room, before fixing her in his gaze.

"You have been summoned," he said, voice warm and inviting like a comfortable bed. It only served to put her off guard.

"Summoned? I am Keara Hallowhill. I'm the one who does the summoning."

He didn't answer. She'd known this was going to happen sooner or later. Hisolda would want an explanation and there was no getting away from it now.

"Fuck," she said under her breath, grabbing a cloak and following the Drake outside. She didn't offer Hesse a second glance. Most likely she'd still be reading that book when Keara got back... *if* she got back.

The Drake led her across the street toward a tower next to the gaol. The scroll sigil crumbling on the wall marked it as a Corwen embassy. Hisolda had requisitioned it for her own use, not that she'd had to throw anyone out. Keara imagined those timid actuaries had been the first to flee the city when the fighting started.

Up a spiral staircase and Keara could see what was happening toward the south through a grimy window. There was a battle at the river, one last push to overwhelm the Viper Battalion positions. No way to tell who was winning, and all she could do was be thankful she wasn't involved.

At the tower's summit was a single door, guarded by the other Drake. He knocked once before opening it, then stood aside to let her enter. The top of the tower consisted of a single huge chamber, windows placed at the cardinal points, letting in the distant sound of fighting. A long table took up most of the room, with Hisolda sitting at one end in a high-backed chair. Opposite her sat Olstrum Garner.

Keara's jaw clenched, the stitches pulling at her cheek. What was this snake doing here? Hisolda was the Archlegate's faithful servant, but Olstrum was his eyes and ears. If she hadn't already known she was in deep shit, it was pretty obvious now.

"Please, take a seat," Hisolda said, as the Drake closed the door behind her.

Keara glanced at the table, at the array of chairs on offer, before choosing to seat herself midway between the pair of them. She glanced at Olstrum, who looked pleased with himself, but then he always did. She then turned to Hisolda.

"What's he doing here?"

The High Legate gazed across the table, allowing Olstrum to speak for himself.

"The Archlegate was growing a little anxious," he said. "As you know he is keen to know the progress of all aspects of his crusade. One might say he obsesses over the details."

"We have everything under control," Keara replied, trying not to sound defensive. "Tyreta Hawkspur is now in our care."

Olstrum's smile widened. "Marvellous. And what of the fabled artificer you were sent to find?"

"He has been eliminated," Hisolda said, before Keara could use the word *murdered*.

Olstrum nodded his understanding. "Not the ideal outcome, but I'm sure the Archlegate will be relieved he is not in Guild hands."

Keara could feel this situation getting away from her. Olstrum and Hisolda were acting like this was their feast, and they'd reserved all the juiciest morsels for themselves. For Keara there were only scraps.

She reclined in her seat, trying to at least look like she was in control. "We have a landship ready to leave for the Anvil in the morning," Keara said. "Tyreta will be transported under Hallowhill guard. She has become quite the sorceress, demonstrating potent talents. I'm sure the Archlegate will—"

"None of that will be necessary," Hisolda said.

Olstrum raised an eyebrow. "Really? Why not?"

"Because we are going to burn her."

Keara's chair almost tipped backward. "You're what?"

Hisolda regarded her with narrowed eyes. "That…thing is an abomination. Whatever heretical powers she has manifested cannot be allowed to persist. She is a danger to us all while she lives, and most of all to the Archlegate. You've seen firsthand what she can do." Hisolda raised a finger to point at Keara's cheek. "It's written all over your face."

Keara could feel this all slipping right through her fingers. If Tyreta died, her one link to Rosomon was gone. If the Guildmaster of Hawkspur heard Keara had been involved in Tyreta's death, there was no way they could form an alliance. Then where would she be?

Olstrum leaned forward. "Heretical sorceress or not, she could be the key to bringing Rosomon's resistance to an end. The Archlegate will want to see his cousin at least. Speak with her. Find out what she knows."

"You have no idea what the Archlegate wants, Olstrum," Hisolda replied. "You are an adviser, nothing more."

Keara placed her hands on the table, trying to stay calm. "You can't do this."

"Don't presume to tell me what I can and can't do. I am the divine hand of the Wyrms. In the absence of the Archlegate, *I* represent the Ministry's will. And the Ministry's will takes precedence over all else."

This was slipping yet further from her grasp. Keara's fingers pressed into the tabletop lest she clench them into fists. "Olstrum is right—the Archlegate needs her. She could be a key factor in ending all this."

"Tyreta Hawkspur is a danger to everyone around her. She has already proven that much. Just last night she managed to escape from her chains, release her fellow rebels and almost succeeded in retrieving her familiar. Killing two battalion troopers in the process. The demonic sorceries at her disposal must be eradicated. The girl will burn."

Keara rose to her feet, hands still pressed on the table. "No. This cannot happen. I will not allow it."

Hisolda's eyes narrowed and she too stood, though at a much more measured pace. "And exactly how do you intend to stop me?"

Keara could think of a dozen ways, but none of them would end well for her. There was no answer she could give.

Hisolda took a step toward her. Was she trying to intimidate? It was kind of working.

"Your relevance already dangles by a gossamer thread, girl. The Hallowhills serve their purpose...for now. If you know what's good for you and your Guild, you'll do as you're told. Then perhaps, when this sorry business is all over, the Archlegate will still have a use for you."

Hisolda was right. For years she had done as she was ordered—by her father, by Sanctan—and in that time she had watched helplessly as the sand emptied through its hourglass. Again and again her usefulness had been eroded. She was being manipulated like a wind-up toy, and every time the key was cranked the mainspring wore away just a little more. Soon that old toy would break and be thrown in the trash with the rest.

"If there's nothing else," Hisolda said, adjusting her robe, "I have a pyre to build."

Keara's hand was at her hip, touching the knife in its sheath—just an ordinary knife since the pyrestones had been destroyed and not replaced. She closed her fist around it, her mind roiling at the edge of panic. Before Hisolda could take a step toward the door, Keara pulled the knife from its sheath and plunged it in her throat.

There they stood, neither of them quite believing what had happened as Hisolda's eyes stared furiously. Keara could only stare back as she dragged the blade free, watching as a red tide gushed down onto that stark blue robe. Hisolda opened her mouth to speak, spewing crimson across her chin, not even raising a hand to stanch the flow. Then, like a curtain cut free of its rail, she collapsed in a heap of stained blue.

Keara stared at that body, realisation fast dawning that she had most definitely fucked things up. The knife was still in her hand—the straight one, a symbol of her Guild. An heirloom that had now most likely damned the Hallowhills to extermination.

In a daze, she turned away from the corpse to see Olstrum standing, hand clapped over his mouth, looking at her as though she'd just grown an extra head. He'd witnessed it all. There was no escaping this now.

She moved toward him, and he stumbled back, toppling the chair behind him, only just managing to stay on his feet. Keara tightened her grip on the knife. What did one more murder matter? Her fate was already sealed anyway.

He was backed against the wall as she approached, knife drawn back to strike.

"I can help you," he blurted.

She should have ignored him, the devious little toad. Just stuck that knife in him and worried about the consequences later, but instead she stopped. Maybe this time he wasn't lying. Might there really be something he could do?

"Sit down," she demanded.

He offered no word of complaint as he slowly inched his way along the wall and slipped into one of the vacant chairs. She picked a chair close by, positioning it to face him before slumping down into it. Slowly she placed the bloody knife on the table, but kept her hand close to it.

"So tell me, Olstrum, what can you do for me?"

With a trembling hand he reached for a decanter on the table, then two glasses. He filled both, then slid one toward her.

"I think it's safe to say you want an end to all this hostility and uncertainty as much as I do."

"What the fuck do you think?" She picked up the glass and tasted it. Surprisingly it was much worse than the vintage she'd tried at that little house. Wherever this wine had come from, it hadn't travelled well.

"And you want Tyreta Hawkspur to stay very much alive?"

Gently she placed the glass back on the table. "Personally I couldn't give a shit one way or the other, but right now it serves my purpose if she lives."

Olstrum finished his wine before pouring himself another. He was trying to look calm, but couldn't hide the tremor in his hand as he poured. "I would suggest it's best for us both. If Rosomon Hawkspur finds out her daughter has been executed, this war might never end."

Keara could well believe it. "And if she's given to the Archlegate, the Guilds will be buried once and for all. Including mine."

"So she has to live," Olstrum said. "And the Hallowhills will have to swap their allegiance."

She had already thought that would have to happen, but as Olstrum said it she realised it was the only option. "And we go back to acting as servants to more powerful Guilds."

"Not necessarily. If you offer Rosomon the use of your webwainers to end this conflict, you can broker a deal that will see your Guild rise. You never struck me as someone who lacked ambition, Keara."

She narrowed her eyes, trying to work out his angle in all this. He was a sly old dog for sure, but could she even trust him?

"You've betrayed the Guilds, and now seem willing to betray the Ministry. What's in this for you?"

For a moment he seemed so very tired, and sighed like a man done with the world. "For too long now I have been dancing a jig like a jester with two kings. It's time for that to end."

"Squirming on a hook more like." He nodded his agreement. "But why? Why have you not just picked a side?"

"Why haven't you?" Olstrum said, a hint of a wry smile.

That was a pretty good question, one she didn't feel the desire to answer. "I asked first."

He stared off wistfully through one of the windows as the distant sound of battle drifted in. "Maybe, in the beginning, I thought I could keep everyone alive. That I could stave off the inevitable. That I was clever enough to play all angles and still win. But the inevitable always comes to get you in the end."

"But why?" Keara said, growing tired of his ambiguity.

When he looked at her, there was a tear in his eye. "Because I was always loyal to Sullivar. He treated me with respect and raised me to a position of importance I could never have dreamed of. But... Sanctan has my family. And all this time I have tried to keep their heads above water, but they could drown at any moment. And so I have had to swim against an ever-rising tide, just to keep them safe. Can you imagine what that's like? Striving to achieve something even though you know it will damn you in the end?"

"Of course," she said, before she could stop herself.

"So tell me. What is it you want?"

She looked at Olstrum as he sat there with his wineglass. He was a traitor. A spy. And yet Keara still felt the need to unburden herself. If half of what he said was true, he was in this up to his neck. And if she was going to survive, she needed someone as desperate as she was.

"Sanctan made promises to the Hallowhills. To my father. Early on it seemed to make sense. Bring down the Guilds and the Hallowhills will rise. Now I know all that was just cowshit. Sanctan doesn't want to change the old guard to the new. He wants to harrow the field and regrow it, so that his is the only crop. There'll be no place for us in that new order. We will become so much chaff."

Olstrum nodded. "It's good that you finally understand that."

Keara felt a little hope begin to creep in. A chink of light through all that dark.

She gazed down at the corpse of Hisolda. "So what do we do about our dear departed friend here?"

"I will take care of it," he replied.

"And how do you intend to do that?" She gestured to the corpse. "Performing divine miracles was her thing, and it looks like she's all out."

Olstrum drained his glass and slowly stood. "You'll just have to trust me."

He quickly backed away from her to the other side of the table. Before she could even stand up, he opened his mouth and bellowed for help.

The door burst open. Both Drakes rushed in, one stopping by the High Legate's body, the other surveying the scene, seeing them both—him standing in a panic, she next to the bloody knife. He made his assessment in an instant and dragged her from the chair.

She glared at Olstrum as she was bundled out of the room, but couldn't read the look on his face. He truly was lower than a snake. Or was he?

That was the problem, she supposed, you never could tell with devious bastards like Olstrum where their loyalty truly lay. Despite the grim fate that might await, she could only admire him for that.

CONALL

His boot sank into the dried earth, almost tripping him. Looking down, he saw his foot had crunched through the desiccated rib cage of some long-dead animal. Or at least he hoped it was an animal. Could have been human. Almost made him want to apologise.

Conall pulled his foot free and staggered on. It wasn't hot—this wasn't the baking extremes of the Karna desert—but thirst still gnawed at him with such wrath he had all but forgotten how hungry he was.

The sword at his back was silent at least. One small mercy to be thankful for. No matter how lonely he felt out here in the wilds, he was still grateful that voice was no longer taunting him.

Though the ground undulated, drifts of dust and broken remnants of masonry rising in his path, he could still see to the far eastern horizon. At least he hoped it was east. Perhaps here, in the bewitched environs of the Drift, the sun and constellations worked differently. Driving him in ever-increasing circles.

Before he could lament further on that, something moved in the distance. At first he thought it might be a mirage, his one remaining eye deceiving him, but as he glared through the haze he became more certain it was real.

Could it be a wagon, moving along some distant road?

His stumbling gait sped to a walk, then a trot, then he was running for all he was worth. The dust cloud wasn't that far away, perhaps half a mile across the blasted landscape. He called out, his voice
hoarse. No way they would hear him.

On he ran, hunting down that wagon, not caring that he might
never catch it. His breath came in ragged gasps as he chased, watching forlornly as the dust cloud disappeared over the next ridge. But
he had to keep moving, had to catch up, even if that wagon was
driven by someone malevolent.

Of course it was. Where would he find any benevolence out here
in the Drift?

When he reached the top of the ridge, he came to a stuttering stop.
A road ran down into a valley, and clustered at the bottom was...a
city? Conall squeezed his eye shut then opened it, girding himself
for this to be a hallucination brought on by fatigue—surely there
were no cities in this Wyrm-forsaken place. But when he opened his
eye again, it was still there, a bustling metropolis, if it could even be
called that. Structures carved out of the wasteland and running off
into the far distance. People teeming among the makeshift streets.

He almost laughed as he stumbled his way down the slope, feeling
the relief of having a road underfoot rather than the rough ground
he had shambled along for so many miles. There was a gate of sorts
at one end of the city, and as he got closer he could see there were no
guards to stop him strolling right in.

Hooded travellers made their way in and out, laden with sacks. A
bull-drawn wagon trundled by, filthy canvas flapping as the driver
clutched the reins in clawlike hands. Some of the people he passed
were armed, looking fearsome and dangerous. Many others not so
much—more bedraggled waifs, barely surviving in the wilds.

No one paid him much heed as he made his way through a makeshift marketplace. Noisy vendors waved dubious-looking meat on
skewers. Despite his hunger, the stench still turned Conall's stomach, and he ignored them as they wafted their charred wares. Here
was a rotted table covered in rusted weapons, there a stall standing
aslant, packed with rusted artifice and broken pieces of armour. A

hooded man stood at the market's epicentre surrounded by piles of dusty old tomes, telling all who would listen that they had been written by ancient sorcerers and would teach magics undreamed of. No one seemed interested in his wild claims.

A hand reached out to him, yellowed fingernails clawing at his tattered tunic. Conall reeled away, seeing a line of beggars in the shadow of a crumbling wall. They moaned and beseeched, but he had nothing to give them. One woman even held up a spindly-armed baby, its belly bloated in starvation, begging him to buy it from her.

Conall quickened his pace, desperate to leave the pitiful show behind, almost staggering into a tall armoured figure. The giant must have been seven feet, leering down from within the shadow of his hood. Conall quickly made his apologies and hurried on, as the beast of a man glared.

Beyond the marketplace a row of tables had been positioned beneath a flapping awning. As he drew closer he realised it was some kind of primitive tavern, a few patrons sitting in the shade, drinking from rusted pewter cups. The more of the city he took in, the more he realised this place was a nightmarish mirror of his home. Markets, taverns, traders and beggars. He could easily have been back in Wyke, but for the menagerie of outlandish figures stalking the place like vultures. He wanted to run from here as fast as his aching legs would carry him, but he was thirsty—so bloody thirsty—and it was unlikely he'd find a drink between here and the border with Torwyn.

A bar of rotted wood stood at the far end of the awning in the shadow of a crumbling wall of grey masonry. A man stood behind it, staring off into the distance as though he'd rather be anywhere else. His hair hung in lank strands, beard patchy, clothes looking like he'd just found them in the street.

"Water?" Conall managed to ask.

The man looked him up and down. "What you got to pay with?"

That was a good question. "I have nothing. But I'm dying of thirst. Just one cup of wat—"

"Half this outpost is dying. Giving shit away doesn't help me survive. That sword at your back looks worth a cup or two though."

For a moment, Conall considered it might be a fair trade. And he might rid himself of this infernal curse into the bargain. But it had kept him alive so far, and the prospect of trying to make it the rest of the way to Torwyn unarmed was worse than dying of thirst.

"I—I can't give you the sword."

"Can't be that thirsty then," the tavernkeeper replied with a shrug. "Best fuck off, hadn't you."

Conall didn't have the will to argue. Though the dryness was biting like a rat at his throat, what would he do? Kill this man and take what he wanted? What might be the consequences of that? Whatever they were, he didn't have the strength or the will to face them.

Instead he turned, walking back beneath the awning until he reached the far table. Conall slumped down in one of the chairs, watching as the woeful folk of this lost and damned city went about their business. It was obvious none of them cared if he lived or died—they had their own hardships to think on. Despite being surrounded by more people than he'd seen in weeks, he was truly on his own.

If he set off now, would he make it home before he expired? There was no way of knowing how far Torwyn was. Conall had gambled often enough, but the stakes had never been this high.

He had to pull himself together—he was a Hawkspur, damn it. This was no time for weeping. He had to rouse what little strength he had left. An Armiger fortress might only be a few miles away.

Reaching behind, he unstrapped the sword from his back and laid it on the table in front of him. He'd bound the cross-guard tight to conceal the baleful jewel, not that it kept the demon quiet. So far though, it had not spoken a word since he'd run screaming from that city of the dead.

Perhaps he should rid himself of it. Hand it over for a canister of water and take his chances. If he knew how far his journey would be, it would help make up his mind.

Before he could think to ask someone, a cup was placed down in front of him. Instead of looking up to see who had offered such a precious gift, Conall just stared. It was filled to the brim with crystal-clear water.

When eventually he looked up and saw Nylia standing over him, he wasn't surprised, but still his hand strayed to the sword laid on the table. She made no move in response—smiling down at him expectantly.

"Why don't you drink?" she asked.

He glanced again at the cup filled to the brim. "Maybe because I don't know what's in it."

"Oh, so suspicious, Conall. It's just water."

"You could have poisoned it for all I know."

She raised an eyebrow. "You're right. I could."

He grasped the cup and pressed it to his mouth, pausing for the briefest moment before glugging down the contents. It was cold on his cracked lips, the most delicious cup of water he'd ever tasted.

When he slammed it back down on the table with a gasp, Nylia took a seat opposite him. Her own sword was strapped to her back and she didn't seem overly concerned his hand was still on the hilt of his.

"You can't escape," she said. "You know that, don't you?"

He regarded her across the table. But for the patch over her right eye she looked like much the same woman he'd first met in that cage in Argon Kyne. Though perhaps now she was much more self-assured. More comfortable in that skin.

"Who am I talking to? Is that Nylia? Or is it the thing inside her head?"

"Does it matter?"

Conall wasn't entirely sure it did. Then again, if it was Nylia, perhaps he would receive at least a modicum of compassion. If it were the demon...not so much.

"You can try and stop me, but I will fight you."

She gestured over one shoulder. "You should know that I am not alone."

Across the busy road Mikal stood leaning against the wall. He grinned, then grimaced, twitching at the passersby, hands flexing as though he were afflicted with a palsy.

"I'm not going back. I don't care how many of you there are. I'm free now, and I'll bloody well die free if I have to."

She scratched her chin as she thought on that. "Are any of us really free? If you were no longer a slave to Senmonthis, then you would just be enslaved by your Guild."

"That's not the same."

"You're right, it is not. The Guilds cannot provide the gift Senmonthis has offered you. The power and majesty. You would never rise to such heights in your homeland. Only back in Arcturius can you fulfil your potential."

"Tempting offer, but I tried that once, and I'm not interested. Whatever Senmonthis is selling, I'm not bloody buying."

Nylia pursed her lips in a grotesque parody of coyness. "Come now. I don't believe that any more than you do. Remember I've tasted it, just like you have. We both know the rapture this gift can give." She tapped a finger to the eyepatch over her right eye.

"I remember being forced to murder those people on the road. Slaughter for slaughter's sake. That's not my way. You can keep your fucking rapture."

"You're talking like this is a choice, Conall."

"You might not have a choice, but I ripped that bastard jewel from my own head. It doesn't control me anymore. I can choose any damn thing I please, and that includes how I die."

He tightened his grip on the sword in front of him but Nylia didn't seem concerned.

"You don't understand. You've been touched by it. Embraced by it. Whether you accept it or not, you will always belong to her."

"Like fuck I will. I am no one's slave. So draw your blade and strike me down, at least I will die free. That's more than you'll ever get."

Nylia sighed. "If dying free is the limit of your ambition, then I pity you."

It wasn't the limit of his ambition. Survival was. But as he looked about this city, desperate for an escape, it appeared that survival might be an ambition too far. Mikal still stood across the road. Nylia sat only a few feet away. There were plenty of places to flee to in this woebegone place, but there might also be dangers worse than these two.

"I know what you're thinking," she said. "But you can't run forever. Eventually it will take hold and consume the man you were, no matter how you try and resist it."

"What's that supposed to mean? I've already beaten it."

She grinned. "This is not something you can resist, no matter how far you flee. One way or another you will be forced to give in. The Scions do not take well to rejection."

"I've already resisted. Senmonthis does not control me anymore. I won."

She laughed like an innocent girl at a summer fayre. It was almost infectious. "No, Conall. You have already lost. You just don't realise it yet."

His fist tightened around the hilt so much it hurt his fingers. "Don't you fucking laugh at me. I'm not as pathetic as I might look."

"Really? I must admit, I'm glad to see you show some steel. But I want you to prove it."

He tore the sword from its sheath, no longer caring what it was, what it stood for, what it might do to him if he succumbed to the temptation. Nylia backed away, her chair toppling as she dodged from the first swipe of the blade.

She didn't reach for her own weapon, as though goading him into attacking. The urge to call upon that demon, to allow it to infuse him with its skill, was overwhelming, but he managed to resist. Over her shoulder, he could see Mikal pushing his way through the crowded street.

"Why can't you just let me go? I'm no use to you now. No use to Senmonthis."

Nylia shook her head. "Not entirely true. But even if you were of no use, you cannot be allowed to return home. Not now. Not when you know so much of her intentions. Were you to warn your mother of what is coming, who knows the lengths she might go to in order to stop us."

He could have argued, could have tried to persuade her that he'd keep his mouth shut, that he'd swear it on any gods she wanted. But there was no time left—Mikal had almost reached them. Better that he just run.

Conall had no idea where he was going. He almost tripped over a chair as he sprinted from beneath the awning, surprised at how much energy he still had in his legs. An empty street beckoned to his left and he raced down it, not daring to look back and see how close Nylia and Mikal were.

A wall stood at the end of the alley, crumbled to rubble, and he vaulted it, landing in a backyard. Tearing down a hide sheet affixed to the doorframe, he stumbled inside. The house was dark, abandoned, detritus on the ground crunching beneath his feet. At the far end of the room he saw another sheet over another door. The only way out. Light beamed beneath it, and Conall did not pause, grabbing the sheet and wrenching it aside.

Mikal stood there, blocking his escape. They regarded one another for a moment, surprise written all over Mikal's twitchy face. Conall was frozen, staring at the man he had once been imprisoned with. Had tried to escape with. It was only then he realised he had sunk his demonic blade in Mikal's gut, almost to the hilt.

Slowly Mikal slid back off the blade, falling to the ground in a puff of dirt.

"Shit," Conall breathed, crouching over him as blood poured from the mortal wound in Mikal's stomach. "Shit."

"Thank you...my friend," Mikal whispered, before the light in that one eye of his went out.

Conall looked up in time to see Nylia race to a stuttering stop nearby. She regarded Mikal's corpse with little emotion, before drawing her own blade. Conall could see the white jewel at its cross-guard just visible beneath the wrapping. It glowed, dull and malignant in the sunlight. He could have run, tried to lose her in this maze of dereliction, but that seemed futile now.

Conall leapt at her, and she danced away as their swords clashed. There was no one to see them in the backstreet. No witnesses that might watch one of them die.

Nylia thrust low and he barely managed to parry, her blade nicking his thigh and forcing a grunt through his gritted teeth. He swung a counter, but she batted it aside with little effort, that wry smile returning to her lips. Then she was on him.

No time to think of a counter. All he could do was twist and parry in the face of her onslaught. It didn't take long to realise she was just toying with him.

She gashed his shoulder, and he snarled in pain, almost losing his footing. Another swipe and she opened a cut in his chest. He went cold with the pain and anticipation—she would kill him or he would surrender. But he could not surrender. Not to her.

"Help me," he growled. "Just do it."

In the far distance he was sure he heard an answer, like a lover's sigh of satisfaction.

Nylia danced a step closer, her blade aimed at his throat. His sword moved with shocking speed, meeting her strike, and Nylia snarled as her weapon was knocked from her grip. Before he could stop it, Conall's sword thrust upward, slashing her face from chin to forehead.

She fell back to the dirt, and Conall danced forward, sword raised. Nylia glared up at him, eyepatch lost, face pouring blood. Her right eye shone baleful and red.

"No," he bellowed.

The sword paused mid-strike. That death blow halted.

He took a step back, breathing heavily as Nylia raised a hand to stem the blood pouring from her face. It would have been so easy to end this. To end her. But what would that have made him? Worse than he had already become.

Conall felt all that frustration well up inside. The notion he had no control terrified him. And all because of the blade he now held. His one last connection to Senmonthis and the demon she had placed inside him.

He drew back his arm and flung the sword as far as he could, not even looking to see where it landed. All he could offer Nylia was one last look of sorrow, before he turned heel and ran. With any luck, he'd find the way east before he collapsed.

ROSOMON

She had woken before dawn in a bedchamber of Jarlath's opulent tower. The sun was rising on a perfect morning, but for the bitter stench of woodsmoke that permeated the air. It was crisp, birds singing from the surrounding forest. Despite all the blood spilled in this city, they still happily chirruped their dawn chorus. Rosomon would have liked to think it was in honour of the Guilds.

Two Armiger Battalions had been defeated. Two barriers toppled. It was a start, at least, and little to do with her planning. If Rawlin had not come in time, if Maugar had not brought his Blackshields, the result might have been much different. She would be dead or captive, instead of victor. Not that the word meant anything when victory still seemed so far away.

She dressed quickly, donning the Hawkspur blue that made her so noticeable. Of course Kassian had advised her against it—that colour would only make her an easier mark for assassins—but she had insisted. She doubted Sanctan would ever abandon his Draconate white, and in return she would not shirk her Guild colours.

A brief look at her reflection in the mirror and she knew she was ready. Perhaps a little more stern about the eyes than before, but for what she had to do that was only appropriate. She was still the

Hawkspur everyone knew. Now she would become the Hawkspur everyone feared.

When she reached the bottom of the tower, Ianto was waiting patiently. Her Imperator was weary about the eyes, that young face marred by cuts and bruises. Though his gaze looked troubled, he stood proudly, bowing as soon as she appeared.

"How are you?" she asked quietly. As soon as she said it, she realised how matronly that must have sounded. Ianto was a warrior, and being mothered would only discomfit him. Nevertheless he shrugged his answer.

"I will live," he replied.

She could see his ribs had been bandaged, his arm stitched. Reminders of how much Rosomon owed this man, barely out of boyhood. She could only offer him a conciliatory pat on the shoulder, desperately trying to ignore how much he reminded her of Conall.

They left the tower and stepped out into the bright sunshine. Workers were still clearing away rubble and charred lumber. Still carrying corpses to mass graves south of the city. It seemed so prosaic, as though this happened every day. Rosomon wondered how many more scenes like this she would have to endure before she had driven Sanctan from her brother's throne. Was five too many? Ten? No, there would never be a number high enough, not now. Not after what she had suffered. Rosomon would endure as much horror as it took to see Sanctan destroyed. Before she could think further on that grim prospect, she saw Kassian Maine approaching.

He wore two swords, the pommels adorned with the sigils of Archwind and Hawkspur. One of them had been Lancelin's blade, if only for a short time. How she needed him now, when she was to perform this darkest of deeds. Would he have advised her against it? Urged caution? Mercy? It did not matter. He was not here.

"My lady," Kassian said with a nod.

"Are the prisoners prepared?" she asked.

"As you have ordered. The survivors of the Corvus Battalion are to the east awaiting the long march to Wyke under the guard of the Mantid. The Ursus are..." He paused, as though finding the right words. "...Where you commanded."

Did Kassian have his doubts about this? He had not expressed his concerns before now. They all knew there was no way she could release any of these battalion troopers lest she have to fight them again in another arena. The Corvus prisoners would be put to use back in Wyke to rebuild her city. She had decided an altogether more appropriate fate for the Ursus.

"Do we have a full casualty report yet?" she asked as they made their way toward the southern gate of Oakhelm.

"On our side," Ianto replied, "surprisingly low considering the inexperience of the vanguard. Oleksig's miners are to be commended. As for the enemy, the Corvus Battalion took a heavy toll, but the Ursus surrendered when the battle went against them. Those who did not flee, anyway. There were no Hallowhill survivors, and but a single Drake."

Rosomon knew who he referred to, remembering that relentless mass of armour pursuing her. But she had managed to persuade him to yield. If only she could do so with the rest of Sanctan's servants.

When they crossed beneath the huge oaken gate to the south, she saw Marshal Rawlin in conversation with his men and those of the Mantid Battalion. Always planning for war. Always on the hunt. She could only admire him for that, relieved that he was on her side rather than standing opposite. Without his timely arrival the battle would have been much different, and she was mindful of what she owed.

He stopped his conversation as she walked by, and she offered a nod of recognition. In turn, he bowed low to her. She was reminded of their first meeting at the Anvil's Cogwheel, when he had shown her little respect at all. Things had changed much since then.

A familiar voice barked orders to the south. By the tree line she saw the hulking figure of Maugar Ironfall marshalling his men to greater effort as they felled trees for Oakhelm's restoration. Xorya stood some feet away, her eyes watchful as the Blackshields laboured with their axes.

"General Hawkspur," Maugar said, as she and her two bodyguards came closer.

She couldn't tell whether he was mocking her with that title, but no one was laughing.

"Maugar," she replied. "You're up early."

"There is much to do, Rosomon."

"You are right, much indeed. And thanks to your daughter we are able to begin."

Xorya had found her father as he journeyed south from Wyrm-head. He had already abandoned his siege days before and was making his way back to the Forge. Had he still been in the north he would never have arrived in time.

"Thanks to many, and the sacrifices they have made," he replied. "So what next? I am eager to take the fight to the enemy and avenge the outrage in my city."

"As am I, Maugar. But first we must see Oakhelm strengthened. We will move on to the Anvil soon enough, but we need a bastion to retreat to in case we fail."

He snorted air from his nose. Indignation or amusement, it was difficult to tell. "For Ironfall, failure means death. There will be no retreat."

"If you insist," she replied. "For the rest of us, we will at least have a contingency."

Ianto leaned in. "They are waiting, my lady."

She nodded before offering Maugar a brief bow he didn't reciprocate. The three of them continued through the trees toward the supply canal that ran to the south of the city. Beyond the wood was a huge lock to raise and lower trade barges on their journey to and from the Anvil. Scores of miners and militia lined the way, bowing at Rosomon as she made her way past. These ordinary folk had fought like lions, defeating an army of trained killers. Now more than ever she thought that perhaps they could win this war, but first there would be justice.

Oleksig stood atop the lock gate that overlooked the water chamber below. Beside him was Borys, gazing down into it. His eyes burned with hate, and Rosomon could well understand his fury.

Before she could join them, two of her Talon came toward her, bundling a prisoner in between them. Rosomon felt a surge of anger as she recognised the woman they had captured, gripping her fists tight lest she display it in front of her followers. Faiza looked desperate, her face bruised. The scouts who had found her had clearly dispatched some justice of their own.

Rosomon felt her stomach churn, but she fought back her emotion. This woman had betrayed her. Had betrayed Wyke. How fateful that she was now in their grasp. But Rosomon couldn't display her hate, this had to be clinical.

"My lady," said one of the scouts, grasping Faiza's arm. "We found her a few miles east, abandoned by the retreating enemy."

Before she could speak, Faiza fell to her knees. "Please, Lady Rosomon, have mercy. I had no idea what they would do, I swear it on the Wyrms."

At the mention of those cursed dragons, Rosomon almost abandoned her reserve. How she would have loved to claw this traitor's eyes out, but there was a much more fitting punishment.

"Swear on your Wyrms all you wish," Rosomon replied. "You will get to meet them soon enough. Put her with the others."

Faiza shrieked in panic, begging, pleading, as the scouts dragged her toward the lock. At the edge they thrust her over the side and into the chamber below.

Rosomon climbed the stairs at the side of the lock to stand beside Oleksig. Inside the vast flood chamber was what remained of the Ursus Battalion, bound hand and foot. She had allowed them to keep their armour at least, there was no need to draw this out any more than necessary. On seeing her, some of them cursed, while others sat in silence, awaiting their fate.

Oleksig's pipe was still in his pocket, his face a solemn mask. "Are you sure you want to go through with this?" he asked under his breath.

"Not losing your nerve are you, Marrlock?" she answered.

But she wasn't sure. She hadn't been sure of anything since this whole thing started, but this was the decision she had come to. They were faced with a ruthless enemy. If she had learned one thing, the only way to fight it was to be more ruthless in return. *Now she would become the Hawkspur everyone feared.*

"Lady Rosomon." The voice echoed up from the base of the flood chamber. She looked down, seeing the youthful features of Captain Ultan glaring up at her. His armour was tarnished with mud, face cut and grazed from the recent battle. He was a much sorrier sight than the one that had greeted her at Wyke those days ago. "I would remind you of the military codes the Armiger are bound by. There are long-standing protocols for the treatment of prisoners. Whatever you're planning is in breach—"

"I hear you, Captain," she replied. "Your objections are noted."

"You cannot do this!" he cried, voice almost breaking.

Panic. Fear. Now he might know how the thousands in Wyke felt just before they perished in the flood. It brought her little solace but it was just, nevertheless.

"I am bound by no Armiger code, Captain Ultan. I am bound by the law of the Guilds. And in the absence of the Justiciers, I am the sole voice of that law. It therefore falls on me to pass sentence. The one most fitting is death."

Ultan shouted back but his voice was lost amid the chorus of protests from his troopers. Rosomon dragged her eyes away to the Titanguard who stood at the gate wheel. A nod of her head and they began to turn it.

The water started as a trickle, the wheel creaking, gears and chains clacking as they opened the gates to the flood chamber. The floor became awash with river water, and those shouts of protest turned to cries of alarm. Another turn of the gate wheel and the gap widened to let in a flood that quickly rose, foot after foot.

Rosomon forced herself to watch as panic set in below them. There might have been a hundred troopers in that pit, crammed together in their heavy armour. At first they shuffled away from the water, desperate to avoid the rising tide, but there was nothing they could do but shout in anger and fear as it rose to knee, waist, chest.

Some begged for mercy, howling their regret. Others stood stalwart, knowing this was the end. Ultan, to his credit, looked resigned to his fate. Did he bear any shame in those last moments? Rosomon would never know.

The water was up to their necks now, and for a fleeting moment Rosomon thought perhaps she should end this madness. She had proven her point, hadn't she? Taught the Ursus the error of their ways? She glanced across at Borys, at Oleksig, at Kassian. Not one of them questioned her. They merely stood watching as dozens perished. Surely if they thought this was wrong, they would have spoken up. But would she have listened?

Maugar Ironfall glared into the water as it rose above their heads. She could see the glee in that toothy grin of his. His daughter Xorya tried to look away, and he grasped her by the arm, forcing her to witness what was happening. Would that harden her to the reality of what they had to do? Rosomon could only hope it would. This was just the beginning.

The last of the Ursus disappeared beneath the surface, the rush of water gradually subsiding as the flood chamber filled. The surface bubbled as the troopers were held underwater by their heavy armour. Only one head still stared, eyes wide in panic. Faiza kicked and gasped, her heavy cloak dragging her down. Rosomon had a moment to wonder if she'd had the sense to kick off her heavy boots, before her head submerged. She managed to struggle her way to the top again, gasping, choking, before she went down once more. One final time she surfaced, shouting something unintelligible before ducking back under. She didn't surface again.

Rosomon dragged her eyes from the flood chamber, gazing at the crowd surrounding it, at the witnesses to a mass execution. If she had made the wrong decision, there was no one here to complain of it. Then her eyes fell on the solemn features of Thalleus Brisco. He held firmly to the arm of her nephew Lorens, who still stared in horror at the drowning pool.

Thalleus looked back at her, and she gestured for him to follow. "Bring him."

She made her way back down from the lock to an open patch of ground. It had been cleared of trees but for a single stump, planed smooth like a tabletop. Several of Oleksig's miners stood nearby, one of them holding a woodcutter's axe.

Rosomon waited as Lorens was urged nearer by Thalleus. Beside her stood Ianto, Kassian, the Marrlocks and Ironfalls. All were silent. All knew what was coming.

"Is this supposed to frighten me, Aunt Rosomon?" Lorens snarled.

He was scared, trying to mask it with anger. "It's a little late in the day for threats, don't you think?"

She forced herself to look at him, unable to quell the memories of the little boy she had known. Her brother's child, once so sweet. Once so loyal.

"You raised your hand to me, Lorens. I told you then it would not happen again."

"Of course not," he replied. "I would never...It was a mistake. I never meant you any harm, Aunt Rosomon. You know that."

"Really? So you have seen the error of your ways? You will turn your back on those Wyrms you hold in such high regard?"

She could see the fight in him. His fear over his faith. He glanced at the block and then the axe, before making his decision.

"Never," he said with surprising resolve. "If you want to behead me, then you'd best get on with it."

Rosomon could only admire his bravery. "I could never do that, Lorens. But still, there has to be justice for what you have done."

She signalled to Thalleus and Borys, who now held Lorens between them. They dragged him to the stump, forcing him to kneel, before Borys stretched Lorens's arm across the smooth wooden surface.

"Wait," he blurted. "What are you doing?"

Kassian was already holding the hilt of the Hawkspur sword toward her. Rosomon grasped it and unsheathed that blade, surprised at how heavy it was. Lancelin had always wielded a sword with such ease. She should have let him kill Lorens when he had the chance, then perhaps none of this would be necessary.

"Aunt Rosomon, please—"

She raised the sword in both hands, bringing it down with all her might to hack his hand off at the wrist. The blade sliced through flesh and bone, and she suddenly realised how real warriors must have felt— to wield the power of life and death in the single swing of a sword.

Lorens howled. Reeling back, leaving his right hand behind. Thalleus grasped him, Borys taking hold of the stump as Oleksig approached with a flaming torch. There was a crackling sound as he burned that wound, a sudden stink of acridity, of charring meat. The howl from Lorens only grew louder.

When they had finished, all he could do was cry and whimper, barely able to stand on his own two feet from the pain and the shock. Rosomon took a step forward, making sure she was all he could see, all he could focus on.

"I said you would never raise your hand to me again, Lorens. And I meant it. This time, I suggest you listen when I tell you to go back to the Anvil. Tell your master what happened here. Let him know the Guilds will not stand idly by while that snake slithers in our midst. We will root him out, and when I raise my blade again, it will be his head that's taken."

Lorens sobbed. "This is not you. Rosomon Hawkspur would never—"

"She would now," Rosomon said, before turning back toward Oakhelm.

After handing Kassian back that heavy blade, it was all she could do to keep walking. To not fall to her knees and weep. But that would have been the act of another woman. A weaker woman. She had just proven who she was. Rosomon Hawkspur had shouted it to the morning sky, loud enough that they would hear her at the Anvil.

KEARA

It was the last tower on the northern extent of the city. The windows were narrow but she could still see out across the city, like some damsel in a fairy tale waiting for her prince to come and rescue her. No one was coming. This was her fucking mess and she'd get herself out of it.

Before a suitably cunning idea could manifest, there was a dull boom from the south. The Armigers were on the move again. Wouldn't be long before they crossed the river and brought the Viper Battalion to its knees. One less obstacle in Sanctan's path. One more obstacle in hers. A path that now looked more treacherous than ever.

Cunning ideas be damned. It wasn't like her schemes had got her anywhere other than a locked room at the top of a tower. But now what? Even if she could escape, where would she go? The Guilds would murder her on sight, and the prospect of returning to her father felt like a fate worse than death.

The thought of explaining her failure to old Ingelram was much more daunting than execution. And yet this was all his doing. He had sent her on this impossible mission with nothing more than a pair of antique daggers. How was she supposed to stand against the might of the Ministry on her own? He had doomed her as surely as that bastard Olstrum.

And where was he, the duplicitous little shit? When he'd spoken in such heartfelt terms on the fate of his family, she had almost felt sympathy for him. Almost. Those words had resonated, to the point she had even considered helping him, and now she was a prisoner because of it. Of all the scheming rats in this nest of treachery, it was obvious Olstrum was the one to fear the most.

As the dull booming rose in intensity she tried to breathe more steadily. All was not lost. She had to believe that, but damn she could use some red drop right now, if only to stymie the relentless noise.

Maybe even now Hesse was hatching a plan for her escape. Formulating a daring rescue with a ruthless efficiency only she could muster.

A fanciful thought.

More likely she was lurking in some dark corner pulling the wings off flies, waiting for someone to tell her what to do. Sending word to her father might be a good bloody start, but she doubted Hesse had even bothered to think of that. If only Keara had thought to surround herself with more competent allies, maybe that would have served her better. Too late to think about recruiting them now.

The door to the chamber opened, making her flinch. She hadn't heard the key turn. Was it even locked? Olstrum didn't look like he had a care in the world as he strolled in. His entrance was heralded by more explosions from the south, but he didn't bat an eyelid as he greeted her with a welcoming smile.

No sooner had he stepped inside than the door closed behind him. Shut by an Armiger trooper or one of the Drakes, Keara couldn't quite see as she quashed her instinct to attack him. To at least leave a mark on that smug face. It might have been satisfying, but it would ultimately make her position even more perilous, if that was possible.

"I hope you're being comfortably accommodated?" he asked.

Keara resisted the urge to gesture around the bare room, pointing out the lack of comforts. She hadn't even been given a blanket, and if there was food or drink on offer, no one had told her.

"Exactly as comfortable as it looks, Olstrum."

He nodded his understanding, but didn't seem to give a shit. "That's nice."

It wasn't nice. It was pretty far from fucking nice, but there was no use in complaining to this bastard.

"So what now?" she asked. "Imminent execution, I would warrant?"

He gazed south through that slit of a window. "Right now Tyreta Hawkspur is being prepared for her journey back to the Anvil. The landship is almost ready."

Not quite what she was asking. "I mean what now for *me*?"

He looked surprised she'd asked. "That…is very much down to you."

Keara resisted the urge to grab him and shake out an answer. "You're going to have to be a lot less cryptic, Olstrum. I'm a webwainer, not a mind reader."

He gave a long sigh, as though this whole thing bored him. An affectation for her benefit, she was sure. Olstrum Garner didn't seem the kind of man who had time to be bored.

"I have persuaded the Drakes who were protecting the High Legate that their priority should be Tyreta. Obviously they were very keen for you to face justice at their hands. I won't go into the details, but they were quite graphic in their description of the punishment you deserved. I pointed out that executing an heir to the Hallowhill Guild might put us on sticky ground…diplomacy-wise. Of course I assured them that it would be handled. Discreetly."

"You mean *I* would be handled," she said, trying not to think on the grisly fate awaiting her at the hands of those Drakes.

"Indeed," he replied, still staring from that window.

He wore a self-assured air about him. A man in complete control of his environment. But the more she watched the more she saw that mask for what it was. His jaw worked frenetically, his back teeth grinding together. The fingernails on his right hand were bitten down to nubs. All the signs of a man under extreme pressure. A gambler locked in a game he could not control, but still forced to wager for the highest of stakes.

"And have you made your decision?" she asked.

He turned to her as though seeing her for the first time. As though his thoughts had been wandering elsewhere.

"My mind has not altered since the last time we spoke. Tyreta cannot be allowed to reach the Anvil."

"And what do you intend to do about it?"

He shrugged. "Me? I intend to do nothing. However, you will stop that landship from ever arriving. Instead, you will take Tyreta Hawkspur back to her mother as a show of good faith."

"You're going to release me? Just like that?"

"I am."

"If something sounds too good to be true, it's usually because it is. Why should I trust you? Why should I believe this isn't one of your games?"

The arrogant disregard had sloughed from his face now. Olstrum's eyes were possibly the saddest she had ever seen.

"I've already told you, I need your help. And now we need each other. Do you think I was lying about my family? About what danger they're in?"

"I'll admit—I had my doubts."

His gaze drifted to the floor. Once again Olstrum looked like his thoughts were miles away. "I've lied about many things over the years. Sometimes for the benefit of my emperor. Sometimes to facilitate Sanctan's rise. Sometimes to protect myself. Right now, the truth is all that remains. And trust..."

Keara took a step forward, placing a hand on his arm. It seemed the right thing to do, but as she touched him she could feel him trembling ever so subtly.

"We'll have to trust one another. Whether we like it or not."

A smile reached his face, but a pained one. In that moment she felt for him. Was she weak from lack of food, lack of red drop, from this whole shitty situation? She couldn't tell, but whatever it was, it made her feel more sympathy for Olstrum than she'd ever thought possible.

He reached into his jacket, taking something wrapped in sackcloth. "Here. You might need these."

She took it, unfolding the cloth to reveal the elaborate hilts of two daggers. Her daggers, now with the pyrestones replaced.

"I'll make sure they're put to good use," she replied.

The smile spread a little further across his face. "I'm sure you will."

ANSELL

The chamber's function was unknown to him. Perhaps lost to memory. It was bare, no windows, one table, one chair. Perhaps a dungeon? Maybe an administrative cell? Whatever it was, it served as his prison now. Not that he couldn't simply walk out of the door; it was not locked after all. But he would not flee. Ansell would face his fate.

A temple serf had brought him food and water, but it sat untouched on the table. He didn't feel the need to eat with such uncertainty ahead.

They had treated his wounds—more bandages, more salves—but the pain of them was numb to him now. Just a dull ache to stack with the rest. More unwelcome reminders of what he had suffered.

But he had saved Grace, and that almost made the pain worth enduring. Where she was now, he had no idea, but at least she was safe in the Mount. Since he had been attacked in the yard the temple was more like a fortress, his brothers posted at every entrance. He could only imagine how his fellow knights had risen in rage at the thought one of their own had been attacked on the grounds of their sacred demesne.

Despite knowing Grace was safe here, he still felt the need to find her. To watch over her and see she was protected. Of all the uncommon feelings he had experienced in recent days, that was the strangest. Perhaps it was simply the will of the Wyrms working through him. Urging him to defend the innocent at all costs. With his fate hanging in the balance he might never understand.

The door to the chamber creaked open and Ansell saw the familiar sight of Falcar and Regenwulf. Both his brothers ducked beneath the low lintel, dragon helms held in the crooks of their arms. He suddenly felt naked without his own armour. Would he ever have the honour of donning it again? Right now he wasn't sure if he even cared.

"It is time," Regenwulf said. "The Archlegate will see you now."

He looked and sounded stern, but then Ansell had never known him to be anything else. Nevertheless, a sense of dread crept up inside, no matter how hard he tried to quash it. He was about to be judged for his disobedience. Though it was rare, he had heard tales of brother knights executed for less. The best he could hope for was to be cast out of the temple, to have the Draconate turn its back on him and be removed from the sight of the Great Wyrms. A short time ago he would have considered that a fate worse than execution, but now...

"Am I to be stained with the name of traitor?" he asked.

"That's not for me to say," Regenwulf replied. "I am only a servant. Not a judge."

Of course he was. And it was an answer that Ansell would normally have accepted, but now, in light of all he had seen and done, it was not enough.

"I would ask that you tell me anyway, brother?" Ansell said.

Regenwulf's brow creased. He had not expected such a question, any more than Ansell would have thought to ask it mere days ago.

"I would say I have always trusted your judgement, and I trust it still. You must have had your reasons to disobey an edict. You are no traitor in my eyes."

Ansell looked to handsome Falcar. "And you?"

In contrast to Regenwulf's stern visage, Falcar flashed that disarming smile of his. "Who is to say that any of us would have acted differently in your position, brother. But it is not we who will measure you. That privilege is for the Archlegate alone. He who presides over us all."

Their words of support meant much. Ansell wanted to ask if they too had their doubts. If they thought they were following a madman on a dark path. But he would never have given them so compromising a choice.

"Where is the girl now?"

"She is safe," Regenwulf replied. "Won't stop asking after you."

That almost brought a smile to his face. Made him want to watch over her more than ever.

"If my fate is a dire one, I would ask that you take care of her. See she comes to no harm."

Regenwulf dropped his gaze as though he was uncomfortable with the prospect, and he could not answer. It was a foolish thing to ask anyway—his brothers were warriors, not nursemaids.

"No matter," Ansell continued. "I am sure she will be well cared for in the Mount."

"I would ask," said Falcar. "Why? Why did you defy the Archlegate's explicit instruction? To disobey his order is as great a sin as any of us could commit."

Ansell regarded his brother with the deepest of sorrow. If only he could have told him. Unburdened himself of what he had seen, what he had done in that man's name. Sanctan Egelrath was a slaughterer of innocent women. A duplicitous wretch. But Ansell could not shatter the illusions of his order. Could not lay doubts before his brothers, as they had been laid before him.

"Because it was the right thing to do," he replied.

Regenwulf straightened. "We should not keep the Archlegate waiting."

He shifted from the doorway, and he and Falcar placed their helms over their heads. As Ansell followed them from the room he was grateful they had not chained him. Allowing him his dignity was at least one mercy. Still, as they walked the corridors of the Mount he could see every eye fall on him with suspicion, before the serfs and legates bowed in respect at their passing. Respect for his brothers, more likely. For a moment he wondered if he would ever see such deference again, before he remembered he barely cared.

It did not take long for him to work out where they were going.

The tower of Ravenothrax stood at the southern extent of the Mount—a grim, black monument to the Great Wyrm of Death. He wondered for a moment if this was a portent of his fate. The black marble and jet that adorned the tower might have intimidated a lesser man, but not Ansell Beckenrike. He had always been prepared for this, always known he would die in service to the Draconate. That death might now be an ignominious one, but at least his conscience would be clear when he stepped through the gate to the Five Lairs.

When they reached the summit of the tower, Sanctan was already waiting. He stood in the shadow of a huge statue, the Great Wyrm of Death dominating the chamber. The Archlegate had his back to them, gazing up at the obsidian carving as it glared down with bejewelled eyes.

Falcar and Regenwulf stopped at the archway. If they were standing guard, prepared to stop him from fleeing his fate, they needn't have bothered. He would not run like a coward, no matter how he was judged.

Ansell walked to the centre of the room, hands by his sides, unarmoured and unadorned like a beggar before his king. Red-tinged light streamed in through the panes of glass on a high circular window, casting an ominous hue across the room, and causing the statue to glow angrily.

"Beautiful, isn't he," Sanctan said, still staring up at the face of their dragon god.

Ansell had never considered any depiction of the Wyrms to be beautiful. Certainly not Ravenothrax. Fearsome perhaps, intimidating, but not beautiful. But then, aesthetics had never been something he paid much heed to.

"Ravenothrax always terrified me as a boy," Sanctan continued. "Even as a lowly legate—a servant of these majestic idols—I was fearful of his wrath. But I learned along the way that there was nothing to fear from the Great Wyrm of Death. He is our protector. Our guide to the next world. There is nothing to fear from him as long as one is pious." He turned to face Ansell, his face a mask of benevolence. "Tell me, do you consider yourself pious?"

"Yes, Archlegate."

It was the only answer to give, whether he still believed it or not.

His words were greeted with a nod of acknowledgment. "Yes. That's what I always believed. That Ansell Beckenrike was the most pious of all my knights. And with that piety would come obedience. Steadfastness. Was I wrong with that assumption?"

"No, Archlegate. You were not wrong."

Sanctan leaned in closer. "Then can you explain to me why you chose to disobey my very specific instructions?"

Because it was the right thing to do. He had already said it once, but he knew that reasoning would not be good enough for the Archlegate.

"Saphenodon teaches us that children are the most innocent of souls. That they are to be protected at all cost. That they must—"

"Saphenodon teaches?" Sanctan said, a sudden edge to his voice. "Do you think to lecture me on scripture, Ansell?"

"No, Archlegate. But you asked me—"

"I asked you why you disobeyed me. Not to parrot lines from the Draconate Prophesies I already know by rote."

Ansell knew what this was now. He was being forced to reveal himself. To disclose his doubts and fears—the ones that had led to his disobedience. The ones that would demonstrate his growing scorn for the Archlegate and his Ministry, and expose him as the heretic he was.

"Grace needed help. And there was no one else to give it."

Sanctan nodded his understanding. "No one other than you? And so you took it upon yourself to go on down to the Burrows? To seek her out? To murder and brutalise in the name of the Draconate in order to save an innocent child?"

"Yes."

Again, Sanctan nodded as though the logic was perfectly clear to him. "That's very admirable. But what do you think the biggest consequence of that might be?"

Ansell thought that was fairly obvious, but if he was forced to say it, he would. "I set out to liberate an innocent child from evildoers. There would inevitably be death in order to see it done. What other consequence could there be?"

Sanctan took a cleansing breath as though quelling his fury. "The consequence is that you have put my already precarious position in yet more jeopardy. The scurrilous rumours about that girl's heritage now have yet more fuel. Had she been left to her fate, those rumours would have faded to embers. She would just have been another dead urchin in the Burrows. But why would anyone murder half a dozen kidnappers to release a worthless orphan, unless she was important somehow?"

Ansell felt himself bristle at the notion Grace was worthless. He struggled to stop his hands clenching into fists, forced himself to endure the slight.

"Before you decided to go on a one-man crusade," Sanctan continued, "people might have suspected the child was mine. Now they know it, beyond any doubt. Why would you take it upon yourself to do that when I told you not to? That child is nothing to you. She's not your daughter. You're not even her uncle, or her ward."

"I am..." He wasn't sure what he was anymore.

Sanctan leaned in close to his ear. "You are my hammer, Ansell Beckenrike. You exist only to smite my enemies. Is that clear?"

"I thought I was a servant of the Ministry."

"I *am* the fucking Ministry!"

Sanctan's scream echoed through the tower. It took all Ansell's will not to flinch at the bellow in his ear. He had seen Sanctan's anger before, but it had always been the petulant dramatics of a child grown. Now he bore all the fury of a zealous priest wronged by his brood.

It would be so easy for him to tip over. To order Ansell executed right here and now, in the sight of the Wyrm of Death. Would Regenwulf obey such an order? Would Falcar? Even after all their earlier talk of brotherhood, Ansell knew it would be impossible for them to defy the word of their master.

"Archlegate."

The word resounded through the tower, shattering the tension. Sanctan looked over Ansell's broad shoulder toward the entrance. The fury faded on his face, back to that look of serenity. That mask.

"Prince Lorens," he said.

Ansell turned to see the son of the emperor he had slain make his way into the chamber. Lorens glanced at Regenwulf and Falcar, a glimmer of fear in his eyes. His arm was heavily bandaged and strapped to his chest. Even with such thick bindings Ansell could tell his hand was severed.

Sanctan ignored Lorens's obvious discomfort. "I was not expecting to see you. What word from Oakhelm?"

Despite Sanctan's friendly greeting, it seemed Lorens was in no mood for pleasantries. "Oakhelm still stands, Archlegate."

A brief twitch of displeasure on Sanctan's cheek, gone as soon as it came. "And what of our aunt, Lady Rosomon?"

Lorens gently fingered the stump of his arm. "She...that bitch took my frigging hand."

"I can see that," Sanctan replied, desperately hanging on to his calm exterior. "But what of the Guilds?"

"They also still stand. Hawkspur, Marrlock, Ironfall. All united against us."

"Where?" snapped Sanctan. Ansell could sense his desperation now, his fear, and could only imagine how dangerous that might make him.

"Still at Oakhelm, I believe. But not for long. As soon as they have consolidated their forces, the Anvil will be in their sights."

Sanctan greeted that news with silence. The mask was slipping gradually, his every muscle tensed as he tried to stay in control. Eventually his eyes fell on Ansell.

"It seems there is still much more work to be done," he said. "A chance, perhaps, for you to redeem yourself."

"Yes, Archlegate."

"Then I suggest you go and prepare. Polish your armour, sharpen your blade, or whatever it is you do. I will call upon you when I am ready."

Ansell bowed before making his way from the chamber. He ignored Lorens, who he could see was sweating heavily, in obvious discomfort. As he passed his brothers he paused for the briefest second. Regenwulf glanced his way from within his helm. It was enough for him to realise he still had one friend here.

As he made his way back down the tower he could not help but wonder whether he was right back where he started. He had been offered a reprieve at least, but did he even want such mercy? Then again, did he still want to leave? To abandon his brothers when they would need him at their side more than they ever had?

He reached his chamber, and opened the door. The first thing to greet him was his armour, standing untouched. It gave him a sense of relief that it was still here, along with a faint tinge of guilt that he had thought to abandon it at all. Then he saw her.

Grace sat on his pallet bed, his copy of the Draconate Prophesies lying open on her lap. She glanced up at him, then went back to the book.

"What are you doing here?" he asked, not quite comprehending how relieved he felt at seeing her.

"Waiting for you," she replied. "You've been gone ages."

He closed the door and sat beside her on the bed. "You're reading? Can you even understand the words in that book?"

"I can try," she replied. So matter-of-fact. So plain and obvious, it made him wonder why everything else had become so complicated. Of course she could try. What else could anyone do?

"Stone," she said suddenly.

"What?" he replied.

"Stone." Grace reached out a tiny hand and touched him on the arm, her finger tracing where all those years ago he had carved a name into his flesh. A name he had soon after abandoned. "What does it mean?"

A good question. Did it mean anything at all anymore?

"I guess it's just a reminder."

She looked up at him, her brow creasing, wrinkles forming on her tiny nose. "Of what?"

"Of how we can all change. If we have to."

That seemed a good enough answer for her, and she went back to the book. Let her read it for now. Ansell had no idea if he would have any further use for it.

TYRETA

They bundled her through the old building, holding tight to her manacled arms. She would have struggled, made them work for it, but after crouching in a dank cell for so long it was all she could do to stand.

The sunlight was blinding, and she squinted, taking in as much of her surroundings as she could. Battalion troopers stood with their splintbows raised, even a couple of steamlock carbines, but nothing powered by pyrestone. There were maybe a dozen of them. Even if her wrists hadn't been locked in manacles, fingers bound tight in case she tried to use her claws, she doubted she'd get far before being stuck like a pincushion.

She could sense no pyrestone in the vicinity. Nothing she might use to her advantage. Before she could figure another way out of this, she heard a clattering of metal. Half a dozen troopers struggled with a cage, dragging it from a nearby alley in a vain attempt to lift it onto a cart. Cat was pawing and scratching, hissing her fury at those troopers, and Tyreta began to share that ire, feeling her own anger match that of the panther.

As they shifted the cage one of them slipped. Shouts of alarm echoing across the open yard as the cage clattered to the stone walkway. The door buckled, its lock snapping under the weight.

Cat smashed her bulk against the door, and it burst open. Troopers yelled for help as the panther leapt into their midst, staggering back out of reach of those rending claws. As keen as she was for Cat to attack, Tyreta saw half a dozen splintbows levelled, ready to unleash a volley of bolts.

"No!" she screamed.

Cat paused, hackles raised, crouched and ready to strike. A low growl issued from her throat as she glared around at the troopers.

Tyreta closed her eyes, desperate not to panic as she reached out across the web. In an instant she was seeing through Cat's eyes, sur-rounded by those troopers and their deadly weapons. She could feel the panther's fear and anger, the desperation to escape tempered by the need to protect Tyreta.

Quickly she quelled those emotions, soothing the fire within. Cat turned obediently, padding back to the cage and climbing inside. No sooner had she done so than one of the troopers slammed the door shut, sliding the bolt back across and securing it with a length of rope.

"Get that thing loaded up," one of the captains ordered.

As Tyreta was pushed forward across the yard she saw Olstrum approaching from the edge of the path. It took all her will not to bare her teeth at that treacherous bastard.

"Deftly done," he said, keeping pace with her as she was led to whatever fate awaited her. "You Hawkspurs never fail to impress me."

"You'd be a lot more impressed if I was out of these chains," she replied, suddenly thinking of all the ways she could hurt him.

"Oh, I'm certain you're right about that. If what I've heard is true, you've turned into quite the killer since I last saw you at the Anvil."

She was bored of his prattling already. How her uncle managed to be in the same room for so long was beyond her. "Have you just come to gloat?"

He held up a hand to the guards holding her. "I'll take it from here."

The troopers stepped back, as Olstrum took her gently by the arm and led her on. She was surprised at how obedient they were, but then Olstrum had a different master now. He was servant to the Archlegate himself, and with it he'd inherited more than a modi-cum of the respect the Ministry inspired.

"I have not come to gloat," Olstrum said quietly. "In fact I thought I might ask a favour of you."

"Really? Do you want me to tell Sanctan what a nice chap you are? Because I'll be honest, I doubt my cousin cares much about what I think anymore."

"No, I'd just like you to remember who sent you on this journey."

"Why is that?"

Olstrum pulled her to halt, regarding her with those narrow eyes of his. He looked deathly serious. "So that when you see your mother, you can pass on my sincerest regards."

"When I see my mother? I don't know if you've been keeping up with events, but I doubt I'll be seeing her for some time."

Olstrum gave a subtle shake of his head. "Anything can happen, Tyreta. You never know your luck."

Had he decided to change his allegiance again? To help her escape? Tyreta found that hard to believe, but even if it were true, she was doubtful she'd persuade her mother of his good intentions. "You... want me to send her your regards? The man who betrayed her brother? The Guilds? Have you been on the red drop?"

Olstrum let out a long weary sigh. "If only I had."

"Let's go," an Armiger captain shouted from up ahead, before she could ask Olstrum what in the Lairs he was talking about.

She followed, seeing the landship waiting at its platform up ahead. It wasn't so long ago she had left Donan and Sted at this platform, and followed her instincts to rescue Cat. Had that been the wrong decision? It certainly seemed so now, but at the time she had not been able to fight that animal urge. Now it seemed her rashness had damned them both. Although from what Olstrum was suggesting, maybe not.

Two Drakes were waiting for her beside the landship, the side of a freight carriage yawning open in anticipation of her arrival. Tyreta glanced back, seeing Olstrum watching from the edge of the terminal. He offered her an almost imperceptible nod, before one of the Drakes took her arm and led her into the yawning chasm of the carriage.

As the Drake forced her to her knees, securing the manacles at her wrist to a ring plate bolted to the floor, she reached out with her power. There was no pyrestone here, nothing to manipulate or overload. She could barely detect the power core of the engine it was so far away. There was nothing she could do to escape.

She heard a howling and thrashing as Cat's cage was wheeled into the carriage. Armiger troopers secured it to the roof and walls with chains, looking relieved when they could eventually leave the ferocious panther behind. With the cage loaded, the Drakes slid the door closed and secured the bolts, moving to the far side of the carriage as the distant engines powered up. With a jolt and a hiss of pistons, the landship began its journey.

It would not take them long to reach the Anvil. Less than a day, and Tyreta would meet her fate. Her only solace was that she would get to face her cousin soon. She would only need one opportunity— one strike—and Sanctan would die. Hopefully with him gone, all this would be over. It was a slim chance, but still a chance nonetheless.

So far all she had done was let her mother down. Perhaps the great Lady Rosomon had been right about her errant daughter all along. Tyreta should have listened, should have done as she was told for once. How she wanted to say sorry, to make amends, but now, in chains, it looked like that chance would never come. Then again, if what Olstrum said was true...

Could she trust him though? Was it wise to rely on the word of such a man? Of course not. If the opportunity came for her to escape, she would have to take it. And soon.

Cat had calmed within her cage, but Tyreta could sense her unease. It would have been so easy to drift into her mind, but the panther was useless to her behind those bars. Likewise there was no pyrestone nearby to manipulate. It was just her and those Drakes. Might they be of use? Could she overwhelm their minds as she could with other animals?

As the landship cruised along its rails, Tyreta closed her eyes. The strands of the web spread through the carriage, but they were wispy and indistinct. Still she reached out, sending her consciousness along those ethereal threads, creeping invisibly toward the knights.

No sooner had she tried to enter the first one's mind than she was repelled, as though a wall of darkness had been thrown up in her path. Was it because they were human? Did it make them more difficult to influence? Or were the Drakes so stalwart in their will that it made them impossible to infect? Either way, it was clear her powers wouldn't help her now.

She opened her eyes, taking a deep breath. Resignation began to dawn as the landship carried on its journey. The grim reality that she was helpless, powerless. Just as she felt she might wallow in that despair for the whole journey, the landship began to slow.

Wheels squealed on their rails, the distant sound of the grinding engine growing shrill as it protested. The Drakes glanced at one another, holding on to the loading straps as the vessel decelerated. When it finally came to a stop, they both drew their blades.

Silence filled the carriage but for the faint hum of the engine. The entire landship had been rendered immobile. Tyreta strained her senses, trying to perceive what was happening, some clue, any clue. Outside there was a trace of pyrestone energy drawing ever closer. She could feel it intensifying until something slammed against the side of the carriage.

That energy began to bloom, building with every heartbeat, rising to a crescendo. Tyreta lowered her head, squeezing her eyes tight a moment before an explosion rocked through the carriage. She was deafened momentarily, before her ears started to ring a long high-pitched note. When she opened her eyes, she was surrounded by dust and smoke. A huge breach had been blown open in the side of the carriage, letting in the bright daylight.

One of the Drakes crawled from shards of broken wood, groggily finding his sword before rising unsteadily to his feet. He staggered toward the yawning gap, raising his sword defensively. Before he could charge, he was showered with tiny metal devices, each one adhering to his tarnished armour, winking with the light of a yellow pyrestone.

There was a staccato drum of popping explosions as the devices triggered, blowing the Drake to pieces where he stood. By now the second knight had risen from the dust, sword already in hand. He charged through the breach to the sound of panicked voices from outside. There was a ring of metal, a cry of alarm, before the unmistakable voltaic hum of a pyrestone weapon. Then silence.

Cat hunkered in the corner of her cage, hackles raised, teeth bared. Tyreta yanked at the manacles about her wrist, but she was still bolted tight to the base of the carriage.

Someone stepped through the breach, and amid the settling dust Tyreta recognised Keara's scarred face. She looked pleased with herself, hair immaculate, Hallowhill tunic pressed and clean. Distinctly out of place amid such carnage.

"Here we are again," Keara said, kneeling down beside Tyreta. "Anyone would think you liked being chained up."

It looked like Olstrum hadn't been lying after all. "Why am I not surprised to see you?"

Keara shrugged. "I guess trouble just tends to follow me around."

"Olstrum gave me the impression I wouldn't be going to the Anvil."

"And he was right." Keara grinned. "You most definitely won't. That would be an absolute waste."

Her sidekick, the rake-thin woman with her dark eyeglasses, entered the carriage with half a dozen other webwainers. They unshackled the cage and began to wheel Cat through the breach.

"Be careful with that," Tyreta said.

"Oh, we will be," Keara replied. "We'll treat your little pet with the utmost care."

"And what about me?" Tyreta lifted her manacled hands as high as she could. "Are you going to get me out of here?"

"Not just yet," Keara replied.

"What do you mean? Are you going to deliver me to my mother in chains? I can't imagine that will go down too well."

Keara lifted a finger to her cheek, tracing the line of stitches. "About that...there's been a slight change of plan. You won't be going back to your mother."

"Then where?"

"I thought it might be nice for you to come back with me to the Web. Unfortunately, your little pet is bound for a slightly different destination."

Tyreta began to get a sinking feeling in her gut. A feeling that this was not quite the rescue she thought it might be. "What are you doing, Keara? What's going on? Is this part of Olstrum's plan?"

Two of the webwainers approached, one of them uncorking a vial. Red drop, from the smell of it.

Keara's grin widened, but her eyes hardened. "Olstrum's plan didn't quite match up with mine. So I've decided to make a few adjustments. Don't worry though, you'll be well taken care of. As long as you remain useful."

One of the webwainers grabbed Tyreta by the hair, dragging her head back. She tried to resist, but manacled to the floor she could barely move. The second webwainer placed a thumb on her eyelid, forcing it open. She tried to blink as they poured in the drop but it was hopeless.

"What are you doing?" she managed to snarl, instantly feeling the effects of the narcotic.

They let go of her, and she felt the carriage spin. Her eyes began to mist, a red sheen covering everything.

"That's a special blend," Keara said. "Much stronger than I'm used to. It should make the rest of your journey a little more comfortable. And it'll make sure those claws of yours are clipped until we get to the Web."

Other colours mixed in with the red—blues and yellows, swirling like ink in water before her eyes. Keara's face began to contort as though Tyreta were staring into the warped surface of a mirror. Then black coloured it all . . .

FULREN

The wagon rolled ever onward, buffeting him out of his hunger and fatigue. His days had been spent shivering in a cloak, cursing the wind that blew through the clear wilderness. Nights were little better, wrapped in that same cloak but with at least a fire for comfort. There was little life out here, wherever *here* was. Occasionally he would sense the fleeting outline of a frightened hare dashing from the undergrowth, or the whispering wings of a bird flying far above. Other than that, it was just Verlyn and a numb arse for company.

At first their horses had been agitated, whickering more nervously with every passing mile. They were steeds bred for riding, unused to the labour of being yoked to a wagon, but within a couple of days they had grown used to it. But then Fulren knew better than most that, given enough time, you could get used to anything. Though he wasn't quite there yet, he had become accustomed to the fleeting senses his blindness gave him. One arm and no legs would be a much greater burden to accept, but he would get there. Eventually.

Right now his greatest foe was boredom. He'd never considered himself the best conversationalist, but Verlyn took introspection to a whole new level. If she wasn't huffing or sighing, she was grunting at the horses, at the road, at the wind. He could see her aura turn an angry red on occasion, but mostly it was a faded and languid green against the blackness. Fulren could only imagine what she was going through. With Ashe gone and the farmhouse burned she had lost everything. He would have sympathised, tried to offer some solace, but he didn't know what to say. And so they said nothing.

Even that voice in his head was quiet. That alluring whisper from beyond the veil of darkness. Throughout the journey he had been expecting it, dreading it, cringing in wait as though it might burst in his head like a firecracker. Despite the silence, he knew it must be there, watching, waiting, choosing the right time to taunt him with its promise. He could only hope that this time he would have the strength to resist.

"Are we close?" he asked, if only to divert his thoughts from that dread whisper.

A sigh and a grumble from his travelling companion. Clearly she was as tired of this journey as he was.

"Are you going to ask me that with every passing hour?"

Fulren hadn't realised he had been so troublesome. "I'm sorry."

He felt her nudge him playfully with her elbow. "You'll be as relieved as I am to know we're very nearly there."

Relieved wasn't the word. "You haven't told me much about the man we're travelling to meet. Is there anything I need to know?"

"Yeah, I guess I should have prepared you a little bit better for this. Let's just say that Lysander Merigot is a man not to be messed with. He'll come across as kindly enough, but don't mistake his amiable manner for weakness. He's one dangerous bastard."

"Dangerous how?" Fulren asked, beginning to wonder if this had been such a good idea.

"Back in the dim and distant he was hunted by both Guild and Ministry alike. You might not believe it, but the Guilds can be as ruthless as the Ministry when it suits them."

Fulren could well believe it. He had been exiled by the Guilds for a crime that wasn't his, despite his mother's efforts. "What did he do to deserve that?"

A pause. She was thinking how best to put this. "As well as being a talented artificer, he might have . . . dabbled."

"In what?"

"As you know, there's a lot more to sorcery than webwaining. Much of it forbidden. He mainly dabbled in the forbidden stuff."

"So dark sorcery? That's basically what you're saying. What kind? Blood magics? Demonism? Something worse?"

"I don't really know. And I'll be honest, I don't really want to."

For the first time Fulren began to realise what danger he was being led into. Outcast artificers were one thing, but fugitive sorcerers quite another. This Lysander might be a monster for all he knew.

"So why are we doing this?"

"Because if half the rumours about Lysander are true, he's the only person who knows what's happening to you. That makes him the only one who can help."

"So how well do you know him, exactly?"

Another pause. More choosing of the right words. "I mean... it's been a while, but I'm sure he'd remember me."

"In a good way?"

"In a *way*. That's better than nothing, right?"

Fulren wasn't so sure. This was sounding like a worse idea with every turn of that wagon's wheels.

"Look," Verlyn continued. "What choice do you have right now? Live out your sorry life in the dark, being looked after by a bitter old woman?"

"Or choose to throw my lot in with a dark magus I know nothing about. I'll be honest, Verlyn, I'm not so bloody sure."

"I hate to break it to you, but you don't have any more time to make up your mind."

"What do you mean?

"I mean, we're here," she said, tugging back on the reins and pulling the horses to a stop.

Fulren sat for a moment, listening to the wind. He wasn't sure what to expect at the dwelling of an infamous magician, but this most definitely wasn't it. There was a faint smell of woodsmoke, but otherwise nothing. No birds singing. No rustling of creatures in the undergrowth.

"Well?" Verlyn asked. "What's your decision? I can turn us around and ride us right out of here, but who knows what's waiting for us on the road."

Fulren knew there was really no choice at all. "All right. Let's get this over with."

Verlyn climbed from the wagon to unload his wheeled chair and then helped him down, making sure he was comfortable before pushing him across the rough ground. They came to a stop, before she knocked at a solid wooden door. More silence as they waited, almost too long, before the sliding of bolts—two, three, four. The door opened without so much as a creak, and whoever answered it had no kind of aura at all. They were just a blank space against the blackness of his vision.

"Hello, Verlyn." A man's voice. No discernible accent, perhaps middle-aged. It was like a ghost had come to receive them.

"Lysander," Verlyn replied.

It was quiet as the two of them stood there. Fulren could only imagine them regarding one another. Was there tension? Were they pleased to be reunited? The disquiet made him almost squirm in his chair.

"So are you going to invite us in?" Verlyn asked eventually.

"Yes," Lysander replied, as though that was his intention all along.

Verlyn wheeled him inside out of the cold. There was a fire burning nearby, but other than that he could sense no great power, nor source of pyrestone. Someone murmured in one corner. An old man perhaps, so old he could no longer speak sense.

The door closed and Fulren turned his head, but still couldn't make out any trace of Lysander. Considering Verlyn had told him this was a great artificer, it seemed odd that he had neither artifice nor pyrestone in his home.

"It's been a long time," Verlyn said, as she wheeled Fulren closer to the fire.

"Has it?" Lysander said. "I hadn't really noticed. Where's Ashe?"

There was a pause as Verlyn worked out how to tell him, but there was only one way in the end. "She's dead."

Lysander sighed. "That's a shame. I always liked Ashe. She had a kind spirit, no matter what the world threw at her. Was it the Ministry?"

"Revocaters. But they're one and the same thing now."

"Yes," Lysander breathed. "Times are indeed changing."

"Do you even know what's going on out there?"

Fulren could hear Lysander moving but still couldn't see him. Not even a shadow being cast over the dull grey of his vision. "One side fights the other. Sometimes the sides shift allegiance, as they always have. It's none of my concern."

"You can't run from this forever," Verlyn snapped. "Can't hide away and hope they'll just ignore you. With the Guilds gone it won't be long before you're found."

"Let them come." His voice sounded grave, but there was also a note of relish in it, as though he looked forward to the confrontation.

That old man, or whoever it was, began to murmur. Lysander moved across the room toward him. "It's all right, Uncle. These are friends." It seemed to calm the old man's muttering. "Or at least I think they are. Who have you brought to see me, Verlyn?"

"He can speak well enough for himself," she replied.

Fulren guessed it was his turn. But what to say? Could he trust this Lysander with the truth? Then again, what did it matter if he couldn't? This was their last place of refuge and his only choices were to trust Lysander or take his chances on the road.

"My name is Fulren... Fulren Hawkspur."

More silence as Lysander considered the words. "You brought an actual Hawkspur to my house?"

"He's not just any Hawkspur, Lysander."

"No?" he replied, a hint of anger in his voice. "He's not a member of the family that had me exiled to this backwater?"

"He has a gift," Verlyn replied. "A powerful one."

"He doesn't look particularly gifted," Lysander snapped. Fulren knew how pitiful he must have appeared, but still the reminder stung. "I am sorry, boy. You didn't deserve that."

"No, he didn't," said Verlyn. "And I'm not just talking about the webwainer gift. This one is special. He has been blessed by the sorcerers of Nyrakkis."

"Has he now," Lysander replied, moving closer.

"A necroglyph," said Fulren. "It's a—"

Lysander began to laugh. "I know what it is, boy. And whether it's a blessing or a curse is debatable. May I see it?"

"Yes," Fulren replied, unbuttoning his shirt. Verlyn helped him pull it down so Lysander could see the markings on the back of his neck and shoulders.

Strong hands probed his flesh. He could smell Lysander's warm breath as he examined him closely.

"That's a glyph all right," he said finally. "And one of ancient design, if I haven't missed my guess."

"You know about necroglyphs?" Fulren asked.

"I've lived a long time, boy. To survive that many years, with the enemies I've got, you learn much or you die. Eh, Uncle?"

There was more unintelligible murmuring from the old man in the corner. Fulren could barely see him there, his outline vague against the black. He wondered if he was so indistinct due to the loss of his faculties—all the vigour gone out of him, leaving few traces for Fulren's mage-sight to detect.

Verlyn pulled the shirt back over Fulren's shoulders. "He needs your help. There must be something you can do for him."

"I'm not sure what," Lysander replied. "This boy has been marked, yes, but look at him."

"This *boy* killed three Revocaters with nothing but a crude rig of artifice strapped to his legs. He has power."

"Power indeed. Are you sure you're no webwainer?"

"No," Fulren replied.

"Interesting. It shows promise, I suppose, but I'm not sure what you want me to do about it."

"I want you to help him," Verlyn bit in frustration. "Make him walk. Make him fight. They killed Ashe. *My* Ashe. Like she was nothing."

"And now you want revenge," Lysander said. "But what about this boy? Do you think he wants to fight, just so you can have your reckoning?"

"I want to fight for me," Fulren said, eager to speak for himself. "The Ministry has to be stopped, and I can't help from this damned chair."

More silence. Verlyn's outline slowly dimmed from red to purple to blue as her anger calmed. Lysander was still nothing more than a shadow against the dark.

"Then perhaps there is something I can do," he said. "Come, boy. I have something to show you." Verlyn moved to push Fulren's wheelchair but Lysander said, "No. I'll take him alone."

She stepped aside, giving Fulren's shoulder a reassuring squeeze. Was that supposed to make him feel better? Right now, all he felt was terrified of this strange man in his strange little house with his enfeebled uncle.

With no idea what to expect, he allowed Lysander to wheel him toward the rear of the tiny hovel, past a heavy curtain and down a narrow corridor. The air was cloying at first, but the further they got from the warmness of the fire, the chillier it became. He heard a final wordless call from the old man, perhaps a last shout of caution, before all went silent. The wheeled chair juddered along the uneven passage, the floor undulating up and down. At times Lysander had to give it a firm shove to keep it moving.

"Where are we going?" Fulren asked.

"Every artificer must have his workshop," Lysander replied.

"I've heard you're more than just an artificer."

Lysander laughed a deep rumble from his throat. "Heard what? That I'm a deviant? A sorcerer? A meddler in the forbidden arts?"

Fulren couldn't think of any politer way of putting it. "Something like that."

Lysander drew the chair to a stop. Fulren could see nothing but the black, though it felt less oppressive, as though they had finally come out of the passage.

"We are here," said Lysander.

Though Fulren tried to spy something, anything in the blackness that might suggest this was a workshop, he could detect nothing. "This feels like a cave."

"It is much more than that, boy. Reach out. Use that gift of yours and let me see what the fuss is about."

Though it sounded a foolish idea, Fulren did as he was asked. He concentrated, trying to tap into whatever power he had used days before to fight the Revocaters. No sooner did he try than the necroglyph began to heat up at the nape of his neck.

Lights danced before him—pinpricks of energy glowing in the dark.

This place was filled with pyrestone energy, he just hadn't detected it until he tapped into the source. More and more lights began to shine until there was a starscape of pyrestone energy illuminating a sea of artifice.

Tables were strewn with it. Machinery standing idle—devices to bevel, bore and bend metal. Grinders, cutters, tappers and finishers. An artificer's dream.

"This is amazing," Fulren breathed, trying to supress his sudden feeling of nostalgia at those innocent days he had spent in the Archwind workshops. "What do you use this for? With such equipment you could perform a great service for Torwyn."

"I owe Torwyn nothing," Lysander replied. "They may have taught me the ways of artifice, but the Archwinds gave me no gifts worth keeping. That was for others to do."

"What are you talking about? What gifts?"

Fulren could sense Lysander moving, that dark silhouette filling up his field of vision and blocking out much of the pyrestone light.

"You think you are the only eastlander to be offered the blessing of a necroglyph?"

The black space that Lysander took up began to fizzle with energy. Though the silhouette darkened, turning black as the void, a pattern began to appear, picked out in deep red. Wings of sparking light sprouted from the blackness like those of an eagle. They spread, unfurling to reveal a scintillating necroglyph that grew beyond Lysander's broad back.

Fulren pressed himself into the chair as the man's body was slowly revealed; a tall humanoid figure that grew to resemble a creature of myth, flesh molten, wings colossal within the limits of the cave. Lysander rose, hovering several feet above the floor, and it was all Fulren could do to not cry out in terror.

"Do you see, Fulren Hawkspur?" Lysander's voice was resonant, echoing through the cave like a god returned to this mortal realm.

Fulren nodded, unable to speak. In response, the wings furled, dissipating like snowflakes in the sun. Lysander's body shrank back to human proportions, but Fulren could still see him framed in the dark of the cave. A bald man, face aged but with a tall athletic build.

"As you see, a necroglyph can imbue its gifts just as readily as curse its user."

"So do you...?" Fulren wasn't sure he should even mention the demon within. The spectre that haunted everyone who was imbued with the dark power of Nyrakkis. "Do you hear those voices too?"

A grin spread on Lysander's face. "At first I did. But I have learned to quiet that whisper, and turn the demon to my will. *My* voice is the only one that matters now. And, given enough time, so will yours. You will fight again, boy. I will show you the way."

"But...how? How can I fight when I..." He didn't want to say the words. It all seemed so hopeless.

Lysander took a step forward. "When you can't even walk?"

"Yes," Fulren whispered. "When I can't even walk."

Lysander laid a hand on his shoulder. "Not yet, Fulren Hawkspur. But you will."

KEARA

The Web always looked better after dark. It hid the decay, the filth, the essence of rot that hung about the place. A tram droned past her on its rails, reminding her that there were quicker ways around the city. This time though, as she made her way toward the manse of the Hallowhills, Keara had chosen to walk. It might help gather her thoughts. Help her see more clearly.

At least she was free of the fighting now. The Web had escaped the conflict that had riven almost every other major city in Torwyn. A haven spared the degradations of war. Perhaps now, more than ever, it was time for her city to join.

Not that war would make this place any worse. It already looked as though it might collapse under the weight of its own misery. By the Lairs, she could have done with Hesse here to lift her mood, but she had sent her off on a grim task of her own. Hesse hadn't liked the prospect of acting the messenger, but once Keara had told her the reasoning it had been easy to persuade her, despite the danger.

A couple walked past her on the street. Well-dressed, and well-to-do, but then despite the state of their surroundings, this was a more affluent area than any other in the city. The man tipped his hat as he walked by. Not recognising her of course, but he would soon. Everyone would know her.

The streets themselves seemed much different than the last time she had been here, but she was thinking much clearer now. A lack of red drop had given her a fresh perspective on things. A new focus. For the first time in so long her path was clear. Or at least she knew her route along it—there were still obstacles to move, but now she could recognise them, identify their weaknesses: They would not stay in her way for long.

The manse looked much the same as she reached the end of the avenue. Autumn leaves had fallen and turned to mulch, with no one bothering to sweep them up. If anything, the stark branches made the place more foreboding as she paused at the end of the path. The iron gate with its missing prongs was already open. One sharp push and they might fall off their hinges.

Two guards loitered with disinterest at the doorway. At least they recognised her as she approached, and made a cursory effort to look vigilant. Neither of them wore Hallowhill colours—most likely free-lance mercenaries hired with what little coin was left in her father's coffers.

"You're dismissed," she said as she stood at the foot of the stairs.

The men glanced at one another, considering whether it was best to stay, before one of them shrugged and they made their way from the grounds. The door wasn't locked and she strolled right in to the stink of mould.

For a moment she paused in the lobby, waiting for Gloster to come shuffling out to greet her, before remembering he had left long ago. Whoever his replacement was, he clearly wasn't here either. Most likely dismissed for some minor infringement like those before him.

Still, she could hear a lilting tune being played from a grammahorn somewhere in the building. The device was old, the tune scratchy, as though it only remembered a shade of the music it had recorded a century before.

She mounted the staircase, careful not to touch the filth-strewn banister. The music got louder as she approached the sitting room and the fire was blazing, her father's chair positioned closer to it to ward off the autumn cold.

He stared into the flames as she came to stand next to him.

Nothing was said. All the while her loathing simmered like a slowly brewing poison. She looked across the room, seeing once again the empty space where her mother's portrait had hung above the mantel. Her long-lost mother. For the first time in her life, Keara allowed herself to believe that the rumours might be true—that it really was her father who'd had Lucasta murdered. It might make what Keara had to do that little bit easier.

"Well?" he said finally in that phlegmy voice. "What do you have to say for yourself? Are the Guilds suitably curbed?"

There was no answer to give but the truth. "No. As far as I know, Rosomon Hawkspur still leads her forces in the north."

"As far as you know." The mockery in his tone would have stung her a few weeks ago, but the need to please this bag of bones was long gone. "If that's the case, what are you doing back here?"

"I just thought I would visit my loving father."

Now it was her turn to adopt a mocking tone, but if old Ingelram detected it, he showed no reaction. Instead he turned to her, mouth widening in a grin that revealed almost every one of his rotting teeth.

"Always as loving as I ever needed to be, daughter. Not that it was ever offered in return."

If Ingelram had ever shown any affection, Keara had not seen it. A sneering old bastard was what he was, and always had been.

"I guess we always knew what this was, Father. An arrangement. Clinical and hollow."

"Please. Spare me the overwrought theatrics. What do you want? For me to confess my regrets? Tears?"

"I want to know my loyalty to this Guild has been appreciated. I want respect."

A cackle from his wrinkled throat. "If you want appreciation, go perform tricks for street urchins. If you want my respect...show me results. But you never could. And you still can't." He waved her off with a withered hand. "Go. Leave me in peace. Scuttle off back to whatever hole you came from and carry on dosing yourself with the drop. You're good for that at least."

Keara felt a well forming in the pit of her stomach. A void into which she had to pour all her resentment. This had to be approached without emotion. This had to be cold as the tundra.

"Those days are gone, Father. From today I am making a change."

"Oh yes? What kind of a change? A more potent narcotic for you to pour into your body?"

She ignored the gibe. "I will take responsibility for my Guild. And I know exactly how."

The crack-toothed grin melted from his face. "*Your* Guild? Really? So do tell, how exactly will you do that? Have you found some secret way to oust that dog Sanctan and bring the other Guildmasters to heel?"

"I have made a start."

His rheumy eyes narrowed to slits, before he reclined back in his seat. Now she had his interest, perhaps for the first time in her life.

"Have you indeed?" he asked.

"Yes. I have taken Tyreta Hawkspur."

That opened his eyes in surprise, before they narrowed in pleasure. "And what do you intend to do with her?"

Should she even bother wasting her breath in telling him? After all, he was an irrelevance now. But no, she should humour him. At least take some pleasure from his reaction before she quashed him to nothing.

"I will use her to bargain with, of course. Lady Rosomon will give me anything I ask in return for the safe delivery of her one remaining child. And I will hand her over as a show of good faith for the truce I will manufacture. Then, when the Guilds are united once more, we will crush this religious coup and retake our rightful position."

She could see him growing less enthused as she spoke, until that sneer was back on his face.

"So you would crawl back into the grimy, filth-ridden bed of the Guilds? You would present yourself as their equal? We are their superiors! Once again, all you can demonstrate is a distinct lack of ambition."

"It would give us more stature than you have ever brought the Hallowhills," she bit back, before desperately trying to calm herself. She had to remember that pit inside her where she had gathered her hate.

In turn, her father looked as though he was about to boil over, lip trembling, hands clasped into ever-whitening fists.

"Don't presume to bark at me, girl. I am Ingelram Hallowhill. And I am still your Guildmaster."

Any other time his ire might have inspired fear in her. Now all she felt was contempt. This had gone far enough. It was now or never.

"I am playing a long game, Father. But you wouldn't appreciate that. Not a man who has decided to play no game at all, other than to sit and wallow, and send others off to do his bidding. Taking no risks. Seeing no reward."

"I warn you, Keara, I am still Guildmaster here."

"No. You're an old man, dead on the inside, who has achieved nothing in his long and miserable life."

"How dare you!" he screamed, squirming in that huge chair. "I will see you driven out. You will be dispossessed. A pariah among the webwainers. No one in the whole of Torwyn will take you in."

She reached down to her side, slowly drawing one of those antique knives. It held the yellow pyrestone, now back in its setting at the hilt. It truly was a beautiful thing. A thing to be treasured.

"You know nothing of webwainers. Nothing of their power, Father. So let me show you."

Before he could bark at her anymore, she plunged the knife through his wrist, skewering it to the arm of the chair he gripped on to so tightly. His shriek of pain and alarm sounded so delicious to her ears, but she could not savour it. Not yet.

"Your ambition always exceeded your ability," she said over the sound of his sobbing cries. "But you were never a webwainer." She stepped around the back of his chair, finger tracing the threadbare upholstery, as her father desperately tried to dislodge the blade from his arm. "Never felt the rapture of using our gift."

She grasped his free hand, slamming it down on the other armrest and unsheathing the second blade, the one with the blue pyrestone. As she plunged it through his left wrist he howled again, spittle running down his chin, tears pouring from his eyes.

"You were never a true Hallowhill like my mother. Never even deserving of the title."

"Are you mad?" he crowed. "You will never get away with this."

His pitiful plea turned to little more than a slobbering moan as he sat, trapped in his rotting throne.

"Oh, but I will, Father. I already have the loyalty of the webwainers. Do you think they care about what happens to one old man? An old man who never really knew them? I know them. And they are mine now. But I will have so much more, the day I am empress of Torwyn."

"You will burn for this," Ingelram screamed, calling on his reserves of strength to curse her one last time.

"You first," Keara whispered.

At her will, the blue pyrestone flared, electric current coursing through Ingelram's bony old body. His jaw clamped shut as he spasmed, rotten teeth spurting forth as they shattered in his mouth.

She ignited the yellow stone, and fire burst from the blade, setting light to Ingelram's sleeve, fast spreading to the chair, flames rising as though she'd doused him in pitch. He howled in pain and fear, a loathsome bellow rising to a screech as he was immolated and wreathed in lightning all at once. Keara squinted against the intense heat and light, but forced herself to watch as the ceiling above him blackened, the air filling with smoke and the stink of charred flesh. She stood for as long as she could before it became overwhelming, her nostrils and lungs filled with it, her mouth tasting that acridity, savouring it until she could take no more.

Ingelram had gone silent now, dead in that chair he loved so much. The fire was spreading to the curtains, the carpet already aflame.

In the distance the grammahorn still played as she walked from the room, its tune now slowed as though mourning her father with a dolorous lament. Smoke was billowing, the fire raging through that dried husk of a building. By the time she stepped out into the fresh night air, she could just see flames starting to lick through the broken tiles of the rooftop.

Strange how she felt nothing much of anything as she watched her childhood home burn. It seemed without the red drop to stimulate her senses, she was left with no sensation at all.

"Fire," someone yelled.

Keara looked along the road to see that couple who had passed her earlier. The man with the hat stopped at the end of the path.

"I should get someone to help," he yelled in a panic. "We should try and save something."

She walked past him as he gawped up at the inferno now running rampant throughout the manse.

"Let it burn," she said. "All of it."

CONALL

Not a single star to show him the way as he stumbled along, probably in circles, probably the wrong direction entirely. Best not worry on that, best just carry on, try to ignore the cold, the danger, keep one foot moving after the other.

Something rustled in the dark. He turned his head, glaring through the black, but couldn't see a damn thing. No baleful eyes staring, no bared teeth. Still his heart was pounding against his chest, reminding him he should never have thrown that sword away, his one salvation out here in the most dangerous place in all Hyreme.

Fuck it. Just keep going. Balking at shadows wouldn't get him anywhere.

The ground rose steeply, until he had to crawl up a ridge on hands and knees. Sharp and rusted metal dug into his palms, the decay of this place still prevalent after a thousand years. When finally he reached the top, he stopped, not quite able to believe what he could see through his one remaining eye.

A fortress was framed against the dark horizon. Torches flickering atop those ominous battlements. Had he made it? For the first time in so long, Conall allowed himself to hope he might actually live through this.

He scrambled over the ridge, almost falling flat on his face, gritting his teeth, pushing himself on. A moan issued from his throat, one he couldn't quell, all his supressed emotions rising to the fore now he saw salvation ahead. As he rushed through the darkness, his foot caught on something that sent him sprawling. He landed hard, hitting his head, but he ignored the pain as he dragged himself to his feet, focusing on the looming edifice ahead.

The ground sloped up to a huge portcullis, brightly lit so the guards atop its battlement could see anyone approaching from the Drift. It was with some relief he heard a bell ring and a voice call out as he staggered closer.

"Someone's coming!"

Conall fell to his knees, crawling the last few feet to the gate, gripping the iron of the portcullis as though it were flotsam, and he back at sea, left to the vagaries of the waves.

"Help me," he tried to cry. It was little more than a mumble from his cracked lips.

There was a clack of chains in the windlass as the iron gate rose. He fell back as half a dozen armoured figures surrounded him— Armiger troopers with their splintbows levelled.

"Looks like a drifter," one of them said. "Must be desperate to have ranged so close to the fort."

"Well, he can't stay here," said another. "Do we put him out of his misery? Make it quick like?"

"Hang on," said a third. "That's . . . No, it can't be."

"What?"

"That's . . . Conall bastard Hawkspur."

Conall could barely see in the light of those torches, and he raised a hand to shield his eye. "Please. He's right. I am him. I am Conall bastard Hawkspur."

Two of them took him under the arms. Now that he'd been rescued, all his energy fled. They carried him inside, the gate closing with a resounding clang behind. In the courtyard were yet more figures viewing him with concern, and one of them shouted to bring water, as someone else knelt down by his side.

"What the fuck have they done to you?"

That was pretty obvious, all things considered.

"Easy boy," said a deep voice, as a man bigger than the rest pushed through the gathered crowd. He reached for Conall's face, lifting that bandage with unexpected gentleness to view the ruin of his eye. "This needs treating. Right now. Get the surgeon."

Conall had made it. Untold days in the Drift and he was finally safe. He should have whooped for joy, punched the air, cursed his hunters for the fools they were. All he could do was shake uncontrollably and fight the urge to weep.

His teeth chattered as one of the troopers lifted a canteen to his dry lips. He sipped at first, feeling the cool water relieve his throat before he snatched it from the man's hands, chugging it like the last tankard of ale he'd ever drink.

"We have to send word to Lady Rosomon," someone said.

"All in good time," said that deep voice. "Right now we have to make sure he lives. Better we deliver good news regarding her son than the worst."

They picked him up again, wrapping a blanket around his shoulders as they carried him across the courtyard. A quick glance around the fort and he could see it was manned by a skeleton crew of around twenty. Hardly the triumphant return he'd envisioned, but twenty would just have to do.

Once inside he was led to a table, one of many lining a huge hall. Bread and cured meat were placed in front of him along with a jug of more sweet-tasting water. The surgeon bustled into the hall, laying a satchel down on the table before regarding his eye with concern. From the pained expression on his face, it was in a bad way.

"Where is everyone?" asked Conall.

The healer rustled in his bag of tricks, looking for bandages and liniment. "Most of the Mantid Battalion have headed north to join your mother's forces."

"They're still fighting? Who else has joined them?"

"Some of the battalions," said the surgeon, wiping away the dried blood on Conall's face. "Bloodwolf, Viper, Kraken. Most of the Ironfall Guild were slaughtered in a massacre and the Forge has fallen. The Rock along with it."

It appeared things hadn't just got worse for him once he'd left Agavere. "What news of my mother?"

The surgeon sighed, as though reluctant to convey bad news. "After the destruction of Wyke she made her way to Oakhelm. It was besieged by the Archlegate's forces but they were repelled. Last thing we heard she still holds the city."

"I have to get to her," he said, trying to stand on legs reluctant to obey. "I have to tell her—"

A firm hand pushed him back to his seat. "You need to rest, boy."

Conall looked up to see the owner of that deep voice, the one who had commanded the men outside. It was a stern visage, just like Beringer's, but there was some sympathy in his grey eyes. He sat his broad frame down opposite Conall, running a meaty hand through his red beard.

"If you insist," Conall replied. For all his talk of reaching his mother, he doubted he could have reached the other side of the room.

"I do, lad. My name is Draga—captain of Fort Karvan in the Drift marshal's absence. You're safe here. Try and relax, and let the surgeon take care of you. Rest the night. Then we'll talk about what to do next."

Conall was happy to do as he was bid, as the surgeon dressed his wound after lathering it with a tincture that stank of poppy essence and something much fouler. He was given a drink that tasted bitter and made his head spin, before Draga and his men helped him to an empty chamber. The bed was basic, but it felt more comfortable than anything he'd ever laid in.

As he rested his head on the pillow he began to feel more faint.

"In a couple of days," said Draga, "I'll have a unit take you north to join up with your mother. In the meantime, get some sleep, Hawkspur. You look like you need it."

Conall barely had a chance to thank him, to ponder how much his fortunes had changed, to think on the battles ahead, before he drifted off...

He strode the coastline as it stretched away beneath a red sky. From the headland he could see miles to the north, the furious waves crashing against the cliffs, vast rocks collapsing into the ocean to be consumed by the inky waters.

The armour that encased him was like a black iron skin, the blade in his hand humming in anticipation, desperate to sing. Behind him waited his army, their fury barely contained, ready to be unleashed in a frenzy.

Turning, he saw that there was not a valiant warrior among them, for the host he had brought was far from human—each one a demon of blackened sinew and cloven hoof. Teeth bared, staring with fury through a shining red eye.

He raised his blade, and on that signal his horde bellowed its glee to the crimson sky. It filled the air with more than noise, casting a hate-filled cloud upon the land, thrilling him to his core, raising a rictus grin within his helm.

The enemy was already rushing from the north, the sound of their approach thunderous, shaking the earth like a tempest raging along the coastline. This too was no army of mortals. It was fell beasts that galloped toward them. A menagerie of claws and hooves and gnashing teeth. Eyes keen for the hunt.

He charged, eating up the ebon ground, racing to meet them with an army of demons at his heels, a snarl of unfettered malice on his slavering lips.

The sword in his hand cut a bloody swathe. A bestial head sent flying, a clawed limb lopped from its torso. Every swing hacked divots in flesh, and in an instant his dark armour was bathed in gore as the bodies began to pile. In turn his army unleashed talon and fang, devouring the animals that had dared to face them.

A rumble of thunderous hooves and he looked across from the coast. To the west galloped flaming steeds, their hooves cracking the earth. Atop each one rode a knight clad in silver, shield and lance shining despite the sun being hidden behind a curtain of ash.

He cut his way through the slaughter, hacking down both friend and foe if they blocked his route to these interlopers. When the first of those fiery destriers came into range, he leapt, striking down the horse and sending its rider tumbling to the earth. The knight was on his feet in an instant, armour almost blinding in its radiance. Their blades clashed, ringing a gong across the battle. With a cry of hate he hacked down, the knight raising his shield only for it to shatter under the weight of the blow. His second strike skewered that lustrous breastplate, spattering the mirror sheen with red.

A howl issued from within his helm as the sword in his hand began to consume the knight's soul, feeding him with forbidden succour. As it did so, that silver armour warped and bent, crushing the wearer within, blood spewing from every vent and breach as he screamed his final terror to the sky.

There was little time to gloat as a roar pierced the air. The sounds of violence ebbing, lulled to silence by that cry. He looked up to see a beast on wings of steel, its eyes two molten orbs, probing the battlefield for a worthy foe.

A wyrm of the most diabolical origin.

The one beast he had come to face.

It opened its great maw, spewing fire across the ranks of his demon host, immolating them in righteous flame. It was all he could do to dive aside and avoid the conflagration, feeling it sear his armour, the dark iron glowing white.

When he rose to his feet, his cloak was aflame, and he tore it from his back, casting it aside before facing that ancient wyrm. The ground rumbled as its four great limbs touched down to the earth, and a cloud of dust billowed with a beat of those great wings.

It roared again, spittle flying forth to hiss on the ground at his feet. In his hand the sword mewled its desire, yearning to cut that steel hide asunder. Oh, how he would give the blade its due.

He charged, gripping the sword in both hands, raising it high, but before he could reach his foe, more beasts cast their shadows across the battlefield.

The wyrms had come in force—the red, black, green and blue.

There was no way he could vanquish them all. No way he could survive the day against these fell beasts. But he cared little for survival. Pain was all that mattered. Violence and death were both master and mistress to him now.

As the steel wyrm opened its maw to greet him, he charged relentlessly onward . . .

The air smelled sweet as he awoke. A candle near the window had burned down to a stump, and he felt the chill keenly. It was hard to breathe as he shivered in the dark, pulling the blanket about him to ward off the cold and the memory of that nightmare. But it was already fading fast, and with all he had endured Conall knew bad dreams were the least that could hurt him.

His eye stung, the tincture and balm administered to it now wearing off. Still he resisted the urge to raise a hand to his face lest he upset the binding over his eye. Let it ache. He could only hope it meant that in time it would heal. Not that he'd ever see from it again, but better blindness than to be cursed with that red jewel.

Conall swung his legs over the edge of the bed, feeling the cold tiles beneath his feet. There was a plain tunic hanging over a chair nearby, and he stood on shaky legs before donning it. A glass pitcher and a cup had been left on a table, and he eagerly tried to cure his relentless thirst. Three cups and the jug was empty, leaving him gasping, but it was still not enough.

It was only then he noticed the door to his chamber lay open. Was it so the surgeon could check on him? Seemed considerate enough, but even with the door open he couldn't hear any sounds from within the garrison.

He moved to the doorway. Out in the corridor there was still no noise—no one wandering the fort, no banal conversation from the troopers. The hour was late, but even in the disciplined confines of Fort Tarkis there had been some life after dark. Here at Karvan it seemed there was nothing.

A sense of unease began to niggle at him. As he made his way along the torchlit corridor he could not shake the feeling that something was wrong. It was as though the entire fort had been abandoned, its skeleton crew having fled and left him to wander the place alone.

The corridor led to an arch, beyond which lay the courtyard. Still no life. When he stepped out into the predawn light, there were no sentries wandering the battlement, no one watching for any more vagabonds to come wandering in off the Drift. Two more steps out into the open, and his foot set down in something warm.

Even in the scant torchlight he could tell it was blood. A trail led to a dark corner of the yard, and he didn't have to peer too hard before he recognised a corpse lying there in the shadows.

Conall turned in panic, glaring toward the portcullis. It was still lowered—no marauding horde had breached the fort's defences, but there was no doubt they were under attack.

He raced toward the alarm bell that hung at the opposite corner of the yard, seeing yet another corpse lying a few feet away, glassy eyes staring at the dark sky. Before he could reach it, a lithe figure stepped into his path.

Nylia glared at him, red jewel of an eye glowing in the black, blood caked to her face where he had struck her with his cursed blade. Even in the dark he could see her body was in poor condition, flesh torn and limbs withered from her relentless pursuit of him across the waste. Despite all that, she still looked ready to kill.

In her hand was her demon sword, its white stone glowing with nauseating light.

"I warned you, Conall. It is impossible to run from this. There is nowhere you can go that I will not follow."

Those were familiar words to him now, but this time they were different. He could sense Nylia was no longer trying to break free of the demon within. All trace of her humanity was lost. Conall knew beyond doubt that this time she would slay him if he refused to go with her.

He felt like pleading. In his weakened state there was no way he could fight. Even if he had a weapon to hand, she could have cut him down without a thought. But still...

"I will not go with you. You're going to have to kill me."

"That is a shame." She raised the sword, gripping it tight in both hands. "But if that is what you ask..."

She swung the blade, but her strike was sluggish, and he managed to duck back out of range. Despite the demon's hold on her, she had been weakened by her journey across the Drift. Nevertheless, he doubted he'd get far if he turned and ran. Was there even anywhere to run to? Anyone left who could help him? Maybe he should just give in—let her cut him down and end all this.

I can still help you.

The voice was clear and crisp in his ear, as though someone were standing right next to him. Conall felt dread at that familiar tone. He had thought himself free of it when he flung away his sword, but it was clear this curse went deeper than a mere weapon.

"No," he snarled, dodging away from another swing of Nylia's blade.

Just reach out for me, Conall. I await you in the shadow.

He stumbled back as Nylia advanced, feeling the solid bulk of the yard wall at his back. Nowhere left to run.

Reach for me.

Conall knew this was it. Nylia would not stop, and he would die here if he didn't reach out for help.

He stretched out his right arm, grasping in the dark, his desperation winning out at the prospect of Nylia's killing strike. His fist closed around a solid hilt, comfortable in his grip, as though it had been crafted for his hand alone.

She raised that blade, swinging it down at his head, as he brought his arm up. Their demon swords clashed, ringing out through the courtyard. For a moment, he saw the uncertainty in her human eye, the red one dulling slightly as though reflecting her reluctance to obey.

"You don't have to die," he said desperately. "I can help you."

She glared in fury, before the light in the red pyrestone died. Nylia backed away, shaking her head, an all-too-human gesture of helplessness.

"Strike, Conall," she whispered. "Swiftly."

His blade moved with such speed it caught him off guard. Before he could try to stop it, he had run her through. Conall let out a bark of anguish as he wrenched his sword free, seeing the white jewel at the cross-guard pulsate, bloating with light.

As Nylia collapsed, he cast that cursed weapon aside, barely noticing it disappear into the shadows once more. Conall dropped to his knees beside her, cradling her head, helpless but to watch as blood ran from the side of her mouth.

"I'm sorry," he said.

She reached up, as though she might touch his face, but her strength left her. Conall caught her hand as it fell, the light extinguishing in the red jewel of her right eye.

At the edge of the yard someone yelled in alarm. In an instant the bell rang, filling the fort with its clangour, drawing more bodies to the scene of wanton murder.

Don't be sorry, boy. We have only just begun.

As the Mantid troopers came running to the alarm, and the one friend he had left in the Drift died, Conall knew the curse he had struggled against still remained. His right hand, now anointed in blood, could summon that sword back at any moment.

He was safely home in Torwyn...but he was still damned.

ROSOMON

Oakhelm looked more like a fort on the Karna Frontier than a city in the midst of a forest. Oleksig and Maugar had pooled their talents and their workforce, their miners and Blackshields, to build the city anew. Its wooden boundary was now reinforced with steel taken from the landship line. Stone blocks had been dug up from around the city, and barricaded the roads that led to every gate. Trees had been felled, stripped, and crafted into great bastions from which archers could shoot and artillery be launched. It might not be enough to hold back the tide of Sanctan's followers, but it was all they had.

Oakhelm would be their last line of defence. A sanctuary to which they would retreat if the attack on the Anvil failed. An attack which Rosomon would have to lead with this ragtag army. But their last battle had ended in victory, and she could have asked no more of them.

They were already mustered in the morning sun. It was a bright day, a good day to start a crusade, but as she walked past the gathered ranks toward the eastern gate, Rosomon felt anything but the noble general.

The statue that had stood in Oakhelm's square was gone now, hacked up and used to bolster the walls. She could only wonder what would replace it in the weeks ahead. Would it be a symbol of the Guilds—a reminder of all they had achieved—or would their enemies eventually erect the likeness of a Great Wyrm?

"We are ready," said Oleksig, striking a match and lighting his pipe. It sent wisps of smoke into the morning air, which blew away on the breeze.

"More than ready," Maugar grunted, taking a step forward, determined not to be outdone by the Guildmaster of Marrlock.

Rosomon wasn't sure they looked ready. Her army was made up of men and women who had toiled as miners all their lives, or worked the fields and manufactories of the Hawkspur Guildlands. Their numbers were strengthened by a few Blackshields, stout and brave as they were, alongside troopers of the Bloodwolf and Mantid, but there were less of them than she'd have liked.

"Have we received any word from other battalions?" she asked.

Ianto shook his head. "Perhaps we will receive word soon, my lady. The road to the Anvil is a long one. There is still time."

She regarded the ranks of her followers again. Few warriors among them. Not much of an army to take on the might of the Ministry, but she had already beaten them once. To take on the Anvil though...

Rosomon dismissed the thought as she strode east, ignoring the horse that had been saddled for her. She would not ride imperiously like the general they proclaimed her to be. She would walk among them as an equal—at least for today.

The gate lay open, and when she reached her Titanguard standing at the edge of the newly reinforced wall, her new flag was unfurled. Someone had taken a great amount of care to weave it—the winged-talon symbol over the cog. A symbol of resistance. Of hope? How long it would last before it was burned to ash, she could not say. Her intention was for it to fly over the highest steeple of Archwind Palace, and she had to keep that goal in mind. Had to disregard the prospect of any other outcome.

Beyond the gate stood Kassian. Behind him were Thalleus, Xorya, Borys, swordwrights all. *Her* swordwrights, each one worth ten battalion troopers. Perhaps a hundred? Unlikely, but they were all paragons of the blade, and she was grateful for their loyalty. Still, the one swordwright she needed the most was not among them. But he would be avenged, as would so many others.

Her hand drifted to the blade she now wore at her side. She had only swung it once, but it was not her skill with it that mattered. It was what the weapon symbolised. As her finger teased the Hawk-spur symbol on the pommel she felt a strange kind of comfort from it. It was the weapon her lover had wielded at the end, and now it would act as her talisman. She could only hope it would bring her more fortune than it had Lancelin.

As those warriors watched her approach, Rosomon couldn't help but think they regarded her with a different aspect. Was it wariness? Respect? Her actions in the aftermath of the battle had most likely surprised them, not that anyone had questioned it. Per-haps her ruthlessness had inspired them, shown them a side to her they never knew existed. It was, after all, a side Rosomon had not known was there, hiding in the shadows, waiting for something to draw it out.

They bowed their respect as she walked past them, well drilled, disciplined. It reminded her of what was expected of her. Reminded her that they could not tarry, not for anything. Not even for Tyreta.

Rosomon tried not to think on that. On the fact she had sent her daughter into danger on a flight of whimsy. She had to focus on tak-ing the initiative in this war. So far she had reacted. Now she would provoke her enemy, draw him out. There would be no more run-ning, no more hiding.

Rawlin stood at the vanguard of their column, his dark armoured troopers waiting to march, lining the road with their wolf stan-dards flying. At the opposite side were the few Mantid Battalion troopers who had chosen to join them.

More pennants flew than she could count—the crossed hammers, the forge flame, the myriad pennants of the mining leagues. It was a proud day for them all. And she could barely shake the feeling she was leading them to their doom.

The road ahead looked long, the landship rail snaking away through the forest, but there was no turning back now. As though to labour the notion, Oleksig took the pipe from his mouth before shouting, "Mining leagues. Prepare to march."

Maugar looked a little disgruntled at Oleksig's presumptuous order, turning to his Blackshields and opening his mouth to bark orders. Before he could, a trumpet blared, followed by the banging of a drum as a hundred musicians of the Marrlock Guild struck up their instruments.

It was a rousing tune. Rosomon almost forgot her trepidation as the music resounded through the forest, but in the distance she could hear another noise that suddenly put her ill at ease. The tracks began to vibrate beneath her feet, and to the west she saw an ominous trail of smoke that heralded an engine approaching through the forest.

The noise grew louder as the sound of the band receded. They could all hear it now, rumbling along, but it was no landship that appeared. Instead it was a strange pyrestone-fuelled contraption, a single seat raised on an iron palanquin, with metal steps at the front so the lone pilot could reach it. On that seat sat a woman, reclining languidly as her engine drew ever closer. When she was within a few yards, the engine slowed, finally coming to a stop.

The army watched as the woman uncrossed her legs and slowly stood. She wore a fur cloak, dark glasses covering her eyes. Everyone was silent as she descended, the heels of her boots clanging with each step until she reached the ground. It was only then Rosomon recognised the purple uniform of the Hallowhill Guild beneath the pelt about her shoulders.

Splintbows were levelled, swords drawn and shields braced as she approached. Rosomon moved to meet her, showing no fear, not while her army was watching. She hadn't taken two steps before Kassian moved up beside her. Rosomon gently raised a hand to keep him in his place, before advancing to within a few feet of the webwainer.

"Lady Rosomon Hawkspur," the woman said, before offering a theatrical bow.

"And you are?"

The webwainer placed a hand to her chest as though she was

flattered at being asked. "Me? That's not important. It's who I represent that matters. And so we're clear, if any harm comes to me, your daughter will not see another dawn."

Rosomon felt the chill of the morning more keenly. Her hand gripped the sword at her side all the tighter, but she knew it was pointless drawing it. Even were she appropriately trained in its use, killing this woman would be a mistake.

"Where is she?"

"Oh, she's quite safe. At the pleasure of the Hallowhill Guild."

"Why should I believe you?"

The webwainer raised a finger, as though struck by an ingenious idea. Then she swept the animal pelt from her shoulders before laying it at Rosomon's feet. It took her a moment before she recognised the pattern on the hide, the subtle spots against the dark fur. Those rending claws were still attached to the limbs, though the head was missing. Tyreta's panther.

She suddenly felt sick, but not at what had been done to this noble beast.

"You have my attention."

The webwainer grinned, all white teeth and black lenses. "Good. Tyreta is at the Web. Guildmaster Keara Hallowhill is keeping her entertained."

"Keara? What has happened to Ingelram?"

The webwainer's grin faded, her bottom lip jutting in feigned remorse. "Alas, he is no longer with us."

"And I assume his daughter demands my immediate surrender?"

It was the only demand that made sense, and one Rosomon had no idea how to answer, but the webwainer shook her head as though it were a preposterous idea.

"Oh, on the contrary. She wishes you every success in the battles to come, and hopes to arrange a meeting. But she is not a patient woman. You are expected at the Web within five days. Or Tyreta might meet with an unfortunate...well..."

She gestured down at the pelt still lying on the ground. Rosomon didn't have to look down at it to understand the insinuation. Could she say yes, though? She had an army to lead. Changing her plans to accommodate the demands of one person, even if it was her daughter's gaoler, would show no kind of leadership at all.

"Tell Keara Hallowhill I will consider her invitation."

The webwainer leaned closer. "I'd consider it fast, if I were you."

With another exaggerated bow, she backed away, before climbing the stairs to the pyrestone engine as dramatically as she had stepped down from it. It whined for a moment before chugging away slowly on those rails as she reclined in her seat and wiggled her fingers in a mocking wave goodbye.

"I know I don't need to tell you, but this has trap written all over it," said Kassian as he watched the engine disappear through the trees.

Rosomon knelt, picking up the pelt and holding it close to her chest. She'd hated the animal, feared it, but now its hide was the only thing she had of her daughter.

"Yes," she replied. "But we've faced traps before, and we're still here to tell the tale."

Ianto moved closer. "Perhaps we should send the Titanguard to the Web, my lady. My men will not stop until Tyreta is safe."

That might just work. It might not. But the last time Tyreta had been in danger, missing and alone in the jungles of the Sundered Isles, Rosomon had put her trust in others to save her. Not this time.

Oleksig stomped toward her along the road. "The army awaits your order."

She looked back over her shoulder. All those people, those warriors, waiting on her decision. Relying on their leader. And yet she could not lead them now. Not when her daughter needed her.

"Oleksig, you will take them west."

"I will?" he replied, raising a bushy grey eyebrow. "What about you?"

"I will catch you up. Don't worry. You won't reach the Anvil without me."

Kassian reached out to touch her arm, then thought better of it. "This is unwise."

"Probably."

"The Hallowhills are looking to snare you."

"Most certainly."

"But you're going anyway?"

She looked to the south, across the sea of green toward the city of the webwainers. "Definitely. And there is nothing that will stop me."

EPILOGUE

Obsidian columns surrounded the huge bath. They were flecked with gold, illuminated by the scant torchlight and glittering through the steamy haze. The heat of the room enveloped him like a cloak, gently lulling Bakhan as he stood waist-deep in the pool. It was warm against his naked flesh, stark in contrast to the frigid aloofness given off by his bathing companion. Not that Bakhan would ever complain to her—that would be more than his life was worth.

He had worked in the bathhouse of Mistress Takesh for over a year. It was a Jubaran institution, established for the most privileged of clientele, but Bakhan had managed to work his way up and become an attendant in these private chambers within a few brief months. Only honoured patrons were allowed access to the upper vaults, and the woman he stood behind was among the most honoured of them all.

Wenis was rumoured to have the ear of Queen Meresankh herself. A rare position indeed, but she looked like she had suffered much to attain it. The recently healed scars stood out livid and white on her shoulders: three long stripes on each. Whatever had made them must have been a fearsome beast.

Bakhan rubbed oil into his hands before massaging it into the flesh of her back. She sighed as he teased the knots from her muscles, and he could feel how lithe and frail she was. Not for the first time he wondered how a woman so feeble could have survived wounds so grievous. There was hardly anything of her, just flesh pulled tight over her bones, every vertebra of her spine visible, from the base of her neck to the lean cheeks of her rump. It would have been so easy for him to close his hands around that slender throat and squeeze the life from her, but not before she imbued the power of the necroglyphs on her arms and killed him first.

It was a fleeting thought, but one he'd had many times. Servicing Wenis was a chore he had suffered for too long, but he knew the rewards would be great were he to endure it just a little longer. A dangerous game to play, toying with arcanists, but as a loyal servant of House Duridor, play it he would.

Master Abana had put him to this task personally, and Bakhan was not of a mind to disappoint. He had been sent here to service those of high status within Jubaran society, and put them at their ease. To listen to their woes and learn what secrets he could, before whispering them to his master in Iskinda. Not even Ak-Samtek's inquisitors knew this place was owned by House Duridor, or that his master gathered much information from its powerful patrons. Surely if they did, this place would have been burned to the ground long before now.

Wenis gave out a moan at his firm yet gentle ministrations, and he felt her body begin to relax.

"Is that pleasant, mistress?" Bakhan asked.

"I would order you to stop if it were not."

Of course she would. He took the opportunity to massage more firmly, teasing out the knots in her back, his fingers caressing her blemished flesh as he did so.

"You never told me where you got such scars, mistress."

She tensed slightly—a nerve touched perhaps? "That's because I have no desire for you to know."

Bakhan bit his tongue. Not for the first time he had pressed too far in his pursuit of information. "Apologies, mistress. I should keep my mouth—"

"Don't apologise, Bakhan, and certainly not for your mouth. On occasion it is useful. Just not when you use it to talk."

He quelled his disdain as quickly as it came. Bakhan was willing to tolerate humiliation for his House, and there were some perks to his position after all. When she was not deriding him, Wenis could be most relentless in her lovemaking. Afterward though she would be silent, distant, as though thinking on a past lover she far preferred to him.

Before he could move his hands to a more sensitive area, something shifted at the other side of the steam-filled room. Bakhan squinted through the haze, seeing a figure in the shadows. But the door to the chamber had not opened—had they been there all the time?

Wenis had seen them too, and slowly she moved toward the side of the huge bath. The waters began to glow as she called on the power of her necroglyphs.

Would there be violence? Sorcery? Bakhan did not relish the prospect of either.

"You there," he called out, eager to avoid a confrontation if he could. "This is a private chamber, reserved for Mistress Takesh's most esteemed guests. You are not welcome here."

The figure stepped out of the shadows. In the torchlight Bakhan saw a face of exquisite beauty, dark eyes, raven hair, a crimson robe covering her slender figure. Had he not been struck dumb by awe, he might have gasped at the sight of her. But then the sight of Amosis Makareth could provoke no other emotion than awe.

"Am I not esteemed enough to join you?" she asked, her voice breathy as though whispering in a lover's ear...just before she slit their throat.

The necroglyphs on Wenis's flesh began to dull, that green light beneath the surface of the water dimming to nothing. Without waiting to be invited, Amosis untied the belt of her silken robe and let it slip from her shoulders. Bakhan could only watch, trying his best not to tremble, as she stepped naked into the huge bath.

What should he do? Offer his service to her? Run as fast and far as he could before she turned her attention to him? Instead he did nothing, as Amosis submerged herself in the water up to her shoulders. She smiled with the pleasure of it before reclining her head on the edge of the pool.

"Get out, boy," she said.

Bakhan didn't need asking twice. Neither did he give Wenis a second glance as he waded to the side of the bath and made his way up the steps. He grasped a towel, wrapping it about his waist to hide his modesty, before heading for the welcome concealment of the shadows.

It would have been wise to leave, but he found himself pausing at the door. From his vantage point in the shadow of the pillars, and hidden by the heavy mist, neither woman could see him. What they were about to say might be of great import. Perhaps even something of value to his master, Abana.

He turned the door handle, opened it, and slammed it shut as though he had fled the chamber. Then he turned, pressing himself against one of the obsidian pillars as he squinted through the steam toward the women.

Amosis reclined against the side of the bath, stretching out her arms, enjoying the moment. Wenis just watched her, the tense atmosphere deepening. As the silence stretched on, Bakhan held his breath, watching like a robber in the dark.

"I hope you're feeling better," Amosis said eventually. "Recovered after your terrible ordeal."

Wenis narrowed her eyes. "I doubt you have disturbed my privacy to enquire after my welfare."

That brought a wry smile to Amosis's face. "No, I have not. I am here to talk about something of grave importance. To enlighten you, Wenis."

"What is so important that the Bearer of the Silent Key would come and see me personally? Why do I deserve such an honour?"

"Because events are moving faster by the day. And time is running short. For all of us."

Wenis let out a sigh, and leaned against the side of the bath. "If you are going to talk in riddles all evening, I might have to get someone to bring more hot water."

Amosis giggled, a tinkling laugh that filled the chamber, her face widening in a grin that did not reach her eyes. "War is coming from the south. The Scions are preparing for an invasion. The armies of Iperion Magna will soon swarm across Nyrakkis and consume everything in their path. Then, once they have turned our lands to dust, they will set their eye to the rest of Hyreme."

Bakhan let out the breath he had been holding, his hand trembling as he pressed it to the dark pillar. He could hardly believe what was being said, and from the confused look on Wenis's face, she shared his scepticism.

"Invasion? But I have heard nothing of this."

"Few have," Amosis replied. "And that is the way our queen wants it to stay. For now."

"But the Scions have been at each other's throats for centuries. Their hatred of one another has kept us safe since the Sundering."

"And now they are united, with but a single purpose. Meresankh has known of their alliance for some time now. Why do you think she sent Assenah across the Drift to treat with the eastlanders?"

"Not for trade then?" said Wenis.

"That was the initial plan. But it was meant to be the start of a very different relationship. Once trade links were secured, we could have formed a military union and faced the threat from the Magna together. But when Assenah was murdered by the dragon priest, those plans were trodden to shit."

"I did not know any of this," Wenis replied. "Nor did I know it was not Fulren who murdered her."

"Of course you didn't." Amosis seemed to relish the fact. "You were not yet an arcanist of any note. You were not yet brought into the fold, but now you have risen to a position of importance. It is time you learned the truth."

Bakhan's knees were trembling as he listened. He had heard of the foreign prince, of his imprisonment, of his trial in the arena. He did not know of the conspiracy surrounding his exile. Nor could he have dreamed that the Scions would unite and plan to conquer the whole of Hyreme. His master at House Duridor would surely lavish him with riches were he to pass on such secrets. He would be lauded, perhaps even gifted with his freedom and a slave boy of his own.

"Such a shame about the Hawkspur boy," Amosis continued.

"The queen was hoping he could be of some use. Might have acted as a bridge between Nyrakkis and Torwyn. But you managed to lose him, just as you lost Assenah."

Wenis glared, her brow creasing in annoyance. "If she thought he would be of use, then why did she condemn him to the trial?"

Amosis splayed her fingers, showing the array of rings that adorned them. "She thought him guilty, of course. And there was pressure from her council. To see justice done, he had to face the Trial of Ghobeq, but she did everything she could to ensure he was successful. Why else would she have allowed you to help him? To grant him the gift of the necroglyph? To craft the magnificent weapon with which he defeated the God of the Rivers? Justice was seen to be done, and that is all that matters."

Wenis looked crestfallen at the news. Bakhan could only feel pity for the Hawkspur—he had been caught up in a game beyond his understanding. Used like a pawn. But then in Nyrakkis you were the puppet or the puppet master—there was no in between.

Amosis moved from the edge of the bath, closer to Wenis. "Poor girl. Do you miss your little prince? You wear such a sad face just at the merest mention of him."

Wenis raised her gaze, fire in those eyes of hers. "Do not mock me, Amosis. I am not part of your cabal, to be toyed with like a fly in your web."

Amosis found her show of steel amusing as she ran a hand though her damp hair. "Cheer up, Wenis, you are to be honoured. Queen Meresankh has a particular task for you. One that will allow you to atone for your past failures."

Wenis narrowed her eyes, her interest piqued. "Go on."

"She would have you return to the land of Torwyn. Find the Mistress of Hawkspur and offer her an alliance. Nyrakkis will assist in her fight against the dragon priest. In return, she will join us in the wars to come. Bring her armies and machines across the Drift so that we might face the Scions together."

Wenis regarded her with a look of disbelief before she barked a humourless laugh across the bath. "Are you insane? We took her precious son away. Threw him into our arena and blinded him. She would never agree to any such proposal. And especially not delivered by the very woman who took him in the first place."

All the mirth had gone from Amosis now, and she leaned closer. "Then you will have a difficult task persuading her."

"More likely she will have me killed on sight."

Amosis dismissed her fears with a curt shake of the head. "I think you are underestimating your powers of persuasion, Wenis."

"Am I? Not even all the dark powers of Malador could sway the vengeful heart of a mother who has lost her son."

Again, Amosis focused her dark eyes on Wenis. "You talk as though you have a choice. Queen Meresankh has made her decision. This is not a request, it is a command."

The grim reminder failed to quell the defiance in Wenis, and she faced Amosis with as much steel as was offered. "You are talking to someone who has travelled across the Drift, who has seen the Hawkspur woman, the love she bore her child. I know she would never—"

"Perhaps you can explain your fears to the queen. I am sure she will take them into account."

That final statement was enough to silence Wenis. She shrank deeper into the water, as though she wanted it to consume her. As though drowning in that pool were a preferable fate over the one that awaited her across the Drift.

Bakhan had heard enough. He knew he should leave, but there was no way of exiting the bath chamber without being discovered. Instead he stepped a little farther into the shadows, hoping to bide his time and escape when the women had finished their conversation.

"Do not feel bad," Amosis continued. "Queen Meresankh would not have selected you for this task if she did not think you had some chance of success."

"Will I at least have someone to accompany me? Warriors of the Medjai or the Caste?"

Amosis raised her arms in a nonchalant shrug. "You may take whomever you wish. Just be careful which of them you take into your confidence."

Wenis's brow furrowed in confusion. "Why?"

The smile returned to Amosis's face as she turned toward where Bakhan was concealed in the shadow. "Come out, boy."

He felt the cold grip of terror. Despite the urge to dash for the door, he could not run. Even if he escaped the chamber, there would be no place he could flee where the Bearer of the Silent Key would not find him.

As he stepped out from behind the obsidian pillar, he saw Wenis glare accusingly. Bakhan would have apologised, would have begged, but knew it would do him no good now.

"Join us," Amosis said.

Bakhan let the towel drop from his waist before stepping down the steps into the bath. As he waded into the pool, he wondered if Amosis would demand he service them both, before he immediately dismissed the thought. Besides, there was no way he would be anything but a flaccid disappointment, such was his dread.

"Is this your latest plaything, Wenis?" Amosis teased with a grin. "You can't miss the Prince of Torwyn that much if you have found his replacement so quickly. Or perhaps he is just to help you overcome your loss."

"Who are you?" Wenis asked him, ignoring the comment. "Who is your master, that you would risk so much to spy on us?"

Bakhan could not speak, so stricken was he with fear, but Amosis was happy to do it for him. "He is in thrall to the House of Duridor. That maggot Abana has a swarm of flies buzzing their way all across the great cities of Nyrakkis. Listening. Whispering. This one was on your shoulder all along, and you didn't even notice. You know, you really should be more vigilant in future. Especially if you are to survive in Torwyn."

"I should kill you," Wenis hissed, as she glared right at him.

Bakhan might have pleaded for his life, told them both that he was happy to betray his master in return for mercy, but before he had the chance Amosis brushed his neck with a ringed finger.

He lifted a hand, touching it to the flesh of his throat. Looking down, he saw the slightest smear of crimson on his fingertip. It grew suddenly cold in the pool, despite the warmth of the water.

Bakhan lost feeling in his fingers, in his toes. He opened his mouth to speak, but no words could escape him as paralysis began to grip his entire body. His legs gave way, and there was nothing he could do to stop it.

"Deep breath, boy," Amosis said, as he began to sink beneath the surface.

Bakhan's eyes shifted to Wenis. She displayed no pleasure as he slowly submerged, but no remorse either. As he was embraced by the water, and the last breath escaped his lungs, the women turned back to one another and continued their conversation as though he wasn't even there.

The story continues in...

Engines of War

Book Three of The Age of Uprising

Keep reading for a sneak peek!

CREDITS

Writer
R. S. Ford
Publisher
Tim Holman
Editorial
Bradley Englert
Tiana Coven
Agent
John Jarrold
Production Editor
Rachel Goldstein
Copyeditor
Kelley Frodel
Proofreaders
Roland Ottewell
Janine Barlow
Production
Erin Cain

Design
Mike Heath | Magnus Creative
Marketing
Natassja Haught
Publicity
Angela Man
Audio
Thomas Mis
Alison Campbell
Phoebe McIntosh
Ciaran Saward
Andrew Kingston
Martin Reeve
Mark Meadows
Katie Villa
Diana Croft

extras

orbit

meet the author

R. S. FORD is a writer of fantasy from Leeds in the heartland of Yorkshire. As well as epic fantasy, he also writes historical fiction as Richard Cullen, and his novel *Oath Bound* was longlisted for the Wilbur Smith Adventure Writing Prize in 2022. If you'd like to learn more about his books and read FREE exclusive content, you can visit his website at wordhog.co.uk, follow him on Twitter at @rich4ord, or join him on Instagram and TikTok at @thewordhog.

Find out more about R. S. Ford and other Orbit authors by registering for the free monthly newsletter at orbitbooks.net.

if you enjoyed
ENGINES OF CHAOS

look out for

ENGINES OF WAR

Book Three of
The Age of Uprising

by

R. S. Ford

Prologue

An unholy wind whipped down from the Dolur Peaks as Gylbard stood at the summit of Wyrmhead, looking out at the vista. The cold air blew through his white-and-gold robes, but the old man had long since learned to ignore the discomfort. His joints would chide him for it later, despite his position as Archlegate—but age did not care for titles.

From the top of the fortress he could look out onto the northern extents of Torwyn from Kalur's Fist, rising from amid the mountain range in the north, to the Drift, falling away in the west. South and east were miles of flat country, crisscrossed by winding rivers that fed each of the Guildlands. Wyrmhead was at the apex providing succour, both literal and spiritual, to the whole of Torwyn.

As Gylbard looked out over the white stone parapet, Tapfoot stalked toward him along the balustrade. The cat paused when she reached him, rubbing her head against his hand. Gylbard lifted her gently from the edge, cradling her against him and hearing her purr softly into his chest.

"How many times must I tell you?" he whispered. "There is much danger here. You must be more careful."

He turned from the balcony, making his way back inside the vestibule that was perched at the summit of the great tower. Inside, Ansell was waiting for him.

The knight commander of the Drakes stood well over six feet, his dragon helm making him appear even taller. His armour was polished to a mirror sheen, tabard bearing the symbol of the Draconate: a dragon rampant surrounded by five stars, each of a different hue. Gylbard might have been intimidated, but the Drakes were faithful servants of the Draconate Ministry, raised from childhood to serve the Archlegate and his priests.

Bowing his head, Ansell dropped to one knee as Gylbard approached.

"Archlegate," he said, his deep voice made even more resonant from within the close-faced helm. "High Legate Egelrath is here to speak with you."

"Ah yes," Gylbard replied. "Then I suppose we should get this over with. Send him in."

As Ansell left, Gylbard sat in one of the high-backed chairs beside the winnowing fire. He absently stroked Tapfoot's back, letting her gentle purring soothe him. For many months now Egelrath had been visiting Wyrmhead. He had voiced his concerns ever louder and more frequently, entreating the Archlegate to act against the constant erosion of the Ministry's powers. But what was Gylbard to do? The Guilds ran Torwyn now, their industry feeding its people and protecting its borders. The Ministry's authority was waning, and there was little any of them could do about it.

"Archlegate."

Gylbard turned to see Sanctan Egelrath kneeling, head bowed. Ansell stood beside him, towering over the priest. A wicked thought entered Gylbard's head that it would have been so easy to have Ansell rid him of this troublesome upstart, but the notion was gone as soon as it came.

"Please, Sanctan, take a seat," Gylbard said.

Egelrath rose, moving beside the fire. "If you don't mind, I will stand. The ride north has left me somewhat sore about the buttocks."

Gylbard smirked. More wicked thoughts entering his head. "Thank you, Ansell. You may leave," he said.

"No, Archlegate," Sanctan said. "Please, let him stay. There is nothing I have to say that a Knight of the Draconate may not hear."

Gylbard shrugged. "Very well. What may I do for you this time?"

Sanctan smiled. His teeth were white, jaw square, hair thick and well groomed. It made Gylbard all the more conscious of how old he was—of his own bald pate and the white of his beard. Sanctan Egelrath was barely thirty, and already he had gained the position of High Legate. It was unheard of in the annals of the Draconate Ministry, but then Sanctan was a testament to how far and how quickly an ambitious man could rise. He was popular among both the legates and Drakes—Gylbard had been left with little choice but to approve the man's ordainment.

"Firstly, you might allow me to stoke this fire," Sanctan said, approaching the hearth. "It's freezing in here." He grabbed a poker, hitching up the red robes that marked him as an adherent of the great Wyrm Undometh, before he knelt by the fire and put some life back into the flames.

"I appreciate your concern, Sanctan, but I doubt you've come all this way to see after my comfort."

"Indeed not," Sanctan replied. He turned and fixed Gylbard with his usual serious visage. "I assume you have heard about the impending arrival of an emissary from Malador?"

Gylbard sighed, tousling Tapfoot's ears, trying to take comfort from the cat's purring. "Of course."

"And?"

Gylbard fought to keep himself calm. He had to show patience. "And what, Sanctan?"

"What do you intend to do about it? Malador is a threat to the freedom of all Torwyn. Those demon worshippers want nothing less than the destruction of everything we have built. They will not stop until the kingdom is in flames and our idols consumed. And now Sullivar welcomes an emissary. It cannot stand."

"It can and it will," Gylbard replied, keeping his voice calm and even in contrast with Sanctan's ranting. "Sullivar only wants peace, as do we all. Receiving an emissary is the first step toward that guarantee. The first step after a thousand years."

"He is capitulating. We have faced a constant threat from the west. Our borders have been tested innumerable times. Malador is not our friend and never will be, no matter how many emissaries they send."

"I disagree," said Gylbard. He stared at Sanctan, as though willing him to defy the word of the Archlegate. The priest remained silent. "A treaty is exactly what we need. The emissary does not represent the whole of Malador, only Nyrakkis, a nation I believe wants peace."

"And Iperion Magna? You believe they want peace too?"

Gylbard shook his head. "One thing at a time, Sanctan. Once a treaty is signed with Nyrakkis, Iperion Magna will follow."

"And you believe that?"

"I have had assurances from Sullivar himself. There is no reason to doubt him."

Sanctan turned to stare into the flames that had now responded to his attentions. The flickering fire bestowed a devilish aspect to his handsome face. Tapfoot gave a low mewl, signalling to Gylbard he had stopped stroking her.

"You know he has proclaimed himself 'emperor'?" Sanctan said, still staring into the fire. "His power grows while ours still dwindles."

"I have heard," Gylbard replied, his patience wearing thin.

"And that soon he will proclaim that the Guildlands are to be known as 'princedoms'? *Princedoms*, Gylbard. And he seated above them? What next? Are we to be renamed too? Cast out? Reduced to mere tokens?"

Gylbard rose to his feet, feeling a shooting pain in his knee, which he tried his best to ignore. He cradled Tapfoot in his arms, stroking her gently, reassuring her all the while.

"Your belief in the notion we are powerless does you no justice, Sanctan. Sullivar is not half the man his father was. Compared to Treon Archwind, Sullivar is but a boy playing a man's game. The Ministry has always been the sole ecclesial authority in Torwyn. The Guilds still pay fealty to the Draconate. Your fears are unfounded."

"By your own words Sullivar is weak. And a weak ruler is worse than any tyrant. Sullivar will lead Torwyn to ruin."

"You are fearful over nothing, Sanctan. You must calm yourself."

The heat from the fire was cloying now. Gylbard turned and made his way back onto the high terrace. Once again he looked out over the view of Torwyn, drawing some comfort from it.

Sanctan followed him out, coming to stand beside him.

"If we do not rise, if we do not retake what was once ours, all this will be gone," Sanctan said, gesturing at the beautiful sight of their homeland. "We have to show the Guilds who holds the real power in Torwyn. For far too long we have allowed them to govern unchecked."

"And what would you have me do? Order a coup? A revolt against the Guilds? Rise up and usurp their power by force?"

"If that's what it takes. Many of the Armiger Battalions serve their own interests in Karna Uzan protecting the flow of pyrestone. There has never been a better time—"

"No!" Gylbard shouted. Tapfoot squirmed in his grip, but he held on tight to her, feeling the cat dig a claw into his arm. More pain to ignore. "I've suffered enough of this impertinence. Now you go too far. Have you forgotten your scripture, Sanctan? Only when the Draconate return shall we rise again. Only when we have a sign."

"More talk of prophecy," Sanctan said. "You would wait for drag-ons to return to Torwyn before you act? Meanwhile the Ministry is reduced to what? A gaggle of petty preachers? We were once revered in Torwyn. We ruled these lands and protected them. The threat from Malador is real. We have to do something. We cannot wait for a sign prophesied in some crumbling old tome."

Gylbard felt his ire rising. He could barely quell it, yearning to rage at his underling, but Sanctan was young. Surely this boy could be curbed without resorting to extreme measures.

"I will forgive your heresy this time, Sanctan. One more word and I will not. The High Legates answer to me, and I will be the one to dictate the actions of the Ministry. I am still the Archlegate."

"And what use are you, old man?"

Gylbard could supress his fury no longer. He held on tight to Tapfoot, trembling at the words of his subordinate.

"Enough," he spat through gritted teeth. "You are done, Egelrath. I will summon the High Legates. You will regret the way you have spoken to me."

"I doubt that, Gylbard."

Before he could redress Sanctan further, something hit him in the back. Tapfoot fell from his grip as he staggered forward, his hands grasping the balustrade. Gylbard tried to stand, but his legs would no longer hold him up and he crumpled to the floor. He looked up to see Ansell standing there, sword unsheathed, blood on the blade.

"No," Gylbard managed to whisper.

"Yes," Sanctan replied. He was cradling Tapfoot, and the cat seemed comfortable in his grip. "Your time is at an end, old man. Mine has just begun."

"No," Gylbard said again, reaching out a trembling hand toward Tapfoot.

Sanctan looked down at the cat, content in his arms. "A treach-erous creature," he said. "Once yours, and now clearly mine. Such a fickle little thing, and you were blind to it all this time. But fear not, Gylbard. The cat will be safe with me. As will Torwyn's future."

"This is not the way, Sanctan," Gylbard tried to say, but his words were lost on the wind. Sanctan had already turned away, was already relaying his orders to Ansell.

Gylbard could only watch helplessly as the chill seeped into his bones and the world darkened.

if you enjoyed
ENGINES OF CHAOS

look out for

THE SWORD DEFIANT

Book One of
Lands of the Firstborn

by

Gareth Hanrahan

Set in a world of dark myth and dangerous prophecy,
The Sword Defiant *launches an epic tale of daring warriors,*
living weapons, and bloodthirsty vengeance.

The sword cares not who it cuts.

Many years ago, Sir Aelfric and his nine companions saved the world,
seizing the Dark Lord's cursed weapons along with his dread city of
Necrad. That was the easy part.

Now, when Aelfric—keeper of the cursed sword Spellbreaker—learns
of a new and terrifying threat, he seeks the nine heroes once again. But
they are wandering adventurers no longer. Yesterday's eager heroes
are today's weary leaders—and some have turned to the darkness,
becoming monsters themselves.

If there's one thing Aelfric knows, it's slaying monsters. Even if they used to be his friends.

Chapter One

No good story ever began in a tavern, but Alf had ended up in one anyway.

"An ogre," proclaimed the old man from the corner by the hearth, "a fearsome ogre! Iron-toothed, yellow-eyed, arms like oak branches!" He wobbled as he crossed the room towards the table of adventurers. "I saw it not three days ago, up on the High Moor. The beast must be slain, lest it find its way down to our fields and flocks!"

One of the young lads was beefy and broad-shouldered, Mulladale stock. He fancied himself a fighter, with that League-forged sword and patchwork armour. "I'll wager it's one of Lord Bone's minions, left over from the war," he declared loudly. "We'll hunt it down!"

"I can track it!" This was a woman in green, her face tattooed. A Wilder-woman of the northern woods – or dressed as one, anyway. "We just need to find its trail."

"There are places of power up on the High Moor," said a third, face shadowed by his hood. He spoke with the refined tones of a Crownland scholar. An apprentice mage, cloak marked with the sign of the Lord who'd sponsored him. He probably had a star-trap strung outside in the bushes. "Ancient temples, shrines to forgotten spirits. Such an eldritch beast might..."

He paused, portentously. Alf bloody hated it when wizards did that, leaving pauses like pit traps in the conversation. Just get on with it, for pity's sake.

Life was too short.

"...be drawn to such places. As might other...legacies of Lord Bone."

"We'll slay it," roared the Mulladale lad, "and deliver this village from peril!"

That won a round of applause from the locals, more for the boy's enthusiasm than any prospect of success. The adventurers huddled over the table, talking ogre-lore, talking about the dangers of the High Moor and the virtues of leaving at first light.

Alf scowled, irritated but unable to say why. He'd finish his drink, he decided, and then turn in. Maybe he'd be drunk enough to fall straight asleep. The loon had disturbed a rare evening of forgetfulness. He'd enjoyed sitting there, listening to village gossip and tall tales and the crackling of the fire. Now, the spell was broken and he had to think about monsters again.

He'd been thinking about monsters for a long time.

The old man sat down next to Alf. Apparently, he wasn't done. He wasn't that old, either – Alf realised he was about the same age. They'd both seen the wrong side of forty-five winters. "Ten feet tall it was," he exclaimed, sending spittle flying into Alf's tankard, "and big tusks, like a bull's horns, at the side of its mouth." He stuck his fingers out to illustrate. "It had the stink of Necrad about it. They have the right of it – it's one of Bone's creatures that escaped! The Nine should have put them all to the sword!"

"Bone's ogres," said Alf, "didn't have tusks." His voice was croaky from disuse. "They cut 'em off. Your ogre didn't come out of Necrad."

"You didn't see the beast! I did! Only the Pits of Necrad could spawn such—"

"You haven't seen the sodding Pits, either," said Alf. He felt the cold rush of anger, and stood up. He needed to be away from people. He stumbled across the room towards the stairs.

Another of the locals caught his arm. "Bit of luck for you, eh?" The fool was grinning and red-cheeked. *Twist, break the wrist. Grab his neck, slam his face into the table. Kick him into the two behind him. Then grab a weapon.* Alf fought against his honed instincts. The evening's drinking had not dulled his edge enough.

He dug up words. "What do you mean?"

"You said you were going off up the High Moor tomorrow. You'd run straight into that ogre's mouth. Best you stay here another few days, 'til it's safe."

"Safe," echoed Alf. He pulled his arm free. "I can't stay. I have to go and see an old friend."

The inn's only private room was upstairs. Sleeping in the common room was a copper a night, the private room an exorbitant six for a poky attic room and the pleasure of hearing the innkeeper snore next door.

Alf locked the door and took Spellbreaker from its hiding place under the bed. The sword slithered in his grasp, metal twisting beneath the dragonhide.

"I could hear them singing about you." Its voice was a leaden whisper. "About the siege of Necrad."

"Just a drinking song," said Alf, "nothing more. They didn't know it was me."

"They spoke the name of my true wielder, and woke me from dreams of slaughter."

"It rhymes with rat-arsed, that's all."

"No, it doesn't."

"It does the way they say it. *Acra-sed*."

"It's pronounced with a hard 't'," said the sword. "Acrai-*st* the Wraith-Captain, Hand of Bone."

"Well," said Alf, "I killed him, so I get to say how it's said. And it's rat-arsed. And so am I."

He shoved the sword back under the bed, then threw himself down, hoping to fall into oblivion. But the same dream caught him again, as it had for a month, and it called him up onto the High Moor to see his friend.

The adventurers left at first light.

Alf left an hour later, after a leisurely breakfast. *Getting soft*, he muttered to himself, but he still caught up with them at the foot of a steep cliff, arguing over which of the goat paths would bring them up onto the windy plateau of the High Moor. Alf marched past them, shoulders hunched against the cold of autumn.

"Hey! Old man!" called one of them. "There's a troll out there!"

Alf grunted as he studied the cliff ahead. It was steep, but not insurmountable. Berys and he had scaled the Wailing Tower in the middle of a howling necrostorm. This was nothing. He found a handhold and hauled himself up the rock face, ignoring the cries of the adventurers below. The Wilder girl followed him a little way, but gave up as Alf rapidly outdistanced her.

His shoulders, his knees ached as he climbed. *Old fool.* Showing off for what? To impress some village children? Why not wave Spellbreaker around? Or carry Lord Bone's skull around on a pole? *If you want glory, you're twenty years too late*, he thought to himself. He climbed on, stretching muscles grown stiff from disuse.

At the top, he sat down on a rock to catch his breath. He'd winded himself. The Wailing Tower, too, was twenty years ago.

He pulled his cloak around himself to ward off the breeze, and lingered there for a few minutes. He watched the adventurers as they debated which path to take, and eventually decided on the wrong one, circling south-east along the cliffs until they vanished into the broken landscape below the moor. He looked out west, across the Mulladales, a patchwork of low hills and farmlands and wooded coppices. Little villages, little lives. All safe.

Twenty years ago? Twenty-one? Whenever it was, Lord Bone's armies came down those goat paths. Undead warriors scuttling down the cliffs head first like bony lizards. Wilder scouts with faces painted pale as death. Witch Elf knights mounted on winged dreadworms. Golems, furnaces blazing with balefire. Between all those horrors and the Mulladales stood just nine heroes.

"It was twenty-two years ago," said Spellbreaker. The damn sword was listening to his thoughts again – or had he spoken out loud? "Twenty-two years since I ate the soul of the Illuminated."

"We beat you bastards good," said Alf. "And chased you out of the temple. Peir nearly slew Acraist then, do you remember?"

"Vividly," replied the sword.

Peir, his hammer blazing with the fire of the Intercessors. Berys, flinging vials of holy water she'd filched from the temple. Gundan, bellowing a war cry as he swung Chopper. Gods, they were so young then. Children, really, only a few years older than the idiot ogre-hunters. The battle of the temple was where they'd first proved themselves heroes. The start of a long, bitter war against Lord Bone. Oh, they'd got side-tracked – there'd been prophecies and quests and strife aplenty to lead them astray – but the path to Necrad began right here, on the edge of the High Moor.

He imagined his younger self struggling up those cliffs, that cheap pig-sticker of a sword clenched in his teeth. What would he have done, if that young warrior reached to the top and saw his future sitting there? Old, tired, tough as old boots. Still had all his limbs, but plenty of scars.

"We won," he whispered to the shade of the past, "and it's still bloody hard."

"You," said the sword, "are going crazy. You should get back to Necrad, where you belong."

"When I'm ready."

"I can call a dreadworm. Even here."

"No."

"Anything could be happening there. We've been away for more than two years, *moping*." There was an unusual edge to the sword's plea. Alf reached down and pulled Spellbreaker from its scabbard, so he could look the blade in the gemstone eye on its hilt and—

—Reflected in the polished black steel as it crept up behind him. Grey hide, hairy, iron-tusked maw drooling. Ogre.

Alf threw himself forward as the monster lunged at him and rolled to the edge of the cliff. Pebbles and dirt tumbled down the precipice, but he caught himself before he followed them over. He hoisted Spellbreaker, but the sword suddenly became impossibly heavy and threatened to tug him backwards over the cliff.

One of the bastard blade's infrequent bouts of treachery. Fine.

He flung the heavy sword at the onrushing ogre, and the monster stumbled over it. Its ropy arms reached for him, but Alf dodged along the cliff edge, seized the monster's wrist and pulled with all his might. The ogre, abruptly aware of the danger that they'd both fall to their deaths, scrambled away from the edge. It was off balance, and vulnerable. Alf leapt on the monster's back and drove one elbow into its ear. The ogre bellowed in pain and fell forward onto the rock he'd been sitting on. Blood gushed from its nose, and the sight sparked unexpected joy in Alf. For a moment, he felt young again, and full of purpose. This, this was what he was meant for!

The ogre tried to dislodge him, but Alf wrapped his legs around its chest, digging his knees into its armpits, his hands clutching shanks of the monster's hair. He bellowed into the ogre's ear in the creature's own language.

"Do you know who I am? I'm the man who killed the Chieftain of the Marrow-Eaters!"

The ogre clawed at him, ripping at his cloak. Its claws scrabbled against the dwarven mail Alf wore beneath his shirt. Alf got his arm locked across the ogre's throat and squeezed.

"I killed Acraist the Wraith-Captain!"

The ogre reared up and threw itself back, crushing Alf against the rock. The impact knocked the air from his lungs, and he felt one of his ribs crack, but he held firm – and sank his teeth into his foe's ear. He bit off a healthy chunk, spat it out and hissed:

"I killed Lord Bone."

It was probably the pain of losing an earlobe, and not his threat, that made the ogre yield, but yield it did. The monster fell to the ground, whimpering.

Alf released his grip on the ogre's neck and picked up Spell-breaker. Oh, *now* the magic sword was perfectly light and balanced in his hand. One swing, and the ogre's head would go rolling across the ground. One cut, and the monster would be slain.

He slapped the ogre with the flat of the blade.

"Look at me."

Yellow terror-filled eyes stared at him.

"There are adventurers hunting for you. They went south-east. You, run north. That way." He pointed with the blade, unsure if the ogre even spoke this dialect. It was the tongue he'd learned in Necrad, the language the Witch Elves used to order their war-beasts around. "Run north!" he added in common, and he shoved the ogre again. The brute got the message and ran, loping on all

fours away from Alf. It glanced back in confusion, unsure of what
had just happened.

Alf lifted Spellbreaker, glared into the sword's eye.

"I was testing you," said the sword. "You haven't had a proper fight
in months. Tournies don't count – no opponent has the courage to
truly test you, and it's all for show anyway. Your strength dwindles.
My wielder must—"

"I'm not your bloody wielder. I'm your gaoler."

"I am *bored*, wielder. Two years of wandering the forests and
back-roads. Two years of hiding and lurking. And when you finally
pluck up the courage to go anywhere, it's to an even duller village.
I tell you, those people should have welcomed the slaughter my
master brought, to relieve them of the tedium of their pathetic—"

"Try that again, and I'll throw you off a cliff."

"Do it. Someone will find me. Some*thing*. I'm a weapon of darkness, and I call to—"

"I'll drop you," said Alf wearily, "into a volcano."

Last time, they'd reached the temple in two days. He'd spent twice
as long already, trudging over stony ground, pushing through
thorns and bracken, clambering around desolate tors and outcrops
of bare rock. He'd known that finding the hidden ravine of the
temple would be tricky, but it took him longer than he'd expected
to reach Giant's Rock, and that was at least a day's travel from the
ravine.

That big pillar of stone, one side covered with shaggy grey-green
moss – that was Giant's Rock, right? In his memory it was bigger.
Alf squinted at the rock, trying to imagine how it might be mistaken for a hunched giant. He'd seen real giants, and they were a
lot bigger.

If this was Giant's Rock, he should turn south there to reach the
valley. If it wasn't, then turning south would bring him into the
empty lands of the fells where no one lived.

Maybe they'd come from a more northerly direction, last time.
He walked around the pillar of stone. It remained obstinately

un-giant-like. No one ever accused Alf of having the soul of a poet. A rock pile was a rock pile to him. The empty sky above him, the empty land all around. He regretted letting that ogre run off; maybe he should have forced it to guide him to the valley. Turn south, or continue east?

The valley was well hidden. There'd been wars fought in these parts, hundreds of years ago, in the dark days after...after...after some kingdom had fallen. The Old Kingdom. Alf's grasp of history was as good as could be expected of a Mulladale farm boy who'd could barely write his name, and twenty-odd years of adventuring hadn't taught him much more. Oh, he could tell you the best way to *fight* an animated skeleton, or loot an ancient tomb, but "whence came the skeleton" or "who built the tomb" were matters for cleverer heads. He remembered Blaise lecturing him on this battlefield, the wizard wasting his breath on talking when he should have been keeping it for walking. Different factions in the Old Kingdom clashed here. Rival cults, Blaise told him, fighting until both sides were exhausted and the Illuminated were driven into hiding. The green grass swallowed up the battlefields and the barrow tombs, and everything was forgotten until Lord Bone had called up those long-dead warriors. Skeletons crawled out of the dirt and took up their rusty swords, and roamed the High Moors again.

Last time, Thurn the Wilder led them. He could track anything and anyone, even the dead. He'd brought them straight to the secret path, following Lord Bone's forces into the hidden heart of the temple. All Alf had to do was fight off the flying dreadworms sent to slow them down. Even then, Acraist had seen that the Nine of them were dangerous.

"No, he didn't," said the sword. It was the first time it had spoken since the cliff top.

"Stop that."

"If Acraist thought you were a threat, he'd have sent more than a few riderless worms. He was intent on breaking the aegis of the temple, not worrying about you bandits. You were an irrelevant nuisance. You got lucky."

"Well, he got killed. And so did Lord Bone, and you can't say that was luck."

A quiver ran through the sword. The blade's equivalent of a derisive snort.

He took another step east, and the sword quivered again.

"What is it?"

"Nothing, O Lammergeier," said Spellbreaker sullenly. Alf hated that nickname, given to him in the songs by some stupid poet drunk on metaphor. He'd never even seen one of the ugly vultures of the mountains beyond Westermarch. They were bone-breaking birds, feasters on marrow. And while Alf might be old and ugly enough now to resemble a vulture, the bloody song had given him that name fifteen or so years ago. He'd broken Bone, hence – Sir Lammergeier.

Poetry was almost as bad as prophecy.

The sword only used the name when it wanted to annoy him – or distract him. What had that pretentious apprentice said in the inn, about creatures of Lord Bone sensing places of power? Alf drew the sword again and took a step forward. The jewelled eye seemed to wince, eldritch light flaring deep within the ruby.

He shook Spellbreaker. "Can you detect the temple?"

"No."

Another step. Another wince.

"You bloody well can," said Alf.

"It's sanctified," admitted Spellbreaker reluctantly. "Acraist protected me from the radiance, last time."

Alf looked around at the moorland. No radiance was visible, at least none he had eyes to see.

"Well then." He set off east, and only turned south when prompted by the twisting of the demonic sword.

Another day, and the terrain became familiar. Some blessing in the temple softened the harshness of the moor. Wildflowers grew all around. Streams cascaded down the rocks, chiming like silver bells. Alf felt weariness fall from his bones, sloughing away like he'd sunk into a warm bath.

Spellbreaker shrieked and rattled in its scabbard.

"It's too bright. I cannot go in there. It will shatter me."

"I'm not leaving you here."

"Wielder, I cannot..."

Alf hesitated. Spellbreaker was among the most dangerous things to come out of Necrad, a weapon of surpassing evil. It could shatter any spell, break any ward. In the hands of a monster, it could wreak terrible harm upon the world. Even that ogre could become something dangerous under the blade's tutelage. But maybe the sword was right – dragging it into the holy place might damage it. When they'd fought Acraist that first time, down in the valley, the Wraith-Captain wasn't half as tough as when they battled him seven years later. The valley burned things of darkness.

Would it burn Alf if he carried the sword down there?

"Look," sneered Spellbreaker. "You're expected."

A tiny candle flame of light danced in the air ahead of Alf. And then another kindled, and another, and another, a trail of sparks leading down into the valley.

Alf drew the sword and drove it deep into the earth. "Stay," he said to it, scolding it like a dog.

Then down, into the hidden valley of the Illuminated One.